Laurence Sterne

LAURENCE STERNE was born on November 24, 1713 at Clonmel, Ireland, where his father, an English Army officer, was stationed. Sterne studied at Jesus College, Cambridge, and was awarded his degree in 1737. Although he had little inclination toward the clergy he became Vicar of Sutton-in-the-Forest in 1738 through the efforts of his uncle, an influential churchman at York. In 1741 Sterne married Elizabeth Lumley, by whom he had a daughter. After spending twenty uneventful years at Sutton, Sterne was catapulted to fame with the appearance of the first two volumes of his sensational *Tristram Shandy* (1760). The acclamation he received prompted Sterne to continue writing his history of the Shandy family, the ninth and final volume being completed in 1767. For more than thirty years Sterne was plagued with a severe lung condition, and, as his health diminished, he traveled through Southern Europe in a futile effort to regain his strength. He died in London on March 18, 1768, just three weeks after the publication of *A Sentimental Journey through France and Italy*.

THE
LIFE
AND
OPINIONS
OF
TRISTRAM SHANDY,
GENTLEMAN

by

Laurence Sterne

Ταράσσει τὼς ᾿Ανθρώπος ὡ τὰ Πραγματα,
ἀλλὰ τὰ περὶ τῶν Πραγμάτων, Δόγματα.

**WITH AN AFTERWORD BY
GERALD WEALES**

A SIGNET CLASSIC
PUBLISHED BY THE NEW AMERICAN LIBRARY

AFTERWORD COPYRIGHT © 1960 WAYNE STATE UNIVERSITY PRESS

First Printing, October, 1962

SIGNET TRADEMARK REG. U.S. PAT. OFF. AND FOREIGN COUNTRIES
REGISTERED TRADEMARK—MARCA REGISTRADA
HECHO EN CHICAGO, U.S.A.

SIGNET CLASSICS *are published by*
The New American Library of World Literature, Inc.
501 Madison Avenue, New York 22, New York

PRINTED IN THE UNITED STATES OF AMERICA

CONTENTS

CONTENTS

To the Right Honourable

Mr. PITT

SIR,

Never poor Wight of a Dedicator had less hopes from his Dedication than I have from this of mine; for it is written in a bye corner of the kingdom, and in a retired thatched house, where I live in a constant endeavour to fence against the infirmities of ill health, and other evils of life, by mirth; being firmly persuaded that every time a man smiles,—— but much more so, when he laughs, that it adds something to this Fragment of Life.

I humbly beg, Sir, that you will honour this book by taking it——(not under your Protection,——it must protect itself, but)——into the country with you; where, if I am ever told it has made you smile, or can conceive it has beguiled you of one moment's pain——I shall think myself as happy as a minister of state;——perhaps much happier than any one (one only excepted) that I have ever read or heard of.

I am, great Sir
(and what is more to your Honour),
I am, good Sir,
Your Well-wisher,
and most humble Fellow-subject,

THE AUTHOR

VOLUME I

CHAPTER 1

I wish either my father or my mother, or indeed both of them, as they were in duty both equally bound to it, had minded what they were about when they begot me; had they duly considered how much depended upon what they were then doing;—that not only the production of a rational Being was concerned in it, but that possibly the happy formation and temperature of his body, perhaps his genius and the very cast of his mind;—and, for aught they knew to the contrary, even the fortunes of his whole house might take their turn from the humours and dispositions which were then upper-most:——Had they duly weighed and considered all this, and proceeded accordingly,——I am verily persuaded I should have made a quite different figure in the world from that in which the reader is likely to see me.——Believe me, good folks, this is not so inconsiderable a thing as many of you may think it;——you have all, I dare say, heard of the animal spirits, as how they are transfused from father to son, &c., &c.——and a great deal to that purpose:——Well, you may take my word that nine parts in ten of a man's sense or his nonsense, his successes and miscarriages in this world, depend upon their motions and activity, and the different tracks and trains you put them into, so that when they are once set a-going, whether right or wrong, 'tis not a halfpenny matter;——away they go cluttering like hey-go-mad; and by treading the same steps over and over again, they presently make a road of it, as plain and as smooth as a garden walk, which, when they are once used to, the devil himself sometimes shall not be able to drive them off it.

Pray, my dear, quoth my mother, *have you not forgot to wind up the clock?*————*Good G——!* cried my father, making an exclamation, but taking care to moderate his voice at the same time,————*Did ever woman, since the creation of the world, interrupt a man with such a silly question?* Pray, what was your father saying?————Nothing.

CHAPTER II

————Then, positively, there is nothing in the question, that I can see, either good or bad.————Then let me tell you, Sir, it was a very unseasonable question at least,————because it scattered and dispersed the animal spirits, whose business it was to have escorted and gone hand-in-hand with the *HOMUNCULUS*, and conducted him safe to the place destined for his reception.

The HOMUNCULUS, Sir, in however low and ludicrous a light he may appear, in this age of levity, to the eye of folly or prejudice:————to the eye of reason in scientific research, he stands confessed————a BEING guarded and circumscribed with rights:————The minutest philosophers, who, by the bye, have the most enlarged understandings (their souls being inversely as their enquiries), show us incontestably, That the HOMUNCULUS is created by the same hand,————engendered in the same course of nature,————endowed with the same locomotive powers and faculties with us:————That he consists, as we do, of skin, hair, fat, flesh, veins, arteries, ligaments, nerves, cartilages, bones, marrow, brains, glands, genitals, humours, and articulations;————is a Being of as much activity,————and, in all senses of the word, as much and as truly our fellow-creature as my Lord Chancellor of England.————He may be benefited, he may be injured,———— he may obtain redress;————in a word, he has all the claims and rights of humanity which Tully, Puffendorff, or the best ethic writers allow to arise out of that state and relation.

Now, dear Sir, what if any accident had befallen him in his way alone?————or that, through terror of it, natural to so young a traveller, my little gentleman had got to his journey's end miserably spent;————his muscular strength and virility worn down to a thread;——his own animal spirits ruffled beyond description;——and that in this sad disordered state of nerves, he had laid down a prey to sudden starts, or a series of melancholy dreams and fancies for nine long, long months together.——I tremble to think what a foundation had been laid for a thousand weaknesses both of body and mind, which no skill of the physician or the philosopher could ever afterwards have set thoroughly to rights.

CHAPTER III

To my uncle Mr. Toby Shandy do I stand indebted for the preceding anecdote, to whom my father, who was an excellent natural philosopher, and much given to close reasoning upon the smallest matters, had oft, and heavily, complained of the injury; but once more particularly, as my uncle Toby well remembered, upon his observing a most unaccountable obliquity (as he called it) in my manner of setting up my top, and justifying the principles upon which I had done it, ——the old gentleman shook his head, and in a tone more expressive by half of sorrow than reproach,——he said his heart all along foreboded, and he saw it verified in this, and from a thousand other observations he had made upon me, That I should neither think nor act like any other man's child:——*But alas!* continued he, shaking his head a second time, and wiping away a tear which was trickling down his cheeks, *My Tristram's misfortunes began nine months before ever he came into the world.*

——My mother, who was sitting by, looked up,——but she knew no more than her backside what my father meant, ——but my uncle, Mr. Toby Shandy, who had been often informed of the affair,——understood him very well.

CHAPTER IV

I know there are readers in the world, as well as many other good people in it, who are no readers at all,——who find themselves ill at ease, unless they are let into the whole secret from first to last, of everything which concerns you.

It is in pure compliance with this humour of theirs, and from a backwardness in my nature to disappoint any one soul living, that I have been so very particular already. As my life and opinions are likely to make some noise in the world, and, if I conjecture right, will take in all ranks, professions, and denominations of men whatever,——be no less read than the *Pilgrim's Progress* itself——and, in the end, prove the very thing which Montaigne dreaded his essays should turn out, that is, a book for a parlour window; I find it necessary to consult everyone a little in his turn; and therefore must beg pardon for going on a little further in the same way: For which cause, right glad I am that I have begun the history of myself in the way I have done; and that I am able to go on tracing everything in it, as Horace says, *ab Ovo*.

Horace, I know, does not recommend this fashion altogether: But that gentleman is speaking only of an epic poem or a tragedy——(I forget which)——besides, if it was not so, I should beg Mr. Horace's pardon;——for in writing what I have set about, I shall confine myself neither to his rules, nor to any man's rules that ever lived.

To such, however, as do not choose to go so far back into these things, I can give no better advice than that they skip over the remaining part of this Chapter; for I declare beforehand, 'tis wrote only for the curious and inquisitive. ——————————— Shut the door. ———————————
I was begot in the night, betwixt the first Sunday and the first Monday in the month of March, in the year of our Lord one thousand seven hundred and eighteen. I am positive I was.——But how I came to be so very particular in my account of a thing which happened before I was born is owing to another small anecdote known only in our own family, but now made public for the better clearing up this point.

My father, you must know, who was originally a Turkey merchant, but had left off business for some years, in order

to retire to, and die upon, his paternal estate in the county of
————, was, I believe, one of the most regular men in everything he did, whether 'twas matter of business, or matter of
amusement, that ever lived. As a small specimen of this extreme exactness of his, to which he was in truth a slave,——
he had made it a rule for many years of his life,——on the
first Sunday night of every month throughout the whole year,
——as certain as ever the Sunday night came,——to wind
up a large house clock which we had standing upon the back-
stairs head, with his own hands:——And being somewhere
between fifty and sixty years of age at the time I have been
speaking of,——he had likewise gradually brought some
other little family concernments to the same period, in order,
as he would often say to my uncle Toby, to get them all out
of the way at one time, and be no more plagued and pestered
with them the rest of the month.

It was attended but with one misfortune, which, in a great
measure, fell upon myself, and the effects of which I fear I
shall carry with me to my grave; namely, that, from an unhappy association of ideas which have no connection in nature, it so fell out at length that my poor mother could never
hear the said clock wound up,——but the thoughts of some
other things unavoidably popped into her head,——and *vice
versa*:——which strange combination of ideas the sagacious
Locke, who certainly understood the nature of these things
better than most men, affirms to have produced more wry
actions than all other sources of prejudice whatsoever.

But this by the bye.

Now it appears, by a memorandum in my father's pocketbook, which now lies upon the table, "That on Lady Day,
which was on the 25th of the same month in which I date my
geniture,——my father set out upon his journey to London
with my eldest brother, Bobby, to fix him at Westminster
school;" and, as it appears from the same authority, "That he
did not get down to his wife and family till the second week
in May following"——it brings the thing almost to a certainty.
However, what follows in the beginning of the next chapter
puts it beyond all possibility of doubt.

————But pray, Sir, What was your father doing all December,——January, and February?——Why, Madam,——he
was all that time afflicted with a Sciatica.

13

CHAPTER V

On the fifth day of November, 1718, which to the era fixed on was as near nine calendar months as any husband could in reason have expected,——was I, Tristram Shandy, Gentleman, brought forth into this scurvy and disastrous world of ours.——I wish I had been born in the Moon, or in any of the planets (except Jupiter or Saturn, because I never could bear cold weather), for it could not well have fared worse with me in any of them (though I will not answer for Venus) than it has in this vile, dirty planet of ours,——which o' my conscience, with reverence be it spoken, I take to be made up of the shreds and clippings of the rest;——not but the planet is well enough, provided a man could be born in it to a great title or to a great estate; or could anyhow contrive to be called up to public charges, and employments of dignity or power;——but that is not my case;——and therefore every man will speak of the fair as his own market has gone in it;——for which cause I affirm it over again to be one of the vilest worlds that ever was made;——for I can truly say that from the first hour I drew my breath in it, to this, that I can now scarce draw it at all, for an asthma I got in skating against the wind in Flanders,——I have been the continual sport of what the world calls fortune; and though I will not wrong her by saying, She has ever made me feel the weight of any great or signal evil,——yet with all the good temper in the world, I affirm it of her that in every stage of my life, and at every turn and corner where she could get fairly at me, the ungracious Duchess has pelted me with a set of as pitiful misadventures and cross accidents as ever small HERO sustained.

CHAPTER VI

In the beginning of the last chapter, I informed you exactly *when* I was born;——but I did not inform you *how*. No; that particular was reserved entirely for a chapter by itself; ——besides, Sir, as you and I are in a manner perfect strangers to each other, it would not have been proper to have let you into too many circumstances relating to myself all at once.——You must have a little patience. I have undertaken, you see, to write not only my life, but my opinions also; hoping and expecting that your knowledge of my character, and of what kind of a mortal I am, by the one, would give you a better relish for the other: As you proceed further with me, the slight acquaintance which is now beginning betwixt us will grow into familiarity; and that, unless one of us is in fault, will terminate in friendship.——*O diem praeclarum!*——then nothing which has touched me will be thought trifling in its nature, or tedious in its telling. Therefore, my dear friend and companion, if you should think me somewhat sparing of my narrative on my first setting out, ——bear with me,——and let me go on, and tell my story my own way:——or if I should seem now and then to trifle upon the road,——or should sometimes put on a fool's cap with a bell to it, for a moment or two as we pass along,—— don't fly off,——but rather courteously give me credit for a little more wisdom than appears upon my outside;——and as we jog on, either laugh with me, or at me, or in short, do anything,——only keep your temper.

CHAPTER VII

In the same village where my father and my mother dwelt, dwelt also a thin, upright, motherly, notable, good old body of a midwife, who, with the help of a little plain good sense, and some years' full employment in her business, in which

15

she had all along trusted little to her own efforts, and a great deal to those of dame Nature,——had acquired, in her way, no small degree of reputation in the world;——by which word *world,* need I in this place inform your Worship that I would be understood to mean no more of it than a small circle described upon the circle of the great world, of four English miles diameter, or thereabouts, of which the cottage where the good old woman lived is supposed to be the centre.——She had been left, it seems, a widow in great distress, with three or four small children, in her forty-seventh year; and as she was at that time a person of decent carriage, ——grave deportment,——a woman moreover of few words, and withal an object of compassion, whose distress and silence under it called out the louder for a friendly lift: the wife of the parson of the parish was touched with pity; and having often lamented an inconvenience to which her husband's flock had for many years been exposed, inasmuch as there was no such thing as a midwife of any kind or degree to be got at, let the case have been never so urgent, within less than six or seven long miles riding; which said seven long miles in dark nights and dismal roads, the country thereabouts being nothing but a deep clay, was almost equal to fourteen; and that in effect was sometimes next to having no midwife at all; it came into her head that it would be doing as seasonable a kindness to the whole parish, as to the poor creature herself, to get her a little instructed in some of the plain principles of the business, in order to set her up in it. As no woman thereabouts was better qualified to execute the plan she had formed than herself, the Gentlewoman very charitably undertook it; and having great influence over the female part of the parish, she found no difficulty in effecting it to the utmost of her wishes. In truth, the parson joined his interest with his wife's in the whole affair; and in order to do things as they should be, and give the poor soul as good a title by law to practise, as his wife had given by institution, ——he cheerfully paid the fees for the ordinary's licence himself, amounting, in the whole, to the sum of eighteen shillings and fourpence; so that, betwixt them both, the good woman was fully invested in the real and corporal possession of her office, together with all its *rights, members, and appurtenances whatsoever.*

These last words, you must know, were not according to the old form in which such licences, faculties, and powers usually ran, which in like cases had heretofore been granted to the sisterhood. But it was according to a neat *Formula* of

16

Didius his own devising, who having a particular turn for taking to pieces, and new-framing over again, all kind of instruments in that way, not only hit upon this dainty amendment, but coaxed many of the old licensed matrons in the neighbourhood to open their faculties afresh, in order to have this whimwham of his inserted.

I own I never could envy Didius in these kinds of fancies of his:——But every man to his own taste.——Did not Dr. Kunastrokius, that great man, at his leisure hours, take the greatest delight imaginable in combing of asses' tails, and plucking the dead hairs out with his teeth, though he had tweezers always in his pocket? Nay, if you come to that, Sir, have not the wisest of men in all ages, not excepting Solomon himself,——have they not had their HOBBY-HORSES;——their running horses,——their coins and their cockleshells, their drums and their trumpets, their fiddles, their pallets,—— their maggots and their butterflies?——and so long as a man rides his HOBBY-HORSE peaceably and quietly along the king's highway, and neither compels you or me to get up behind him,——pray, Sir, what have either you or I to do with it?

CHAPTER VIII

——*De gustibus non est disputandum;*——that is, there is no disputing against HOBBY-HORSES; and, for my part, I seldom do; nor could I with any sort of grace, had I been an enemy to them at the bottom; for happening, at certain intervals and changes of the Moon, to be both fiddler and painter, according as the fly stings:——Be it known to you that I keep a couple of pads myself, upon which, in their turns (nor do I care who knows it), I frequently ride out and take the air;——though sometimes, to my shame be it spoken, I take somewhat longer journeys than what a wise man would think altogether right.——But the truth is,——I am not a wise man;——and besides am a mortal of so little consequence in the world, it is not much matter what I do; so I seldom fret or fume at all about it: Nor does it much disturb my rest when I see such great Lords and tall Personages as hereafter follow;——such, for instance, as my Lord A, B, C, D, E, F, G, H, I, K, L, M, N, O, P, Q,

and so on, all of a row, mounted upon their several horses;
——some with large stirrups, getting on in a more grave
and sober pace;——others on the contrary, tucked up to their
very chins, with whips across their mouths, scouring and
scampering it away like so many little party-coloured devils
astride a mortgage,——and as if some of them were resolved
to break their necks.——So much the better——say I to myself;——for in case the worst should happen, the world will
make a shift to do excellently well without them;——and
for the rest,——why,——God speed them,——e'en let them
ride on without opposition from me; for were their lordships
unhorsed this very night,——'tis ten to one but that many
of them would be worse mounted by one half before tomorrow morning.

Not one of these instances therefore can be said to break in
upon my rest.——But there is an instance which I own puts
me off my guard, and that is when I see one born for great
actions, and, what is still more for his honour, whose nature
ever inclines him to good ones;——when I behold such a
one, my Lord, like yourself, whose principles and conduct
are as generous and noble as his blood, and whom, for that
reason, a corrupt world cannot spare one moment;——when
I see such a one, my Lord, mounted, though it is but for a
minute beyond the time which my love to my country has
prescribed to him, and my zeal for his glory wishes,—then,
my Lord, I cease to be a philosopher, and in the first transport of an honest impatience, I wish the HOBBY-HORSE, with
all his fraternity, at the devil.

"My Lord,
"I maintain this to be a dedication, notwithstanding its
singularity in the three great essentials of matter, form, and
place: I beg, therefore, you will accept it as such, and that
you will permit me to lay it, with the most respectful humility, at your Lordship's feet,——when you are upon them,——
which you can be when you please:——and that is, my Lord,
whenever there is occasion for it, and I will add, to the best
purposes too. I have the honour to be,

My Lord,
Your Lordship's most obedient,
and most devoted,
and most humble servant,
TRISTRAM SHANDY"

CHAPTER IX

I solemnly declare to all mankind that the above dedication was made for no one Prince, Prelate, Pope, or Potentate, ——Duke, Marquis, Earl, Viscount, or Baron of this or any other Realm in Christendom;——nor has it yet been hawked about, or offered publicly or privately, directly or indirectly, to any one person or personage, great or small; but is honestly a true Virgin Dedication, untried on upon any soul living.

I labour this point so particularly merely to remove any offence or objection which might arise against it, from the manner in which I propose to make the most of it;—— which is the putting it up fairly to public sale; which I now do.

——Every author has a way of his own in bringing his points to bear;——for my own part, as I hate chaffering and higgling for a few guineas in a dark entry,——I resolved within myself, from the very beginning, to deal squarely and openly with your Great Folks in this affair, and try whether I should not come off the better by it.

If therefore there is any one Duke, Marquis, Earl, Viscount, or Baron, in these his Majesty's dominions, who stands in need of a tight, genteel dedication, and whom the above will suit (for by the bye, unless it suits in some degree, I will not part with it),——it is much at his service for fifty guineas;——which I am positive is twenty guineas less than it ought to be afforded for, by any man of genius.

My Lord, if you examine it over again, it is far from being a gross piece of daubing, as some dedications are. The design, your Lordship sees, is good, the colouring transparent,——the drawing not amiss;——or to speak more like a man of science,——and measure my piece in the painter's scale, divided into 20,——I believe, my Lord, the outlines will turn out as 12,——the composition as 9,——the colouring as 6,——the expression 13 and a half,——and the design,——if I may be allowed, my Lord, to understand my own *design,* and supposing absolute perfection in designing to be as 20,——I think it cannot well fall short of 19. Besides all this,——there is keeping in it, and the dark strokes in the HOBBY-HORSE (which is a secondary figure, and a kind of background to the whole) give great force to the principal lights in your own figure, and make it come off wonderfully;——and besides, there is an air of originality in the *tout ensemble*.

Be pleased, my good Lord, to order the sum to be paid into the hands of Mr. Dodsley, for the benefit of the author; and in the next edition care shall be taken that this chapter be expunged, and your Lordship's titles, distinctions, arms, and good actions be placed at the front of the preceding chapter: All which, from the words, *De gustibus non est disputandum,* and whatever else in this book relates to HOBBY-HORSES, but no more, shall stand dedicated to your Lordship.——The rest I dedicate to the MOON, who, by the bye, of all the PATRONS or MATRONS I can think of, has most power to set my book a-going, and make the world run mad after it.

Bright Goddess,

If thou art not too busy with CANDIDE and Miss CUNÉGONDE's affairs,——take Tristram Shandy's under thy protection also.

CHAPTER X

Whatever degree of small merit the act of benignity in favour of the midwife might justly claim, or in whom that claim truly rested,——at first sight seems not very material to this history;——certain however it was that the gentle-woman, the parson's wife, did run away at that time with the whole of it: And yet, for my life, I cannot help thinking but that the parson himself, though he had not the good fortune to hit upon the design first,——yet, as he heartily concurred in it the moment it was laid before him, and as heartily parted with his money to carry it into execution, had a claim to some share of it,——if not to a full half of whatever honour was due to it.

The world at that time was pleased to determine the matter otherwise.

Lay down the book, and I will allow you half a day to

give a probable guess at the grounds of this procedure.

Be it known then that, for about five years before the date of the midwife's licence, of which you have had so circumstantial an account,——the parson we have to do with had made himself a country talk by a breach of all decorum, which he had committed against himself, his station, and his office;——and that was in never appearing better, or otherwise, mounted than upon a lean, sorry jackass of a horse, value about one pound fifteen shillings; who, to shorten all description of him, was full brother to Rosinante, as far as similitude congenial could make him; for he answered his description to a hairbreadth in everything,——except that I do not remember 'tis anywhere said that Rosinante was broken-winded; and that, moreover, Rosinante, as is the happiness of most Spanish horses, fat or lean,——was undoubtedly a horse at all points.

I know very well that the HERO's horse was a horse of chaste deportment, which may have given grounds for a contrary opinion: But it is as certain at the same time that Rosinante's continency (as may be demonstrated from the adventure of the Yanguesian carriers) proceeded from no bodily defect or cause whatsoever, but from the temperance and orderly current of his blood.——And let me tell you, Madam, there is a great deal of very good chastity in the world, in behalf of which you could not say more for your life.

Let that be as it may, as my purpose is to do exact justice to every creature brought upon the stage of this dramatic work,——I could not stifle this distinction in favour of Don Quixote's horse;——in all other points the parson's horse, I say, was just such another,——for he was as lean, and as lank, and as sorry a jade as HUMILITY herself could have bestrided.

In the estimation of here and there a man of weak judgment, it was greatly in the parson's power to have helped the figure of this horse of his,——for he was master of a very handsome demipeaked saddle, quilted on the seat with green plush, garnished with a double row of silver-headed studs, and a noble pair of shining brass stirrups, with a housing altogether suitable, of grey superfine cloth, with an edging of black lace, terminating in a deep, black, silk fringe, *poudré d'or,*——all which he had purchased in the pride and prime of his life, together with a grand embossed bridle, ornamented at all points as it should be.——But not caring to banter his beast, he had hung all these up behind his study door;———and, in lieu of them, had seriously befitted him with just such a bridle and such a saddle as the figure and value of such a steed might well and truly deserve.

In the several sallies about his parish, and in the neighbouring visits to the gentry who lived around him,———you will easily comprehend that the parson, so appointed, would both hear and see enough to keep his philosophy from rusting. To speak the truth, he never could enter a village but he caught the attention of both old and young.———Labour stood still as he passed,———the bucket hung suspended in the middle of the well,———the spinning wheel forgot its round,———even chuck-farthing and shuffle-cap themselves stood gaping till he had got out of sight; and as his movement was not of the quickest, he had generally time enough upon his hands to make his observations,———to hear the groans of the serious,———and the laughter of the lighthearted;———all which he bore with excellent tranquility.———His character was———he loved a jest in his heart———and as he saw himself in the true point of ridicule, he would say he could not be angry with others for seeing him in a light in which he so strongly saw himself: So that to his friends, who knew his foible was not the love of money, and who therefore made the less scruple in bantering the extravagance of his humour,———instead of giving the true cause,———he chose rather to join in the laugh against himself; and as he never carried one single ounce of flesh upon his own bones, being altogether as spare a figure as his beast,———he would sometimes insist upon it that the horse was as good as the rider deserved;———that they were, centaur-like,———both of a piece. At other times, and in other moods, when his spirits were above the temptation of false wit,———he would say he found himself going off fast in a consumption; and, with great gravity, would pretend he could not bear the sight of a fat horse without a dejection of heart, and a sensible alteration in his pulse; and that he had made choice of the lean one he rode upon not only to keep himself in countenance, but in spirits.

At different times he would give fifty humorous and opposite reasons for riding a meek-spirited jade of a broken-winded horse, preferably to one of mettle;———for on such a one he could sit mechanically, and meditate as delightfully *de vanitate mundi et fugâ saeculi,* as with the advantage of a death's head before him;———that, in all other exercitations, he could spend his time, as he rode slowly along,———to as much account as in his study;———that he could draw

22

up an argument in his sermon,——or a hole in his breeches, as steadily on the one as in the other;——that brisk trotting and slow argumentation, like wit and judgment, were two incompatible movements.——But that upon his steed——he could unite and reconcile everything,——he could compose his sermon,——he could compose his cough,——and, in case nature gave a call that way, he could likewise compose himself to sleep.——In short, the parson upon such encounters would assign any cause but the true cause,——and he withheld the true one only out of a nicety of temper, because he thought it did honour to him.

But the truth of the story was as follows: In the first years of this gentleman's life, and about the time when the superb saddle and bridle were purchased by him, it had been his manner, or vanity, or call it what you will,——to run into the opposite extreme.——In the language of the county where he dwelt, he was said to have loved a good horse, and generally had one of the best in the whole parish standing in his stable always ready for saddling; and as the nearest midwife, as I told you, did not live nearer to the village than seven miles, and in a vile country,——it so fell out that the poor gentleman was scarce a whole week together without some piteous application for his beast; and as he was not an unkind-hearted man, and every case was more pressing and more distressful than the last,——as much as he loved his beast, he had never a heart to refuse him; the upshot of which was generally this, that his horse was either clapped, or spavined, or greased;——or he was twitter-boned, or broken-winded, or something, in short, or other had befallen him which would let him carry no flesh;——so that he had every nine or ten months a bad horse to get rid of,——and a good horse to purchase in his stead.

What the loss in such a balance might amount to, *communibus annis,* I would leave to a special jury of sufferers in the same traffic to determine;——but let it be what it would, the honest gentleman bore it for many years without a murmur, till at length, by repeated ill accidents of the kind, he found it necessary to take the thing under consideration; and upon weighing the whole, and summing it up in his mind, he found it not only disproportioned to his other expenses, but withal so heavy an article in itself as to disable him from any other act of generosity in his parish: Besides this he considered that with half the sum thus galloped away, he could do ten times as much good;——and what still weighed more with him than all other considerations put together was this, that it confined all his charity into one particular channel, and where, as he fancied, it was the least wanted, namely, to the childbearing and child-getting part of his parish; reserving nothing for the impotent,——nothing for the aged,——nothing for the many comfortless scenes he was hourly called forth to visit, where poverty, and sickness, and affliction dwelt together.

For these reasons he resolved to discontinue the expense; and there appeared but two possible ways to extricate him clearly out of it;——and these were either to make it an irrevocable law never more to lend his steed upon any application whatever,——or else be content to ride the last poor devil, such as they had made him, with all his aches and infirmities, to the very end of the chapter.

As he dreaded his own constancy in the first,——he very cheerfully betook himself to the second; and though he could very well have explained it, as I said, to his honour,—— yet, for that very reason, he had a spirit above it; choosing rather to bear the contempt of his enemies, and the laughter of his friends, than undergo the pain of telling a story which might seem a panegyric upon himself.

I have the highest idea of the spiritual and refined sentiments of this reverend gentleman, from this single stroke in his character, which I think comes up to any of the honest refinements of the peerless knight of La Mancha, whom, by the bye, with all his follies, I love more, and would actually have gone further to have paid a visit to, than the greatest hero of antiquity.

But this is not the moral of my story: The thing I had in view was to show the temper of the world in the whole of this affair.——For you must know that so long as this explanation would have done the parson credit,——the devil a soul could find it out;——I suppose his enemies would not, and that his friends could not.——But no sooner did he bestir himself in behalf of the midwife, and pay the expenses of the ordinary's licence to set her up,——but the whole secret came out; every horse he had lost, and two horses more than ever he had lost, with all the circumstances of their destruction, were known and distinctly remembered. ——The story ran like wildfire.——"The parson had a returning fit of pride which had just seized him; and he was going to be well mounted once again in his life; and if it was so, 'twas plain as the sun at noonday, he would pocket the expense of the licence, ten times told the very first year:——so that everybody was left to judge what were his views in this act of charity."

What were his views in this, and in every other action of his life,——or rather what were the opinions which floated in the brains of other people concerning it, was a thought which too much floated in his own, and too often broke in upon his rest, when he should have been sound asleep.

About ten years ago, this gentleman had the good fortune to be made entirely easy upon that score,——it being just so long since he left his parish,——and the whole world at the same time behind him,——and stands accountable to a judge of whom he will have no cause to complain.

But there is a fatality attends the actions of some men: Order them as they will, they pass through a certain medium which so twists and refracts them from their true directions ——that, with all the titles to praise which a rectitude of heart can give, the doers of them are nevertheless forced to live and die without it.

Of the truth of which this gentleman was a painful example.——But to know by what means this came to pass, ——and to make that knowledge of use to you, I insist upon it that you read the two following chapters, which contain such a sketch of his life and conversation as will carry its moral along with it.——When this is done, if nothing stops us in our way, we will go on with the midwife.

CHAPTER XI

Yorick was this parson's name, and, what is very remarkable in it (as appears from a most ancient account of the family, wrote upon strong vellum, and now in perfect preservation), it had been exactly so spelt for near,——I was within an ace of saying nine hundred years;——but I would not shake my credit in telling an improbable truth, however indisputable in itself;——and therefore I shall content myself with only saying,——It had been exactly so spelt, without the least variation or transposition of a single letter, for I do not know how long; which is more than I would venture to say of one half of the best surnames in the kingdom; which, in a course of years, have generally undergone as many chops and changes as their owners.——Has this been owing to the pride or to the shame of the respective proprietors?——In honest truth, I think, sometimes to the one, and sometimes to the other, just as the temptation has wrought. But a villainous affair it is, and will one day so blend and confound us all together that no one shall be able to stand up and swear, "That his own great-grandfather was the man who did either this or that."

This evil had been sufficiently fenced against by the prudent care of the Yorick family, and their religious preservation of these records I quote, which do further inform us, That the family was originally of Danish extraction, and had been transplanted into England as early as in the reign of Horwendillus, King of Denmark, in whose court, it seems, an ancestor of this Mr. Yorick's, and from whom he was lineally descended, held a considerable post to the day of his death. Of what nature this considerable post was, this record saith not;——it only adds, That, for near two centuries, it had been totally abolished as altogether unnecessary, not only in that court, but in every other court of the Christian world.

It has often come into my head that this post could be no other than that of the king's chief Jester;——and that Hamlet's Yorick, in our Shakespeare, many of whose plays, you know, are founded upon authenticated facts,——was certainly the very man.

I have not the time to look into Saxo-Grammaticus's Danish history, to know the certainty of this;——but if you have leisure, and can easily get at the book, you may do it full as well yourself.

I had just time, in my travels through Denmark with Mr. Noddy's eldest son, whom, in the year 1741, I accompanied as governor, riding along with him at a prodigious rate through most parts of Europe, and of which original journey performed by us two a most delectable narrative will be given in the progress of this work. I had just time, I say, and that was all, to prove the truth of an observation made by a long sojourner in that country;——namely, "That Nature was neither very lavish, nor was she very stingy in her gifts of genius and capacity to its inhabitants;——but, like a discreet parent, was moderately kind to them all; observing such an equal tenor in the distribution of her favours as to bring them, in those points, pretty near to a level with each other; so that you will meet with few instances in that kingdom of refined parts; but a great deal of good plain household understanding amongst all ranks of people, of which everybody has a share;" which is, I think, very right.

With us, you see, the case is quite different;——we are all

26

ups and downs in this matter;———you are a great genius;———or 'tis fifty to one, Sir, you are a great dunce and a blockhead;———not that there is a total want of intermediate steps;———no,———we are not so irregular as that comes to;———but the two extremes are more common, and in a greater degree in this unsettled island, where nature, in her gifts and dispositions of this kind, is most whimsical and capricious; fortune herself not being more so in the bequest of her goods and chattels than she.

This is all that ever staggered my faith in regard to Yorick's extraction, who, by what I can remember of him, and by all the accounts I could ever get of him, seemed not to have had one single drop of Danish blood in his whole crasis; in nine hundred years, it might possibly have all run out:———I will not philosophize one moment with you about it; for happen how it would, the fact was this:———That instead of that cold phlegm and exact regularity of sense and humours you would have looked for in one so extracted, ———he was, on the contrary, as mercurial and sublimated a composition,———as heteroclite a creature in all his declensions,———with as much life and whim, and *gaieté de coeur* about him, as the kindliest climate could have engendered and put together. With all this sail, poor Yorick carried not one ounce of ballast; he was utterly unpractised in the world; and, at the age of twenty-six, knew just about as well how to steer his course in it as a romping, unsuspicious girl of thirteen: So that upon his first setting out, the brisk gale of his spirits, as you will imagine, ran him foul ten times in a day of somebody's tackling; and as the grave and more slow-paced were oftenest in his way,——— you may likewise imagine 'twas with such he had generally the ill luck to get the most entangled. For aught I know there might be some mixture of unlucky wit at the bottom of such *Fracas:*———For, to speak the truth, Yorick had an invincible dislike and opposition in his nature to gravity; ———not to gravity as such,———for where gravity was wanted, he would be the most grave or serious of mortal men for days and weeks together;———but he was an enemy to the affectation of it, and declared open war against it, only as it appeared a cloak for ignorance, or for folly; and then, whenever it fell in his way, however sheltered and protected, he seldom gave it much quarter.

Sometimes, in his wild way of talking, he would say, That gravity was an errant scoundrel; and he would add,———of the most dangerous kind too,———because a sly one; and that, he verily believed, more honest, well-meaning people were bubbled out of their goods and money by it in one twelvemonth, than by pocket-picking and shoplifting in seven. In the naked temper which a merry heart discovered, he would say, There was no danger,——but to itself:—— whereas the very essence of gravity was design, and consequently deceit;——'twas a taught trick to gain credit of the world for more sense and knowledge than a man was worth; and that, with all its pretensions,——it was no better, but often worse, than what a French wit had long ago defined it,——*viz., A mysterious carriage of the body to cover the defects of the mind;*——which definition of gravity, Yorick, with great imprudence, would say, deserved to be wrote in letters of gold.

But, in plain truth, he was a man unhackneyed and unpractised in the world, and was altogether as indiscreet and foolish on every other subject of discourse where policy is wont to impress restraint. Yorick had no impression but one, and that was what arose from the nature of the deed spoken of; which impression he would usually translate into plain English without any periphrasis,——and too oft without much distinction of either personage, time, or place;——so that when mention was made of a pitiful or an ungenerous proceeding,——he never gave himself a moment's time to reflect who was the Hero of the piece,——what his station, ——or how far he had power to hurt him hereafter;——but if it was a dirty action,——without more ado,——The man was a dirty fellow,——and so on:——And as his comments had usually the ill fate to be terminated either in a *bon mot,* or to be enlivened throughout with some drollery or humour of expression, it gave wings to Yorick's indiscretion. In a word, though he never sought, yet, at the same time, as he seldom shunned occasions of saying what came uppermost, and without much ceremony;——he had but too many temptations in life of scattering his wit and his humour,——his gibes and his jests about him.——They were not lost for want of gathering.

What were the consequences, and what was Yorick's catastrophe thereupon, you will read in the next chapter.

CHAPTER XII

The *Mortgager* and *Mortgagee* differ the one from the other not more in length of purse, than the *Jester* and *Jestee* do in that of memory. But in this the comparison between them runs, as the scholiasts call it, upon all four; which, by the bye, is upon one or two legs more than some of the best of Homer's can pretend to;——namely, That the one raises a sum and the other a laugh at your expense, and think no more about it. Interest, however, still runs on in both cases; ——the periodical or accidental payments of it just serving to keep the memory of the affair alive; till, at length, in some evil hour,——pop comes the creditor upon each, and by demanding principal upon the spot, together with full interest to the very day, makes them both feel the full extent of their obligations.

As the reader (for I hate your *ifs*) has a thorough knowledge of human nature, I need not say more to satisfy him that my Hero could not go on at this rate without some slight experience of these incidental mementos. To speak the truth, he had wantonly involved himself in a multitude of small book debts of this stamp, which, notwithstanding Eugenius's frequent advice, he too much disregarded; thinking that as not one of them was contracted through any malignancy,——but, on the contrary, from an honesty of mind, and a mere jocundity of humour, they would all of them be crossed out in course.

Eugenius would never admit this; and would often tell him that one day or other he would certainly be reckoned with; and he would often add, in an accent of sorrowful apprehension,——to the uttermost mite. To which Yorick, with his usual carelessness of heart, would as often answer with a pshaw!——and if the subject was started in the fields, ——with a hop, skip, and a jump at the end of it; but if close pent up in the social chimney corner, where the culprit was barricadoed in with a table and a couple of armchairs, and could not so readily fly off in a tangent,——Eugenius would then go on with his lecture upon discretion, in words to this purpose, though somewhat better put together.

Trust me, dear Yorick, this unwary pleasantry of thine will

sooner or later bring thee into scrapes and difficulties which no afterwit can extricate thee out of.——In these sallies, too oft, I see, it happens that a person laughed at considers himself in the light of a person injured, with all the rights of such a situation belonging to him; and when thou viewest him in that light too, and reckons up his friends, his family, his kindred and allies,——and musters up with them the many recruits which will list under him from a sense of common danger;——'tis no extravagant arithmetic to say that for every ten jokes,——thou hast got a hundred enemies; and till thou hast gone on, and raised a swarm of wasps about thy ears, and art half stung to death by them, thou wilt never be convinced it is so.

I cannot suspect it, in the man whom I esteem, that there is the least spur from spleen or malevolence of intent in these sallies.——I believe and know them to be truly honest and sportive:——But consider, my dear lad, that fools cannot distinguish this,——and that knaves will not; and thou knowest not what it is either to provoke the one, or to make merry with the other;——whenever they associate for mutual defence, depend upon it, they will carry on the war in such a manner against thee, my dear friend, as to make thee heartily sick of it, and of thy life too.

REVENGE from some baneful corner shall level a tale of dishonour at thee, which no innocence of heart or integrity of conduct shall set right.——The fortunes of thy house shall totter,——thy character, which led the way to them, shall bleed on every side of it,——thy faith questioned, ——thy works belied,——thy wit forgotten,——thy learning trampled on. To wind up the last scene of thy tragedy, CRUELTY and COWARDICE, twin ruffians, hired and set on by MALICE in the dark, shall strike together at all thy infirmities and mistakes:——the best of us, my dear lad, lie open there,——and trust me,——trust me, Yorick, *When, to gratify a private appetite, it is once resolved upon that an innocent and an helpless creature shall be sacrificed, 'tis an easy matter to pick up sticks enough from any thicket where it has strayed, to make a fire to offer it up with.*

Yorick scarce ever heard this sad vaticination of his destiny read over to him but with a tear stealing from his eye, and a promissory look attending it that he was resolved, for the time to come, to ride his tit with more sobriety.——But, alas, too late!——a grand confederacy, with ***** and ***** at the head of it, was formed before the first prediction of it.——The whole plan of the attack, just as Eugenius had

30

foreboded, was put in execution all at once,——with so little mercy on the side of the allies,——and so little suspicion in Yorick of what was carrying on against him,—— that when he thought, good easy man! full surely preferment was o' ripening,——they had smote his root, and then he fell, as many a worthy man had fallen before him.

Yorick, however, fought it out with all imaginable gallantry for some time; till, overpowered by numbers, and worn out at length by the calamities of the war,——but more so by the ungenerous manner in which it was carried on,——he threw down the sword; and though he kept up his spirits in appearance to the last,——he died, nevertheless, as was generally thought, quite brokenhearted.

What inclined Eugenius to the same opinion was as follows:

A few hours before Yorick breathed his last, Eugenius stept in with an intent to take his last sight and last farewell of him: Upon his drawing Yorick's curtain, and asking how he felt himself, Yorick, looking up in his face, took hold of his hand,——and, after thanking him for the many tokens of his friendship to him, for which, he said, if it was their fate to meet hereafter,——he would thank him again and again,——he told him he was within a few hours of giving his enemies the slip forever.——I hope not, answered Eugenius, with tears trickling down his cheeks, and with the tenderest tone that ever man spoke,——I hope not, Yorick, said he.——Yorick replied with a look up, and a gentle squeeze of Eugenius's hand, and that was all,——but it cut Eugenius to his heart.——Come,——come, Yorick, quoth Eugenius, wiping his eyes, and summoning up the man within him,——my dear lad, be comforted,——let not all thy spirits and fortitude forsake thee at this crisis when thou most wants them;——who knows what resources are in store, and what the power of God may yet do for thee?——Yorick laid his hand upon his heart, and gently shook his head;—— for my part, continued Eugenius, crying bitterly as he uttered the words,——I declare I know not, Yorick, how to part with thee,——and would gladly flatter my hopes, added Eugenius, cheering up his voice, that there is still enough left of thee to make a bishop,——and that I may live to see it.——I beseech thee, Eugenius, quoth Yorick, taking off his nightcap as well as he could with his left hand,——his right being still grasped close in that of Eugenius,——I beseech thee to take a view of my head.——I see nothing that ails it, replied Eugenius. Then, alas! my friend, said Yorick, let me tell you that 'tis so bruised and misshapened with the blows which ***** and *****, and some others, have so unhandsomely given me in the dark, that I might say with Sancho Panza that should I recover, and "Mitres thereupon be suffered to rain down from heaven as thick as hail, not one of 'em would fit it."——Yorick's last breath was hanging upon his trembling lips ready to depart as he uttered this:——yet still it was uttered with something of a Cervantic tone;——and as he spoke it, Eugenius could perceive a stream of lambent fire lighted up for a moment in his eyes;——faint picture of those flashes of his spirit which (as Shakespeare said of his ancestor) were wont to set the table in a roar!

Eugenius was convinced from this that the heart of his friend was broke; he squeezed his hand,——and then walked softly out of the room, weeping as he walked. Yorick followed Eugenius with his eyes to the door,——he then closed them,——and never opened them more.

He lies buried in a corner of his churchyard, in the parish of ————, under a plain marble slab, which his friend Eugenius, by leave of his executors, laid upon his grave, with no more than these three words of inscription serving both for his epitaph and elegy.

Alas, poor YORICK!

Ten times in a day has Yorick's ghost the consolation to hear his monumental inscription read over with such a variety of plaintive tones as denote a general pity and esteem for him;——a footway crossing the churchyard close by the side of his grave,——not a passenger goes by without stopping to cast a look upon it,——and sighing as he walks on,

Alas, poor Y O R I C K !

CHAPTER XIII

It is so long since the reader of this rhapsodical work has been parted from the midwife, that it is high time to mention her again to him, merely to put him in mind that there is such a body still in the world, and whom, upon the best judgment I can form upon my own plan at present,——I am going to introduce to him for good and all: But as fresh matter may be started, and much unexpected business fall out betwixt the reader and myself, which may require immediate dispatch,——'twas right to take care that the poor woman should not be lost in the meantime;——because when she is wanted, we can no way do without her.

I think I told you that this good woman was a person of no small note and consequence throughout our whole village and township;——that her fame has spread itself to the very outedge and circumference of that circle of importance of which kind every soul living, whether he has a shirt to his back or no,——has one surrounding him;——which said circle, by the way, whenever 'tis said that such a one is of great weight and importance in the *world*,——I desire may be enlarged or contracted in your Worship's fancy, in a compound ratio of the station, profession, knowledge, abilities, height, and depth (measuring both ways) of the personage brought before you.

In the present case, if I remember, I fixed it at about four or five miles, which not only comprehended the whole parish, but extended itself to two or three of the adjacent hamlets in the skirts of the next parish; which made a considerable thing of it. I must add, That she was, moreover, very well looked on at one large grange house and some other odd houses and farms within two or three miles, as I said, from the smoke of her own chimney:——But I must here, once for all, inform you that all this will be more exactly delineated and explained in a map, now in the hands of the engraver, which, with many other pieces and developments to this work, will be added to the end of the twentieth volume,——not to swell the work,——I detest the thought of such a thing,——but by way of commentary, scholium, illustration, and key to such passages, incidents, or innuendos as shall be thought to be either of private interpretation or of dark or doubtful meaning after my life and my opinions shall have been read over (now don't forget the meaning of the word) by all the *world;*——which, betwixt you and me, and in spite of all the gentlemen reviewers in Great Britain, and of all that their Worships shall undertake to write or say to the contrary,——I am determined shall be the case.——I need not tell your Worship that all this is spoke in confidence.

CHAPTER XIV

Upon looking into my mother's marriage settlement, in order to satisfy myself and reader in a point necessary to be cleared up before we could proceed any further in this history,——I had the good fortune to pop upon the very thing I wanted before I had read a day and a half straight forwards;——it might have taken me up a month;——which shows plainly that when a man sits down to write a history, ——though it be but the history of Jack Hickathrift or Tom Thumb, he knows no more than his heels what lets and confounded hinderances he is to meet with in his way,——or what a dance he may be led, by one excursion or another, before all is over. Could a historiographer drive on his history, as a muleteer drives on his mule,——straight forwards, ——for instance, from Rome all the way to Loreto, without ever once turning his head aside either to the right hand or to the left,——he might venture to foretell you to an hour when he should get to his journey's end;——but the thing is, morally speaking, impossible: For, if he is a man of the least spirit, he will have fifty deviations from a straight line to make with this or that party as he goes along, which he can no ways avoid. He will have views and prospects to himself perpetually soliciting his eye, which he can no more help standing still to look at than he can fly; he will moreover have various

Accounts to reconcile:
Anecdotes to pick up:
Inscriptions to make out:
Stories to weave in:
Traditions to sift:

Personages to call upon:

Panegyrics to paste up at this door:

Pasquinades at that:——All which both the man and his mule are quite exempt from. To sum up all; there are archives at every stage to be looked into, and rolls, records, documents, and endless genealogies, which justice ever and anon calls him back to stay the reading of:——In short, there is no end of it;——for my own part, I declare I have been at it these six weeks, making all the speed I possibly could,——and am not yet born:——I have just been able, and that's all, to tell you *when* it happened, but not *how;*——so that you see the thing is yet far from being accomplished.

These unforeseen stoppages, which I own I had no conception of when I first set out,——but which, I am convinced now, will rather increase than diminish as I advance,——have struck out a hint which I am resolved to follow;——and that is,——not to be in a hurry,——but to go on leisurely, writing and publishing two volumes of my life every year;——which, if I am suffered to go on quietly, and can make a tolerable bargain with my bookseller, I shall continue to do as long as I live.

CHAPTER XV

The article in my mother's marriage settlement which I told the reader I was at the pains to search for, and which, now that I have found it, I think proper to lay before him,——is so much more fully expressed in the deed itself than ever I can pretend to do it, that it would be barbarity to take it out of the lawyer's hand:——It is as follows.

"𝕬𝖓𝖉 𝖙𝖍𝖎𝖘 𝕴𝖓𝖉𝖊𝖓𝖙𝖚𝖗𝖊 𝖋𝖚𝖗𝖙𝖍𝖊𝖗 𝖜𝖎𝖙𝖓𝖊𝖘𝖘𝖊𝖙𝖍, That the said Walter Shandy, merchant, in consideration of the said intended marriage to be had, and, by God's blessing, to be well and truly solemnized and consummated between the said Walter Shandy and Elizabeth Mollineux aforesaid, and divers other good and valuable causes and considerations him thereunto specially moving,——doth grant, covenant, condescend, consent, conclude, bargain, and fully agree to and with John Dixon and James Turner, Esqrs., the above-named trustees, &c., &c.——to wit,——That in case it should hereafter so fall out, chance, happen, or otherwise come to pass,——That the said Walter Shandy, merchant, shall have left off business before the time, or times, that the said Elizabeth Mollineux shall, according to the course of nature, or otherwise, have left off bearing and bringing forth children;——and that, in consequence of the said Walter Shandy having so left off business, he shall, in despite, and against the free will, consent, and good-liking of the said Elizabeth Mollineux,——make a departure from the city of London, in order to retire to, and dwell upon, his estate at Shandy Hall, in the county of ——, or at any other country seat, castle, hall, mansion house, messuage, or grange house now purchased, or hereafter to be purchased, or upon any part or parcel thereof:——That then, and as often as the said Elizabeth Mollineux shall happen to be *enceinte* with child or children severally and lawfully begot, or to be begotten, upon the body of the said Elizabeth Mollineux during her said coverture,——he the said Walter Shandy shall, at his own proper cost and charges, and out of his own proper monies, upon good and reasonable notice, which is hereby agreed to be within six weeks of her the said Elizabeth Mollineux's full reckoning, or time of supposed and computed delivery,——pay, or cause to be paid, the sum of one hundred and twenty pounds of good and lawful money to John Dixon and James Turner, Esqrs., or assigns,——upon TRUST and confidence, and for and unto the use and uses, intent, end, and purpose following:——That is to say, That the said sum of one hundred and twenty pounds shall be paid into the hands of the said Elizabeth Mollineux, or to be otherwise applied by them the said trustees, for the well and truly hiring of one coach, with able and sufficient horses, to carry and convey the body of the said Elizabeth Mollineux and the child or children which she shall be then and there *enceinte* and pregnant with,——unto the city of London; and for the further paying and defraying of all other incidental costs, charges, and expenses whatsoever,——in and about, and for, and relating to her said intended delivery and lying in, in the said city or suburbs thereof. And that the said Elizabeth Mollineux shall and may, from time to time, and at all such time and times as are here convenanted and agreed upon,——peaceably and quietly hire the said coach and horses, and have free ingress, egress, and regress throughout her journey, in and from the said coach, according to the tenor, true intent, and meaning of these presents, without any let, suit, trouble, disturbance, molestation, discharge, hinderance, forfeiture, eviction, vexation, interruption, or encumbrance whatsoever.——And that it shall moreover be lawful to and for the said Elizabeth Mollineux, from time to time, and as oft or often as she shall well and truly be advanced in her said pregnancy, to the time heretofore stipulated and agreed upon,——to live and reside in such place or places, and in such family or families, and with such relations, friends, and other persons within the said city of London, as she, at her own will and pleasure, notwithstanding her present coverture, and as if she was a *femme sole* and unmarried,——shall think fit.—— 𝔄𝔫𝔡 𝔱𝔥𝔦𝔰 𝔍𝔫𝔡𝔢𝔫𝔱𝔲𝔯𝔢 𝔣𝔲𝔯𝔱𝔥𝔢𝔯 𝔴𝔦𝔱𝔫𝔢𝔰𝔰𝔢𝔱𝔥, That for the most effectually carrying of the said covenant into execution, the said Walter Shandy, merchant, doth hereby grant, bargain, sell, release, and confirm unto the said John Dixon and James Turner, Esqrs., their heirs, executors, and assigns, in their actual possession now being, by virtue of an indenture of bargain and sale for a year to them the said John Dixon and James Turner, Esqrs., by him the said Walter Shandy, merchant, thereof made; which said bargain and sale for a year bears date the day next before the date of these presents, and by force and virtue of the statute for transferring of uses into possession,——𝔄𝔩𝔩 that the manor and lordship of Shandy in the county of ———, with all the rights, members, and appurtenances thereof; and all and every the messuages, houses, buildings, barns, stables, orchards, gardens, backsides, tofts, crofts, garths, cottages, lands, meadows, feedings, pastures, marshes, commons, woods, underwoods, drains, fisheries, waters, and watercourses;——together with all rents, reversions, services, annuities, fee farms, knight's fees, views of frankpledge, escheats, reliefs, mines, quarries, goods and chattels of felons and fugitives, felons of themselves, and put in exigent, deodands, free warrens, and all other royalties and seigniories, rights and jurisdictions, privileges and hereditaments whatsoever.——𝔄𝔫𝔡 𝔞𝔩𝔰𝔬 the advowson, donation, presentation, and free disposition of the rectory or parsonage of Shandy aforesaid, and all and every the tenths, tithes, glebe lands"——In three words,——"My mother was to lay in (if she chose it) in London."

But in order to put a stop to the practise of any unfair play on the part of my mother, which a marriage article of this nature too manifestly opened a door to, and which indeed had never been thought of at all, but for my uncle Toby Shandy,——a clause was added in security of my

father, which was this:———"That in case my mother hereafter should, at any time, put my father to the trouble and
expense of a London journey upon false cries and tokens,
———that for every such instance she should forfeit all the
right and title which the covenant gave her to the next turn;
———but to no more,———and so on, *toties quoties,* in as ef-
fectual a manner as if such a covenant betwixt them had not
been made."———This, by the way, was no more than what was
reasonable;———and yet, as reasonable as it was, I have ever
thought it hard that the whole weight of the article should
have fallen entirely, as it did, upon myself.

But I was begot and born to misfortunes;———for my poor
mother, whether it was wind or water,———or a compound of
both,———or neither;———or whether it was simply the mere
swell of imagination and fancy in her;———or how far a
strong wish and desire to have it so might mislead her judgment;———in short, whether she was deceived or deceiving
in this matter, it no way becomes me to decide. The fact was
this, That, in the latter end of September, 1717, which was
the year before I was born, my mother having carried my
father up to town much against the grain,———he peremptorily insisted upon the clause;———so that I was doomed,
by marriage articles, to have my nose squeezed as flat to
my face as if the destinies had actually spun me without one.

How this event came about,———and what a train of vexatious disappointments, in one stage or other of my life, have
pursued me from the mere loss, or rather compression, of
this one single member,———shall be laid before the reader all
in due time.

CHAPTER XVI

My father, as anybody may naturally imagine, came down
with my mother into the country in but a pettish kind of a
humour. The first twenty or five-and-twenty miles he did
nothing in the world but fret and tease himself, and indeed
my mother too, about the cursed expense, which he said
might every shilling of it have been saved;———then what
vexed him more than everything else was the provoking time
of the year,———which, as I told you, was towards the end

of September, when his wall fruit, and greengages especially, in which he was very curious, were just ready for pulling: ——"Had he been whistled up to London upon a Tom Fool's errand in any other month of the whole year, he should not have said three words about it."

For the next two whole stages, no subject would go down but the heavy blow he had sustained from the loss of a son, whom it seems he had fully reckoned upon in his mind, and registered down in his pocketbook, as a second staff for his old age, in case Bobby should fail him. "The disappointment of this," he said, "was ten times more to a wise man than all the money which the journey, &c., had cost him, put together;——rot the hundred and twenty pounds,——he did not mind it a rush."

From Stilton all the way to Grantham, nothing in the whole affair provoked him so much as the condolences of his friends, and the foolish figure they should both make at church the first Sunday;——of which, in the satirical vehemence of his wit, now sharpened a little by vexation, he would give so many humorous and provoking descriptions, ——and place his rib and self in so many tormenting lights and attitudes in the face of the whole congregation,——that my mother declared these two stages were so truly tragicomical that she did nothing but laugh and cry in a breath, from one end to the other of them all the way.

From Grantham till they had crossed the Trent, my father was out of all kind of patience at the vile trick and imposition which he fancied my mother had put upon him in this affair. ——"Certainly," he would say to himself, over and over again, "the woman could not be deceived herself;——if she could,——what weakness!"——tormenting word! which led his imagination a thorny dance, and, before all was over, played the deuce and all with him;——for sure as ever the word *weakness* was uttered, and struck full upon his brain, ——so sure it set him upon running divisions upon how many kinds of weaknesses there were;——that there was such a thing as weakness of the body,——as well as weakness of the mind,——and then he would do nothing but syllogize within himself for a stage or two together, How far the cause of all these vexations might, or might not, have arisen out of himself.

In short, he had so many little subjects of disquietude springing out of this one affair, all fretting successively in his mind as they rose up in it, that my mother, whatever was her journey up, had but an uneasy journey of it down.

———In a word, as she complained to my uncle Toby, he would have tired out the patience of any flesh alive.

CHAPTER XVII

Though my father travelled homewards, as I told you, in none of the best of moods,———pshawing and pishing all the way down,———yet he had the complaisance to keep the worst part of the story still to himself;———which was the resolution he had taken of doing himself the justice which my uncle Toby's clause in the marriage settlement empowered him; nor was it till the very night in which I was begot, which was thirteen months after, that she had the least intimation of his design; when my father, happening, as you remember, to be a little chagrined and out of temper, ———took occasion as they lay chatting gravely in bed afterwards, talking over what was to come,———to let her know that she must accommodate herself as well as she could to the bargain made between them in their marriage deeds; which was to lie in of her next child in the country to balance the last year's journey.

My father was a gentleman of many virtues,———but he had a strong spice of that in his temper which might, or might not, add to the number.———'Tis known by the name of perseverance in a good cause,———and of obstinacy in a bad one: Of this my mother had so much knowledge that she knew 'twas to no purpose to make any remonstrance,———so she e'en resolved to sit down quietly, and make the most of it.

CHAPTER XVIII

As the point was that night agreed, or rather determined, that my mother should lie in of me in the country, she took her measures accordingly; for which purpose, when she was three days, or thereabouts, gone with child, she began to cast her eyes upon the midwife, whom you have so often heard me mention; and before the week was well got round, as the famous Dr. Maningham was not to be had, she had come to a final determination in her mind,——notwithstanding there was a scientific operator within so near a call as eight miles of us, and who, moreover, had expressly wrote a five-shilling book upon the subject of midwifery, in which he had exposed not only the blunders of the sisterhood itself, ——but had likewise superadded many curious improvements for the quicker extraction of the foetus in cross births, and some other cases of danger which belay us in getting into the world; notwithstanding all this, my mother, I say, was absolutely determined to trust her life, and mine with it, into no soul's hand but this old woman's only.——Now this I like;——when we cannot get at the very thing we wish, ——never to take up with the next best in degree to it;—— no; that's pitiful beyond description;——it is no more than a week from this very day in which I am now writing this book for the edification of the world,——which is March 9, 1759, ——that my dear, dear Jenny, observing I looked a little grave, as she stood cheapening a silk of five-and-twenty shillings a yard,——told the mercer she was sorry she had given him so much trouble;——and immediately went and bought herself a yard-wide stuff of tenpence a yard.——'Tis the duplication of one and the same greatness of soul; only what lessened the honour of it somewhat, in my mother's case, was that she could not heroine it into so violent and hazardous an extreme as one in her situation might have wished, because the old midwife had really some little claim to be depended upon;——as much, at least, as success could give her; having, in the course of her practice of near twenty years in the parish, brought every mother's son of them into the world without any one slip or accident which could fairly be laid to her account.

These facts, though they had their weight, yet did not altogether satisfy some few scruples and uneasinesses which hung upon my father's spirits in relation to this choice.—— To say nothing of the natural workings of humanity and justice,——or of the yearnings of parental and connubial love, all which prompted him to leave as little to hazard as possible in a case of this kind;——he felt himself concerned in a particular manner that all should go right in the present case,——from the accumulated sorrow he lay open to, should any evil betide his wife and child in lying in at Shandy Hall.——He knew the world judged by events, and would add to his afflictions in such a misfortune by loading him with the whole blame of it.——"Alas o' day;——had Mrs. Shandy, poor gentlewoman! had but her wish in going up to town just to lie in and come down again;——which, they say, she begged and prayed for upon her bare knees, ——and which, in my opinion, considering the fortune which Mr. Shandy got with her,——was no such mighty matter to have complied with, the lady and her babe might both of 'em have been alive at this hour."

This exclamation, my father knew, was unanswerable;—— and yet, it was not merely to shelter himself,——nor was it altogether for the care of his offspring and wife that he seemed so extremely anxious about this point;——my father had extensive views of things,——and stood, moreover, as he thought, deeply concerned in it for the public good, from the dread he entertained of the bad uses an ill-fated instance might be put to.

He was very sensible that all political writers upon the subject had unanimously agreed and lamented, from the beginning of Queen Elizabeth's reign down to his own time, that the current of men and money towards the metropolis, upon one frivolous errand or another,——set in so strong, ——as to become dangerous to our civil rights;——though, by the bye,——a *current* was not the image he took most delight in,——a *distemper* was here his favourite metaphor, and he would run it down into a perfect allegory, by maintaining it was identically the same in the body national as in the body natural, where blood and spirits were driven up into the head faster than they could find their ways down; ——a stoppage of circulation must ensue, which was death in both cases.

There was little danger, he would say, of losing our liberties by French politics or French invasions;——nor was he so much in pain of a consumption from the mass of corrupted matter and ulcerated humours in our constitution, ——which he hoped was not so bad as it was imagined;—— but he verily feared that in some violent push, we should go off, all at once, in a state apoplexy;——and then he would say, *The Lord have mercy upon us all.*

My father was never able to give the history of this distemper,——without the remedy along with it.

"Was I an absolute prince," he would say, pulling up his breeches with both his hands, as he rose from his armchair, "I would appoint able judges at every avenue of my metropolis, who should take cognizance of every fool's business who came there;——and if, upon a fair and candid hearing, it appeared not of weight sufficient to leave his own home, and come up, bag and baggage, with his wife and children, farmers' sons, &c., &c., at his backside, they should be all sent back, from constable to constable, like vagrants as they were, to the place of their legal settlements. By this means I shall take care that my metropolis tottered not through its own weight;——that the head be no longer too big for the body;——that the extremes, now wasted and pined in, be restored to their due share of nourishment, and regain, with it, their natural strength and beauty:——I would effectually provide, That the meadows and cornfields of my dominions should laugh and sing;——that good cheer and hospitality flourish once more;——and that such weight and influence be put thereby into the hands of the Squirality of my kingdom, as should counterpoise what I perceive my Nobility are now taking from them.

"Why are there so few palaces and gentlemen's seats," he would ask, with some emotion, as he walked across the room, "throughout so many delicious provinces in France? Whence is it that the few remaining *Châteaus* amongst them are so dismantled,——so unfurnished, and in so ruinous and desolate a condition?——Because, Sir," he would say, "in that kingdom no man has any country interest to support; ——the little interest of any kind which any man has any-where in it is concentrated in the court, and the looks of the Grand Monarch; by the sunshine of whose countenance, or the clouds which pass across it, every Frenchman lives or dies."

Another political reason which prompted my father so strongly to guard against the least evil accident in my mother's lying in in the country——was, That any such instance would infallibly throw a balance of power, too great already, into the weaker vessels of the gentry, in his own or higher stations;——which, with the many other usurped rights which that part of the constitution was hourly establishing,——would, in the end, prove fatal to the monarchical system of domestic government established in the first creation of things by God.

In this point he was entirely of Sir Robert Filmer's opinion, That the plans and institutions of the greatest monarchies in the eastern parts of the world were, originally, all stolen from that admirable pattern and prototype of this household and paternal power;——which, for a century, he said, ? more, had gradually been degenerating away into a ?

45

government;———the form of which, however desirable in great combinations of the species,———was very troublesome in small ones,———and seldom produced anything, that he saw, but sorrow and confusion.

For all these reasons, private and public, put together,——— my father was for having the man midwife by all means,——— my mother by no means. My father begged and intreated she would for once recede from her prerogative in this matter, and suffer him to choose for her;———my mother, on the contrary, insisted upon her privilege in this matter to choose for herself,———and have no mortal's help but the old woman's.———What could my father do? He was almost at his wit's end;———talked it over with her in all moods;——— placed his arguments in all lights;———argued the matter with her like a Christian,———like a heathen,———like a husband,———like a father,———like a patriot,———like a man:——— My mother answered everything only like a woman; which was a little hard upon her;———for as she could not assume and fight it out behind such a variety of characters,——— 'twas no fair match;———'twas seven to one.———What could my mother do?———She had the advantage (otherwise she had been certainly overpowered) of a small reinforcement of chagrin personal at the bottom which bore her up, and enabled her to dispute the affair with my father with so equal an advantage,———that both sides sung *Te Deum*. In a word, my mother was to have the old woman,———and the operator was to have licence to drink a bottle of wine with my father and my uncle Toby Shandy in the back parlour, ———for which he was to be paid five guineas.

I must beg leave, before I finish this chapter, to enter a caveat in the breast of my fair reader;———and it is this:——— Not to take it absolutely for granted from an unguarded word or two which I have dropped in it,———"That I am a married man."———I own the tender appellation of my dear, dear Jenny,———with some other strokes of conjugal knowledge, interspersed here and there, might, naturally enough, have misled the most candid judge in the world into such a determination against me.———All I plead for, in this case, Madam, is strict justice, and that you do so much of it, to me as well as to yourself,———as not to prejudice or receive ession of me till you have better evidence than , at present, can be produced against me:——— be so vain or unreasonable, Madam, as to de-ld therefore think that my dear, dear Jenny is tress;———no,———that would be flattering my

46

character in the other extreme, and giving it an air of freedom which, perhaps, it has no kind of right to. All I contend for is the utter impossibility, for some volumes, that you, or the most penetrating spirit upon earth, should know how this matter really stands.——It is not impossible but that my dear, dear Jenny! tender as the appellation is, may be my child.——Consider,——I was born in the year Eighteen.—— Nor is there anything unnatural or extravagant in the supposition that my dear Jenny may be my friend.——Friend! ——My friend.——Surely, Madam, a friendship between the two sexes may subsist, and be supported without———Fie! Mr. Shandy:——Without anything, Madam, but that tender and delicious sentiment which ever mixes in friendship, where there is a difference of sex. Let me intreat you to study the pure and sentimental parts of the best French Romances;——it will really, Madam, astonish you to see with what a variety of chaste expression this delicious sentiment, which I have the honour to speak of, is dressed out.

CHAPTER XIX

I would sooner undertake to explain the hardest problem in Geometry than pretend to account for it that a gentleman of my father's great good sense,——knowing, as the reader must have observed him, and curious too in philosophy,—— wise also in political reasoning,——and in polemical (as he will find) no way ignorant,——could be capable of entertaining a notion in his head so out of the common track,—— that I fear the reader, when I come to mention it to him, if he is the least of a choleric temper, will immediately throw the book by; if mercurial, he will laugh most heartily at it;——and if he is of a grave and saturnine cast, he will, at first sight, absolutely condemn as fanciful and extravagant; and that was in respect to the choice and imposition of Christian names, on which he thought a great deal more depended than what superficial minds were capable of conceiving.

His opinion in this matter was, That there was a strange kind of magic bias, which good or bad names, as he called them, irresistibly impressed upon our characters and conduct.

The Hero of Cervantes argued not the point with more seriousness,——nor had he more faith,——or more to say on the powers of Necromancy in dishonouring his deeds,—— or on DULCINEA's name in shedding lustre upon them, than my father had on those of TRISMEGISTUS or ARCHIMEDES on the one hand,——or of NYKY and SIMKIN on the other. How many CAESARS and POMPEYS, he would say, by mere inspiration of the names, have been rendered worthy of them? And how many, he would add, are there who might have done exceeding well in the world, had not their characters and spirits been totally depressed and NICODEMUSED into nothing.

I see plainly, Sir, by your looks (or as the case happened, my father would say),——that you do not heartily subscribe to this opinion of mine,——which to those, he would add, who have not carefully sifted it to the bottom,——I own has an air more of fancy than of solid reasoning in it;—— and yet, my dear Sir, if I may presume to know your character, I am morally assured I should hazard little in stating a case to you,——not as a party in the dispute,——but as a judge, and trusting my appeal upon it to your own good sense and candid disquisition in this matter;——you are a person free from as many narrow prejudices of education as most men;——and, if I may presume to penetrate further into you,——of a liberality of genius above bearing down an opinion, merely because it wants friends. Your son!—— your dear son,——from whose sweet and open temper you have so much to expect.——Your BILLY, Sir!——would you, for the world, have called him JUDAS?——Would you, my dear Sir, he would say, laying his hand upon your breast, with the genteelest address,——and in that soft and irresistible *piano* of voice which the nature of the *argumentum ad hominem* absolutely requires,——Would you, Sir, if a Jew of a godfather had proposed the name for your child, and offered you his purse along with it, would you have consented to such a desecration of him?——O my God! he would say, looking up, if I know your temper right, Sir,——you are incapable of it;——you would have trampled upon the offer; ——you would have thrown the temptation at the tempter's head with abhorrence.

Your greatness of mind in this action, which I admire, with that generous contempt of money which you show me in the whole transaction, is really noble;——and what renders it more so is the principle of it;——the workings of a parent's love upon the truth and conviction of this very hypothesis,

48

namely, That was your son called JUDAS,——the sordid and treacherous idea so inseparable from the name would have accompanied him through life like his shadow, and, in the end, made a miser and a rascal of him, in spite, Sir, of your example.

I never knew a man able to answer this argument.——But, indeed, to speak of my father as he was,——he was certainly irresistible, both in his orations and disputations;——he was born an orator:——Θεοδίδακτος.——Persuasion hung upon his lips, and the elements of Logic and Rhetoric were so blended up in him,——and, withal, he had so shrewd a guess at the weaknesses and passions of his respondent,——that NATURE might have stood up and said,——"This man is eloquent." In short, whether he was on the weak or the strong side of the question, 'twas hazardous in either case to attack him:——And yet, 'tis strange, he had never read Cicero nor Quintilian *de Oratore,* nor Isocrates, nor Aristotle, nor Longinus amongst the ancients;——nor Vossius, nor Skioppius, nor Ramus, nor Farnaby amongst the moderns;——and what is more astonishing, he had never in his whole life the least light or spark of subtilty struck into his mind, by one single lecture upon Crackenthorp or Burgersdicius, or any Dutch logician or commentator;——he knew not so much as in what the difference of an argument *ad ignorantiam* and an argument *ad hominem* consisted; so that I well remember, when he went up along with me to enter my name at Jesus College in ****,——it was a matter of just wonder with my worthy tutor, and two or three fellows of that learned society,——that a man who knew not so much as the names of his tools should be able to work after that fashion with 'em.

To work with them in the best manner he could was what my father was, however, perpetually forced upon;——for he had a thousand little sceptical notions of the comic kind to defend,——most of which notions, I verily believe, at first entered upon the footing of mere whims, and of a *vive la Bagatelle;* and as such he would make merry with them for half an hour or so, and having sharpened his wit upon 'em, dismiss them till another day.

I mention this not only as matter of hypothesis or conjecture upon the progress and establishment of my father's many odd opinions,——but as a warning to the learned reader against the indiscreet reception of such guests who, after a free and undisturbed entrance, for some years, into our brains,——at length claim a kind of settlement there,

49

———working sometimes like yeast;———but more generally after the manner of the gentle passion, beginning in jest,——— but ending in downright earnest.

Whether this was the case of the singularity of my father's notions,———or that his judgment, at length, became the dupe of his wit;———or how far, in many of his notions, he might, though odd, be absolutely right;———the reader, as he comes at them, shall decide. All that I maintain here is that in this one, of the influence of Christian names, however it gained footing, he was serious;———he was all uniformity;———he was systematical, and, like all systematic reasoners, he would move both heaven and earth, and twist and torture everything in nature to support his hypothesis. In a word, I repeat it over again;———he was serious;———and, in consequence of it, he would lose all kind of patience whenever he saw people, especially of condition, who should have known better,———as careless and as indifferent about the name they imposed upon their child,———or more so, than in the choice of *Ponto* or *Cupid* for their puppy dog.

This, he would say, looked ill;———and had, moreover, this particular aggravation in it, *viz.*, That when once a vile name was wrongfully or injudiciously given, 'twas not like the case of a man's character, which, when wronged, might hereafter be cleared;———and possibly, sometime or other, if not in the man's life, at least after his death,———be, somehow or other, set to rights with the world: But the injury of this, he would say, could never be undone;———nay, be doubted even whether an act of parliament could reach it:———He knew as well as you that the legislature assumed a power over surnames;———but for very strong reasons, which he could give, it had never yet adventured, he would say, to go a step further.

It was observable that though my father, in consequence of this opinion, had, as I have told you, the strongest likings and dislikings towards certain names,———that there were still numbers of names which hung so equally in the balance before him that they were absolutely indifferent to him. *Jack, Dick,* and *Tom* were of this class: These my father called neutral names;———affirming of them, without a satire, That there had been as many knaves and fools, at least, as wise and good men, since the world began, who had indifferently borne them;———so that, like equal forces acting against each other in contrary directions, he thought they mutually destroyed each other's effects; for which reason, he would often declare, He would not give a cherry stone to choose

50

amongst them. *Bob,* which was my brother's name, was another of these neutral kinds of Christian names which operated very little either way; and as my father happened to be at Epsom when it was given him,——he would ofttimes thank heaven it was no worse. *Andrew* was something like a negative quantity in Algebra with him;——'twas worse, he said, than nothing.——*William* stood pretty high:——*Numps* again was low with him;——and *Nick,* he said, was the DEVIL.

But of all the names in the universe, he had the most unconquerable aversion for TRISTRAM;——he had the lowest and most contemptible opinion of it of anything in the world,——thinking it could possibly produce nothing, in *rerum natura,* but what was extremely mean and pitiful: So that in the midst of a dispute on the subject, in which, by the bye, he was frequently involved,——he would sometimes break off in a sudden and spirited EPIPHONEMA, or rather EROTESIS, raised a third, and sometimes a full fifth, above the key of the discourse,——and demand it categorically of his antagonist, Whether he would take upon him to say he had ever remembered,——whether he had ever read,——or even whether he had ever heard tell of a man called *Tristram* performing anything great or worth recording?—— No——, he would say,——TRISTRAM!——The thing is impossible.

What could be wanting in my father but to have wrote a book to publish this notion of his to the world? Little boots it to the subtle speculatist to stand single in his opinions,—— unless he gives them proper vent:——It was the identical thing which my father did;——for in the year Sixteen, which was two years before I was born, he was at the pains of writing an express DISSERTATION simply upon the word *Tristram,*——showing the world, with great candour and modesty, the grounds of his great abhorrence to the name.

When this story is compared with the title page,——Will not the gentle reader pity my father from his soul?——to see an orderly and well-disposed gentleman who, though singular, ——yet inoffensive in his notions,——so played upon in them by cross purposes;——to look down upon the stage, and see him baffled and overthrown in all his little systems and wishes; to behold a train of events perpetually falling out against him, and in so critical and cruel a way as if they had purposely been planned and pointed against him, merely to insult his speculations.——In a word, to behold such a one, in his old age, ill fitted for troubles, ten times in a day suffering sorrow;——ten times in a day calling the child of his prayers TRISTRAM!——Melancholy dissyllable of sound! which, to his ears, was unison to *Nincompoop*, and every name vituperative under heaven.——By his ashes! I swear it,——if ever malignant spirit took pleasure, or busied itself in traversing the purposes of mortal man,——it must have been here;——and if it was not necessary I should be born before I was christened, I would this moment give the reader an account of it.

CHAPTER XX

——How could you, Madam, be so inattentive in reading the last chapter? I told you in it, *That my mother was not a Papist.*——Papist! You told me no such thing, Sir. Madam, I beg leave to repeat it over again, That I told you as plain, at least, as words, by direct inference, could tell you such a thing.——Then, Sir, I must have missed a page.——No, Madam,——you have not missed a word.——Then I was asleep, Sir.——My pride, Madam, cannot allow you that refuge.——Then, I declare, I know nothing at all about the matter.——That, Madam, is the very fault I lay to your charge; and as a punishment for it, I do insist upon it that you immediately turn back, that is as soon as you get to the next full stop, and read the whole chapter over again.

I have imposed this penance upon the lady neither out of wantonness or cruelty, but from the best of motives; and therefore shall make her no apology for it when she returns back:——'Tis to rebuke a vicious taste which has crept into thousands besides herself,——or reading straight forwards, more in quest of the adventures than of the deep erudition and knowledge which a book of this cast, if read over as it should be, would infallibly impart with them.——The mind should be accustomed to make wise reflections, and draw curious conclusions as it goes along; the habitude of which made Pliny the younger affirm, "That he never read a book so bad but he drew some profit from it." The stories of Greece and Rome, run over without this turn and application,——do less service, I affirm it, than the history of

Parismus and Parismenus, or of the Seven Champions of England, read with it.

————But here comes my fair Lady. Have you read over again the chapter, Madam, as I desired you?——You have: And did you not observe the passage, upon the second reading, which admits the inference?——Not a word like it! Then, Madam, be pleased to ponder well the last line but one of the chapter, where I take upon me to say, "It was *necessary* I should be born before I was christened." Had my mother, Madam, been a Papist, that consequence did not follow.*

It is a terrible misfortune for this same book of mine, but more so to the Republic of Letters,——so that my own is quite swallowed up in the consideration of it,——that this selfsame vile pruriency for fresh adventures in all things has got so strongly into our habit and humours,——and so wholly intent are we upon satisfying the impatience of our concupiscence that way,——that nothing but the gross and more carnal parts of a composition will go down:——The subtle hints and sly communications of science fly off, like spirits, upwards;——the heavy moral escapes downwards; and both the one and the other are as much lost to the world as if they were still left in the bottom of the inkhorn.

I wish the male reader has not passed by many a one as quaint and curious as this one in which the female reader has been detected. I wish it may have its effects;——and that all good people, both male and female, from her example, may be taught to think as well as read.

* The Romish Rituals direct the baptizing of the child, in cases of danger, *before* it is born;——but upon this proviso, That some part or other of the child's body be seen by the baptizer: ——But the Doctors of the Sorbonne, by a deliberation held amongst them, April 10, 1733,——have enlarged the powers of the midwives, by determining, That though no part of the child's body should appear,——that baptism shall, nevertheless, be administered to it by injection,——*par le moyen d'une petite Canulle,*——Anglicè *a squirt.*——'Tis very strange that St. Thomas Aquinas, who had so good a mechanical head, both for tying and untying the knots of school divinity,——should, after so much pains bestowed upon this,——give up the point at last, as a second *La chose impossible,*——"*Infantes in maternis uteris existentes* (quoth St. Thomas) *baptizari possunt nullo modo.*" ——O Thomas! Thomas!

If the reader has the curiosity to see the question upon baptism *by injection,* as presented to the Doctors of the Sorbonne, with their consultation thereupon, it is as follows.

MEMOIRE presenté à Messieurs les Docteurs de SORBONNE.*

Un Chirurgien Accoucheur, represente à Messieurs les Docteurs de Sorbonne, qu'il y a des cas, quoique très rares, où une mère ne sçauroit accoucher, & même où l'enfant est tellement renfermé dans le sein de sa mère, qu'il ne fait paroître aucune partie de son corps, ce qui seroit un cas, suivant les Rituels, de lui conférer, du moins sous condition, le baptême. Le Chirurgien, qui consulte, prétend, par le moyen d'une petite canulle, de pouvoir baptiser immediatement l'enfant, sans faire aucun tort à la mere.——Il demande si ce moyen, qu'il vient de proposer, est permis & légitime, et s'il peut s'en servir dans le cas qu'il vient d'exposer.

REPONSE

Le Conseil estime, que la question proposée souffre de grandes difficultés. Les Théologiens posent d'un côté pour principe, que le baptême, qui est une naissance spirituelle, suppose une première naissance; il faut être né dans le monde, pour renaître en Jesus Christ, comme ils l'enseignent. S. Thomas, 3 part, quaest. 68. artic. 11. suit cette doctrine comme une verité constante; l'on ne peut, dit ce S. Docteur, baptiser les enfans qui sont renfermés dans le sein de leurs Mères, et S. Thomas est fondé sur ce, que les enfans ne sont point nés, & ne peuvent être comptés parmi les autres hommes; d'où il conclud, qu'ils ne peuvent être l'object d'une action extérieure, pour recevoir par leur ministère, les sacremens nécessaires au salut: Pueri in maternis uteris existentes nondum prodierunt in lucem ut cum aliis hominibus vitam ducant; unde non possunt subjici actioni humanae, ut per eorum ministerium sacramenta recipiant ad salutem. *Les rituels ordonnent dans la pratique ce que les théologiens ont établi sur les mêmes matières, & ils deffendent tous d'une manière uniforme de baptiser les enfans qui sont renfermés dans le sein de leurs mères, s'ils ne font paroître quelque partie de leurs corps. Le concours des théologiens, & des rituels, qui sont les règles des diocèses, paroît former une autorité qui termine la question présente; cependant le conseil de conscience considérant d'un côte, que le raisonnement des théologiens est uniquement fondé sur une raison de convenance, & que la deffense des rituels, suppose que l'on ne peut baptiser immediatement les enfans*

* Vide Deventer, Paris edit., 4to, 1734, p. 366.

54

ainsi renfermés dans le sein de leurs mères, ce qui est contre la supposition présente; & d'un autre côté, considérant que les mêmes théologiens enseignent, que l'on peut risquer les sacremens qu Jésus Christ a établis comme des moyens faciles, mais nécessaires pour sanctifier les hommes; & d'ailleurs estimant, que les enfans renfermés dans le sein de leurs mères, pourroient être capables de salut, parce qu'ils sont capables de damnation;———pour ces considerations, & en égard à l'exposé, suivant lequel on assure avoir trouvé un moyen certain de baptiser ces enfans ainsi renfermés, sans faire aucun tort à la mère, le Conseil estime que l'on pourroit se servir du moyen proposé, sans la confiance qu'il a, que Dieu n'a point laissé ces sortes d'enfans sans aucuns secours, & supposant, comme il est exposé, que le moyen dont il s'agit est propre à leur procurer le baptême; cependant comme il s'agiroit, en autorisant la pratique proposée, de changer une règle universellement établie, le Conseil croit que celui qui consulte doit s'addresser à son évêque, & à qui il appartient de juger de l'utilité, & du danger du moyen proposé, & comme, sous le bon plaisir de l'évêque, le conseil estime qu'il faudroit recourir au Pape, qui a le droit d'expliquer les règles de l'église, et d'y déroger dans le cas, où la loi ne sçauroit obliger, quelque sage & quelque utile que paroisse la manière de baptiser dont il s'agit, le conseil ne pourroit l'approuver sans le concours de ces deux autorités. On conseille au moins à celui qui consulte, de s'addresser à son évêque, & de lui faire part de la présente décision, afin que, si le prelat entre dans les raisons sur lesquelles les docteurs soussignés s'appuyent, il puisse être autorisé dans le cas de nécessité, où il risqueroit trop d'attendre que la permission fût demandée & accordée d'employer le moyen qu'il propose si avantageux au salut de l'enfant. Au reste le conseil, en estimant que l'on pourroit s'en servir croit cependant, que si les enfans dont il s'agit, venoient au monde, contre l'espérance de ceux qui se seroient servis du même moyen, il seroit nécessaire de les baptiser sous condition, & en cela le conseil se conforme à tous les rituels, qui en autorisant le baptême d'un enfant qui fait paroître quelque partie de son corps, enjoignent néantmoins, & ordonnent de le baptiser sous condition, s'il vient heureusement au monde.

Déliberé en Sorbonne, le 10 Avril, 1733.

A. Le Moyne,
L. De Romigny,
De Marcilly

55

Mr. Tristram Shandy's compliments to Messrs. Le Moyne, De Romigny, and De Marcilly, hopes they all rested well the night after so tiresome a consultation.——He begs to know whether, after the ceremony of marriage, and before that of consummation, the baptizing all the HOMUNCULI at once, slapdash, by *injection*, would not be a shorter and safer cut still; on condition, as above, That if the HOMUNCULI do well and come safe into the world after this, That each and every of them shall be baptized again (*sous condition.*)——And provided, in the second place, That the thing can be done, which Mr. Shandy apprehends it may, *par le moyen d'une* petite canulle, and *sans faire aucun tort au père*.

CHAPTER XXI

——I wonder what's all that noise, and running backwards and forwards for, abovestairs, quoth my father, addressing himself, after an hour and a half's silence, to my uncle Toby,——who you must know, was sitting on the opposite side of the fire, smoking his social pipe all the time, in mute contemplation of a new pair of black plush breeches which he had got on;——What can they be doing, brother? quoth my father;——we can scarce hear ourselves talk.

I think, replied my uncle Toby, taking his pipe from his mouth, and striking the head of it two or three times upon the nail of his left thumb, as he began his sentence,——I think, says he:——But to enter rightly into my uncle Toby's sentiments upon this matter, you must be made to enter first a little into his character, the outlines of which I shall just give you, and then the dialogue between him and my father will go on as well again.

——Pray what was the man's name,——for I write in such a hurry, I have no time to recollect or look for it,——who first made the observation, "That there was great inconstancy in our air and climate"? Whoever he was, 'twas a just and good observation in him.——But the corollary drawn from it, namely, "That it is this which has furnished us with such a variety of odd and whimsical characters,"——that was not his;——it was found out by another man, at least a century and a half after him:——Then again,——that this copious storehouse of original materials is the true and natural cause that our Comedies are so much better than those of France, or any others that either have, or can be wrote upon the Continent;——that discovery was not fully made till about the middle of King William's reign,——when the great Dryden, in writing one of his long prefaces (if I mistake not), most fortunately hit upon it. Indeed towards the latter end of Queen Anne, the great Addison began to patronize the notion, and more fully explained it to the world in one or two of his Spectators;——but the discovery was not his.——Then, fourthly and lastly, that this strange irregularity in our climate, producing so strange an irregularity in our characters,——doth thereby, in some sort, make us amends, by giving us somewhat to make us merry with when the weather will not suffer us to go out of doors,——that observation is my own;——and was struck out by me this very rainy day, March 26, 1759, and betwixt the hours of nine and ten in the morning.

Thus,——thus my fellow-labourers and associates in this great harvest of our learning, now ripening before our eyes; thus it is, by slow steps of casual increase, that our knowledge physical, metaphysical, physiological, polemical, nautical, mathematical, enigmatical, technical, biographical, romantical, chemical, and obstetrical, with fifty other branches of it (most of 'em ending, as these do, in *ical*), have, for these two last centuries and more, gradually been creeping upwards towards that Ακμὴ of their perfections, from which, if we may form a conjecture from the advances of these last seven years, we cannot possibly be far off.

When that happens, it is to be hoped, it will put an end to all kind of writings whatsoever;——the want of all kind of writing will put an end to all kind of reading;——and that in time, *As war begets poverty, poverty peace,*——must, in course, put an end to all kind of knowledge,——and then ——we shall have all to begin over again; or, in other words, be exactly where we started.

——Happy! thrice happy Times! I only wish that the era of my begetting, as well as the mode and manner of it, had been a little altered,——or that it could have been put off with any convenience to my father or mother, for some twenty or five-and-twenty years longer, when a man in the literary world might have stood some chance.——

But I forget my uncle Toby, whom all this while we have left knocking the ashes out of his tobacco pipe.

His humour was of that particular species which does honour to our atmosphere; and I should have made no scruple of ranking him amongst one of the first-rate productions of it, had not there appeared too many strong lines in it of a family likeness, which showed that he derived the singularity of his temper more from blood than either wind or water, or any modifications or combinations of them whatever: And I have, therefore, ofttimes wondered that my father, though I believe he had his reasons for it, upon his observing some tokens of eccentricity in my course when I was a boy,——— should never once endeavour to account for them in this way; for all the SHANDY FAMILY were of an original character throughout;———I mean the males,———the females had no character at all,———except, indeed, my great aunt DINAH, who, about sixty years ago, was married and got with child by the coachman, for which my father, according to his hypothesis of Christian names, would often say, She might thank her godfathers and godmothers.

It will seem very strange,——— and I would as soon think of dropping a riddle in the reader's way, which is not my interest to do, as set him upon guessing how it could come to pass that an event of this kind, so many years after it had happened, should be reserved for the interruption of the peace and unity, which otherwise so cordially subsisted, between my father and my uncle Toby. One would have thought that the whole force of the misfortune should have spent and wasted itself in the family at first,———as is generally the case:———But nothing ever wrought with our family after the ordinary way. Possibly at the very time this happened, it might have something else to afflict it; and as afflictions are sent down for our good, and that as this had never done the SHANDY FAMILY any good at all, it might lie waiting till apt times and circumstances should give it an opportunity to discharge its office.———Observe, I determine nothing upon this.———My way is ever to point out to the curious, different tracts of investigation, to come at the first springs of the events I tell;———not with a pedantic *Fescue*,———or in the decisive Manner of Tacitus, who outwits himself and his reader;———but with the officious humility of a heart devoted to the assistance merely of the inquisitive;———to them I write,———and by them I shall be read,———if any such reading as this could be supposed to hold out so long, to the very end of the world.

Why this cause of sorrow, therefore, was thus reserved for my father and uncle is undetermined by me. But how and in what direction it exerted itself, so as to become the cause of dissatisfaction between them after it began to operate, is what I am able to explain with great exactness, and is as follows:

My uncle TOBY SHANDY, Madam, was a gentleman who, with the virtues which usually constitute the character of a man of honour and rectitude,——possessed one in a very eminent degree which is seldom or never put into the catalogue; and that was a most extreme and unparalleled modesty of nature;——though I correct the word *nature*, for this reason, that I may not prejudge a point which must shortly come to a hearing; and that is, Whether this modesty of his was natural or acquired.——Whichever way my uncle Toby came by it, 'twas nevertheless modesty in the truest sense of it; and that is, Madam, not in regard to words, for he was so unhappy as to have very little choice in them,——but to things;——and this kind of modesty so possessed him, and it arose to such a height in him, as almost to equal, if such a thing could be, even the modesty of a woman: That female nicety, Madam, and inward cleanliness of mind and fancy in your sex which makes you so much the awe of ours.

You will imagine, Madam, that my uncle Toby had contracted all this from this very source;——that he had spent a great part of his time in converse with your sex; and that, from a thorough knowledge of you, and the force of imitation which such fair examples render irresistible,——he had acquired this amiable turn of mind.

I wish I could say so,——for unless it was with his sister-in-law, my father's wife and my mother,——my uncle Toby scarce exchanged three words with the sex in as many years;——no, he got it, Madam, by a blow.——A blow!—— Yes, Madam, it was owing to a blow from a stone, broke off by a ball from the parapet of a hornwork at the siege of Namur, which struck full upon my uncle Toby's groin.— Which way could that effect it? The story of that, Madam, is long and interesting;——but it would be running my history all upon heaps to give it you here.——'Tis for an episode hereafter; and every circumstance relating to it in its proper place, shall be faithfully laid before you:——Till then, it is not in my power to give further light into this matter, or say more than what I have said already,——That my uncle Toby was a gentleman of unparalleled modesty, which happening to be somewhat subtilized and rarefied by the constant heat of a little family pride,——they both so wrought together within him that he could never bear to hear the affair of my aunt DINAH touched upon, but with the greatest emotion.———The least hint of it was enough to make the blood fly into his face;———but when my father enlarged upon the story in mixed companies, which the illustration of his hypothesis frequently obliged him to do,——— the unfortunate blight of one of the fairest branches of the family would set my uncle Toby's honour and modesty o' bleeding; and he would often take my father aside, in the greatest concern imaginable, to expostulate and tell him he would give him anything in the world, only to let the story rest.

My father, I believe, had the truest love and tenderness for my uncle Toby that ever one brother bore towards another, and would have done anything in nature, which one brother in reason could have desired of another, to have made my uncle Toby's heart easy in this, or any other point. But this lay out of his power.

———My father, as I told you, was a philosopher in grain, ———speculative,———systematical;———and my aunt Dinah's affair was a matter of as much consequence to him as the retrogradation of the planets to Copernicus:———The back-slidings of Venus in her orbit fortified the Copernican system, called so after his name; and the backslidings of my aunt Dinah in her orbit did the same service in establishing my father's system, which, I trust will forever hereafter be called the *Shandean System,* after his.

In any other family dishonour, my father, I believe, had as nice a sense of shame as any man whatever;———and neither he nor, I dare say, Copernicus, would have divulged the affair in either case, or have taken the least notice of it to the world, but for the obligations they owed, as they thought, to truth.———*Amicus Plato,* my father would say, construing the words to my uncle *Toby,* as he went along, *Amicus Plato;* that is, DINAH was my aunt;———*sed magis amica veritas*———but TRUTH is my sister.

This contrariety of humours betwixt my father and my uncle was the source of many a fraternal squabble. The one could not bear to hear the tale of family disgrace recorded, ———and the other would scarce ever let a day pass to an end without some hint at it.

For God's sake, my uncle Toby would cry,———and for my sake, and for all our sakes, my dear brother Shandy,———do let this story of our aunt's and her ashes sleep in peace;——— how can you,———how can you have so little feeling and compassion for the character of our family:———What is the character of a family to an hypothesis? my father would reply.——Nay, if you come to that——what is the life of a family:——The life of a family!——my uncle Toby would say, throwing himself back in his armchair, and lifting up his hands, his eyes, and one leg.——Yes, the life,——my father would say, maintaining his point. How many thousands of 'em are there every year that come cast away (in all civilized countries at least)——and considered as nothing but common air, in competition of an hypothesis. In my plain sense of things, my uncle Toby would answer,—— every such instance is downright MURDER, let who will commit it.——There lies your mistake, my father would reply; ——for, in *Foro Scientiae*, there is no such thing as MURDER, ——'tis only DEATH, brother.

My uncle Toby would never offer to answer this by any other kind of argument than that of whistling half a dozen bars of *Lillabullero*.——You must know it was the usual channel through which his passions got vent, when anything shocked or surprised him;——but especially when anything which he deemed very absurd was offered.

As not one of our logical writers, nor any of the commentators upon them, that I remember, have thought proper to give a name to this particular species of argument,——I here take the liberty to do it myself, for two reasons. First, That, in order to prevent all confusion in disputes, it may stand as much distinguished forever from every other species of argument,——as the *Argumentum ad Verecundiam, ex Absurdo, ex Fortiori,* or any other argument whatsoever:——And, secondly, That it may be said by my children's children, when my head is laid to rest,——that their learned grandfather's head had been busied to as much purpose, once, as other people's:——That he had invented a name,——and generously thrown it into the TREASURY of the *Ars Logica,* for one of the most unanswerable arguments in the whole science. And if the end of disputation is more to silence than convince,——they may add, if they please, to one of the best arguments too.

I do therefore, by these presents, strictly order and command, That it be known and distinguished by the name and title of the *Argumentum Fistulatorium,* and no other;—— and that it rank hereafter with the *Argumentum Baculinum,* and the *Argumentum ad Crumenam,* and forever hereafter be treated of in the same chapter.

As for the *Argumentum Tripodium,* which is never used but by the woman against the man;——and the *Argumentum ad Rem,* which, contrariwise, is made use of by the man only against the woman:——As these two are enough in conscience for one lecture;——and, moreover, as the one is the best answer to the other,——let them likewise be kept apart, and be treated of in a place by themselves.

CHAPTER XXII

The learned Bishop Hall, I mean the famous Dr. Joseph Hall, who was Bishop of Exeter in King James the First's reign, tells us in one of his *Decads,* at the end of his divine art of meditation, imprinted at London, in the year 1610, by John Beal, dwelling in Aldersgate Street, "That it is an abominable thing for a man to commend himself;"——and I really think it is so.

And yet, on the other hand, when a thing is executed in a masterly kind of a fashion, which thing is not likely to be found out;——I think it is full as abominable that a man should lose the honour of it, and go out of the world with the conceit of it rotting in his head.

This is precisely my situation.

For in this long digression which I was accidentally led into, as in all my digressions (one only excepted), there is a master stroke of digressive skill the merit of which has all along, I fear, been overlooked by my reader,——not for want of penetration in him,——but because 'tis an excellence seldom looked for, or expected, indeed, in a digression;—— and it is this: That though my digressions are all fair, as you observe,——and that I fly off from what I am about, as far and as often too as any writer in Great Britain; yet I constantly take care to order affairs so, that my main business does not stand still in my absence.

I was just going, for example, to have given you the great outlines of my uncle Toby's most whimsical character,—— when my aunt Dinah and the coachman came across us, and led us a vagary some millions of miles into the very heart of the planetary system: Notwithstanding all this you perceive that the drawing of my uncle Toby's character went on gently all the time;——not the great contours of it,——that was impossible,——but some familiar strokes and faint designations of it were here and there touched in, as we went along, so that you are much better acquainted with my uncle Toby now than you was before.

By this contrivance the machinery of my work is of a species by itself; two contrary motions are introduced into it, and reconciled, which were thought to be at variance with each other. In a word, my work is digressive, and it is progressive too,——and at the same time.

This, Sir, is a very different story from that of the earth's moving round her axis in her diurnal rotation, with her progress in her elliptic orbit which brings about the year, and constitutes that variety and vicissitude of seasons we enjoy;——though I own it suggested the thought,——as I believe the greatest of our boasted improvements and discoveries have come from some such trifling hints.

Digressions, incontestably, are the sunshine;——they are the life, the soul of reading;——take them out of this book, for instance,——you might as well take the book along with them;——one cold eternal winter would reign in every page of it; restore them to the writer,——he steps forth like a bridegroom,——bids All hail, brings in variety, and forbids the appetite to fail.

All the dexterity is in the good cookery and management of them, so as to be not only for the advantage of the reader, but also of the author, whose distress, in this matter, is truly pitiable: For if he begins a digression,——from that moment, I observe, his whole work stands stock still;—— and if he goes on with his main work,——then there is an end of his digression.

——This is vile work.——For which reason, from the beginning of this, you see, I have constructed the main work and the adventitious parts of it with such intersections, and have so complicated and involved the digressive and progressive movements, one wheel within another, that the whole machine, in general, has been kept a-going;——and, what's more, it shall be kept a-going these forty years, if it pleases the fountain of health to bless me so long with life and good spirits.

CHAPTER XXIII

I have a strong propensity in me to begin this chapter very nonsensically, and I will not balk my fancy.——Accordingly I set off thus.

If the fixture of Momus's glass in the human breast, according to the proposed emendation of that archcritic, had taken place,——first, This foolish consequence would certainly have followed,——That the very wisest and the very gravest of us all, in one coin or other, must have paid window money every day of our lives.

And, secondly, That had the said glass been there set up, nothing more would have been wanting, in order to have taken a man's character, but to have taken a chair and gone softly, as you would to a dioptrical beehive, and looked in, ——viewed the soul stark naked;——observed all her motions,——her machinations;——traced all her maggots from their first engendering to their crawling forth;——watched her loose in her frisks, her gambols, her capriccios; and after some notice of her more solemn deportment, consequent upon such frisks, &c.——then taken your pen and ink and set down nothing but what you had seen, and could have sworn to:——But this is an advantage not to be had by the biographer in this planet;——in the planet Mercury (belike) it may be so, if not better still for him;——for there the intense heat of the country, which is proved by computators, from its vicinity to the sun, to be more than equal to that of red-hot iron,——must, I think, long ago have vitrified the bodies of the inhabitants (as the efficient cause) to suit them for the climate (which is the final cause); so that, betwixt them both, all the tenements of their souls, from top to bottom, may be nothing else, for aught the soundest philosophy can show to the contrary, but one fine transparent body of clear glass (bating the umbilical knot);——so that, till the inhabitants grow old and tolerably wrinkled, whereby the rays of light, in passing through them, become so monstrously refracted,——or return reflected from their surfaces in such transverse lines to the eye, that a man cannot be seen through;——his soul might as well, unless for mere ceremony,——or the trifling advantage which the umbilical point gave her,——might, upon all other accounts, I say, as well play the fool out o' doors as in her own house.

But this, as I said above, is not the case of the inhabitants of this earth;——our minds shine not through the body, but are wrapt up here in a dark covering of uncrystallized flesh and blood; so that if we would come to the specific characters of them, we must go some other way to work.

Many, in good truth, are the ways which human wit has been forced to take to do this thing with exactness.

Some, for instance, draw all their characters with wind

instruments.——Virgil takes notice of that way in the affair of Dido and Aeneas;——but it is as fallacious as the breath of fame;——and, moreover, bespeaks a narrow genius. I am not ignorant that the Italians pretend to a mathematical exactness in their designations of one particular sort of character among them, from the *forte* or *piano* of a certain wind instrument they use,——which they say is infallible.——I dare not mention the name of the instrument in this place; ——'tis sufficient we have it amongst us,——but never think making a drawing by it;——this is enigmatical, and intended to be so, at least *ad populum*.——And therefore I beg, Madam, when you come here, that you read on as fast as you can, and never stop to make any inquiry about it.

There are others, again, who will draw a man's character from no other helps in the world but merely from his evacuations;—but this often gives a very incorrect outline,—— unless, indeed, you take a sketch of his repletions too; and by correcting one drawing from the other, compound one good figure out of them both.

I should have no objection to this method, but that I think it must smell too strong of the lamp,——and be rendered still more operose by forcing you to have an eye to the rest of his *Non-Naturals*.——Why the most natural actions of a man's life should be called his Non-Naturals——is another question.

There are others, fourthly, who disdain every one of these expedients;——not from any fertility of their own, but from the various ways of doing it, which they have borrowed from the honourable devices which the Pentagraphic Brethren * of the brush have shown in taking copies.——These, you must know, are your great historians.

One of these you will see drawing a full-length character *against the light;*——that's illiberal,——dishonest,——and hard upon the character of the man who sits.

Others, to mend the matter, will make a drawing of you in the *Camera;*——that is most unfair of all,——because *there* you are sure to be represented in some of your most ridiculous attitudes.

To avoid all and every one of these errors, in giving you my uncle Toby's character, I am determined to draw it by no mechanical help whatever;——nor shall my pencil be guided by any one wind instrument which ever was blown upon, either on this or on the other side of the Alps;——nor will I

---

* Pentagraph, an instrument to copy prints and pictures mechanically, and in any proportion.

consider either his repletions or his discharges,——or touch upon his Non-Naturals;——but, in a word, I will draw my uncle Toby's character from his HOBBY-HORSE.

CHAPTER XXIV

If I was not morally sure that the reader must be out of all patience for my uncle Toby's character,——I would here previously have convinced him that there is no instrument so fit to draw such a thing with, as that which I have pitched upon.

A man and his HOBBY-HORSE, though I cannot say that they act and react exactly after the same manner in which the soul and body do upon each other: Yet doubtless there is a communication between them of some kind, and my opinion rather is that there is something in it more of the manner of electrified bodies,——and that by means of the heated parts of the rider, which come immediately into contact with the back of the HOBBY-HORSE.——By long journeys and much friction, it so happens that the body of the rider is at length filled as full of HOBBY-HORSICAL matter as it can hold; ——so that if you are able to give but a clear description of the nature of the one, you may form a pretty exact notion of the genius and character of the other.

Now the HOBBY-HORSE which my uncle Toby always rode upon was, in my opinion, an HOBBY-HORSE well worth giving a description of, if it was only upon the score of his great singularity; for you might have travelled from York to Dover, ——from Dover to Penzance in Cornwall, and from Penzance to York back again, and not have seen such another upon the road; or if you had seen such a one, whatever haste you had been in, you must infallibly have stopped to have taken a view of him. Indeed, the gait and figure of him was so strange, and so utterly unlike was he, from his head to his tail, to any one of the whole species, that it was now and then made a matter of dispute,——whether he was really a HOBBY-HORSE or no: But as the Philosopher would use no other argument to the sceptic who disputed with him against the reality of motion, save that of rising up upon his legs, and walking across the room;——so would my uncle Toby use no other argument to prove his HOBBY-HORSE was a

HOBBY-HORSE indeed, but by getting upon his back and riding him about;——leaving the world after that to determine the point as it thought fit.

In good truth, my uncle Toby mounted him with so much pleasure, and he carried my uncle Toby so well,——that he troubled his head very little with what the world either said or thought about it.

It is now high time, however, that I give you a description of him:——But to go on regularly, I only beg you will give me leave to acquaint you first how my uncle Toby came by him.

CHAPTER XXV

The wound in my uncle Toby's groin, which he received at the siege of Namur, rendering him unfit for the service, it was thought expedient he should return to England, in order, if possible, to be set to rights.

He was four years totally confined,——part of it to his bed, and all of it to his room; and in the course of his cure, which was all that time in hand, suffered unspeakable miseries,——owing to a succession of exfoliations from the *os pubis*, and the outward edge of that part of the *coxendix* called the *os ilium*,——both which bones were dismally crushed, as much by the irregularity of the stone, which I told you was broke off the parapet,——as by its size—— (though it was pretty large), which inclined the surgeon all along to think that the great injury which it had done my uncle Toby's groin was more owing to the gravity of the stone itself than to the projectile force of it,——which he would often tell him was a great happiness.

My father at that time was just beginning business in London, and had taken a house;——and as the truest friendship and cordiality subsisted between the two brothers,——and that my father thought my uncle Toby could nowhere be so well nursed and taken care of as in his own house,——he assigned him the very best apartment in it.——And what was a much more sincere mark of his affection still, he would never suffer a friend or an acquaintance to step into the house on any occasion, but he would take him by the hand,

and lead him upstairs to see his brother Toby, and chat an hour by his bed side.

The history of a soldier's wound beguiles the pain of it; ——my uncle's visitors at least thought so, and in their daily calls upon him, from the courtesy arising out of that belief, they would frequently turn the discourse to that subject,—— and from that subject the discourse would generally roll on to the siege itself.

These conversations were infinitely kind; and my uncle Toby received great relief from them, and would have received much more, but that they brought him into some unforeseen perplexities, which, for three months together, retarded his cure greatly; and if he had not hit upon an expedient to extricate himself out of them, I verily believe they would have laid him in his grave.

What these perplexities of my uncle Toby were——'tis impossible for you to guess;——if you could,——I should blush; not as a relation,——not as a man,——nor even as a woman,——but I should blush as an author; inasmuch as I set no small store by myself upon this very account, that my reader has never yet been able to guess at anything. And in this, Sir, I am of so nice and singular a humour that if I thought you was able to form the least judgment or probable conjecture to yourself of what was to come in the next page,——I would tear it out of my book.

VOLUME II

CHAPTER I

I have begun a new book, on purpose that I might have room enough to explain the nature of the perplexities in which my uncle Toby was involved, from the many discourses and interrogations about the siege of Namur, where he received his wound.

I must remind the reader, in case he has read the history of King William's wars,——but if he has not,——I then inform him that one of the most memorable attacks in that seige was that which was made by the English and Dutch upon the point of the advanced counterscarp before the gate of St. Nicolas, which inclosed the great sluice or water stop where the English were terribly exposed to the shot of the counterguard and demibastion of St. Roch: The issue of which hot dispute, in three words, was this, That the Dutch lodged themselves upon the counterguard,——and that the English made themselves masters of the covered way before St. Nicolas's gate, notwithstanding the gallantry of the French officers, who exposed themselves upon the glacis, sword in hand.

As this was the principal attack of which my uncle Toby was an eyewitness at Namur,——the army of the besiegers being cut off, by the confluence of the Maas and Sambre, from seeing much of each other's operations,——my uncle Toby was generally more eloquent and particular in his account of it; and the many perplexities he was in arose out of the almost insurmountable difficulties he found in telling his story intelligibly, and giving such clear ideas of the differences and distinctions between the scarp and counterscarp,

——the glacis and covered way,——the half-moon and ravelin,——as to make his company fully comprehend where and what he was about.

Writers themselves are too apt to confound these terms;——so that you will the less wonder if in his endeavours to explain them, and in opposition to many misconceptions, that my uncle Toby did ofttimes puzzle his visitors, and sometimes himself too.

To speak the truth, unless the company my father led upstairs were tolerably clearheaded, or my uncle Toby was in one of his best explanatory moods, 'twas a difficult thing, do what he could, to keep the discourse free from obscurity.

What rendered the account of this affair the more intricate to my uncle Toby was this,——that in the attack of the counterscarp before the gate of St. Nicolas, extending itself from the bank of the Maas quite up to the great water stop,—— the ground was cut and cross-cut with such a multitude of dykes, drains, rivulets, and sluices, on all sides,——and he would get so sadly bewildered and set fast amongst them, that frequently he could neither get backwards or forwards to save his life; and was ofttimes obliged to give up the attack upon that very account only.

These perplexing rebuffs gave my uncle Toby Shandy more perturbations than you would imagine; and as my father's kindness to him was continually dragging up fresh friends and fresh inquirers,——he had but a very uneasy task of it.

No doubt my uncle Toby had great command of himself, ——and could guard appearances, I believe, as well as most men;——yet anyone may imagine that when he could not retreat out of the ravelin without getting into the half-moon, or get out of the covered way without falling down the counterscarp, nor cross the dyke without danger of slipping into the ditch, but that he must have fretted and fumed inwardly:——He did so;——and these little and hourly vexations, which may seem trifling and of no account to the man who has not read Hippocrates, yet, whoever has read Hippocrates, or Dr. James Mackenzie, and has considered well the effects which the passions and affections of the mind have upon the digestion——(Why not of a wound as well as of a dinner?)——may easily conceive what sharp paroxysms and exacerbations of his wound my uncle Toby must have undergone upon that score only.

——My uncle Toby could not philosophize upon it;—— 'twas enough he felt it was so,——and having sustained the pain and sorrows of it for three months together, he was resolved some way or other to extricate himself.

He was one morning lying upon his back in his bed, the anguish and nature of the wound upon his groin suffering him to lie in no other position, when a thought came into his head that if he could purchase such a thing, and have it pasted down upon a board, as a large map of the fortifications of the town and citadel of Namur, with its environs, it might be a means of giving him ease.——I take notice of his desire to have the environs along with the town and citadel for this reason,——because my uncle Toby's wound was got in one of the traverses, about thirty toises from the returning angle of the trench, opposite to the salient angle of the demibastion of St. Roch;——so that he was pretty confident he could stick a pin upon the identical spot of ground where he was standing in when the stone struck him.

All this succeeded to his wishes, and not only freed him from a world of sad explanations, but, in the end, it proved the happy means, as you will read, of procuring my uncle Toby his HOBBY-HORSE.

CHAPTER II

There is nothing so foolish, when you are at the expense of making an entertainment of this kind, as to order things so badly as to let your critics and gentry of refined taste run it down: Nor is there anything so likely to make them do it as that of leaving them out of the party, or, what is full as offensive, of bestowing your attention upon the rest of your guests in so particular a way, as if there was no such thing as a critic (by occupation) at table.

——I guard against both; for, in the first place, I have left half a dozen places purposely open for them;——and, in the next place, I pay them all court,——Gentlemen, I kiss your hands,——I protest no company could give me half the pleasure,——by my soul I am glad to see you,——I beg only you will make no strangers of yourselves, but sit down without any ceremony, and fall on heartily.

I said I had left six places, and I was upon the point of

71

carrying my complaisance so far as to have left a seventh open for them,——and in this very spot I stand on;—— but being told by a critic (though not by occupation,—— but by nature) that I had acquitted myself well enough, I shall fill it up directly, hoping, in the meantime, that I shall be able to make a great deal of more room next year.

——How, in the name of wonder! could your uncle Toby, who, it seems, was a military man, and whom you have represented as no fool,——be at the same time such a confused, puddingheaded, muddleheaded fellow as——Go look.

So, Sir Critic, I could have replied; but I scorn it.——'Tis language unurbane,——and only befitting the man who cannot give clear and satisfactory accounts of things, or dive deep enough into the first causes of human ignorance and confusion. It is moreover the reply valiant,——and therefore I reject it; for though it might have suited my uncle Toby's character as a soldier excellently well,——and had he not accustomed himself, in such attacks, to whistle the *Lillabullero,*——as he wanted no courage, 'tis the very answer he would have given; yet it would by no means have done for me. You see as plain as can be that I write as a man of erudition;——that even my similes, my allusions, my illustrations, my metaphors, are erudite,——and that I must sustain my character properly, and contrast it properly too,——else what would become of me? Why, Sir, I should be undone;——at this very moment that I am going here to fill up one place against a critic,——I should have made an opening for a couple.

——Therefore I answer thus:

Pray, Sir, in all the reading which you have ever read, did you ever read such a book as Locke's Essay upon the Human Understanding?——Don't answer me rashly,——because many, I know, quote the book who have not read it,——and many have read it who understand it not:——If either of these is your case, as I write to instruct, I will tell you in three words what the book is.——It is a history.——A history! of who? what? where? when? Don't hurry yourself. ——It is a history book, Sir (which may possibly recommend it to the world), of what passes in a man's own mind; and if you will say so much of the book, and no more, believe me, you will cut no contemptible figure in a metaphysic circle.

But this by the way.

Now if you will venture to go along with me, and look down into the bottom of this matter, it will be found that the cause of obscurity and confusion in the mind of man is threefold.

Dull organs, dear Sir, in the first place. Secondly, slight and transient impressions made by objects when the said organs are not dull. And, thirdly, a memory like unto a sieve, not able to retain what it has received.——Call down Dolly, your chambermaid, and I will give you my cap and bell along with it, if I make not this matter so plain that Dolly herself shall understand it as well as Malebranche.—— When Dolly has indited her epistle to Robin and has thrust her arm into the bottom of her pocket hanging by her right side;——take that opportunity to recollect that the organs and faculties of perception can by nothing in this world be so aptly typified and explained as by that one thing which Dolly's hand is in search of.——Your organs are not so dull that I should inform you,——'tis an inch, Sir, of red seal wax.

When this is melted and dropped upon the letter, if Dolly fumbles too long for her thimble, till the wax is over-hardened, it will not receive the mark of her thimble from the usual impulse which was wont to imprint it. Very well: If Dolly's wax, for want of better, is beeswax, or of a temper too soft,——though it may receive,——it will not hold the impression, how hard soever Dolly thrusts against it; and last of all, supposing the wax good, and eke the thimble, but applied thereto in careless haste, as her mistress rings the bell;——in any one of these three cases, the print left by the thimble will be as unlike the prototype as a brass jack.

Now you must understand that not one of these was the true cause of the confusion in my uncle Toby's discourse; and it is for that very reason I enlarge upon them so long, after the manner of great physiologists,——to show the world what it did *not* arise from.

What it did arise from I have hinted above, and a fertile source of obscurity it is,——and ever will be,——and that is the unsteady uses of words which have perplexed the clearest and most exalted understandings.

It is ten to one (at Arthur's) whether you have ever read the literary histories of past ages;——if you have,——what terrible battles, y-clept logomachies, have they occasioned and perpetuated with so much gall and inkshed,——that a good-natured man cannot read the accounts of them without tears in his eyes.

Gentle critic! when thou hast weighed all this, and considered within thyself how much of thy own knowledge, discourse, and conversation has been pestered and disordered, at one time or other, by this, and this only:——What a pudder and racket in COUNCILS about οὐσία and ὑπόστασις; and in the SCHOOLS of the learned about power and about spirit;——about essences, and about quintessences;——about substances, and about space.——What confusion in greater THEATRES from words of little meaning, and as indeterminate a sense;——when thou considers this, thou wilt not wonder at my uncle Toby's perplexities;——thou wilt drop a tear of pity upon his scarp and his counterscarp,——his glacis and his covered way,——his ravelin and his half-moon: 'Twas not by ideas,——by heaven! his life was put in jeopardy by words.

CHAPTER III

When my uncle Toby got his map of Namur to his mind, he began immediately to apply himself, and with the utmost diligence, to the study of it; for nothing being of more importance to him that his recovery, and his recovery depending, as you have read, upon the passions and affections of his mind, it behoved him to take the nicest care to make himself so far master of his subject as to be able to talk upon it without emotion.

In a fortnight's close and painful application, which, by the bye, did my uncle Toby's wound upon his groin no good, ——he was enabled, by the help of some marginal documents at the feet of the elephant, together with Gobesius's military architecture and pyroballogy, translated from the Flemish, to form his discourse with passable perspicuity; and before he was two full months gone,——he was right eloquent upon it, and could make not only the attack of the advanced counterscarp with great order;——but having, by that time, gone much deeper into the art than what his first motive made necessary,——my uncle Toby was able to cross the Maas and Sambre; make diversions as far as Vauban's line, the abbey of Salsines, &c., and give his visitors as distinct a history of each of their attacks as of that of the gate of St. Nicholas, where he had the honour to receive his wound.

But the desire of knowledge, like the thirst of riches, increases ever with the acquisition of it. The more my uncle Toby pored over his map, the more he took a liking to it; ——by the same process and electrical assimilation, as I told you, through which I ween the souls of connoisseurs themselves, by long friction and incumbition, have the happiness, at length, to get all bevirtued,——bepictured,——bebutterflied, and befiddled.

The more my uncle Toby drank of this sweet fountain of science, the greater was the heat and impatience of his thirst, so that, before the first year of his confinement had well gone round, there was scarce a fortified town in Italy or Flanders of which, by one means or other, he had not procured a plan, reading over as he got them, and carefully collating therewith the histories of their sieges, their demolitions, their improvements, and new works, all which he would read with that intense application and delight, that he would forget himself, his wound, his confinement, his dinner.

In the second year my uncle Toby purchased Ramelli and Cataneo, translated from the Italian;——likewise Stevinus, Marolis, the Chevalier de Ville, Lorini, Coehorn, Sheeter, the Count de Pagan, the Marshal Vauban, Mons. Blondel, with almost as many more books of military architecture as Don Quixote was found to have of chivalry, when the curate and barber invaded his library.

Towards the beginning of the third year, which was in August, Ninety-nine, my uncle Toby found it necessary to understand a little of projectiles:——And having judged it best to draw his knowledge from the fountainhead, he began with N. Tartaglia, who it seems was the first man who detected the imposition of a cannon ball's doing all that mischief under the notion of a right line.——This N. Tartaglia proved to my uncle Toby to be an impossible thing.

——Endless is the Search of Truth!

No sooner was my uncle Toby satisfied which road the cannon ball did not go, but he was insensibly led on, and resolved in his mind to enquire and find out which road the ball did go: For which purpose he was obliged to set off afresh with old Maltus, and studied him devoutly.——He proceeded next to Galileo and Torricellius, wherein, by certain geometrical rules, infallibly laid down, he found the recise path to be a PARABOLA,——or else an HYPERBOLA,—— and that the parameter, or *latus rectum,* of the conic section of the said path was to the quantity and amplitude in a direct *ratio* as the whole line to the sine of double the angle of incidence, formed by the breech upon an horizontal plan$_e$;——and that the semiparameter,——stop! my dear uncle Toby,——stop!——go not one foot further into this thorny and bewildered track;——intricate are the steps! intricate are the mazes of this labyrinth! intricate are the troubles which the pursuit of this bewitching phantom, KNOWLEDGE, will bring upon thee.——O my uncle! fly—fly—fly from it as from a serpent.——Is it fit, good-natured man! thou shouldst sit up, with the wound upon thy groin, whole nights baking thy blood with hectic watchings?——Alas! 'twill exasperate thy symptoms,——check thy perspirations,——evaporate thy spirits,——waste thy animal strength,——dry up thy radical moisture,——bring thee into a costive habit of body, impair thy health,——and hasten all the infirmities of thy old age.——O my uncle! my uncle Toby!

CHAPTER IV

I would not give a groat for that man's knowledge in pencraft who does not understand this,——That the best plain narrative in the world, tacked very close to the last spirited apostrophe to my uncle Toby,——would have felt both cold and vapid upon the reader's palate;——therefore I forthwith put an end to the chapter,——though I was in the middle of my story.

——Writers of my stamp have one principle in common with painters.——Where an exact copying makes our pictures less striking, we choose the less evil; deeming it even more pardonable to trespass against truth than beauty.——This is to be understood *cum grano salis;* but be it as it will,——as the parallel is made more for the sake of letting the apostrophe cool than anything else,——'tis not very material whether upon any other score the reader approves of it or not.

In the latter end of the third year, my uncle Toby perceiving that the parameter and semiparameter of the conic section angered his wound, he left off the study of projectiles in a kind of a huff, and betook himself to the practical part of fortification only; the pleasure of which, like a spring held back, returned upon him with redoubled force.

It was in this year that my uncle began to break in upon
the daily regularity of a clean shirt,——to dismiss his
barber unshaven,——and to allow his surgeon scarce time
sufficient to dress his wound, concerning himself so little
about it as not to ask him once in seven times' dressing
how it went on: When, lo!——all of a sudden, for the change
was as quick as lightning, he began to sigh heavily for his
recovery,——complained to my father, grew impatient with
the surgeon;——and one morning as he heard his foot coming upstairs, he shut up his books, and thrust aside his instruments, in order to expostulate with him upon the pro-
traction of his cure, which, he told him, might surely have
been accomplished at least by that time:——He dwelt long
upon the miseries he had undergone, and the sorrows of
his four years' melancholy imprisonment;——adding that had
it not been for the kind looks and fraternal cheerings of the
best of brothers,——he had long since sunk under his misfortunes.——My father was by: My uncle Toby's eloquence
brought tears into his eyes;——'twas unexpected.——My
uncle Toby, by nature, was not eloquent;——it had the
greater effect.——The surgeon was confounded;——not that
there wanted grounds for such, or greater, marks of impatience,——but 'twas unexpected too; in the four years he
had attended him, he had never seen anything like it in my
uncle Toby's carriage; he had never once dropped one fretful or discontented word;——he had been all patience,——
all submission.

——We lose the right of complaining sometimes by for-
bearing it;——but we oftener treble the force:——The surgeon was astonished;——but much more so when he heard
my uncle Toby go on and peremptorily insist upon his healing up the wound directly,——or sending for Monsieur
Ronjat, the king's serjeant-surgeon, to do it for him.

The desire of life and health is implanted in man's nature;——the love of liberty and enlargement is a sister passion to it: These my uncle Toby had in common with his
species;——and either of them had been sufficient to account
for his earnest desire to get well and out of doors;——but
I have told you before that nothing wrought with our family
after the common way;——and from the time and manner
in which this eager desire showed itself in the present case,
the penetrating reader will suspect there was some other
cause or crotchet for it in my uncle Toby's head:——There
was so, and 'tis the subject of the next chapter to set forth
what that cause and crotchet was. I own, when that's done,

'twill be time to return back to the parlour fireside, where we left my uncle Toby in the middle of his sentence.

CHAPTER V

When a man gives himself up to the government of a ruling passion,——or, in other words, when his HOBBY-HORSE grows headstrong,——farewell cool reason and fair discretion!

My uncle Toby's wound was near well, and as soon as the surgeon recovered his surprise, and could get leave to say as much——he told him 'twas just beginning to incarnate; and that if no fresh exfoliation happened, which there was no signs of,——it would be dried up in five or six weeks. The sound of as many olympiads twelve hours before would have conveyed an idea of shorter duration to my uncle Toby's mind.——The succession of his ideas was now rapid; ——he broiled with impatience to put his design in execution;——and so, without consulting further with any soul living,——which, by the bye, I think is right when you are predetermined to take no one soul's advice,——he privately ordered Trim, his man, to pack up a bundle of lint and dressings, and hire a chariot and four to be at the door exactly by twelve o'clock that day, when he knew my father would be upon 'Change.——So leaving a banknote upon the table for the surgeon's care of him, and a letter of tender thanks for his brother's,——he packed up his maps, his books of fortification, his instruments, &c.——and, by the help of a crutch on one side, and Trim on the other,—— my uncle Toby embarked for Shandy Hall.

The reason, or rather the rise, of this sudden demigration was as follows:

The table in my uncle Toby's room, and at which, the night before this change happened, he was sitting with his maps, &c., about him,——being somewhat of the smallest, for that infinity of great and small instruments of knowledge which usually lay crowded upon it,——he had the accident, in reaching over for his tobacco box, to throw down his compasses, and in stooping to take the compasses up, with his sleeve he threw down his case of instruments and snuffers;——and as the dice took a run against him, in his endeavouring to catch the snuffers in falling,——he thrust Monsieur Blondel off the table and Count de Pagan o' top of him.

'Twas to no purpose for a man lame as my uncle Toby was to think of redressing all these evils by himself;——he rung his bell for his man Trim;——Trim! quoth my uncle Toby, prithee see what confusion I have here been making. ——I must have some better contrivance, Trim.——Canst not thou take my rule and measure the length and breadth of this table, and then go and bespeak me one as big again? ——Yes, an' please your Honour, replied Trim, making a bow;——but I hope your Honour will be soon well enough to get down to your country seat, where,——as your Honour takes so much pleasure in fortification, we could manage this mater to a T.

I must here inform you that this servant of my uncle Toby's, who went by the name of Trim, had been a corporal in my uncle's own company,—his real name was James Butler,——but having got the nickname of Trim in the regiment, my uncle Toby, unless when he happened to be very angry with him, would never call him by any other name.

The poor fellow had been disabled for the service by a wound on his left knee by a musket bullet, at the battle of Landen, which was two years before the affair of Namur;—— and as the fellow was well beloved in the regiment, and a handy fellow into the bargain, my uncle Toby took him for his servant, and of excellent use was he, attending my uncle Toby in the camp and in his quarters as valet, groom, barber, cook, seamster, and nurse; and indeed, from first to last, waited upon him and served him with great fidelity and affection.

My uncle Toby loved the man in return, and what attached him more to him still was the similitude of their knowledge:——For Corporal Trim (for so, for the future, I shall call him), by four years' occasional attention to his master's discourse upon fortified towns, and the advantage of prying and peeping continually into his master's plans, &c., exclusive and besides what he gained HOBBY-HORSICALLY, as a body servant, *Non-Hobby-Horsical per se*,——had become no mean proficient in the science; and was thought, by the cook and chambermaid. to know as much of the nature of strongholds as my uncle Toby himself.

I have but one more stroke to give to finish Corporal Trim's character,——and it is the only dark line in it.—— The fellow loved to advise,——or rather to hear himself

79

talk; his carriage, however, was so perfectly respectful, 'twas easy to keep him silent when you had him so; but set his tongue a-going,——you had no hold of him;——he was voluble;——the eternal interlardings of *your Honour,* with the respectfulness of Corporal Trim's manner, interceding so strong in behalf of his elocution,——that though you might have been incommoded,——you could not well be angry. My uncle Toby was seldom either the one or the other with him,——or, at least, this fault, in Trim, broke no squares with 'em. My uncle Toby, as I said, loved the man;——and besides, as he ever looked upon a faithful servant,——but as a humble friend,——he could not bear to stop his mouth.——Such was Corporal Trim.

If I durst presume, continued Trim, to give your Honour my advice, and speak my opinion in this matter.—— Thou art welcome, Trim, quoth my uncle Toby,——speak,——speak what thou thinkst upon the subject, man, without fear. Why then, replied Trim (not hanging his ears and scratching his head like a country lout, but) stroking his hair back from his forehead, and standing erect as before his division.——I think, quoth Trim, advancing his left, which was his lame leg, a little forwards,——and pointing with his right hand open towards a map of Dunkirk, which was pinned against the hangings,——I think, quoth Corporal Trim, with humble submission to your Honour's better judgment,——that these ravelins, bastions, curtains, and hornworks make but a poor, contemptible, fiddle-faddle piece of work of it here upon paper, compared to what your Honour and I could make of it, were we in the country by ourselves, and had but a rood, or a rood and a half of ground to do what we pleased with. As summer is coming on, continued Trim, your Honour might sit out of doors, and give me the nography——(call it ichnography, quoth my uncle)——of the town or citadel your Honour was pleased to sit down before,——and I will be shot by your Honour upon the glacis of it, if I did not fortify it to your Honour's mind.——I dare say thou wouldst, Trim, quoth my uncle.——For if your Honour, continued the corporal, could but mark me the polygon, with its exact lines and angles.—— That I could do very well, quoth my uncle.——I would begin with the fosse, and if your Honour could tell me the proper depth and breadth,——I can to a hairsbreadth, Trim, replied my uncle,——I would throw out the earth upon this hand towards the town for the scarp,——and on that hand towards the campaign for the counterscarp.—— Very right, Trim, quoth my uncle Toby.——And when I had sloped them to your mind,——an' please your Honour, I would face the glacis, as the finest fortifications are done in Flanders, with sods,——and as your Honour knows they should be,——and I would make the walls and parapets with sods too;——The best engineers call them gazons, Trim, said my uncle Toby;——Whether they are gazons or sods is not much matter, replied Trim; your Honour knows they are ten times beyond a facing either of brick or stone;——I know they are, Trim, in some respects,——quoth my uncle Toby, nodding his head;——for a cannon ball enters into the gazon right onwards, without bringing any rubbish down with it, which might fill the fosse (as was the case at St. Nicolas's Gate) and facilitate the passage over it.

Your Honour understands these matters, replied Corporal Trim, better than any officer in his Majesty's service;——but would your Honour please to let the bespeaking of the table alone, and let us but go into the country, I would work under your Honour's directions like a horse, and make fortifications for you something like a tansy, with all their batteries, saps, ditches, and palisadoes, that it should be worth all the world's riding twenty miles to go and see it.

My uncle Toby blushed as red as scarlet as Trim went on;——but it was not a blush of guilt,——of modesty,——or of anger;——it was a blush of joy;——he was fired with Corporal Trim's project and description.——Trim! said my uncle Toby, thou hast said enough.——We might begin the campaign, continued Trim, on the very day that his Majesty and the Allies take the field, and demolish them town by town as fast as——Trim, quoth my uncle Toby, say no more. ——Your Honour, continued Trim, might sit in your arm-chair (pointing to it) this fine weather, giving me your orders, and I would——Say no more, Trim, quoth my uncle Toby. ——Besides, your Honour would get not only pleasure and good pastime,——but good air, and good exercise, and good health,——and your Honour's wound would be well in a month. Thou hast said enough, Trim,——quoth my uncle Toby (putting his hand into his breeches pocket)——I like thy project mightily;——And if your Honour pleases, I'll this moment go and buy a pioneer's spade to take down with us, and I'll bespeak a shovel and a pickaxe, and a couple of—— Say no more, Trim, quoth my uncle Toby, leaping up upon one leg, quite overcome with rapture,——and thrusting a guinea into Trim's hand;——Trim, said my uncle Toby, say no more; ——but go down, Trim, this moment, my lad, and bring up my supper this instant.

Trim ran down and brought up his master's supper,——to

no purpose:——Trim's plan of operation ran so in my uncle Toby's head, he could not taste it.——Trim, quoth my uncle Toby, get me to bed;——'twas all one.——Corporal Trim's description had fired his imagination;——my uncle Toby could not shut his eyes.——The more he considered it, the more bewitching the scene appeared to him;——so that, two full hours before daylight, he had come to a final determination, and had concerted the whole plan of his and Corporal Trim's decampment.

My uncle Toby had a little neat country house of his own in the village where my father's estate lay at Shandy, which had been left him by an old uncle, with a small estate of about one hundred pounds a year. Behind this house, and contiguous to it, was a kitchen garden of about half an acre;——and at the bottom of the garden, and cut off from it by a tall yew hedge, was a bowling green, containing just about as much ground as Corporal Trim wished for;——so that as Trim uttered the words, "A rood and a half of ground to do what they would with:"——this identical bowling green instantly presented itself, and became curiously painted, all at once, upon the retina of my uncle Toby's fancy;——which was the physical cause of making him change colour, or at least of heightening his blush to that immoderate degree I spoke of.

Never did lover post down to a beloved mistress with more heat and expectation than my uncle Toby did to enjoy this selfsame thing in private;——I say in private;——for it was sheltered from a house, as I told you, by a tall yew hedge, and was covered on the other three sides, from mortal sight, by rough holly and thick-set flowering shrubs;——so that the idea of not being seen did not a little contribute to the idea of pleasure preconceived in my uncle Toby's mind. ——Vain thought! however thick it was planted about,—— or private soever it might seem,——to think, dear uncle Toby, of enjoying a thing which took up a whole rood and a half of ground,——and not have it known!

How my uncle Toby and Corporal Trim managed this matter,——with the history of their campaigns, which were no way barren of events,——may make no uninteresting underplot in the epitasis and working up of this drama.——At present the scene must drop,——and change for the parlour fireside.

CHAPTER VI

——What can they be doing, brother? said my father.——I think, replied my uncle Toby,——taking, as I told you, his pipe from his mouth, and striking the ashes out of it as he began his sentence;——I think, replied he,——it would not be amiss, brother, if we rung the bell.

Pray, what's all that racket over our heads, Obadiah?—— quoth my father;——my brother and I can scarce hear ourselves speak.

Sir, answered Obadiah, making a bow towards his left shoulder,——my Mistress is taken very badly;——and where's Susannah running down the garden there, as if they were going to ravish her?——Sir, she is running the shortest cut into the town, replied Obadiah, to fetch the old midwife.—— Then saddle a horse, quoth my father, and do you go directly for Dr. Slop, the man midwife, with all our services,——and let him know your mistress is fallen into labour,——and that I desire he will return with you with all speed.

It is very strange, says my father, addressing himself to my uncle Toby, as Obadiah shut the door,——as there is so expert an operator as Dr. Slop so near——that my wife should persist to the very last in this obstinate humour of hers, in trusting the life of my child, who has had one misfortune already, to the ignorance of an old woman;——and not only the life of my child, brother,——but her own life, and with it the lives of all the children I might, peradventure, have begot out of her hereafter.

Mayhap, brother, replied my uncle Toby, my sister does it to save the expense:——A pudding's end,——replied my father;——the doctor must be paid the same for inaction as action,——if not better,——to keep him in temper.

——Then it can be out of nothing in the whole world, quoth my uncle Toby, in the simplicity of his heart,——but MODESTY:——My sister, I dare say, added he, does not care to let a man come so near her ****. I will not say whether my uncle Toby had completed the sentence or not;——'tis for his advantage to suppose he had,——as, I think, he could have added no ONE WORD which would have improved it.

If, on the contrary, my uncle Toby had not fully arrived at his period's end,——then the world stands indebted to the sudden snapping of my father's tobacco pipe for one of the neatest examples of that ornamental figure in oratory which Rhetoricians style the *Aposiopesis*.——Just heaven! how does the *Poco più* and the *Poco meno* of the Italian artists,——the insensible MORE or LESS, determine the precise line of beauty in the sentence, as well as in the statue! How do the slight touches of the chisel, the pencil, the pen, the fiddlestick, *et cetera*,——give the true swell, which gives the true pleasure!——O my countrymen!——be nice;——be cautious of your language;——and never, O! never let it be forgotten upon what small particles your eloquence and your fame depend.

——"My sister, mayhap," quoth my uncle Toby, "does not choose to let a man come so near her ****." Make this dash, ——'tis an Aposiopesis.——Take the dash away, and write *Backside*,——'tis Bawdy.——Scratch Backside out, and put *Covered way* in,——'tis a Metaphor;——and, I dare say, as fortification ran so much in my uncle Toby's head, that if he had been left to have added one word to the sentence,—— that word was it.

But whether that was the case or not the case,——or whether the snapping of my father's tobacco pipe so critically happened through accident or anger,——will be seen in due time.

CHAPTER VII

Though my father was a good natural philosopher,——yet he was something of a moral philosopher too; for which reason, when his tobacco pipe snapped short in the middle, ——he had nothing to do,——as such,——but to have taken hold of the two pieces, and thrown them gently upon the back of the fire.——He did no such thing;——he threw them with all the violence in the world;——and, to give the action still more emphasis,——he started up upon both his legs to do it.

This looked something like heat;——and the manner of his reply to what my uncle Toby was saying proved it was so.

——"Not choose," quoth my father (repeating my uncle Toby's words), "to let a man come so near her."——By heaven, brother Toby! you would try the patience of a Job; ——and I think I have the plagues of one already, without it. ——Why?——Where?——Wherein?——Wherefore?——Upon what account, replied my uncle Toby, in the utmost astonishment.——To think, said my father, of a man living to your age, brother, and knowing so little about women!—— I know nothing at all about them,——replied my uncle Toby; and I think, continued he, that the shock I received the year after the demolition of Dunkirk, in my affair with widow Wadman;——which shock you know I should not have received, but from my total ignorance of the sex;——has given me just cause to say, That I neither know, nor do pretend to know, anything about 'em, or their concerns either.——Methinks, brother, replied my father, you might, at least, know so much as the right end of a woman from the wrong.

It is said in Aristotle's *Master-Piece*, "That when a man doth think of anything which is past,——he looketh down upon the ground;——but that when he thinketh of something which is to come, he looketh up towards the heavens."

My uncle Toby, I suppose, thought of neither,——for he looked horizontally.——Right end,——quoth my uncle Toby, muttering the two words low to himself, and fixing his two eyes insensibly, as he muttered them, upon a small crevice formed by a bad joint in the chimney piece.—— Right end of a woman!——I declare, quoth my uncle, I know no more which it is than the man in the moon;——and if I was to think, continued my uncle Toby (keeping his eye still fixed upon the bad joint), this month together, I am sure I should not be able to find it out.

Then brother Toby, replied my father, I will tell you. Everything in this world, continued my father (filling a fresh pipe),——everything in this earthly world, my dear brother Toby, has two handles.——Not always, quoth my uncle Toby.——At least, replied my father, every one has two hands,——which comes to the same thing.——Now, if a man was to sit down coolly, and consider within himself the make, the shape, the construction, come-at-ability, and convenience of all the parts which constitute the whole of that animal called Woman, and compare them analogically.—— I never understood rightly the meaning of that word,—— quoth my uncle Toby.——ANALOGY, replied my father, is the certain relation and agreement, which different——Here a devil of a rap at the door snapped my father's definition (like his tobacco pipe) in two,——and, at the same time, crushed the head of as notable and curious a dissertation as ever was engendered in the womb of speculation;——it was some months before my father could get an opportunity to be safely delivered of it:——And, at this hour, it is a thing full as problematical as the subject of the dissertation itself—— (considering the confusion and distresses of our domestic misadventures, which are now coming thick one upon the back of another) whether I shall be able to find a place for it in the third volume or not.

CHAPTER VIII

It is about an hour and a half's tolerable good reading since my uncle Toby rung the bell, when Obadiah was ordered to saddle a horse, and go for Dr. Slop, the man midwife;—— so that no one can say, with reason, that I have not allowed Obadiah time enough, poetically speaking, and considering the emergency too, both to go and come;——though, morally and truly speaking, the man, perhaps, has scarce had time to get on his boots.

If the hypercritic will go upon this; and is resolved after all to take a pendulum, and measure the true distance betwixt the ringing of the bell and the rap at the door;—— and, after finding it to be no more than two minutes, thirteen seconds, and three fifths,——should take upon him to insult over me for such a breach in the unity, or rather probability, of time;——I would remind him that the idea of duration and of its simple modes is got merely from the train and succession of our ideas,——and is the true scholastic pendulum,——and by which, as a scholar, I will be tried in this matter,——abjuring and detesting the jurisdiction of all other pendulums whatever.

I would, therefore, desire him to consider that it is but poor eight miles from Shandy Hall to Dr. Slop the man midwife's house;——and that whilst Obadiah has been going those said miles and back, I have brought my uncle Toby from Namur, quite across all Flanders, into England:—— That I have had him ill upon my hands near four years;—— and have since travelled him and Corporal Trim, in a chariot and four, a journey of near two hundred miles down into Yorkshire;———all which put together must have prepared the reader's imagination for the entrance of Dr. Slop upon the stage,———as much at least (I hope) as a dance, a song, or a concerto between the acts.

If my hypercritic is intractable, alleging that two minutes and thirteen seconds are no more than two minutes and thirteen seconds,———when I have said all I can about them; ———and that this plea, though it might save me dramatically, will damn me biographically, rendering my book, from this very moment, a professed ROMANCE, which before was a book apocryphal:———If I am thus pressed———I then put an end to the whole objection and controversy about it all at once,——— by acquainting him that Obadiah had not got above three-score yards from the stable yard before he met with Dr. Slop; ———and indeed he gave a dirty proof that he had met with him,———and was within an ace of giving a tragical one too.

Imagine to yourself;———but this had better begin a new chapter.

CHAPTER IX

Imagine to yourself a little, squat, uncourtly figure of a Dr. Slop, of about four feet and a half perpendicular height, with a breadth of back, and a sesquipedality of belly, which might have done honour to a serjeant in the horse guards.

Such were the outlines of Dr. Slop's figure, which,———if you have read Hogarth's analysis of beauty, and if you have not, I wish you would,———you must know, may as certainly be caricatured and conveyed to the mind by three strokes as three hundred.

Imagine such a one,———for such, I say, were the outlines of Dr. Slop's figure, coming slowly along, foot by foot, waddling through the dirt upon the vertebrae of a little diminutive pony, of a pretty colour;———but of strength,——— alack!———scarce able to have made an amble of it, under such a fardel, had the roads been in an ambling condition. ———They were not.———Imagine to yourself Obadiah, mounted upon a strong monster of a coach horse, pricked into a full gallop, and making all practicable speed the adverse way.

Pray, Sir, let me interest you a moment in this description.

Had Dr. Slop beheld Obadiah a mile off, posting in a narrow lane directly towards him, at that monstrous rate,——splashing and plunging like a devil through thick and thin, as he approached, would not such a phenomenon, with such a vortex of mud and water moving along with it round its axis, ——have been a subject of juster apprehension to Dr. Slop in his situation than the *worst* of Whiston's comets?——To say nothing of the NUCLEUS; that is, of Obadiah and the coach horse.——In my idea, the vortex alone of 'em was enough to have involved and carried, if not the doctor, at least the doctor's pony quite away with it. What then do you think must the terror and hydrophobia of Dr. Slop have been, when you read (which you are just going to do) that he was advancing thus warily along towards Shandy Hall and had approached to within sixty yards of it, and within five yards of a sudden turn, made by an acute angle of the garden wall,—— and in the dirtiest part of a dirty lane,——when Obadiah and his coach horse turned the corner, rapid, furious,——pop, ——full upon him!——Nothing, I think, in nature can be supposed more terrible than such a Rencounter,——so imprompt! so ill prepared to stand the shock of it as Dr. Slop was!

What could Dr. Slop do?——He crossed himself + —— Pugh!——but the doctor, Sir, was a Papist.——No matter; he had better have kept hold of the pummel.——He had so;——nay, as it happened, he had better have done nothing at all;——for in crossing himself, he let go his whip,——and in attempting to save his whip betwixt his knee and his saddle's skirt, as it slipped, he lost his stirrup;——in losing which, he lost his seat;——and in the multitude of all these losses (which, by the bye, shows what little advantage there is in crossing), the unfortunate doctor lost his presence of mind. So that, without waiting for Obadiah's onset, he left his pony to its destiny, tumbling off it diagonally, something in the style and manner of a pack of wool, and without any other consequence from the fall save that of being left (as it would have been) with the broadest part of him sunk about twelve inches deep in the mire.

Obadiah pulled off his cap twice to Dr. Slop;——once as he was falling,——and then again when he saw him seated. ——Ill-timed complaisance!——had not the fellow better have stopped his horse, and got off and helped him?——Sir, he did all that his situation would allow;——but the MoMENTUM of the coach horse was so great that Obadiah could not do it all at once;——he rode in a circle three times round Dr. Slop before he could fully accomplish it anyhow; ——and at the last, when he did stop his beast, 'twas done with such an explosion of mud that Obadiah had better have been a league off. In short, never was a Dr. Slop so beluted, and so transubstantiated, since that affair came into fashion.

CHAPTER X

When Dr. Slop entered the back parlour, where my father and my uncle Toby were discoursing upon the nature of women,——it was hard to determine whether Dr. Slop's figure, or Dr. Slop's presence, occasioned more surprise to them; for as the accident happened so near the house as not to make it worth while for Obadiah to remount him,——Obadiah had led him in as he was, *unwiped, unappointed, unaneled,* with all his stains and blotches on him.——He stood like Hamlet's ghost, motionless and speechless for a full minute and a half at the parlour door (Obadiah still holding his hand), with all the majesty of mud. His hinder parts, upon which he had received his fall, totally besmeared,——and in every other part of him, blotched over in such a manner with Obadiah's explosion that you would have sworn (without mental reservation) that every grain of it had taken effect.

Here was a fair opportunity for my uncle Toby to have triumphed over my father in his turn;——for no mortal who had beheld Dr. Slop in that pickle could have dissented from so much, at least, of my uncle Toby's opinion, "That mayhap his sister might not care to let such a Dr. Slop come so near her ****" But it was the *Argumentum ad hominem;* and if my uncle Toby was not very expert at it, you may think, he might not care to use it.——No; the reason was——'twas not his nature to insult.

Dr. Slop's presence, at that time, was no less problematical than the mode of it; though, it is certain, one moment's reflection in my father might have solved it; for he had apprized Dr. Slop but the week before that my mother was at her full reckoning; and as the doctor had heard nothing since, 'twas natural and very political too in him to have taken a ride to Shandy Hall, as he did, merely to see how matters went on.

But my father's mind took unfortunately a wrong turn in the investigation; running, like the hypercritic's, altogether upon the ringing of the bell and the rap upon the door,—— measuring their distance,——and keeping his mind so intent upon the operation as to have power to think of nothing else,——commonplace infirmity of the greatest mathematicians! working with might and main at the demonstration, and so wasting all their strength upon it, that they have none left in them to draw the corollary, to do good with.

The ringing of the bell and the rap upon the door struck likewise strong upon the sensorium of my uncle Toby,—— but it excited a very different train of thoughts;——the two irreconcilable pulsations instantly brought Stevinus, the great engineer, along with them into my uncle Toby's mind:—— What business Stevinus had in this affair——is the greatest problem of all;——it shall be solved,——but not in the next chapter.

CHAPTER XI

Writing, when properly managed (as you may be sure I think mine is), is but a different name for conversation: As no one who knows what he is about in good company would venture to talk all;——so no author who understands the just boundaries of decorum and good breeding would presume to think all: The truest respect which you can pay to the reader's understanding is to halve this matter amicably, and leave him something to imagine, in his turn, as well as yourself.

For my own part, I am eternally paying him compliments of this kind, and do all that lies in my power to keep his imagination as busy as my own.

'Tis his turn now;——I have given an ample description of Dr. Slop's sad overthrow, and of his sad appearance in the back parlour;——his imagination must now go on with it for a while.

Let the reader imagine, then, that Dr. Slop has told his tale;——and in what words, and with what aggravations his fancy chooses:——Let him suppose that Obadiah has told his tale also, and with such rueful looks of affected concern as he thinks will best contrast the two figures as they stand by each other:——Let him imagine that my father has stepped upstairs to see my mother:——And, to conclude this work of imagination,——let him imagine the doctor washed,——rubbed down,——condoled with,——felicitated,——got into a pair of Obadiah's pumps, stepping forwards towards the door, upon the very point of entering upon action.

Truce!——truce, good Dr. Slop!——stay thy obstetric hand;——return it safe into thy bosom to keep it warm;——little dost thou know what obstacles,——little dost thou think what hidden causes retard its operation!——Hast thou, Dr. Slop,——hast thou been intrusted with the secret articles of this solemn treaty which has brought thee into this place? ——Art thou aware that, at this instant, a daughter of Lucina is put obstetrically over thy head? Alas! 'tis too true.—— Besides, great son of Pilumnus! what canst thou do?—— Thou hast come forth unarmed;——thou hast left thy *tire tête*,——thy new-invented *forceps*,——thy *crotchet*,—— thy *squirt*, and all thy instruments of salvation and deliverance behind thee.——By heaven! at this moment they are hanging up in a green baize bag, betwixt thy two pistols, at thy bed's head!——Ring;——call;——send Obadiah back upon the coach horse to bring them with all speed.

——Make great haste, Obadiah, quoth my father, and I'll give thee a crown;——and, quoth my uncle Toby, I'll give him another.

CHAPTER XII

Your sudden and unexpected arrival, quoth my uncle Toby, addressing himself to Dr. Slop (all three of them sitting down to the fire together, as my uncle Toby began to speak)—— instantly brought the great Stevinus into my head, who, you must know, is a favourite author with me.——Then, added my father, making use of the argument *Ad Crumenam*, ——I will lay twenty guineas to a single crown piece (which will serve to give away to Obadiah when he gets back) that this same Stevinus was some engineer or other,——or has wrote something or other, either directly or indirectly, upon the science of fortification.

He has so,——replied my uncle Toby.——I knew it, said

91

my father;——though, for the soul of me, I cannot see what kind of connection there can be betwixt Dr. Slop's sudden coming and a discourse upon fortification;——yet I feared it.
——Talk of what we will, brother,——or let the occasion be never so foreign or unfit for the subject,——you are sure to bring it in: I would not, brother Toby, continued my father,——I declare I would not have my head so full of curtains and hornworks.——That, I dare say, you would not, quoth Dr. Slop, interrupting him, and laughing most immoderately at his pun.

Dennis, the critic, could not detest and abhor a pun, or the insinuation of a pun, more cordially than my father;——he would grow testy upon it at any time;——but to be broke in upon by one, in a serious discourse, was as bad, he would say, as a fillip upon the nose;——he saw no difference.

Sir, quoth my uncle Toby, addressing himself to Dr. Slop,——the curtains my brother Shandy mentions here have nothing to do with bedsteads;——though, I know, Du Cange says, "That bed curtains, in all probability, have taken their name from them;"——nor have the horn works he speaks of anything in the world to do with the horn works of cuckoldom:——But the *curtain*, Sir, is the word we use in fortification for that part of the wall or rampart which lies between the two bastions and joins them.——Besiegers seldom offer to carry on their attacks directly against the curtain for this reason, because they are so well *flanked*. ('Tis the case of other curtains, quoth Dr. Slop, laughing.) However, continued my uncle Toby, to make them sure, we generally choose to place ravelins before them, taking care only to extend them beyond the fosse or ditch:——The common men, who know very little of fortification, confound the ravelin and the half-moon together,——though they are very different things;——not in their figure or construction, for we make them exactly alike in all points;——for they always consist of two faces, making a salient angle, with the gorges not straight, but in form of a crescent.——Where then lies the difference? (quoth my father, a little testily).——In their situations, answered my uncle Toby:——For when a ravelin, brother, stands before the curtain, it is a ravelin; and when a ravelin stands before a bastion, then the ravelin is not a ravelin;——it is a half-moon;——a half-moon likewise is a half-moon, and no more, so long as it stands before its bastion;——but was it to change place, and get before the curtain,——'twould be no longer a half-moon; a half-moon, in that case, is not a half-moon;——'tis no more than a ravelin.——I think, quoth my father, that the noble science of defence has its weak sides,——as well as others.

——As for the hornworks (high! ho! sighed my father) which, continued my uncle Toby, my brother was speaking of, they are a very considerable part of an outwork;——they are called by the French engineers *Ouvrage à corne*, and we generally make them to cover such places as we suspect to be weaker than the rest;——'tis formed by two epaulements or demibastions;——they are very pretty, and if you will take a walk, I'll engage to show you one well worth your trouble. ——I own, continued my uncle Toby, when we crown them, ——they are much stronger, but then they are very expensive, and take up a great deal of ground; so that, in my opinion, they are most of use to cover or defend the head of a camp; otherwise the double tenaille——By the mother who bore us! ——brother Toby, quoth my father, not able to hold out any longer,——you would provoke a saint;——here have you got us, I know not how, not only souse into the middle of the old subject again:——But so full is your head of these con-founded works, that though my wife is this moment in the pains of labour,——and you hear her cry out,——yet noth-ing will serve you but to carry off the man midwife.—— *Accoucheur*,——if you please, quoth Dr. Slop.——With all my heart, replied my father, I don't care what they call you,——but I wish the whole science of fortification, with all its inventors, at the devil;——it has been the death of thou-sands,——and it will be mine, in the end.——I would not, I would not, brother Toby, have my brains so full of saps, mines, blinds, gabions, palisadoes, ravelins, half-moons, and such trumpery, to be proprietor of Namur, and of all the towns in Flanders with it.

My uncle Toby was a man patient of injuries;——not from want of courage;——I have told you in the fifth chapter of this second book, "That he was a man of courage:"——And will add here that where just occasions presented, or called it forth,——I know no man under whose arm I would sooner have taken shelter; nor did this arise from any insensibility or obtuseness of his intellectual parts;——for he felt this insult of my father's as feelingly as a man could do;——but he was of a peaceful, placid nature,——no jarring element in it,——all was mixed up so kindly within him; my uncle Toby had scarce a heart to retaliate upon a fly.

——Go——says he, one day at dinner, to an overgrown one which had buzzed about his nose, and tormented him cruelly all dinnertime,——and which, after infinite attempts, he had caught at last, as it flew by him;——I'll not hurt thee, says my uncle Toby, rising from his chair, and going across the room, with the fly in his hand,——I'll not hurt a hair of thy head:——Go, says he, lifting up the sash, and opening his hand as he spoke, to let it escape;——go, poor devil, get thee gone, why should I hurt thee?——This world surely is wide enough to hold both thee and me.

I was but ten years old when this happened; but whether it was that the action itself was more in unison to my nerves at that age of pity, which instantly set my whole frame into one vibration of most pleasurable sensation;——or how far the manner and expression of it might go towards it;——or in what degree, or by what secret magic,——a tone of voice and harmony of movement, attuned by mercy, might find a passage to my heart, I know not;——this I know, that the lesson of universal good will then taught and imprinted by my uncle Toby has never since been worn out of my mind: And though I would not depreciate what the study of the *Literae humaniores,* at the university, have done for me in that respect, or discredit the other helps of an expensive education bestowed upon me both at home and abroad since;——yet I often think that I owe one half of my philanthropy to that one accidental impression.

☞ This is to serve for parents and governors instead of a whole volume upon the subject.

I could not give the reader this stroke in my uncle Toby's picture by the instrument with which I drew the other parts of it,——that taking in no more than the mere HOBBY-HORSICAL likeness;——this is a part of his moral character. My father, in this patient endurance of wrongs which I mention, was very different, as the reader must long ago have noted; he had a much more acute and quick sensibility of nature, attended with a little soreness of temper; though this never transported him to anything which looked like malignancy;——yet, in the little rubs and vexations of life, 'twas apt to show itself in a drollish and witty kind of peevishness:——He was, however, frank and generous in his nature;——at all times open to conviction; and in the little ebullitions of this subacid humour towards others, but particularly towards my uncle Toby, whom he truly loved,——he would feel more pain, ten times told (except in the affair of my aunt Dinah, or where an hypothesis was concerned) than what he ever gave.

The characters of the two brothers, in this view of them, reflected light upon each other, and appeared with great advantage in this affair which arose about Stevinus.

I need not tell the reader, if he keeps a HOBBY-HORSE,——that a man's HOBBY-HORSE is as tender a part as he has about him; and that these unprovoked strokes at my uncle Toby's could not be unfelt by him.——No;——as I said above, my uncle Toby did feel them, and very sensibly too.

Pray, Sir, what said he?——How did he behave?——O, Sir!——it was great: For as soon as my father had done insulting his HOBBY-HORSE,——he turned his head, without the least emotion, from Dr. Slop, to whom he was addressing his discourse, and looked up into my father's face with a countenance spread over with so much good nature;——so placid;——so fraternal;——so inexpressibly tender towards him;——it penetrated my father to his heart: He rose up hastily from his chair, and seizing hold of both my uncle Toby's hands as he spoke:——Brother Toby, said he,——I beg thy pardon;——forgive, I pray thee, this rash humour which my mother gave me.——My dear, dear brother, answered my uncle Toby, rising up by my father's help, say no more about it;——you are heartily welcome, had it been ten times as much, brother. But 'tis ungenerous, replied my father, to hurt any man;——a brother worse;——but to hurt a brother of such gentle manners,——so unprovoking,——and so unresenting;——'tis base:——By heaven, 'tis cowardly.——You are heartily welcome, brother, quoth my uncle Toby,——had it been fifty times as much.——Besides, what have I to do, my dear Toby, cried my father, either with your amusements or your pleasures, unless it was in my power (which it is not) to increase their measure?

——Brother Shandy, answered my uncle Toby, looking wistfully in his face,——you are much mistaken in this point;——for you do increase my pleasure very much, in begetting children for the Shandy family at your time of life.——But, by that, Sir, quoth Dr. Slop, Mr. Shandy increases his own.——Not a jot, quoth my father.

CHAPTER XIII

My brother does it, quoth my uncle Toby, out of *principle.* ——In a family way, I suppose, quoth Dr. Slop.——Pshaw! ——said my father,——'tis not worth talking of.

CHAPTER XIV

At the end of the last chapter, my father and my uncle Toby were left both standing, like Brutus and Cassius at the close of the scene making up their accounts.

As my father spoke the three last words,——he sat down;——my uncle Toby exactly followed his example, only that before he took his chair, he rung the bell, to order Corporal Trim, who was in waiting, to step home for Stevinus;——my uncle Toby's house being no further off than the opposite side of the way.

Some men would have dropped the subject of Stevinus;——but my uncle Toby had no resentment in his heart, and he went on with the subject, to show my father that he had none.

Your sudden appearance, Dr. Slop, quoth my uncle, resuming the discourse, instantly brought Stevinus into my head. (My father, you may be sure, did not offer to lay any more wagers upon Stevinus's head)——Because, continued my uncle Toby, the celebrated sailing chariot which belonged to Prince Maurice, and was of such wonderful contrivance and velocity as to carry half a dozen people thirty German miles in I don't know how few minutes,——was invented by Stevinus, that great mathematician and engineer.

You might have spared your servant the trouble, quoth Dr. Slop, (as the fellow is lame) of going for Stevinus's account of it, because, in my return from Leyden through the Hague, I walked as far as Schevling, which is two long miles, on purpose to take a view of it.

——That's nothing, replied my uncle Toby, to what the learned Peireskius did, who walked a matter of five hundred miles, reckoning from Paris to Schevling, and from Schevling to Paris back again, in order to see it,——and nothing else.

Some men cannot bear to be outgone.

The more fool Peireskius, replied Dr. Slop. But mark, 'twas out of no contempt of Peireskius at all;——but that Peireskius's indefatigable labour in trudging so far on foot out of love for the sciences reduced the exploit of Dr.

Slop, in that affair, to nothing;——the more fool Peireskius, said he again:——Why so?——replied my father, taking his brother's part, not only to make reparation as fast as he could for the insult he had given him, which sat still upon my father's mind;——but partly that my father began really to interest himself in the discourse.——Why so?——said he. Why is Peireskius, or any man else, to be abused for an appetite for that or any other morsel of sound knowledge? For, notwithstanding I know nothing of the chariot in question, continued he, the inventor of it must have had a very mechanical head; and though I cannot guess upon what principles of philosophy he has achieved it,——yet certainly his machine has been constructed upon solid ones, be they what they will, or it could not have answered at the rate my brother mentions.

It answered, replied my uncle Toby, as well, if not better; for, as Peireskius elegantly expresses it, speaking of the velocity of its motion, *Tam citus erat, quam erat ventus;* which, unless I have forgot my Latin, is *that it was as swift as the wind itself.*

But pray, Dr. Slop, quoth my father, interrupting my uncle (though not without begging pardon for it, at the same time), upon what principles was this selfsame chariot set a-going?——Upon very pretty principles to be sure, replied Dr. Slop;——and I have often wondered, continued he, evading the question, why none of our gentry, who live upon large plains like this of ours——(especially they whose wives are not past childbearing), attempt nothing of this kind; for it would not only be infinitely expeditious upon sudden calls, to which the sex is subject,——if the wind only served,——but would be excellent good husbandry to make use of the winds, which cost nothing, and which eat nothing, rather than horses, which (the devil take 'em) both cost and eat a great deal.

For that very reason, replied my father, "Because they cost nothing, and because they eat nothing,"——the scheme is bad;——it is the consumption of our products, as well as the manufactures of them, which gives bread to the hungry, circulates trade,——brings in money, and supports the value of our lands;——and though, I own, if I was a prince, I would generously recompense the scientific head which brought forth such contrivances,——yet I would as peremptorily suppress the use of them.

My father here had got into his element,——and was going on as prosperously with his dissertation upon trade as

97

my uncle Toby had before upon his of fortification;——but, to the loss of much sound knowledge, the destinies in the morning had decreed that no dissertation of any kind should be spun by my father that day;——for as he opened his mouth to begin the next sentence,

CHAPTER XV

In popped Corporal Trim with Stevinus:——But 'twas too late;——all the discourse had been exhausted without him, and was running into a new channel.

——You may take the book home again, Trim, said my uncle Toby, nodding to him.

But prithee, corporal, quoth my father, drolling,——look first into it, and see if thou canst spy aught of a sailing chariot in it.

Corporal Trim, by being in the service, had learned to obey,——and not to remonstrate;——so taking the book to a side table, and running over the leaves; an' please your Honour, said Trim, I can see no such thing;——however, continued the corporal, drolling a little in his turn, I'll make sure work of it, an' please your Honour;——so taking hold of the two covers of the book, one in each hand, and letting the leaves fall down, as he bent the covers back, he gave the book a good sound shake.

There is something fallen out, however, said Trim, an' please your Honour; but it is not a chariot, or anything like one:——Prithee, corporal, said my father, smiling, what is it then?——I think, answered Trim, stooping to take it up,——'tis more like a sermon,——for it begins with a text of Scripture, and the chapter and verse;——and then goes on, not as a chariot,——but like a sermon directly.

The company smiled.

I cannot conceive how it is possible, quoth my uncle Toby, for such a thing as a sermon to have got into my Stevinus.

I think 'tis a sermon, replied Trim;——but if it please your Honours, as it is a fair hand, I will read you a page;——for Trim, you must know, loved to hear himself read almost as well as talk.

I have ever a strong propensity, said my father, to look

into things which cross my way by such strange fatalities as these;——and as we have nothing better to do, at least till Obadiah gets back, I should be obliged to you, brother, if Dr. Slop has no objection to it, to order the corporal to give us a page or two of it,——if he is as able to do it as he seems willing. An' please your Honour, quoth Trim, I officiated two whole campaigns in Flanders as clerk to the chaplain of the regiment.——He can read it, quoth my uncle Toby, as well as I can.——Trim, I assure you, was the best scholar in my company, and should have had the next halberd, but for the poor fellow's misfortune. Corporal Trim laid his hand upon his heart, and made an humble bow to his master;——then laying down his hat upon the floor, and taking up the sermon in his left hand, in order to have his right at liberty,——he advanced, nothing doubting, into the middle of the room, where he could best see, and be best seen by, his audience.

CHAPTER XVI

——If you have any objection,——said my father, addressing himself to Dr. Slop. Not in the least, replied Dr. Slop; ——for it does not appear on which side of the question it is wrote;——it may be a composition of a divine of our church, as well as yours,——so that we run equal risks.——'Tis wrote upon neither side, quoth Trim, for 'tis only upon *Conscience*, an' please your Honours.

Trim's reason put his audience into good humour,——all but Dr. Slop, who, turning his head about towards Trim, looked a little angry.

Begin, Trim,——and read distinctly, quoth my father;—— I will, an' please your Honour, replied the corporal, making a bow, and bespeaking attention with a slight movement of his right hand.

CHAPTER XVII

——But before the corporal begins, I must first give you a description of his attitude;——otherwise he will naturally stand represented, by your imagination, in an uneasy posture,

——stiff,——perpendicular,——dividing the weight of his body equally upon both legs;——his eye fixed, as if on duty;——his look determined;——clinching the sermon in his left hand, like his firelock:——In a word, you would be apt to paint Trim as if he was standing in his platoon ready for action:——His attitude was as unlike all this as you can conceive.

He stood before them with his body swayed, and bent forwards just so far as to make an angle of 85 degrees and a half upon the plane of the horizon;——which sound orators, to whom I address this, know very well to be the true persuasive angle of incidence;——in any other angle you may talk and preach;——'tis certain,——and it is done every day;——but with what effect,——I leave the world to judge!

The necessity of this precise angle of 85 degrees and a half to a mathematical exactness,——does it not show us, by the way,——how the arts and sciences mutually befriend each other?

How the deuce Corporal Trim, who knew not so much as an acute angle from an obtuse one, came to hit it so exactly;——or whether it was chance or nature, or good sense or imitation, &c., shall be commented upon in that part of this cyclopaedia of arts and sciences where the instrumental parts of the eloquence of the senate, the pulpit, the bar, the coffeehouse, the bedchamber and fireside fall under consideration.

He stood,——for I repeat it, to take the picture of him in at one view, with his body swayed, and somewhat bent forwards,——his right leg firm under him, sustaining seven eighths of his whole weight,——the foot of his left leg, the defect of which was no disadvantage to his attitude, advanced a little,——not laterally, nor forwards, but in a line betwixt them;——his knee bent, but that not violently,——but so as to fall within the limits of the line of beauty;——and I add, of the line of science too;——for consider, it had one eighth part of his body to bear up;——so that in this case the position of the leg is determined,——because the foot could be no further advanced, or the knee more bent, than what would allow him mechanically to receive an eighth part of his whole weight under it,——and to carry it too.

☞ This I recommend to painters:——need I add,——to orators?——I think not; for, unless they practise it,——they must fall upon their noses.

So much for Corporal Trim's body and legs.——He held

the sermon loosely,——not carelessly, in his left hand, raised
something above his stomach, and detached a little from his
breast;——his right arm falling negligently by his side, as
nature and the laws of gravity ordered it,——but with the
palm of it open and turned towards his audience, ready
to aid the sentiment, in case it stood in need.

Corporal Trim's eyes and the muscles of his face were in
full harmony with the other parts of him;——he looked
frank,——unconstrained,——something assured,——but not
bordering upon assurance.

Let not the critic ask how Corporal Trim could come by all
this; I've told him it shall be explained;——but so he stood
before my father, my uncle Toby, and Dr. Slop,——so swayed
his body, so contrasted his limbs, and with such an oratorical
sweep throughout the whole figure,——a statuary might have
modelled from it;——nay, I doubt whether the oldest Fellow
of a College,——or the Hebrew Professor himself, could
have much mended it.

Trim made a bow, and read as follows:

The SERMON

HEBREWS xiii: 18

——*For we* trust *we have a good Conscience.*——

"TRUST!——Trust we have a good conscience!"

[Certainly, Trim, quoth my father, interrupting him, you
give that sentence a very improper accent; for you curl up
your nose, man, and read it with such a sneering tone, as if
the Parson was going to abuse the Apostle.

He is, an' please your Honour, replied Trim. Pugh! said
my father, smiling.

Sir, quoth Dr. Slop, Trim is certainly in the right; for the
writer (who I perceive is a Protestant), by the snappish manner in which he takes up the Apostle, is certainly going to
abuse him,——if this treatment of him has not done it already.
But from whence, replied my father, have you concluded so
soon, Dr. Slop, that the writer is of our church?——for aught
I can see yet,——he may be of any church:——Because, answered Dr. Slop, if he was of ours,——he durst no more
take such a licence,——than a bear by his beard:——If, in
our communion, Sir, a man was to insult an Apostle,——a

101

saint,——or even the paring of a saint's nail,——he would have his eyes scratched out.——What, by the saint? quoth my uncle Toby. No, replied Dr. Slop,——he would have an old house over his head. Pray, is the Inquisition an ancient building, answered my uncle Toby, or is it a modern one? ——I know nothing of architecture, replied Dr. Slop.——An' please your Honours, quoth Trim, the Inquisition is the vilest——Prithee spare thy description, Trim; I hate the very name of it, said my father.——No matter for that, answered Dr. Slop;——it has its uses; for though I'm no great advocate for it, yet in such a case as this, he would soon be taught better manners; and I can tell him, if he went on at that rate, would be flung into the Inquisition for his pains. God help him then, quoth my uncle Toby. Amen, added Trim; for, heaven above knows, I have a poor brother who has been fourteen years a captive in it.——I never heard one word of it before, said my uncle Toby, hastily:——How came he there, Trim?——O, Sir! the story will make your heart bleed,——as it has made mine a thousand times;——but it is too long to be told now;——your Honour shall hear it from first to last someday when I am working beside you in our fortifications;——but the short of the story is this:—— That my brother Tom went over a servant to Lisbon,—— and then married a Jew's widow, who kept a small shop, and sold sausages, which, somehow or other, was the cause of his being taken in the middle of the night out of his bed, where he was lying with his wife and two small children, and carried directly to the Inquisition, where, God help him, continued Trim, fetching a sigh from the bottom of his heart, ——the poor honest lad lies confined at this hour;——he was as honest a soul, added Trim (pulling out his handkerchief), as ever blood warmed.——

——The tears trickled down Trim's cheeks faster than he could well wipe them away.——A dead silence in the room ensued for some minutes.——Certain proof of pity!

Come, Trim, quoth my father, after he saw the poor fellow's grief had got a little vent,——read on,——and put this melancholy story out of thy head:——I grieve that I interrupted thee;——but prithee begin the sermon again;——for if the first sentence in it is matter of abuse, as thou sayest, I have a great desire to know what kind of provocation the Apostle has given.

Corporal Trim wiped his face, and returning his handkerchief into his pocket, and making a bow as he did it,——he began again.]

The SERMON

HEBREWS xiii: 18

——For we trust we have a good Conscience.——

"TRUST! trust we have a good conscience! Surely if there is anything in this life which a man may depend upon, and to the knowledge of which he is capable of arriving upon the most indisputable evidence, it must be this very thing, ——whether he has a good conscience or no."

[I am positive I am right, quoth Dr. Slop.]

"If a man thinks at all, he cannot well be a stranger to the true state of this account;——he must be privy to his own thoughts and desires;——he must remember his past pursuits, and know certainly the true springs and motives which, in general, have governed the actions of his life."

[I defy him, without an assistant, quoth Dr. Slop.]

"In other matters we may be deceived by false appearances; and, as the wise man complains, *hardly do we guess aright at the things that are upon the earth, and with labour do we find the things that are before us.* But here the mind has all the evidence and facts within herself;——is conscious of the web she has wove;——knows its texture and fineness, and the exact share which every passion has had in working upon the several designs which virtue or vice had planned before her."

[The language is good, and I declare Trim reads very well, quoth my father.]

"Now,——as conscience is nothing else but the knowledge which the mind has within herself of this; and the judgment, either of approbation or censure, which it unavoidably makes upon the successive actions of our lives; 'tis plain you will say, from the very terms of the proposition,——whenever this inward testimony goes against a man, and he stands self-accused,——that he must necessarily be a guilty man.—— And, on the contrary, when the report is favourable on his side, and his heart condemns him not,——that it is not a matter of *trust*, as the Apostle intimates,——but a matter of *certainty* and fact that the conscience is good, and that the man must be good also."

[Then the Apostle is altogether in the wrong, I suppose, quoth Dr. Slop, and the Protestant divine is in the right. Sir, have patience, replied my father, for I think it will presently appear that St. Paul and the Protestant divine are both of an opinion.——As nearly so, quoth Dr. Slop, as east is to west; ——but this, continued he, lifting both hands, comes from the liberty of the press.

It is no more, at the worst, replied my uncle Toby, than the liberty of the pulpit; for it does not appear that the sermon is printed, or ever likely to be.

Go on, Trim, quoth my father.]

"At first sight this may seem to be a true state of the case; and I make no doubt but the knowledge of right and wrong is so truly impressed upon the mind of man,——that did no such thing ever happen as that the conscience of a man, by long habits of sin, might (as the Scripture assures it may) insensibly become hard;——and, like some tender parts of his body, by much stress and continual hard usage, lose, by degrees, that nice sense and perception with which God and nature endowed it:——Did this never happen;——or was it certain that self-love could never hang the least bias upon the judgment;——or that the little interests below could rise up and perplex the faculties of our upper regions, and encompass them about with clouds and thick darkness:——Could no such thing as favour and affection enter this sacred COURT: ——Did WIT disdain to take a bribe in it;——or was ashamed to show its face as an advocate for an unwarrantable enjoyment:——Or, lastly, were we assured that INTEREST stood always unconcerned whilst the cause was hearing,—— and that passion never got into the judgment seat, and pronounced sentence in the stead of reason, which is supposed always to preside and determine upon the case:——Was this truly so, as the objection must suppose;——no doubt then, the religious and moral state of a man would be exactly what he himself esteemed it;——and the guilt or innocence of every man's life could be known, in general, by no better measure than the degrees of his own approbation and censure.

"I own, in one case, whenever a man's conscience does accuse him (as it seldom errs on that side) that he is guilty; and, unless in melancholy and hypochondriac cases, we may safely pronounce upon it that there is always sufficient grounds for the accusation.

"But the converse of the proposition will not hold true; ——namely, that whenever there is guilt, the conscience must accuse; and if it does not, that a man is therefore innocent.——This is not fact:——So that the common consolation which some good Christian or other is hourly administering to himself,——that he thanks God his mind does not misgive him; and that, consequently, he has a good conscience, because he has a quiet one,——is fallacious;—— and as current as the inference is, and as infallible as the rule appears at first sight, yet, when you look nearer to it, and try the truth of this rule upon plain facts,——you see it liable to so much error from a false application;——the principle upon which it goes so often perverted;——the whole force of it lost, and sometimes so vilely cast away, that it is painful to produce the common examples from human life which confirm the account.

"A man shall be vicious and utterly debauched in his principles;——exceptionable in his conduct to the world; shall live shameless, in the open commission of a sin which no reason or pretence can justify;——a sin by which, contrary to all the workings of humanity, he shall ruin forever the deluded partner of his guilt;——rob her of her best dowry; and not only cover her own head with dishonour,——but involve a whole virtuous family in shame and sorrow for her sake.—— Surely, you will think, conscience must lead such a man a troublesome life;——he can have no rest night or day from its reproaches.

"Alas! CONSCIENCE had something else to do, all this time, than break in upon him; as Elijah reproached the god Baal,——this domestic God *was either talking, or pursuing, or was in a journey, or peradventure he slept and could not be awoke.*

"Perhaps HE was gone out in company with HONOUR to fight a duel; to pay off some debt at play;——or dirty annuity, the bargain of his lust: Perhaps CONSCIENCE all this time was engaged at home, talking loud against petty larceny, and executing vengeance upon some such puny crimes as his fortune and rank in life secured him against all temptation of committing; so that he lives as merrily" [If he was of our church though, quoth Dr. Slop, he could not],——"sleeps as soundly in his bed;——and at last meets death as unconcernedly;——perhaps much more so than a much better man."

[All this is impossible with us, quoth Dr. Slop, turning to my father;——the case could not happen in our church. ——It happens in ours, however, replied my father, but too often.——I own, quoth Dr. Slop (struck a little with my father's frank acknowledgment)——that a man in the Romish church may live as badly;——but then he cannot easily die so.——'Tis little matter, replied my father, with an air of indifference,——how a rascal dies.——I mean, answered Dr. Slop, he would be denied the benefits of the last sacraments.

——Pray, how many have you in all, said my uncle Toby, ——for I always forget?——Seven, answered Dr. Slop.—— Humph!——said my uncle Toby; though not accented as a note of acquiescence,——but as an interjection of that particular species of surprise when a man, in looking into a drawer, finds more of a thing than he expected.——Humph! replied my uncle Toby. Dr. Slop, who had an ear, understood my uncle Toby as well as if he had wrote a whole volume against the seven sacraments.——Humph! replied Dr. Slop (stating my uncle Toby's argument over again to him)——Why, Sir, are there not seven cardinal virtues?—— Seven mortal sins?——Seven golden candlesticks?——Seven heavens?——'Tis more than I know, replied my uncle Toby. ——Are there not seven wonders of the world?——Seven days of the creation?——Seven planets?——Seven plagues? ——That there are, quoth my father, with a most affected gravity. But prithee, continued he, go on with the rest of thy characters, Trim.]

"Another is sordid, unmerciful" [here Trim waved his right hand], "a straithearted, selfish wretch, incapable either of private friendship or public spirit. Take notice how he passes by the widow and orphan in their distress, and sees all the miseries incident to human life without a sigh or a prayer." [And please your Honours, cried Trim, I think this a viler man than the other.]

"Shall not conscience rise up and sting him on such occasions?——No; thank God there is no occasion; *I pay every man his own;——I have no fornication to answer to my conscience;——no faithless vows or promises to make up;——I have debauched no man's wife or child; thank God, I am not as other men, adulterers, unjust, or even as this libertine who stands before me.*

"A third is crafty and designing in his nature. View his whole life;——'tis nothing but a cunning contexture of dark arts and unequitable subterfuges, basely to defeat the true intent of all laws,——plain dealing and the safe enjoyment of our several properties.——You will see such a one working out a frame of little designs upon the ignorance and perplexities of the poor and needy man;——shall raise a fortune upon the inexperience of a youth, or the unsuspecting temper of his friend, who would have trusted him with his life.

"When old age comes on, and repentance calls him to look back upon this black account, and state it over again with his conscience,——CONSCIENCE looks into the STATUTES at LARGE;——finds no express law broken by what he has done;

——perceives no penalty or forfeiture of goods and chattels incurred;——sees no scourge waving over his head, or prison opening his gates upon him:——What is there to affright his conscience?——Conscience has got safely entrenched behind the Letter of the Law; sits there invulnerable, fortified with **Cases** and **Reports** so strongly on all sides,——that it is not preaching can dispossess it of its hold."

[Here Corporal Trim and my uncle Toby exchanged looks with each other.——Aye,——aye, Trim! quoth my uncle Toby, shaking his head,——these are but sorry fortifications, Trim.——O! very poor work, answered Trim, to what your Honour and I make of it.——The character of this last man, said Dr. Slop, interrupting Trim, is more detestable than all the rest;——and seems to have been taken from some pettifogging Lawyer amongst you:——Amongst us, a man's conscience could not possibly continue so long *blinded;*——three times in a year, at least, he must go to confession. Will that restore it to sight? quoth my uncle Toby.——Go on, Trim, quoth my father, or Obadiah will have got back before thou hast got to the end of thy sermon;——'tis a very short one, replied Trim.——I wish it was longer, quoth my uncle Toby, for I like it hugely.——Trim went on.]

"A fourth man shall want even this refuge;——shall break through all this ceremony of slow chicane;——scorns the doubtful workings of secret plots and cautious trains to bring about his purpose:——See the barefaced villain, how he cheats, lies, perjures, robs, murders.——Horrid!——But indeed much better was not to be expected, in the present case;——the poor man was in the dark!——his priest had got the keeping of his conscience;——and all he would let him know of it was, That he must believe in the Pope;——go to Mass;——cross himself;——tell his beads;——be a good Catholic, and that this, in all conscience, was enough to carry him to heaven. What——if he perjures!——Why,——he had a mental reservation in it.——But if he is so wicked and abandoned a wretch as you represent him;——if he robs,——if he stabs;——will not conscience, on every such act, receive a wound itself? Aye,—but the man has carried it to confession;——the wound digests there, and will do well enough, and in a short time be quite healed up by absolution. O Popery! what hast thou to answer for?——when, not content with the too many natural and fatal ways through which the heart of man is every day thus treacherous to itself above all things,——thou hast wilfully set open this wide gate of deceit before the face of this unwary traveller, too apt, God knows, to go astray of himself; and confidently speak peace to himself, when there is no peace.

"Of this the common instances which I have drawn out of life are too notorious to require much evidence. If any man doubts the reality of them, or thinks it impossible for a man to be such a bubble to himself,——I must refer him a moment to his own reflections, and will then venture to trust my appeal with his own heart.

"Let him consider in how different a degree of detestation numbers of wicked actions stand *there,* though equally bad and vicious in their own natures;——he will soon find that such of them as strong inclination and custom have prompted him to commit are generally dressed out and painted with all the false beauties which a soft and a flattering hand can give them;——and that the others, to which he feels no propensity, appear at once naked and deformed, surrounded with all the true circumstances of folly and dishonour.

"When David surprised Saul sleeping in the cave, and cut off the skirt of his robe,——we read his heart smote him for what he had done:——But in the matter of Uriah, where a faithful and gallant servant, whom he ought to have loved and honoured, fell to make way for his lust,—— where conscience had so much greater reason to take the alarm, his heart smote him not. A whole year had almost passed from the first commission of that crime to the time Nathan was sent to reprove him; and we read not once of the least sorrow or compunction of heart which he testified, during all that time, for what he had done.

"Thus conscience, this once able monitor,——placed on high as a judge within us, and intended by our maker as a just and equitable one too,——by an unhappy train of causes and impediments, takes often such imperfect cognizance of what passes,——does its office so negligently,——sometimes so corruptly,——that it is not to be trusted alone; and therefore we find there is a necessity, an absolute necessity of joining another principle with it to aid, if not govern, its determinations.

"So that if you would form a just judgment of what is of infinite importance to you not to be misled in,——namely, in what degree of real merit you stand either as an honest man, an useful citizen, a faithful subject to your king, or a good servant to your God,——call in religion and morality.—— Look,——What is written in the law of God?——How read-

108

est thou?——Consult calm reason and the unchangeable obligations of justice and truth;——what say they?

"Let CONSCIENCE determine the matter upon these reports;——and then if thy heart condemns thee not, which is the case the Apostle supposes,——the rule will be infallible" [Here Dr. Slop fell asleep]; *"thou wilt have confidence towards God;*——that is, have just grounds to believe the judgment thou has passed upon thyself is the judgment of God; and nothing else but an anticipation of that righteous sentence which will be pronounced upon thee hereafter by that Being, to whom thou art finally to give an account of thy actions.

"Blessed is the man indeed, then, as the author of the book of Ecclesiasticus expresses it, *who is not pricked with the multitude of his sins: Blessed is the man whose heart hath not condemned him; whether he be rich, or whether he be poor, if he have a good heart* (a heart thus guided and informed) *he shall at all times rejoice in a cheerful countenance; his mind shall tell him more than seven watchmen that sit above upon a tower on high."*——[A tower has no strength, quoth my uncle Toby, unless 'tis flanked.] "In the darkest doubts it shall conduct him safer than a thousand casuists, and give the state he lives in a better security for his behaviour than all the clauses and restrictions put together which lawmakers are forced to multiply:——*Forced,* I say, as things stand; human laws not being a matter of original choice, but of pure necessity, brought in to fence against the mischievous effects of those consciences which are no law unto themselves; well intending, by the many provisions made,——that in all such corrupt and misguided cases, where principles and the checks of conscience will not make us upright,——to supply their force, and, by the terrors of goals and halters, oblige us to it."

[I see plainly, said my father, that this sermon has been composed to be preached at the Temple——or at some Assize.——I like the reasoning,——and am sorry that Dr. Slop has fallen asleep before the time of his conviction;——for it is now clear that the Parson, as I thought at first, never insulted St. Paul in the least;——nor has there been, brother, the least difference between them.——A great matter, if they had differed, replied my uncle Toby;——the best friends in the world may differ sometimes.——True,——brother Toby, quoth my father, shaking hands with him;——we'll fill our pipes, brother, and then Trim shall go on.

Well,——what dost thou think of it? said my father,

speaking to Corporal Trim, as he reached his tobacco box.

I think, answered the corporal, that the seven watchmen upon the tower, who, I suppose, are all sentinels there,——are more, an' please your Honour, than were necessary;——and to go on at that rate would harass a regiment all to pieces, which a commanding officer who loves his men will never do, if he can help it; because two sentinels, added the corporal, are as good as twenty.——I have been a commanding officer myself in the *Corps de Garde* a hundred times, continued Trim, rising an inch higher in his figure, as he spoke,——and all the time I had the honour to serve his Majesty King William, in relieving the most considerable posts, I never left more than two in my life.——Very right, Trim, quoth my uncle Toby,——but you do not consider, Trim, that the towers in Solomon's days were not such things as our bastions, flanked and defended by other works;——this, Trim, was an invention since Solomon's death; nor had they hornworks, or ravelins before the curtain, in his time;——or such a fosse as we make with a cuvette in the middle of it, and with covered ways and counterscarps pallisadoed along it, to guard against a *Coup de main:*——So that the seven men upon the tower were a party, I dare say, from the *Corps de Garde,* set there, not only to look out, but to defend it.——They could be no more, an' please your Honour, than a Corporal's Guard.——My father smiled inwardly,——but not outwardly;——the subject between my uncle Toby and Corporal Trim being rather too serious, considering what had happened, to make a jest of:——So putting his pipe into his mouth, which he had just lighted,——he contented himself with ordering Trim to read on. He read on as follows:]

"To have the fear of God before our eyes, and, in our mutual dealings with each other, to govern our actions by the eternal measures of right and wrong:——The first of these will comprehend the duties of religion;——the second, those of morality, which are so inseparably connected together that you cannot divide these two *tables,* even in imagination (though the attempt is often made in practice), without breaking and mutually destroying them both.

"I said the attempt is often made, and so it is;——there being nothing more common than to see a man who has no sense at all of religion,——and indeed has so much honesty as to pretend to none, who would take it as the bitterest affront, should you but hint at a suspicion of his moral character,——or imagine he was not conscientiously just and scrupulous to the uttermost mite.

"When there is some appearance that it is so,——though one is unwilling even to suspect the appearance of so amiable a virtue as moral honesty, yet were we to look into the grounds of it, in the present case, I am persuaded we should find little reason to envy such a one the honour of his motive.

"Let him declaim as pompously as he chooses upon the subject, it will be found to rest upon no better foundation than either his interest, his pride, his ease, or some such little and changeable passion as will give us but small dependence upon his actions in matters of great stress.

"I will illustrate this by an example.

"I know the banker I deal with, or the physician I usually call in" [There is no need, cried Dr. Slop (waking), to call in any physician in this case], "to be neither of them men of much religion: I hear them make a jest of it every day, and treat all its sanctions with so much scorn as to put the matter past doubt. Well;——notwithstanding this, I put my fortune into the hands of the one;——and what is dearer still to me, I trust my life to the honest skill of the other.

"Now, let me examine what is my reason for this great confidence.——Why, in the first place, I believe there is no probability that either of them will employ the power I put into their hands to my disadvantage;——I consider that honesty serves the purposes of this life:——I know their success in the world depends upon the fairness of their characters. ——In a word,——I'm persuaded that they cannot hurt me, without hurting themselves more.

"But put it otherwise, namely, that interest lay, for once, on the other side; that a case should happen wherein the one, without stain to his reputation, could secrete my fortune, and leave me naked in the world;——or that the other could send me out of it, and enjoy an estate by my death, without dishonour to himself or his art:——In this case, what hold have I of either of them?——Religion, the strongest of all motives, is out of the question:——Interest, the next most powerful motive in the world, is strongly against me:——What have I left to cast into the opposite scale to balance this temptation?——Alas! I have nothing,—— nothing but what is lighter than a bubble——I must lay at the mercy of HONOUR, or some such capricious principle. ——Strait security for two of my most valuable blessings! ——my property and my life.

"As, therefore, we can have no dependence upon morality without religion;——so, on the other hand, there is nothing better to be expected from religion without morality; nevertheless, 'tis no prodigy to see a man whose real moral character stands very low, who yet entertains the highest notion of himself in the light of a religious man.

"He shall not only be covetous, revengeful, implacable, ——but even wanting in points of common honesty; yet, inasmuch as he talks aloud against the infidelity of the age, ——is zealous for some points of religion,——goes twice a day to church,——attends the sacraments,——and amuses himself with a few instrumental parts of religion,——shall cheat his conscience into a judgment that, for this, he is a religious man, and has discharged truly his duty to God: And you will find that such a man, through force of this delusion, generally looks down with spiritual pride upon every other man who has less affectation of piety,——though, perhaps, ten times more moral honesty than himself.

"*This likewise is a sore evil under the sun;* and I believe there is no one mistaken principle which, for its time, has wrought more serious mischiefs.————For a general proof of this,——examine the history of the Romish church"—— [Well, what can you make of that? cried Dr. Slop];—— "see what scenes of cruelty, murders, rapines, bloodshed" [They may thank their own obstinacy, cried Dr. Slop] "have all been sanctified by a religion not strictly governed by morality.

"In how many kingdoms of the world" [Here Trim kept waving his right hand from the sermon to the extent of his arm, returning it backwards and forwards to the conclusion of the paragraph.]

"In how many kingdoms of the world has the crusading sword of this misguided saint-errant spared neither age, or merit, or sex, or condition?——and, as he fought under the banners of a religion which set him loose from justice and humanity, he showed none; mercilessly trampled upon both, ——heard neither the cries of the unfortunate, nor pitied their distresses."

[I have been in many a battle, an' please your Honour, quoth Trim, sighing, but never in so melancholy a one as this.——I would not have drawn a trigger in it, against these poor souls,——to have been made a general officer.——Why? what do you understand of the affair? said Dr. Slop, looking towards Trim with something more of contempt than the corporal's honest heart deserved.——What do you know, friend, about this battle you talk of?——I know, replied Trim, that I never refused quarter in my life to any man who cried out for it;——but to a woman or a child, continued

Trim, before I would level my musket at them, I would lose my life a thousand times.——Here's a crown for thee, Trim, to drink with Obadiah tonight, quoth my uncle Toby, and I'll give Obadiah another too.——God bless your Honour, replied Trim,——I had rather these poor women and children had it.——Thou art an honest fellow, quoth my uncle Toby.——My father nodded his head,——as much as to say,——and so he is.——

But prithee, Trim, said my father, make an end,——for I see thou hast but a leaf or two left.]

Corporal Trim read on.

"If the testimony of past centuries in this matter is not sufficient,——consider at this instant how the votaries of that religion are every day thinking to do service and honour to God, by actions which are a dishonour and scandal to themselves.

"To be convinced of this, go with me for a moment into the prisons of the inquisition."——[God help my poor brother Tom.]——"Behold Religion, with Mercy and Justice chained down under her feet,——there sitting ghastly upon a black tribunal, propped up with racks and instruments of torment. Hark!——hark! what a piteous groan!" [Here Trim's face turned as pale as ashes.] "See the melancholy wretch who uttered it"——[Here the tears began to trickle down], "just brought forth to undergo the anguish of a mock trial, and endure the utmost pains that a studied system of cruelty has been able to invent."——[D—n them all, quoth Trim, his colour returning into his face as red as blood.]——"Behold this helpless victim delivered up to his tormentors,——his body so wasted with sorrow and confinement."——[Oh! 'tis my brother, cried poor Trim in a most passionate exclamation, dropping the sermon upon the ground, and clapping his hands together——I fear 'tis poor Tom. My father's and my uncle Toby's hearts yearned with sympathy for the poor fellow's distress;——even Slop himself acknowledged pity for him.——Why, Trim, said my father, this is not a history,——'tis a sermon thou art reading;——prithee begin the sentence again.]——"Behold this helpless victim delivered up to his tormentors,——his body so wasted with sorrow and confinement, you will see every nerve and muscle as it suffers.

"Observe the last movement of that horrid engine!" [I would rather face a cannon, quoth Trim, stamping.]—— "See what convulsions it has thrown him into!——Consider the nature of the posture in which he now lies stretched——

what exquisite tortures he endures by it!"——[I hope 'tis not in Portugal.]——" 'Tis all nature can bear! Good God! see how it keeps his weary soul hanging upon his trembling lips!" [I would not read another line of it, quoth Trim, for all this world;——I fear, an' please your Honours, all this is in Portugal, where my poor brother Tom is. I tell thee, Trim, again, quoth my father, 'tis not an historical account,——'tis a description.——'Tis only a description, honest man, quoth Slop, there's not a word of truth in it.——That's another story, replied my father.——However, as Trim reads it with so much concern,——'tis cruelty to force him to go on with it.——Give me hold of the sermon, Trim;——I'll finish it for thee, and thou mayest go. I must stay and hear it too, replied Trim, if your Honour will allow me;——though I would not read it myself for a colonel's pay.——Poor Trim! quoth my uncle Toby. My father went on.]

"——Consider the nature of the posture in which he now lies stretched,——what exquisite torture he endures by it!——'Tis all nature can bear!——Good God! See how it keeps his weary soul hanging upon his trembling lips,—— willing to take its leave,——but not suffered to depart!—— Behold the unhappy wretch led back to his cell!" [Then, thank God, however, quoth Trim, they have not killed him] ——"See him dragged out of it again to meet the flames, and the insults in his last agonies, which this principle,——this principle that there can be religion without mercy has prepared for him." [Then, thank God,——he is dead, quoth Trim,——he is out of his pain,——and they have done their worst at him.——O Sirs!——Hold your peace, Trim, said my father, going on with the sermon, lest Trim should incense Dr. Slop,——we shall never have done at this rate.]

"The surest way to try the merit of any disputed notion is to trace down the consequences such a notion has produced, and compare them with the spirit of Christianity;——'tis the short and decisive rule which our Saviour hath left us, for these and suchlike cases, and it is worth a thousand arguments——*By their fruits ye shall know them.*

"I will add no further to the length of this sermon than by two or three short and independent rules deducible from it.

"*First,* Whenever a man talks loudly against religion,—— always suspect that it is not his reason, but his passions which have got the better of his CREED. A bad life and a good belief are disagreeable and troublesome neighbours, and where they separate, depend upon it, 'tis for no other cause but quietness' sake.

114

"*Secondly,* When a man, thus represented, tells you in any particular instance,——That such a thing goes *against* his conscience,——always believe he means exactly the same thing as when he tells you such a thing goes *against* his stomach;——a present want of appetite being generally the true cause of both.

"In a word,——trust that man in nothing who has not a CONSCIENCE in everything.

"And, in your own case, remember this plain distinction, a mistake in which has ruined thousands,——that your conscience is not a law:——No, God and reason made the law, and have placed conscience within you to determine;—— not like an Asiatic cadi, according to the ebbs and flows of his own passions,——but like a British judge in this land of liberty and good sense, who makes no new law, but faithfully declares that law which he knows already written."

FINIS

Thou hast read the sermon extremely well, Trim, quoth my father.——If he had spared his comments, replied Dr. Slop, he would have read it much better. I should have read it ten times better, Sir, answered Trim, but that my heart was so full.——That was the very reason, Trim, replied my father, which has made thee read the sermon as well as thou hast done; and if the clergy of our church, continued my father, addressing himself to Dr. Slop, would take part in what they deliver as deeply as this poor fellow has done;——as their compositions are fine (I deny it, quoth Dr. Slop),—I maintain it that the eloquence of our pulpits, with such subjects to inflame it,——would be a model for the whole world: ——But, alas! continued my father, and I own it, Sir, with sorrow, that, like French politicians in this respect, what they gain in the cabinet they lose in the field.——'Twere a pity, quoth my uncle, that this should be lost. I like the sermon well, replied my father;——'tis dramatic,——and there is something in that way of writing, when skilfully managed, which catches the attention.——We preach much in that way with us, and Dr. Slop.——I know that very well, said my father,——but in a tone and manner which disgusted Dr. Slop, full as much as his assent, simply, could have pleased him. ——But in this, added Dr. Slop, a little piqued,——our sermons have greatly the advantage, that we never introduce any character into them below a patriarch or a patriarch's

115

wife, or a martyr or a saint.——There are some very bad
characters in this, however, said my father, and I do not
think the sermon a jot the worse for 'em.——But pray, quoth
my uncle Toby,——whose can this be?——How could it get
into my Stevinus? A man must be as great a conjurer as
Stevinus, said my father, to resolve the second question:——
The first, I think, is not so difficult;——for unless my judgment greatly deceives me,——I know the author, for 'tis
wrote, certainly, by the parson of the parish.

The similitude of the style and manner of it with those my
father constantly had heard preached in his parish church
was the ground of his conjecture,——proving it as strongly,
as an argument *a priori* could prove such a thing to a philosophic mind, That it was Yorick's and no one's else:——It
was proved to be so *a posteriori* the day after, when Yorick
sent a servant to my uncle Toby's house to enquire after
it.

It seems that Yorick, who was inquisitive after all kinds of
knowledge, had borrowed Stevinus of my uncle Toby, and
had carelessly popped his sermon, as soon as he had made it,
into the middle of Stevinus; and, by an act of forgetfulness,
to which he was ever subject, he had sent Stevinus home,
and his sermon to keep him company.

Ill-fated sermon! Thou wast lost, after this recovery of
thee, a second time, dropped through an unsuspected fissure
in thy master's pocket, down into a treacherous and a tattered lining,——trod deep into the dirt by the left hind foot
of his Rosinante, inhumanly stepping upon thee as thou fall-
edst;——buried ten days in the mire,——raised up out of it
by a beggar, sold for a halfpenny to a parish clerk,——
transferred to his parson,——lost forever to thy own, the
remainder of his days,——nor restored to his restless MANES
till this very moment, that I tell the world the story.

Can the reader believe that this sermon of Yorick's was
preached at an assize, in the cathedral of York, before a
thousand witnesses, ready to give oath of it, by a certain
prebendary of that church, and actually printed by him
when he had done,——and within so short a space as two
years and three months after Yorick's death.——Yorick, indeed, was never better served in his life!——but it was a little hard to maltreat him before, and plunder him after he
was laid in his grave.

However, as the gentleman who did it was in perfect charity with Yorick,——and, in conscious justice, printed but a
few copies to give away;——and that, I am told, he could

moreover have made as good a one himself, had he thought fit,——I declare I would not have published this anecdote to the world;——nor do I publish it with an intent to hurt his character and advancement in the church;——I leave that to others;——but I find myself impelled by two reasons, which I cannot withstand.

The first is, That, in doing justice, I may give rest to Yorick's ghost;——which, as the country people,——and some others, believe,——*still walks.*

The second reason is, That, by laying open this story to the world, I gain an opportunity of informing it,——That in case the character of Parson Yorick and this sample of his sermons is liked,——that there are now in the possession of the Shandy family as many as will make a handsome volume, at the world's service,——and much good may they do it.

CHAPTER XVIII

Obadiah gained the two crowns without dispute; for he came in jingling, with all the instruments in the green baize bag we spoke of, slung across his body, just as Corporal Trim went out of the room.

It is now proper, I think, quoth Dr. Slop (clearing up his looks), as we are in a condition to be of some service to Mrs. Shandy, to send upstairs to know how she goes on.

I have ordered, answered my father, the old midwife to come down to us upon the least difficulty;——for you must know, Dr. Slop, continued my father, with a perplexed kind of a smile upon his countenance, that by express treaty, solemnly ratified between me and my wife, you are no more than an auxiliary in this affair,——and not so much as that, ——unless the lean old mother of a midwife abovestairs cannot do without you.——Women have their particular fancies, and in points of this nature, continued my father, where they bear the whole burden, and suffer so much acute pain for the advantage of our families, and the good of the species,—— they claim a right of deciding, *en Souverains,* in whose hands, and in what fashion, they choose to undergo it.

They are in the right of it,——quoth my uncle Toby. But, Sir, replied Dr. Slop, not taking notice of my uncle Toby's opinion, but turning to my father,——they had better govern in other points;——and a father of a family, who wished its perpetuity, in my opinion, had better exchange this prerogative with them, and give up some other rights in lieu of it. ——I know not, quoth my father, answering a little too testily, to be quite dispassionate in what he said,——I know not, quoth he, what we have left to give up, in lieu of who shall bring our children into the world,——unless that——of who shall beget them.————One would almost give up anything, replied Dr. Slop.——I beg your pardon,——answered my uncle Toby.——Sir, replied Dr. Slop, it would astonish you to know what Improvements we have made of late years in all branches of obstetrical knowledge, but particularly in that one single point of the safe and expeditious extraction of the *foetus*,——which has received such lights that, for my part (holding up his hands), I declare I wonder how the world has——I wish, quoth my uncle Toby, you had seen what prodigious armies we had in Flanders.

CHAPTER XIX

I have dropped the curtain over this scene for a minute,—— to remind you of one thing,——and to inform you of another.

What I have to inform you comes, I own, a little out of its due course;——for it should have been told a hundred and fifty pages ago, but that I foresaw then 'twould come in pat hereafter, and be of more advantage here than elsewhere. ——Writers had need look before them to keep up the spirit and connection of what they have in hand.

When these two things are done,——the curtain shall be drawn up again, and my uncle Toby, my father, and Dr. Slop shall go on with their discourse, without any more interruption.

First, then, the matter which I have to remind you of is this;——that from the specimens of singularity in my father's notions in the point of Christian names, and that other point previous thereto,——you was led, I think, into an opinion (and I am sure I said as much) that my father was a gentleman altogether as odd and whimsical in fifty other opinions.

In truth, there was not a stage in the life of man, from the very first act of his begetting,——down to the lean and slippered pantaloon in his second childishness, but he had some favourite notion to himself springing out of it, as sceptical, and as far out of the highway of thinking, as these two which have been explained.

——Mr. Shandy, my father, Sir, would see nothing in the light in which others placed it;——he placed things in his own light;——he would weigh nothing in common scales;——no,——he was too refined a researcher to lay open to so gross an imposition.——To come at the exact weight of things in the scientific steel yard, the fulcrum, he would say, should be almost invisible, to avoid all friction from popular tenets;——without this the minutiae of philosophy, which should always turn the balance, will have no weight at all.

——Knowledge, like matter, he would affirm, was divisible *in infinitum*,——that the grains and scruples were as much a part of it as the gravitation of the whole world.——In a word, he would say, error was error,——no matter where it fell,——whether in a fraction,——or a pound,——'twas alike fatal to truth, and she was kept down at the bottom of her well as inevitably by a mistake in the dust of a butterfly's wing,——as in the disk of the sun, the moon, and all the stars of heaven put together.

He would often lament that it was for want of considering this properly, and of applying it skilfully to civil matters, as well as to speculative truths, that so many things in this world were out of joint;——that the political arch was giving way;——and that the very foundations of our excellent constitution in church and state were so sapped as estimators had reported.

You cry out, he would say, we are a ruined, undone people.——Why? he would ask, making use of the sorites or syllogism of Zeno and Chrysippus, without knowing it belonged to them.——Why? why are we a ruined people?—— Because we are corrupted.——Whence is it, dear Sir, that we are corrupted?——Because we are needy;——our poverty, and not our wills, consent.——And wherefore, he would add, are we needy?——From the neglect, he would answer, of our pence and our halfpence:——Our banknotes, Sir, our guineas,——nay our shillings, take care of themselves.

'Tis the same, he would say, throughout the whole circle of the sciences;——the great, the established points of them are not to be broke in upon.——The laws of nature will defend themselves;——but error——(he would add, looking earnestly at my mother),——error, Sir, creeps in through the minute holes, and small crevices, which human nature leaves unguarded.

This turn of thinking in my father is what I had to remind you of:——The point you are to be informed of, and which I have reserved for this place, is as follows:

Amongst the many and excellent reasons with which my father had urged my mother to accept of Dr. Slop's assistance preferably to that of the old woman,——there was one of a very singular nature; which, when he had done arguing the matter with her as a Christian, and came to argue it over again with her as a philosopher, he had put his whole strength to, depending indeed upon it as his sheet anchor. ——It failed him; though from no defect in the argument itself; but that, do what he could, he was not able for his soul to make her comprehend the drift of it.——Cursed luck!——said he to himself, one afternoon, as he walked out of the room, after he had been stating it for an hour and a half to her, to no manner of purpose;——cursed luck! said he, biting his lip as he shut the door,——for a man to be master of one of the finest chains of reasoning in nature,——and have a wife at the same time with such a headpiece that he cannot hang up a single inference within-side of it, to save his soul from destruction.

This argument, though it was entirely lost upon my mother,——had more weight with him than all his other arguments joined together:——I will therefore endeavour to do it justice,——and set it forth with all the perspicuity I am master of.

My father set out upon the strength of these two following axioms:

First, That an ounce of a man's own wit was worth a tun of other peoples; and,

Secondly (Which, by the bye, was the groundwork of the first axiom,——though it comes last), That every man's wit must come from every man's own soul,——and no other body's.

Now, as it was plain to my father that all souls were by nature equal,——and that the great difference between the most acute and the most obtuse understanding——was from no original sharpness or bluntness of one thinking substance above or below another,——but arose merely from the lucky or unlucky organization of the body, in that part where the soul principally took up her residence,——he had made it the subject of his enquiry to find out the identical place.

Now, from the best accounts he had been able to get of

this matter, he was satisfied it could not be where Descartes had fixed it, upon the top of the *pineal* gland of the brain; which, as he philosophised, formed a cushion for her about the size of a marrow pea; though to speak the truth, as so many nerves did terminate all in that one place,——'twas no bad conjecture;——and my father had certainly fallen with that great philosopher plumb into the centre of the mistake, had it not been for my uncle Toby, who rescued him out of it by a story he told him of a Walloon officer at the battle of Landen, who had one part of his brain shot away by a musket ball,——and another part of it taken out after by a French surgeon; and, after all, recovered, and did his duty very well without it.

If death, said my father, reasoning with himself, is nothing but the separation of the soul from the body;——and if it is true that people can walk about and do their business without brains,——then certes the soul does not inhabit there. Q. E. D.

As for that certain very thin, subtle, and very fragrant juice which Coglionissimo Borri, the great Milanese physician, affirms, in a letter to Bartholine, to have discovered in the cellulae of the occipital parts of the cerebellum, and which he likewise affirms to be the principal seat of the reasonable soul (for, you must know, in these latter and more enlightened ages, there are two souls in every man living,—— the one, according to the great Metheglingius, being called the *Animus,* the other the *Anima*);——as for this opinion, I say, of Borri,——my father could never subscribe to it by any means; the very idea of so noble, so refined, so immaterial, and so exalted a being as the *Anima,* or even the *Animus,* taking up her residence, and sitting dabbling, like a tadpole, all day long, both summer and winter, in a puddle, ——or in a liquid of any kind, how thick or thin soever, he would say, shocked his imagination; he would scarce give the doctrine a hearing.

What, therefore, seemed the least liable to objections of any was that the chief sensorium, or headquarters of the soul, and to which place all intelligences were referred, and from whence all her mandates were issued,——was in, or near, the cerebellum,——or rather somewhere about the *medulla oblongata,* wherein it was generally agreed by Dutch anatomists that all the minute nerves from all the organs of the seven senses concentred, like streets and winding alleys, into a square.

So far there was nothing singular in my father's opinion; ——he had the best of philosophers, of all ages and climates, to go along with him.——But here he took a road of his own, setting up another Shandean hypothesis upon these cornerstones they had laid for him;——and which said hypothesis equally stood its ground; whether the subtilty and fineness of the soul depended upon the temperature and clearness of the said liquor, or of the finer network and texture in the cerebellum itself, which opinion he favoured.

He maintained that next to the due care to be taken in the act of propagation of each individual, which required all the thought in the world, as it laid the foundation of this incomprehensible contexture in which wit, memory, fancy, eloquence, and what is usually meant by the name of good natural parts, do consist;——that next to this and his Christian name, which were the two original and most efficacious causes of all,——that the third cause, or rather what logicians call the *Causa sine qua non,* and without which all that was done was of no manner of significance,——was the preservation of this delicate and fine-spun web from the havoc which was generally made in it by the violent compression and crush which the head was made to undergo by the nonsensical method of bringing us into the world by that part foremost.

——This requires explanation.

My father, who dipped into all kinds of books, upon looking into *Lithopaedus Senonesis de Partu difficili,** published by Adrianus Smelvgot, had found out, That the lax and pliable state of a child's head in parturition, the bones of the cranium having no sutures at that time, was such——that by force of the woman's efforts, which, in strong labour pains, was equal, upon an average, to a weight of 470 pounds avoirdupois acting perpendicularly upon it;——it so happened that, in 49 instances out of 50, the said head was compressed and moulded into the shape of an oblong conical piece of dough, such as a pastry cook generally rolls up in order to make a pie of.——Good God! cried my father, what havoc and destruction must this make in the infinitely fine and tender texture of the cerebellum!——Or if there is

* The author is here twice mistaken;——for *Lithopaedus* should be wrote thus, *Lithopaedii Senonensis Icon.* The second mistake is that this *Lithopaedus* is not an author, but a drawing of a petrified child. The account of this, published by Albosius, 1580, may be seen at the end of Cordaeus's works in Spachius. Mr. Tristram Shandy has been led into this error either from seeing Lithopaedus's name of late in a catalogue of learned writers in Dr. ——, or by mistaking *Lithopaedus* for *Trinecavellius,*——from the too great similitude of the names.

such a juice as Borri pretends,——is it not enough to make the clearest liquor in the world both feculent and mothery?

But how great was his apprehension when he further understood that this force, acting upon the very vertex of the head, not only injured the brain itself, or cerebrum,—— but that it necessarily squeezed and propelled the cerebrum towards the cerebellum, which was the immediate seat of the understanding.——Angels and ministers of grace defend us! cried my father,——can any soul withstand this shock?—— No wonder the intellectual web is so rent and tattered as we see it; and that so many of our best heads are no better than a puzzled skein of silk,——all perplexity,——all confusion withinside.

But when my father read on, and was let into the secret that when a child was turned topsy-turvy, which was easy for an operator to do, and was extracted by the feet;——that instead of the cerebrum being propelled towards the cerebellum, the cerebellum, on the contrary, was propelled simply towards the cerebrum, where it could do no manner of hurt: ——By heavens! cried he, the world is in a conspiracy to drive out what little wit God has given us,——and the professors of the obstetric art are listed into the same conspiracy.——What is it to me which end of my son comes foremost into the world, provided all goes right after, and his cerebellum escapes uncrushed?

It is the nature of an hypothesis, when once a man has conceived it, that it assimilates everything to itself as proper nourishment; and, from the first moment of your begetting it, it generally grows the stronger by everything you see, hear, read, or understand. This is of great use.

When my father was gone with this about a month, there was scarce a phenomenon of stupidity or of genius which he could not readily solve by it;——it accounted for the eldest son being the greatest blockhead in the family.—— Poor devil, he would say,——he made way for the capacity of his younger brothers.——It unriddled the observations of drivellers and monstrous heads,——showing, *a priori*, it could not be otherwise,——unless * * * * I don't know what. It wonderfully explained and accounted for the acumen of the Asiatic genius, and that sprightlier turn, and a more penetrating intuition of minds, in warmer climates; not from the loose and commonplace solution of a clearer sky, and a more perpetual sunshine, &c.——which, for aught he knew, might as well rarefy and dilute the faculties of the soul into nothing, by one extreme,——as they are condensed in colder climates by the other;——but he traced the affair up to its springhead;——showed that, in warmer climates, nature had laid a lighter tax upon the fairest parts of the creation;——their pleasures more;——the necessity of their pains less, insomuch that the pressure and resistance upon the vertex was so slight that the whole organization of the cerebellum was preserved;——nay, he did not believe, in natural births, that so much as a single thread of the network was broke or displaced,——so that the soul might just act as she liked.

When my father had got so far,——what a blaze of light did the accounts of the Caesarian section, and of the towering geniuses who had come safe into the world by it, cast upon this hypothesis! Here you see, he would say, there was no injury done to the sensorium;——no pressure of the head against the pelvis;——no propulsion of the cerebrum towards the cerebellum, either by the *os pubis* on this side, or the *os coxcygis* on that;——and, pray, what were the happy consequences? Why, Sir, your Julius Caesar, who gave the operation a name;——and your Hermes Trismegistus, who was born so before ever the operation had a name;——your Scipio Africanus; your Manlius Torquatus; our Edward the Sixth,——who, had he lived, would have done the same honour to the hypothesis:——These, and many more, who figured high in the annals of fame,——all came *sideway,* Sir, into the world.

This incision of the *abdomen* and *uterus* ran for six weeks together in my father's head;——he had read, and was satisfied, that wounds in the *epigastrium,* and those in the *matrix,* were not mortal;——so that the belly of the mother might be opened extremely well to give a passage to the child.——He mentioned the thing one afternoon to my mother,——merely as a matter of fact;——but seeing her turn as pale as ashes at the very mention of it, as much as the operation flattered his hopes,——he thought it as well to say no more of it,—— contenting himself with admiring——what he thought was to no purpose to propose.

This was my father Mr. Shandy's hypothesis; concerning which I have only to add that my brother Bobby did as great honour to it (whatever he did to the family) as any one of the great heroes we spoke of:——For happening not only to be christened, as I told you, but to be born too, when my father was at Epsom,——being moreover my mother's *first* child,——coming into the world with his head *foremost,*—— and turning out afterwards a lad of wonderful slow parts,

——my father spelt all these together into his opinion; and as he had failed at one end,——he was determined to try the other.

This was not to be expected from one of the sisterhood, who are not easily to be put out of their way,——and was therefore one of my father's great reasons in favour of a man of science, whom he could better deal with.

Of all men in the world, Dr. Slop was the fittest for my father's purpose;——for though his new-invented forceps was the armour he had proved, and what he maintained, to be the safest instrument of deliverance,——yet, it seems, he had scattered a word or two in his book in favour of the very thing which ran in my father's fancy;——though not with a view to the soul's good in extracting by the feet, as was my father's system,——but for reasons merely obstetrical.

This will account for the coalition betwixt my father and Dr. Slop, in the ensuing discourse, which went a little hard against my uncle Toby.——In what manner a plain man, with nothing but common sense, could bear up against two such allies in science——is hard to conceive.——You may conjecture upon it, if you please,——and whilst your imagination is in motion, you may encourage it to go on, and discover by what causes and effects in nature it could come to pass that my uncle Toby got his modesty by the wound he received upon his groin.——You may raise a system to account for the loss of my nose by marriage articles,——and show the world how it could happen that I should have the misfortune to be called TRISTRAM, in opposition to my father's hypothesis, and the wish of the whole family, godfathers and godmothers not excepted.——These, with fifty other points left yet unraveled, you may endeavour to solve if you have time;——but I tell you beforehand it will be in vain, for not the sage Alquife, the magician in Don Belianis of Greece, nor the no less famous Urganda, the sorceress his wife (were they alive), could pretend to come within a league of the truth.

The reader will be content to wait for a full explanation of these matters till the next year,——when a series of things will be laid open which he little expects.

VOLUME III

Multitudinis imperitae non formido judicia; meis
tamen, rogo, parcant opusculis—in quibus fuit
propositi semper, a jocis ad seria, a seriis vicissim
ad jocos transire.

—JOAN. SARESBERIENSIS,
Episcopus Lugdun.

CHAPTER I

——"I *wish*, Dr. Slop," quoth my uncle Toby (repeating
his wish for Dr. Slop a second time, and with a degree of
more zeal and earnestness in his manner of wishing than he
had wished it at first) *——"*I wish*, Dr. Slop," quoth my
uncle Toby, "*you had seen what prodigious armies we had
in Flanders.*"

My uncle Toby's wish did Dr. Slop a disservice which his
heart never intended any man;——Sir, it confounded him
——and thereby putting his ideas first into confusion, and
then to flight, he could not rally them again for the soul of
him.

In all disputes,——male or female,——whether for
honour, for profit, or for love,——it makes no difference in
the case;——nothing is more dangerous, Madam, than a wish
coming sideways in this unexpected manner upon a man:
the safest way in general to take off the force of the wish is
for the party wished at instantly to get up upon his legs——
and wish the *wisher* something in return, of pretty near the
same value,——so balancing the account upon the spot,

* Vid. Vol. II, p. 118.

you stand as you were——nay sometimes gain the advantage of the attack by it.

This will be fully illustrated to the world in my chapter of wishes.——

Dr. Slop did not understand the nature of this defence; ——he was puzzled with it, and it put an entire stop to the dispute for four minutes and half;——five had been fatal to it:——my father saw the danger——the dispute was one of the most interesting disputes in the world, "Whether the child of his prayers and endeavours should be born without a head or with one:"——he waited to the last moment to allow Dr. Slop, in whose behalf the wish was made, his right of returning it; but perceiving, I say, that he was confounded, and continued looking with that perplexed vacuity of eye which puzzled souls generally stare with,——first in my uncle Toby's face——then in his——then up——then down——then east——east and by east, and so on,—— coasting it along by the plinth of the wainscot till he had got to the opposite point of the compass,——and that he had actually begun to count the brass nails upon the arm of his chair——my father thought there was no time to be lost with my uncle Toby, so took up the discourse as follows.

CHAPTER II

"——What prodigious armies you had in Flanders!"—— Brother Toby, replied my father, taking his wig from off his head with his right hand, and with his *left* pulling out a striped India handkerchief from his right coat pocket, in order to rub his head, as he argued the point with my uncle Toby.——

——Now, in this I think my father was much to blame; and I will give you my reasons for it.

Matters of no more seeming consequence in themselves than *"Whether my father should have taken off his wig with his right hand or with his left"*——have divided the greatest kingdoms, and made the crowns of the monarchs who governed them to totter upon their heads.——But need I tell you, Sir, that the circumstances with which everything in this world is begirt give everything in this world its size and shape;——and by tightening it, or relaxing it, this way or that, make the thing to be what it is——great——little—— good——bad——indifferent or not indifferent, just as the case happens.

As my father's India handkerchief was in his right coat pocket, he should by no means have suffered his right hand to have got engaged: on the contrary, instead of taking off his wig with it, as he did, he ought to have committed that entirely to the left; and then, when the natural exigency my father was under of rubbing his head called out for his hand-kerchief, he would have had nothing in the world to have done, but to have put his right hand into his right coat pocket and taken it out;——which he might have done without any violence, or the least ungraceful twist in any one tendon or muscle of his whole body.

In this case (unless, indeed, my father had been resolved to make a fool of himself by holding the wig stiff in his left hand——or by making some nonsensical angle or other at his elbow joint, or armpit),——his whole attitude had been easy——natural——unforced: Reynolds himself, as great and gracefully as he paints, might have painted him as he sat.

Now, as my father managed this matter,——consider what a devil of a figure my father made of himself.

——In the latter end of Queen Anne's reign, and in the beginning of the reign of King George the First——"*Coat pockets were cut very low down in the skirt.*"——I need say no more——the father of mischief, had he been hammering at it a month, could not have contrived a worse fashion for one in my father's situation.

CHAPTER III

It was not an easy matter in any king's reign (unless you were as a lean a subject as myself) to have forced your hand diagonally, quite across your whole body, so as to gain the bottom of your opposite coat pocket.——In the year one thousand seven hundred and eighteen, when this happened, it was extremely difficult; so that when my uncle Toby dis-covered the transverse zigzaggery of my father's approaches towards it, it instantly brought into his mind those he had done duty in, before the gate of St. Nicolas;——the idea of which drew off his attention so entirely from the subject in debate, that he had got his right hand to the bell to ring up Trim, to go and fetch his map of Namur, and his compasses and sector along with it, to measure the returning angles of the traverses of that attack,——but particularly of that one where he received his wound upon his groin.

My father knit his brows, and as he knit them, all the blood in his body seemed to rush up into his face——my uncle Toby dismounted immediately.

——I did not apprehend your uncle Toby was o' horse-back.——

CHAPTER IV

A man's body and his mind, with the utmost reverence to both I speak it, are exactly like a jerkin, and a jerkin's lining;——rumple the one——you rumple the other. There is one certain exception however in this case, and that is when you are so fortunate a fellow as to have had your jerkin made of a gum taffeta, and the body lining to it of a sarcenet or thin Persian.

Zeno, Cleanthes, Diogenes Babylonius, Dionysius Hera-cleotes, Antipater, Panaetius, and Posidonius amongst the Greeks;——Cato and Varro and Seneca amongst the Ro-mans;——Pantenus and Clemens Alexandrinus and Mon-taigne amongst the Christians; and a score and a half of good honest, unthinking, Shandean people as ever lived, whose names I can't recollect,——all pretended that their jerkins were made after this fashion;——you might have rumpled and crumpled, and doubled and creased, and fretted and fridged the outsides of them all to pieces;——in short, you might have played the very devil with them, and at the same time, not one of the insides of 'em would have been one but-ton the worse, for all you had done to them.

I believe in my conscience that mine is made up some-what after this sort:——for never poor jerkin has been tickled off at such a rate as it has been these last nine months together,——and yet I declare the lining to it,——as far as I am a judge of the matter, it is not a threepenny piece the

worse;——pell-mell, helter-skelter, ding-dong, cut and thrust,
back stroke and fore stroke, side way and long way, have
they been trimming it for me:——had there been the least
gumminess in my lining,——by heaven! it had all of it
long ago been frayed and fretted to a thread.

——You, Messrs. the monthly Reviewers!——how could
you cut and slash my jerkin as you did?——how did you
know but you would cut my lining too?

Heartily and from my soul, to the protection of that Being
who will injure none of us, do I recommend you and your
affairs,——so God bless you;——only next month, if any one
of you should gnash his teeth, and storm and rage at me, as
some of you did last MAY (in which I remember the weather
was very hot),——don't be exasperated if I pass it by again
with good temper,——being determined as long as I live or
write (which in my case means the same thing) never to give
the honest gentleman a worse word or a worse wish than my
uncle Toby gave the fly which buzzed about his nose all
dinnertime,——"Go,——go poor devil," quoth he, "——get
thee gone,——why should I hurt thee? This world is surely
wide enough to hold both thee and me."

CHAPTER V

Any man, Madam, reasoning upwards, and observing the
prodigious suffusion of blood in my father's countenance,
——by means of which (as all the blood in his body seemed
to rush up into his face, as I told you) he must have red-
dened, pictorically and seientintically speaking, six whole
tints and a half, if not a full octave above his natural
colour:——any man, Madam, but my uncle Toby, who had
observed this, together with the violent knitting of my father's
brows, and the extravagant contortion of his body during
the whole affair,——would have concluded my father in a
rage; and taking that for granted,——had he been a lover of
such kind of concord as arises from two such instruments
being put into exact tune,——he would instantly have
screwed up his, to the same pitch;——and then the devil and
all had broke loose;——the whole piece, Madam, must have
been played off like the sixth of Avison Scarlatti——*con*

furia,——like mad.——Grant me patience!——What has *con furia,*——*con strepito,*——or any other hurly-burly word whatever to do with harmony?

Any man, I say, Madam, but my uncle Toby, the benignity of whose heart interpreted every motion of the body in the kindest sense the motion would admit of, would have concluded my father angry and blamed him too. My uncle Toby blamed nothing but the tailor who cut the pocket hole;—— so sitting still till my father had got his handkerchief out of it, and looking all the time up in his face with inexpressible good will——my father at length went on as follows.

CHAPTER VI

——"What prodigious armies you had in Flanders!"—— Brother Toby, quoth my father, I do believe thee to be as honest a man, and with as good and as upright a heart, as ever God created;——nor is it thy fault if all the children which have been, may, can, shall, will, or ought to be begotten come with their heads foremost into the world:——but believe me, dear Toby, the accidents which unavoidably waylay them, not only in the article of our begetting 'em,—— though these, in my opinion, are well worth considering,—— but the dangers and difficulties our children are beset with, after they are got forth into the world, are enow;——little need is there to expose them to unnecessary ones in their passage to it.——Are these dangers, quoth my uncle Toby, laying his hand upon my father's knee, and looking up seriously in his face for an answer,——are these dangers greater now o' days, brother, than in times past? Brother Toby, answered my father, if a child was but fairly begot, and born alive, and healthy, and the mother did well after it,——our forefathers never looked further.——My uncle Toby instantly withdrew his hand from off my father's knee, reclined his body gently back in his chair, raised his head till he could just see the cornice of the room, and then, directing the buccinatory muscles along his cheeks, and the orbicular muscles around his lips, to do their duty,——he whistled *Lillabullero.*

CHAPTER VII

Whilst my uncle Toby was whistling *Lillabullero* to my father,——Dr. Slop was stamping and cursing and damning at Obadiah at a most dreadful rate;——it would have done your heart good, and cured you, Sir, forever, of the vile sin of swearing to have heard him.——I am determined therefore to relate the whole affair to you.

When Dr. Slop's maid delivered the green baize bag, with her master's instruments in it, to Obadiah, she very sensibly exhorted him to put his head and one arm through the strings, and ride with it slung across his body: so undoing the bowknot, to lengthen the strings for him, without any more ado, she helped him on with it. However, as this, in some measure, unguarded the mouth of the bag, lest anything should bolt out in galloping back at the speed Obadiah threatened, they consulted to take it off again; and in the great care and caution of their hearts, they had taken the two strings and tied them close (pursing up the mouth of the bag first) with half a dozen hard knots, each of which Obadiah, to make all safe, had twitched and drawn together with all the strength of his body.

This answered all that Obadiah and the maid intended; but was no remedy against some evils which neither he or she foresaw. The instruments, it seems, as tight as the bag was tied above, had so much room to play in it, towards the bottom (the shape of the bag being conical), that Obadiah could not make a trot of it but with such a terrible jingle, what with the *tire-tête*, *forceps*, and *squirt*, as would have been enough, had Hymen been taking a jaunt that way, to have frightened him out of the country; but when Obadiah accelerated this motion, and from a plain trot assayed to prick his coach horse into a full gallop——by heaven! Sir, ——the jingle was incredible.

As Obadiah had a wife and three children——the turpitude of fornication, and the many other political ill consequences of this jingling, never once entered his brain;——he had however his objection, which came home to himself, and weighed with him, as it has ofttimes done with the greatest

133

patriots.——*"The poor fellow, Sir, was not able to hear himself whistle."*

CHAPTER VIII

As Obadiah loved wind music preferably to all the instrumental music he carried with him,——he very considerately set his imagination to work, to contrive and to invent by what means he should put himself in a condition of enjoying it.

In all distresses (except musical) where small cords are wanted,——nothing is so apt to enter a man's head as his hatband:——the philosophy of this is so near the surface—— I scorn to enter into it.

As Obadiah's was a mixed case;——mark, Sirs,——I say a mixed case, for it was obstetrical,——*scrip*-tical, squirtical, Papistical,——and as far as the coach horse was concerned in it,——caball-istical——and only partly musical;——Obadiah made no scruple of availing himself of the first expedient which offered;——so taking hold of the bag and instruments, and griping them hard together with one hand, and with the finger and thumb of the other, putting the end of the hatband betwixt his teeth, and then slipping his hand down to the middle of it,——he tied and cross-tied them all fast together from one end to the other (as you would cord a trunk) with such a multiplicity of roundabouts and intricate cross turns, with a hard knot at every intersection or point where the strings met,——that Dr. Slop must have had three fifths of Job's patience at least to have unloosed them.——I think, in my conscience, that had NATURE been in one of her nimble moods, and in humour for such a contest——and she and Dr. Slop both fairly started together——there is no man living who had seen the bag with all that Obadiah had done to it,——and known likewise the great speed the goddess can make when she thinks proper, who would have had the least doubt remaining in his mind——which of the two would have carried off the prize. My mother, Madam, had been delivered sooner than the green bag infallibly——at least by twenty *knots*.——Sport of small accidents, Tristram Shandy! that thou art, and ever will be! had that trial been made for thee, and it was fifty to one but it had,——thy affairs had

134

not been so depressed——(at least by the depression of thy nose) as they have been; nor had the fortunes of thy house and the occasions of making them, which have so often presented themselves in the course of thy life to thee, been so often, so vexatiously, so tamely, so irrecoverably abandoned ——as thou hast been forced to leave them!——but 'tis over, ——all but the account of 'em, which cannot be given to the curious till I am got out into the world.

CHAPTER IX

Great wits jump: for the moment Dr. Slop cast his eyes upon his bag (which he had not done till the dispute with my uncle Toby about midwifery put him in mind of it),——the very same thought occurred.——'Tis God's mercy, quoth he (to himself), that Mrs. Shandy has had so bad a time of it;—— else she might have been brought to bed seven times told, before one half of these knots could have got untied.——But here, you must distinguish——the thought floated only in Dr. Slop's mind, without sail or ballast to it, as a simple proposition; millions of which, as your Worship knows, are every day swimming quietly in the middle of the thin juice of a man's understanding, without being carried backwards or forwards, till some little gusts of passion or interest drive them to one side.

A sudden trampling in the room above, near my mother's bed, did the proposition the very service I am speaking of. By all that's unfortunate, quoth Dr. Slop, unless I make haste, the thing will actually befall me as it is.

CHAPTER X

In the case of *knots*,——by which, in the first place, I would not be understood to mean slipknots,——because in the course of my life and opinions,——my opinions concerning

135

them will come in more properly when I mention the catastrophe of my great-uncle Mr. Hammond Shandy,——a little man,——but of high fancy:——he rushed into the Duke of Monmouth's affair:——nor, secondly, in this place, do I mean that particular species of knots called bowknots;——there is so little address, or skill, or patience required in the unloosing them, that they are below my giving any opinion at all about them.——But by the knots I am speaking of, may it please your Reverences to believe that I mean good, honest, devilish tight, hard knots, made *bona fide,* as Obadiah made his;——in which there is no quibbling provision made by the duplication and return of the two ends of the strings through the annulus or noose made by the second *implication* of them——to get them slipped and undone by——I hope you apprehend me.

In the case of these *knots* then, and of the several obstructions which, may it please your Reverences, such knots cast in our way in getting through life——every hasty man can whip out his penknife and cut through them.——'Tis wrong. Believe me, Sirs, the most virtuous way, and which both reason and conscience dictate,——is to take our teeth or our fingers to them.——Dr. Slop had lost his teeth;——his favourite instrument, by extracting in a wrong direction, or by some misapplication of it unfortunately slipping, he had formerly, in a hard labour, knocked out three of the best of them, with the handle of it:——he tried his fingers——alas! the nails of his fingers and thumbs were cut close.——The deuce take it! I can make nothing of it either way, cried Dr. Slop.—— The trampling overhead near my mother's bedside increased. ——Pox take the fellow! I shall never get the knots untied as long as I live.——My mother gave a groan——Lend me your penknife——I must e'en cut the knots at last - - - - - pugh! - - - psha! - - - Lord! I have cut my thumb quite across to the very bone——curse the fellow——if there was not another man midwife within fifty miles——I am undone for this bout——I wish the scoundrel hanged——I wish he was shot——I wish all the devils in hell had him for a blockhead——

My father had a great respect for Obadiah, and could not bear to hear him disposed of in such a manner——he had moreover some little respect for himself——and could as ill bear with the indignity offered to himself in it.

Had Dr. Slop cut any part about him but his thumb——my father had passed it by——his prudence had triumphed: as it was, he was determined to have his revenge.

Small curses, Dr. Slop, upon great occasions, quoth my father (condoling with him first upon the accident), are but so much waste of our strength and soul's health to no manner of purpose.——I own it, replied Dr. Slop.——They are like sparrow shot, quoth my uncle Toby (suspending his whistling), fired against a bastion.——They serve, continued my father, to stir the humours——but carry off none of their acrimony:——for my own part, I seldom swear or curse at all——I hold it bad——but if I fall into it, by surprise, I generally retain so much presence of mind (right, quoth my uncle Toby) as to make it answer my purpose——that is, I swear on, till I find myself easy. A wise and a just man however would always endeavour to proportion the vent given to these humours, not only to the degree of them stirring within himself——but to the size and ill intent of the offence upon which they are to fall.——*"Injuries come only from the heart,"*——quoth my uncle Toby. For this reason, continued my father, with the most Cervantic gravity, I have the greatest veneration in the world for that gentleman who, in distrust of his own discretion in this point, sat down and composed (that is at his leisure) fit forms of swearing suitable to all cases, from the lowest to the highest provocations which could possibly happen to him;——which forms being well considered by him, and such moreover as he could stand to, he kept them ever by him on the chimney piece, within his reach, ready for use.——I never apprehended, replied Dr. Slop, that such a thing was ever thought of,——much less executed. I beg your pardon——answered my father; I was reading, though not using, one of them to my brother Toby this morning, whilst he poured out the tea——'tis here upon the shelf over my head;——but if I remember right, 'tis too violent for a cut of the thumb.——Not at all, quoth Dr. Slop ——the devil take the fellow.——Then, answered my father, 'Tis much at your service, Dr. Slop——on condition you will read it aloud;——so rising up and reaching down a form of excommunication of the church of Rome, a copy of which my father (who was curious in his collections) had procured out of the leger book of the church of Rochester, writ by ERNULPHUS the bishop——with a most affected seriousness of look and voice, which might have cajoled ERNULPHUS himself,——he put it into Dr. Slop's hands.——Dr. Slop wrapt his thumb up in the corner of his handkerchief, and with a wry face, though without any suspicion, read aloud, as follows,——my uncle Toby whistling *Lillabullero,* as loud as he could, all the time.

Textus de Ecclesiâ Roffensi, per Ernulfum Episcopum.

CAP. XI.

EXCOMMUNICATIO*

Ex auctoritate Dei omnipotentis, Patris, et Filij, et Spiritus Sancti, et sanctorum canonum, sanctaeque et intemeratae Virginis Dei genetricis Mariae,

---

* As the genuineness of the consultation of the Sorbonne upon the question of baptism was doubted by some, and denied by others,——'twas thought proper to print the original of this excommunication; for the copy of which Mr. Shandy returns thanks to the chapter clerk of the dean and chapter of Rochester.

CHAPTER XI

"By the authority of God Almighty, the Father, Son, and Holy Ghost, and of the holy canons, and of the undefiled Virgin Mary, mother and patroness of our Saviour." [I think there is no necessity, quoth Dr. Slop, dropping the paper down to his knee, and addressing himself to my father,——as you have read it over, Sir, so lately, to read it aloud;——and as Captain Shandy seems to have no great inclination to hear it,——I may as well read it to myself. That's contrary to treaty, replied my father;——besides, there is something so whimsical, especially in the latter part of it, I should grieve to lose the pleasure of a second reading. Dr. Slop did not altogether like it,——but my uncle Toby offering at that instant to give over whistling, and read it himself to them,——Dr. Slop thought he might as well read it under the cover of my uncle Toby's whistling,——as suffer my uncle Toby to read it alone;——so raising up the paper to his face, and holding it quite parallel to it, in order to hide his chagrin, ——he read it aloud as follows,——my uncle Toby whistling *Lillabullero,* though not quite so loud as before.]

————Atque omnium coelestium virtutum, angelorum, archangelorum, thronorum, dominationum, potestatuum, cherubin ac seraphin, & sanctorum patriarchum, prophetarum, & omnium apostolorum et evangelistarum, & sanctorum innocentum, qui in conspectu Agni soli digni inventi sunt canticum cantare novum, et sanctorum martyrum, et sanctorum confessorum, et sanctarum virginum, atque omnium simul sanctorum et electorum Dei,————Excommunicamus, et anathe-

vel os   s   *vel* os   s

matizamus hunc furem, vel hunc malefactorem, N. N. et a liminibus sanctae Dei ecclesiae sequestramus et aeternis sup-

vel i   n

pliciis excruciandus, mancipetur, cum Dathan et Abiram, et cum his qui dixerunt Domino Deo, Recede à nobis, scientiam viarum tuarum nolumus: et sicut aquâ ignis extinguitur, sic

vel eorum   n

extinguatur lucerna ejus in secula seculorum nisi respuerit, et

n

ad satisfactionem venerit. Amen.

os

Maledicat illum Deus Pater qui hominem creavit. Maledicat

os   os

illum Dei Filius qui pro homine passus est. Maledicat illum

os

Spiritus Sanctus qui in baptismo effusus est. Maledicat illum sancta crux, quam Christus pro nostrâ salute hostem triumphans, ascendit.

os

Maledicat illum sancta Dei genetrix et perpetua Virgo

os

Maria. Maledicat illum sanctus Michael, animarum susceptor

os

sacrarum. Maledicant illum omnes angeli et archangeli, principatus et potestates, omnisque militia coelestis.

os

Maledicat illum patriarcharum et prophetarum laudabilis

os

numerus. Maledicat illum sanctus Johannes praecursor et Baptista Christi, et sanctus Petrus, et sanctus Paulus, atque sanctus Andreas, omnesque Christi apostoli, simul et caeteri discipuli, quatuor quoque evangelistae, qui sua praedicatione

os

mundum universum converterunt. Maledicat illum cuneus martyrum et confessorum mirificus, qui Deo bonis operibus placitus inventus est.

"By the authority of God Almighty, the Father, Son, and Holy Ghost, and of the undefiled Virgin Mary, mother and patroness of our Saviour, and of all the celestial virtues, angels, archangels, thrones, dominions, powers, cherubins and seraphins, and of all the holy patriarchs, prophets, and of all the apostles and evangelists, and of the holy innocents, who in the sight of the holy Lamb are found worthy to sing the new song of the holy martyrs and holy confessors, and of the holy virgins, and of all the saints together with the holy and elect of God.——May he [Obadiah] be damned [for tying these knots].——We excommunicate and anathematise him, and from the thresholds of the holy church of God Almighty we sequester him, that he may be tormented, disposed, and delivered over with Dathan and Abiram, and with those who say unto the Lord God, Depart from us, we desire none of thy ways. And as fire is quenched with water, so let the light of him be put out forevermore, unless it shall repent him [Obadiah, of the knots which he has tied] and make satisfaction [for them]. Amen.

"May the Father who created man curse him.——May the Son who suffered for us curse him.——May the Holy Ghost who was given to us in baptism curse him [Obadiah].—— May the holy cross which Christ for our salvation, triumphing over his enemies, ascended——curse him.

"May the holy and eternal Virgin Mary, mother of God, curse him.——May St. Michael, the advocate of holy souls, curse him.——May all the angels and archangels, principalities and powers, and all the heavenly armies, curse him." [Our armies swore terribly in Flanders, cried my uncle Toby,—— but nothing to this.——For my own part, I could not have a heart to curse my dog so.]

"May St. John the precursor, and St. John the Baptist, and St. Peter and St. Paul, and St. Andrew, and all other Christ's apostles, together curse him. And may the rest of his disciples and four evangelists, who by their preaching converted the universal world,——and may the holy and wonderful company of martyrs and confessors, who by their holy works are found pleasing to God Almighty, curse him" [Obadiah].

141

os
Maledicant illum sacrarum virginum chori, quae mundi vana causa honoris Christi respuenda contempserunt. Male-

os
dicant illum omnes sancti qui ab initio mundi usque in finem seculi Deo dilecti inveniuntur.

os
Maledicant illum coeli et terra, et omnia sancta in eis manentia.

i n   n
Maledictus sit ubicunque fuerit, sive in domo, sive in agro, sive in viâ, sive in semitâ, sive in silvâ, sive in aquâ, sive in ecclesiâ.

i n
Maledictus sit vivendo, moriendo,———————————————

————— ————— ————— ————— —————
————— ————— ————— ————— —————
————— ————— ————— ————— —————
————— ————— ————— ————— —————

manducando, bibendo, esuriendo, sitiendo, jejunando, dormi-tando, dormiendo, vigilando, ambulando, stando, sedendo, jacendo, operando, quiescendo, mingendo, cacando, fleboto-mando.

i n
Maledictus sit in totis viribus corporis.

i n
Maledictus sit intus et exterius.
i n   i n
Maledictus sit in capillis; maledictus sit in cerebro. Male-
i n
dictus sit in vertice, in temporibus, in fronte, in auriculis, in superciliis, in oculis, in genis, in maxillis, in naribus, in den-tibus, mordacibus sive molaribus, in labiis, in guttere, in humeris, in harnis, in brachiis, in manubus, in digitis, in pec-tore, in corde, et in omnibus interioribus stomacho tenus, in renibus, in inguinibus, in femore, in genitalibus, in coxis, in genubus, in cruribus, in pedibus, et in unguibus.

Maledictus sit in totis compagibus membrorum, a vertice capitis, usque ad plantam pedis———non sit in eo sanitas.

142

"May the holy choir of the holy virgins, who for the honour of Christ have despised the things of the world, damn him.——May all the saints, who from the beginning of the world to everlasting ages are found to be beloved of God, damn him.——May the heavens and earth, and all the holy things remaining therein, damn him [Obadiah] or her [or whoever else had a hand in tying these knots].

"May he [Obadiah] be damned wherever he be,——whether in the house or the stables, the garden or the field, or the highway, or in the path, or in the wood, or in the water, or in the church.——May he be cursed in living, in dying." [Here my uncle Toby, taking the advantage of a *minim* in the second bar of his tune, kept whistling one continual note to the end of the sentence——Dr. Slop with his division of curses moving under him, like a running bass all the way.] "May he be cursed in eating and drinking, in being hungry, in being thirsty, in fasting, in sleeping, in slumbering, in walking, in standing, in sitting, in lying, in working, in resting, in pissing, in shitting, and in bloodletting.

"May he [Obadiah] be cursed in all the faculties of his body.

"May he be cursed inwardly and outwardly.——May he be cursed in the hair of his head.——May he be cursed in his brains, and in his vertex" [that is a sad curse, quoth my father], "in his temples, in his forehead, in his ears, in his eyebrows, in his cheeks, in his jawbones, in his nostrils, in his foreteeth and grinders, in his lips, in his throat, in his shoulders, in his wrists, in his arms, in his hands, in his fingers.

"May he be damned in his mouth, in his breast, in his heart and purtenance, down to the very stomach.

"May he be cursed in his reins, and in his groin" [God in heaven forbid, quoth my uncle Toby],——"in his thighs, in his genitals" [my father shook his head], "and in his hips, and in his knees, his legs, and feet, and toenails.

"May he be cursed in all the joints and articulations of his members, from the top of his head to the sole of his foot, may there be no soundness in him.

Maledicat illum Christus Filius Dei vivi toto suae majestatis imperio

———et insurgat adversus illum coelum cum omnibus virtuti-bus quae in eo moventur ad *damnandum* eum, nisi penituerit et ad satisfactionem venerit. Amen. Fiat, fiat. Amen.

"May the Son of the living God, with all the glory of his Majesty"——[Here my uncle Toby, throwing back his head, gave a monstrous, long, loud Whew——w——w——something betwixt the interjectional whistle of *Hey day!* and the word itself.——

——By the golden beard of Jupiter——and of Juno (if her majesty wore one), and by the beards of the rest of your heathen worships, which by the bye was no small number, since what with the beards of your celestial gods, and gods aerial and aquatic,——to say nothing of the beards of town-gods and country gods, or of the celestial goddesses your wives, or of the infernal goddesses your whores and concubines (that is in case they wore 'em),——all which beards, as Varro tells me, upon his word and honour, when mustered up together, made no less than thirty thousand effective beards upon the pagan establishment;——every beard of which claimed the rights and privileges of being stroked and sworn by,——by all these beards together then,——I vow and protest that of the two bad cassocks I am worth in the world, I would have given the better of them, as freely as ever Cid Hamet offered his,——only to have stood by, and heard my uncle Toby's accompaniment.]

——"Curse him," continued Dr. Slop,——"and may heaven with all the powers which move therein rise up against him, curse and damn him [Obadiah] unless he repent and make satisfaction. Amen. So be it,——so be it. Amen."

I declare, quoth my uncle Toby, my heart would not let me curse the devil himself with so much bitterness.——He is the father of curses, replied Dr. Slop.——So am not I, replied my uncle.——But he is cursed, and damned already, to all eternity,——replied Dr. Slop.

I am sorry for it, quoth my uncle Toby.

Dr. Slop drew up his mouth, and was just beginning to return my uncle Toby the compliment of his Whu——u——u——or interjectional whistle,——when the door hastily opening in the next chapter but one——put an end to the affair.

CHAPTER XII

Now don't let us give ourselves a parcel of airs, and pretend that the oaths we make free with in this land of liberty of ours are our own; and because we have the spirit to swear them,——imagine that we have had the wit to invent them too.

I'll undertake this moment to prove it to any man in the world, except to a connoisseur;——though I declare I object only to a connoisseur in swearing,——as I would do to a connoisseur in painting, &c., &c., the whole set of 'em are so hung round and *befetished* with the bobs and trinkets of criticism;——or to drop my metaphor, which by the bye is a pity,——for I have fetched it as far as from the coast of Guinea;——their heads, Sir, are stuck so full of rules and compasses, and have that eternal propensity to apply them upon all occasions, that a work of genius had better go to the devil at once, than stand to be pricked and tortured to death by 'em.

——And how did Garrick speak the soliloquy last night? ——Oh, against all rule, my Lord,——most ungrammatically! betwixt the substantive and the adjective, which should agree together in *number, case,* and *gender,* he made a breach thus,——stopping, as if the point wanted settling;——and betwixt the nominative case, which your Lordship knows should govern the verb, he suspended his voice in the epilogue a dozen times, three seconds and three fifths by a stop watch, my Lord, each time.——Admirable grammarian!——But in suspending his voice——was the sense suspended likewise? Did no expression of attitude or countenance fill up the chasm?——Was the eye silent? Did you narrowly look?—— I looked only at the stop watch, my Lord.——Excellent observer!

And what of this new book the whole world makes such a rout about?——Oh! 'tis out of all plumb, my Lord,—— quite an irregular thing!——not one of the angles at the four corners was a right angle.——I had my rule and compasses, &c., my Lord, in my pocket.——Excellent critic!

——And for the epic poem your Lordship bid me look at;

——upon taking the length, breadth, height, and depth of it, and trying them at home upon an exact scale of Bossu's,—— 'tis out, my Lord, in every one of its dimensions.——Admirable connoisseur!

——And did you step in, to take a look at the grand picture, in your way back.——'Tis a melancholy daub! my Lord; not one principle of the *pyramid* in any one group! ——and what a price!——for there is nothing of the colouring of Titian,——the expression of Rubens,——the grace of Raphael,——the purity of Domenichino,——the *corregiescity* of Correggio,——the learning of Poussin,——the airs of Guido,——the taste of the Carraccis,——or the grand contour of Angelo.——Grant me patience, just heaven!—— Of all the cants which are canted in this canting world,—— though the cant of hypocrites may be the worst,——the cant of criticism is the most tormenting!

I would go fifty miles on foot, for I have not a horse worth riding on, to kiss the hand of that man whose generous heart will give up the reins of his imagination into his author's hands,——be pleased he knows not why, and cares not wherefore.

Great Apollo! if thou art in a giving humour,——give me, ——I ask no more, but one stroke of native humour, with a single spark of thy own fire along with it,——and send Mercury, with the *rules and compasses*, if he can be spared, with my compliments to——no matter.

Now to anyone else, I will undertake to prove that all the oaths and imprecations which we have been puffing off upon the world for these two hundred and fifty years last past, as originals,——except *St. Paul's thumb*,——*God's flesh and God's fish*, which were oaths monarchical, and, considering who made them, not much amiss; and as kings' oaths, 'tis not much matter whether they were fish or flesh;——else, I say, there is not an oath, or at least a curse amongst them, which has not been copied over and over again out of Ernulphus, a thousand times: but, like all other copies, how infinitely short of the force and spirit of the original!——It is thought to be no bad oath,——and by itself passes very well—— *"G—d damn you."*——Set it beside Ernulphus's——"God Almighty the Father damn you,——God the Son damn you, ——God the Holy Ghost damn you,"——you see 'tis nothing.——There is an Orientality in his we cannot rise up to: besides, he is more copious in his invention,——possessed more of the excellencies of a swearer,——had such a thorough knowledge of the human frame, its membranes, nerves, ligaments, knittings of the joints, and articulations,——that when Ernulphus cursed,——no part escaped him.——'Tis true, there is something of a *hardness* in his manner,—— and, as in Michelangelo, a want of *grace*,——but then there is such a greatness of *gusto!*

My father, who generally looked upon everything in a light very different from all mankind,——would, after all, never allow this to be an original.——He considered rather Ernulphus's anathema as an institute of swearing, in which, as he suspected, upon the decline of *swearing* in some milder pontificate, Ernulphus, by order of the succeeding pope, had with great learning and diligence collected together all the laws of it;——for the same reason that Justinian, in the decline of the empire, had ordered his chancellor Tribonian to collect the Roman or civil laws all together into one code or digest,——lest through the rust of time,——and the fatality of all things committed to oral tradition, they should be lost to the world forever.

For this reason my father would ofttimes affirm there was not an oath, from the great and tremendous oath of William the Conqueror (*By the splendour of God*), down to the lowest oath of a scavenger (*Damn your eyes*), which was not to be found in Ernulphus.——In short, he would add,——I defy a man to swear *out* of it.

The hypothesis is, like most of my father's, singular and ingenious too;——nor have I any objection to it but that it overturns my own.

CHAPTER XIII

——Bless my soul!——my poor mistress is ready to faint, ——and her pains are gone,——and the drops are done, ——and the bottle of julep is broke,——and the nurse has cut her arm——(and I, my thumb, cried Dr. Slop), and the child is where it was, continued Susannah,——and the midwife has fallen backwards upon the edge of the fender, and bruised her hip as black as your hat.——I'll look at it, quoth Dr. Slop.——There is no need of that, replied Susannah;—— you had better look at my mistress;——but the midwife would gladly first give you an account how things are, so desires you would go upstairs and speak to her this moment.

Human nature is the same in all professions.

The midwife had just before been put over Dr. Slop's head. ——He had not digested it.——No, replied Dr. Slop, 'twould be full as proper if the midwife came down to me.——I like subordination, quoth my uncle Toby,——and but for it, after the reduction of Lille, I know not what might have become of the garrison of Ghent, in the mutiny for bread, in the year Ten.——Nor, replied Dr. Slop (parodying my uncle Toby's hobby-horsical reflection, though full as hobby-horsically himself),——do I know, Captain Shandy, what might have become of the garrison abovestairs, in the mutiny and confusion I find all things are in at present, but for the subordination of fingers and thumbs to ******—— the application of which, Sir, under this accident of mine, comes in so *a propos* that without it, the cut upon my thumb might have been felt by the Shandy family, as long as the Shandy family had a name.

CHAPTER XIV

Let us go back to the ******——in the last chapter.

It is a singular stroke of eloquence (at least it was so when eloquence flourished at Athens and Rome, and would be so now, did orators wear mantles) not to mention the name of a thing, when you had the thing about you, *in petto,* ready to produce, pop, in the place you want it. A scar, an axe, a sword, a pinked doublet, a rusty helmet, a pound and a half of potashes in an urn, or a three-halfpenny pickle pot, ——but above all, a tender infant royally accoutred.—— Though if it was too young, and the oration as long as Tully's second Philippic,——it must certainly have beshit the orator's mantle.——And then again, if too old,——it must have been unwieldy and incommodious to his action,——so as to make him lose by his child almost as much as he could gain by it.——Otherwise, when a state orator has hit the precise age to a minute,——hid his BAMBINO in his mantle so cunningly that no mortal could smell it,——and produced it so critically that no soul could say it came in by head and shoulders,——Oh, Sirs! it has done wonders.——It has

149

opened the sluices, and turned the brains, and shook the principles, and unhinged the politics of half a nation.

These feats however are not to be done, except in those states and times, I say, where orators wore mantles,——and pretty large ones too, my brethren, with some twenty or five-and-twenty yards of good purple, superfine, marketable cloth in them,——with large flowing folds and doubles, and in a great style of design.——All which plainly shows, may it please your Worships, that the decay of eloquence, and the little good service it does at present, both within and without doors, is owing to nothing else in the world but short coats, and the disuse of *trunk hose.*——We can conceal nothing under ours, Madam, worth showing.

CHAPTER XV

Dr. Slop was within an ace of being an exception to all this argumentation: for happening to have his green baize bag upon his knees, when he began to parody my uncle Toby, ——'twas as good as the best mantle in the world to him: for which purpose, when he foresaw the sentence would end in his new-invented *forceps,* he thrust his hand into the bag in order to have them ready to clap in, where your Reverences took so much notice of the ******, which had he managed, ——my uncle Toby had certainly been overthrown: the sentence and the argument in that case jumping closely in one point, so like the two lines which form the salient angle of a ravelin,——Dr. Slop would never have given them up;—— and my uncle Toby would as soon have thought of flying, as taking them by force: but Dr. Slop fumbled so vilely in pulling them out, it took off the whole effect, and what was a ten times' worse evil (for they seldom come alone in this life), in pulling out his *forceps,* his *forceps* unfortunately drew out the *squirt* along with it.

When a proposition can be taken in two senses,——'tis a law in disputation, That the respondent may reply to which of the two he pleases, or finds most convenient for him.——This threw the advantage of the argument quite on my uncle Toby's side.——"Good God!" cried my uncle Toby, *"are children brought into the world with a squirt?"*

CHAPTER XVI

——Upon my honour, Sir, you have tore every bit of the skin quite off the back of both my hands with your forceps, cried my uncle Toby,——and you have crushed all my knuckles into the bargain with them, to a jelly. 'Tis your own fault, said Dr. Slop;——you should have clinched your two fists together into the form of a child's head, as I told you, and sat firm.——I did so, answered my uncle Toby.—— Then the points of my forceps have not been sufficiently armed, or the rivet wants closing——or else the cut on my thumb has made me a little awkward,——or possibly—— 'Tis well, quoth my father, interrupting the detail of possibilities,——that the experiment was not first made upon my child's headpiece.——It would not have been a cherry stone the worse, answered Dr. Slop. I maintain it, said my uncle Toby, it would have broke the cerebellum (unless indeed the skull had been as hard as a grenado), and turned it all into a perfect posset. Pshaw! replied Dr. Slop, a child's head is naturally as soft as the pap of an apple;——the sutures give way,——and besides, I could have extracted by the feet after.——Not you, said she.——I rather wish you would begin that way, quoth my father.

Pray do, added my uncle Toby.

CHAPTER XVII

——And pray, good woman, after all, will you take upon you to say it may not be the child's hip, as well as the child's head?——'Tis most certainly the head, replied the midwife. Because, continued Dr. Slop (turning to my father), as positive as these old ladies generally are,——'tis a point very difficult to know,——and yet of the greatest consequence to be known;——because, Sir, if the hip is mistaken for the head,——there is a possibility (if it is a boy) that the forceps ***************

——What the possibility was, Dr. Slop whispered very low to my father, and then to my uncle Toby.——There is no such danger, continued he, with the head.——No, in truth, quoth my father,——but when your possibility has taken place at the hip,——you may as well take off the head too.

——It is morally impossible the reader should understand this;——'tis enough Dr. Slop understood it;——so taking the green baize bag in his hand, with the help of Obadiah's pumps he tripped pretty nimbly, for a man of his size, across the room to the door,———and from the door was shown the way, by the good old midwife, to my mother's apartment.

CHAPTER XVIII

It is two hours, and ten minutes,——and no more,——cried my father, looking at his watch, since Dr. Slop and Obadiah arrived,——and I know not how it happens, brother Toby,——but to my imagination it seems almost an age.

——Here——pray, Sir, take hold of my cap,——nay, take the bell along with it, and my pantofles too.——

Now, Sir, they are all at your service; and I freely make you a present of 'em, on condition you give me all your attention to this chapter.

Though my father said, *"he knew not how it happened,"* ——yet he knew very well how it happened;——and at the instant he spoke it, was predetermined in his mind to give my uncle Toby a clear account of the matter by a metaphysical dissertation upon the subject of *duration and its simple modes,* in order to show my uncle Toby by what mechanism and mensurations in the brain it came to pass that the rapid succession of their ideas, and the eternal scampering of discourse from one thing to another, since Dr. Slop had come into the room, had lengthened out so short a period to so inconceivable an extent.——I know not how it happens,——cried my father,——but it seems an age.

——'Tis owing, entirely, quoth my uncle Toby, to the succession of our ideas.

My father, who had an itch in common with all philoso-

phers of reasoning upon everything which happened, and ac-
counting for it too,——proposed infinite pleasure to himself
in this of the succession of ideas, and had not the least apprehension of having it snatched out of his hands by my
uncle Toby, who (honest man!) generally took everything as
it happened;——and who, of all men in the world, troubled
his brain the least with abstruse thinking;——the ideas of
time and space,——or how we came by those ideas,——or of
what stuff they were made,——or whether they were born
with us,——or we picked them up afterwards as we went
along,——or whether we did it in frocks,——or not till we
had got into breeches,——with a thousand other inquiries
and disputes about INFINITY, PRESCIENCE, LIBERTY, NECES-
SITY, and so forth, upon whose desperate and unconquerable
theories so many fine heads have been turned and cracked,
——never did my uncle Toby's the least injury at all; my
father knew it,——and was no less surprised than he was disappointed with my uncle's fortuitous solution.

Do you understand the theory of that affair? replied my
father.

Not I, quoth my uncle.

——But you have some ideas, said my father, of what you
talk about.——

No more than my horse, replied my uncle Toby.

Gracious heaven! cried my father, looking upwards, and
clasping his two hands together,——there is a worth in thy
honest ignorance, brother Toby;——'twere almost a pity to
exchange it for a knowledge.——But I'll tell thee.——

To understand what *time* is aright, without which we never
can comprehend *infinity*, insomuch as one is a portion of the
other,——we ought seriously to sit down and consider what
idea it is we have of *duration*, so as to give a satisfactory account how we came by it.——What is that to anybody?
quoth my uncle Toby.* *For if you will turn your eyes inwards upon your mind,* continued my father, *and observe attentively, you will perceive, brother, that whilst you and I are
talking together, and thinking and smoking our pipes; or
whilst we receive successively ideas in our minds; we know
that we do exist, and so we estimate the existence or the con-
tinuation of the existence of ourselves, or anything else com-
mensurate to the succession of any ideas in our minds, the
duration of ourselves, or any such other thing coexisting with
our thinking,*——*and so according to that preconceived*——

* Vid. Locke.

You puzzle me to death, cried my uncle Toby.——

——'Tis owing to this, replied my father, that in our computations of *time,* we are so used to minutes, hours, weeks, and months,——and of clocks (I wish there was not a clock in the kingdom), to measure out their several portions to us, and to those who belong to us,——that 'twill be well, if in time to come, the *succession of our ideas* be of any use or service to us at all.

Now, whether we observe it or no, continued my father, in every sound man's head, there is a regular succession of ideas of one sort or other, which follow each other in train just like——A train of artillery? said my uncle Toby.—— A train of a fiddlestick!——quoth my father,——which follow and succeed one another in our minds at certain distances, just like the images in the inside of a lantern turned round by the heat of a candle.——I declare, quoth my uncle Toby, mine are like a smokejack.——Then, brother Toby, I have nothing more to say to you upon the subject, said my father.

CHAPTER XIX

——What a conjuncture was here lost!——My father in one of his best explanatory moods,——in eager pursuit of a metaphysic point into the very regions where clouds and thick darkness would soon have encompassed it about;—— my uncle Toby in one of the finest dispositions for it in the world;——his head like a smokejack;——the funnel unswept, and the ideas whirling round and round about in it, all obfuscated and darkened over with fuliginous matter! ——By the tombstone of Lucian——if it is in being;—— if not, why then, by his ashes! by the ashes of my dear Rabelais, and dearer Cervantes;——my father and my uncle Toby's discourse upon TIME and ETERNITY——was a discourse devoutly to be wished for! and the petulancy of my father's humour in putting a stop to it, as he did, was a robbery of the *Ontologic treasury,* of such a jewel as no coalition of great occasions and great men are ever likely to restore to it again.

CHAPTER XX

Though my father persisted in not going on with the discourse,——yet he could not get my uncle Toby's smokejack out of his head,——piqued as he was at first with it;—— there was something in the comparison at the bottom which hit his fancy; for which purpose, resting his elbow upon the table, and reclining the right side of his head upon the palm of his hand,——but looking first steadfastly in the fire,—— he began to commune with himself and philosophize about it: but his spirits being wore out with the fatigues of investigating new tracts, and the constant exertion of his faculties upon that variety of subjects which had taken their turn in the discourse,——the idea of the smokejack soon turned all his ideas upside down,——so that he fell asleep almost before he knew what he was about.

As for my uncle Toby, his smokejack had not made a dozen revolutions before he fell aleep also.——Peace be with them both.——Dr. Slop is engaged with the midwife and my mother abovestairs.——Trim is busy in turning an old pair of jack boots into a couple of mortars to be employed in the siege of Messina next summer,——and is this instant boring the touchholes with the point of a hot poker. ——All my heroes are off my hands;——'tis the first time I have had a moment to spare,——and I'll make use of it, and write my preface.

THE

Author's PREFACE

No, I'll not say a word about it,——here it is;——in publishing it,——I have appealed to the world,——and to the world I leave it;——it must speak for itself.

All I know of the matter is,——when I sat down, my intent was to write a good book; and as far as the tenuity of my understanding would hold out,——a wise, aye, and a discreet,——taking care only, as I went along, to put into it all the wit and the judgment (be it more or less) which the great author and bestower of them had thought fit originally to give me,——so that, as your Worships see,——'tis just as God pleases.

Now, Agelastes (speaking dispraisingly) sayeth, That there may be some wit in it, for aught he knows,——but no judgment at all. And Triptolemus and Phutatorius, agreeing thereto, ask, How is it possible there should? for that wit and judgment in this world never go together; inasmuch as they are two operations differing from each other as wide as east is from west.——So says Locke;——so are farting and hiccuping, say I. But in answer to this, Didius, the great church lawyer, in his code *de fartandi et illustrandi fallaciis,* doth maintain and make fully appear, That an illustration is no argument,——nor do I maintain the wiping of a looking glass clean to be a syllogism;——but you all, may it please your Worships, see the better for it,——so that the main good these things do is only to clarify the understanding, previous to the application of the argument itself, in order to free it from any little motes, or specks of opacular matter, which, if left swimming therein, might hinder a conception and spoil all.

Now, my dear Anti-Shandeans, and thrice-able critics, and fellow-labourers (for to you I write this Preface),——and to you, most subtle statesmen and discreet doctors (do——pull off your beards) renowned for gravity and wisdom;—— Monopolus, my politician;——Didius, my counsel; Kysarcius, my friend;——Phutatorius, my guide;——Gastripheres, the preserver of my life; Somnolentius, the balm and repose of it,——not forgetting all others as well sleeping as waking, ——ecclesiastical as civil, whom for brevity, but out of no resentment to you, I lump all together.——Believe me, right worthy,

My most zealous wish and fervent prayer in your behalf, and in my own too, in case the thing is not done already for us,——is that the great gifts and endowments both of wit and judgment, with everything which usually goes along with them,——such as memory, fancy, genius, eloquence, quick parts, and whatnot, may this precious moment without stint or measure, let or hinderance, be poured down warm as each of us could bear it,——scum and sediment an' all (for I would not have a drop lost) into the several receptacles, cells, cellules, domiciles, dormitories, refectories, and spare places of our brains,——in such sort, that they might continue to be injected and tunned into, according to the true intent and meaning of my wish, until every vessel of them, both great and small, be so replenished, saturated, and filled up therewith, that no more, would it save a man's life, could possibly be got either in or out.

Bless us!——what noble work we should make!——how should I tickle it off!——and what spirits should I find myself in, to be writing away for such readers!——and you, ——just heaven!——with what raptures would you sit and read,——but oh!——'tis too much,——I am sick,——I faint away deliciously at the thoughts of it!——'tis more than nature can bear!——lay hold of me,——I am giddy,——I am stone blind,——I'm dying,——I am gone.——Help! Help! Help!——But hold,——I grow something better again, for I am beginning to foresee, when this is over, that as we shall all of us continue to be great wits,——we should never agree amongst ourselves, one day to an end:——there would be so much satire and sarcasm,——scoffing and flouting, with raillying and reparteeing of it,——thrusting and parrying in one corner or another,——there would be nothing but mischief amongst us.——Chaste stars! what biting and scratching, and what a racket and a clatter we should make, what with breaking of heads, and rapping of knuckles, and hitting of sore places,——there would be no such thing as living for us.

But then again, as we should all of us be men of great judgment, we should make up matters as fast as ever they went wrong; and though we should abominate each other, ten times worse than so many devils or devilesses, we should nevertheless, my dear creatures, be all courtesy and kindness, ——milk and honey,——'twould be a second land of promise,——a paradise upon earth, if there was such a thing to be had,——so that upon the whole we should have done well enough.

All I fret and fume at, and what most distresses my invention at present, is how to bring the point itself to bear; for as your Worships well know, that of these heavenly emanations of *wit* and *judgment,* which I have so bountifully wished both for your Worships and myself,——there is but a certain *quantum* stored up for us all, for the use and behoof of the whole race of mankind; and such small *modicums* of 'em are only sent forth into this wide world, circulating here and there in one by corner or another,——and in such narrow streams, and at such prodigious intervals from each other, that one would wonder how it holds out, or could be sufficient for the wants and emergencies of so many great states, and populous empires.

Indeed there is one thing to be considered, that in Nova Zembla, North Lapland, and in all those cold and dreary tracts of the globe, which lie more directly under the arctic and antarctic circles,——where the whole province of a man's concernments lies for near nine months together within the narrow compass of his cave,——where the spirits are compressed almost to nothing,——and where the passions of a man, with everything which belongs to them, are as frigid as the zone itself;——there the least quantity of *judgment* imaginable does the business,——and of *wit*——there is a total and an absolute saving,——for as not one spark is wanted,——so not one spark is given. Angels and ministers of grace defend us! What a dismal thing would it have been to have governed a kingdom, to have fought a battle, or made a treaty, or run a match, or wrote a book, or got a child, or held a provincial chapter there, with so *plentiful a lack* of wit and judgment about us! for mercy's sake! let us think no more about it, but travel on as fast as we can southwards into Norway,——crossing over Swedeland, if you please, through the small triangular province of Angermania to the lake of Bothnia, coasting along it through east and west Bothnia, down to Karelia, and so on, through all those states and provinces which border upon the far side of the Gulf of Finland, and the northeast of the Baltic, up to Petersburg, and just stepping into Ingria;——then stretching over directly from thence through the north parts of the Russian empire——leaving Siberia a little upon the left hand till we get into the very heart of Russian and Asiatic Tartary.

Now throughout this long tour which I have led you, you observe the good people are better off by far than in the polar countries which we have just left:——for if you hold your hand over your eyes, and look very attentively, you may perceive some small glimmerings (as it were) of wit, with a comfortable provision of good plain *household* judgment, which taking the quality and quantity of it together, they make a very good shift with,——and had they more of either the one or the other, it would destroy the proper balance betwixt them, and I am satisfied moreover they would want occasions to put them to use.

Now, Sir, if I conduct you home again into this warmer and more luxuriant island, where you perceive the spring tide of our blood and humours runs high,——where we have more ambition, and pride, and envy, and lechery, and other whoreson passions upon our hands to govern and subject to reason,——the *height* of our wit and the *depth* of our judgment, you see, are exactly proportioned to the *length* and *breadth* of our necessities,——and accordingly, we have them sent down amongst us in such a flowing kind of decent and creditable plenty, that no one thinks he has any cause to complain.

It must however be confessed on this head that, as our air blows hot and cold,——wet and dry, ten times in a day, we have them in no regular and settled way;——so that sometimes, for near half a century together, there shall be very little wit or judgment either to be seen or heard of amongst us:——the small channels of them shall seem quite dried up;——then all of a sudden the sluices shall break out, and take a fit of running again like fury;——you would think they would never stop:——and then it is that in writing and fighting, and twenty other gallant things, we drive all the world before us.

It is by these observations, and a wary reasoning by analogy in that kind of argumentative process which Suidas calls *dialectic induction*,——that I draw and set up this position as most true and veritable.

That of these two luminaries, so much of their irradiations are suffered from time to time to shine down upon us as he, whose infinite wisdom which dispenses everything in exact weight and measure, knows will just serve to light us on our way in this night of our obscurity; so that your Reverences and Worships now find out, nor is it a moment longer in my power to conceal it from you, That the fervent wish in your behalf with which I set out was no more than the first insinuating *How d'ye* of a caressing prefacer stifling his reader, as a lover sometimes does a coy mistress into silence. For alas! could this effusion of light have been as easily procured as the exordium wished it——I tremble to think how many thousands, for it, of benighted travellers (in the learned sciences at least) must have groped and blundered on in the dark, all the nights of their lives,——running their heads against posts, and knocking out their brains, without ever getting to their journey's end;——some falling with their noses perpendicularly into sinks,——others horizontally with their tails into kennels. Here one half of a learned profession tilting full butt against the other half of it, and then tumbling and rolling one over the other in the dirt like hogs.——Here the brethren of another profession, who should have run in opposition to each other, flying on the contrary like a flock of wild geese, all in a row the same way.——What confusion!——what mistakes!——fiddlers and painters judging by their eyes and ears,——admirable!—— trusting to the passions excited in an air sung, or a story painted to the heart,——instead of measuring them by a quadrant.

In the foreground of this picture, a *statesman* turning the political wheel, like a brute, the wrong way round——*against* the stream of corruption,——by heaven!——instead of *with* it.

In this corner, a son of the divine Aesculapius, writing a book against predestination; perhaps worse,——feeling his patient's pulse, instead of his apothecary's;——a brother of the faculty in the background, upon his knees in tears,—— drawing the curtains of a mangled victim to beg his forgiveness;——offering a fee,——instead of taking one.

In that spacious HALL, a coalition of the gown, from all the bars of it, driving a damned, dirty, vexatious cause before them, with all their might and main, the wrong way; ——kicking it *out* of the great doors, instead of *in,*——and with such fury in their looks, and such a degree of inveteracy in their manner of kicking it, as if the laws had been originally made for the peace and preservation of mankind:——perhaps a more enormous mistake committed by them still, ——a litigated point fairly hung up;——for instance, Whether John o' Nokes his nose could stand in Tom o' Stiles his face, without a trespass, or not,——rashly determined by them in five-and-twenty minutes, which, with the cautious pros and cons required in so intricate a proceeding, might have taken up as many months,——and if carried on upon a military plan, as your Honours know an ACTION should be, with all the stratagems practicable therein,——such as feints, ——forced marches,——surprises,——ambuscades,——mask batteries, and a thousand other strokes of generalship which consist in catching at all advantages on both sides,——might reasonably have lasted them as many years, finding food and raiment all that term for a centumvirate of the profession.

As for the clergy——No——If I say a word against them, I'll be shot.——I have no desire,——and besides, if I had,——I durst not for my soul touch upon the subject; ——with such weak nerves and spirits, and in the condition I am in at present, 'twould be as much as my life was worth, to deject and contrist myself with so sad and melancholy an account,——and therefore, 'tis safer to draw a curtain across, and hasten from it, as fast as I can, to the main and principal point I have undertaken to clear up,——and that is,

How it comes to pass that your men of least *wit* are reported to be men of most *judgment.*——But mark,——I say, *reported to be,*——for it is no more, my dear Sirs, than a report, and which, like twenty others taken up every day upon trust, I maintain to be a vile and malicious report into the bargain.

This, by the help of the observations already premised, and I hope already weighed and perpended by your Reverences and Worships, I shall forthwith make appear.

I hate set dissertations,——and above all things in the world, 'tis one of the silliest things in one of them to darken your hypothesis by placing a number of tall, opaque words, one before another, in a right line, betwixt your own and your reader's conception,——when in all likelihood, if you had looked about, you might have seen something standing, or hanging up, which would have cleared the point at once; ——"for what hinderance, hurt, or harm doth the laudable desire of knowledge bring to any man, if even from a sot, a pot, a fool, a stool, a winter mittain, a truckle for a pully, the lid of a goldsmith's crucible, an oil bottle, an old slipper, or a cane chair?"——I am this moment sitting upon one. Will you give me leave to illustrate this affair of wit and judgment by the two knobs on the top of the back of it;——they are fastened on, you see, with two pegs stuck slightly into two gimlet holes, and will place what I have to say in so clear a light as to let you see through the drift and meaning of my whole preface, as plainly as if every point and particle of it was made up of sunbeams.

I enter now directly upon the point.

——Here stands *wit,*——and there stands *judgment,* close beside it, just like the two knobs I'm speaking of upon the back of this selfsame chair on which I am sitting.

——You see, they are the highest and most ornamental parts of its *frame,*——as wit and judgment are of *ours,*—— and like them too, indubitably both made and fitted to go together, in order, as we say in all such cases of duplicated embellishments,——*to answer one another.*

Now for the sake of an experiment, and for the clearer illustrating this matter,——let us for a moment take off one of these two curious ornaments (I care not which) from the point or pinnacle of the chair it now stands on;——nay, don't laugh at it.——But did you ever see in the whole course of your lives such a ridiculous business as this has made of it?——Why, 'tis as miserable a sight as a sow with one ear; and there is just as much sense and symmetry in the one as in the other:——do,——pray, get off your seats, only to take a view of it.——Now would any man who valued his character a straw have turned a piece of work out of his hand in such a condition?——nay, lay your hands upon your hearts, and answer this plain question, Whether this one single knob which now stands here like a blockhead by itself can serve any purpose upon earth but to put one in mind of the want of the other;——and let me further ask, in case the chair was your own, if you would not in your consciences think, rather than be as it is, that it would be ten times better without any knob at all?

Now these two knobs,——or top ornaments of the mind of man, which crown the whole entablature,——being, as I said, wit and judgment, which of all others, as I have proved it, are the most needful,——the most prized,——the most calamitous to be without, and consequently the hardest to come at,——for all these reasons put together, there is not a mortal amongst us so destitute of a love of good fame or feeding,——or so ignorant of what will do him good therein,——who does not wish and steadfastly resolve in his own mind to be, or to be thought, at least, master of the one or the other, and indeed of both of them, if the thing seems any way feasible, or likely to be brought to pass.

Now your graver gentry having little or no kind of chance in aiming at the one,——unless they laid hold of the other,——pray what do you think would become of them?——Why, Sirs, in spite of all their *gravities*, they must e'en have been contented to have gone with their insides naked:——this was not to be borne, but by an effort of philosophy not to be supposed in the case we are upon,——so that no one could well have been angry with them, had they been satisfied with what little they could have snatched up and secreted under their cloaks and great perriwigs, had they not raised a *hue* and *cry* at the same time against the lawful owners.

I need not tell your Worships that this was done with so much cunning and artifice——that the great Locke, who was seldom outwitted by false sounds,——was nevertheless bubbled here. The cry, it seems, was so deep and solemn a one, and what with the help of great wigs, grave faces, and other implements of deceit, was rendered so general a one against the *poor wits* in this matter, that the philosopher himself was deceived by it;——it was his glory to free the world from the lumber of a thousand vulgar errors,——but this was not of the number; so that instead of sitting down coolly, as such a philosopher should have done, to have examined the matter of fact before he philosophised upon it;——on the contrary, he took the fact for granted, and so joined in with the cry, and hallooed it as boisterously as the rest.

This has been made the *Magna Charta* of stupidity ever since,——but your Reverences plainly see it has been obtained in such a manner that the title to it is not worth a groat;——which by the bye is one of the many and vile impositions which gravity and grave folks have to answer for hereafter.

As for great wigs, upon which I may be thought to have spoken my mind too freely,——I beg leave to qualify whatever has been unguardedly said to their dispraise or prejudice, by one general declaration——That I have no abhorrence whatever, nor do I detest and abjure either great wigs or long beards,——any further than when I see they are bespoke and let grow on purpose to carry on this selfsame imposture——for any purpose,——peace be with them;—— ☞ mark only,——I write not for them.

CHAPTER XXI

Every day for at least ten years together did my father resolve to have it mended;——'tis not mended yet;——no family but ours would have borne with it an hour,——and what is most astonishing, there was not a subject in the world upon which my father was so eloquent as upon that of door hinges.——And yet at the same time, he was certainly one of the greatest bubbles to them, I think, that history can produce: his rhetoric and conduct were at perpetual handicuffs. ——Never did the parlour door open——but his philosophy or his principles fell a victim to it;——three drops of oil with a feather, and a smart stroke of a hammer, had saved his honour forever.

——Inconsistent soul that man is!——languishing under wounds which he has the power to heal!——his whole life a contradiction to his knowledge!——his reason, that precious gift of God to him——(instead of pouring in oil), serving but to sharpen his sensibilities,——to multiply his pains and render him more melancholy and uneasy under them!—— poor unhappy creature, that he should do so!——are not the necessary causes of misery in this life enow, but he must add

163

voluntary ones to his stock of sorrow;——struggle against evils which cannot be avoided, and submit to others which a tenth part of the trouble they create him would remove from his heart forever?

By all that is good and virtuous! if there are three drops of oil to be got, and a hammer to be found within ten miles of Shandy Hall,——the parlour-door hinge shall be mended this reign.

CHAPTER XXII

When Corporal Trim had brought his two mortars to bear, he was delighted with his handiwork above measure; and knowing what a pleasure it would be to his master to see them, he was not able to resist the desire he had of carrying them directly into his parlour.

Now next to the moral lesson I had in view in mentioning the affair of *hinges*, I had a speculative consideration arising out of it, and it is this.

Had the parlour door opened and turned upon its hinges, as a door should do——

——Or for example, as cleverly as our government has been turning upon its hinges——(that is, in case things have all along gone well with your Worship,——otherwise I give up my simile),——in this case, I say, there had been no danger either to master or man in Corporal Trim's peeping in: the moment he had beheld my father and my uncle Toby fast asleep,——the respectfulness of his carriage was such, he would have retired as silent as death, and left them both in their armchairs, dreaming as happy as he had found them: but the thing was morally speaking so very impracticable that for the many years in which this hinge was suffered to be out of order, and amongst the hourly grievances my father submitted to upon its account,——this was one; that he never folded his arms to take his nap after dinner, but the thoughts of being unavoidably awakened by the first person who should open the door was always uppermost in his imagination, and so incessantly stepped in betwixt him and the first balmy presage of his repose as to rob him, as he often declared, of the whole sweets of it.

"When things move upon bad hinges, an' please your Lordships, *how can it be otherwise?"*

Pray, what's the matter? Who is there? cried my father, waking, the moment the door began to creak.——I wish the smith would give a peep at that confounded hinge.——'Tis nothing, an' please your Honour, said Trim, but two mortars I am bringing in.——They shan't make a clatter with them here, cried my father hastily.——If Dr. Slop has any drugs to pound, let him do it in the kitchen.——May it please your Honour, cried Trim,——they are two mortar pieces for a siege next summer, which I have been making out of a pair of jack boots which Obadiah told me your Honour had left off wearing.——By heaven! cried my father, springing out of his chair, as he swore,——I have not one appointment belonging to me which I set so much store by as I do by these jack boots;——they were our great-grandfather's, brother Toby,——they were *hereditary.* Then I fear, quoth my uncle Toby, Trim has cut off the entail.——I have only cut off the tops, an' please your Honour, cried Trim.——I hate *perpetuities* as much as any man alive, cried my father, ——but these jack boots, continued he (smiling, though very angry at the same time), have been in the family, brother, ever since the civil wars;——Sir Roger Shandy wore them at the battle of Marston Moor.——I declare I would not have taken ten pounds for them.——I'll pay you the money, brother Shandy, quoth my uncle Toby, looking at the two mortars with infinite pleasure, and putting his hand into his breeches pocket as he viewed them.——I'll pay you the ten pounds this moment with all my heart and soul.——

Brother Toby, replied my father, altering his tone, you care not what money you dissipate and throw away, provided, continued he, 'tis but upon a SIEGE.——Have I not a hundred and twenty pounds a year, besides my half-pay? cried my uncle Toby.——What is that,——replied my father, hastily,——to ten pounds for a pair of jack boots?——twelve guineas for your *pontoons;*——half as much for your *Dutch* drawbridge;——to say nothing of the train of little brass artillery you bespoke last week, with twenty other preparations for the siege of Messina; believe me, dear brother Toby, continued my father, taking him kindly by the hand,——these military operations of yours are above your strength;—— you mean well, brother,——but they carry you into greater expenses than you were first aware of,——and take my word, ——dear Toby, they will in the end quite ruin your fortune, and make a beggar of you.——What signifies it if they do,

165

brother, replied my uncle Toby, so long as we know 'tis for the good of the nation.——

My father could not help smiling for his soul;——his anger at the worst was never more than a spark,——and the zeal and simplicity of Trim,——and the generous (though hobby-horsical) gallantry of my uncle Toby, brought him into perfect good humour with them in an instant.

Generous souls!——God prosper you both, and your mortar pieces too, quoth my father to himself.

CHAPTER XXIII

All is quiet and hush, cried my father, at least abovestairs, ——I hear not one foot stirring.——Prithee, Trim, who is in the kitchen? There is no one soul in the kitchen, answered Trim, making a low bow as he spoke, except Dr. Slop.—— Confusion! cried my father (getting up upon his legs a second time),——not one single thing has gone right this day! had I faith in astrology, brother (which, by the bye, my father had), I would have sworn some retrograde planet was hanging over this unfortunate house of mine, and turning every individual thing in it out of its place.——Why, I thought Dr. Slop had been abovestairs with my wife, and so said you. ——What can the fellow be puzzling about in the kitchen? ——He is busy, an' please your Honour, replied Trim, in making a bridge.——'Tis very obliging in him, quoth my uncle Toby;——pray give my humble service to Dr. Slop Trim, and tell him I thank him heartily.

You must know, my uncle Toby mistook the bridge as widely as my father mistook the mortars;——but to understand how my uncle Toby could mistake the bridge,——I fear I must give you an exact account of the road which led to it;——or to drop my metaphor (for there is nothing more dishonest in an historian than the use of one),——in order to conceive the probability of this error in my uncle Toby aright, I must give you some account of an adventure of Trim's, though much against my will. I say much against my will, only because the story, in one sense, is certainly out of its place here; for by right it should come in either amongst the anecdotes of my uncle Toby's amours with widow Wadman, in which Corporal Trim was no mean actor,——or else in the middle of his and my uncle Toby's campaigns on the bowling green,——for it will do very well in either place;——but then if I reserve it for either of those parts of my story,——I ruin the story I'm upon,——and if I tell it here,——I anticipate matters, and ruin it there.

——What would your Worships have me to do in this case?

——Tell it, Mr. Shandy, by all means.——You are a fool, Tristram, if you do.

O ye Powers! (for powers ye are, and great ones too)——which enable mortal man to tell a story worth the hearing,——that kindly show him where he is to begin it,——and where he is to end it,——what he is to put into it,——and what he is to leave out,——how much of it he is to cast into shade,——and whereabouts he is to throw his light!——Ye who preside over this vast empire of biographical freebooters, and see how many scrapes and plunges your subjects hourly fall into;——will you do one thing?

I beg and beseech you (in case you will do nothing better for us) that wherever, in any part of your dominions it so falls out, that three several roads meet in one point, as they have done just here,——that at least you set up a guidepost, in the center of them, in mere charity to direct an uncertain devil which of the three he is to take.

CHAPTER XXIV

Though the shock my uncle Toby received the year after the demolition of Dunkirk, in his affair with widow Wadman, had fixed him in a resolution never more to think of the sex,——or of aught which belonged to it;——yet Corporal Trim had made no such bargain with himself. Indeed in my uncle Toby's case there was a strange and unaccountable concurrence of circumstances which insensibly drew him in, to lay siege to that fair and strong citadel.——In Trim's case there was a concurrence of nothing in the world but of him and Bridget in the kitchen;——though in truth, the love and veneration he bore his master was such, and so fond was he of imitating him in all he did, that had my uncle Toby employed his time and genius in tagging of points,——I am persuaded the honest corporal would have laid down his arms, and followed his example with pleasure. When therefore my uncle Toby sat down before the mistress,——Corporal Trim incontinently took ground before the maid.

Now, my dear friend Garrick, whom I have so much cause to esteem and honour——(why, or wherefore, 'tis no matter), ——can it escape your penetration,——I defy it,——that so many playwrights, and opificers of chitchat have ever since been working upon Trim's and my uncle Toby's pattern.—— I care not what Aristotle, or Pacuvius, or Bossu, or Ricaboni say——(though I never read one of them);——there is not a greater difference between a single-horse chair and Madam Pompadour's *vis-à-vis*, then betwixt a single amour and an amour thus nobly doubled, and going upon all four, prancing throughout a grand drama.——Sir, a simple, single, silly affair of that kind——is quite lost in five acts,——but that is neither here or there.

After a series of attacks and repulses in a course of nine months on my uncle Toby's quarter, a most minute account of every particular of which shall be given in its proper place, my uncle Toby, honest man! found it necessary to draw off his forces, and raise the siege somewhat indignantly.

Corporal Trim, as I said, had made no such bargain either with himself——or with anyone else;——the fidelity however of his heart not suffering him to go into a house which his master had forsaken with disgust,——he contented himself with turning his part of the siege into a blockade;—— that is, he kept others off,——for though he never after went to the house, yet he never met Bridget in the village but he would either nod, or wink, or smile, or look kindly at her, ——or (as circumstances directed) he would shake her by the hand,——or ask her lovingly how she did,——or would give her a ribband,——and now and then, though never but when it could be done with decorum, would give Bridget a ——————

Precisely in this situation did these things stand for five years; that is, from the demolition of Dunkirk in the year 13, to the latter end of my uncle Toby's campaign in the year 18, which was about six or seven weeks before the time I'm speaking of.——When Trim, as his custom was, after he had put my uncle Toby to bed, going down one moonshiny night to see that everything was right at his fortifications,——in the lane separated from the bowling green with flowering shrubs and holly,——he espied his Bridget.

As the corporal thought there was nothing in the world so well worth showing as the glorious works which he and my uncle Toby had made, Trim courteously and gallantly took her by the hand, and led her in: this was not done so privately but that the foul-mouthed trumpet of Fame carried it from ear to ear, till at length it reached my father's, with this untoward circumstance along with it, that my uncle Toby's curious drawbridge, constructed and painted after the Dutch fashion, and which went quite across the ditch,——was broke down, and somehow or other crushed all to pieces that very night.

My father, as you have observed, had no great esteem for my uncle Toby's hobby-horse,——he thought it the most ridiculous horse that ever gentleman mounted, and indeed unless my uncle Toby vexed him about it, could never think of it once without smiling at it;——so that it never could get lame or happen any mischance but it tickled my father's imagination beyond measure; but this being an accident much more to his humour than any one which had yet befallen it, it proved an inexhaustible fund of entertainment to him.——Well,——but dear Toby! my father would say, do tell us seriously how this affair of the bridge happened.——How can you tease me so much about it? my uncle Toby would reply;——I have told it you twenty times, word for word as Trim told it me.——Prithee how was it then, corporal? my father would cry, turning to Trim.——It was a mere misfortune, an' please your Honour,——I was showing Mrs. Bridget our fortifications, and in going too near the edge of the fosse, I unfortunately slipped in.——Very well, Trim! my father would cry——(smiling mysteriously, and giving a nod,——but without interrupting him);——and being linked fast, an' please your Honour, arm in arm with Mrs. Bridget, I dragged her after me, by means of which she fell backwards soss against the bridge;——and Trim's foot (my uncle Toby would cry, taking the story out of his mouth) getting into the cuvette, he tumbled full against the bridge too.——It was a thousand to one, my uncle Toby would add, that the poor fellow did not break his leg.——Ay truly! my father would say,——a limb is soon broke, brother Toby, in such encounters.——And so, an' please your Honour, the bridge, which your Honour knows was a very slight one, was broke down betwixt us, and splintered all to pieces.

At other times, but especially when my uncle Toby was so unfortunate as to say a syllable about cannons, bombs, or petards,——my father would exhaust all the stores of his eloquence (which indeed were very great) in a panegyric upon the BATTERING RAMS of the ancients,——the VINEA, which Alexander made use of at the siege of Tyre.——He would tell my uncle Toby of the CATAPULTAE of the Syrians, which threw such monstrous stones so many hundred feet, and shook the strongest bulwarks from their very foundation;——he would go on and describe the wonderful mechanism of the BALLISTA, which Marcellinus makes so much rout about,——the terrible effects of the PYRABOLI,——which cast fire,——the danger of the TEREBRA and SCORPIO, which cast javelins.——But what are these, he would say, to the destructive machinery of Corporal Trim?——Believe me, brother Toby, no bridge, or bastion, or sally port that ever was constructed in this world can hold out against such artillery.

My uncle Toby would never attempt any defence against the force of this ridicule but that of redoubling the vehemence of smoking his pipe; in doing which, he raised so dense a vapour one night after supper that it set my father, who was a little phthisical, into a suffocating fit of violent coughing: my uncle Toby leaped up without feeling the pain upon his groin,—— and, with infinite pity, stood beside his brother's chair, tapping his back with one hand, and holding his head with the other, and from time to time, wiping his eyes with a clean cambric handkerchief, which he pulled out of his pocket.——The affectionate and endearing manner in which my uncle Toby did these little offices——cut my father through his reins for the pain he had just been giving him.——May my brains be knocked out with a battering ram or a catapulta, I care not which, quoth my father to himself, ——if ever I insult this worthy soul more.

CHAPTER XXV

The drawbridge being held irreparable, Trim was ordered directly to set about another,——but not upon the same model; for Cardinal Alberoni's intrigues at that time being discovered, and my uncle Toby rightly foreseeing that a flame would inevitably break out betwixt Spain and the Empire, and that the operations of the ensuing campaign must in all likelihood be either in Naples or Sicily,——he determined upon an Italian bridge——(my uncle Toby, by the bye, was not far out in his conjectures),——but my father, who was infinitely the better politician, and took the lead as far of my uncle Toby in the cabinet as my uncle Toby took it of him in the field,——convinced him that if the King of Spain and the Emperor went together by the ears, that England and France and Holland must, by force of their pre-engagements, all enter the lists too;——and if so, he would say, the combatants, brother Toby, as sure as we are alive, will fall to it again, pell-mell, upon the old prize-fighting stage of Flanders;——then what will you do with your Italian bridge?

——We will go on with it then, upon the old model, cried my uncle Toby.

When Corporal Trim had about half finished it in that style,——my uncle Toby found out a capital defect in it, which he had never thoroughly considered before. It turned, it seems, upon hinges at both ends of it, opening in the middle, one half of which turning to one side of the fosse, and the other, to the other; the advantage of which was this, that by dividing the weight of the bridge into two equal portions, it impowered my uncle Toby to raise it up or let it down with the end of his crutch, and with one hand, which, as his garrison was weak, was as much as he could well spare; ——but the disadvantages of such a construction were insurmountable,——for by this means, he would say, I leave one half of my bridge in my enemy's possession,——and pray of what use is the other?

The natural remedy for this was no doubt to have his bridge fast only at one end with hinges, so that the whole might be lifted up together, and stand bolt upright,——but that was rejected for the reason given above.

For a whole week after he was determined in his mind to have one of that particular construction which is made to draw back horizontally to hinder a passage, and to thrust forwards again to gain a passage,——of which sorts your Worships might have seen three famous ones at Spires before its destruction,——and one now at Breisach, if I mistake not;——but my father advising my uncle Toby, with great earnestness, to have nothing more to do with thrusting bridges,——and my uncle foreseeing moreover that it would but perpetuate the memory of the corporal's misfortune,—— he changed his mind, for that of the Marquis d'Hôpital's in-

171

vention, which the younger Bernouilli has so well and learn-edly described, as your Worships may see,———*Act. Erud. Lips.* an. 1695;———to these a lead weight is an eternal bal-ance, and keeps watch as well as a couple of sentinels, inas-much as the construction of them was a curve line approxi-mating to a cycloid,———if not a cycloid itself.

My uncle Toby understood the nature of a parabola as well as any man in England,———but was not quite such a master of the cycloid;———he talked however about it every day;———the bridge went not forwards.———We'll ask some-body about it, cried my uncle Toby to Trim.

CHAPTER XXVI

When Trim came in and told my father that Dr. Slop was in the kitchen, and busy in making a bridge,———my uncle Toby,———the affair of the jack boots having just then raised a train of military ideas in his brain,———took it instantly for granted that Dr. Slop was making a model of the Marquis d'Hôpital's bridge.———'Tis very obliging in him, quoth my uncle Toby;———pray give my humble service to Dr. Slop, Trim, and tell him I thank him heartily.

Had my uncle Toby's head been a Savoyard's box, and my father peeping in all the time at one end of it,———it could not have given him a more distinct conception of the opera-tions in my uncle Toby's imagination than what he had; so notwithstanding the catapulta and battering ram, and his bit-ter imprecation about them, he was just beginning to tri-umph.———

When Trim's answer, in an instant, tore the laurel from his brows, and twisted it to pieces.

CHAPTER XXVII

———This unfortunate drawbridge of yours, quoth my father ———God bless your Honour, cried Trim, 'tis a bridge for Master's nose.———In bringing him into the world with his vile instruments, he has crushed his nose, Susannah says, as flat as a pancake to his face, and he is making a false bridge with a piece of cotton and a thin piece of whalebone out of Susannah's stays, to raise it up.

——Lead me, brother Toby, cried my father, to my room this instant.

CHAPTER XXVIII

From the first moment I sat down to write my life for the amusement of the world, and my opinions for its instruction, has a cloud insensibly been gathering over my father.——A tide of little evils and distresses has been setting in against him.——Not one thing, as he observed himself, has gone right: and now is the storm thickened, and going to break, and pour down full upon his head.

I enter upon this part of my story in the most pensive and melancholy frame of mind that ever sympathetic breast was touched with.——My nerves relax as I tell it.——Every line I write, I feel an abatement of the quickness of my pulse, and of that careless alacrity with it, which every day of my life prompts me to say and write a thousand things I should not.——And this moment that I last dipped my pen into my ink, I could not help taking notice what a cautious air of sad composure and solemnity there appeared in my manner of doing it.——Lord! how different from the rash jerks, and harebrained squirts thou art wont, Tristram! to transact it with in other humours,——dropping thy pen,——spurting thy ink about thy table and thy books,——as if thy pen and thy ink, thy books and thy furniture cost thee nothing.

CHAPTER XXIX

——I won't go about to argue the point with you;——'tis so,——and I am persuaded of it, Madam, as much as can be, "That both man and woman bear pain or sorrow (and, for

173

aught I know, pleasure too) best in a horizontal position."

The moment my father got up into his chamber, he threw himself prostrate across his bed in the wildest disorder imaginable, but at the same time, in the most lamentable attitude of a man borne down with sorrows that ever the eye of pity dropped a tear for.——The palm of his right hand, as he fell upon the bed, receiving his forehead, and covering the greatest part of both his eyes, gently sunk down with his head (his elbow giving way backwards) till his nose touched the quilt;——his left arm hung insensible over the side of the bed, his knuckles reclining upon the handle of the chamber pot, which peeped out beyond the valance;——his right leg (his left being drawn up towards his body) hung half over the side of the bed, the edge of it pressing upon his shinbone. ——He felt it not. A fixed, inflexible sorrow took possession of every line of his face.——He sighed once,——heaved his breast often,——but uttered not a word.

An old set-stitched chair, valanced and fringed around with parti-coloured worsted bobs, stood at the bed's head, opposite to the side where my father's head reclined.——My uncle Toby sat him down in it.

Before an affliction is digested,——consolation ever comes too soon;——and after it is digested,——it comes too late: so that you see, Madam, there is but a mark between these two, as fine almost as a hair, for a comforter to take aim at: my uncle Toby was always either on this side or on that of it, and would often say, He believed in his heart, he could as soon hit the longitude; for this reason, when he sat down in the chair, he drew the curtain a little forwards, and having a tear at everyone's service,——he pulled out a cambric handkerchief,——gave a low sigh,——but held his peace.

CHAPTER XXX

——*"All is not gain that is got into the purse."*——So that notwithstanding my father had the happiness of reading the oddest books in the universe, and had moreover, in himself, the oddest way of thinking that ever man in it was blessed with, yet it had this drawback upon him after all,——that it laid him open to some of the oddest and most whimsical distresses; of which this particular one which he sunk under at present is as strong an example as can be given.

No doubt, the breaking down of the bridge of a child's nose by the edge of a pair of forceps,——however scientifically applied,——would vex any man in the world who was at so much pains in begetting a child as my father was;—— yet it will not account for the extravagance of his affliction, or will it justify the un-Christian manner he abandoned and surrendered himself up to it.

To explain this, I must leave him upon the bed for half an hour,——and my good uncle Toby in his old fringed chair sitting beside him.

CHAPTER XXXI

——I think it a very unreasonable demand,——cried my great-grandfather, twisting up the paper, and throwing it upon the table.——By this account, Madam, you have but two thousand pounds' fortune, and not a shilling more,——and you insist upon having three hundred pounds a year jointure for it.——

——"Because," replied my great-grandmother, "you have little or no nose, Sir."——

Now, before I venture to make use of the word *Nose* a second time,——to avoid all confusion in what will be said upon it, in this interesting part of my story, it may not be amiss to explain my own meaning, and define, with all possible exactness and precision, what I would willingly be understood to mean by the term: being of opinion that 'tis owing to the negligence and perverseness of writers, in despising this precaution, and to nothing else,——That all the polemical writings in divinity are not as clear and demonstrative as those upon a *Will-o'-the-Wisp,* or any other sound part of philosophy, and natural pursuit; in order to which, what have you to do, before you set out, unless you intend to go puzzling on to the day of judgment,——but to give the world a good definition, and stand to it, of the main word you have most occasion for,——changing it, Sir, as you would a guinea, into small coin?——which done,——let the father of confusion puzzle you, if he can; or put a different idea either into your head, or your reader's head, if he knows how.

In books of strict morality and close reasoning, such as this I am engaged in,——the neglect is inexcusable; and heaven is witness, how the world has revenged itself upon me for leaving so many openings to equivocal strictures,—— and for depending so much as I have done, all along, upon the cleanliness of my readers' imaginations.

——Here are two senses, cried Eugenius, as we walked along, pointing with the forefinger of his right hand to the word *Crevice*, in the fifty-second page of the second volume of this book of books,*——here are two senses,——quoth he.——And here are two roads, replied I, turning short upon him,——a dirty and a clean one;——which shall we take?

——The clean,——by all means, replied Eugenius. Eugenius, said I, stepping before him, and laying my hand upon his breast,——to define——is to distrust.——Thus I triumphed over Eugenius; but I triumphed over him as I always do, like a fool.——'Tis my comfort, however, I am not an obstinate one; therefore

I define a nose as follows,——intreating only beforehand, and beseeching my readers, both male and female, of what age, complexion, and condition soever, for the love of God and their own souls, to guard against the temptations and suggestions of the devil, and suffer him by no art or wile to put any other ideas into their minds than what I put into my definition.——For by the word *Nose*, throughout all this long chapter of noses, and in every other part of my work where the word *Nose* occurs,——I declare, by that word I mean a Nose, and nothing more, or less.

CHAPTER XXXII

——"Because," quoth my great-grandmother, repeating the words again,——"you have little or no nose, Sir"———

S'death! cried my great-grandfather, clapping his hand upon his nose,——'tis not so small as that comes to;——'tis a full inch longer than my father's.——Now, my great-grandfather's nose was for all the world like unto the noses of all the men, women, and children whom Pantagruel found

* In this edition, page 85.

dwelling upon the island of ENNASIN.————By the way, if you would know the strange way of getting akin amongst so flat-nosed a people,————you must read the book;————find it out yourself, you never can.————

————'Twas shaped, Sir, like an ace of clubs.

————'Tis a full inch, continued my great-grandfather, pressing up the ridge of his nose with his finger and thumb; and repeating his assertion,————'tis a full inch longer, Madam, than my father's————.You must mean your uncle's, replied my great-grandmother.

————My great-grandfather was convinced.————He untwisted the paper, and signed the article.

CHAPTER XXXIII

————What an unconscionable jointure, my dear, do we pay out of this small estate of ours, quoth my grandmother to my grandfather.

My father, replied my grandfather, had no more nose, my dear, saving the mark, than there is upon the back of my hand.————

————Now, you must know that my great-grandmother outlived my grandfather twelve years; so that my father had the jointure to pay, a hundred and fifty pounds half-yearly———— (on Michaelmas and Lady Day)————during all that time.

No man discharged pecuniary obligations with a better grace than my father.————And as far as the hundred pounds went, he would fling it upon the table, guinea by guinea, with that spirited jerk of an honest welcome which generous souls, and generous souls only, are able to fling down money: but as soon as ever he entered upon the odd fifty,————he generally gave a loud *Hem!*————rubbed the side of his nose leisurely with the flat part of his forefinger,———— inserted his hand cautiously betwixt his head and the caul of his wig,————looked at both sides of every guinea, as he parted with it,————and seldom could get to the end of the fifty pounds without pulling out his handkerchief, and wiping his temples.

Defend me, gracious heaven! from those persecuting spirits who make no allowances for these workings within us.———— Never,————O never may I lay down in their tents, who cannot relax the engine, and feel pity for the force of education, and the prevalance of opinions long derived from ancestors!

For three generations at least, this *tenet* in favour of long noses had gradually been taking root in our family.———— TRADITION was all along on its side, and INTEREST was every half year stepping in to strengthen it; so that the whimsicality of my father's brain was far from having the whole honour of this, as it had of almost all his other strange notions.————For in a great measure he might be said to have sucked this in with his mother's milk. He did his part however.————If education planted the mistake (in case it was one), my father watered it, and ripened it to perfection.

He would often declare, in speaking his thoughts upon the subject, that he did not conceive how the greatest family in England could stand it out against an uninterrupted succession of six or seven short noses.————And for the contrary reason, he would generally add, That it must be one of the greatest problems in civil life, where the same number of long and jolly noses following one another in a direct line did not raise and hoist it up into the best vacancies in the kingdom.————He would often boast that the Shandy family ranked very high in King Harry the VIIIth's time, but owed its rise to no state engine,————he would say,————but to that only;————but that, like other families, he would add,————it had felt the turn of the wheel, and had never recovered the blow of my great-grandfather's nose.————It was an ace of clubs, indeed, he would cry, shaking his head,————and as vile a one for an unfortunate family as ever turned up trumps.

————Fair and softly, gentle reader!————where is thy fancy carrying thee?————If there is truth in man, by my great-grandfather's nose, I mean the external organ of smelling, or that part of man which stands prominent in his face, ————and which painters say, in good jolly noses and well-proportioned faces, should comprehend a full third,————that is, measuring downwards from the setting on of the hair.————

————What a life of it has an author, at this pass!

CHAPTER XXXIV

It is a singular blessing that nature has formed the mind of man with the same happy backwardness and renitency against conviction which is observed in old dogs,——"of not learning new tricks."

What a shuttlecock of a fellow would the greatest philosopher that ever existed be whisked into at once, did he read such books, and observe such facts, and think such thoughts, as would eternally be making him change sides!

Now, my father, as I told you last year, detested all this. ——He picked up an opinion, Sir, as a man in a state of nature picks up an apple.——It becomes his own,——and if he is a man of spirit, he would lose his life rather than give it up.——

I am aware that Didius, the great civilian, will contest this point; and cry out against me, Whence comes this man's right to this apple? *ex confesso,* he will say,——things were in a state of nature.——The apple as much Frank's apple as John's. Pray, Mr. Shandy, what patent has he to show for it? and how did it begin to be his? was it when he set his heart upon it? or when he gathered it? or when he chewed it? or when he roasted it? or when he peeled? or when he brought it home? or when he digested?——or when he —— — ? ——. For 'tis plain, Sir, if the first picking up of the apple made it not his,——that no subsequent act could.

Brother Didius, Tribonius will answer——(now Tribonius the civilian and church lawyer's beard being three inches and a half and three eighths longer than Didius his beard,—— I'm glad he takes up the cudgels for me, so I give myself no further trouble about the answer.)——Brother Didius, Tribonius will say, it is a decreed case, as you may find it in the fragments of Gregorius and Hermogenes's codes, and in all the codes from Justinian's down to the codes of Louis and Des Eaux,——That the sweat of a man's brows, and the exudations of a man's brains, are as much a man's own property as the breeches upon his backside;——which said exudations, &c., being dropped upon the said apple by the labour of finding it, and picking it up; and being moreover indissolubly wasted, and as indissolubly annexed by the picker up, to the thing picked up, carried home, roasted, peeled, eaten, digested, and so on;——'tis evident that the gatherer of the apple, in so doing, has mixed up something which was his own with the apple which was not his own, by which means he has acquired a property;——or, in other words, the apple is John's apple.

By the same learned chain of reasoning my father stood up for all his opinions: he had spared no pains in picking them up, and the more they lay out of the common way, the better still was his title.——No mortal claimed them: they had cost him moreover as much labour in cooking and digesting as in the case above, so that they might well and truly be said to be of his own goods and chattels.——Accordingly he held fast by 'em, both by teeth and claws,—— would fly to whatever he could lay his hands on,——and in a word, would intrench and fortify them round with as many circumvallations and breastworks as my uncle Toby would a citadel.

There was one plaguy rub in the way of this,——the scarcity of materials to make anything of a defence with, in case of a smart attack; inasmuch as few men of great genius had exercised their parts in writing books upon the subject of great noses: by the trotting of my lean horse, the thing is incredible! and I am quite lost in my understanding when I am considering what a treasure of precious time and talents together has been wasted upon worse subjects,——and how many millions of books in all languages, and in all possible types and bindings, have been fabricated upon points not half so much tending to the unity and peacemaking of the world. What was to be had, however, he set the greater store by; and though my father would ofttimes sport with my uncle Toby's library,——which, by the bye, was ridiculous enough, ——yet at the very same time he did it, he collected every book and treatise which had been systematically wrote upon noses, with as much care as my honest uncle Toby had done those upon military architecture.——'Tis true, a much less table would have held them,——but that was not thy transgression, my dear uncle.——

Here,——but why here,——rather than in any other part of my story,——I am not able to tell;——but here it is, ————my heart stops me to pay to thee, my dear uncle Toby, once for all, the tribute I owe thy goodness.——Here let me thrust my chair aside, and kneel down upon the ground, whilst I am pouring forth the warmest sentiments of love for thee, and veneration for the excellency of thy character, that

ever virtue and nature kindled in a nephew's bosom.——
Peace and comfort rest forevermore upon thy head!——
Thou enviedst no man's comforts,——insultedst no man's
opinions.——Thou blackenedst no man's character,——de-
vouredst no man's bread: gently, with faithful Trim behind
thee, didst thou amble round the little circle of thy pleasures,
jostling no creature in thy way;——for each one's sorrows,
thou hadst a tear,——for each man's need, thou hadst a
shilling.

Whilst I am worth one, to pay a weeder,——thy path
from thy door to thy bowling green shall never be grown
up.——Whilst there is a rood and a half of land in the
Shandy family, thy fortifications, my dear uncle Toby, shall
never be demolished.

CHAPTER XXXV

My father's collection was not great, but to make amends,
it was curious; and consequently, he was some time in making it; he had the great good fortune however to set off well,
in getting Bruscambille's prologue upon long noses, almost
for nothing,——for he gave no more for Bruscambille than
three half crowns; owing indeed to the strong fancy which
the stallman saw my father had for the book the moment he
laid his hands upon it.——There are not three Bruscambilles
in Christendom,——said the stallman, except what are
chained up in the libraries of the curious. My father flung
down the money as quick as lightning,——took Bruscambille
into his bosom,——hied home from Piccadilly to Coleman
Street with it, as he would have hied home with a treasure,
without taking his hand once off from Bruscambille all the
way.

To those who do not yet know of which gender Bruscambille is,——inasmuch as a prologue upon long noses might
easily be done by either,——'twill be no objection against
the simile——to say, That when my father got home, he
solaced himself with Bruscambille after the manner in which,
'tis ten to one, your Worship solaced yourself with your first
mistress,——that is, from morning even unto night: which
by the bye, how delightful soever it may prove to the

inamorato,——is of little or no entertainment at all to by-standers.——Take notice, I go no farther with the simile;——my father's eye was greater than his appetite,——his zeal greater than his knowledge,——he cooled——his affections became divided,——he got hold of Prignitz,——purchased Scroderus, Andrea Paraeus, Bouchet's Evening Conferences, and above all, the great and learned Hafen Slawkenbergius; of which, as I shall have much to say by and bye,——I will say nothing now.

CHAPTER XXXVI

Of all the tracts my father was at the pains to procure and study in support of his hypothesis, there was not any one wherein he felt a more cruel disappointment at first than in the celebrated dialogue between Pamphagus and Cocles, written by the chaste pen of the great and venerable Erasmus, upon the various uses and seasonable applications of long noses.——Now don't let Satan, my dear girl, in this chapter, take advantage of any one spot of rising ground to get astride of your imagination, if you can any ways help it; or if he is so nimble as to slip on,——let me beg of you, like an unbacked filly, *to frisk it, to squirt it, to jump it, to rear it, to bound it,——and to kick it, with long kicks and short kicks,* till like Tickletoby's mare, you break a strap or a crupper, and throw his worship into the dirt.——You need not kill him.——

——And pray who was Tickletoby's mare?——'tis just as discreditable and unscholar-like a question, Sir, as to have asked what year (*ab urb. con.*) the second Punic war broke out.——Who was Tickletoby's mare!——Read, read, read, read, my unlearned reader! read,——or by the knowledge of the great saint Paraleipomenon——I tell you beforehand, you had better throw down the book at once; for without *much reading,* by which your Reverence knows I mean *much knowledge,* you will no more be able to penetrate the moral of the next marbled page (motley emblem of my work!) than the world with all its sagacity has been able to unravel the many opinions, transactions, and truths which still lie mystically hid under the dark veil of the black one.

184

CHAPTER XXXVII

"Nihil me poenitet hujus nasi," quoth Pamphagus;——that is,——"My nose has been the making of me."——
"Nec est cur poeniteat," replies Cocles; that is, "How the deuce should such a nose fail?"

The doctrine, you see, was laid down by Erasmus, as my father wished it, with the utmost plainness; but my father's disappointment was in finding nothing more from so able a pen but the bare fact itself; without any of that speculative subtilty or ambidexterity of argumentation upon it which heaven had bestowed upon man on purpose to investigate truth and fight for her on all sides.——My father pished and pughed at first most terribly;——'tis worth something to have a good name. As the dialogue was of Erasmus, my father soon came to himself, and read it over and over again with great application, studying every word and every syllable of it through and through in its most strict and literal interpretation;——he could still make nothing of it that way. Mayhaps there is more meant than is said in it, quoth my father.—— Learned men, brother Toby, don't write dialogues upon long noses for nothing.——I'll study the mystic and the allegoric sense;——here is some room to turn a man's self in, brother. My father read on.——

Now, I find it needful to inform your Reverences and Worships that besides the many nautical uses of long noses enumerated by Erasmus, the dialogist affirmeth that a long nose is not without its domestic conveniences also, for that in a case of distress,——and for want of a pair of bellows, it will do excellently well, *ad excitandum focum* (to stir up the fire).

Nature had been prodigal in her gifts to my father beyond measure, and had sown the seeds of verbal criticism as deep within him as she had done the seeds of all other knowledge,——so that he had got out his penknife, and was trying experiments upon the sentence, to see if he could not scratch some better sense into it.——I've got within a single letter, brother Toby, cried my father, of Erasmus his mystic meaning.——You are near enough, brother, replied my uncle, in all conscience.——Pshaw! cried my father, scratching on,

———I might as well be seven miles off.———I've done it,——— said my father, snapping his fingers.———See, my dear brother Toby, how I have mended the sense.———But you have marred a word, replied my uncle Toby.———My father put on his spectacles,———bit his lip,———and tore out the leaf in a passion.

CHAPTER XXXVIII

O Slawkenbergius! thou faithful analyzer of my *Disgrázias,* ———thou sad foreteller of so many of the whips and short turns which in one stage or other of my life have come slap upon me from the shortness of my nose, and no other cause that I am conscious of.———Tell me, Slawkenbergius! what secret impulse was it? what intonation of voice? whence came it? how did it sound in thy ears?———art thou sure thou heardst it?———which first cried out to thee,———go,———go, Slawkenbergius! dedicate the labours of thy life,———neglect thy pastimes,———call forth all the powers and faculties of thy nature,———macerate thyself in the service of mankind, and write a grand FOLIO for them, upon the subject of their noses.

How the communication was conveyed into Slawkenbergius's sensorium,———so that Slawkenbergius should know whose finger touched the key,———and whose hand it was that blew the bellows,———as Hafen Slawkenbergius has been dead and laid in his grave above fourscore and ten years,———we can only raise conjectures.

Slawkenbergius was played upon, for aught I know, like one of Whitefield's disciples,———that is, with such a distinct intelligence, Sir, of which of the two *masters* it was that had been practising upon his *instrument,*———as to make all reasoning upon it needless.

———For in the account which Hafen Slawkenbergius gives the world of his motives and occasions for writing, and spending so many years of his life upon this one work———towards the end of his prolegomena, which by the bye should have come first,———but the bookbinder has most injudiciously placed it betwixt the analytical contents of the book, and the book itself,———he informs his reader that ever since he had arrived at the age of discernment, and was able to sit down coolly, and consider within himself the true state and condition of man, and distinguish the main end and design of his being;——or,——to shorten my translation, for Slawkenbergius's book is in Latin, and not a little prolix in this passage,——ever since I understood, quoth Slawkenbergius, any thing,——or rather what was what,——and could perceive that the point of long noses had been too loosely handled by all who had gone before,——have I, Slawkenbergius, felt a strong impulse, with a mighty and unresistible call within me, to gird up myself to this undertaking.

And to do justice to Slawkenbergius, he has entered the list with a stronger lance, and taken a much larger career in it, than any one man who had ever entered it before him,—— and indeed, in many respects, deserves to be *enniched* as a prototype for all writers, of voluminous works at least, to model their books by,——for he has taken in, Sir, the whole subject,——examined every part of it, *dialectically*,——then brought it into full day; dilucidating it with all the light which either the collision of his own natural parts could strike,——or the profoundest knowledge of the sciences had impowered him to cast upon it,——collating, collecting, and compiling,——begging, borrowing, and stealing, as he went along, all that had been wrote or wrangled thereupon in the schools and porticos of the learned: so that Slawkenbergius his book may properly be considered, not only as a model, ——but as a thorough-stitched DIGEST and regular institute of *noses;* comprehending in it all that is or can be needful to be known about them.

For this cause it is that I forbear to speak of so many (otherwise) valuable books and treatises of my father's collecting, wrote either plump upon noses,——or collaterally touching them;——such for instance as Prignitz, now lying upon the table before me, who with infinite learning, and from the most candid and scholar-like examination of above four thousand different skulls, in upwards of twenty charnel houses in Silesia, which he had rummaged,——has informed us that the mensuration and configuration of the osseous or bony parts of human noses, in any *given* tract of country, except Crim Tartary, where they are all crushed down by the thumb, so that no judgment can be formed upon them,—— are much nearer alike than the world imagines;——the difference amongst them being, he says, a mere trifle, not worth taking notice of,——but that the size and jollity of every individual nose, and by which one nose ranks above another,

187

and bears a higher price, is owing to the cartilaginous and muscular parts of it, into whose ducts and sinuses the blood and animal spirits being impelled, and driven by the warmth and force of the imagination, which is but a step from it (bating the case of idiots, whom Prignitz, who had lived many years in Turkey, supposes under the more immediate tutelage of heaven),——it so happens, and ever must, says Prignitz, that the excellency of the nose is in a direct arithmetical proportion to the excellency of the wearer's fancy.

It is for the same reason, that is, because 'tis all comprehended in Slawkenbergius, that I say nothing likewise of Scroderus (Andrea) who all the world knows set himself to oppugn Prignitz with great violence,——proving it in his own way, first *logically* and then by a series of stubborn facts, "That so far was Prignitz from the truth, in affirming that the fancy begat the nose, that on the contrary,——the nose begat the fancy."

——The learned suspected Scroderus of an indecent sophism in this,——and Prignitz cried out aloud in the dispute that Scroderus had shifted the idea upon him,——but Scroderus went on, maintaining his thesis.——

My father was just balancing within himself which of the two sides he should take in this affair, when Ambrose Paraeus decided it in a moment, and by overthrowing the systems both of Prignitz and Scroderus, drove my father out of both sides of the controversy at once.

Be witness——

I don't acquaint the learned reader,——in saying it, I mention it only to show the learned I know the fact myself——

That this Ambrose Paraeus was chief surgeon and nosemender to Francis the Ninth of France, and in high credit with him and the two preceding, or succeeding, kings (I know not which)——and that except in the slip he made in his story of Taliacotius's noses, and his manner of setting them on,——he was esteemed by the whole college of physicians at that time as more knowing in matters of noses than anyone who had ever taken them in hand.

Now Ambrose Paraeus convinced my father that the true and efficient cause of what had engaged so much the attention of the world, and upon which Prignitz and Scroderus had wasted so much learning and fine parts,——was neither this nor that,——but that the length and goodness of the nose was owing simply to the softness and flaccidity in the nurse's breast,——as the flatness and shortness of *puisne*

188

noses was to the firmness and elastic repulsion of the same organ of nutrition in the hale and lively,——which, though happy for the woman, was the undoing of the child, inasmuch as his nose was so snubbed, so rebuffed, so rebated, and so refrigerated thereby, as never to arrive *ad mensuram suam legitimam;*——but that in case of the flaccidity and softness of the nurse or mother's breast,——by sinking into it, quoth Paraeus, as into so much butter, the nose was comforted, nourished, plumped up, refreshed, refocillated, and set a-growing forever.

I have but two things to observe of Paraeus; first, that he proves and explains all this with the utmost chastity and decorum of expression:——for which may his soul forever rest in peace!

And, secondly, that besides the systems of Prignitz and Scroderus, which Ambrose Paraeus his hypothesis effectually overthrew,——it overthrew at the same time the system of peace and harmony of our family; and for three days together, not only embroiled matters between my father and my mother, but turned likewise the whole house and everything in it, except my uncle Toby, quite upside down.

Such a ridiculous tale of a dispute between a man and his wife never surely in any age or country got vent through the keyhole of a street door!

My mother, you must know,——but I have fifty things more necessary to let you know first;——I have a hundred difficulties which I have promised to clear up, and a thousand distresses and domestic misadventures crowding in upon me thick and threefold, one upon the neck of another;——a cow broke in (to-morrow morning) to my uncle Toby's fortifications, and eat up two rations and a half of dried grass, tearing up the sods with it which faced his hornwork and covered way.——Trim insists upon being tried by a court-martial,——the cow to be shot,——Slop to be *crucifixed,* ——myself to be *tristramed,* and at my very baptism made a martyr of;——poor unhappy devils that we all are!——I want swaddling,——but there is no time to be lost in exclamations.——I have left my father lying across his bed, and my uncle Toby in his old fringed chair, sitting beside him, and promised I would go back to them in half an hour, and five-and-thirty minutes are lapsed already.——Of all the perplexities a mortal author was ever seen in,——this certainly is the greatest,——for I have **Hafen Sl**awkenbergius's folio, Sir, to finish——a dialogue between my father and my uncle Toby, upon the solution of Prignitz, Scroderus,

Ambrose Paraeus, Ponocrates, and Grangousier to relate,——
a tale out of Slawkenbergius to translate, and all this in five
minutes less than no time at all;——such a head!——would
to heaven! my enemies only saw the inside of it!

CHAPTER XXXIX

There was not any one scene more entertaining in our
family,——and to do it justice in this point,——and I here
put off my cap and lay it upon the table close beside my
inkhorn, on purpose to make my declaration to the world
concerning this one article the more solemn,——that I believe in my soul (unless my love and partiality to my understanding blinds me) the hand of the supreme Maker and
first Designer of all things never made or put a family together (in that period at least of it, which I have sat down to
write the story of)——where the characters of it were cast
or contrasted with so dramatic a felicity as ours was, for this
end; or in which the capacities of affording such exquisite
scenes, and the powers of shifting them perpetually from
morning to night, were lodged and intrusted with so unlim-
ited a confidence, as in the SHANDY FAMILY.

Not any one of these was more diverting, I say, in this
whimsical theatre of ours,——than what frequently arose out
of this selfsame chapter of long noses,——especially when
my father's imagination was heated with the enquiry, and
nothing would serve him but to heat my uncle Toby's
too.

My uncle Toby would give my father all possible fair play
in this attempt; and with infinite patience would sit smoking
his pipe for whole hours together, whilst my father was practising upon his head, and trying every accessible avenue to
drive Prignitz and Scroderus's solutions into it.

Whether they were above my uncle Toby's reason,——or
contrary to it,——or that his brain was like wet tinder,
and no spark could possibly take hold,——or that it was so
full of saps, mines, blinds, curtains, and such military disquali-
fications to his seeing clearly into Prignitz and Scroderus's
doctrines,——I say not,——let schoolmen——scullions, anatomists, and engineers fight for it amongst themselves.——

'Twas some misfortune, I make no doubt, in this affair, that my father had every word of it to translate for the benefit of my uncle Toby, and render out of Slawkenbergius's Latin, of which, as he was no great master, his translation was not always of the purest,——and generally least so where 'twas most wanted;——this naturally opened a door to a second misfortune,——that in the warmer paroxysms of his zeal to open my uncle Toby's eyes,——my father's ideas run on as much faster than the translation as the translation outmoved my uncle Toby's;——neither the one or the other added much to the perspicuity of my father's lecture.

CHAPTER XL

The gift of ratiocination and making syllogisms,——I mean in man,——for in superior classes of beings, such as angels and spirits,——'tis all done, may it please your Worships, as they tell me, by INTUITION;——and beings inferior, as your Worships all know,——syllogize by their noses: though there is an island swimming in the sea, though not altogether at its ease, whose inhabitants, if my intelligence deceives me not, are so wonderfully gifted as to syllogize after the same fashion, and ofttimes to make very well out too:——but that's neither here nor there——

The gift of doing it as it should be, amongst us,——or the great and principal act of ratiocination in man, as logicians tell us, is the finding out the agreement or disagreement of two ideas one with another, by the intervention of a third (called the *medius terminus*); just as a man, as Locke well observes, by a yard finds two men's ninepin alleys to be of the same length, which could not be brought together, to measure their equality, by *juxta-position*.

Had the same great reasoner looked on, as my father illustrated his systems of noses, and observed my uncle Toby's deportment,——what great attention he gave to every word, ——and as oft as he took his pipe from his mouth, with what wonderful seriousness he contemplated the length of it,—— surveying it transversely as he held it betwixt his finger and his thumb,——then foreright,——then this way, and then that, in all its possible directions and foreshortenings,——he would have concluded my uncle Toby had got hold of the *medius terminus;* and was syllogizing and measuring with it the truth of each hypothesis of long noses, in order as my father laid them before him. This, by the bye, was more than my father wanted;——his aim in all the pains he was at in these philosophic lectures——was to enable my uncle Toby not to *discuss,*——but *comprehend;*——to *hold* the grains and scruples of learning,——not to *weigh* them.—— My uncle Toby, as you will read in the next chapter, did neither the one or the other.

CHAPTER XLI

'Tis a pity, cried my father one winter's night, after a three hours' painful translation of Slawkenbergius,——'tis a pity, cried my father, putting my mother's thread paper into the book for a mark, as he spoke——that truth, brother Toby, should shut herself up in such impregnable fastnesses, and be so obstinate as not to surrender herself sometimes up upon the closest siege.——

Now it happened then, as indeed it had often done before, that my uncle Toby's fancy, during the time of my father's explanation of Prignitz to him,——having nothing to stay it there, had taken a short flight to the bowling green;——his body might as well have taken a turn there too,——so that with all the semblance of a deep schoolman intent upon the *medius terminus,*——my uncle Toby was in fact as ignorant of the whole lecture, and all its pros and cons, as if my father had been translating Hafen Slawkenbergius from the Latin tongue into the Cherokee. But the word *siege,* like a talismanic power, in my father's metaphor, wafting back my uncle Toby's fancy, quick as a note could follow the touch, ——he opened his ears,——and my father observing that he took his pipe out of his mouth, and shuffled his chair nearer the table, as with a desire to profit,——my father with great pleasure began his sentence again,——changing only the plan, and dropping the metaphor of the siege of it, to keep clear of some dangers my father apprehended from it.

'Tis a pity, said my father, that truth can only be on one side, brother Toby,——considering what ingenuity these

learned men have all shown in their solutions of noses.——
Can noses be dissolved? replied my uncle Toby.——

——My father thrust back his chair,——rose up,——put
on his hat,——took four long strides to the door,——jerked it
open,——thrust his head halfway out,——shut the door again,
——took no notice of the bad hinge,——returned to the
table,——plucked my mother's thread paper out of Slawkenbergius's book,——went hastily to his bureau,——walked
slowly back, twisting my mother's thread paper about his
thumb,——unbuttoned his waistcoat,——threw my mother's
thread paper into the fire,——bit her satin pincushion in
two, filled his mouth with bran,——confounded it;——but
mark!——the oath of confusion was levelled at my uncle
Toby's brain,——which was e'en confused enough already;
——the curse came charged only with the bran;——the
bran, may it please your Honours,——was no more than
powder to the ball.

'Twas well my father's passions lasted not long; for so long
as they did last, they led him a busy life on't, and it is one
of the most unaccountable problems that ever I met with in
my observations of human nature, that nothing should prove
my father's mettle so much, or make his passions go off so
like gunpowder, as the unexpected strokes his science met
with from the quaint simplicity of my uncle Toby's questions.——Had ten dozen of hornets stung him behind in so
many different places all at one time,——he could not have
exerted more mechanical functions in fewer seconds,——or
started half so much, as with one single *quaere* of three
words unseasonably popping in full upon him in his hobby-
horsical career.

'Twas all one to my uncle Toby;——he smoked his pipe
on, with unvaried composure;——his heart never intended
offence to his brother,——and as his head could seldom find
out where the sting of it lay,——he always gave my father
the credit of cooling by himself.——He was five minutes
and thirty-five seconds about it in the present case.

By all that's good! said my father, swearing, as he came to
himself, and taking the oath out of Ernulphus's digest of
curses——(though to do my father justice, it was a fault (as
he told Dr. Slop in the affair of Ernulphus) which he as seldom committed as any man upon earth).——By all that's good
and great! brother Toby, said my father, if it was not for
the aids of philosophy, which befriend one so much as they do,
——you would put a man beside all temper.——Why, by the
solutions of noses, of which I was telling you, I meant, as you

193

might have known had you favoured me with one grain of attention, the various accounts which learned men of different kinds of knowledge have given the world of the causes of short and long noses.——There is no cause but one, replied my uncle Toby,——why one man's nose is longer than another's, but because that God pleases to have it so.——That is Grangousier's solution, said my father.——'Tis he, continued my uncle Toby, looking up, and not regarding my father's interruption, who makes us all, and frames and puts us together in such forms and proportions, and for such ends, as is agreeable to his infinite wisdom.——'Tis a pious account, cried my father, but not philosophical;——there is more religion in it than sound science. 'Twas no inconsistent part of my uncle Toby's character——that he feared God, and reverenced religion.——So the moment my father finished his remark,——my uncle Toby fell a-whistling *Lilla-bullero*, with more zeal (though more out of tune) than usual.——

What is become of my wife's thread paper?

CHAPTER XLII

No matter;——as an appendage to seamstressy, the thread paper might be of some consequence to my mother;——of none to my father, as a mark in Slawkenbergius. Slawkenbergius in every page of him was a rich treasury of inexhaustible knowledge to my father;——he could not open him amiss, and he would often say, in closing the book, that if all the arts and sciences in the world, with the books which treated of them, were lost,——should the wisdom and policies of governments, he would say, through disuse, ever happen to be forgot, and all that statesmen had wrote, or caused to be written, upon the strong or the weak sides of courts and kingdoms, should they be forgot also,——and Slawkenbergius only left,——there would be enough in him in all conscience, he would say, to set the world a-going again. A treasure therefore was he indeed! an institute of all that was necessary to be known of noses, and everything else,——at *matin*, noon, and vespers was Hafen Slawkenbergius his recreation and delight: 'twas forever in his hands;——you would have sworn, Sir, it had been a canon's prayerbook,——so worn, so glazed, so contrited, and attrited was it with fingers and with thumbs in all its parts, from one end even unto the other.

I am not such a bigot to Slawkenbergius as my father;—— there is a fund in him, no doubt; but in my opinion, the best, I don't say the most profitable, but the most amusing part of Hafen Slawkenbergius is his tales,——and, considering he was a German, many of them told not without fancy:—— these take up his second book, containing nearly one half of his folio, and are comprehended in ten decads, each decad containing ten tales.——Philosophy is not built upon tales; and therefore 'twas certainly wrong in Slawkenbergius to send them into the world by that name;——there are a few of them in his eighth, ninth, and tenth decads which I own seem rather playful and sportive than speculative,——but in general they are to be looked upon by the learned as a detail of so many independent facts, all of them turning round somehow or other upon the main hinges of his subject, and collected by him with great fidelity, and added to his work as so many illustrations upon the doctrines of noses.

As we have leisure enough upon our hands,——if you give me leave, Madam, I'll tell you the ninth tale of his tenth decad.

VOLUME IV

SLAWKENBERGII
Fabella*

Vespera quâdam frigidulâ, posteriori in parte mensis Augusti, peregrinus, mulo fusco colore insidens, manticâ a tergo, paucis indusijs, binis calceis, braccisque sericis coccinejs repletâ, Argentoratum ingressus est.

Militi eum percontanti, quum portus intraret, dixit, se apud Nasorum promontorium fuisse, Francofurtum proficisci, et Argentoratum, transitu ad fines Sarmatiae mensis intervallo, reversurum.

Miles peregrini in faciem suspexit——Di boni, nova forma nasi!

At multum mihi profuit, inquit peregrinus, carpum amento extrahens, e quo pependit acinaces: Loculo manum inseruit; & magnâ cum urbanitate, pilei parte anteriore tactâ manu sinistrâ, ut extendit dextram, militi florinum dedit et processit.

Dolet mihi, ait miles, tympanistam nanum et valgum alloquens, virum adeo urbanum vaginam perdidisse; itinerari haud poterit nudâ acinaci, neque vaginam toto Argentorato, habilem inveniet.——Nullam unquam habui, respondit peregrinus

---

* As Hafen Slawkenbergius *de Nasis* is extremely scarce, it may not be unacceptable to the learned reader to see the specimen of a few pages of his original; I will make no reflection upon it, but that his storytelling Latin is much more concise than his philosophic——and, I think, has more of Latinity in it.

VOLUME IV

SLAWKENBERGIUS'S
TALE

It was one cool refreshing evening, at the close of a very
sultry day, in the latter end of the month of August, when a
stranger, mounted upon a dark mule, with a small cloak bag
behind him, containing a few shirts, a pair of shoes, and
a crimson satin pair of breeches, entered the town of Strasburg.

He told the sentinel who questioned him as he entered the
gates that he had been at the Promontory of Noses——was
going on to Frankfort——and should be back again at Strasburg that day month, in his way to the borders of Crim
Tartary.

The sentinel looked up into the stranger's face——never
saw such a nose in his life!

——I have made a very good venture of it, quoth the
stranger——so slipping his wrist out of the loop of a black
ribband, to which a short scimitar was hung: He put his hand
into his pocket, and with great courtesy touching the forepart of his cap with his left hand, as he extended his right
——he put a florin into the sentinel's hand, and passed on.

It grieves me, said the sentinel, speaking to a little dwarf-
ish bandy-legged drummer, that so courteous a soul should
have lost his scabbard——he cannot travel without one to
his scimitar, and will not be able to get a scabbard to fit it in
all Strasburg.——I never had one, replied the stranger,

197

*respiciens,——seque comiter inclinans——hoc more gesto,
nudam acinacem elevans, mulo lentè progrediente, ut nasum
tueri possim.*

*Non immerito, benigne peregrine, respondit miles.
Nihili aestimo, ait ille tympanista, e pergamenâ factitius est.*

*Prout christianus sum, inquit miles, nasus ille, ni sexties
major sit, meo esset conformis.
Crepitare audivi ait tympanista.
Mehercule! sanguinem emisit, respondit miles.
Miseret me, inquit tympanista, qui non ambo tetigimus!*

*Eodem temporis puncto, quo haec res argumentata fuit inter
militem et tympanistam, disceptabatur ibidem tubicine &
uxore suâ, qui tunc accesserunt, et peregrino praetereunte, res-
titerunt.
Quantus nasus! aeque longus est, ait tubicina, ac tuba.*

*Et ex eodem metallo, ait tubicen, velut sternutamento
audias.
Tantum abest, respondit illa, quod fistulam dulcedine
vincit.
Aeneus est, ait tubicen.
Nequaquam, respondit uxor.
Rursum affirmo, ait tubicen, quod aeneus est.
Rem penitus explorabo; prius, enim digito tangam, ait uxor,
quam dormivero.
Mulus peregrini, gradu lento progressus est, ut unum-
quodque verbum controversiae, non tantum inter militem et
tympanistam, verum etiam inter tubicinem et uxorem ejus,
audiret.
Nequaquam, ait ille, in muli collum fraena demittens, &
manibus ambabus in pectus positis (mulo lentè progrediente),
nequaquam, ait ille, respiciens, non necesse est ut res isthaec
dilucidata foret. Minime gentium! meus nasus nunquam tangetur, dum spiritus hos reget artus——ad quid agendum? ait
uxor burgomagistri.
Peregrinus illi non respondit. Votum faciebat tunc temporis sancto Nicolao, quo facto, sinum dextram inserens, e*

looking back to the sentinel, and putting his hand up to his cap as he spoke——I carry it, continued he, thus——holding up his naked scimitar, his mule moving on slowly all the time, on purpose to defend my nose.

It is well worth it, gentle stranger, replied the sentinel.

——'Tis not worth a single stiver, said the bandy-legged drummer;——'tis a nose of parchment.

As I am a true Catholic——except that it is six times as big——'tis a nose, said the sentinel, like my own.

——I heard it crackle, said the drummer.

By dunder, said the sentinel, I saw it bleed.

What a pity, cried the bandy-legged drummer, we did not both touch it!

At the very time that this dispute was maintaining by the sentinel and the drummer——was the same point debating betwixt a trumpeter and a trumpeter's wife, who were just then coming up, and had stopped to see the stranger pass by.

Benedicity!——What a nose! 'tis as long, said the trumpeter's wife, as a trumpet.

And of the same metal, said the trumpeter, as you hear by its sneezing.

——'Tis as soft as a flute, said she.

——'Tis brass, said the trumpeter.

——'Tis a pudding's end——said his wife.

I tell thee again, said the trumpeter, 'tis a brazen nose.

I'll know the bottom of it, said the trumpeter's wife, for I will touch it with my finger before I sleep.

The stranger's mule moved on at so slow a rate that he heard every word of the dispute, not only betwixt the sentinel and the drummer, but betwixt the trumpeter and the trumpeter's wife.

No! said he, dropping his reins upon his mule's neck, and laying both his hands upon his breast, the one over the other in a saintlike position (his mule going on easily all the time), No! said he, looking up,——I am not such a debtor to the world——slandered and disappointed as I have been——as to give it that conviction——no! said he, my nose shall never be touched whilst heaven gives me strength——To do what? said a burgomaster's wife.

The stranger took no notice of the burgomaster's wife——he was making a vow to St. Nicolas; which done, having uncrossed his arms with the same solemnity with which he crossed them, he took up the reins of his bridle with his left hand, and putting his right hand into his bosom, with his

quâ negligenter pependit acinaces, lento gradu processit per plateam Argentorati latam quae ad diversorium templo ex adversum ducit.

Peregrinus mulo descendens stabulo includi, & manticam inferri jussit: quâ apertâ et coccineis sericis femoralibus extractis cum argenteo laciniato Περιζωματὲ, his sese induit, statimque, acinaci in manu, ad forum deambulavit.

Quod ubi peregrinus esset ingressus, uxorem tubicinis obviam euntem aspicit; illico cursum flectit, metuens ne nasus suus exploraretur, atque ad diversorium regressus est——exuit se vestibus; braccas coccineas sericas manticae imposuit mulumque educi jussit.

Francofurtum proficiscor, ait ille, et Argentoratum quatuor abhinc hebdomadis revertar.

Bene curasti hoc jumentum (ait) muli faciem manu demulcens——me, manticamque meam, plus sexcentis mille passibus portavit.

Longa via est! respondet hospes, nisi plurimum esset negoti.——Enimvero ait peregrinus a nasorum promontorio redij, et nasum speciosissimum, egregiosissimumque quem unquam quisquam sortitus est acquisivi!

Dum peregrinus hanc miram rationem, de seipso reddit, hospes et uxor ejus, oculis intentis, peregrini nasum contemplantur——Per sanctos, sanctasque omnes, ait hospitis uxor, nasis duodecim maximis, in toto Argentorato major est!—— estne, ait illa mariti in aurem insusurrans, nonne est nasus praegrandis?

Dolus inest, anime mi, ait hospes—nasus est falsus.——

Verus est, respondit uxor.——
Ex abiete factus est, ait ille, terebinthinum olet——

Carbunculus inest, ait uxor.
Mortuus est nasus, respondit hospes.
Vivus est, ait illa,——& si ipsa vivam tangam.

scimitar hanging loosely to the wrist of it, he rode on as slowly as one foot of the mule could follow another through the principal streets of Strasburg, till chance brought him to the great inn in the market place over against the church.

The moment the stranger alighted, he ordered his mule to be led into the stable, and his cloak bag to be brought in; then opening, and taking out of it, his crimson satin breeches, with a silver-fringed——(appendage to them, which I dare not translate)——he put his breeches, with his fringed codpiece, on and forthwith, with his short scimitar in his hand, walked out to the grand parade.

The stranger had just taken three turns upon the parade, when he perceived the trumpeter's wife at the opposite side of it—so turning short, in pain lest his nose should be attempted, he instantly went back to his inn—undressed himself, packed up his crimson satin breeches, &c., in his cloak-bag, and called for his mule.

I am going forwards, said the stranger, for Frankfort—— and shall be back at Strasburg this day month.

I hope, continued the stranger, stroking down the face of his mule with his left hand as he was going to mount it, that you have been kind to this faithful slave of mine——it has carried me and my cloak bag, continued he, tapping the mule's back, above six hundred leagues.

——'Tis a long journey, Sir, replied the master of the inn ——unless a man has great business.——Tut! tut! said the stranger, I have been at the Promontory of Noses; and have got me one of the goodliest and jolliest, thank heaven, that ever fell to a single man's lot.

Whilst the stranger was giving this odd account of himself, the master of the inn and his wife kept both their eyes fixed full upon the stranger's nose——By St. Radagunda, said the innkeeper's wife to herself, there is more of it than in any dozen of the largest noses put together in all Strasburg! is it not, said she, whispering her husband in his ear, is it not a noble nose?

'Tis an imposture, my dear, said the master of the inn—— 'tis a false nose.——

'Tis a true nose, said his wife.——

'Tis made of fir tree, said he;——I smell the turpentine.——

There's a pimple on it, said she.

'Tis a dead nose, replied the innkeeper.

'Tis a live nose, and if I am alive myself, said the innkeeper's wife, I will touch it.

Votum feci sancto Nicolao, ait peregrinus, nasum meum intactum fore usque ad——Quodnam tempus? illico respondit illa.

Minime tangetur, inquit ille (manibus in pectus compositis) usque ad illam horam——Quam horam? ait illa.——Nullam, respondit peregrinus, donec pervenio, ad——Quem locum, ——obsecro? ait illa——Peregrinus nil respondens mulo conscenso discessit.

I have made a vow to St. Nicolas this day, said the stranger, that my nose shall not be touched till——Here the stranger, suspending his voice, looked up——Till when? said she hastily.

It never shall be touched, said he, clasping his hands and bringing them close to his breasts, till that hour——What hour? cried the innkeeper's wife.——Never!——never! said the stranger, never till I am got——For heaven sake into what place? said she.——The stranger rode away without saying a word.

The stranger had not got half a league on his way towards Frankfort, before all the city of Strasburg was in an uproar about his nose. The *Compline* bells were just ringing to call the Strasburgers to their devotions, and shut up the duties of the day in prayer:——no soul in all Strasburg heard 'em——the city was like a swarm of bees——men, women, and children (the *Compline* bells tinkling all the time) flying here and there——in at one door, out at another——this way and that way——long ways and cross ways——up one street, down another street——in at this alley, out at that——did you see it? did you see it? did you see it? O! did you see it? ——who saw it? who did see it? for mercy's sake, who saw it?

Alack o' day! I was at vespers!——I was washing, I was starching, I was scouring, I was quilting——God help me! I never saw it——I never touched it!——would I had been a sentinel, a bandy-legged drummer, a trumpeter, a trumpeter's wife, was the general cry and lamentation in every street and corner of Strasburg.

Whilst all this confusion and disorder triumphed throughout the great city of Strasburg, was the courteous stranger going on as gently upon his mule in his way to Frankfort, as if he had had no concern at all in the affair——talking all the way he rode in broken sentences, sometimes to his mule ——sometimes to himself——sometimes to his Julia.

O Julia, my lovely Julia!——nay, I cannot stop to let thee bite that thistle——that ever the suspected tongue of a rival should have robbed me of enjoyment when I was upon the point of tasting it.——

——Pugh!——'tis nothing but a thistle——never mind it ——thou shalt have a better supper at night.——

——Banished from my country——my friends——from thee.——

Poor devil, thou'rt sadly tired with thy journey!——come ——get on a little faster——there's nothing in my cloak bag but two shirts——a crimson satin pair of breeches, and a fringed——Dear Julia!

——But why to Frankfort?——is it that there is a hand unfelt, which secretly is conducting me through these meanders and unsuspected tracts——

——Stumbling! by St. Nicolas! every step——why, at this rate we shall be all night in getting in——

——To happiness——or am I to be the sport of fortune and slander——destined to be driven forth unconvicted——unheard——untouched——if so, why did I not stay at Strasburg, where justice——but I had sworn!——Come, thou shalt drink——to St. Nicolas——O Julia!——What dost thou prick up thy ears at?——'tis nothing but a man, &c.——

The stranger rode on, communing in this manner with his mule and Julia——till he arrived at his inn, where, as soon as he arrived, he alighted——saw his mule, as he had promised it, taken good care of——took off his cloak bag, with his crimson satin breeches, &c., in it——called for an omelet to his supper, went to his bed about twelve o'clock, and in five minutes fell fast asleep.

It was about the same hour when, the tumult in Strasburg being abated for that night,——the Strasburgers had all got quietly into their beds——but not like the stranger, for the rest either of their minds or bodies; Queen Mab, like an elf as she was, had taken the stranger's nose, and without reduction of its bulk, had that night been at the pains of slitting and dividing it into as many noses of different cuts and fashions as there were heads in Strasburg to hold them. The Abbess of Quedlinburg, who, with the four great dignitaries of her chapter, the prioress, the deaness, the subchantress, and senior canoness, had that week come to Strasburg to consult the university upon a case of conscience relating to their placket holes——was ill all the night.

The courteous stranger's nose had got perched upon the top of the pineal gland of her brain, and made such rousing work in the fancies of the four great dignitaries of her chapter, they could not get a wink of sleep the whole night through for it——there was no keeping a limb still amongst them——in short, they got up like so many ghosts.

The penitentiaries of the third order of St. Francis——the nuns of Mt. Calvary——the Praemonstratenses——the Clunienses *——the Carthusians, and all the severer orders of nuns who lay that night in blankets or haircloth, were

* Hafen Slawkenbergius means the Benedictine nuns of Cluny, founded in the year 940, by Odo, abbé de Cluny.

still in a worse condition than the Abbess of Quedlinburg ——by tumbling and tossing, and tossing and tumbling from one side of their beds to the other the whole night long—— the several sisterhoods had scratched and mauled themselves all to death——they got out of their beds almost flayed alive——everybody thought St. Antony had visited them for probation with his fire——they had never once, in short, shut their eyes the whole night long from vespers to matins.

The nuns of St. Ursula acted the wisest——they never attempted to go to bed at all.

The dean of Strasburg, the prebendaries, the capitulars and domiciliars (capitularly assembled in the morning to consider the case of buttered buns) all wished they had followed the nuns of St. Ursula's example.———In the hurry and confusion everything had been in the night before, the bakers had all forgot to lay their leaven——there were no buttered buns to be had for breakfast in all Strasburg—— the whole close of the cathedral was in one eternal commotion——such a cause of restlessness and disquietude, and such a zealous inquiry into the cause of that restlessness, had never happened in Strasburg since Martin Luther, with his doctrines, had turned the city upside down.

If the stranger's nose took this liberty of thrusting itself thus into the dishes * of religious orders, &c., what a carnival did his nose make of it in those of the laity!——'tis more than my pen, worn to the stump as it is, has power to describe; though I acknowledge (*cries Slawkenbergius, with more gaiety of thought than I could have expected from him*) that there is many a good simile now subsisting in the world which might give my countrymen some idea of it; but at the close of such a folio as this, wrote for their sakes, and in which I have spent the greatest part of my life——though I own to them the simile is in being, yet would it not be unreasonable in them to expect I should have either time or inclination to search for it? Let it suffice to say that the riot and disorder it occasioned in the Strasburgers' fantasies was so general——such an overpowering mastership had it got of all the faculties of the Strasburgers' minds——so many strange things, with equal confidence on all sides, and with equal eloquence in all places, were spoken and sworn

---

* Mr. Shandy's compliments to orators——is very sensible that Slawkenbergius has here changed his metaphor———which he is very guilty of;——that as a translator, Mr. Shandy has all along done what he could to make him stick to it——but that here 'twas impossible.

to concerning it, that turned the whole stream of all discourse and wonder towards it;——every soul, good and bad ——rich and poor——learned and unlearned——doctor and student——mistress and maid——gentle and simple—— nun's flesh and woman's flesh in Strasburg spent their time in hearing tidings about it——every eye in Strasburg languished to see it——every finger——every thumb in Strasburg burned to touch it.

Now what might add, if anything may be thought necessary to add to so vehement a desire——was this, that the sentinel, the bandy-legged drummer, the trumpeter, the trumpeter's wife, the burgomaster's widow, the master of the inn, and the master of the inn's wife, how widely soever they all differed every one from another in their testimonies and descriptions of the stranger's nose——they all agreed together in two points——namely, that he was gone to Frankfort, and would not return to Strasburg till that day month; and secondly, whether his nose was true or false, that the stranger himself was one of the most perfect paragons of beauty——the finest-made man!——the most genteel!—— the most generous of his purse——the most courteous in his carriage that had ever entered the gates of Strasburg—— that as he rode, with his scimitar slung loosely to his wrist, through the streets——and walked with his crimson satin breeches across the parade——'twas with so sweet an air of careless modesty, and so manly withal——as would have put the heart in jeopardy (had his nose not stood in his way) of every virgin who had cast her eyes upon him.

I call not upon that heart which is a stranger to the throbs and yearnings of curiosity so excited to justify the Abbess of Quedlinburg, the prioress, the deaness and sub-chantress for sending at noonday for the trumpeter's wife: she went through the streets of Strasburg with her husband's trumpet in her hand,——the best apparatus the straitness of the time would allow her for the illustration of her theory;——she stayed no longer than three days.

The sentinel and the bandy-legged drummer!——nothing on this side of old Athens could equal them! they read their lectures under the city gates to comers and goers, with all the pomp of a Chrysippus and a Crantor in their porticos.

The master of the inn, with his ostler on his left hand, read his also in the same style,——under the portico or gateway of his stable yard——his wife, hers more privately in a back room: all flocked to their lectures; not promiscuously——but to this or that, as is ever the way, as faith and credulity marshaled them——in a word, each Strasburger came crowding for intelligence——and every Strasburger had the intelligence he wanted.

'Tis worth remarking, for the benefit of all demonstrators in natural philosophy, &c., that as soon as the trumpeter's wife had finished the Abbess of Quedlinburg's private lecture, and had begun to read in public, which she did upon a stool in the middle of the great parade——she incommoded the other demonstrators mainly, by gaining incontinently the most fashionable part of the city of Strasburg for her auditory——But when a demonstrator in philosophy (cries Slawkenbergius) has a *trumpet* for an apparatus, pray what rival in science can pretend to be heard besides him?

Whilst the unlearned, through these conduits of intelligence, were all busied in getting down to the bottom of the well, where TRUTH keeps her little court,——were the learned in their way as busy in pumping her up through the conduits of dialect induction——they concerned themselves not with facts——they reasoned——

Not one profession had thrown more light upon this subject than the faculty——had not all their disputes about it run into the affair of *Wens* and oedematous swellings, they could not keep clear of them for their blood and souls—— the stranger's nose had nothing to do either with wens or oedematous swellings.

It was demonstrated however very satisfactorily that such a ponderous mass of heterogeneous matter could not be congested and conglomerated to the nose whilst the infant was *in Utero,* without destroying the statical balance of the foetus, and throwing it plump upon its head nine months before the time.——

——The opponents granted the theory——they denied the consequences.

And if a suitable provision of veins, arteries, &c., said they, was not laid in, for the due nourishment of such a nose, in the very first stamina and rudiments of its formation before it came into the world (bating the case of wens), it could not regularly grow and be sustained afterwards.

This was all answered by a dissertation upon nutriment, and the effect which nutriment had in extending the vessels, and in the increase and prolongation of the muscular parts to the greatest growth and expansion imaginable——In the triumph of which theory, they went so far as to affirm that there was no cause in nature why a nose might not grow to the size of the man himself.

The respondents satisfied the world this event could never happen to them so long as a man had but one stomach and one pair of lungs——For the stomach, said they, being the only organ destined for the reception of food, and turning it into chyle,——and the lungs the only engine of sanguification,——it could possibly work off no more than what the appetite brought it: or admitting the possibility of a man's overloading his stomach, nature had set bounds however to his lungs——the engine was of a determined size and strength, and could elaborate but a certain quantity in a given time——that is, it could produce just as much blood as was sufficient for one single man, and no more; so that, if there was as much nose as man——they proved a mortification must necessarily ensue; and forasmuch as there could not be a support for both, that the nose must either fall off from the man, or the man inevitably fall off from his nose.

Nature accommodates herself to these emergencies, cried the opponents—else what do you say to the case of a whole stomach——a whole pair of lungs, and but *half* a man, when both his legs have been unfortunately shot off?——

He dies of a plethora, said they——or must spit blood, and in a fortnight or three weeks go off in a consumption——

——It happens otherways——replied the opponents.——

It ought not, said they.

The more curious and intimate inquirers after Nature and her doings, though they went hand in hand a good way together, yet they all divided about the nose at last, almost as much as the faculty itself.

They amicably laid it down that there was a just and geometrical arrangement and proportion of the several parts of the human frame to its several destinations, offices, and functions, which could not be transgressed but within certain limits——that Nature, though she sported——she sported within a certain circle;——and they could not agree about the diameter of it.

The logicians stuck much closer to the point before them than any of the classes of the literati;——they began and ended with the word *Nose*; and had it not been for a *petitio principii*, which one of the ablest of them ran his head against in the beginning of the combat, the whole controversy had been settled at once.

A nose, argued the logician, cannot bleed without blood——and not only blood——but blood circulating in it to supply the phenomenon with a succession of drops——(a stream being but a quicker succession of drops that is in-

cluded, said he)——Now death, continued the logician, being
nothing but the stagnation of the blood——

I deny the definition——Death is the separation of the
soul from the body, said his antagonist——Then we don't
agree about our weapon, said the logician——Then there
is an end of the dispute, replied the antagonist.

The civilians were still more concise; what they offered
being more in the nature of a decree——than a dispute.

——Such a monstrous nose, said they, had it been a true
nose, could not possibly have been suffered in civil society
——and if false——to impose upon society with such false
signs and tokens was a still greater violation of its rights,
and must have had still less mercy shown it.

The only objection to this was that if it proved anything,
it proved the stranger's nose was neither true nor false.

This left room for the controversy to go on. It was maintained by the advocates of the ecclesiastic court that there
was nothing to inhibit a decree, since the stranger *ex mero
motu* had confessed he had been at the Promontory of
Noses, and had got one of the goodliest, &c.——To this it
was answered, it was impossible there should be such a
place as the Promontory of Noses, and the learned be ignorant where it lay. The commissary of the Bishop of
Strasburg undertook the advocates, explained this matter in
a treatise upon proverbial phrases, showing them that the
Promontory of Noses was a mere allegoric expression, im-
porting no more than that Nature had given him a long
nose: in proof of which, with great learning, he cited the
underwritten authorities,* which had decided the point incontestably, had it not appeared that a dispute about some
franchises of dean and chapter lands had been determined
by it nineteen years before.

* Nonnulli ex nostratibus eadem loquendi formulâ utun.
Quinimo et Logistae & Canonistae——Vid. Parce Barne Jas in d.
L. Provincial. Constitut. de conjec. vid. Vol. Lib. 4. Titul. 1. N. 7.
quâ etiam in re conspir. Om. de Promontorio Nas. Tichmak.
ff. d. tit. 3. fol. 189 passim. Vid. Glos. de contrahend. empt. &c.
nec non J. Scrudr. in cap. §. refut. ff. per totum Cum his
cons. Rever. J. Tubal, Sentent. & Prov. cap. 9. ff. 11, 12 obiter.
V. et. Librum, cui Tit. de Terris & Phras. Belg. ad finem, cum
Comment. N. Bardy Belg. Vid. Scrip. Argentotarens. de Antiq.
Ecc. in Episc. Archiv. fid. coll. per Von Jacobum Koinshoven
Folio Argent. 1583, praecip. ad finem. Quibus add. Rebuff in L.
obvenire de Signif. Nom. ff. fol. & de Jure, Gent. & Civil. de
protib. aliena feud. per federa, test. Joha. Luxius in prolegom.
quem velim videas, de Analy. Cap. 1, 2, 3. Vid. Idea.

It happened——I must not say unluckily for Truth, because they were given her a lift another way in so doing; that the two universities of Strasburg——the Lutheran, founded in the year 1538 by Jacobus Sturmius, counsellor of the senate,——and the Popish, founded by Leopold, Archduke of Austria, were, during all this time, employing the whole depth of their knowledge (except just what the affair of the Abbess of Quedlinburg's placket holes required)——in determining the point of Martin Luther's damnation.

The Popish doctors had undertaken to demonstrate *a priori* that from the necessary influence of the planets on the twenty-second day of October, 1483,——when the moon was in the twelfth house——Jupiter, Mars, and Venus in the third, the Sun, Saturn, and Mercury all got together in the fourth——that he must in course, and unavoidably, be a damned man——and that his doctrines, by a direct corollary, must be damned doctrines too.

By inspection into his horoscope, where five planets were in coition all at once with Scorpio * (in reading this my father would always shake his head) in the ninth house, which the Arabians allotted to religion——it appeared that Martin Luther did not care one stiver about the matter——and that from the horoscope directed to the conjunction of Mars—— they made it plain likewise he must die cursing and blaspheming——with the blast of which his soul (being steeped in guilt) sailed before the wind, into the lake of hellfire.

The little objection of the Lutheran doctors to this was that it must certainly be the soul of another man, born Oct. 22, '83, which was forced to sail down before the wind in that manner——inasmuch as it appeared from the register of Islaben, in the county of Mansfelt, that Luther was not born in the year 1483, but in '84; and not on the 22d day of October, but on the 10th of November, the eve of Martinmas Day, from whence he had the name of Martin.

[——I must break off my translation for a moment; for if I did not, I know I should no more be able to shut my

---

* Haec mira, satisque horrenda. [5] Planetarum coitio sub Scorpio Asterismo in nonâ coeli statione, quam Arabes religioni deputabant efficit Martinum Lutherum sacrilegum hereticum, christianae religionis hostem acerrimum atque prophanum, ex horoscopi directione ad Martis coitum, [ir]religiosissimus obiit, ejus Anima scelestissima ad infernos navigavit——ab Alecto, Tisiphone, et Megaera flagellis igneis cruciata perenniter.

——Lucas Gauricus in Tractatu astrologico de praeteritis multorum hominum accidentibus per genituras examinatis.

eyes in bed than the Abbess of Quedlinburg——It is to tell the reader that my father never read this passage of Slawkenbergius to my uncle Toby but with triumph——not over my uncle Toby, for he never opposed him in it——but over the whole world.

——Now you see, brother Toby, he would say, looking up, "that Christian names are not such indifferent things;"—— had Luther here been called by any other name but Martin, he would have been damned to all eternity——Not that I look upon Martin, he would add, as a good name——far from it——'tis something better than a neutral, and but a little ——yet little as it is, you see it was of some service to him.

My father knew the weakness of this prop to his hypothesis, as well as the best logician could show him——yet so strange is the weakness of man at the same time, as it fell in his way, he could not for his life but make use of it; and it was certainly for this reason that though there are many stories in Hafen Slawkenbergius's Decads full as entertaining as this I am translating, yet there is not one amongst them which my father read over with half the delight——it flattered two of his strangest hypotheses together——his NAMES and his NOSES——I will be bold to say, he might have read all the books in the Alexandrian library, had not fate taken other care of them, and not have met with a book or a passage in one which hit two such nails as these upon the head at one stroke.]

The two universities of Strasburg were hard tugging at this affair of Luther's navigation. The Protestant doctors had demonstrated that he had not sailed right before the wind, as the Popish doctors had pretended; and as everyone knew there was no sailing full in the teeth of it,——they were going to settle, in case he had sailed, how many points he was off; whether Martin had doubled the cape, or had fallen upon a leeshore; and no doubt, as it was an enquiry of much edification, at least to those who understood this sort of NAVIGATION, they had gone on with it in spite of the size of the stranger's nose, had not the size of the stranger's nose drawn off the attention of the world from what they were about——it was their business to follow.——

The Abbess of Quedlinburg and her four dignitaries was no stop; for the enormity of the stranger's nose running full as much in their fancies as their case of conscience——The affair of their placket holes kept cold——In a word, the printers were ordered to distribute their types——all controversies dropped.

'Twas a square cap with a silk tassel upon the crown of it ——to a nutshell——to have guessed on which side of the nose the two universities would split.

'Tis above reason, cried the doctors on one side.

'Tis below reason, cried the others.

'Tis faith, cried one.

'Tis a fiddlestick, said the other.

'Tis possible, cried the one.

'Tis impossible, said the other.

God's power is infinite, cried the Nosarians; he can do anything.

He can do nothing, replied the Antinosarians, which implies contradictions.

He can make matter think, said the Nosarians.

As certainly as you can make a velvet cap out of a sow's ear, replied the Antinosarians.

He can make two and two five, replied the Popish doctors. ——'Tis false, said their opponents.——

Infinite power is infinite power, said the doctors who maintained the *reality* of the nose.——It extends only to all possible things, replied the Lutherans.

By God in heaven, cried the Popish doctors, he can make a nose, if he thinks fit, as big as the steeple of Strasburg.

Now the steeple of Strasburg being the biggest and the tallest church steeple to be seen in the whole world, the Antinosarians denied that a nose of 575 geometrical feet in length could be worn, at least by a middle-sized man——The Popish doctors swore it could——The Lutheran doctors said No;——it could not.

This at once started a new dispute, which they pursued a great way, upon the extent and limitation of the moral and natural attributes of God——That controversy led them naturally into Thomas Aquinas, and Thomas Aquinas to the devil.

The stranger's nose was no more heard of in the dispute ——it just served as a frigate to launch them into the gulf of school divinity,——and then they all sailed before the wind.

Heat is in proportion to the want of true knowledge.

The controversy about the attributes, &c., instead of cooling, on the contrary had inflamed the Strasburgers' imaginations to a most inordinate degree——The less they understood of the matter, the greater was their wonder about it ——they were left in all the distresses of desire unsatisfied ——saw their doctors, the Parchmentarians, the Brassarians, the Turpentarians, on one side——the Popish doctors on the other, like Pantagruel and his companions in quest of the oracle of the bottle, all embarked and out of sight.

——The poor Strasburgers left upon the beach!

——What was to be done?——No delay——the uproar increased——everyone in disorder——the city gates set open.——

Unfortunate Strasburgers! was there in the storehouse of nature——was there in the lumber rooms of learning—— was there in the great arsenal of chance, one single engine left undrawn forth to torture your curiosities, and stretch your desires, which was not pointed by the hand of fate to play upon your hearts?——I dip not my pen into my ink to excuse the surrender of yourselves——'tis to write your pane-gyric. Show me a city so macerated with expectation—— who neither eat, or drank, or slept, or prayed, or hearkened to the calls either of religion or nature for seven-and-twenty days together, who could have held out one day longer.

On the twenty-eighth the courteous stranger had promised to return to Strasburg.

Seven thousand coaches (Slawkenbergius must certainly have made some mistake in his numerical characters) 7000 coaches——15000 single-horse chairs——20000 waggons, crouded as full as they could all hold with senators, counsellors, syndics——Beguines, widows, wives, virgins, canons, concubines, all in their coaches——The Abbess of Quedlinburg, with the prioress, the deaness and subchantress leading the procession in one coach, and the Dean of Stras-burg, with the four great dignitaries of his chapter on her left hand——the rest following higglety-pigglety as they could; some on horseback——some on foot——some led ——some driven——some down the Rhine——some this way——some that——all set out at sunrise to meet the courteous stranger on the road.

Haste we now towards the catastrophe of my tale——I say *Catastrophe* (cries Slawkenbergius) inasmuch as a tale, with parts rightly disposed, not only rejoiceth (*gaudet*) in the *Catastrophe* and *Peripetia* of a DRAMA, but rejoiceth more-over in all the essential and integrant parts of it——it has its *Protasis, Epitasis, Catastasis,* its *Catastrophe* or *Peripetia* growing one out of the other in it, in the order Aristotle first planted them——without which a tale had better never be told at all, says Slawkenbergius, but be kept to a man's self.

In all my ten tales, in all my ten decads, have I, Slawken-bergius, tied down every tale of them as tightly to this rule, as I have done this of the stranger and his nose.

——From his first parley with the sentinel, to his leaving the city of Strasburg, after pulling off his crimson satin pair of breeches, is the *Protasis* or first entrance——where the characters of the *Personae Dramatis* are just touched in, and the subject slightly begun.

The *Epitasis*, wherein the action is more fully entered upon and heightened, till it arrives at its state or height called the *Catastasis*, and which usually takes up the 2d and 3d act, is included within that busy period of my tale betwixt the first night's uproar about the nose, to the conclusion of the trumpeter's wife's lectures upon it in the middle of the grand parade; and from the first embarking of the learned in the dispute——to the doctors finally sailing away, and leaving the Strasburgers upon the beach in distress, is the *Catastasis* or the ripening of the incidents and passions for their bursting forth in the fifth act.

This commences with the setting out of the Strasburgers in the Frankfort road, and terminates in unwinding the labyrinth and bringing the hero out of a state of agitation (as Aristotle calls it) to a state of rest and quietness.

This, says Hafen Slawkenbergius, constitutes the *Catastrophe* or *Peripetia* of my tale——and that is the part of it I am going to relate.

We left the stranger behind the curtain asleep——he enters now upon the stage.

——What dost thou prick up thy ears at?——'tis nothing but a man upon a horse——was the last word the stranger uttered to his mule. It was not proper then to tell the reader that the mule took his master's word for it; and without any more *if's* or *ands,* let the traveller and his horse pass by.

The traveller was hastening with all diligence to get to Strasburg that night——What a fool am I, said the traveller to himself, when he had rode about a league farther, to think of getting into Strasburg this night——Strasburg!——the great Strasburg!——Strasburg, the capital of all Alsatia! Strasburg, an imperial city! Strasburg, a sovereign state! Strasburg, garrisoned with five thousand of the best troops in all the world!——Alas! if I was at the gates of Strasburg this moment, I could not gain admittance into it for a ducat——nay, a ducat and half——'tis too much——better go back to the last inn I have passed——than lie I know not where——or give I know not what. The traveller, as he made these reflections in his mind, turned his horse's head about, and three minutes after the stranger had been conducted into his chamber, he arrived at the same inn.

———We have bacon in the house, said the host, and bread———and till eleven o'clock this night had three eggs in it———but a stranger, who arrived an hour ago, has had them dressed into an omelet, and we have nothing.———

———Alas! said the traveller, harrassed as I am, I want nothing but a bed———I have one as soft as is in Alsatia, said the host.

———The stranger, continued he, should have slept in it, for 'tis my best bed, but upon the score of his nose———He has got a defluxion, said the traveller———Not that I know, cried the host———But 'tis a camp bed, and Jacinta, said he, looking towards the maid, imagined there was not room in it to turn his nose in———Why so? cried the traveller, starting back———It is so long a nose, replied the host——— The traveller fixed his eyes upon Jacinta, then upon the ground———kneeled upon his right knee———had just got his hand laid upon his breast———Trifle not with my anxiety, said he, rising up again———'Tis no trifle, said Jacinta, 'tis the most glorious nose!———The traveller fell upon his knee again ———laid his hand upon his breast———then said he, looking up to heaven, thou hast conducted me to the end of my pilgrimage———'Tis Diego!

The traveller was the brother of the Julia so often invoked that night by the stranger as he rode from Strasburg upon his mule; and was come, on her part, in quest of him. He had accompanied his sister from Valadolid across the Pyrenean mountains through France, and had many an entangled skein to wind off in pursuit of him through the many meanders and abrupt turnings of a lover's thorny tracks.

———Julia had sunk under it———and had not been able to go a step farther than to Lyons, where, with the many disquietudes of a tender heart, which all talk of———but few feel———she sickened, but had just strength to write a letter to Diego; and having conjured her brother never to see her face till he had found him out, and put the letter into his hands, Julia took to her bed.

Fernandez (for that was her brother's name)———though the camp bed was as soft as any one in Alsace, yet he could not shut his eyes in it.———As soon as it was day he rose, and hearing Diego was risen too, he entered his chamber, and discharged his sister's commission.

The letter was as follows:

"Seig. DIEGO.

"Whether my suspicions of your nose were justly excited

215

or not——'tis not now to inquire——it is enough I have not had firmness to put them to farther trial.

"How could I know so little of myself, when I sent my *Dueña* to forbid your coming more under my lattice? or how could I know so little of you, Diego, as to imagine you would not have stayed one day in Valadolid to have given ease to my doubts?——Was I to be abandoned, Diego, because I was deceived? or was it kind to take me at my word, whether my suspicions were just or no, and leave me, as you did, a prey to much uncertainty and sorrow?

"In what manner Julia has resented this——my brother, when he puts this letter into your hands, will tell you: He will tell you in how few moments she had repented of the rash message she had sent you——in what frantic haste she flew to her lattice, and how many days and nights together she leaned immovably upon her elbow, looking through it towards the way which Diego was wont to come.

"He will tell you, when she heard of your departure ——how her spirits deserted her——how her heart sickened——how piteously she mourned——how low she hung her head. O Diego! how many weary steps has my brother's pity led me by the hand languishing to trace out yours! how far has desire carried me beyond strength——and how oft have I fainted by the way, and sunk into his arms, with only power to cry out——O my Diego!

"If the gentleness of your carriage has not belied your heart, you will fly to me, almost as fast as you fled from me ——haste as you will, you will arrive but to see me expire. ——'Tis a bitter draught, Diego, but O! 'tis embittered still more by dying un————"

She could proceed no farther.

Slawkenbergius supposes the word intended was *unconvinced*, but her strength would not enable her to finish her letter.

The heart of the courteous Diego overflowed as he read the letter——he ordered his mule forthwith and Fernandez's horse to be saddled; and as no vent in prose is equal to that of poetry in such conflicts——chance, which as often directs us to remedies as to *diseases,* having thrown a piece of charcoal into the window——Diego availed himself of it, and whilst the ostler was getting ready his mule, he eased his mind against the wall as follows.

ODE

Harsh and untuneful are the notes of love,
Unless my Julia strikes the key,
Her hand alone can touch the part,
Whose dulcet move-
ment charms the heart,
And governs all the man with sympathetic sway.

2d

O Julia!

The lines were very natural——for they were nothing at all to the purpose, says Slawkenbergius, and 'tis a pity there were no more of them; but whether it was that Seig. Diego was slow in composing verses—or the ostler quick in saddling mules——is not averred; certain it was that Diego's mule and Fernandez's horse were ready at the door of the inn before Diego was ready for his second stanza; so without staying to finish his ode, they both mounted, sallied forth, passed the Rhine, traversed Alsace, shaped their course towards Lyons, and before the Strasburgers and the Abbess of Quedlinburg had set out on their cavalcade, had Fernandez, Diego, and his Julia crossed the Pyrenean mountains, and got safe to Valadolid.

'Tis needless to inform the geographical reader that when Diego was in Spain, it was not possible to meet the courteous stranger in the Frankfort road; it is enough to say that of all restless desires, curiosity being the strongest——the Strasburgers felt the full force of it; and that for three days and nights they were tossed to and fro in the Frankfort road, with the tempestuous fury of this passion, before they could submit to return home——When alas! an event was prepared for them, of all others the most grievous that could befall a free people.

As this revolution of the Strasburgers' affairs is often spoken of, and little understood, I will, in ten words, says Slawkenbergius, give the world an explanation of it, and with it put an end to my tale.

Everybody knows of the grand system of Universal Monarchy, wrote by order of Mons. Colbert, and put in manuscript into the hands of Lewis the Fourteenth, in the year 1664.

'Tis as well known that one branch out of many of that

217

system was the getting possession of Strasburg, to favour an entrance at all times into Swabia, in order to disturb the quiet of Germany——and that in consequence of this plan, Strasburg unhappily fell at length into their hands.

It is the lot of few to trace out the true springs of this and suchlike revolutions——The vulgar look too high for them ——Statesmen look too low——Truth (for once) lies in the middle.

What a fatal thing is the popular pride of a free city! cries one historian——The Strasburgers deemed it a diminution of their freedom to receive an imperial garrison——and so fell a prey to a French one.

The fate, says another, of the Strasburgers may be a warning to all free people to save their money——They anticipated their revenues——brought themselves under taxes, exhausted their strength, and in the end became so weak a people, they had not strength to keep their gates shut, and so the French pushed them open.

Alas! alas! cries Slawkenbergius, 'twas not the French—— 'twas CURIOSITY pushed them open——The French indeed, who are ever upon the catch, when they saw the Strasburgers, men, women, and children, all marched out to follow the stranger's nose——each man followed his own, and marched in.

Trade and manufactures have decayed and gradually grown down ever since——but not from any cause which commercial heads have assigned; for it is owing to this only, that Noses have ever so run in their heads, that the Strasburgers could not follow their business.

Alas! alas! cries Slawkenbergius, making an exclamation ——it is not the first——and I fear will not be the last fortress that has been either won——or lost by NOSES.

The END of

Slawkenbergius's TALE

CHAPTER I

With all this learning upon Noses running perpetually in my father's fancy——with so many family prejudices——and ten decads of such tales running on forever along with them ——how was it possible with such exquisite——was it a true nose?——That a man with such exquisite feelings as my father had could bear the shock at all belowstairs——or indeed abovestairs, in any other posture but the very posture I have described.

——Throw yourself down upon the bed a dozen times ——taking care only to place a looking glass first in a chair on one side of it, before you do it——But was the stranger's nose a true nose——or was it a false one?

To tell that beforehand, Madam, would be to do injury to one of the best tales in the Christian world; and that is the tenth of the tenth decad which immediately follows this.

This tale, crieth Slawkenbergius somewhat exultingly, has been reserved by me for the concluding tale of my whole work; knowing right well that when I shall have told it, and my reader shall have read it through——'twould be even high time for both of us to shut up the book; inasmuch, continues Slawkenbergius, as I know of no tale which could possibly ever go down after it.

——'Tis a tale indeed!

This sets out with the first interview in the inn at Lyons, when Fernandez left the courteous stranger and his sister Julia alone in her chamber, and is overwritten,

The INTRICACIES
of
Diego and Julia

Heavens! thou art a strange creature, Slawkenbergius! what a whimsical view of the involutions of the heart of woman hast thou opened! how this can ever be translated, and yet if this specimen of Slawkenbergius's tales, and the exquisitiveness of his moral, should please the world——

219

translated shall a couple of volumes be.————Else, how this can ever be translated into good English I have no sort of conception.————There seems in some passages to want a sixth sense to do it rightly.————What can he mean by the lambent pupilability of slow, low, dry chat, five notes below the natural tone,————which you know, Madam, is little more than a whisper? The moment I pronounced the words, I could perceive an attempt towards a vibration in the strings, about the region of the heart.————The brain made no acknowledgment.————There's often no good understanding betwixt 'em.————I felt as if I understood it.————I had no ideas. ————The movement could not be without cause.————I'm lost. I can make nothing of it,————unless, may it please your Worships, the voice in that case being little more than a whisper, unavoidably forces the eyes to approach not only within six inches of each other————but to look into the pupils————is not that dangerous?————But it can't be avoided————for to look up to the ceiling, in that case the two chins unavoidably meet————and to look down into each other's laps, the foreheads come into immediate contact, which at once puts an end to the conference————I mean to the sentimental part of it.————What is left, Madam, is not worth stooping for.

CHAPTER II

My father lay stretched across the bed as still as if the hand of death had pushed him down, for a full hour and a half, before he began to play upon the floor with the toe of that foot which hung over the bedside; my uncle Toby's heart was a pound lighter for it.————In a few moments, his left hand, the knuckles of which had all the time reclined upon the handle of the chamber pot, came to its feeling————he thrust it a little more within the valance————drew up his hand, when he had done, into his bosom————gave a hem! ————My good uncle Toby, with infinite pleasure, answered it; and full gladly would have ingrafted a sentence of consolation upon the opening it afforded; but having no talents, as I said, that way, and fearing moreover that he might set out with something which might make a bad matter worse, he contented himself with resting his chin placidly upon the cross of his crutch.

Now whether the compression shortened my uncle Toby's face into a more pleasurable oval,——or that the philanthropy of his heart, in seeing his brother beginning to emerge out of the sea of his afflictions, had braced up his muscles,——so that the compression upon his chin only doubled the benignity which was there before, is not hard to decide.——My father, in turning his eyes, was struck with such a gleam of sunshine in his face, as melted down the sullenness of his grief in a moment.

He broke silence as follows.

CHAPTER III

Did ever man, brother Toby, cried my father, raising himself up upon his elbow, and turning himself round to the opposite side of the bed, where my uncle Toby was sitting in his old fringed chair, with his chin resting upon his crutch—— did ever a poor unfortunate man, brother Toby, cried my father, receive so many lashes?——The most I ever saw given, quoth my uncle Toby (ringing the bell at the bed's head for Trim), was to a grenadier, I think in Mackay's regiment.

——Had my uncle Toby shot a bullet through my father's heart, he could not have fallen down with his nose upon the quilt more suddenly.

Bless me! said my uncle Toby.

CHAPTER IV

Was it Mackay's regiment, quoth my uncle Toby, where the poor grenadier was so unmercifully whipped at Bruges about the ducats?——O Christ! he was innocent! cried Trim with a deep sigh.——And he was whipped, may it please

221

your Honour, almost to death's door.——They had better have shot him outright, as he begged, and he had gone directly to heaven, for he was as innocent as your Honour. ——I thank thee, Trim, quoth my uncle Toby. I never think of his, continued Trim, and my poor brother Tom's misfortunes, for we were all three school fellows, but I cry like a coward.——Tears are no proof of cowardice, Trim. ——I drop them ofttimes myself, cried my uncle Toby.——I know your Honour does, replied Trim, and so am not ashamed of it myself.——But to think, may it please your Honour, continued Trim, a tear stealing into the corner of his eye as he spoke——to think of two virtuous lads with hearts as warm in their bodies, and as honest as God could make them——the children of honest people, going forth with gallant spirits to seek their fortunes in the world——and fell into such evils!——poor Tom! to be tortured upon a rack for nothing——but marrying a Jew's widow who sold sausages——honest Dick Johnson's soul to be scourged out of his body for the ducats another man put into his knapsack! ——O!——these are misfortunes, cried Trim,——pulling out his handkerchief——these are misfortunes, may it please your Honour, worth lying down and crying over.

——My father could not help blushing.

'Twould be a pity, Trim, quoth my uncle Toby, thou shouldst ever feel sorrow of thy own——thou feelest it so tenderly for others.——Alack o' day, replied the corporal, brightening up his face——your Honour knows I have neither wife or child——I can have no sorrows in this world.——My father could not help smiling.——As few as any man, Trim, replied my uncle Toby; nor can I see how a fellow of thy light heart can suffer, but from the distress of poverty in thy old age——when thou art passed all services, Trim,——and hast outlived thy friends——An' please your Honour, never fear, replied Trim cheerily—— But I would have thee never fear, Trim, replied my uncle; and therefore, continued my uncle Toby, throwing down his crutch, and getting up upon his legs as he uttered the word *therefore*——in recompense, Trim, of thy long fidelity to me, and that goodness of thy heart I have had such proofs of——whilst thy master is worth a shilling——thou shalt never ask elsewhere, Trim, for a penny. Trim attempted to thank my uncle Toby,——but had not power——tears trickled down his cheeks faster than he could wipe them off ——He laid his hands upon his breast——made a bow to the ground, and shut the door.

———I have left Trim my bowling green, cried my uncle Toby———My father smiled———I have left him moreover a pension, continued my uncle Toby———My father looked grave.

CHAPTER V

Is this a fit time, said my father to himself, to talk of PEN-SIONS and GRENADIERS?

CHAPTER VI

When my uncle Toby first mentioned the grenadier, my father, I said, fell down with his nose flat to the quilt, and as suddenly as if my uncle Toby had shot him; but it was not added that every other limb and member of my father instantly relapsed with his nose into the same precise atti-tude in which he lay first described; so that when Corporal Trim left the room, and my father found himself disposed to rise off the bed,———he had all the little preparatory move-ments to run over again, before he could do it.———Attitudes are nothing, Madam;———'tis the transition from one at-titude to another———like the preparation and resolution of the discord into harmony, which is all in all.

For which reason my father played the same jig over again with his toe upon the floor———pushed the chamber pot still a little farther within the valance———gave a hem ———raised himself up upon his elbow———and was just be-ginning to address himself to my uncle Toby———when rec-ollecting the unsuccessfulness of his first effort in that at-titude,———he got upon his legs, and in making the third turn across the room, he stopped short before my uncle Toby; and laying the three first fingers of his right hand in the palm of his left, and stooping a little, he addressed himself to my uncle Toby as follows.

CHAPTER VII

When I reflect, brother Toby, upon MAN; and take a view of
that dark side of him which represents his life as open to so
many causes of trouble——when I consider, brother Toby,
how oft we eat the bread of affliction, and that we are born
to it, as to the portion of our inheritance——I was born
to nothing, quoth my uncle Toby, interrupting my father
——but my commission. Zooks! said my father, did not my
uncle leave you a hundred and twenty pounds a year?——
What could I have done without it? replied my uncle Toby.
————That's another concern, said my father testily——
But I say, Toby, when one runs over the catalogue of all the
cross reckonings and sorrowful *items* with which the heart of
man is overcharged, 'tis wonderful by what hidden resources
the mind is enabled to stand it out, and bear itself up, as it
does against the impositions laid upon our nature.————
'Tis by the assistance of Almighty God, cried my uncle Toby,
looking up, and pressing the palms of his hands close together——'tis not from our own strength, brother Shandy
——a sentinel in a wooden sentry box might as well pretend
to stand it out against a detachment of fifty men;——we
are upheld by the grace and the assistance of the best of
Beings.

————That is cutting the knot, said my father, instead of untying it.——But give me leave to lead you, brother Toby, a
little deeper into this mystery.

With all my heart, replied my uncle Toby.

My father instantly exchanged the attitude he was in
for that in which Socrates is so finely painted by Raphael in
his school of Athens; which your Connoisseurship knows is
so exquisitely imagined that even the particular manner of
the reasoning of Socrates is expressed by it——for he holds
the forefinger of his left hand between the forefinger and the
thumb of his right, and seems as if he was saying to the
libertine he is reclaiming——"*You grant me* this——
and this: and this, and this, I don't ask of you——they
follow of themselves in course."

So stood my father, holding fast his forefinger betwixt his
finger and his thumb, and reasoning with my uncle Toby

as he sat in his old fringed chair, valanced around with parti-coloured worsted bobs——O Garrick! what a rich scene of this would thy exquisite powers make! and how gladly would I write such another to avail myself of thy immortality, and secure my own behind it.

CHAPTER VIII

Though man is of all others the most curious vehicle, said my father, yet at the same time 'tis of so slight a frame and so totteringly put together that the sudden jerks and hard jostlings it unavoidably meets with in this rugged journey would overset and tear it to pieces a dozen times a day—— was it not, brother Toby, that there is a secret spring within us——Which spring, said my uncle Toby, I take to be Religion.——Will that set my child's nose on? cried my father, letting go his finger, and striking one hand against the other ——It makes everything straight for us, answered my uncle Toby——Figuratively speaking, dear Toby, it may, for aught I know, said my father; but the spring I am speaking of is that great and elastic power within us of counterbalancing evil, which like a secret spring in a well-ordered machine, though it can't prevent the shock——at least it imposes upon our sense of it.

Now, my dear brother, said my father, replacing his forefinger, as he was coming closer to the point,——had my child arrived safe into the world, unmartyred in that precious part of him——fanciful and extravagant as I may appear to the world in my opinion of Christian names, and of that magic bias which good or bad names irresistably impress upon our characters and conducts——heaven is witness! that in the warmest transports of my wishes for the prosperity of my child, I never once wished to crown his head with more glory and honour than what GEORGE or EDWARD would have spread around it.

But alas! continued my father, as the greatest evil has befallen him——I must counteract and undo it with the greatest good.

He shall be christened Trismegistus, brother.

I wish it may answer——replied my uncle Toby, rising up.

CHAPTER IX

What a chapter of chances, said my father, turning himself about upon the first landing, as he and my uncle Toby were going downstairs——what a long chapter of chances do the events of this world lay open to us! Take pen and ink in hand, brother Toby, and calculate it fairly——I know no more of calculations than this baluster, said my uncle Toby (striking short of it with his crutch, and hitting my father a desperate blow souse upon his shinbone),——'Twas a hundred to one——cried my uncle Toby.——I thought, quoth my father (rubbing his shin), you had known nothing of calculations, brother Toby.——'Twas a mere chance, said my uncle Toby——Then it adds one to the chapter——replied my father.

The double success of my father's repartees tickled off the pain of his shin at once——it was well it so fell out——(chance! again)——or the world to this day had never known the subject of my father's calculation——to guess it—— there was no chance——What a lucky chapter of chances has this turned out! for it has saved me the trouble of writing one express, and in truth I have enough already upon my hands without it——Have not I promised the world a chapter of knots? two chapters upon the right and the wrong end of a woman? a chapter upon whiskers' a chapter upon wishes?——a chapter of noses?——No, I have done that—— a chapter upon my uncle Toby's modesty: to say nothing of a chapter upon chapters, which I will finish before I sleep—— by my great-grandfather's whiskers, I shall never get half of 'em through this year.

Take pen and ink in hand, and calculate it fairly, brother Toby, said my father, and it will turn out a million to one that of all the parts of the body, the edge of the forceps should have the ill luck just to fall upon and break down that one part which should break down the fortunes of our house with it.

It might have been worse, replied my uncle Toby——I don't comprehend, said my father——Suppose the hip had presented, replied my uncle Toby, as Dr. Slop foreboded.

My father reflected half a minute——looked down——
touched the middle of his forehead slightly with his finger——

——True, said he.

CHAPTER X

Is it not a shame to make two chapters of what passed in
going down one pair of stairs? for we are got no farther
yet than to the first landing, and there are fifteen more steps
down to the bottom; and for aught I know, as my father and
my uncle Toby are in a talking humour, there may be as
many chapters as steps;——let that be as it will, Sir, I can
no more help it than my destiny:——A sudden impulse
comes across me——drop the curtain, Shandy——I drop
it——Strike a line here across the paper, Tristram——I strike
it——and hey for a new chapter!

The deuce of any other rule have I to govern myself by in
this affair——and if I had one——as I do all things out of all
rule——I would twist it and tear it to pieces, and throw it
into the fire when I had done——Am I warm? I am, and
the cause demands it——a pretty story! is a man to follow
rules——or rules to follow him?

Now this, you must know, being my chapter upon chapters,
which I promised to write before I went to sleep, I thought
it meet to ease my conscience entirely before I laid down,
by telling the world all I knew about the matter at once: Is
not this ten times better than to set out dogmatically with a
sententious parade of wisdom, and telling the world a story
of a roasted horse——that chapters relieve the mind——
that they assist——or impose upon the imagination——and
that in a work of this dramatic cast they are as necessary
as the shifting of scenes——with fifty other cold conceits,
enough to extinguish the fire which roasted him.——O! but
to understand this, which is a puff at the fire of Diana's
temple——you must read Longinus——read away——if you
are not a jot the wiser by reading him the first time over——
never fear——read him again——Avicenna and Licetus read
Aristotle's metaphysics forty times through apiece, and
never understood a single word.——But mark the conse-

quence——Avicenna turned out a desperate writer at all kinds of writing——for he wrote books *de omni scribili;* and for Licetus (Fortùnio, though all the world knows he was born a foetus,* of no more than five inches and a half in length, yet he grew to that astonishing height in literature as to write a book with a title as long as himself——the learned know I mean his *Gonopsychanthropologia,* upon the origin of the human soul.

So much for my chapter upon chapters, which I hold to be the best chapter in my whole work; and take my word, whoever reads it is full as well employed as in picking straws.

* *Ce Fœtus* n'étoit pas plus grand que la paume de la main; mais son père l'ayant éxaminé en qualité de Médecin, & ayant trouvé que c'étoit quelque chose de plus qu'un Embryon, le fit transporter tout vivant à Rapallo, où il le fit voir à Jerôme Bardi & à d'autres Medecins du lieu. On trouva qu'il ne lui manquoit rien d'essential à la vie; & son père pour faire voir un essai de son expérience, entreprit d'achever l'ouvrage de la Nature, & de travailler à la formation de l'Enfant avec le même artifice que celui dont on se sert pour faire éclorre les Poulets in Egypte. Il instruisit une Nourrice de tout ce qu'elle avoit à faire, & ayant fait mettre son fils dans un four proprement accommodé, il reussit à l'élever et à lui faire prendre ses accroissemens nécessaires, par l'uniformité d'une chaleur étrangére measurée exactement sur les dégrés d'un Thermomètre, ou d'un autre instrument équivalent. (Vide Mich. Giustinian, ne gli Scritt. Liguri à Cart. 223.488.)

On auroit toujours été très satisfait de l'industrie d'un Père si expérimenté dans l'Art de la Génération, quand il n'auroit pû prolonger la vie à son fils que pour quelques mois, ou pour peu d'années.

Mais quand on se represente que l'Enfant a vécu pres de quatrevingts ans, & qu'il a composé quatre-vingts Ouvrages différents tous fruits d'une longue lecture,——il faut convenir que tout ce qui est incroyable n'est pas toujours faux, & que la *Vraisemblance n'est pas toujours du côté de la Vérité*.

Il n'avoit que dix-neuf ans lorsqu'il composa Gonopsychanthropologia de Origine Animae humanae.

(Les Enfans célèbres, revûs & corrigés par M. De la Monnoye de l'Académie Françoise.)

CHAPTER XI

We shall bring all things to rights, said my father, setting his foot upon the first step from the landing——This Trismegistus, continued my father, drawing his leg back, and turning to my uncle Toby——was the greatest, Toby, of all earthly beings——he was the greatest king——the greatest lawgiver——the greatest philosopher——and the greatest priest——and engineer——said my uncle Toby.——
——In course, said my father.

CHAPTER XII

——And how does your mistress? cried my father, taking the same step over again from the landing, and calling to Susannah, whom he saw passing by the foot of the stairs with a huge pincushion in her hand——how does your mistress? As well, said Susannah, tripping by, but without looking up, as can be expected——What a fool am I! said my father, drawing his leg back again——let things be as they will, brother Toby, 'tis ever the precise answer——And how is the child, pray?——No answer. And where is Dr. Slop? added my father, raising his voice aloud, and looking over the balusters——Susannah was out of hearing.

Of all the riddles of a married life, said my father, crossing the landing, in order to set his back against the wall, whilst he propounded it to my uncle Toby——of all the puzzling riddles, said he, in a marriage state,——of which you may trust me, brother Toby, there are more asses' loads than all Job's stock of asses could have carried——there is not one that has more intricacies in it than this——that from the very moment the mistress of the house is brought to bed, every female in it, from my lady's gentlewoman down to the cinder wench, becomes an inch taller for it; and give themselves more airs upon that single inch than all their other inches put together.

I think rather, replied my uncle Toby, that 'tis we who sink an inch lower.——If I meet but a woman with child——I do it——'Tis a heavy tax upon that half of our fellow-creatures, brother Shandy, said my uncle Toby——'Tis a piteous burden upon 'em, continued he, shaking his head. ——Yes, yes, 'tis a painful thing——said my father, shaking his head too——but certainly, since shaking of heads came into fashion, never did two heads shake together, in concert, from two such different springs.

God bless ⎫ 'em all——said my uncle Toby and
Deuce take ⎭ my father, each to himself.

CHAPTER XIII

Holla!——you chairman!——here's sixpence——do step into that bookseller's shop, and call me a *day-tall* critic. I am very willing to give any one of 'em a crown to help me with his tackling, to get my father and my uncle Toby off the stairs, and to put them to bed.——

——'Tis even high time; for except a short nap, which they both got whilst Trim was boring the jack boots——and which, by the bye, did my father no sort of good upon the score of the bad hinge——they have not else shut their eyes since nine hours before the time that Dr. Slop was led into the back parlour in that dirty pickle by Obadiah.

Was every day of my life to be as busy a day as this,—— and to take up,——truce——

I will not finish that sentence till I have made an observation upon the strange state of affairs between the reader and myself, just as things stand at present——an observation never applicable before to any one biographical writer since the creation of the world but to myself——and I believe will never hold good to any other, until its final destruction——and therefore, for the very novelty of it alone, it must be worth your Worships' attending to.

I am this month one whole year older than I was this time twelvemonth; and having got, as you perceive, almost into the middle of my fourth volume——and no farther than to my first day's life——'tis demonstrative that I have three hundred and sixty-four days more life to write just now, than when I first set out; so that instead of advancing, as a common writer, in my work with what I have been doing at it——on the contrary, I am just thrown so many volumes back——was every day of my life to be as busy a day as this——And why not?——and the transactions and opinions of it to take up as much description——And for what reason should they be cut short? as at this rate I should just live 364 times faster than I should write—It must follow, an' please your Worships, that the more I write, the more I shall have to write——and consequently, the more your Worships read, the more your Worships will have to read.

Will this be good for your Worships' eyes?

It will do well for mine; and, was it not that my OPINIONS will be the death of me, I perceive I shall lead a fine life of it out of this selfsame life of mine; or, in other words, shall lead a couple of fine lives together.

As for the proposal of twelve volumes a year, or a volume a month, it no way alters my prospect——write as I will, and rush as I may into the middle of things, as Horace advises,——I shall never overtake myself——whipped and driven to the last pinch, at the worst I shall have one day the start of my pen——and one day is enough for two volumes——and two volumes will be enough for one year.——

Heaven prosper the manufactures of paper under this propitious reign which is now opened to us,——as I trust its providence will prosper everything else in it that is taken in hand.——

As for the propagation of Geese——I give myself no concern——Nature is all bountiful——I shall never want tools to work with.

——So then, friend! you have got my father and my uncle Toby off the stairs, and seen them to bed?——And how did you manage it?——You dropped a curtain at the stairs' foot——I thought you had no other way for it——Here's a crown for your trouble.

CHAPTER XIV

——Then reach me my breeches off the chair, said my father to Susannah——There is not a moment's time to dress you, Sir, cried Susannah——the child is as black in the face as my——As your what? said my father, for like all orators, he was a dear searcher into comparisons—— Bless me, Sir, said Susannah, the child's in a fit——And where's Mr. Yorick——Never where he should be, said Susannah, but his curate's in the dressing room, with the child upon his arm, waiting for the name——and my Mistress bid me run as fast as I could to know, as Captain Shandy is the godfather, whether it should not be called after him.

Were one sure, said my father to himself, scratching his eyebrow, that the child was expiring, one might as well compliment my brother Toby as not——and 'twould be a pity, in such a case, to throw away so great a name as Trismegistus upon him——But he may recover.

No, no,——said my father to Susannah, I'll get up—— There is no time, cried Susannah, the child's as black as my shoe. Trismegistus, said my father——But stay——thou art a leaky vessel, Susannah, added my father; canst thou carry Trismegistus in thy head the length of the gallery without scattering——Can I? cried Susannah, shutting the door in a huff——If she can, I'll be shot, said my father, bouncing out of bed in the dark, and groping for his breeches.

Susannah ran with all speed along the gallery.

My father made all possible speed to find his breeches.

Susannah got the start, and kept it——'Tis *Tris*——something, cried Susannah——There is no Christian name in the world, said the curate, beginning with *Tris*——but Tristram. Then 'tis Tristram-gistus, quoth Susannah.

——There is no *gistus* to it, noodle!——'tis my own name, replied the curate, dipping his hand as he spoke into the basin——Tristram! said he, &c., &c., &c., &c., so Tristram was I called, and Tristram shall I be to the day of my death.

My father followed Susannah with his nightgown across his arm, with nothing more than his breeches on, fastened through haste with but a single button, and that button through haste thrust only half into the buttonhole.

——She has not forgot the name? cried my father, half opening the door——No, no, said the curate, with a tone of intelligence——And the child is better, cried Susannah ——And how does your Mistress? As well, said Susannah, as can be expected——Pish! said my father, the button of his breeches slipping out of the buttonhole——So that whether the interjection was levelled at Susannah, or the button-hole,——whether pish was an interjection of contempt or an interjection of modesty, is a doubt, and must be a doubt till I shall have time to write the three following favorite chapters, that is, my chapter of *chambermaids*——my chapter of *pishes,* and my chapter of *buttonholes.*

All the light I am able to give the reader at present is this, that the moment my father cried Pish! he whisked him-self about——and with his breeches held up by one hand, and his nightgown thrown across the arm of the other, he returned along the gallery to bed, something slower than he came.

CHAPTER XV

I wish I could write a chapter upon sleep.

A fitter occasion could never have presented itself than what this moment offers, when all the curtains of the family are drawn——the candles put out——and no creature's eyes are open but a single one, for the other has been shut these twenty years, of my mother's nurse.

It is a fine subject!

And yet, as fine as it is, I would undertake to write a dozen chapters upon buttonholes, both quicker and with more fame than a single chapter upon this.

Buttonholes!——there is something lively in the very idea of 'em——and trust me, when I get amongst 'em——You gentry with great beards——look as grave as you will——I'll make merry work with my buttonholes——I shall have 'em all to myself——'tis a maiden subject——I shall run foul of no man's wisdom or fine sayings in it.

But for sleep——I know I shall make nothing of it before

I begin——I am no dab at your fine sayings in the first place——and in the next, I cannot for my soul set a grave face upon a bad matter, and tell the world——'tis the refuge of the unfortunate——the enfranchisement of the prisoner ——the downy lap of the hopeless, the weary, and the brokenhearted; nor could I set out with a lie in my mouth, by affirming that of all the soft and delicious functions of our nature, by which the great Author of it, in his bounty, has been pleased to recompense the sufferings wherewith his justice and his good pleasure has wearied us,——that this is the chiefest (I know pleasures worth ten of it), or what a happiness it is to man, when the anxieties and passions of the day are over, and he lays down upon his back, that his soul shall be so seated within him that whichever way she turns her eyes, the heavens shall look calm and sweet above her ——no desire——or fear——or doubt that troubles the air, nor any difficulty past, present, or to come, that the imagination may not pass over without offence, in that sweet secession.

——God's blessing, said Sancho Panza, be upon the man who first invented this selfsame thing called sleep——it covers a man all over like a cloak. Now there is more to me in this, and it speaks warmer to my heart and affections, than all the dissertations squeezed out of the heads of the learned together upon the subject.

——Not that I altogether disapprove of what Montaigne advances upon it——'tis admirable in its way.——(I quote by memory.)

The world enjoys other pleasures, says he, as they do that of sleep, without tasting or feeling it as it slips and passes by ——We should study and ruminate upon it, in order to render proper thanks to him who grants it to us——for this end I cause myself to be disturbed in my sleep, that I may the better and more sensibly relish it——And yet I see few, says he again, who live with less sleep when need requires; my body is capable of a firm, but not of a violent and sudden agitation——I evade of late all violent exercises——I am never weary with walking——but from my youth, I never liked to ride upon pavements. I love to lie hard and alone, and even without my wife——This last word may stagger the faith of the world——but remember, *"La Vraisemblance* [as Baylet says in the affair of Licetus] *n'est pas toujours du Côté la Vérité."* And so much for sleep.

CHAPTER XVI

If my wife will but venture him——brother Toby, Trismegistus shall be dressed and brought down to us, whilst you and I are getting our breakfasts together.——

——Go, tell Susannah, Obadiah, to step here.

She is run upstairs, answered Obadiah, this very instant, sobbing and crying, and wringing her hands as if her heart would break.——

We shall have a rare month of it, said my father, turning his head from Obadiah, and looking wistfully in my uncle Toby's face for some time——we shall have a devilish month of it, brother Toby, said my father, setting his arms akimbo, and shaking his head; fire, water, women, wind—— brother Toby!——'Tis some misfortune, quoth my uncle Toby——That it is, cried my father,——to have so many jarring elements breaking loose, and riding triumph in every corner of a gentleman's house——Little boots it to the peace of a family, brother Toby, that you and I possess ourselves, and sit here silent and unmoved,——whilst such a storm is whistling over our heads.——

——And what's the matter, Susannah? They have called the child Tristram——and my Mistress is just got out of an hysteric fit about it——No!——'tis not my fault, said Susannah——I told him it was Tristram-gistus.

——Make tea for yourself, brother Toby, said my father, taking down his hat——but how different from the sallies and agitations of voice and members which a common reader would imagine!

——For he spake in the sweetest modulation——and took down his hat with the gentlest movement of limbs, that ever affliction harmonized and attuned together.

——Go to the bowling green for Corporal Trim, said my uncle Toby, speaking to Obadiah, as soon as my father left the room.

CHAPTER XVII

When the misfortune of my NOSE fell so heavily upon my father's head,——the reader remembers that he walked instantly upstairs, and cast himself down upon his bed; and from hence, unless he has a great insight into human nature, he will be apt to expect a rotation of the same ascending and descending movements from him upon this misfortune of my NAME;——no.

The different weight, dear Sir,——nay even the different package of two vexations of the same weight,——makes a very wide difference in our manners of bearing and getting through with them.——It is not half an hour ago, when (in the great hurry and precipitation of a poor devil's writing for daily bread) I threw a fair sheet, which I had just finished and carefully wrote out, slap into the fire, instead of the foul one.

Instantly I snatched off my wig, and threw it perpendicularly, with all imaginable violence, up to the top of the room——indeed I caught it as it fell——but there was an end of the matter; nor do I think anything else in Nature would have given such immediate ease: She, dear Goddess, by an instantaneous impulse, in all *provoking cases*, determines us to a sally of this or that member——or else she thrusts us into this or that place, or posture of body, we know not why——But mark, Madam, we live amongst riddles and mysteries——the most obvious things which come in our way have dark sides, which the quickest sight cannot penetrate into; and even the clearest and most exalted understandings amongst us find ourselves puzzled and at a loss in almost every cranny of Nature's works; so that this, like a thousand other things, falls out for us in a way which, though we cannot reason upon it,——yet we find the good of it, may it please your Reverences and your Worships——and that's enough for us.

Now, my father could not lie down with this affliction for his life——nor could he carry it upstairs like the other—— He walked composedly out with it to the fish pond.

Had my father leaned his head upon his hand, and reasoned an hour which way to have gone——reason, with all her force, could not have directed him to anything like it: there is something, Sir, in fish ponds——but what it is, I leave to system builders and fish-pond diggers betwixt 'em to find out——but there is something, under the first disorderly transport of the humours, so unaccountably becalming in an orderly and a sober walk towards one of them, that I have often wondered that neither Pythagoras, nor Plato, nor Solon, nor Lycurgus, nor Mahomet, nor any of your noted lawgivers ever gave order about them.

CHAPTER XVIII

Your Honour, said Trim, shutting the parlour door before he began to speak, has heard, I imagine, of this unlucky accident——O yes, Trim! said my uncle Toby, and it gives me great concern——I am heartily concerned too, but I hope your Honour, replied Trim, will do me the justice to believe that it was not in the least owing to me——To thee ——Trim!——cried my uncle Toby, looking kindly in his face——'twas Susannah's and the curate's folly betwixt them ——What business could they have together, an' please your Honour, in the garden?——In the gallery, thou mean-est, replied my uncle Toby.

Trim found he was upon a wrong scent, and stopped short with a low bow——Two misfortunes, quoth the corporal to himself, are twice as many at least as are needful to be talked over at one time;——the mischief the cow has done in break-ing into the fortifications may be told his Honour hereafter ——Trim's casuistry and address, under the cover of his low bow, prevented all suspicion in my uncle Toby, so he went on with what he had to say to Trim as follows.

————For my own part, Trim, though I can see little or no difference betwixt my nephew's being called Tristram or Trismegistus——yet as the thing sits so near my brother's heart, Trim,——I would freely have given a hundred pounds rather than it should have happened——A hundred pounds, an' please your Honour, replied Trim;——I would not give a cherry stone to boot——Nor would I, Trim, upon my own account, quoth my uncle Toby——but my brother, whom

237

there is no arguing with in this case——maintains that a great deal more depends, Trim, upon Christian names than what ignorant people imagine;——for he says there never was a great or heroic action performed since the world began by one called Tristram——nay, he will have it, Trim, that a man can neither be learned, or wise, or brave——'Tis all a fancy, an' please your Honour——I fought just as well, replied the corporal, when the regiment called me Trim, as when they called me James Butler——And for my own part, said my uncle Toby, though I should blush to boast of myself, Trim,——yet had my name been Alexander, I could have done no more at Namur than my duty——Bless your Honour! cried Trim, advancing three steps as he spoke, does a man think of his Christian name when he goes upon the attack?——Or when he stands in the trench, Trim? cried my uncle Toby, looking firm——Or when he enters a breach? said Trim, pushing in between two chairs——Or forces the lines? cried my uncle, rising up, and pushing his crutch like a pike——Or facing a platoon, cried Trim, presenting his stick like a firelock——Or when he marches up the glacis, cried my uncle Toby, looking warm and setting his foot upon his stool.——

CHAPTER XIX

My father was returned from his walk to the fish pond—— and opened the parlour door in the very height of the attack, just as my uncle Toby was marching up the glacis——Trim recovered his arms——never was my uncle Toby caught riding at such a desperate rate in his life! Alas! my uncle Toby! had not a weightier matter called forth all the ready eloquence of my father——how hadst thou then and thy poor HOBBY-HORSE too have been insulted!

My father hung up his hat with the same air he took it down; and after giving a slight look at the disorder of the room, he took hold of one of the chairs which had formed the corporal's breach, and placing it over against my uncle Toby, he sat down in it, and as soon as the tea things were taken away and the door shut, he broke out in a lamentation as follows.

It is in vain longer, said my father, addressing himself as much to Ernulphus's curse, which was laid upon the corner of the chimney piece,——as to my uncle Toby, who sat under it——it is in vain longer, said my father, in the most querulous monotone imaginable, to struggle as I have done against this most uncomfortable of human persuasions——I see it plainly that either for my own sins, brother Toby, or the sins and follies of the Shandy family, heaven has thought fit to draw forth the heaviest of its artillery against me; and that the prosperity of my child is the point upon which the whole force of it is directed to play——Such a thing would batter the whole universe about our ears, brother Shandy, said my uncle Toby,——if it was so——Unhappy Tristram! child of wrath! child of decrepitude! interruption! mistake! and discontent! What one misfortune or disaster in the book of embryotic evils that could unmechanize thy frame, or entangle thy filaments! which has not fallen upon thy head, ere ever thou camest into the world——what evils in thy passage into it!——What evils since!——produced into being in the decline of thy father's days——when the powers of his imagination and of his body were waxing feeble——when radical heat and radical moisture, the elements which should have tempered thine, were drying up; and nothing left to found thy stamina in but negations——'tis pitiful——brother Toby, at the best, and called out for all the little helps that care and attention on both sides could give it. But how were we defeated! You know the event, brother Toby——'tis too melancholy a one to be repeated now——when the few animal spirits I was worth in the world, and with which memory, fancy, and quick parts should have been conveyed,—— were all dispersed, confused, confounded, scattered, and sent to the devil.——

Here then was the time to have put a stop to this persecution against him;——and tried an experiment at least—— whether calmness and serenity of mind in your sister, with a due attention, brother Toby, to her evacuations and repletions——and the rest of her non-naturals, might not, in a course of nine months' gestation, have set all things to rights. ——My child was bereft of these!——What a teasing life did she lead herself, and consequently her foetus too, with that nonsensical anxiety of hers about lying in in town? I thought my sister submitted with the greatest patience, replied my uncle Toby———I never heard her utter one fretful word about it———She fumed inwardly, cried my father; and that, let me tell you, brother, was ten times worse for the child ———and then! what battles did she fight with me, and what perpetual storms about the midwife———There she gave vent, said my uncle Toby———Vent! cried my father, looking up———

But what was all this, my dear Toby, to the injuries done us by my child's coming head foremost into the world, when all I wished, in this general wreck of his frame, was to have saved this little casket unbroke, unrifled———

With all my precautions, how was my system turned topside-turvy in the womb with my child! his head exposed to the hand of violence, and a pressure of 470 pounds avoirdupois weight acting so perpendicularly upon its apex——— that at this hour 'tis ninety per cent insurance that the fine network of the intellectual web be not rent and torn to a thousand tatters.

———Still we could have done.———Fool, coxcomb, puppy ———give him but a NOSE———Cripple, Dwarf, Driviller, Goose-cap———(shape him as you will) the door of Fortune stands open———O *Licetus! Licetus!* had I been blest with a foetus five inches long and a half, like thee———fate might have done her worst.

Still, brother Toby, there was one cast of the die left for our child after all———O Tristram! Tristram! Tristram!

We will send for Mr. Yorick, said my uncle Toby.

———You may send for whom you will, replied my father.

CHAPTER XX

What a rate have I gone on at, curvetting and frisking it away, two up and two down for four volumes together, without looking once behind, or even on one side of me, to see whom I trod upon!———I'll tread upon no one,———quoth I to myself when I mounted———I'll take a good rattling gallop; but I'll not hurt the poorest jackass upon the road———So off I set———up one lane———down another, through this turnpike ———over that, as if the archjockey of jockeys had got behind me.

Now ride at this rate with what good intention and resolution you may,——'tis a million to one you'll do someone a mischief, if not yourself——He's flung——he's off——he's lost his seat——he's down——he'll break his neck——see!——if he has not galloped full amongst the scaffolding of the undertaking critics!——he'll knock his brains out against some of their posts——he's bounced out!——look——he's now riding like a madcap full tilt through a whole crowd of painters, fiddlers, poets, biographers, physicians, lawyers, logicians, players, schoolmen, churchmen, statesmen, soldiers, casuists, connoisseurs, prelates, popes, and engineers——Don't fear, said I——I'll not hurt the poorest jackass upon the king's highway——But your horse throws dirt; see you've splashed a bishop——I hope in God 'twas only Ernulphus, said I——But you have squirted full in the faces of Mess. Le Moyne, De Romigny, and De Marcilly, doctors of the Sorbonne——That was last year, replied I——But you have trod this moment upon a king.——Kings have bad times on't, said I, to be trod upon by such people as me.

You have done it, replied my accuser.

I deny it, quoth I, and so have got off, and here am I standing with my bridle in one hand, and with my cap in the other, to tell my story——And what is it? You shall hear in the next chapter.

CHAPTER XXI

As Francis the First of France was one winterly night warming himself over the embers of a wood fire, and talking with his first minister of sundry things for the good of the state*——it would not be amiss, said the king, stirring up the embers with his cane, if this good understanding betwixt ourselves and Switzerland was a little strengthened——There is no end, Sire, replied the minister, in giving money to these people——they would swallow up the treasury of France——Poo! poo! answered the king——there are more ways, Mons. *le Premier*, of bribing states, besides that of giving money——I'll pay Switzerland the honour of standing

* Vide Menagiana, vol. 1.

godfather for my next child——Your Majesty, said the minister, in so doing, would have all the grammarians in Europe upon your back;——Switzerland, as a republic, being a female, can in no construction be godfather——She may be godmother, replied Francis, hastily——so announce my intentions by a courier tomorrow morning.

I am astonished, said Francis the First (that day fortnight), speaking to his minister as he entered the closet, that we have had no answer from Switzerland——Sire, I wait upon you this moment, said Mons. *le Premier*, to lay before you my dispatches upon that business.——They take it kindly? said the king——They do, Sire, replied the minister, and have the highest sense of the honour your Majesty has done them—— but the republic, as godmother, claims her right, in this case, of naming the child.

In all reason, quoth the king——she will christen him Francis, or Henry, or Lewis, or some name that she knows will be agreeable to us. Your Majesty is deceived, replied the minister——I have this hour received a dispatch from our resident, with the determination of the republic on that point also——And what name has the republic fixed upon for the dauphin?——Shadrach, Meshach, and Abednego, replied the minister——By St. Peter's girdle, I will have nothing to do with the Swiss, cried Francis the First, pulling up his breeches and walking hastily across the floor.

Your Majesty, replied the minister calmly, cannot bring yourself off.

We'll pay them in money——said the king.

Sire, there are not sixty thousand crowns in the treasury, answered the minister——I'll pawn the best jewel in my crown, quoth Francis the First.

Your Honour stands pawned already in this matter, answered Mons. *le Premier*.

Then, Mons. *le Premier*, said the king, by——we'll go to war with 'em.

CHAPTER XXII

Albeit, gentle reader, I have lusted earnestly, and endeavoured carefully (according to the measure of such slender skill as God has vouchsafed me, and as convenient leisure from other occasions of needful profit and healthful pastime have permitted), that these little books, which I here put into thy hands, might stand instead of many bigger books ——yet have I carried myself towards thee in such fanciful guise of careless disport, that right sore am I ashamed now to entreat thy lenity seriously——in beseeching thee to believe it of me that in the story of my father and his christen names,——I had no thoughts of treading upon Francis the First——nor in the affair of the nose——upon Francis the Ninth——nor in the character of my uncle Toby——of characterizing the militiating spirits of my country——the wound upon his groin is a wound to every comparison of that kind;——nor by Trim,——that I meant the Duke of Ormond——or that my book is wrote against predestination, or free will, or taxes——If 'tis wrote against anything,—— 'tis wrote, an' please your Worships, against the spleen; in order, by a more frequent and a more convulsive elevation and depression of the diaphragm, and the succussations of the intercostal and abdominal muscles in laughter, to drive the *gall* and other *bitter juices* from the gall bladder, liver, and sweetbread of his Majesty's subjects, with all the inimicitious passions which belong to them, down into their duodenums.

CHAPTER XXIII

——But can the thing be undone, Yorick? said my father ——for in my opinion, continued he, it cannot. I am a vile canonist, replied Yorick——but of all evils holding suspense to be the most tormenting, we shall at least know the worst of this matter. I hate these great dinners——said my father ——The size of the dinner is not the point, answered Yorick ——we want, Mr. Shandy, to dive into the bottom of this doubt, whether the name can be changed or not——and as the beards of so many commissaries, officials, advocates, proctors, registers, and of the most able of our school divines, and others, are all to meet in the middle of one table, and Didius has so pressingly invited you,——who in your distress would miss such an occasion? All that is requisite, continued Yorick, is to apprize Didius, and let him manage a

conversation after dinner so as to introduce the subject——
Then my brother Toby, cried my father, clapping his two
hands together, shall go with us.

——Let my old tiewig, quoth my uncle Toby, and my
laced regimentals be hung to the fire all night, Trim.

CHAPTER XXV

——No doubt, Sir——there is a whole chapter wanting here
——and a chasm of ten pages made in the book by it——but
the bookbinder is neither a fool, or a knave, or a puppy——
nor is the book a jot more imperfect (at least upon that
score),——but, on the contrary, the book is more perfect and
complete by wanting the chapter than having it, as I shall
demonstrate to your Reverences in this manner——I question first, by the bye, whether the same experiment might not
be made as successfully upon sundry other chapters——but
there is no end, an' please your Reverences, in trying experiments upon chapters——we have had enough of it——So
there's an end of that matter.

But before I begin my demonstration, let me only tell
you that the chapter which I have torn out, and which otherwise you would all have been reading just now, instead of
this,——was the description of my father's, my uncle Toby's,
Trim's, and Obadiah's setting out and journeying to the visi-
tations at ****.

We'll go in the coach, said my father——Prithee, have the
arms been altered, Obadiah?——It would have made my
story much better to have begun with telling you that at the
time my mother's arms were added to the Shandys', when
the coach was repainted upon my father's marriage, it had so
fallen out that the coach painter, whether by performing all
his works with the left hand, like Turpilius the Roman, or
Hans Holbein of Basel——or whether 'twas more from the
blunder of his head than hand——or whether, lastly, it was
from the sinister turn which everything relating to our family was apt to take——It so fell out, however, to our reproach, that instead of the *bend dexter,* which since Harry
the Eighth's reign was honestly our due——a *bend sinister,*
by some of these fatalities, had been drawn quite across the
field of the Shandy arms. 'Tis scarce credible that the mind of
so wise a man as my father was could be so much incommoded with so small a matter. The word coach——let it be
whose it would——or coachman, or coach horse, or coach
hire, could never be named in the family, but he constantly

complained of carrying this vile mark of Illegitimacy upon the door of his own; he never once was able to step into the coach, or out of it, without turning round to take a view of the arms, and making a vow at the same time that it was the last time he would ever set his foot in it again, till the *bend sinister* was taken out——but like the affair of the hinge, it was one of the many things which the Destinies had set down in their books——ever to be grumbled at (and in wiser families than ours)——but never to be mended.

——Has the *bend sinister* been brushed out, I say? said my father——There has been nothing brushed out, Sir, answered Obadiah, but the lining. We'll go o' horseback, said my father, turning to Yorick——Of all things in the world, except politics, the clergy know the least of heraldry, said Yorick——No matter for that, cried my father——I should be sorry to appear with a blot in my escutcheon before them ——Never mind the *bend sinister*, said my uncle Toby, putting on his tiewig——No, indeed, said my father,——you may go with my aunt Dinah to a visitation with a *bend sinister*, if you think fit——My poor uncle Toby blushed. My father was vexed at himself——No——my dear brother Toby, said my father, changing his tone——but the damp of the coach lining about my loins may give me the Sciatica again, as it did December, January, and February last winter ——so if you please, you shall ride my wife's pad——and as you are to preach, Yorick, you had better make the best of your way before,——and leave me to take care of my brother Toby, and to follow at our own rates.

Now the chapter I was obliged to tear out was the description of this cavalcade, in which Corporal Trim and Obadiah, upon two coach horses abreast, led the way as slow as a patrol——whilst my uncle Toby, in his laced regimentals and tiewig, kept his rank with my father, in deep roads and dissertations alternately upon the advantage of learning and arms, as each could get the start.

——But the painting of this journey, upon reviewing it, appears to be so much above the style and manner of anything else I have been able to paint in this book, that it could not have remained in it without depreciating every other scene; and destroying at the same time that necessary equipoise and balance (whether of good or bad) betwixt chapter and chapter, from whence the just proportions and harmony of the whole work results. For my own part, I am but just set up in the business, so know little about it——but, in my opinion, to write a book is for all the world like humming a song——be but in tune with yourself, Madam, 'tis no matter how high or how low you take it.

——This is the reason, may it please your Reverences, that some of the lowest and flattest compositions pass off very well ——(as Yorick told my uncle Toby one night) by siege—— My uncle Toby looked brisk at the sound of the word *siege*, but could make neither head or tail of it.

I'm to preach at court next Sunday, said Homenas——run over my notes——so I hummed over Dr. Homenas's notes ——the modulation's very well——'twill do, Homenas, if it holds on at this rate——so on I hummed——and a tolerable tune I thought it was; and to this hour, may it please your Reverences, had never found out how low, how flat, how spiritless and jejune it was, but that all of a sudden, up started an air in the middle of it, so fine, so rich, so heavenly ——it carried my soul up with it into the other world; now had I (as Montaigne complained in a parallel accident)—— had I found the declivity easy, or the ascent accessible—— certes I had been outwitted——Your notes, Homenas, I should have said, are good notes,——but it was so perpendicular a precipice——so wholly cut off from the rest of the work, that by the first note I hummed, I found myself flying into the other world, and from thence discovered the vale from whence I came, so deep, so low, and dismal, that I shall never have the heart to descend into it again.

☞A dwarf who brings a standard along with him to measure his own size,——take my word, is a dwarf in more articles than one——And so much for tearing out of chapters.

CHAPTER XXVI

——See if he is not cutting it all into slips, and giving them about him to light their pipes!——'Tis abominable, answered Didius; it should not go unnoticed, said Dr. Kysarcius—— ☞ he was of the Kysarcii of the Low Countries.

Methinks, said Didius, half rising from his chair in order to remove a bottle and a tall decanter, which stood in a direct line betwixt him and Yorick——you might have spared this sarcastic stroke, and have hit upon a more proper place,

Mr. Yorick——or at least upon a more proper occasion to have shown your contempt of what we have been about: If the Sermon is of no better worth than to light pipes with—— 'twas certainly, Sir, not good enough to be preached before so learned a body; and if 'twas good enough to be preached before so learned a body——'twas certainly, Sir, too good to light their pipes with afterwards.

——I have got him fast hung up, quoth Didius to himself, upon one of the two horns of my dilemma—let him get off as he can.

I have undergone such unspeakable torments in bringing forth this sermon, quoth Yorick, upon this occasion,——that I declare, Didius, I would suffer martyrdom——and if it was possible, my horse with me, a thousand times over, before I would sit down and make such another: I was delivered of it at the wrong end of me——it came from my head instead of my heart——and it is for the pain it gave me, both in the writing and preaching of it, that I revenge myself of it in this manner.——To preach, to show the extent of our reading, or the subtleties of our wit——to parade it in the eyes of the vulgar with the beggarly accounts of a little learning, tinseled over with a few words which glitter, but convey little light and less warmth——is a dishonest use of the poor single half hour in a week which is put into our hands—— 'Tis not preaching the gospel——but ourselves——For my own part, continued Yorick, I had rather direct five words point-blank to the heart——

As Yorick pronounced the word *point-blank,* my uncle Toby rose up to say something upon projectiles——when a single word, and no more, uttered from the opposite side of the table, drew everyone's ears towards it——a word, of all others in the dictionary, the last in that place to be expected ——a word I am ashamed to write——yet must be written ——must be read;——illegal——uncanonical——guess ten thousand guesses, multiplied into themselves——rack—— torture your invention forever, you're where you was—— In short, I'll tell it in the next chapter.

CHAPTER XXVII

ZOUNDS! ————————————————

—————————Z——ds! cried Phutatorius, partly to himself
——and yet high enough to be heard——and what seemed
odd, 'twas uttered in a construction of look, and in a tone of
voice, somewhat between that of a man in amazement, and of
one in bodily pain.

One or two who had very nice ears, and could distinguish
the expression and mixture of the two tones as plainly as a
third or a *fifth*, or any other chord in music——were the
most puzzled and perplexed with it——the *concord* was good
in itself——but then 'twas quite out of the key, and no way
applicable to the subject stated;——so that with all their
knowledge, they could not tell what in the world to make of
it.

Others, who knew nothing of musical expression, and
merely lent their ears to the plain import of the *word*, imagined that Phutatorius, who was somewhat of a choleric
spirit, was just going to snatch the cudgels out of Didius's
hands, in order to bemaul Yorick to some purpose——and
that the desperate monosyllable Z——ds was the exordium to
an oration, which, as they judged from the sample, presaged
but a rough kind of handling of him; so that my uncle
Toby's good nature felt a pang for what Yorick was about
to undergo. But seeing Phutatorius stop short, without any
attempt or desire to go on——a third party began to suppose
that it was no more than an involuntary respiration, casually
forming itself into the shape of a twelvepenny oath——
without the sin or substance of one.

Others, and especially one or two who sat next him, looked
upon it, on the contrary, as a real and substantial oath pro-
pensely formed against Yorick, to whom he was known to
bear no good liking——which said oath, as my father phi-
losophized upon it, actually lay fretting and fuming at that
very time in the upper regions of Phutatorius's purtenance;
and so was naturally, and according to the due course of
things, first squeezed out by the sudden influx of blood

which was driven into the right ventricle of Phutatorius's heart by the stroke of surprise which so strange a theory of preaching had excited.

How finely we argue upon mistaken facts!

There was not a soul busied in all these various reasonings upon the monosyllable which Phutatorius uttered——who did not take this for granted, proceeding upon it as from an axiom, namely, that Phutatorius's mind was intent upon the subject of debate which was arising between Didius and Yorick; and indeed as he looked first towards the one, and then towards the other, with the air of a man listening to what was going forwards,——who would not have thought the same? But the truth was that Phutatorius knew not one word or one syllable of what was passing——but his whole thoughts and attention were taken up with a transaction which was going forwards at that very instant within the precincts of his own Galligaskins, and in a part of them where of all others he stood most interested to watch accidents: So that notwithstanding he looked with all the attention in the world, and had gradually screwed up every nerve and muscle in his face to the utmost pitch the instrument would bear, in order, as it was thought, to give a sharp reply to Yorick, who sat over against him——Yet, I say, was Yorick never once in any one domicile of Phutatorius's brain——but the true cause of his exclamation lay at least a yard below.

This I will endeavour to explain to you with all imaginable decency.

You must be informed then, that Gastripheres, who had taken a turn into the kitchen a little before dinner, to see how things went on——observing a wicker basket of fine chesnuts standing upon the dresser, had ordered that a hundred or two of them might be roasted and sent in, as soon as dinner was over——Gastripheres inforcing his orders about them, that Didius, but Phutatorius especially, were particularly fond of 'em.

About two minutes before the time that my uncle Toby interrupted Yorick's harangue——Gastripheres's chesnuts were brought in——and as Phutatorius's fondness for 'em was uppermost in the waiter's head, he laid them directly before Phutatorius, wrapt up hot in a clean damask napkin.

Now whether it was physically impossible, with half a dozen hands all thrust into the napkin at a time——but that some one chesnut, of more life and rotundity than the rest,

260

must be put in motion——it so fell out, however, that one was actually sent rolling off the table; and as Phutatorius sat straddling under——it fell perpendicularly into that particular aperture of Phutatorius's breeches for which, to the shame and indelicacy of our language be it spoke, there is no chaste word throughout all Johnson's dictionary——let it suffice to say——it was that particular aperture which, in all good societies, the laws of decorum do strictly require, like the temple of Janus (in peace at least), to be universally shut up.

The neglect of this punctilio in Phutatorius (which by the bye should be a warning to all mankind) had opened a door to this accident.——

——Accident, I call it, in compliance to a received mode of speaking,——but in no opposition to the opinion either of Acrites or Mythogeras in this matter; I know they were both prepossessed and fully persuaded of it——and are so to this hour, That there was nothing of accident in the whole event——but that the chesnut's taking that particular course, and in a manner of its own accord——and then falling with all its heat directly into that one particular place, and no other——was a real judgment upon Phutatorius, for that filthy and obscene treatise *de Concubinis retinendis,* which Phutatorius had published about twenty years ago——and was that identical week going to give the world a second edition of.

It is not my business to dip my pen in this controversy——much undoubtedly may be wrote on both sides of the question——all that concerns me as an historian is to represent the matter of fact, and render it credible to the reader, that the hiatus in Phutatorius's breeches was sufficiently wide to receive the chesnut;——and that the chesnut, somehow or other, did fall perpendicularly and piping hot into it, without Phutatorius's perceiving it, or anyone else at that time.

The genial warmth which the chesnut imparted was not undelectable for the first twenty or five-and-twenty seconds,——and did no more than gently solicit Phutatorius's attention towards the part:——But the heat gradually increasing, and in a few seconds more getting beyond the point of all sober pleasure, and then advancing with all speed into the regions of pain,——the soul of Phutatorius, together with all his ideas, his thoughts, his attention, his imagination, judgment, resolution, deliberation, ratiocination, memory, fancy, with ten battalions of animal spirits, all tumultuously crowded down, through different defiles and circuits, to the place in danger, leaving all his upper regions, as you may imagine, as empty as my purse.

With the best intelligence which all these messengers could bring him back, Phutatorius was not able to dive into the secret of what was going forwards below, nor could he make any kind of conjecture, what the devil was the matter with it: However, as he knew not what the true cause might turn out, he deemed it most prudent, in the situation he was in at present, to bear it, if possible, like a stoic; which, with the help of some wry faces and compursions of the mouth, he had certainly accomplished, had his imagination continued neuter——but the sallies of the imagination are ungovernable in things of this kind——a thought instantly darted into his mind that though the anguish had the sensation of glowing heat——it might, notwithstanding that, be a bite as well as a burn; and if so, that possibly a *Newt*, or an *Asker*, or some such detested reptile, had crept up, and was fastening his teeth——the horrid idea of which, with a fresh glow of pain arising that instant from the chesnut, seized Phutatorius with a sudden panic, and in the first terrifying disorder of the passion, it threw him, as it has done the best generals upon earth, quite off his guard;—— the effect of which was this, that he leapt incontinently up, uttering as he rose that interjection of surprise so much descanted upon, with the aposiopetic break after it, marked thus, Z——ds——which, though not strictly canonical, was still as little as any man could have said upon the occasion;——and which, by the bye, whether canonical or not, Phutatorius could no more help than he could the cause of it.

Though this has taken up some time in the narrative, it took up little more time in the transaction than just to allow time for Phutatorius to draw forth the chesnut, and throw it down with violence upon the floor——and for Yorick to rise from his chair, and pick the chesnut up.

It is curious to observe the triumph of slight incidents over the mind:——What incredible weight they have in forming and governing our opinions, both of men and things,—— that trifles light as air shall waft a belief into the soul, and plant it so immovably within it,——that Euclid's demonstrations, could they be brought to batter it in breach, should not all have power to overthrow it.

Yorick, I said, picked up the chesnut which Phutatorius's wrath had flung down——the action was trifling——I am ashamed to account for it——he did it for no reason but that he thought the chesnut not a jot worse for the adventure——and that he held a good chesnut worth stooping for.——But this incident, trifling as it was, wrought differently in Phutatorius's head: He considered this act of Yorick's, in getting off his chair, and picking up the chesnut, as a plain acknowledgment in him that the chesnut was originally his,——and in course, that it must have been the owner of the chesnut, and no one else, who could have played him such a prank with it: What greatly confirmed him in this opinion was this, that the table being parallelo-grammical and very narrow, it afforded a fair opportunity for Yorick, who sat directly over against Phutatorius, of slipping the chesnut in——and consequently that he did it. The look of something more than suspicion, which Phutatorius cast full upon Yorick as these thoughts arose, too evidently spoke his opinion——and as Phutatorius was naturally supposed to know more of the matter than any person besides, his opinion at once became the general one; ——and for a reason very different from any which have been yet given——in a little time it was put out of all manner of dispute.

When great or unexpected events fall out upon the stage of this sublunary world——the mind of man, which is an inquisitive kind of a substance, naturally takes a flight, behind the scenes, to see what is the cause and first spring of them——The search was not long in this instance.

It was well known that Yorick had never a good opinion of the treatise which Phutatorius had wrote *de Concubinis retinendis,* as a thing which he feared had done hurt in the world——and 'twas easily found out that there was a mystical meaning in Yorick's prank——and that his chucking the chesnut hot into Phutatorius's ***-***** was a sarcastical fling at his book——the doctrines of which, they said, had inflamed many an honest man in the same place.

This conceit awakened Somnolentius——made Agelastes smile——and if you can recollect the precise look and air of a man's face intent in finding out a riddle——it threw Gastripheres's into that form——and in short was thought by many to be a master stroke of arch-wit.

This, as the reader has seen from one end to the other, was as groundless as the dreams of philosophy: Yorick, no doubt, as Shakespeare said of his ancestor——— *"was a man of jest,"* but it was tempered with something which withheld him from that, and many other ungracious

pranks, of which he as undeservedly bore the blame;——
but it was his misfortune all his life long to bear the im-
putation of saying and doing a thousand things of which
(unless my esteem blinds me) his nature was incapable.
All I blame him for——or rather, all I blame and alternately
like him for, was that singularity of his temper which would
never suffer him to take pains to set a story right with the
world, however in his power. In every ill usage of that
sort, he acted precisely as in the affair of his lean horse
——he could have explained it to his honour, but his
spirit was above it; and besides, he ever looked upon the inventor, the propagator and believer of an illiberal report
alike so injurious to him,——he could not stoop to tell his
story to them——and so trusted to time and truth to do it
for him.

This heroic cast produced him inconveniences in many
respects——in the present, it was followed by the fixed resentment of Phutatorius, who, as Yorick had just made an
end of his chesnut, rose up from his chair a second time, to
let him know it——which indeed he did with a smile; saying
only——that he would endeavour not to forget the obligation.

But you must mark and carefully separate and distinguish
these two things in your mind.

——The smile was for the company.

——The threat was for Yorick.

CHAPTER XXVIII

——Can you tell me, quoth Phutatorius, speaking to Gastripheres, who sat next to him,——for one would not apply to a
surgeon in so foolish an affair,——can you tell me, Gastripheres, what is best to take out the fire?——Ask Eugenius,
said Gastripheres——That greatly depends, said Eugenius,
pretending ignorance of the adventure, upon the nature of the
part——If it is a tender part, and a part which can con-
veniently be wrapt up——It is both the one and the other,
replied Phutatorius, laying his hand as he spoke, with an
emphatical nod of his head, upon the part in question, and
lifting up his right leg at the same time to ease and ventilate

it——If that is the case, said Eugenius, I would advise you, Phutatorius, not to tamper with it by any means; but if you will send to the next printer, and trust your cure to such a simple thing as a soft sheet of paper just come off the press——you need do nothing more than twist it round—— The damp paper, quoth Yorick (who sat next to his friend Eugenius), though I know it has a refreshing coolness in it ——yet I presume is no more than the vehicle——and that the oil and lamp black with which the paper is so strongly impregnated does the business——Right, said Eugenius, and is of any outward application I would venture to recommend the most anodyne and safe.

Was it my case, said Gastripheres, as the main thing is the oil and lamp black, I should spread them thick upon a rag, and clap it on directly. That would make a very devil of it, replied Yorick——And besides, added Eugenius, it would not answer the intention, which is the extreme neatness and elegance of the prescription, which the faculty hold to be half in half——for consider, if the type is a very small one (which it should be), the sanative particles, which come into contact in this form, have the advantage of being spread so infinitely thin and with such a mathematical equality (fresh paragraphs and large capitals excepted) as no art or management of the spatula can come up to. It falls out very luckily, replied Phutatorius, that the second edition of my treatise *de Concubinis retinendis* is at this instant in the press—— You may take any leaf of it, said Eugenius———No matter which——provided, quoth Yorick, there is no bawdry in it——

They are just now, replied Phutatorius, printing off the ninth chapter——which is the last chapter but one in the book——Pray what is the title to that chapter, said Yorick, making a respectful bow to Phutatorius as he spoke———I think, answered Phutatorius, 'tis that *de re concubinaria*.

For heaven's sake keep out of that chapter, quoth Yorick. ——By all means——added Eugenius.

CHAPTER XXIX

——Now, quoth Didius, rising up, and laying his right hand with his fingers spread upon his breast——had such a blunder about a Christian name happened before the Reformation————(It happened the day before yesterday, quoth my uncle Toby to himself) and when baptism was administered in Latin————('Twas all in English, said my uncle)————Many things might have coincided with it, and upon the authority of sundry decreed cases, to have pronounced the baptism null, with a power of giving the child a new name————Had a priest, for instance, which was no uncommon thing, through ignorance of the Latin tongue, baptized a child of Tom o' Stiles *in nomino patriae & filia & spiritum sanctos,*————the baptism was held null————I beg your pardon, replied Kysarcius,————in that case, as the mistake was only in the *terminations,* the baptism was valid———— and to have rendered it null, the blunder of the priest should have fallen upon the first syllable of each noun———— and not, as in your case, upon the last.————

My father delighted in subtleties of this kind, and listened with infinite attention.

Gastripheres, for example, continued Kysarcius, baptizes a child of John Stradling's *in gomine gatris, &c., &c.,* instead of *in nomine patris, &c.*————Is this a baptism? No, ————say the ablest canonists; inasmuch as the radix of each word is hereby torn up, and the sense and meaning of them removed and changed quite to another object; for *gomine* does not signify a name, nor *gatris* a father————What do they signify? said my uncle Toby————Nothing at all———— quoth Yorick————Ergo, such a baptism is null, said Kysarcius————In course, answered Yorick, in a tone two parts jest and one part earnest————

But in the case cited, continued Kysarcius, where *patriae* is put for *patris, filia* for *filii,* and so on————as it is a fault only in the declension, and the roots of the words continue untouched, the inflexions of their branches, either this way or that, does not in any sort hinder the baptism, inasmuch as the same sense continues in the words as before————But then, said Didius, the intention of the priest's pronouncing them grammatically must have been proved to have gone along with it————Right, answered Kysarcius; and of this, brother Didius, we have an instance in a decree of the decretals of Pope Leo the IIId.————But my brother's child, cried my uncle Toby, has nothing to do with the Pope———— 'tis the plain child of a Protestant gentleman, christened Tristram against the wills and wishes both of its father and mother, and all who are akin to it————

If the wills and wishes, said Kysarcius, interrupting my uncle Toby, of those only who stand related to Mr. Shandy's

266

child were to have weight in this matter, Mrs. Shandy, of all people, has the least to do in it——My uncle Toby laid down his pipe, and my father drew his chair still closer to the table to hear the conclusion of so strange an introduction.

It has not only been a question,* Captain Shandy, amongst the best lawyers and civilians in this land, continued Kysarcius, *"Whether the mother be of kin to her child,"*——but after much dispassionate enquiry and jactitation of the arguments on all sides,——it has been adjudged for the negative,—— namely, *"That the mother is not of kin to her child."* † My father instantly clapped his hand upon my uncle Toby's mouth, under colour of whispering in his ear——the truth was, he was alarmed for *Lillabullero*——and having a great desire to hear more of so curious an argument——he begged my uncle Toby, for heaven's sake, not to disappoint him in it——My uncle Toby gave a nod——resumed his pipe, and contenting himself with whistling *Lillabullero* inwardly—— Kysarcius, Didius, and Triptolemus went on with the discourse as follows.

This determination, continued Kysarcius, how contrary soever it may seem to run to the stream of vulgar ideas, yet had reason strongly on its side; and has been put of all manner of dispute from the famous case known commonly by the name of the Duke of Suffolk's case:——It is cited in Brook, said Triptolemus————And taken notice of by Lord Coke, added Didius——And you may find it in Swinburn on Testaments, said Kysarcius.

The case, Mr. Shandy, was this.

In the reign of Edward the Sixth, Charles, Duke of Suffolk, having issue a son by one venter, and a daughter by another venter, made his last will, wherein he devised goods to his son, and died; after whose death the son died also ——but without will, without wife, and without child—— his mother and his sister by the father's side (for she was born of the former venter) then living. The mother took the administration of her son's goods, according to the statute of the 21st of Harry the Eighth, whereby it is enacted, That in case any person die intestate, the administration of his goods shall be committed to the next of kin.

The administration being thus (surreptitiously) granted to the mother, the sister by the father's side commenced a suit before the Ecclesiastical Judge, alleging, 1st, That she her-

* Vid. Swinburn on Testaments, Part 7. §8.
† Vid. Brook Abridg. Tit. Administr. N. 47.

self was next of kin; and 2dly, That the mother was not of kin at all to the party deceased; and therefore prayed the court that the administration granted to the mother might be revoked, and be committed unto her, as next of kin to the deceased, by force of the said statute.

Hereupon, as it was a great cause, and much depending upon its issue——and many causes of great property likely to be decided in times to come by the precedent to be then made——the most learned, as well in the laws of this realm as in the civil law, were consulted together, whether the mother was of kin to her son, or no.——Whereunto not only the temporal lawyers——but the church lawyers——the jurisconsulti——the jurisprudentes——the civilians——the advocates——the commissaries——the judges of the consistory and prerogative courts of Canterbury and York, with the master of the faculties, were all unanimously of opinion, That the mother was not of kin to her child—— *

And what said the Duchess of Suffolk to it? said my uncle Toby.

The unexpectedness of my uncle Toby's question confounded Kysarcius more than the ablest advocate——He stopped a full minute, looking in my uncle Toby's face without replying——and in that single minute Triptolemus put by him, and took the lead as follows.

'Tis a ground and principle in the law, said Triptolemus, that things do not ascend, but descend in it; and I make no doubt 'tis for this cause, that however true it is that the child may be of the blood or seed of its parents——that the parents, nevertheless, are not of the blood and seed of it; inasmuch as the parents are not begot by the child, but the child by the parents——For so they write, *Liberi sunt de sanguine patris & matris, sed pater et mater non sunt de sanguine liberorum.*

——But this, Triptolemus, cried Didius, proves too much——for from this authority cited it would follow, not only what indeed is granted on all sides, that the mother is not of kin to her child——but the father likewise——It is held, said Triptolemus, the better opinion; because the father, the mother, and the child, though they be three persons, yet are they but (*caro una*) † one flesh; and consequently no degree of kindred——or any method of acquiring one *in nature*——There you push the argument again too far,

* Mater non numeratur inter consanguineos. Bald. in ult. C. de Verb. signific.
† Vid. Brook Abridg. Tit. Administr. N. 47.

cried Didius——for there is no prohibition *in nature,* though there is the Levitical law,——but that a man may beget a child upon his grandmother——in which case, supposing the issue a daughter, she would stand in relation both of—— But who ever thought, cried Kysarcius, of laying with his grandmother?——The young gentleman, replied Yorick, whom Selden speaks of——who not only thought of it, but justified his intention to his father by the argument drawn from the law of retaliation——"You laid, Sir, with my mother, said the lad——why may not I lay with yours?"—— 'Tis the *Argumentum commune,* added Yorick.——'Tis as good, replied Eugenius, taking down his hat, as they deserve.

The company broke up——

CHAPTER XXX

——And pray, said my uncle Toby, leaning upon Yorick, as he and my father were helping him leisurely down the stairs ——don't be terrified, Madam, this staircase conversation is not so long as the last——And pray, Yorick, said my uncle Toby, which way is this said affair of Tristram at length settled by these learned men? Very satisfactorily, replied Yorick; no mortal, Sir, has any concern with it——for Mrs. Shandy the mother is nothing at all akin to him——and as the mother's in the surest side——Mr. Shandy, in course, is still less than nothing———In short, he is not as much akin to him, Sir, as I am——

——That may well be, said my father, shaking his head.

——Let the learned say what they will, there must certainly, quoth my uncle Toby, have been some sort of consanguinity betwixt the Duchess of Suffolk and her son——

The vulgar are of the same opinion, quoth Yorick, to this hour.

CHAPTER XXXI

Though my father was hugely tickled with the subtleties of these learned discourses————'twas still but like the anointing of a broken bone————The moment he got home, the weight of his afflictions returned upon him but so much the heavier, as is ever the case when the staff we lean on slips from under us————He became pensive————walked frequently forth to the fish pond————let down one loop of his hat————sighed often————forbore to snap————and, as the hasty sparks of temper, which occasion snapping, so much assist perspiration and digestion, as Hippocrates tells us————he had certainly fallen ill with the extinction of them, had not his thoughts been critically drawn off, and his health rescued, by a fresh train of disquietudes left him with a legacy of a thousand pounds by my aunt Dinah————

My father had scarce read the letter, when taking the thing by the right end, he instantly begun to plague and puzzle his head how to lay it out mostly to the honour of his family————A hundred and fifty odd projects took possession of his brains by turns————he would do this, and that, and t'other————He would go to Rome————he would go to law————he would buy stock————he would buy John Hobson's farm————he would new forefront his house, and add a new wing to make it even————There was a fine water mill on this side, and he would build a windmill on the other side of the river in full view to answer it————But above all things in the world, he would inclose the great Ox-moor, and send out my brother Bobby immediately upon his travels.

But as the sum was *finite*, and consequently could not do everything————and in truth very few of these to any purpose, ————of all the projects which offered themselves upon this occasion, the two last seemed to make the deepest impression; and he would infallibly have determined upon both at once, but for the small inconvenience hinted at above, which absolutely put him under a necessity of deciding in favour either of the one or the other.

This was not altogether so easy to be done; for though 'tis

certain my father had long before set his heart upon this necessary part of my brother's education, and like a prudent man had actually determined to carry it into execution, with the first money that returned from the second creation of actions in the Mississippi scheme, in which he was an adventurer——yet the Ox-moor, which was a fine, large, whinny, undrained, unimproved common, belonging to the Shandy estate, had almost as old a claim upon him: He had long and affectionately set his heart upon turning it likewise to some account.

But having never hitherto been pressed with such a conjuncture of things as made it necessary to settle either the priority or justice of their claims,——like a wise man he had refrained entering into any nice or critical examination about them: So that upon the dismission of every other project at this crisis,———the two old projects, the Ox-moor and my brother, divided him again; and so equal a match were they for each other, as to become the occasion of no small contest in the old gentleman's mind,——which of the two should be set o' going first.

——People may laugh as they will——but the case was this.

It had ever been the custom of the family, and by length of time was almost become a matter of common right, that the eldest son of it should have free ingress, egress, and regress into foreign parts before marriage,——not only for the sake of bettering his own private parts, by the benefit of exercise and change of so much air——but simply for the mere delectation of his fancy, by the feather put into his cap of having been abroad——*tantum valet,* my father would say, *quantum sonat.*

Now as this was a reasonable, and in course a most Christian indulgence——to deprive him of it, without why or wherefore,——and thereby make an example of him, as the first Shandy unwhirled about Europe in a post chaise, and only because he was a heavy lad——would be using him ten times worse than a Turk.

On the other hand, the case of the Ox-moor was full as hard.

Exclusive of the original purchase money, which was eight hundred pounds——it had cost the family eight hundred pounds more in a lawsuit about fifteen years before——besides the Lord knows what trouble and vexation.

It had been moreover in possession of the Shandy family ever since the middle of the last century; and though it lay full in view before the house, bounded on one extremity by the water mill, and on the other by the projected windmill spoken of above,——and for all these reasons seemed to have the fairest title of any part of the estate to the care and protection of the family——yet by an unaccountable fatality, common to men, as well as the ground they tread on, ——it had all along most shamefully been overlooked; and to speak the truth of it, had suffered so much by it, that it would have made any man's heart have bled (Obadiah said), who understood the value of land, to have rode over it and only seen the condition it was in.

However, as neither the purchasing this tract of ground ——nor indeed the placing of it where it lay, were either of them, properly speaking, of my father's doing——he had never thought himself any way concerned in the affair—— till the fifteen years before, when the breaking out of that cursed lawsuit mentioned above (and which had arose about its boundaries)——which being altogether my father's own act and deed, it naturally awakened every other argument in its favour; and upon summing them all up together, he saw not merely in interest, but in honour, he was bound to do something for it——and that now or never was the time.

I think there must certainly have been a mixture of ill luck in it, that the reasons on both sides should happen to be so equally balanced by each other; for though my father weighed them in all humours and conditions——spent many an anxious hour in the most profound and abstracted meditation upon what was best to be done——reading books of farming one day——books of travels another——laying aside all passion whatever——viewing the arguments on both sides in all their lights and circumstances——communing every day with my uncle Toby——arguing with Yorick, and talking over the whole affair of the Ox-moor with Obadiah——yet nothing in all that time appeared so strongly in behalf of the one, which was not either strictly applicable to the other, or at least so far counterbalanced by some consideration of equal weight as to keep the scales even.

For to be sure, with proper helps, and in the hands of some people, though the Ox-moor would undoubtedly have made a different appearance in the world from what it did, or ever would do in the condition it lay——yet every tittle of this was true with regard to my brother Bobby——let Obadiah say what he would.——

In point of interest——the contest, I own, at first sight, did not appear so undecisive betwixt them; for whenever my father took pen and ink in hand, and set about calculating the simple expense of paring and burning, and fencing in the Ox-moor, &c. &c.——with the certain profit it would bring him in return——the latter turned out so prodigiously in his way of working the account, that you would have sworn the Ox-moor would have carried all before it. For it was plain he should reap a hundred lasts of rape, at twenty pounds a last, the very first year——besides an excellent crop of wheat the year following——and the year after that, to speak within bounds, a hundred——but, in all likelihood, a hundred and fifty——if not two hundred quarters of pease and beans ——besides potatoes without end——But then, to think he was all this while breeding up my brother like a hog to eat them——knocked all on the head again, and generally left the old gentleman in such a state of suspense——that, as he often declared to my uncle Toby——he knew no more than his heels what to do.

Nobody but he who has felt it can conceive what a plaguing thing it is to have a man's mind torn asunder by two projects of equal strength, both obstinately pulling in a contrary direction at the same time: For, to say nothing of the havoc which by a certain consequence is unavoidably made by it all over the finer system of the nerves, which you know convey the animal spirits and more subtle juices from the heart to the head, and so on——It is not to be told in what a degree such a wayward kind of friction works upon the more gross and solid parts, wasting the fat and impairing the strength of a man every time as it goes backwards and forwards.

My father had certainly sunk under this evil, as certainly as he had done under that of my CHRISTIAN NAME——had he not been rescued out of it as he was out of that, by a fresh evil——the misfortune of my brother Bobby's death.

What is the life of man! Is it not to shift from side to side?——from sorrow to sorrow?——to button up one cause of vexation!——and unbutton another!

CHAPTER XXXII

From this moment I am to be considered as heir apparent to the Shandy family——and it is from this point properly that the story of my LIFE and my OPINIONS sets out; with all my hurry and precipitation I have but been clearing the ground to raise the building——and such a building do I foresee it will turn out, as never was planned, and as never was executed, since Adam. In less than five minutes I shall have thrown my pen into the fire, and the little drop of thick ink which is left remaining at the bottom of my inkhorn after it ——I have but half a score things to do in the time——I have a thing to name——a thing to lament——a thing to hope——a thing to promise, and a thing to threaten——I have a thing to suppose——a thing to declare——a thing to conceal——a thing to choose, and a thing to pray for.—— This chapter, therefore, I *name* the chapter of THINGS—— and my next chapter to it, that is, the first chapter of my next volume, if I live, shall be my chapter upon WHISKERS, in order to keep up some sort of connection in my works.

The thing I lament is that things have crowded in so thick upon me that I have not been able to get into that part of my work towards which I have all the way looked forwards, with so much earnest desire; and that is the campaigns, but especially the amours, of my uncle Toby, the events of which are of so singular a nature, and so Cervantic a cast, that if I can so manage it as to convey but the same impressions to every other brain which the occurrences themselves excite in my own——I will answer for it the book shall make its way in the world much better than its master has done before it——O Tristram! Tristram! can this but be once brought about——the credit which will attend thee as an author shall counterbalance the many evils which have befallen thee as a man——thou wilt feast upon the one——when thou hast lost all sense and remembrance of the other!——

No wonder I itch so much as I do to get at these amours ——They are the choicest morsel of my whole story! and when I do get at 'em——assure yourselves, good folks—— (nor do I value whose squeamish stomach takes offence at it), I shall not be at all nice in the choice of my words;——and that's the thing I have to *declare*.————I shall never get all through in five minutes, that I fear——and the thing I *hope* is that your Worships and Reverences are not offended—— if you are, depend upon't I'll give you something, my good gentry, next year, to be offended at——that's my dear Jenny's way——but who my Jenny is——and which is the right and which the wrong end of a woman, is the thing to be *concealed*——it shall be told you the next chapter but one to my chapter of buttonholes,——and not one chapter before.

And now that you have just got to the end of these four volumes——the thing I have to *ask* is, how you feel your heads? my own aches dismally——as for your healths, I know they are much better——True Shandeism, think what you will against it, opens the heart and lungs, and like all those affections which partake of its nature, it forces the blood and other vital fluids of the body to run freely through its channels, and makes the wheel of life run long and cheerfully round.

Was I left like Sancho Panza, to choose my kingdom, it should not be maritime——or a kingdom of blacks to make a penny of——no, it should be a kingdom of hearty laughing subjects: And as the bilious and more saturnine passions, by creating disorders in the blood and humours, have as bad an influence, I see, upon the body politic as body natural——and as nothing but a habit of virtue can fully govern those passions, and subject them to reason——I should add to my prayer——that God would give my subjects grace to be as WISE as they were MERRY; and then should I be the happiest monarch, and they the happiest people under heaven——

And so, with this moral for the present, may it please your Worships and your Reverences, I take my leave of you till this time twelvemonth, when (unless this vile cough kills me in the meantime) I'll have another pluck at your beards, and lay open a story to the world you little dream of.

Dixero si quid fortè jocosius, hoc mihi juris Cum venia dabis.——   Hor.

—Si quis calumnietur levius esse quam decet theologum, aut mordacius quam deceat Christianum—non Ego, sed Democritus dixit.—
ERASMUS.

To the Right Honourable

JOHN,

Lord Viscount SPENCER

MY LORD,

I humbly beg leave to offer you these two Volumes; they are the best my talents, with such bad health as I have, could produce:——had providence granted me a larger stock of either, they had been a much more proper present to your Lordship.

I beg your Lordship will forgive me if, at the same time I dedicate this work to you, I join Lady SPENCER, in the liberty I take of inscribing the story of Le Fever in the sixth volume to her name; for which I have no other motive, which my heart has informed me of, but that the story is a humane one.

> *I am,*
> *My Lord,*
> *Your Lordship's*
> *Most Devoted,*
> *And most humble Servant,*
> LAUR. STERNE

VOLUME V

CHAPTER I

If it had not been for those two mettlesome tits, and that madcap of a postillion who drove them from Stilton to Stamford, the thought had never entered my head. He flew like lightning——there was a slope of three miles and a half—— we scarce touched the ground——the motion was most rapid ——most impetuous——'twas communicated to my brain ——my heart partook of it——By the great God of day, said I, looking towards the sun, and thrusting my arm out of the forewindow of the chaise, as I made my vow, "I will lock up my study door the moment I get home, and throw the key of it ninety feet below the surface of the earth, into the draw well at the back of my house."

The London waggon confirmed me in my resolution: it hung tottering upon the hill, scarce progressive, dragged—— dragged up by eight *heavy beasts*——"by main strength!" ——quoth I, nodding——"but your betters draw the same way——and something of everybody's!——O rare!"

Tell me, ye learned, shall we forever be adding so much to the *bulk*——so little to the *stock?*

Shall we forever make new books, as apothecaries make new mixtures, by pouring only out of one vessel into another?

Are we forever to be twisting and untwisting the same rope? forever in the same track——forever at the same pace?

Shall we be destined to the days of eternity, on holy days as well as working days, to be showing the *relics of learning*, as monks do the relics of their saints——without working one——one single miracle with them?

Who made MAN, with powers which dart him from earth to heaven in a moment——that great, that most excellent, and most noble creature of the world——the *miracle* of nature, as Zoroaster in his book περὶ φύσεως called him—— the SHEKINAH of the divine presence, as Chrysostom——the *image* of God, as Moses——the *ray* of divinity, as Plato—— the *marvel* of *marvels,* as Aristotle——to go sneaking on at this pitiful——pimping——pettifogging rate?

I scorn to be as abusive as Horace upon the occasion—— but if there is no catachresis in the wish, and no sin in it, I wish from my soul that every imitator in Great Britain, France, and Ireland had the farcy for his pains; and that there was a good farcical house, large enough to hold——aye ——and sublimate them, *shagrag* and *bobtail,* male and female, all together: and this leads me to the affair of *Whiskers* ——but by what chain of ideas——I leave as a legacy in *mortmain* to Prudes and Tartuffes, to enjoy and make the most of.

Upon Whiskers

I'm sorry I made it——'twas as inconsiderate a promise as ever entered a man's head——A chapter upon whiskers! alas! the world will not bear it——'tis a delicate world——but I knew not of what mettle it was made——nor had I ever seen the underwritten fragment; otherwise, as surely as noses are noses, and whiskers are whiskers still (let the world say what it will to the contrary), so surely would I have steered clear of this dangerous chapter.

The Fragment

* * * * * * * * * *
* * * * * * * * * *

* *——You are half asleep, my good lady, said the old gentleman, taking hold of the old lady's hand and giving it a gentle squeeze, as he pronounced the word *whiskers*——shall we change the subject? By no means, replied the old lady——I like your account of these matters: so throwing a thin gauze handkerchief over her head, and leaning it back upon the chair with her face turned towards him, and advancing her two feet as she reclined herself——I desire, continued she, you will go on.

The old gentleman went on as follows.——Whiskers! cried the Queen of Navarre, dropping her knotting ball, as La Fosseuse uttered the word——Whiskers, Madam, said La Fos-seuse, pinning the ball to the queen's apron, and making a courtesy as she repeated it.

La Fosseuse's voice was naturally soft and low, yet 'twas an articulate voice: and every letter of the word *whiskers* fell distinctly upon the Queen of Navarre's ear——Whiskers! cried the queen, laying a greater stress upon the word, and as if she had still distrusted her ears——Whiskers, replied La Fosseuse, repeating the word a third time——There is not a cavalier, Madam, of his age in Navarre, continued the maid of honour, pressing the page's interest upon the queen, that has so gallant a pair——Of what? cried Margaret, smil-ing——Of whiskers, said La Fosseuse, with infinite modesty.

The word *whiskers* still stood its ground, and continued to be made use of in most of the best companies throughout the little kingdom of Navarre, notwithstanding the indiscreet use which La Fosseuse had made of it: the truth was, La Fosseuse had pronounced the word not only before the queen, but upon sundry other occasions at court, with an accent which always implied something of a mystery——And as the court of Margaret, as all the world knows, was at that time a mixture of gallantry and devotion——and whiskers being as applicable to the one as the other, the word naturally stood its ground——it gained full as much as it lost; that is, the clergy were for it——the laity were against it——and for the women,——*they* were divided.——

The excellency of the figure and mien of the young Sieur De Croix was at that time beginning to draw the attention of the maids of honour towards the terrace before the palace gate, where the guard was mounted. The Lady De Baussiere fell deeply in love with him,——La Battarelle did the same ——it was the finest weather for it that ever was remembered in Navarre——La Guyol, La Maronette, La Sabatiere fell in love with the Sieur De Croix also——La Rebours and La Fos-seuse knew better——De Croix had failed in an attempt to recommend himself to La Rebours; and La Rebours and La Fosseuse were inseparable.

The Queen of Navarre was sitting with her ladies in the painted bow window, facing the gate of the second court, as De Croix passed through it——He is handsome, said the Lady Baussiere.——He has a good mien, said La Battarelle. ——He is finely shaped, said La Guyol.——I never saw an officer of the horse guards in my life, said La Maronette, with two such legs——Or who stood so well upon them, said La Sabatiere——But he has no whiskers, cried La Fosseuse—— Not a pile, said La Rebours.

The queen went directly to her oratory, musing all the way, as she walked through the gallery, upon the subject; turning it this way and that way in her fancy——*Ave Maria* + —— what can La Fosseuse mean? said she, kneeling down upon the cushion.

La Guyol, La Battarelle, La Maronette, La Sabatiere retired instantly to their chambers——Whiskers! said all four of them to themselves, as they bolted their doors on the inside.

The Lady Carnavallette was counting her beads with both hands, unsuspected under her farthingale——from St. Antony down to St. Ursula inclusive, not a saint passed through her fingers without whiskers; St. Francis, St. Dominick, St. Bennet, St. Basil, St. Bridget had all whiskers.

The Lady Baussiere had got into a wilderness of conceits, with moralizing too intricately upon La Fosseuse's text—— She mounted her palfry, her page followed her——the host passed by——the Lady Baussiere rode on.

One denier, cried the order of mercy——one single denier, in behalf of a thousand patient captives, whose eyes look towards heaven and you for their redemption.

——The Lady Baussiere rode on.

Pity the unhappy, said a devout, venerable, hoary-headed man, meekly holding up a box, begirt with iron, in his withered hands——I beg for the unfortunate——good my Lady, 'tis for a prison——for an hospital——'tis for an old man ——a poor man undone by shipwreck, by suretyship, by fire ——I call God and all his angels to witness——'tis to clothe the naked——to feed the hungry——'tis to comfort the sick and the brokenhearted.

——The Lady Baussiere rode on.

A decayed kinsman bowed himself to the ground.

——The Lady Baussiere rode on.

He ran begging bareheaded on one side of her palfry, conjuring her by the former bonds of friendship, alliance, consanguinity, &c.——Cousin, aunt, sister, mother——for virtue's sake, for your own, for mine, for Christ's sake remember me——pity me.

——The Lady Baussiere rode on.

Take hold of my whiskers, said the Lady Baussiere——The page took hold of her palfry. She dismounted at the end of the terrace.

There are some trains of certain ideas which leave prints of themselves about our eyes and eyebrows; and there is a consciousness of it, somewhere about the heart, which serves but to make these etchings the stronger——we see, spell, and put them together without a dictionary.

Ha, ha! he, hee! cried La Guyol and La Sabatiere, looking close at each other's prints——Ho, ho! cried La Battarelle and Maronette, doing the same:——Whist! cried one——st, st,——said a second,——hush, quoth a third——poo, poo, replied a fourth——gramercy! cried the Lady Carnavallette;——'twas she who bewhiskered St. Bridget.

La Fosseuse drew her bodkin from the knot of her hair, and having traced the outline of a small whisker with the blunt end of it, upon one side of her upper lip, put it into La Rebours's hand——La Rebours shook her head.

The Lady Baussiere coughed thrice into the inside of her muff——La Guyol smiled——Fie, said the Lady Baussiere. The Queen of Navarre touched her eye with the tip of her forefinger——as much as to say, I understand you all.

'Twas plain to the whole court the word was ruined: La Fosseuse had given it a wound, and it was not the better for passing through all these defiles——It made a faint stand, however, for a few months; by the expiration of which, the Sieur De Croix, finding it high time to leave Navarre for want of whiskers——the word in course became indecent, and (after a few efforts) absolutely unfit for use.

The best word, in the best language of the best world, must have suffered under such combinations.———The curate of d'Estella wrote a book against them, setting forth the dangers of accessory ideas, and warning the Navarois against them.

Does not all the world know, said the curate d'Estella at the conclusion of his work, that Noses ran the same fate some centuries ago in most parts of Europe which Whiskers have now done in the kingdom of Navarre——The evil indeed spread no further then,——but have not beds and bolsters, and nightcaps and chamber pots, stood upon the brink of destruction ever since? Are not trouse, and placket holes, and pump handles——and spigots and faucets, in danger still, from the same association?——Chastity, by nature the gentlest of all affections——give it but its head——'tis like a ramping and a roaring lion.

The drift of the curate d'Estella's argument was not understood.——They ran the scent the wrong way.——The world bridled his ass at the tail.——And when the *extremes* of DELICACY, and the *beginnings* of CONCUPISCENCE, hold their next provincial chapter together, they may decree that bawdy also.

CHAPTER II

When my father received the letter which brought him the melancholy account of my brother Bobby's death, he was busy calculating the expense of his riding post from Calais to Paris, and so on to Lyons.

'Twas a most inauspicious journey; my father having had every foot of it to travel over again, and his calculation to begin afresh, when he had almost got to the end of it, by Obadiah's opening the door to acquaint him the family was out of yeast——and to ask whether he might not take the great coach horse early in the morning, and ride in search of some.——With all my heart, Obadiah, said my father (pursuing his journey),——take the coach horse, and welcome. ——But he wants a shoe, poor creature! said Obadiah.—— Poor creature! said my uncle Toby, vibrating the note back again, like a string in unison. Then ride the Scotch horse, quoth my father hastily.——He cannot bear a saddle upon his back, quoth Obadiah, for the whole world.——The devil's in that horse; then take PATRIOT, cried my father, and shut the door.——PATRIOT is sold, said Obadiah.——Here's for you! cried my father, making a pause, and looking in my uncle Toby's face, as if the thing had not been a matter of fact.——Your Worship ordered me to sell him last April, said Obadiah.——Then go on foot for your pains, cried my father.——I had much rather walk than ride, said Obadiah, shutting the door.

What plagues! cried my father, going on with his calculation.——But the waters are out, said Obadiah,——opening the door again.

Till that moment, my father, who had a map of Sanson's, and a book of the post roads before him, had kept his hand upon the head of his compasses, with one foot of them fixed upon Nevers, the last stage he had paid for——purposing to go on from that point with his journey and calculation, as soon as Obadiah quitted the room; but this second attack of Obadiah's, in opening the door and laying the whole country under water, was too much.——He let go his compasses—— or rather with a mixed motion betwixt accident and anger, he threw them upon the table; and then there was nothing for him to do but to return back to Calais (like many others), as wise as he had set out.

When the letter was brought into the parlour which contained the news of my brother's death, my father had got forwards again upon his journey to within a stride of the compasses of the very same stage of Nevers.——By your leave, Mons. Sanson, cried my father, striking the point of his compasses through Nevers into the table,——and nodding to my uncle Toby to see what was in the letter,——twice of one night is too much for an English gentleman and his son, Mons. Sanson, to be turned back from so lousy a town as Nevers;——what thinkst thou, Toby, added my father in a sprightly tone.——Unless it be a garrison town, said my uncle Toby,——for then——I shall be a fool, said my father, smiling to himself, as long as I live.——So giving a second nod——and keeping his compasses still upon Nevers with one hand, and holding his book of the post roads in the other——half calculating and half listening, he leaned forwards upon the table with both elbows, as my uncle Toby hummed over the letter.

—— —— —— —— —— —— ——

—— —— —— —— —— —— ——

—— —— —— —— ——he's gone! said my uncle Toby.——Where——Who? cried my father.——My nephew, said my uncle Toby.——What——without leave——without money——without governor? cried my father in amazement. No;——he is dead, my dear brother, quoth my uncle Toby.——Without being ill? cried my father again.——I dare say not, said my uncle Toby, in a low voice, and fetching a deep sigh from the bottom of his heart; he has been ill enough, poor lad! I'll answer for him——for he is dead.

When Agrippina was told of her son's death, Tacitus informs us that not being able to moderate the violence of her passions, she abruptly broke off her work——My father stuck his compasses into Nevers, but so much the faster.——What contrarieties! his, indeed, was matter of calculation——Agrippina's must have been quite a different affair; who else could pretend to reason from history?

How my father went on, in my opinion, deserves a chapter to itself.——

CHAPTER III

———— ———— And a chapter it shall have, and a devil of a one too——so look to yourselves.

'Tis either Plato, or Plutarch, or Seneca, or Xenophon, or Epictetus, or Theophrastus, or Lucian——or someone perhaps of later date——either Cardan, or Budaeus, or Petrarch, or Stella——or possibly it may be some divine or father of the church, St. Austin, or St. Cyprian, or Bernard, who affirms that it is an irresistible and natural passion to weep for the loss of our friends or children——and Seneca (I'm positive) tells us somewhere that such griefs evacuate themselves best by that particular channel.——And accordingly we find that David wept for his son Absalom——Adrian for his Antinoüs——Niobe for her children, and that Apollodorus and Crito both shed tears for Socrates before his death.

My father managed his affliction otherwise; and indeed differently from most men either ancient or modern; for he neither wept it away, as the Hebrews and the Romans——or slept it off, as the Laplanders——or hanged it, as the English, or drowned it, as the Germans——nor did he curse it, or damn it, or excommunicate it, or rhyme it, or *lillabullero* it.——

——He got rid of it, however.

Will your Worships give me leave to squeeze in a story between these two pages?

When Tully was bereft of his dear daughter Tullia, at first he laid it to his heart,——he listened to the voice of Nature, and modulated his own unto it.——O my Tullia! my daughter! my child!——still, still, still,——'twas O my Tullia!——my Tullia! Methinks I see my Tullia, I hear my Tullia, I talk with my Tullia.——But as soon as he began to look into the stores of philosophy, and consider how many excellent things might be said upon the occasion——nobody upon earth can conceive, says the great orator, how happy, how joyful it made me.

My father was as proud of his eloquence as MARCUS TULLIUS CICERO could be for his life, and for aught I am con-

vinced of to the contrary at present, with as much reason: it was indeed his strength——and his weakness too.——His strength——for he was by nature eloquent,——and his weakness—for he was hourly a dupe to it; and provided an occasion in life would but permit him to show his talents, or say either a wise thing, a witty, or a shrewd one——(bating the case of a systematic misfortune)——he had all he wanted.
——A blessing which tied up my father's tongue, and a misfortune which set it loose with a good grace, were pretty equal: sometimes, indeed, the misfortune was the better of the two; for instance, where the pleasure of the harangue was as *ten*, and the pain of the misfortune but as *five*—— my father gained half in half, and consequently was as well again off as it never had befallen him.

This clue will unravel what otherwise would seem very inconsistent in my father's domestic character; and it is this, that in the provocations arising from the neglects and blunders of servants, or other mishaps unavoidable in a family, his anger, or rather the duration of it, eternally ran counter to all conjecture.

My father had a favourite little mare, which he had consigned over to a most beautiful Arabian horse, in order to have a pad out of her for his own riding: he was sanguine in all his projects; so talked about his pad every day with as absolute a security as if it had been reared, broke,——and bridled and saddled at his door ready for mounting. By some neglect or other in Obadiah, it so fell out that my father's expectations were answered with nothing better than a mule, and as ugly a beast of the kind as ever was produced.

My mother and my uncle Toby expected my father would be the death of Obadiah——and that there never would be an end of the disaster.——See here! you rascal, cried my father, pointing to the mule, what you have done!——It was not me, said Obadiah.——How do I know that? replied my father.

Triumph swam in my father's eyes, at the repartee——the Attic salt brought water into them——and so Obadiah heard no more about it.

Now let us go back to my brother's death.

Philosophy has a fine saying for everything.——For *Death* it has an entire set; the misery was, they all at once rushed into my father's head, that 'twas difficult to string them together, so as to make anything of a consistent show out of them.——He took them as they came.

" 'Tis an inevitable chance——the first statute in *Magna*

287

Charta——it is an everlasting act of parliament, my dear brother,——*All must die.*

"If my son could not have died, it had been matter of wonder,——not that he is dead.

"Monarchs and princes dance in the same ring with us.

"——*To die* is the great debt and tribute due unto nature: tombs and monuments, which should perpetuate our memories, pay it themselves; and the proudest pyramid of them all, which wealth and science have erected, has lost its apex, and stands obtruncated in the traveller's horizon." (My father found he got great ease, and went on)——"Kingdoms and provinces, and towns and cities, have they not their periods? and when those principles and powers which at first cemented and put them together have performed their several evolutions, they fall back."——Brother Shandy, said my uncle Toby, laying down his pipe at the word *evolutions* ——Revolutions, I meant, quoth my father,——by heaven! I meant revolutions, brother Toby——evolutions is nonsense. ——'Tis not nonsense——said my uncle Toby.——But is it not nonsense to break the thread of such a discourse, upon such an occasion? cried my father——do not——dear Toby, continued he, taking him by the hand, do not——do not, I beseech thee, interrupt me at this crisis.——My uncle Toby put his pipe into his mouth.

"Where is Troy and Mycenae, and Thebes and Delos, and Persepolis and Agrigentum"——continued my father, taking up his book of post roads, which he had laid down. ——"What is become, brother Toby, of Nineveh and Babylon, of Cyzicus and Mytilene? The fairest towns that ever the sun rose upon are now no more: the names only are left, and those (for many of them are wrong spelt) are falling themselves by piecemeals to decay, and in length of time will be forgotten, and involved with everything in a perpetual night: the world itself, brother Toby, must——must come to an end.

"Returning out of Asia, when I sailed from Aegina towards Megara" (*when can this have been? thought my uncle Toby*), "I began to view the country round about. Aegina was behind me, Megara was before, Piraeus on the right hand, Corinth on the left.——What flourishing towns now prostrate upon the earth! Alas! alas! said I to myself, that man should disturb his soul for the loss of a child, when so much as this lies awfully buried in his presence——Remember, said I to myself again——remember thou art a man."——

Now my uncle Toby knew not that this last paragraph was an extract of Servius Sulpicius's consolatory letter to Tully.

——He had as little skill, honest man, in the fragments, as he had in the whole pieces of antiquity.——And as my father, whilst he was concerned in the Turkey trade, had been three or four different times in the Levant, in one of which he had stayed a whole year and an half at Zante, my uncle Toby naturally concluded that in some one of these periods he had taken a trip across the Archipelago into Asia; and that all this sailing affair with Aegina behind, and Megara before, and Piraeus on the right hand, &c., &c., was nothing more than the true course of my father's voyage and reflections.——'Twas certainly in his *manner,* and many an undertaking critic would have built two stories higher upon worse foundations.——And pray, brother, quoth my uncle Toby, laying the end of his pipe upon my father's hand in a kindly way of interruption——but waiting till he finished the account——what year of our Lord was this?——'Twas no year of our Lord, replied my father.——That's impossible, cried my uncle Toby.——Simpleton! said my father,—— 'twas forty years before Christ was born.

My uncle Toby had but two things for it; either to suppose his brother to be the wandering Jew, or that his misfortunes had disordered his brain.——"May the Lord God of heaven and earth protect him and restore him," said my uncle Toby, praying silently for my father, and with tears in his eyes.

——My father placed the tears to a proper account, and went on with his harangue with great spirit.

"There is not such great odds, brother Toby, betwixt good and evil, as the world imagines"——(this way of setting off, by the bye, was not likely to cure my uncle Toby's suspicions)——"Labour, sorrow, grief, sickness, want, and woe are the sauces of life."——Much good may it do them—— said my uncle Toby to himself.——

"My son is dead!——so much the better;——'tis a shame in such a tempest to have but one anchor.

"But he is gone forever from us!——be it so. He is got from under the hands of his barber before he was bald—— he is but risen from a feast before he was surfeited——from a banquet before he had got drunken.

"The Thracians wept when a child was born"——(and we were very near it, quoth my uncle Toby)——"and feasted and made merry when a man went out of the world; and with reason.——Death opens the gate of fame, and shuts the gate of envy after it;——it unlooses the chain of the captive, and puts the bondsman's task into another man's hands.

"Show me the man, who knows what life is, who dreads it, and I'll show thee a prisoner who dreads his liberty."

Is it not better, my dear brother Toby (for mark——our appetites are but diseases),——is it not better not to hunger at all than to eat?——not to thirst than to take physic to cure it?

Is it not better to be freed from cares and agues, from love and melancholy, and the other hot and cold fits of life, than like a galled traveller, who comes weary to his inn, to be bound to begin his journey afresh?

There is no terror, brother Toby, in its looks, but what it borrows from groans and convulsions——and the blowing of noses, and the wiping away of tears with the bottoms of curtains in a dying man's room.——Strip it of these, what is it——'Tis better in battle than in bed, said my uncle Toby. ——Take away its hearses, its mutes, and its mourning,—— its plumes, scutcheons, and other mechanic aids——What is it?——*Better in battle!* continued my father, smiling, for he has absolutely forgot my brother Bobby——'tis terrible no way——for consider, brother Toby,——when we *are*—— death is *not;*——and when death *is*——we are *not.* My uncle Toby laid down his pipe to consider the proposition; my father's eloquence was too rapid to stay for any man—— away it went,——and hurried my uncle Toby's ideas along with it.——

For this reason, continued my father, 'tis worthy to recollect how little alteration in great men the approaches of death have made.——Vespasian died in a jest upon his close stool——Galba with a sentence——Septimius Severus in a dispatch——Tiberius in dissimulation, and Caesar Augustus in a compliment.——I hope 'twas a sincere one——quoth my uncle Toby.

——'Twas to his wife,——said my father.

CHAPTER IV

——And lastly——for of all the choice anecdotes which history can produce of this matter, continued my father,—— this, like the gilded dome which covers in the fabric,—— crowns all.——

'Tis of Cornelius Gallus, the praetor——which I dare say, brother Toby, you have read.——I dare say I have not, replied my uncle.——He died, said my father, as ********** ——And if it was with his wife, said my uncle Toby—— there could be no hurt in it.——That's more than I know ——replied my father.

CHAPTER V

My mother was going very gingerly in the dark along the passage which led to the parlour, as my uncle Toby pronounced the word *wife*.——'Tis a shrill, penetrating sound of itself, and Obadiah had helped it by leaving the door a little ajar, so that my mother heard enough of it to imagine herself the subject of the conversation: so laying the edge of her finger across her two lips——holding in her breath, and bending her head a little downwards, with a twist of her neck——(not towards the door, but from it, by which means her ear was brought to the chink)——she listened with all her powers:——the listening slave, with the Goddess of Silence at his back, could not have given a finer thought for an intaglio.

In this attitude I am determined to let her stand for five minutes: till I bring up the affairs of the kitchen (as Rapin does those of the church) to the same period.

CHAPTER VI

Though in one sense our family was certainly a simple machine, as it consisted of a few wheels; yet there was thus much to be said for it, that these wheels were set in motion by so many different springs, and acted one upon the other from such a variety of strange principles and impulses,—— that though it was a simple machine, it had all the honour and advantages of a complex one,——and a number of as odd movements within it as ever were beheld in the inside of a Dutch silk mill.

Amongst these there was one I am going to speak of in which, perhaps, it was not altogether so singular as in many others; and it was this, that whatever motion, debate, harangue, dialogue, project, or dissertation was going forwards in the parlour, there was generally another at the same time, and upon the same subject, running parallel along with it in the kitchen.

Now to bring this about, whenever an extraordinary message, or letter, was delivered in the parlour,——or a discourse suspended till a servant went out——or the lines of discontent were observed to hang upon the brows of my father or mother——or, in short, when anything was supposed to be upon the tapis worth knowing or listening to, 'twas the rule to leave the door not absolutely shut, but somewhat ajar—— as it stands just now,——which, under covert of the bad hinge (and that possibly might be one of the many reasons why it was never mended), it was not difficult to manage; by which means, in all these cases, a passage was generally left, not indeed as wide as the Dardanelles, but still wide enough, for all that, to carry on as much of this windward trade as was sufficient to save my father the trouble of governing his house;——my mother at this moment stands profiting by it. ——Obadiah did the same thing, as soon as he had left the letter upon the table which brought the news of my brother's death; so that before my father had well got over his surprise, and entered upon his harangue,——had Trim got upon his legs, to speak his sentiments upon the subject.

A curious observer of nature, had he been worth the inventory of all Job's stock——though, by the bye, *your curious observers are seldom worth a groat*——would have given the half of it to have heard Corporal Trim and my father, two orators so contrasted by nature and education, haranguing over the same bier.

My father a man of deep reading——prompt memory—— with Cato, and Seneca, and Epictetus at his fingers' ends.——

The corporal——with nothing——to remember——of no deeper reading than his muster roll——or greater names at his fingers' end than the contents of it.

The one proceeding from period to period, by metaphor and allusion, and striking the fancy as he went along (as men of wit and fancy do) with the entertainment and pleasantry of his pictures and images.

The other, without wit or antithesis, or point, or turn, this way or that; but leaving the images on one side, and the pictures on the other, going straight forwards as nature could lead him, to the heart. O Trim! would to heaven thou hadst a better historian!——would——thy historian had a better pair of breeches!——O ye critics! will nothing melt you?

CHAPTER VII

——My young Master in London is dead! said Obadiah.——

——A green satin nightgown of my mother's, which had been twice scoured, was the first idea which Obadiah's exclamation brought into Susannah's head.——Well might Locke write a chapter upon the imperfections of words.—— Then, quoth Susannah, we must all go into mourning.—— But note a second time: the word *mourning,* notwithstanding Susannah made use of it herself——failed also of doing its office; it excited not one single idea tinged either with grey or black;——all was green.——The green satin nightgown hung there still.

——O! 'twill be the death of my poor Mistress, cried Susannah.——My mother's whole wardrobe followed.——What a procession! her red damask,——her orange-tawny,——her white and yellow lutestrings,——her brown taffeta,——her bone-laced caps, her bed gowns and comfortable underpetticoats.——Not a rag was left behind.——*"No,——she will never look up again,"* said Susannah.

We had a fat foolish scullion——my father, I think, kept her for her simplicity;——she had been all autumn struggling with a dropsy.——He is dead! said Obadiah,——he is certainly dead!——So am not I, said the foolish scullion.

——Here is sad news, Trim! cried Susannah, wiping her eyes as Trim stepped into the kitchen;——Master Bobby is dead and *buried,*——the funeral was an interpolation of Susannah's,——we shall have all to go into mourning, said Susannah.

I hope not, said Trim.——You hope not! cried Susannah earnestly.——The mourning ran not in Trim's head, whatever it did in Susannah's.——I hope——said Trim, explaining himself, I hope in God the news is not true. I heard the letter read with my own ears, answered Obadiah; and we shall have a terrible piece of work of it in stubbing the Oxmoor.——Oh! he's dead, said Susannah.——As sure, said the scullion, as I am alive.

I lament for him from my heart and my soul, said Trim, fetching a sigh.——Poor creature!——poor boy! poor gentleman!

——He was alive last Whitsuntide, said the coachman. ——Whitsuntide! alas! cried Trim, extending his right arm, and falling instantly into the same attitude in which he read the sermon;——what is Whitsuntide, Jonathan (for that was the coachman's name), or Shrovetide, or any tide or time past, to this? Are we not here now, continued the corporal (striking the end of his stick perpendicularly upon the floor, so as to give an idea of health and stability),——and are we not——(dropping his hat upon the ground) gone! in a moment!——'Twas infinitely striking! Susannah burst into a flood of tears.——We are not stocks and stones.——Jonathan, Obadiah, the cookmaid all melted.——The foolish fat scullion herself, who was scouring a fish kettle upon her knees, was roused with it.——The whole kitchen crowded about the corporal.

Now as I perceive plainly that the preservation of our constitution in church and state,——and possibly the preservation of the whole world——or what is the same thing, the distribution and balance of its property and power, may in time to come depend greatly upon the right understanding of this stroke of the corporal's eloquence——I do demand your attention,——your Worships and Reverences, for any ten pages together, take them where you will in any other part of the work, shall sleep for it at your ease.

I said, "we were not stocks and stones"——'tis very well. I should have added, nor are we angels, I wish we were,—— but men clothed with bodies, and governed by our imaginations;——and what a junketing piece of work of it there is, betwixt these and our seven senses, especially some of them, for my own part, I own it, I am ashamed to confess. Let it suffice to affirm that of all the senses, the eye (for I absolutely deny the touch, though most of your *Barbati,* I know, are for it) has the quickest commerce with the soul,——gives a smarter stroke, and leaves something more inexpressible upon the fancy, than words can either convey——or sometimes get rid of.

——I've gone a little about——no matter, 'tis for health ——let us only carry it back in our mind to the mortality of

Trim's hat.——"Are we not here now,——and gone in a moment?"——There was nothing in the sentence——'twas one of your self-evident truths we have the advantage of hearing every day; and if Trim had not trusted more to his hat than his head——he had made nothing at all of it.

——"Are we not here now,"——continued the corporal, "and are we not"——(dropping his hat plumb upon the ground——and pausing, before he pronounced the word)—— "gone! in a moment?" The descent of the hat was as if a heavy lump of clay had been kneaded into the crown of it. ——Nothing could have expressed the sentiment of mortality, of which it was the type and forerunner, like it;——his hand seemed to vanish from under it,——it fell dead,——the corporal's eye fixed upon it, as upon a corpse,——and Susannah burst into a flood of tears.

Now——Ten thousand, and ten thousand times ten thousand (for matter and motion are infinite) are the ways by which a hat may be dropped upon the ground, without any effect.——Had he flung it, or thrown it, or cast it, or skimmed it, or squirted, or let it slip or fall in any possible direction under heaven,——or in the best direction that could be given to it,——had he dropped it like a goose——like a puppy—— like an ass——or in doing it, or even after he had done, had he looked like a fool,——like a ninny——like a nincompoop ——it had failed, and the effect upon the heart had been lost.

Ye who govern this mighty world and its mighty concerns with the *engines* of eloquence,——who heat it, and cool it, and melt it, and mollify it,——and then harden it again to *your purpose*——

Ye who wind and turn the passions with this great windlass,——and, having done it, lead the owners of them whither ye think meet——

Ye, lastly, who drive——and why not, Ye also who are driven, like turkeys to market, with a stick and a red clout ——meditate——meditate, I beseech you, upon Trim's hat.

CHAPTER VIII

Stay——I have a small account to settle with the reader, before Trim can go on with his harangue.——It shall be done in two minutes.

Amongst many other book debts, all of which I shall discharge in due time,——I own myself a debtor to the world for two items,——a chapter upon *chambermaids and buttonholes,* which, in the former part of my work, I promised and fully intended to pay off this year: but some of your Worships and Reverences telling me that the two subjects, especially so connected together, might endanger the morals of the world,——I pray the chapter upon chambermaids and buttonholes may be forgiven me,——and that they will accept of the last chapter in lieu of it; which is nothing, an't please your reverences, but a chapter of *chambermaids, green gowns, and old hats.*

Trim took his off the ground,——put it upon his head, and then went on with his oration upon death, in manner and form following.

CHAPTER IX

————To us, Jonathan, who know not what want or care is——who live here in the service of two of the best of masters——(bating in my own case his Majesty King William the Third, whom I had the honour to serve both in Ireland and Flanders)——I own it, that from Whitsuntide to within three weeks of Christmas,——'tis not long——'tis like nothing;——but to those, Jonathan, who know what death is, and what havoc and destruction he can make, before a man can well wheel about——'tis like a whole age.——O Jonathan! 'twould make a good-natured man's heart bleed, to consider, continued the corporal (standing perpendicularly), how low many a brave and upright fellow has been laid since that time!——And trust me, Susy, added the corporal, turning to Susannah, whose eyes were swimming in water, ——before that time comes round again,——many a bright eye will be dim.——Susannah placed it to the right side of the page——she wept——but she court'sied too.——Are we not, continued Trim, looking still at Susannah——are we not like a flower of the field——a tear of pride stole in betwixt every two tears of humiliation——else no tongue could have described Susannah's affliction——is not all flesh grass?—— 'Tis clay,——'tis dirt.——They all looked directly at the scullion;——the scullion had just been scouring a fish kettle.——It was not fair.——

——What is the finest face that ever man looked at!——I could hear Trim talk so forever, cried Susannah,——what is it! (Susannah laid her hand upon Trim's shoulder)——but corruption?——Susannah took it off.

——Now I love you for this——and 'tis this delicious mixture within you which makes you dear creatures what you are;——and he who hates you for it——all I can say of the matter is——That he has either a pumpkin for his head——or a pippin for his heart,——and whenever he is dissected 'twill be found so.

CHAPTER X

Whether Susannah, by taking her hand too suddenly from off the corporal's shoulder (by the whisking about of her passions),——broke a little the chain of his reflections——

Or whether the corporal began to be suspicious he had got into the doctor's quarters, and was talking more like the chaplain than himself——

Or whether - - - - - - - - - - - - - - - - - - -

Or whether——for in all such cases a man of invention and parts may with pleasure fill a couple of pages with suppositions——which of all these was the cause, let the curious physiologist, or the curious anybody, determine——'tis certain, at least, the corporal went on thus with his harangue.

For my own part, I declare it, that out of doors, I value not death at all:——not this . . . added the corporal, snapping his fingers,——but with an air which no one but the corporal could have given to the sentiment.——In battle, I value death not this . . . and let him not take me cowardly, like poor Joe Gibbins, in scouring his gun.——What is he? A pull of a trigger——a push of a bayonet an inch this way or that——makes the difference.——Look along the line——to the right——see! Jack's down! well,——'tis worth a regiment of horse to him.——No——'tis Dick. Then Jack's no worse.
——Never mind which,——we pass on,——in hot pursuit the wound itself which brings him is not felt,——the best way is to stand up to him,——the man who flies is in ten

times more danger than the man who marches up into his jaws.——I've looked him, added the corporal, an hundred times in the face,——and know what he is.——He's nothing, Obadiah, at all in the field.——But he's very frightful in a house, quoth Obadiah.——I never mind it myself, said Jonathan, upon a coach box.——It must, in my opinion, be most natural in bed, replied Susannah.——And could I escape him by creeping into the worst calf's skin that ever was made into a knapsack, I would do it there——said Trim——but that is nature.

——Nature is nature, said Jonathan.——And that is the reason, cried Susannah, I so much pity my Mistress.——She will never get the better of it.——Now I pity the Captain the most of anyone in the family, answered Trim.—— Madam will get ease of heart in weeping,——and the Squire in talking about it,——but my poor Master will keep it all in silence to himself.——I shall hear him sigh in his bed for a whole month together, as he did for Lieutenant Le Fever. An' please your Honour, do not sigh so piteously, I would say to him as I laid besides him. I cannot help it, Trim, my Master would say,——'tis so melancholy an accident——I cannot get it off my heart.——Your Honour fears not death yourself.——I hope, Trim, I fear nothing, he would say, but the doing a wrong thing.——Well, he would add, whatever betides, I will take care of Le Fever's boy.——And with that, like a quieting draught, his Honour would fall asleep.

I like to hear Trim's stories about the Captain, said Susannah.——He is a kindly hearted gentleman, said Obadiah, as ever lived.——Aye,——and as brave a one too, said the corporal, as ever stept before a platoon.——There never was a better officer in the king's army,——or a better man in God's world; for he would march up to the mouth of a cannon, though he saw the lighted match at the very touch hole,—— and yet, for all that, he has a heart as soft as a child for other people.——He would not hurt a chicken.——I would sooner, quoth Jonathan, drive such a gentleman for seven pounds a year——than some for eight.——Thank thee, Jonathan! for thy twenty shillings,——as much, Jonathan, said the corporal, shaking him by the hand, as if thou hadst put the money into my own pocket.——I would serve him to the day of my death out of love. He is a friend and a brother to me,——and could I be sure my poor brother Tom was dead,——continued the corporal, taking out his handkerchief,——was I worth ten thousand pounds, I would leave every shilling of it to the Captain.——Trim could not refrain

298

from tears at this testamentary proof he gave of his affection to his master.——The whole kitchen was affected.——Do tell us this story of the poor lieutenant, said Susannah.—— With all my heart, answered the corporal.

Susannah, the cook, Jonathan, Obadiah, and Corporal Trim formed a circle about the fire; and as soon as the scullion had shut the kitchen door,——the corporal begun.

CHAPTER XI

I am a Turk if I had not as much forgot my mother as if Nature had plastered me up, and set me down naked upon the banks of the river Nile, without one.——Your most obedient servant, Madam——I've cost you a great deal of trouble;——I wish it may answer;——but you have left a crack in my back,——and here's a great piece fallen off here before,——and what must I do with this foot?——I shall never reach England with it.

For my own part I never wonder at anything;——and so often has my judgment deceived me in my life, that I always suspect it, right or wrong;——at least I am seldom hot upon cold subjects. For all this, I reverence truth as much as anybody; and when it has slipped us, if a man will but take me by the hand, and go quietly and search for it, as for a thing we have both lost, and can neither of us do well without, ——I'll go to the world's end with him:——But I hate disputes,——and therefore (bating religious points, or such as touch society) I would almost subscribe to anything which does not choke me in the first passage, rather than be drawn into one——But I cannot bear suffocation,——and bad smells worst of all.——For which reasons, I resolved from the beginning, That if ever the army of martyrs was to be augmented,——or a new one raised,——I would have no hand in it, one way or t'other.

CHAPTER XII

————But to return to my mother.

My uncle Toby's opinion, Madam, "that there could be no harm in Cornelius Gallus the Roman praetor's lying with his wife;"————or rather the last word of that opinion————(for it was all my mother heard of it), caught hold of her by the weak part of the whole sex:————You shall not mistake me, ————I mean her curiosity;————she instantly concluded herself the subject of the conversation, and with that prepossession upon her fancy, you will readily conceive every word my father said was accommodated either to herself, or her family concerns.

————Pray, Madam, in what street does the lady live who would not have done the same?

From the strange mode of Cornelius's death, my father had made a transition to that of Socrates, and was giving my uncle Toby an abstract of his pleading before his judges; ————'twas irresistible:————not the oration of Socrates,————but my father's temptation to it.————He had wrote the Life of Socrates * himself the year before he left off trade, which, I fear, was the means of hastening him out of it;————so that no one was able to set out with so full a sail, and in so swelling a tide of heroic loftiness upon the occasion, as my father was. Not a period in Socrates's oration which closed with a shorter word than *transmigration,* or *annihilation,* ————or a worse thought in the middle of it than *to be*———— *or not to be;*————the entering upon a new and untried state of things;————or upon a long, a profound and peaceful sleep, without dreams, without disturbance;————*That we and our children were born to die,————but neither of us born to be slaves.*————No————there I mistake; that was part of Eleazer's oration, as recorded by Josephus (*de Bell. Judaic.*)————Eleazer owns he had it from the philosophers of India; in all likelihood Alexander the Great, in his irruption into India,

---

* This book my father would never consent to publish; 'tis in manuscript, with some other tracts of his, in the family, all or most of which will be printed in due time.

after he had overrun Persia, amongst the many things he stole,——stole that sentiment also; by which means it was carried, if not all the way by himself (for we all know he died at Babylon), at least by some of his marauders, into Greece,——from Greece it got to Rome,——from Rome to France,——and from France to England:——So things come round.——

By land carriage I can conceive no other way.——

By water the sentiment might easily have come down the Ganges into the Sinus Gangeticus, or Bay of Bengal, and so into the Indian Sea; and following the course of trade (the way from India by the Cape of Good Hope being then unknown), might be carried with other drugs and spices up the Red Sea to Joddah, the port of Mecca, or else to Tor or Suez, towns at the bottom of the gulf; and from thence by caravans to Coptos, but three days' journey distant, so down the Nile directly to Alexandria, where the SENTIMENT would be landed at the very foot of the great staircase of the Alexandrian library,——and from that storehouse it would be fetched.————Bless me! what a trade was driven by the learned in those days!

CHAPTER XIII

——Now my father had a way, a little like that of Job's (in case there ever was such a man——if not, there's an end of the matter.——

Though, by the bye, because your learned men find some difficulty in fixing the precise era in which so great a man lived;——whether, for instance, before or after the patriarchs, &c.——to vote, therefore, that he never lived *at all* is a little cruel,——'tis not doing as they would be done by—— happen that as it may)——My father, I say, had a way, when things went extremely wrong with him, especially upon the first sally of his impatience,——of wondering why he was begot,——wishing himself dead;——sometimes worse:—— And when the provocation ran high, and grief touched his lips with more than ordinary powers,——Sir, you scarce could have distinguished him from Socrates himself.—— Every word would breathe the sentiments of a soul disdain-

301

ing life, and careless about all its issues; for which reason, though my mother was a woman of no deep reading, yet the abstract of Socrates's oration, which my father was giving my uncle Toby, was not altogether new to her.——She listened to it with composed intelligence, and would have done so to the end of the chapter, had not my father plunged (which he had no occasion to have done) into that part of the pleading where the great philosopher reckons up his connections, his alliances and children, but renounces a security to be so won by working upon the passions of his judges.——"I have friends——I have relations,——I have three desolate children,"——says Socrates.——

——Then, cried my mother, opening the door,——you have one more, Mr. Shandy, than I know of.

By heaven! I have one less,——said my father, getting up and walking out of the room.

CHAPTER XIV

——They are Socrates's children, said my uncle Toby. He has been dead a hundred years ago, replied my mother.

My uncle Toby was no chronologer——so not caring to advance a step but upon safe ground, he laid down his pipe deliberately upon the table, and rising up, and taking my mother most kindly by the hand, without saying another word, either good or bad, to her, he led her out after my father, that he might finish the eclaircissement himself.

CHAPTER XV

Had this volume been a farce, which, unless everyone's life and opinions are to be looked upon as a farce as well as mine, I see no reason to suppose—the last chapter, Sir, had finished the first act of it, and then this chapter must have set off thus.

Ptr..r..r..ing——twing——twang——prut——trut——
'tis a cursed bad fiddle.——Do you know whether my fiddle's in tune or no?——trut..prut..——They should be
fifths.——'Tis wickedly strung——tr...a.e.i.o.u.-twang.——
The bridge is a mile too high, and the sound post absolutely
down,——else——trut . . prut——hark! 'tis not so bad a
tone.——Diddle diddle, diddle diddle, diddle diddle, dum,
There is nothing in playing before good judges,——but
there's a man there——no——not him with the bundle under
his arm——the grave man in black.——'Sdeath! not the gentleman with the sword on.——Sir, I had rather play a Ca-
priccio to Calliope herself than draw my bow across my fiddle before that very man; and yet, I'll stake my Cremona to
a Jew's trump, which is the greatest musical odds that every
were laid, that I will this moment stop three hundred and
fifty leagues out of tune upon my fiddle, without punishing
one single nerve that belongs to him.——Twaddle diddle,
tweddle diddle,——twiddle diddle,——twoddle diddle,——
twuddle diddle,——prut-trut——krish——krash——krush.
——I've undone you, Sir,——but you see he is no worse,
——and was Apollo to take his fiddle after me, he can make
him no better.

Diddle diddle, diddle diddle, diddle diddle——hum——
dum——drum.

——Your Worships and your Reverences love music——
and God has made you all with good ears——and some of
you play delightfully yourselves——trut-prut,——prut-trut.

O! there is——whom I could sit and hear whole days,——
whose talents lie in making what he fiddles to be felt,——
who inspires me with his joys and hopes, and puts the most
hidden springs of my heart into motion.——If you would
borrow five guineas of me, Sir,——which is generally ten
guineas more than I have to spare——or you, Messrs. Apothecary and Tailor, want your bills paying,——that's your time.

CHAPTER XVI

The first thing which entered my father's head, after affairs
were a little settled in the family, and Susannah had got possession of my mother's green satin nightgown,——was to sit

down coolly, after the example of Xenophon, and write a TRISTRA-*paedia*, or system of education for me; collecting first for that purpose his own scattered thoughts, counsels, and notions; and binding them together, so as to form an INSTITUTE for the government of my childhood and adolescence. I was my father's last stake——he had lost my brother Bobby entirely,——he had lost, by his own computation, full three fourths of me——that is, he had been unfortunate in his three first great casts for me——my geniture, nose, and name,——there was but this one left; and accordingly my father gave himself up to it with as much devotion as ever my uncle Toby had done to his doctrine of projectiles. ——The difference between them was that my uncle Toby drew his whole knowledge of projectiles from Nicholas Tartaglia——My father spun his, every thread of it, out of his own brain,——or reeled and cross-twisted what all other spinners and spinsters had spun before him, that 'twas pretty near the same torture to him.

In about three years, or something more, my father had got advanced almost into the middle of his work.——Like all other writers, he met with disappointments.——He imagined he should be able to bring whatever he had to say into so small a compass that when it was finished and bound, it might be rolled up in my mother's hussif.——Matter grows under our hands.——Let no man say,——"Come—— I'll write a *duodecimo.*"

My father gave himself up to it, however, with the most painful diligence, proceeding step by step in every line with the same kind of caution and circumspection (though I cannot say upon quite so religious a principle) as was used by John de la Casse, the Lord Archbishop of Benevento, in compassing his *Galateo;* in which his Grace of Benevento spent near forty years of his life; and when the thing came out, it was not of above half the size or the thickness of a Rider's Almanac.——How the holy man managed the affair, unless he spent the greatest part of his time in combing his whiskers, or playing at *primero* with his chaplain,——would pose any mortal not let into the true secret;——and therefore 'tis worth explaining to the world, was it only for the encouragement of those few in it who write not so much to be fed—— as to be famous.

I own had John de la Casse, the Archbishop of Benevento, for whose memory (notwithstanding his *Galateo*) I retain the highest veneration,——had he been, Sir, a slender clerk ——of dull wit——slow parts——costive head, and so forth,

———he and his *Galateo* might have jogged on together to the age of Methuselah for me;———the phenomenon had not been worth a parenthesis.———

But the reverse of this was the truth: John de la Casse was a genius of fine parts and fertile fancy; and yet with all these great advantages of nature, which should have pricked him forwards with his *Galateo,* he lay under an impuissance at the same time of advancing above a line and an half in the compass of a whole summer's day: this disability in his Grace arose from an opinion he was afflicted with,———which opinion was this,———*viz.,* that whenever a Christian was writing a book (not for his private amusement, but) where his intent and purpose was *bona fide,* to print and publish it to the world, his first thoughts were always the temptations of the evil one.———This was the state of ordinary writers: but when a personage of venerable character and high station, either in church or state, once turned author,———he maintained that from the very moment he took pen in hand———all the devils in hell broke out of their holes to cajole him.——— 'Twas Termtime with them;———every thought, first and last, was captious;———how specious and good soever,———'twas all one;———in whatever form or colour it presented itself to the imagination,———'twas still a stroke of one or other of 'em levelled at him, and was to be fenced off.———So that the life of a writer, whatever he might fancy to the contrary, was not so much a state of *composition,* as a state of *warfare;* and his probation in it, precisely that of any other man militant upon earth,———both depending alike not half so much upon the degrees of his WIT———as his RESISTANCE.

My father was hugely pleased with this theory of John de la Casse, Archbishop of Benevento; and (had it not cramped him a little in his creed) I believe would have given ten of the best acres in the Shandy estate to have been the broacher of it.———How far my father actually believed in the devil will be seen when I come to speak of my father's religious notions, in the progress of this work: 'tis enough to say here, as he could not have the honour of it, in the literal sense of the doctrine———he took up with the allegory of it;———and would often say, especially when his pen was a little retrograde, there was as much good meaning, truth, and knowledge couched under the veil of John de la Casse's parabolical representation,———as was to be found in any one poetic fiction or mystic record of antiquity.———Prejudice of education, he would say, *is the devil,*———and the multitudes of them which we suck in with our mother's milk———*are the devil and all.*——We are haunted with them, brother Toby, in all our lucubrations and researches; and was a man fool enough to submit tamely to what they obtruded upon him, ——what would his book be? Nothing,——he would add, throwing his pen away with a vengeance,——nothing but a farrago of the clack of nurses, and of the nonsense of the old women (of both sexes) throughout the kingdom.

This is the best account I am determined to give of the slow progress my father made in his *Tristrapaedia;* at which (as I said) he was three years and something more indefatigably at work, and at last, had scarce completed, by his own reckoning, one half of his undertaking: the misfortune was that I was all that time totally neglected and abandoned to my mother; and what was almost as bad, by the very delay, the first part of the work, upon which my father had spent the most of his pains, was rendered entirely useless;—— every day a page or two became of no consequence.——

——Certainly it was ordained as a scourge upon the pride of human wisdom, That the wisest of us all should thus outwit ourselves, and eternally forgo our purposes in the intemperate act of pursuing them.

In short, my father was so long in all his acts of resistance,——or in other words,——he advanced so very slow with his work, and I began to live and get forwards at such a rate, that if an event had not happened,——which, when we get to it, if it can be told with decency, shall not be concealed a moment from the reader——I verily believe I had put by my father, and left him drawing a sundial, for no better purpose than to be buried underground.

CHAPTER XVII

——'Twas nothing,——I did not lose two drops of blood by it——'twas not worth calling in a surgeon, had he lived next door to us——thousands suffer by choice what I did by accident.——Dr. Slop made ten times more of it than there was occasion:——some men rise by the art of hanging great weights upon small wires,——and I am this day (August the 10th, 1761) paying part of the price of this man's reputation. ——O 'twould provoke a stone, to see how things are carried

on in this world!——The chambermaid had left no *******
*** under the bed:——Cannot you contrive, Master, quoth
Susannah, lifting up the sash with one hand, as she spoke,
and helping me up into the window seat with the other,——
cannot you manage, my dear, for a single time to **** ***
** *** *******?

I was five years old.——Susannah did not consider that
nothing was well hung in our family,——so slap came the
sash down like lightning upon us;——Nothing is left,——
cried Susannah,——nothing is left——for me, but to run my
country.——

My uncle Toby's house was a much kinder sanctuary; and
so Susannah fled to it.

CHAPTER XVIII

When Susannah told the corporal the misadventure of the
sash, with all the circumstances which attended the *murder*
of me——(as she called it),——the blood forsook his cheeks;
——all accessories in murder being principals,——Trim's
conscience told him he was as much to blame as Susannah,
——and if the doctrine had been true, my uncle Toby had as
much of the bloodshed to answer for to heaven as either of
'em;——so that neither reason or instinct, separate or together, could possibly have guided Susannah's steps to so proper
an asylum. It is in vain to leave this to the reader's imagination:——to form any kind of hypothesis that will render
these propositions feasible, he must cudgel his brains sore,
——and to do it without,——he must have such brains as no
reader ever had before him.——Why should I put them either
to trial or to torture? 'Tis my own affair: I'll explain it myself.

CHAPTER XIX

'Tis a pity, Trim, said my uncle Toby, resting with his hand
upon the corporal's shoulder, as they both stood surveying
their works,——that we have not a couple of fieldpieces to

mount in the gorge of that new redoubt;——'twould secure the lines all along there, and make the attack on that side quite complete:——get me a couple cast, Trim.

Your Honour shall have them, replied Trim, before tomorrow morning.

It was the joy of Trim's heart,——nor was his fertile head ever at a loss for expedients in doing it, to supply my uncle Toby in his campaigns with whatever his fancy called for; had it been his last crown, he would have sate down and hammered it into a paterero to have prevented a single wish in his master. The corporal had already,——what with cutting off the ends of my uncle Toby's spouts,——hacking and chiseling up the sides of his leaden gutters,——melting down his pewter shaving basin,——and going at last, like Lewis the Fourteenth, on to the top of the church for spare ends, &c.——he had that very campaign brought no less than eight new battering cannons, besides three demiculverins, into the field; my uncle Toby's demand for two more pieces for the redoubt had set the corporal at work again; and no better resource offering, he had taken the two leaden weights from the nursery window: and as the sash pulleys, when the lead was gone, were of no kind of use, he had taken them away also, to make a couple of wheels for one of their carriages.

He had dismantled every sash window in my uncle Toby's house long before, in the very same way,——though not always in the same order; for sometimes the pulleys had been wanted, and not the lead,——so then he began with the pulleys,——and the pulleys being picked out, then the lead became useless,——and so the lead went to pot too.

——A great MORAL might be picked handsomely out of this, but I have not time——'tis enough to say, wherever the demolition began, 'twas equally fatal to the sash window.

CHAPTER XX

The corporal had not taken his measures so badly in this stroke of artilleryship, but that he might have kept the matter entirely to himself, and left Susannah to have sustained the whole weight of the attack as she could;——true courage is not content with coming off so.——The corporal, whether as general or comptroller of the train,——'twas no matter,——had done that without which, as he imagined, the misfortune could never have happened,——*at least in Susannah's hands;*——How would your Honours have behaved?——He determined at once not to take shelter behind Susannah,——but to give it; and with this resolution upon his mind, he marched upright into the parlour, to lay the whole manoeuvre before my uncle Toby.

My uncle Toby had just then been giving Yorick an account of the battle of Steenkerke, and of the strange conduct of Count Solmes in ordering the foot to halt, and the horse to march where it could not act; which was directly contrary to the king's commands, and proved the loss of the day.

There are incidents in some families so pat to the purpose of what is going to follow,——they are scarce exceeded by the invention of a dramatic writer;——I mean of ancient days.——

Trim, by the help of his forefinger, laid flat upon the table, and the edge of his hand striking across it at right angles, made a shift to tell his story so, that priests and virgins might have listened to it;——and the story being told,——the dialogue went on as follows.

CHAPTER XXI

——I would be pickueted to death, cried the corporal, as he concluded Susannah's story, before I would suffer the woman to come to any harm;——'twas my fault, an' please your Honour,——not hers.

Corporal Trim, replied my uncle Toby, putting on his hat which lay upon the table,——if anything can be said to be a fault, when the service absolutely requires it should be done,——'tis I certainly who deserve the blame;——you obeyed your orders.

Had Count Solmes, Trim, done the same at the battle of Steenkerke, said Yorick, drolling a little upon the corporal, who had been run over by a dragoon in the retreat,——he had saved thee;——Saved! cried Trim, interrupting Yorick, and finishing the sentence for him after his own fashion;——

he had saved five battalions, an' please your Reverence, every soul of them:——there was Cutts's——continued the corporal, clapping the forefinger of his right hand upon the thumb of his left, and counting round his hand,——there was Cutts's,——Mackay's,——Angus's,——Graham's,—— and Leven's, all cut to pieces;——and so had the English life guards too, had it not been for some regiments upon the right, who marched up boldly to their relief, and received the enemy's fire in their faces, before any one of their own platoons discharged a musket;——they'll go to heaven for it, ——added Trim.——Trim is right, said my uncle Toby, nodding to Yorick,——he's perfectly right. What signified his marching the horse, continued the corporal, where the ground was so strait, and the French had such a nation of hedges, and copses, and ditches, and felled trees laid this way and that to cover them (as they always have.);——Count Solmes should have sent us;——we would have fired muzzle to muzzle with them for their lives.——There was nothing to be done for the horse:——he had his foot shot off however for his pains, continued the corporal, the very next campaign at Landen.——Poor Trim got his wound there, quoth my uncle Toby.——'Twas owing, an' please your Honour, entirely to Count Solmes;——had we drubbed them soundly at Steenkerke, they would not have fought us at Landen.——Possibly not,——Trim, said my uncle Toby;——though if they have the advantage of a wood, or you give them a moment's time to intrench themselves, they are a nation which will pop and pop forever at you.——There is no way but to march coolly up to them,——receive their fire, and fall in upon them, pell-mell——Ding-dong, added Trim.——Horse and foot, said my uncle Toby.——Helter-skelter, said Trim. ——Right and left, cried my uncle Toby.——Blood an' 'ounds, shouted the corporal;——the battle raged,——Yorick drew his chair a little to one side for safety, and after a moment's pause, my uncle Toby, sinking his voice a note,—— resumed the discourse as follows.

CHAPTER XXII

King William, said my uncle Toby, addressing himself to Yorick, was so terribly provoked at Count Solmes for disobeying his orders that he would not suffer him to come into his presence for many months after.——I fear, answered Yorick, the squire will be as much provoked at the corporal, as the king at the count.——But 'twould be singularly hard in this case, continued he, if Corporal Trim, who has behaved so diametrically opposite to Count Solmes, should have the fate to be rewarded with the same disgrace;——too oft in this world do things take that train.——I would spring a mine, cried my uncle Toby, rising up,——and blow up my fortifications, and my house with them, and we would perish under their ruins, ere I would stand by and see it.——Trim directed a slight——but a grateful bow towards his master, ——and so the chapter ends.

CHAPTER XXIII

——Then, Yorick, replied my uncle Toby, you and I will lead the way abreast,——and do you, corporal, follow a few paces behind us.——And Susannah, an' please your Honour, said Trim, shall be put in the rear.——'Twas an excellent disposition,——and in this order, without either drums beating, or colours flying, they marched slowly from my uncle Toby's house to Shandy Hall.

——I wish, said Trim, as they entered the door,——instead of the sash weights, I had cut off the church spout, as I once thought to have done.——You have cut off spouts enow, replied Yorick.——

CHAPTER XXIV

As many pictures as have been given of my father, how like him soever in different airs and attitudes,——not one, or all of them, can ever help the reader to any kind of preconception of how my father would think, speak, or act, upon any untried occasion or occurrence of life.——There was that infinitude of oddities in him, and of chances along with it, by which handle he would take a thing;——it baffled, Sir, all calculations.——The truth was, his road lay so very far on one side from that wherein most men travelled,——that every object before him presented a face and section of itself to his eye altogether different from the plan and elevation of it seen by the rest of mankind.——In other words, 'twas a different object,——and in course was differently considered:

This is the true reason that my dear Jenny and I, as well as all the world besides us, have such eternal squabbles about nothing.——She looks at her outside,——I, at her in——. How is it possible we should agree about her value?

CHAPTER XXV

'Tis a point settled,——and I mention it for the comfort of Confucius,* who is apt to get entangled in telling a plain story——that provided he keeps along the line of his story, ——he may go backwards and forwards as he will,——'tis still held to be no digression.

This being premised, I take the benefit of the *act of going backwards* myself.

CHAPTER XXVI

Fifty thousand pannier loads of devils——(not of the Archbishop of Benevento's,——I mean of Rabelais's devils), with their tails chopped off by their rumps, could not have made so diabolical a scream of it as I did——when the accident befell me: it summoned up my mother instantly into the nursery,——so that Susannah had but just time to make her escape down the back stairs, as my mother came up the fore.

Now, though I was old enough to have told the story my-

* Mr. Shandy is supposed to mean ***** ***, Esq; member for ******,——and not the Chinese legislator.

self,——and young enough, I hope, to have done it without malignity; yet Susannah, in passing by the kitchen, for fear of accidents, had left it in shorthand with the cook——the cook had told it with a commentary to Jonathan, and Jonathan to Obadiah; so that by the time my father had rung the bell half a dozen times, to know what was the matter above,——was Obadiah enabled to give him a particular account of it, just as it had happened.——I thought as much, said my father, tucking up his nightgown;——and so walked upstairs.

One would imagine from this——(though for my own part I somewhat question it)——that my father, before that time, had actually wrote that remarkable chapter in the *Tristrapaedia* which to me is the most original and entertaining one in the whole book;——and that is the *chapter upon sash windows,* with a bitter philippic at the end of it upon the forgetfulness of chambermaids.——I have but two reasons for thinking otherwise.

First, Had the matter been taken into consideration before the event happened, my father certainly would have nailed up the sash window for good an' all;——which, considering with what difficulty he composed books,——he might have done with ten times less trouble than he could have wrote the chapter: this argument I foresee holds good against his writing the chapter even after the event; but 'tis obviated under the second reason, which I have the honour to offer to the world in support of my opinion that my father did not write the chapter upon sash windows and chamber pots at the time supposed,——and it is this.

——That, in order to render the *Tristrapaedia* complete,——I wrote the chapter myself.

CHAPTER XXVII

My father put on his spectacles,——looked,——took them off,——put them into the case——all in less than a statutable minute; and without opening his lips, turned about, and walked precipitately downstairs: my mother imagined he had stepped down for lint and basilicon; but seeing him return with a couple of folios under his arm, and Obadiah following him with a large reading desk, she took it for granted 'twas an herbal, and so drew him a chair to the bedside, that he might consult upon the case at his ease.

——If it be but right done,——said my father, turning to the Section——*de sede vel subjecto circumcisionis*,——for he had brought up Spencer *de Legibus Hebraeorum Ritualibus*——and Maimonides, in order to confront and examine us altogether.——

——If it be but right done, quoth he:——Only tell us, cried my mother, interrupting him, what herbs.——For that, replied my father, you must send for Dr. Slop.

My mother went down, and my father went on, reading the section as follows.

*   *   *   *   *   *   *   *   *   *   *   *   *   *   *   *
*   *   *   *   *   *   *   *   *   *   *   *   *   *   *   *
*   *   *   *   *   *   *   ——Very well,——said my father,
*   *   *   *   *   *   *   *   *   *   *   *   *   *   *   *
*   *   *   *   *   *   *   *   *   *   *   *   *   *   *   *
*   *   *   ——nay, if it has that convenience——and so without stopping a moment to settle it first in his mind whether the Jews had it from the Egyptians, or the Egyptians from the Jews,——he rose up, and rubbing his forehead two or three times across with the palm of his hand, in the manner we rub out the footsteps of care, when evil has trod lighter upon us than we foreboded,——he shut the book, and walked downstairs.——Nay, said he, mentioning the name of a different great nation upon every step as he set his foot upon it ——if the EGYPTIANS,——the SYRIANS,——the PHOENICIANS, ——the ARABIANS,——the CAPADOCIANS,——if the COLCHI and TROGLODYTES did it,——if SOLON and PYTHAGORAS submitted,——what is TRISTRAM?——Who am I, that I should fret or fume one moment about the matter?

CHAPTER XXVIII

Dear Yorick, said my father, smiling (for Yorick had broke his rank with my uncle Toby in coming through the narrow entry, and so had stept first into the parlour),——this Tristram of ours, I find, comes very hardly by all his religious rites.——Never was the son of Jew, Christian, Turk, or Infidel initiated into them in so oblique and slovenly a

314

manner.——But he is no worse, I trust, said Yorick.——
There has been certainly, continued my father, the deuce and
all to do in some part or other of the ecliptic, when this offspring of mine was formed.——That you are a better judge
of than I, replied Yorick.——Astrologers, quoth my father,
know better than us both:——the trine and sextile aspects
have jumped awry,——or the opposite of their ascendents
have not hit it, as they should,——or the lords of the
genitures (as they call them) have been at *bo-peep*,——or
something has been wrong above, or below with us.

'Tis possible, answered Yorick.——But is the child, cried
my uncle Toby, the worse?——The Troglodytes say not, replied my father.——And your theologists, Yorick, tell us——
Theologically? said Yorick,——or speaking after the manner
of apothecaries? *——statesmen? †——or washerwomen? ‡

——I'm not sure, replied my father,——but they tell us,
brother Toby, he's the better for it.——Provided, said Yorick,
you travel him into Egypt.——Of that, answered my father,
he will have the advantage, when he sees the Pyramids.——

Now every word of this, quoth my uncle Toby, is Arabic
to me.——I wish, said Yorick, 'twas so to half the world.

——ILUS,** continued my father, circumcised his whole
army one morning.——Not without a court-martial? cried my
uncle Toby.——Though the learned, continued he, taking no
notice of my uncle Toby's remark, but turning to Yorick,——
are greatly divided still who Ilus was;——some say Saturn;
——some, the supreme Being;——others, no more than a
brigadier general under Pharaoh-Nechoh.——Let him be who
he will, said my uncle Toby, I know not by what article of
war he could justify it.

The controvertists, answered my father, assign two-and-
twenty different reasons for it:——others indeed, who have
drawn their pens on the opposite side of the question, have
shown the world the futility of the greatest part of them.——
But then again, our best polemic divines——I wish there was
not a polemic divine, said Yorick, in the kingdom;——one
ounce of practical divinity——is worth a painted shipload of
all their Reverences have imported these fifty years.——
Pray, Mr. Yorick, quoth my uncle Toby,——do tell me what
a polemic divine is.——The best description, Captain

---

*Χαλεπῆς νόσου, καὶ δυσιάτου ἀπαλλαγὴ, ἥν ἄνθρακα καλοῦσιν.——PHILO.
†Τὰ τεμνόμενα τῶν ἐθνῶν πολυγονώτατα, καὶ πολυανθρωπότατα εἶναι.
‡Καθαριότητος εἵνεκεν.——BOCHART.
**'Ο Ἴλος, τὰ αἰδοῖα περιτέμνεται, τἀυτὸ ποιῆσαι καὶ τοὺς ἁμ' αὑτῶ συμμά-
χους καταναγκάσας.——SANCHUNIATHO.

Shandy, I have ever read is a couple of 'em, replied Yorick, in the account of the battle fought single hands betwixt Gymnast and Captain Tripet, which I have in my pocket.——I beg I may hear it, quoth my uncle Toby earnestly.——You shall, said Yorick.——And as the corporal is waiting for me at the door,——and I know the description of a battle will do the poor fellow more good than his supper,——I beg, brother, you'll give him leave to come in.——With all my soul, said my father.——Trim came in, erect and happy as an emperor; and having shut the door, Yorick took a book from his right-hand coat pocket, and read, or pretended to read, as follows.

CHAPTER XXIX

——"which words being heard by all the soldiers which were there, divers of them being inwardly terrified, did shrink back and make room for the assailant: all this did Gymnast very well remark and consider; and therefore, making as if he would have alighted from off his horse, as he was poising himself on the mounting side, he most nimbly (with his short sword by his thigh) shifting his feet in the stirrup and performing the stirrup-leather feat, whereby, after the inclining of his body downwards, he forthwith launched himself aloft into the air, and placed both his feet together upon the saddle, standing upright, with his back turned towards his horse's head,——Now (said he) my case goes forward. Then suddenly, in the same posture wherein he was, he fetched a gambol upon one foot, and turning to the left hand, failed not to carry his body perfectly round, just into his former position, without missing one jot.——Ha! said Tripet, I will not do that at this time,——and not without cause. Well, said Gymnast, I have failed,——I will undo this leap; then with a marvellous strength and agility, turning towards the right hand, he fetched another frisking gambol as before; which done, he set his right-hand thumb upon the bow of the saddle, raised himself up, and sprung into the air, poising and upholding his whole weight upon the muscle and nerve of the said thumb, and so turned and whirled himself about three times: at the fourth, reversing his body and overturning it upside down, and foreside back, without *touching anything,* he brought himself betwixt the horse's two ears, and then giving himself a jerking swing, he seated himself upon the crupper——"

(This can't be fighting, said my uncle Toby.——The corporal shook his head at it.——Have patience, said Yorick.)

"Then (Tripet) passed his right leg over his saddle, and placed himself *en croupe.*——But, said he, 'twere better for me to get into the saddle; then putting the thumbs of both hands upon the crupper before him, and thereupon leaning himself, as upon the only supporters of his body, he incontinently turned heels over head in the air, and straight found himself betwixt the bow of the saddle in a tolerable seat; then springing into the air with a somerset, he turned him about like a windmill, and made above a hundred frisks, turns, and demipomadas."——Good God! cried Trim, losing all patience,——one home thrust of a bayonet is worth it all. ——I think so too, replied Yorick.——

——I am of a contrary opinion, quoth my father.

CHAPTER XXX

——No,——I think I have advanced nothing, replied my father, making answer to a question which Yorick had taken the liberty to put to him,——I have advanced nothing in the *Tristrapaedia,* but what is as clear as any one proposition in Euclid.——Reach me, Trim, that book from off the scrutoire: it has ofttimes been in my mind, continued my father, to have read it over both to you, Yorick, and to my brother Toby, and I think it a little unfriendly in myself in not having done it long ago:——shall we have a short chapter or two now,——and a chapter or two hereafter, as occasions serve; and so on, till we get through the whole? My uncle Toby and Yorick made the obeisance which was proper; and the corporal, though he was not included in the compliment, laid his hand upon his breast, and made his bow at the same time.——The company smiled. Trim, quoth my father, has paid the full price for staying out the *entertainment.*——He did not seem to relish the play, replied Yorick.——'Twas a Tom Fool's battle, an' please your Reverence, of Captain

317

Tripet's and that other officer, making so many somersets, as they advanced;——the French come on capering now and then in that way,——but not quite so much.

My uncle Toby never felt the consciousness of his existence with more complacency than what the corporal's and his own reflections made him do at that moment;——he lighted his pipe,——Yorick drew his chair closer to the table,——Trim snuffed the candle,——my father stirred up the fire,——took up the book,——coughed twice, and begun.

CHAPTER XXXI

The first thirty pages, said my father, turning over the leaves, ——are a little dry; and as they are not closely connected with the subject,——for the present we'll pass them by: 'tis a prefatory introduction, continued my father, or an introductory preface (for I am not determined which name to give it) upon political or civil government; the foundation of which being laid in the first conjunction betwixt male and female, for procreation of the species——I was insensibly led into it.——'Twas natural, said Yorick.

The original of society, continued my father, I'm satisfied, is what Politian tells us, *i.e.,* merely conjugal; and nothing more than the getting together of one man and one woman; ——to which (according to Hesiod) the philosopher adds a servant:——but supposing in the first beginning there were no men servants born——he lays the foundation of it in a man,——a woman,——and a bull.——I believe 'tis an ox, quoth Yorick, quoting the passage (οἶκον μὲν πρώτιστα, γυναῖκά τε, βοῦν τ' ἀροτῆρα.)——A bull must have given more trouble than his head was worth.——But there is a better reason still, said my father (dipping his pen into his ink), for, the ox being the most patient of animals, and the most useful withal in tilling the ground for their nourishment,——was the properest instrument, and emblem too, for the new-joined couple that the creation could have associated with them.—— And there is a stronger reason, added my uncle Toby, than them all for the ox.——My father had not power to take his pen out of his inkhorn till he had heard my uncle Toby's reason.——For when the ground was tilled, said my uncle Toby, and made worth inclosing, then they began to secure it by walls and ditches, which was the origin of fortification.——True, true, dear Toby, cried my father, striking out the bull, and putting the ox in his place.

My father gave Trim a nod to snuff the candle, and resumed his discourse.

——I enter upon this speculation, said my father carelessly, and half shutting the book, as he went on,——merely to show the foundation of the natural relation between a father and his child; the right and jurisdiction over whom he acquires these several ways——

1st, by marriage.

2d, by adoption.

3d, by legitimation.

And 4th, by procreation; all which I consider in their order.

I lay a slight stress upon one of them, replied Yorick——the act, especially where it ends there, in my opinion lays as little obligation upon the child as it conveys power to the father. ——You are wrong,——said my father argutely, and for this plain reason   *   *   *   *   *   *   *   *   *   *   *
*   *   *   *   *   *   *   *   *   *   *   *   *   *
*   *   *   *   *   *   *   *   *   *   *   *   . ——I own, added my father, that the offspring, upon this account, is not so under the power and jurisdiction of the *mother.*—— But the reason, replied Yorick, equally holds good for her. ——She is under authority herself, said my father:——and besides, continued my father, nodding his head and laying his finger upon the side of his nose, as he assigned his reason,——*she is not the principal agent,* Yorick.——In what? quoth my uncle Toby, stopping his pipe.——Though by all means, added my father (not attending to my uncle Toby), *"The son ought to pay her respect,"* as you may read, Yorick, at large in the first book of the Institutes of Justinian, at the eleventh title and the tenth section.——I can read it as well, replied Yorick, in the catechism.

CHAPTER XXXII

Trim can repeat every word of it by heart, quoth my uncle Toby.——Pugh! said my father, not caring to be interrupted with Trim's saying his catechism. He can upon my honour, replied my uncle Toby.——Ask him, Mr. Yorick, any question you please.——

——The fifth Commandment, Trim——said Yorick, speaking mildly, and with a gentle nod, as to a modest catechumen. The corporal stood silent.——You don't ask him right, said my uncle Toby, raising his voice, and giving it rapidly like the word of command;——The fifth—— ——cried my uncle Toby.——I must begin with the first, an' please your Honour, said the corporal.——

——Yorick could not forbear smiling.——Your Reverence does not consider, said the corporal, shouldering his stick like a musket, and marching into the middle of the room, to illustrate his position,——that 'tis exactly the same thing as doing one's exercise in the field.——

"Join your right hand to your firelock," cried the corporal, giving the word of command, and performing the motion.——

"Poise your firelock," cried the corporal, doing the duty still of both adjutant and private man.

"Rest your firelock;"——one motion, an' please your Reverence, you see leads into another.——If his Honour will begin but with the *first*——

THE FIRST——cried my uncle Toby, setting his hand upon his side—— * * * * * * * * * * * *
* * * * * * * * * * * *

THE SECOND——cried my uncle Toby, waving his tobacco pipe, as he would have done his sword at the head of a regiment.——The corporal went through his *manual* with exactness; and having *honoured his father and mother,* made a low bow, and fell back to the side of the room.

Everything in this world, said my father, is big with jest, ——and has wit in it, and instruction too,——if we can but find it out.

——Here is the *scaffoldwork* of INSTRUCTION, its true point of folly, without the BUILDING behind it.——

——Here is the glass for pedagogues, preceptors, tutors, governors, gerund-grinders and bear-leaders to view themselves in, in their true dimensions.——

Oh! there is a husk and shell, Yorick, which grows up with learning, which their unskilfulness knows not how to fling away!

——SCIENCES MAY BE LEARNED BY ROTE, BUT WISDOM NOT.

Yorick thought my father inspired.——I will enter into obligations this moment, said my father, to lay out all my aunt Dinah's legacy in charitable uses (of which, by the bye,

320

my father had no high opinion), if the corporal has any one determinate idea annexed to any one word he has repeated.——Prithee, Trim, quoth my father, turning round to him,——What dost thou mean by *"honouring thy father and mother"*?

Allowing them, an' please your Honour, three halfpence a day out of my pay, when they grew old.——And didst thou do that, Trim? said Yorick.——He did indeed, replied my uncle Toby.——Then, Trim, said Yorick, springing out of his chair, and taking the corporal by the hand, thou art the best commentator upon that part of the Decalogue; and I honour thee more for it, corporal Trim, than if thou hadst had a hand in the Talmud itself.

CHAPTER XXXIII

O blessed health! cried my father, making an exclamation, as he turned over the leaves to the next chapter,——thou art above all gold and treasure; 'tis thou who enlargest the soul,——and openest all its powers to receive instruction and to relish virtue.——He that has thee has little more to wish for;——and he that is so wretched as to want thee ——wants everything with thee.

I have concentrated all that can be said upon this important head, said my father, into a very little room, therefore we'll read the chapter quite through.

My father read as follows.

"The whole secret of health depending upon the due contention for mastery betwixt the radical heat and the radical moisture"——You have proved that matter of fact, I suppose, above, said Yorick. Sufficiently, replied my father.

In saying this, my father shut the book,——not as if he resolved to read no more of it, for he kept his forefinger in the chapter:——nor pettishly,——for he shut the book slowly, his thumb resting, when he had done it, upon the upper side of the cover, as his three fingers supported the lower side of it, without the least compressive violence.——

I have demonstrated the truth of that point, quoth my father, nodding to Yorick, most sufficiently in the preceding chapter.

Now could the man in the moon be told that a man in

the earth had wrote a chapter sufficiently demonstrating,
That the secret of all health depended upon the due contention for mastery betwixt the *radical heat* and the *radical moisture,*——and that he had managed the point so well that
there was not one single word wet or dry upon radical heat
or radical moisture, throughout the whole chapter,——or a
single syllable in it, pro or con, directly or indirectly, upon
the contention betwixt these two powers in any part of the
animal economy——

"O thou eternal maker of all beings!"——he would cry,
striking his breast with his right hand (in case he had one),
——"Thou whose power and goodness can enlarge the faculties of thy creatures to this infinite degree of excellence and
perfection,——What have we MOONITES done?"

CHAPTER XXXIV

With two strokes, the one at Hippocrates, the other at Lord
Verulam, did my father achieve it.

The stroke at the prince of physicians, with which he
began, was no more than a short insult upon his sorrowful
complaint of the *Ars longa*——and *Vita brevis.*——Life
short, cried my father,——and the art of healing tedious!
And who are we to thank for both, the one and the other,
but the ignorance of quacks themselves,——and the stage-
loads of chemical nostrums, and peripatetic lumber, with
which, in all ages, they have first flattered the world, and at
last deceived it.

——O my Lord Verulam! cried my father, turning from
Hippocrates, and making his second stroke at him, as the
principal of nostrum-mongers, and the fittest to be made an
example of to the rest,——What shall I say to thee, my great
Lord Verulam? What shall I say to thy internal spirit,——
thy opium,——thy saltpetre,——thy greasy unctions,——thy
daily purges,——thy nightly clysters and succedaneums?

——My father was never at a loss what to say to any
man, upon any subject; and had the least occasion for the
exordium of any man breathing: how he dealt with his Lordship's opinion,——you shall see;——but when,——I know
not;——we must first see what his Lordship's opinion was.

CHAPTER XXXV

"The two great causes which conspire with each other to shorten life, says Lord Verulam, are first——

"The internal spirit, which, like a gentle flame, wastes the body down to death:——And secondly, the external air, that parches the body up to ashes:——which two enemies attacking us on both sides of our bodies together, at length destroy our organs, and render them unfit to carry on the functions of life."

This being the state of the case, the road to Longevity was plain; nothing more being required, says his Lordship, but to repair the waste committed by the internal spirit, by making the substance of it more thick and dense, by a regular course of opiates on one side, and by refrigerating the heat of it on the other, by three grains and a half of saltpetre every morning before you got up.——

Still this frame of ours was left exposed to the inimical assaults of the air without;——but this was fenced off again by a course of greasy unctions, which so fully saturated the pores of the skin that no spicula could enter;——nor could any one get out.——This put a stop to all perspiration, sensible and insensible, which being the cause of so many scurvy distempers——a course of clysters was requisite to carry off redundant humours,——and render the system complete.

What my father had to say to my Lord of Verulam's opiates, his saltpetre, and greasy unctions and clysters, you shall read,——but not today—or tomorrow: time presses upon me ——my reader is impatient——I must get forwards.——You shall read the chapter at your leisure (if you choose it), as soon as ever the *Tristrapaedia* is published.——

Sufficeth it at present to say, my father levelled the hypothesis with the ground, and in doing that, the learned know, he built up and established his own.——

CHAPTER XXXVI

The whole secret of health, said my father, beginning the sentence again, depending evidently upon the due contention betwixt the radical heat and radical moisture within us;—— the least imaginable skill had been sufficient to have maintained it, had not the schoolmen confounded the task, merely (as Van Helmont, the famous chemist, has proved) by all along mistaking the radical moisture for the tallow and fat of animal bodies.

Now the radical moisture is not the tallow or fat of animals, but an oily and balsamous substance; for the fat and tallow, as also the phlegm or watery parts, are cold; whereas the oily and balsamous parts are of a lively heat and spirit, which accounts for the observation of Aristotle, *"Quod omne animal post coitum est* triste."

Now it is certain that the radical heat lives in the radical moisture, but whether *vice versa* is a doubt: however, when the one decays, the other decays also; and then is produced either an unnatural heat, which causes an unnatural dryness ——or an unnatural moisture, which causes dropsies.——So that if a child, as he grows up, can but be taught to avoid running into fire or water, as either of 'em threaten his destruction,——'twill be all that is needful to be done upon that head.——

CHAPTER XXXVII

The description of the siege of Jericho itself could not have engaged the attention of my uncle Toby more powerfully than the last chapter;——his eyes were fixed upon my father, throughout it;——he never mentioned radical heat and radical moisture, but my uncle Toby took his pipe out of his mouth, and shook his head; and as soon as the chapter was finished, he beckoned to the corporal to come close to his

chair, to ask him the following question,——*aside.*—— * * *
* * * * * * * * * * * * * * . It was at the siege of Limerick, an' please your Honour, replied the corporal, making
a bow.

The poor fellow and I, quoth my uncle Toby, addressing
himself to my father, were scarce able to crawl out of our
tents, at the time the siege of Limerick was raised, upon the
very account you mention.——Now what can have got into
that precious noodle of thine, my dear brother Toby? cried
my father, mentally.——By heaven! continued he, communing still with himself, it would puzzle an Oedipus to bring it
in point.——

I believe, an' please your Honour, quoth the corporal, that
if it had not been for the quantity of brandy we set fire to
every night, and the claret and cinnamon with which I plied
your Honour off;——And the geneva, Trim, added my uncle
Toby, which did us more good than all——I verily believe,
continued the corporal, we had both, an' please your Honour,
left our lives in the trenches, and been buried in them too.
——The noblest grave, corporal! cried my uncle Toby, his
eyes sparkling as he spoke, that a soldier could wish to lie
down in.——But a pitiful death for him! an' please your
Honour, replied the corporal.

All this was as much Arabic to my father as the rites of
the Colchi and Troglodytes had been before to my uncle
Toby, my father could not determine whether he was to
frown or smile.——

My uncle Toby, turning to Yorick, resumed the case at
Limerick, more intelligibly than he had begun it,——and so
settled the point for my father at once.

CHAPTER XXXVIII

It was undoubtedly, said my uncle Toby, a great happiness
for myself and the corporal that we had all along a burning
fever, attended with a most raging thirst, during the whole
five-and-twenty days the flux was upon us in the camp; otherwise what my brother calls the radical moisture must, as I
conceive it, inevitably have got the better.——My father
drew in his lungs top-full of air, and looking up, blew it
forth again, as slowly as he possibly could.——

————It was heaven's mercy to us, continued my uncle Toby, which put it into the corporal's head to maintain that due contention betwixt the radical heat and the radical moisture, by reinforcing the fever, as he did all along, with hot wine and spices; whereby the corporal kept up (as it were) a continual firing, so that the radical heat stood its ground from the beginning to the end, and was a fair match for the moisture, terrible as it was.————Upon my honour, added my uncle Toby, you might have heard the contention within our bodies, brother Shandy, twenty toises.————If there was no firing, said Yorick.

Well————said my father, with a full aspiration, and pausing awhile after the word————Was I a judge, and the laws of the country which made me one permitted it, I would condemn some of the worst malefactors, provided they had had their clergy ———— ———— ———— ———— ———— ———— ————

————Yorick, foreseeing the sentence was likely to end with no sort of mercy, laid his hand upon my father's breast, and begged he would respite it for a few minutes, till he asked the corporal a question.————Prithee, Trim, said Yorick, without staying for my father's leave,————tell us honestly———— what is thy opinion concerning this selfsame radical heat and radical moisture?

With humble submission to his Honour's better judgment, quoth the corporal, making a bow to my uncle Toby———— Speak thy opinion freely, corporal, said my uncle Toby.———— The poor fellow is my servant,————not my slave,————added my uncle Toby, turning to my father.————

The corporal put his hat under his left arm, and with his stick hanging upon the wrist of it, by a black thong split into a tassel about the knot, he marched up to the ground where he had performed his catechism; then touching his under jaw with the thumb and fingers of his right hand before he opened his mouth,————he delivered his notion thus.

CHAPTER XXXIX

Just as the corporal was humming, to begin————in waddled Dr. Slop.————'Tis not twopence matter————the corporal shall go on in the next chapter, let who will come in.————

Well, my good doctor, cried my father sportively, for the transitions of his passions were unaccountably sudden,——— and what has this whelp of mine to say to the matter?———

Had my father been asking after the amputation of the tail of a puppy dog———he could not have done it in a more careless air: the system which Dr. Slop had laid down to treat the accident by no way allowed of such a mode of enquiry. ———He sat down.

Pray, Sir, quoth my uncle Toby, in a manner which could not go unanswered,———in what condition is the boy?——— 'Twill end in a *phimosis,* replied Dr. Slop.

I am no wiser than I was, quoth my uncle Toby,———returning his pipe into his mouth.———Then let the corporal go on, said my father, with his medical lecture.———The corporal made a bow to his old friend, Dr. Slop, and then delivered his opinion concerning radical heat and radical moisture, in the following words.

CHAPTER XL

The city of Limerick, the siege of which was begun under his Majesty King William himself, the year after I went into the army———lies, an' please your Honours, in the middle of a devilish wet, swampy country.———'Tis quite surrounded, said my uncle Toby, with the Shannon, and is, by its situation, one of the strongest fortified places in Ireland.———

I think this is a new fashion, quoth Dr. Slop, of beginning a medical lecture.———'Tis all true, answered Trim.———Then I wish the faculty would follow the cut of it, said Yorick. ———'Tis all cut through, an' please your Reverence, said the corporal, with drains and bogs; and besides, there was such a quantity of rain fell during the siege, the whole country was like a puddle;———'twas that, and nothing else, which brought on the flux, and which had like to have killed both his Honour and myself; now there was no such thing, after the first ten days, continued the corporal, for a soldier to lie dry in his tent, without cutting a ditch round it, to draw off the water;———nor was that enough, for those who could afford it, as his Honour could, without setting fire every night to a pewter dish full of brandy, which took off the damp of the air, and made the inside of the tent as warm as a stove.——

And what conclusion dost thou draw, Corporal Trim, cried my father, from all these premises?

I infer, an' please your Worship, replied Trim, that the radical moisture is nothing in the world but ditch water—— and that the radical heat, of those who can go to the expense of it, is burnt brandy——the radical heat and moisture of a private man, an' please your Honours, is nothing but ditch water——and a dram of geneva——and give us but enough of it, with a pipe of tobacco, to give us spirits, and drive away the vapours——we know not what it is to fear death.

I am at a loss, Captain Shandy, quoth Dr. Slop, to determine in which branch of learning your servant shines most, whether in physiology, or divinity.——Slop had not forgot Trim's comment upon the sermon.——

It is but an hour ago, replied Yorick, since the corporal was examined in the latter, and passed muster with great honour.——

The radical heat and moisture, quoth Dr. Slop, turning to my father, you must know, is the basis and foundation of our being,——as the root of a tree is the source and principle of its vegetation.——It is inherent in the seeds of all animals, and may be preserved sundry ways, but principally in my opinion by *consubstantials, impriments,* and *occludents.* ——Now this poor fellow, continued Dr. Slop, pointing to the corporal, has had the misfortune to have heard some superficial empiric discourse upon this nice point.——That he has,——said my father.——Very likely, said my uncle.—— I'm sure of it——quoth Yorick.——

CHAPTER XLI

Dr. Slop being called out to look at a cataplasm he had ordered, it gave my father an opportunity of going on with another chapter in the *Tristrapaedia.*——Come! cheer up, my lads: I'll show you land——for when we have tugged through that chapter, the book shall not be opened again this twelve-month.——Huzza!——

CHAPTER XLII

——Five years with a bib under his chin;

Four years in travelling from christcross-row to Malachi;

A year and a half in learning to write his own name;

Seven long years and more τύπω-ing it, at Greek and Latin;

Four years at his *probations* and his *negations*——the fine statue still lying in the middle of the marble block,——and nothing done, but his tools sharpened to hew it out!——'Tis a piteous delay!——Was not the great Julius Scaliger within an ace of never getting his tools sharpened at all?—— Forty-four years old was he before he could manage his Greek;——and Peter Damianus, Lord Bishop of Ostia, as all the world knows, could not so much as read, when he was of man's estate.——And Baldus himself, as eminent as he turned out after, entered upon the law so late in life that everybody imagined he intended to be an advocate in the other world: no wonder, when Eudamidas, the son of Archidamas, heard Xenocrates at seventy-five disputing about *wisdom,* that he asked gravely,——*If the old man be yet disputing and enquiring concerning wisdom,——what time will he have to make use of it?*

Yorick listened to my father with great attention; there was a seasoning of wisdom unaccountably mixed up with his strangest whims, and he had sometimes such illuminations in the darkest of his eclipses, as almost attoned for them:——be wary, Sir, when you imitate him.

I am convinced, Yorick, continued my father, half reading and half discoursing, that there is a northwest passage to the intellectual world; and that the soul of man has shorter ways of going to work, in furnishing itself with knowledge and instruction, than we generally take with it.——But alack! all fields have not a river or a spring running besides them;—— every child, Yorick! has not a parent to point it out.

——The whole entirely depends, added my father, in a low voice, upon the *auxiliary verbs,* Mr. Yorick.

Had Yorick trod upon Virgil's snake, he could not have looked more surprised.——I am surprised too, cried my father, observing it,——and I reckon it as one of the greatest

329

calamities which ever befell the republic of letters, That those who have been entrusted with the education of our children, and whose business it was to open their minds, and stock them early with ideas, in order to set the imagination loose upon them, have made so little use of the auxiliary verbs in doing it, as they have done——So that, except Raymond Lullius, and the elder Pelegrini, the last of which arrived to such perfection in the use of 'em, with his topics, that in a few lessons, he could teach a young gentleman to discourse with plausibility upon any subject, pro and con, and to say and write all that could be spoken or written concerning it, without blotting a word, to the admiration of all who beheld him.——I should be glad, said Yorick, interrupting my father, to be made to comprehend this matter. You shall, said my father.

The highest stretch of improvement a single word is capable of is a high metaphor,——for which, in my opinion, the idea is generally the worse, and not the better;——but be that as it may,——when the mind has done that with it—— there is an end,——the mind and the idea are at rest,—— until a second idea enters;——and so on.

Now the use of the *Auxiliaries* is at once to set the soul a-going by herself upon the materials as they are brought her; and by the versability of this great engine, round which they are twisted, to open new tracks of enquiry, and make every idea engender millions.

You excite my curiosity greatly, said Yorick.

For my own part, quoth my uncle Toby, I have given it up. ——The Danes, an' please your Honour, quoth the corporal, who were on the left at the siege of Limerick, were all auxiliaries.——And very good ones, said my uncle Toby.——But the auxiliaries, Trim, my brother is talking about,——I conceive to be different things.——

——You do? said my father, rising up.

CHAPTER XLIII

My father took a single turn across the room, then sat down and finished the chapter.

The verbs auxiliary we are concerned in here, continued

my father, are, *am; was; have; had; do; did; make; made; suffer; shall; should; will; would; can; could; owe; ought; used;* or *is wont.*——And these varied with tenses, *present, past, future,* and conjugated with the verb *see,*——or with these questions added to them,——*Is it? Was it? Will it be? Would it be? May it be? Might it be?* And these again put negatively, *Is it not? Was it not? Ought it not?*——Or affirmatively,——*It is; It was; It ought to be.* Or chronologically, *Has it been always? Lately? How long ago?*——Or hypothetically,——*If it was; If it was not?* What would follow? ——If the French should beat the English? If the Sun go out of the Zodiac?

Now, by the right use and application of these, continued my father, in which a child's memory should be exercised, there is no one idea can enter his brain, how barren soever, but a magazine of conceptions and conclusions may be drawn forth from it.——Didst thou ever see a white bear? cried my father, turning his head round to Trim, who stood at the back of his chair:——No, an' please your Honour, replied the corporal.——But thou couldst discourse about one, Trim, said my father, in case of need?——How is it possible, brother, quoth my uncle Toby, if the corporal never saw one?——'Tis the fact I want, replied my father,——and the possibility of it is as follows.

A WHITE BEAR! Very well. Have I ever seen one? Might I ever have seen one? Am I ever to see one? Ought I ever to have seen one? Or can I ever see one?

Would I had seen a white bear! (for how can I imagine it?)

If I should see a white bear, what should I say? If I should never see a white bear, what then?

If I never have, can, must, or shall see a white bear alive, have I ever seen the skin of one? Did I ever see one painted? —described? Have I never dreamed of one?

Did my father, mother, uncle, aunt, brothers, or sisters ever see a white bear? What would they give? How would they behave? How would the white bear have behaved? Is he wild? Tame? Terrible? Rough? Smooth?

——Is the white bear worth seeing?——

——Is there no sin in it?——

Is it better than a BLACK ONE?

VOLUME VI

CHAPTER I

———We'll not stop two moments, my dear Sir,———only, as we have got through these five volumes (do, Sir, sit down upon a set———they are better than nothing), let us just look back upon the country we have passed through.———

———What a wilderness has it been! and what a mercy that we have not both of us been lost, or devoured by wild beasts, in it.

Did you think the world itself, Sir, had contained such a number of Jack Asses?———How they viewed and reviewed us as we passed over the rivulet at the bottom of that little valley!———and when we climbed over that hill, and were just getting out of sight———good God! what a braying did they all set up together!

———Prithee, shepherd! who keeps all those Jack Asses? * * *

———Heaven be their comforter———What! are they never curried?———Are they never taken in in winter?———Bray bray ———bray. Bray on,———the world is deeply your debtor;——— louder still———that's nothing;———in good sooth, you are ill-used:———Was I a Jack Ass, I solemnly declare, I would bray in g sol re ut from morning even unto night.

CHAPTER II

When my father had danced his white bear backwards and forwards through half a dozen pages, he closed the book for good an' all,——and in a kind of triumph redelivered it into Trim's hand, with a nod to lay it upon the scrutoire where he found it.——Tristram, said he, shall be made to conjugate every word in the dictionary, backwards and forwards, the same way;——every word, Yorick, by this means, you see, is converted into a thesis or an hypothesis;——every thesis and hypothesis have an offspring of propositions;——and each proposition has its own consequences and conclusions; every one of which leads the mind on again, into fresh tracks of enquiries and doubtings.——The force of this engine, added my father, is incredible, in opening a child's head.——'Tis enough, brother Shandy, cried my uncle Toby, to burst it into a thousand splinters.——

I presume, said Yorick, smiling,——it must be owing to this——(for let logicians say what they will, it is not to be accounted for sufficiently from the bare use of the ten predicaments)——that the famous Vincent Quirino, amongst the many other astonishing feats of his childhood, of which the Cardinal Bembo has given the world so exact a story,—— should be able to paste up in the public schools at Rome, so early as in the eighth year of his age, no less than four thousand five hundred and sixty different theses, upon the most abstruse points of the most abstruse theology;——and to defend and maintain them in such sort as to cramp and dumfound his opponents.——What is that, cried my father, to what is told us of Alphonsus Tostatus, who, almost in his nurse's arms, learned all the sciences and liberal arts without being taught any one of them?——What shall we say of the great Peireskius?——That's the very man, cried my uncle Toby, I once told you of, brother Shandy, who walked a matter of five hundred miles, reckoning from Paris to Schevling, and from Schevling back again, merely to see Stevinus's flying chariot.——He was a very great man! added my uncle Toby (meaning Stevinus);——He was so, brother Toby, said my father (meaning Peireskius),——and had multiplied his ideas so fast, and increased his knowledge to such a prodigious stock, that, if we may give credit to an anecdote concerning him, which we cannot withhold here, without shaking the authority of all anecdotes whatever——at seven years of age, his father committed entirely to his care the education of his younger brother, a boy of five years old,——with the sole management of all his concerns.——Was the father as wise as the son? quoth my uncle Toby:——I should think not, said Yorick:——But what are these, continued my father—— (breaking out in a kind of enthusiasm)——what are these, to those prodigies of childhood in Grotius, Scioppius, Heinsius, Politian, Pascal, Joseph Scaliger, Ferdinand de Cordouè, and others——some of which left off their *substantial forms* at nine years old, or sooner, and went on reasoning without them;——others went through their classics at seven;—— wrote tragedies at eight;——Ferdinand de Cordouè was so wise at nine,——'twas thought the devil was in him;——and at Venice gave such proofs of his knowledge and goodness that the monks imagined he was Antichrist, or nothing.—— Others were masters of fourteen languages at ten,——finished the course of their rhetoric, poetry, logic, and ethics at eleven,——put forth their commentaries upon Servius and Martianus Capella at twelve,——and at thirteen received their degrees in philosophy, laws, and divinity:——But you forget the great Lipsius, quoth Yorick, who composed a work * the day he was born;——They should have wiped it up, said my uncle Toby, and said no more about it.

CHAPTER III

When the cataplasm was ready, a scruple of *decorum* had unseasonably rose up in Susannah's conscience about holding the candle, whilst Slop tied it on; Slop had not treated

---

* Nous aurions quelque intérêt, says Baillet, de montrer qu'il n' a rien de ridicule s'il étoit véritable, au moins dans le sense énigmatique que Nicius Erythraeus a tâché de lui donner. Cet auteur dit que pour comprendre comme Lipse, a pû composer un ouvrage le premier jour de sa vie, il faut s'imaginer, que ce premier jour n'est pas celui de sa naissance charnelle, mais celui au quel il a commencé d'user de la raison; il veut que ç'ait été à l'age de *neuf* ans; et il nous veut persuader que ce fut en cet âge, que Lipse fit un poème.——Le tour est ingenieux, etc. etc.

Susannah's distemper with anodynes,——and so a quarrel had ensued betwixt them.

——Oh! oh!——said Slop, casting a glance of undue freedom in Susannah's face, as she declined the office;——then I think I know you, Madam——You know me, Sir! cried Susannah fastidiously, and with a toss of her head, levelled, evidently, not at his profession, but at the doctor himself, ——you know me! cried Susannah again.——Dr. Slop clapped his finger and his thumb instantly upon his nostrils; ——Susannah's spleen was ready to burst at it;——'Tis false, said Susannah.——Come, come, Mrs. Modesty, said Slop, not a little elated with the success of his last thrust,——if you won't hold the candle and look——you may hold it and shut your eyes:——That's one of your popish shifts, cried Susannah:——'Tis better, said Slop, with a nod, than no shift at all, young woman;——I defy you, sir, cried Susannah, pulling her shift sleeve below her elbow.

It was almost impossible for two persons to assist each other in a surgical case with a more splenetic cordiality.

Slop snatched up the cataplasm,——Susannah snatched up the candle;——a little this way, said Slop; Susannah, looking one way, and rowing another, instantly set fire to Slop's wig, which being somewhat bushy and unctuous withal, was burnt out before it was well kindled.——You impudent whore! cried Slop——(for what is passion, but a wild beast),——you impudent whore, cried Slop, getting upright, with the cataplasm in his hand;——I never was the destruction of anybody's nose, said Susannah,——which is more than you can say:——Is it? cried Slop, throwing the cataplasm in her face; ——Yes, it is, cried Susannah, returning the compliment with what was left in the pan.——

CHAPTER IV

Dr. Slop and Susannah filed cross bills against each other in the parlour; which done, as the cataplasm had failed, they retired into the kitchen to prepare a fomentation for me; ——and whilst that was doing, my father determined the point as you will read.

CHAPTER V

You see 'tis high time, said my father, addressing himself equally to my uncle Toby and Yorick, to take this young creature out of these women's hands, and put him into those of a private governor. Marcus Antoninus provided fourteen governors all at once to superintend his son Commodus's education,——and in six weeks he cashiered five of them; ——I know very well, continued my father, that Commodus's mother was in love with a gladiator at the time of her conception, which accounts for a great many of Commodus's cruelties when he became emperor;——but still I am of opinion that those five whom Antoninus dismissed did Commodus's temper in that short time more hurt than the other nine were able to rectify all their lives long.

Now as I consider the person who is to be about my son as the mirror in which he is to view himself from morning to night, and by which he is to adjust his looks, his carriage, and perhaps the inmost sentiments of his heart;——I would have one, Yorick, if possible, polished at all points, fit for my child to look into.——This is very good sense, quoth my uncle Toby to himself.

——There is, continued my father, a certain mien and motion of the body and all its parts, both in acting and speaking, which argues a man *well within;* and I am not at all surprised that Gregory of Nazianzum, upon observing the hasty and untoward gestures of Julian, should foretell he would one day become an apostate;——or that St. Ambrose should turn his *Amanuensis* out of doors, because of an indecent motion of his head, which went backwards and forwards like a flail;——or that Democritus should conceive Protagoras to be a scholar, from seeing him bind up a faggot, and thrusting, as he did it, the small twigs inwards.——There are a thousand unnoticed openings, continued my father, which let a penetrating eye at once into a man's soul; and I maintain it, added he, that a man of sense does not lay down his hat in coming into a room,——or take it up in going out of it, but something escapes, which discovers him.

It is for these reasons, continued my father, that the governor I make choice of shall neither * lisp, or squint, or wink,

* Vid. Pellegrina.

or talk loud, or look fierce or foolish;——or bite his lips, or grind his teeth, or speak through his nose, or pick it, or blow it with his fingers.——

He shall neither walk fast,——or slow, or fold his arms, ——for that is laziness;——or hang them down,——for that is folly; or hide them in his pocket, for that is nonsense.——

He shall neither strike, or pinch, or tickle,——or bite, or cut his nails, or hawk, or spit, or snift, or drum with his feet or fingers in company;——nor (according to Erasmus) shall he speak to anyone in making water,——nor shall he point to carrion or excrement.——Now this is all nonsense again, quoth my uncle Toby to himself.——

I will have him, continued my father, cheerful, facete, jovial; at the same time, prudent, attentive to business, vigilant, acute, argute, inventive, quick in resolving doubts and speculative questions;——he shall be wise and judicious, and learned:——And why not humble, and moderate, and gentle-tempered, and good? said Yorick:——And why not, cried my uncle Toby, free, and generous, and bountiful, and brave? ——He shall, my dear Toby, replied my father, getting up and shaking him by his hand.——Then, brother Shandy, answered my uncle Toby, raising himself off the chair, and laying down his pipe to take hold of my father's other hand,—— I humbly beg I may recommend poor Le Fever's son to you; ——a tear of joy of the first water sparkled in my uncle Toby's eye,——and another, the fellow to it, in the corporal's, as the proposition was made;——you will see why when you read Le Fever's story:——fool that I was! nor can I recollect (nor perhaps you), without turning back to the place, what it was that hindered me from letting the corporal tell it in his own words;——but the occasion is lost;——I must tell it now in my own.

CHAPTER VI

The Story of LE FEVER

It was some time in the summer of that year in which Dendermond was taken by the allies,——which was about seven years before my father came into the country,——and about as many after the time that my uncle Toby and Trim had privately decamped from my father's house in town, in order to lay some of the finest sieges to some of the finest fortified cities in Europe——when my uncle Toby was one evening getting his supper, with Trim sitting behind him at a small sideboard,——I say, sitting——for in consideration of the corporal's lame knee (which sometimes gave him exquisite pain)——when my uncle Toby dined or supped alone, he would never suffer the corporal to stand; and the poor fellow's veneration for his master was such that, with a proper artillery, my uncle Toby could have taken Dendermond itself with less trouble than he was able to gain this point over him; for many a time when my uncle Toby supposed the corporal's leg was at rest, he would look back, and detect him standing behind him with the most dutiful respect: this bred more little squabbles betwixt them than all other causes for five-and-twenty years together——But this is neither here nor there——why do I mention it?——Ask my pen,——it governs me,——I govern not it.

He was one evening sitting thus at his supper, when the landlord of a little inn in the village came into the parlour with an empty phial in his hand, to beg a glass or two of sack; 'Tis for a poor gentleman,——I think, of the army, said the landlord, who has been taken ill at my house four days ago, and has never held up his head since, or had a desire to taste anything, till just now, that he has a fancy for a glass of sack and a thin toast,——*I think,* says he, taking his hand from his forehead, *it would comfort me.*——

——If I could neither beg, borrow, or buy such a thing, ——added the landlord,——I would almost steal it for the poor gentleman, he is so ill.——I hope in God he will still mend, continued he——we are all of us concerned for him.

Thou art a good-natured soul, I will answer for thee, cried my uncle Toby; and thou shalt drink the poor gentleman's health in a glass of sack thyself,——and take a couple of bottles with my service, and tell him he is heartily welcome to them, and to a dozen more if they will do him good.

Though I am persuaded, said my uncle Toby, as the landlord shut the door, he is a very compassionate fellow——Trim,——yet I cannot help entertaining a high opinion of his guest too; there must be something more than common in him that in so short a time should win so much upon the affections of his host;——And of his whole family, added the corporal, for they are all concerned for him.——Step after him, said my uncle Toby,——do Trim,——and ask if he knows his name.

——I have quite forgot it, truly, said the landlord, coming

back into the parlour with the corporal,——but I can ask his son again:——Has he a son with him then? said my uncle Toby.——A boy, replied the landlord, of about eleven or twelve years of age;——but the poor creature has tasted almost as little as his father; he does nothing but mourn and lament for him night and day:——He has not stirred from the bedside these two days.

My uncle Toby laid down his knife and fork, and thrust his plate from before him, as the landlord gave him the account; and Trim, without being ordered, took away without saying one word, and in a few minutes after brought him his pipe and tobacco.

——Stay in the room a little, said my uncle Toby.——

Trim!——said my uncle Toby, after he lighted his pipe, and smoked about a dozen whiffs.——Trim came in front of his master and made his bow;——my uncle Toby smoked on, and said no more.——Corporal! said my uncle Toby ——the corporal made his bow.——My uncle Toby proceeded no farther, but finished his pipe.

Trim! said my uncle Toby, I have a project in my head, as it is a bad night, of wrapping myself up warm in my roquelaure, and paying a visit to this poor gentleman.—— Your Honour's roquelaure, replied the corporal, has not once been had on since the night before your Honour received your wound, when we mounted guard in the trenches before the gate of St. Nicolas;——and besides it is so cold and rainy a night, that what with the roquelaure, and what with the weather, 'twill be enough to give your Honour your death, and bring on your Honour's torment in your groin. I fear so, replied my uncle Toby, but I am not at rest in my mind, Trim, since the account the landlord has given me.—— I wish I had not known so much of this affair,——added my uncle Toby,——or that I had known more of it:—— How shall we manage it? Leave it, an't please your Honour, to me, quoth the corporal;——I'll take my hat and stick and go to the house and reconnoitre, and act accordingly; and I will bring your Honour a full account in an hour.——Thou shalt go, Trim, said my uncle Toby, and here's a shilling for thee to drink with his servant.——I shall get it all out of him, said the corporal, shutting the door.

My uncle Toby filled his second pipe; and had it not been that he now and then wandered from the point, with considering whether it was not full as well to have the curtain of the tenaille a straight line, as a crooked one,—— he might be said to have thought of nothing else but poor Le Fever and his boy the whole time he smoked it.

CHAPTER VII

The Story of LE FEVER, continued

It was not till my uncle Toby had knocked the ashes out of his third pipe that Corporal Trim returned from the inn, and gave him the following account.

I despaired at first, said the corporal, of being able to bring back your Honour any kind of intelligence concerning the poor sick lieutenant——Is he in the army then? said my uncle Toby——He is, said the corporal——And in what regiment? said my uncle Toby——I'll tell your Honour, replied the corporal, everything straight forwards, as I learnt it. ——Then, Trim, I'll fill another pipe, said my uncle Toby, and not interrupt thee till thou hast done; so sit down at thy ease, Trim, in the window seat, and begin thy story again. The corporal made his old bow, which generally spoke as plain as a bow could speak it——*Your Honour is good:* ——And having done that, he sat down, as he was ordered, ——and begun the story to my uncle Toby over again in pretty near the same words.

I despaired at first, said the corporal, of being able to bring back any intelligence to your Honour about the lieutenant and his son; for when I asked where his servant was, from whom I made myself sure of knowing everything which was proper to be asked,——That's a right distinction, Trim, said my uncle Toby——I was answered, an' please your Honour, that he had no servant with him;——that he had come to the inn with hired horses, which, upon finding himself unable to proceed (to join, I suppose, the regiment), he had dismissed the morning after he came.——If I get better, my dear, said he, as he gave his purse to his son to pay the man,——we can hire horses from hence.——But alas! the poor gentleman will never get from hence, said the landlady to me,——for I heard the deathwatch all night long; ——and when he dies, the youth, his son, will certainly die with him; for he is brokenhearted already.

I was hearing this account, continued the corporal, when the youth came into the kitchen, to order the thin toast the landlord spoke of;——but I will do it for my father myself, said the youth.——Pray let me save you the trouble, young gentleman, said I, taking up a fork for the purpose, and offering him my chair to sit down upon by the fire, whilst I did it.——I believe, Sir, said he, very modestly, I can please him best myself.——I am sure, said I, his Honour will not like the toast the worse for being toasted by an old soldier.—— The youth took hold of my hand, and instantly burst into tears.——Poor youth! said my uncle Toby,——he has been bred up from an infant in the army, and the name of a soldier, Trim, sounded in his ears like the name of a friend; ——I wish I had him here.

——I never in the longest march, said the corporal, had so great a mind to my dinner as I had to cry with him for company:——What could be the matter with me, an' please your Honour? Nothing in the world, Trim, said my uncle Toby, blowing his nose,——but that thou art a good-natured fellow.

When I gave him the toast, continued the corporal, I thought it was proper to tell him I was Captain Shandy's servant, and that your Honour (though a stranger) was extremely concerned for his father;——and that if there was anything in your house or cellar——(And thou mightst have added my purse too, said my uncle Toby)——he was heartily welcome to it:——He made a very low bow (which was meant to your Honour) but no answer,——for his heart was full——so he went upstairs with the toast:——I warrant you, my dear, said I, as I opened the kitchen door, your father will be well again.——Mr. Yorick's curate was smoking a pipe by the kitchen fire,——but said not a word good or bad to comfort the youth.——I thought it wrong, added the corporal ——I think so too, said my uncle Toby.

When the lieutenant had taken his glass of sack and toast, he felt himself a little revived, and sent down into the kitchen, to let me know that in about ten minutes he should be glad if I would step upstairs.——I believe, said the landlord, he is going to say his prayers,——for there was a book laid upon the chair by his bedside, and as I shut the door, I saw his son take up a cushion.——

I thought, said the curate, that you gentlemen of the army, Mr. Trim, never said your prayers at all.——I heard the poor gentleman say his prayers last night, said the landlady, very devoutly, and with my own ears, or I could not have believed it.——Are you sure of it? replied the curate.——A soldier, an' please your Reverence, said I, prays as often (of his own accord) as a parson;——and when he is fighting for his king, and for his own life, and for his honour too, he has the most reason to pray to God of anyone in the whole world——'Twas well said of thee, Trim, said my uncle Toby. ——But when a soldier, said I, an' please your Reverence, has been standing for twelve hours together in the trenches, up to his knees in cold water,——or engaged, said I, for months together in long and dangerous marches;——harassed, perhaps, in his rear today;——harassing others tomorrow;——detached here;——countermanded there;——resting this night out upon his arms;——beat up in his shirt the next;——benumbed in his joints;——perhaps without straw in his tent to kneel on;——must say his prayers *how* and *when* he can.——I believe, said I,——for I was piqued, quoth the corporal, for the reputation of the army,——I believe, an' please your Reverence, said I, that when a soldier gets time to pray,——he prays as heartily as a parson,—— though not with all his fuss and hypocrisy.——Thou shouldst not have said that, Trim, said my uncle Toby,——for God only knows who is a hypocrite, and who is not:——At the great and general review of us all, corporal, at the day of judgment (and not till then),——it will be seen who has done their duties in this world,——and who has not; and we shall be advanced, Trim, accordingly.——I hope we shall, said Trim.——It is in the Scripture, said my uncle Toby; and I will show it thee tomorrow:——In the meantime we may depend upon it, Trim, for our comfort, said my uncle Toby, that God Almighty is so good and just a governor of the world that if we have but done our duties in it,——it will never be enquired into whether we have done them in a red coat or a black one:——I hope not, said the corporal—— But go on, Trim, said my uncle Toby, with thy story.

When I went up, continued the corporal, into the lieutenant's room, which I did not do till the expiration of the ten minutes,——he was lying in his bed with his head raised upon his hand, with his elbow upon the pillow, and a clean white cambric handkerchief beside it:——The youth was just stooping down to take up the cushion, upon which I supposed he had been kneeling,——the book was laid upon the bed, ——and as he rose, in taking up the cushion with one hand, he reached out his other to take it away at the same time.—— Let it remain there, my dear, said the lieutenant.

He did not offer to speak to me, till I had walked up close to his bedside:——If you are Captain Shandy's servant, said he, you must present my thanks to your master, with my little boy's thanks along with them, for his courtesy to me;—— if he was of Levens's——said the lieutenant.——I told him your Honour was——Then, said he, I served three campaigns with him in Flanders, and remember him,——but 'tis most likely, as I had not the honour of any acquaintance with him, that he knows nothing of me.——You will tell him, however, that the person his good nature has laid under obligations to him is one Le Fever, a lieutenant in Angus's ——but he knows me not,——said he, a second time, musing;——possibly he may my story——added he——pray tell the captain I was the ensign at Breda whose wife was most unfortunately killed with a musket shot, as she lay in my arms in my tent.——I remember the story, an't please your Honour, said I, very well.——Do you so? said he, wiping his eyes with his handkerchief,——then well may I.—— In saying this, he drew a little ring out of his bosom, which seemed tied with a black ribband about his neck, and kissed it twice——Here, Billy, said he;——the boy flew across the room to the bedside,——and falling down upon his knee, took the ring in his hand, and kissed it too,——then kissed his father, and sat down upon the bed and wept.

I wish, said my uncle Toby, with a deep sigh,——I wish, Trim, I was asleep.

Your Honour, replied the corporal, is too much concerned; ——shall I pour your Honour out a glass of sack to your pipe?——Do, Trim, said my uncle Toby.

I remember, said my uncle Toby, sighing again, the story of the ensign and his wife, with a circumstance his modesty omitted;——and particularly well that he, as well as she, upon some account or other (I forget what), was universally pitied by the whole regiment;——but finish the story thou art upon:——'Tis finished already, said the corporal,——for I could stay no longer,——so wished his Honour a good night; young Le Fever rose from off the bed, and saw me to the bottom of the stairs; and as we went down together, told me they had come from Ireland, and were on their route to join the regiment in Flanders.——But alas! said the corporal, ——the lieutenant's last day's march is over.——Then what is to become of his poor boy? cried my uncle Toby.

344

CHAPTER VIII

The Story of LE FEVER, continued

It was to my uncle Toby's eternal honour,——though I tell it only for the sake of those who, when cooped in betwixt a natural and a positive law, know not for their souls which way in the world to turn themselves——That notwithstanding my uncle Toby was warmly engaged at that time in carrying on the siege of Dendermond, parallel with the allies, who pressed theirs on so vigorously that they scarce allowed him time to get his dinner——that nevertheless he gave up Dendermond, though he had already made a lodgment upon the counterscarp,——and bent his whole thoughts towards the private distresses at the inn; and, except that he ordered the garden gate to be bolted up, by which he might be said to have turned the siege of Dendermond into a blockade, ——he left Dendermond to itself,——to be relieved or not by the French king, as the French king thought good; and only considered how he himself should relieve the poor lieutenant and his son.

——That kind BEING who is a friend to the friendless shall recompense thee for this.

Thou hast left this matter short, said my uncle Toby to the corporal, as he was putting him to bed,——and I will tell thee in what, Trim.——In the first place, when thou madest an offer of my services to Le Fever,——as sickness and travelling are both expensive, and thou knowest he was but a poor lieutenant, with a son to subsist as well as himself, out of his pay,——that thou didst not make an offer to him of my purse; because, had he stood in need, thou knowest, Trim, he had been as welcome to it as myself.——Your Honour knows, said the corporal, I had no orders;——True, quoth my uncle Toby,——thou didst very right, Trim, as a soldier,——but certainly very wrong as a man.

In the second place, for which, indeed, thou hast the same excuse, continued my uncle Toby,——when thou offeredst him whatever was in my house,——thou shouldst have offered him my house too:——A sick brother officer should have the best quarters, Trim, and if we had him with us,—— we could tend and look to him:——Thou art an excellent nurse thyself, Trim,——and what with thy care of him, and the old woman's, and his boy's, and mine together, we might recruit him again at once, and set him upon his legs.——

——In a fortnight or three weeks, added my uncle Toby, smiling,——he might march.——He will never march, an' please your Honour, in this world, said the corporal:——He will march, said my uncle Toby, rising up from the side of the bed, with one shoe off:——An' please your Honour, said the corporal, he will never march, but to his grave:——He shall march, cried my uncle Toby, marching the foot which had a shoe on, though without advancing an inch,——he shall march to his regiment.——He cannot stand it, said the corporal;——He shall be supported, said my uncle Toby;——He'll drop at last, said the corporal, and what will become of his boy?——He shall not drop, said my uncle Toby, firmly.——A-well-o'-day,——do what we can for him, said Trim, maintaining his point,——the poor soul will die:—— He shall not die, by G——, cried my uncle Toby.

——The ACCUSING SPIRIT which flew up to heaven's chancery with the oath blushed as he gave it in;——and the RECORDING ANGEL, as he wrote it down, dropped a tear upon the word, and blotted it out forever.

CHAPTER IX

——My uncle Toby went to his bureau,——put his purse into his breeches pocket, and having ordered the corporal to go early in the morning for a physician,——he went to bed, and fell asleep.

CHAPTER X

The Story of LE FEVER, concluded

The sun looked bright the morning after, to every eye in the village but Le Fever's and his afflicted son's; the hand of death pressed heavy upon his eyelids,——and hardly could the wheel at the cistern turn round its circle,——when my uncle Toby, who had rose up an hour before his wonted time, entered the lieutenant's room, and without preface or apology, sat himself down upon the chair by the bedside, and independently of all modes and customs, opened the curtain in the manner an old friend and brother officer would have done it, and asked him how he did,——how he had rested in the night,——what was his complaint,——where was his pain,——and what he could do to help him:——and without giving him time to answer any one of the enquiries, went on and told him of the little plan which he had been concerting with the corporal the night before for him.——

——You shall go home directly, Le Fever, said my uncle Toby, to my house,——and we'll send for a doctor to see what's the matter,——and we'll have an apothecary,——and the corporal shall be your nurse;——and I'll be your servant, Le Fever.

There was a frankness in my uncle Toby,——not the *effect* of familiarity,——but the *cause* of it,——which let you at once into his soul, and showed you the goodness of his nature; to this, there was something in his looks, and voice, and manner, superadded, which eternally beckoned to the unfortunate to come and take shelter under him; so that before my uncle Toby had half finished the kind offers he was making to the father, had the son insensibly pressed up close to his knees, and had taken hold of the breast of his coat, and was pulling it towards him.——The blood and spirits of Le Fever, which were waxing cold and slow within him, and were retreating to their last citadel, the heart,——rallied back,——the film forsook his eyes for a moment,——he looked up wishfully in my uncle Toby's face,——then cast a look upon his boy,——and that *ligament*, fine as it was, ——was never broken.——

Nature instantly ebbed again,——the film returned to its place,——the pulse fluttered——stopped——went on—— throbbed——stopped again——moved——stopped——shall I go on?——No.

CHAPTER XI

I am so impatient to return to my own story, that what remains of young Le Fever's, that is, from this turn of his fortune to the time my uncle Toby recommended him for my preceptor, shall be told in a very few words, in the next chapter.——All that is necessary to be added to this chapter is as follows.——

That my uncle Toby, with young Le Fever in his hand, attended the poor lieutenant, as chief mourners, to his grave.

That the governor of Dendermond paid his obsequies all military honours,——and that Yorick, not to be behindhand ——paid him all ecclesiastic——for he buried him in his chancel:——And it appears, likewise, he preached a funeral sermon over him——I say it *appears,*——for it was Yorick's custom, which I suppose a general one with those of his profession, on the first leaf of every sermon which he composed, to chronicle down the time, the place, and the occasion of its being preached: to this he was ever wont to add some short comment or stricture upon the sermon itself, seldom, indeed, much to its credit:——For instance, *This sermon upon the Jewish dispensation——I don't like it at all;——Though I own there is a world of* WATER-LANDISH *knowledge in it,——but 'tis all tritical, and most tritically put together.* ————*This is but a flimsy kind of a composition; what was in my head when I made it?*

————N.B. *The excellency of this text is that it will suit any sermon,——and of this sermon,——that it will suit any text.——*

————*For this sermon I shall be hanged,——for I have stolen the greatest part of it. Dr. Paidagunes found me out.* ☞ *Set a thief to catch a thief.*

On the back of half a dozen I find written, *So-so,* and no more——and upon a couple *Moderato;* by which, as far as one may gather from Altieri's Italian dictionary,——but mostly from the authority of a piece of green whipcord, which seemed to have been the unravelling of Yorick's whiplash, with which he has left us the two sermons marked *Moderato,* and the half dozen of *So-so,* tied fast together in one bundle by themselves,——one may safely suppose he meant pretty near the same thing.

348

There is but one difficulty in the way of this conjecture, which is this, that the *moderato*'s are five times better than the *so-so*'s;——show ten times more knowledge of the human heart;——have seventy times more wit and spirit in them; ——(and, to rise properly in my climax)——discover a thousand times more genius;——and to crown all, are infinitely more entertaining than those tied up with them;——for which reason, whene'er Yorick's *dramatic* sermons are offered to the world, though I shall admit but one out of the whole number of the *so-so*'s, I shall, nevertheless, adventure to print the two *moderato*'s without any sort of scruple.

What Yorick could mean by the words *lentamente,*——*tenuto,*——*grave,*——and sometimes *adagio,*——as applied to theological compositions, and with which he has characterized some of these sermons, I dare not venture to guess. ——I am more puzzled still upon finding *a l'octava alta!* upon one;——*Con strepito* upon the back of another;—— *Siciliana* upon a third;——*Alla capella* upon a fourth;—— *Con l'arco* upon this;——*Senza l'arco* upon that.——All I know is that they are musical terms, and have a meaning; ——and as he was a musical man, I will make no doubt but that by some quaint application of such metaphors to the compositions in hand, they impressed very distinct ideas of their several characters upon his fancy,——whatever they may do upon that of others.

Amongst these, there is that particular sermon which has unaccountably led me into this digression——The funeral sermon upon poor Le Fever, wrote out very fairly, as if from a hasty copy.——I take notice of it the more because it seems to have been his favourite composition——It is upon mortality; and is tied lengthways and crossways with a yarn thrum, and then rolled up and twisted round with a half sheet of dirty blue paper, which seems to have been once the cast cover of a general review, which to this day smells horribly of horse drugs.——Whether these marks of humiliation were designed,——I something doubt;——because at the end of the sermon (and not at the beginning of it),—— very different from his way of treating the rest, he had wrote——

Bravo!

——Though not very offensively,——for it is at two inches, at least, and a half's distance from, and below, the concluding line of the sermon, at the very extremity of the page, and in that right-hand corner of it which, you know, is generally covered with your thumb; and, to do it justice, it is wrote besides with a crow's quill so faintly in a small

Italian hand, as scarce to solicit the eye towards the place, whether your thumb is there or not,——so that from the *manner of it*, it stands half excused; and being wrote moreover with very pale ink, diluted almost to nothing,——'tis more like a *ritratto* of the shadow of vanity, than of VANITY herself——of the two; resembling rather a faint thought of transient applause, secretly stirring up in the heart of the composer, than a gross mark of it, coarsely obtruded upon the world.

With all these extenuations, I am aware that in publishing this, I do no service to Yorick's character as a modest man; ——but all men have their failings! and what lessens this still farther, and almost wipes it away, is this, that the word was struck through sometime afterwards (as appears from a different tint of the ink) with a line quite across it in this manner, ~~BRAVO~~—— as if he had retracted, or was ashamed of, the opinion he had once entertained of it.

These short characters of his sermons were always written, excepting in this one instance, upon the first leaf of his sermon, which served as a cover to it; and usually upon the inside of it, which was turned towards the text;——but at the end of his discourse, where, perhaps, he had five or six pages, and sometimes, perhaps, a whole score to turn himself in, ——he took a larger circuit, and, indeed, a much more mettlesome one;——as if he had snatched the occasion of unlacing himself with a few more frolicsome strokes at vice than the straitness of the pulpit allowed.——These, though hussar-like they skirmish lightly and out of all order, are still auxiliaries on the side of virtue;——tell me then, Mynheer Vander Blonederdondergewdenstronke, why they should not be printed together?

CHAPTER XII

When my uncle Toby had turned everything into money, and settled all accounts betwixt the agent of the regiment and Le Fever, and betwixt Le Fever and all mankind,—— there remained nothing more in my uncle Toby's hands than an old regimental coat and a sword; so that my uncle Toby found little or no opposition from the world in taking administration. The coat my uncle Toby gave the corporal;——Wear it, Trim, said my uncle Toby, as long as it will hold together, for the sake of the poor lieutenant——And this,——said my uncle Toby, taking up the sword in his hand, and drawing it out of the scabbard as he spoke——and this, Le Fever, I'll save for thee;——'tis all the fortune, continued my uncle Toby, hanging it up upon a crook, and pointing to it,——'tis all the fortune, my dear Le Fever, which God has left thee; but if he has given thee a heart to fight thy way with it in the world,——and thou doest it like a man of honour,——'tis enough for us.

As soon as my uncle Toby had laid a foundation, and taught him to inscribe a regular polygon in a circle, he sent him to a public school, where, excepting Whitsuntide and Christmas, at which times the corporal was punctually dispatched for him,——he remained to the spring of the year Seventeen; when, the stories of the emperor's sending his army into Hungary against the Turks kindling a spark of fire in his bosom, he left his Greek and Latin without leave, and throwing himself upon his knees before my uncle Toby, begged his father's sword, and my uncle Toby's leave to go along with it, to go and try his fortune under Eugene.——Twice did my uncle Toby forget his wound, and cry out, Le Fever! I will go with thee, and thou shalt fight beside me——And twice he laid his hand upon his groin, and hung down his head in sorrow and disconsolation.——

My uncle Toby took down the sword from the crook, where it had hung untouched ever since the lieutenant's death, and delivered it to the corporal to brighten up;——and having detained Le Fever a single fortnight to equip him, and contract for his passage to Leghorn,——he put the sword into his hand;——If thou art brave, Le Fever, said my uncle Toby, this will not fail thee,——but Fortune, said he (musing a little),——Fortune may——And if she does,——added my uncle Toby, embracing him, come back again to me, Le Fever, and we will shape thee another course.

The greatest injury could not have oppressed the heart of Le Fever more than my uncle Toby's paternal kindness;——he parted from my uncle Toby as the best of sons from the best of fathers——both dropped tears——and as my uncle Toby gave him his last kiss, he slipped sixty guineas, tied up in an old purse of his father's, in which was his mother's ring, into his hand,——and bid God bless him.

CHAPTER XIII

Le Fever got up to the imperial army just time enough to try what metal his sword was made of, at the defeat of the Turks before Belgrade; but a series of unmerited mischances had pursued him from that moment, and trod close upon his heels for four years together after: he had withstood these buffetings to the last, till sickness overtook him at Marseilles, from whence he wrote my uncle Toby word he had lost his time, his services, his health, and, in short, everything but his sword;——and was waiting for the first ship to return back to him.

As this letter came to hand about six weeks before Susannah's accident, Le Fever was hourly expected; and was uppermost in my uncle Toby's mind all the time my father was giving him and Yorick a description of what kind of a person he would choose for a preceptor to me: but as my uncle Toby thought my father at first somewhat fanciful in the accomplishments he required, he forebore mentioning Le Fever's name,——till the character, by Yorick's interposition, ending unexpectedly in one who should be gentle-tempered, and generous, and good, it impressed the image of Le Fever and his interest upon my uncle Toby so forceably, he rose instantly off his chair; and laying down his pipe, in order to take hold of both my father's hands——I beg, brother Shandy, said my uncle Toby, I may recommend poor Le Fever's son to you——I beseech you, do, added Yorick——He has a good heart, said my uncle Toby——And a brave one too, an' please your Honour, said the corporal.

——The best hearts, Trim, are ever the bravest, replied my uncle Toby.——And the greatest cowards, an' please your Honour, in our regiment, were the greatest rascals in it. ——There was Serjeant Kumbur, and Ensign——

——We'll talk of them, said my father, another time.

CHAPTER XIV

What a jovial and a merry world would this be, may it please your Worships, but for that inextricable labyrinth of debts, cares, woes, want, grief, discontent, melancholy, large jointures, impositions, and lies!

Dr. Slop, like a son of a w——, as my father called him for it,——to exalt himself,——debased me to death,—— and made ten thousand times more of Susannah's accident than there was any grounds for; so that in a week's time, or less, it was in everybody's mouth, *That poor Master Shandy* * * * * * * * * * * * * * entirely.——And FAME, who loves to double everything,——in three days more, had sworn positively she saw it,——and all the world, as usual, gave credit to her evidence——"That the nursery window had not only * ;——but that *'s also."

Could the world have been sued like a BODY CORPORATE, ——my father had brought an action upon the case, and trounced it sufficiently; but to fall foul of individuals about it——as every soul who had mentioned the affair did it with the greatest pity imaginable;——'twas like flying in the very face of his best friends:——And yet to acquiesce under the report in silence——was to acknowledge it openly,——at least in the opinion of one half of the world; and to make a bustle again, in contradicting it,——was to confirm it as strongly in the opinion of the other half.——

——Was ever poor devil of a country gentleman so hampered? said my father.

I would show him publicly, said my uncle Toby, at the market cross.

——'Twill have no effect, said my father.

CHAPTER XV

——I'll put him, however, into breeches, said my father,
——let the world say what it will.

CHAPTER XVI

There are a thousand resolutions, Sir, both in church and
state, as well as in matters, Madam, of a more private concern,——which, though they have carried all the appearance
in the world of being taken, and entered upon, in a hasty,
harebrained, and unadvised manner, were, notwithstanding
this (and could you or I have got into the cabinet, or stood
behind the curtain, we should have found it was so),
weighed, poised, and perpended——argued upon——can-
vassed through——entered into, and examined on all sides
with so much coolness, that the GODDESS of COOLNESS herself
(I do not take upon me to prove her existence) could neither
have wished it, or done it better.

Of the number of these was my father's resolution of putting me into breeches; which, though determined at once,
——in a kind of huff, and a defiance of all mankind, had,
nevertheless, been pro'd and conned, and judicially talked
over betwixt him and my mother about a month before, in
two several *beds of justice*, which my father had held for that
purpose. I shall explain the nature of these beds of justice
in my next chapter; and in the chapter following that, you
shall step with me, Madam, behind the curtain, only to hear
in what kind of manner my father and my mother debated
between themselves this affair of the breeches,——from which
you may form an idea, how they debated all lesser matters.

CHAPTER XVII

The ancient Goths of Germany, who (the learned Cluverius is positive) were first seated in the country between the Vistula and the Oder, and who afterwards incorporated the Herculi, the Bugians, and some other Vandalic clans to 'em, ——had all of them a wise custom of debating everything of importance to their state twice; that is,——once drunk, and once sober:——Drunk——that their counsels might not want vigour;——and sober——that they might not want discretion.

Now my father, being entirely a water drinker,——was a long time gravelled almost to death, in turning this as much to his advantage as he did every other thing which the ancients did or said; and it was not till the seventh year of his marriage, after a thousand fruitless experiments and devices, that he hit upon an expedient which answered the purpose;——and that was when any difficult and momentous point was to be settled in the family, which required great sobriety, and great spirit too, in its determination,——he fixed and set apart the first Sunday night in the month, and the Saturday night which immediately preceded it, to argue it over, in bed, with my mother: By which contrivance, if you consider, Sir, with yourself, * * * * * * * *
* * * * * * * * * * * * * * *
* * * * * * * * * * * * * * *
* * * * * * * * * * * * * * *
* * * * * * * * *

These my father, humourously enough, called his *beds of justice;*——for from the two different counsels taken in these two different humours, a middle one was generally found out, which touched the point of wisdom as well as if he had got drunk and sober a hundred times.

It must not be made a secret of to the world, that this answers full as well in literary discussions, as either in military or conjugal; but it is not every author that can try the experiment as the Goths and Vandals did it——or if he can, may it be always for his body's health; and to do it as my father did it,——am I sure it would be always for his soul's.——

My way is this:——

In all nice and ticklish discussions——(of which, heaven knows, there are but too many in my book),——where I find I cannot take a step without the danger of having either their Worships or their Reverences upon my back——I write one half *full*,——and t'other *fasting;*——or write it all full,—— and correct it fasting;——or write it fasting,——and correct it full, for they all come to the same thing:——So that with a less variation from my father's plan than my father's from the Gothic——I feel myself upon a par with him in his first bed of justice,——and no way inferior to him in his second. ——These different and almost irreconcilable effects flow uniformly from the wise and wonderful mechanism of Nature,——of which——be hers the honour.——All that we can do is to turn and work the machine to the improvement and better manufactory of the arts and sciences.——

Now, when I write full,——I write as if I was never to write fasting again as long as I live;——that is, I write free from the cares, as well as the terrors, of the world.——I count not the number of my scars,——nor does my fancy go forth into dark entries and bye corners to antedate my stabs.——In a word, my pen takes its course; and I write on as much from the fullness of my heart, as my stomach.——

But when, an' please your Honours, I indite fasting, 'tis a different history.——I pay the world all possible attention and respect,——and have as great a share (whilst it lasts) of that understrapping virtue of discretion as the best of you. ——So that betwixt both, I write a careless kind of a civil, nonsensical, good-humoured Shandean book, which will do all your hearts good——

——And all your heads too,——provided you understand it.

CHAPTER XVIII

We should begin, said my father, turning himself half round in bed, and shifting his pillow a little towards my mother's, as he opened the debate——We should begin to think, Mrs. Shandy, of putting this boy into breeches.——

We should so,——said my mother.——We defer it, my dear, quoth my father, shamefully.——

I think we do, Mr. Shandy,——said my mother.

———Not but the child looks extremely well, said my father, in his vests and tunics.———

———He does look very well in them,———replied my mother.———

———And for that reason it would be almost a sin, added my father, to take him out of 'em.———

———It would so,———said my mother:———But indeed he is growing a very tall lad,———rejoined my father.

———He is very tall for his age, indeed,———said my mother.———

———I can not (making two syllables of it) imagine, quoth my father, who the deuce he takes after.———

I cannot conceive, for my life,———said my mother.———

Humph!———said my father.

(The dialogue ceased for a moment.)

———I am very short myself,———continued my father, gravely.

You are very short, Mr. Shandy,———said my mother.

Humph! quoth my father to himself, a second time: in muttering which, he plucked his pillow a little further from my mother's,———and turning about again, there was an end of the debate for three minutes and a half.

———When he gets these breeches made, cried my father in a higher tone, he'll look like a beast in 'em.

He will be very awkward in them at first, replied my mother.———

———And 'twill be lucky if that's the worst on't, added my father.

It will be very lucky, answered my mother.

I suppose, replied my father,———making some pause first, ———he'll be exactly like other people's children.———

Exactly, said my mother.———

———Though I should be sorry for that, added my father: and so the debate stopped again.

———They should be of leather, said my father, turning him about again.———

They will last him, said my mother, the longest.

But he can have no linings to 'em, replied my father.———

He cannot, said my mother.

'Twere better to have them of fustian, quoth my father.

Nothing can be better, quoth my mother.———

———Except dimity,———replied my father:———'Tis best of all,———replied my mother.

———One must not give him his death, however,———interrupted my father.

By no means, said my mother:——and so the dialogue stood still again.

I am resolved, however, quoth my father, breaking silence the fourth time, he shall have no pockets in them.——

——There is no occasion for any, said my mother.——

I mean in his coat and waistcoat,——cried my father.

——I mean so too,——replied my mother.

——Though if he gets a gig or a top——Poor souls! it is a crown and a scepter to them;——They should have where to secure it.——

Order it as you please, Mr. Shandy, replied my mother.——

——But don't you think it right? added my father, pressing the point home to her.

Perfectly, said my mother, if it pleases you, Mr. Shandy.——

——There's for you! cried my father, losing temper——Pleases me!——You never will distinguish, Mrs. Shandy, nor shall I ever teach you to do it, betwixt a point of pleasure and a point of convenience.——This was on the Sunday night;——and further this chapter sayeth not.

CHAPTER XIX

After my father had debated the affair of the breeches with my mother,——he consulted Albertus Rubenius upon it; and Albertus Rubenius used my father ten times worse in the consultation (if possible) than even my father had used my mother: For as Rubenius had wrote a quarto *express, De re Vestiaria Veterum,*——it was Rubenius's business to have given my father some lights.——On the contrary, my father might as well have thought of extracting the seven cardinal virtues out of a long beard,——as of extracting a single word out of Rubenius upon the subject.

Upon every other article of ancient dress, Rubenius was very communicative to my father;——gave him a full and satisfactory account of

The Toga, or loose gown.

The Chlamys.

The Ephod.

The Tunica, or Jacket.

The Synthesis.

The Paenula.

The Lacema, with its Cucullus.

The Paludamentum.

The Praetexta.

The Sagum, or soldier's jerkin.

The Trabea: of which, according to Suetonius, there were three kinds.——

——But what are all these to the breeches? said my father. Rubenius threw him down upon the counter all kinds of shoes which had been in fashion with the Romans.—— There was,

> The open shoe.
>
> The close shoe.
>
> The slip shoe.
>
> The wooden shoe.
>
> The sock.
>
> The buskin.

And The military shoe with hobnails in it, which Juvenal takes notice of.

There were, The clogs.

> The pattens.
>
> The pantofles.
>
> The brogues.
>
> The sandals, with latchets to them.

There was, The felt shoe.

> The linen shoe.
>
> The laced shoe.
>
> The braided shoe.
>
> The calceus incisus.

And The calceus rostratus.

Rubenius showed my father how well they all fitted,——in what manner they laced on,——with what points, straps, thongs, latchets, ribbands, jags, and ends.——

——But I want to be informed about the breeches, said my father.

Albertus Rubenius informed my father that the Romans manufactured stuffs of various fabrics,——some plain,—— some striped,——others diapered throughout the whole contexture of the wool with silk and gold——That linen did not begin to be in common use till towards the declension of the empire, when the Egyptians coming to settle amongst them brought it into vogue.

——That persons of quality and fortune distinguished themselves by the fineness and whiteness of their clothes;

which colour (next to purple, which was appropriated to the great offices) they most affected and wore on their birthdays and public rejoicings.——That it appeared from the best historians of those times that they frequently sent their clothes to the fuller, to be cleaned and whitened;——but that the inferior people, to avoid that expense, generally wore brown clothes, and of a something coarser texture,——till towards the beginning of Augustus's reign, when the slave dressed like his master, and almost every distinction of habiliment was lost, but the *latus clavus*.

And what was the *latus clavus?* said my father.

Rubenius told him that the point was still litigating amongst the learned:——That Egnatius, Sigonius, Bossius Ticinensis, Bayfius, Budaeus, Salmasius, Lipsius, Lazius, Isaac Casaubon, and Joseph Scaliger all differed from each other,——and he from them: That some took it to be the button,——some the coat itself,——others only the colour of it:——That the great Bayfius, in his Wardrobe of the Ancients, chap. 12——honestly said, he knew not what it was,——whether a tibula,——a stud,——a button,——a loop,——a buckle,——or clasps and keepers.——

——My father lost the horse, but not the saddle——They are *hooks and eyes,* said my father——and with hooks and eyes he ordered my breeches to be made.

CHAPTER XX

We are now going to enter upon a new scene of events.——

——Leave we then the breeches in the tailor's hands, with my father standing over him with his cane, reading him as he sat at work a lecture upon the *latus clavus,* and pointing to the precise part of the waistband where he was determined to have it sewed on.——

Leave we my mother——(truest of all the *pococurantes* of her sex!)——careless about it, as about everything else in the world which concerned her;——that is,——indifferent whether it was done this way or that,——provided it was but done at all.——

Leave we Slop likewise to the full profits of all my dishonours.——

Leave we poor Le Fever to recover, and get home from Marseilles as he can.——And last of all,——because the hardest of all——

Let us leave, if possible, *myself:*——But 'tis impossible,——I must go along with you to the end of the work.

CHAPTER XXI

If the reader has not a clear conception of the rood and the half of ground which lay at the bottom of my uncle Toby's kitchen garden, and which was the scene of so many of his delicious hours,——the fault is not in me,——but in his imagination;——for I am sure I gave him so minute a description, I was almost ashamed of it.

When FATE was looking forwards one afternoon, into the great transactions of future times,——and recollected for what purposes this little plot, by a decree fast bound down in iron, had been destined,——she gave a nod to NATURE——'twas enough——Nature threw half a spadeful of her kindliest compost upon it, with just so *much* clay in it as to retain the forms of angles and indentings,——and so *little* of it too as not to cling to the spade, and render works of so much glory nasty in foul weather.

My uncle Toby came down, as the reader has been informed, with plans along with him, of almost every fortified town in Italy and Flanders; so let the Duke of Marlborough, or the allies, have set down before what town they pleased, my uncle Toby was prepared for them.

His way, which was the simplest one in the world, was this: as soon as ever a town was invested——(but sooner when the design was known) to take the plan of it (let it be what town it would) and enlarge it upon a scale to the exact size of his bowling green; upon the surface of which, by means of a large role of packthread, and a number of small pickets driven into the ground, at the several angles and redans, he transferred the lines from his paper; then taking the profile of the place, with its works, to determine the depths and slopes of the ditches,——the talus of the glacis, and the precise height of the several banquettes, parapets, &c.——he set the corporal to work——and sweetly went it on:——

The nature of the soil,——the nature of the work itself,—— and above all, the good nature of my uncle Toby sitting by from morning to night, and chatting kindly with the corporal upon past-done deeds,——left LABOUR little else but the ceremony of the name.

When the place was finished in this manner, and put into a proper posture of defence,——it was invested,——and my uncle Toby and the corporal began to run their first parallel. ——I beg I may not be interrupted in my story, by being told, *That the first parallel should be at least three hundred toises distant from the main body of the place,——and that I have not left a single inch for it;*——for my uncle Toby took the liberty of incroaching upon his kitchen garden, for the sake of enlarging his works on the bowling green, and for that reason generally ran his first and second parallels betwixt two rows of his cabbages and his cauliflowers; the conveniences and inconveniences of which will be considered at large in the history of my uncle Toby's and the corporal's campaigns, of which this I'm now writing is but a sketch, and will be finished, if I conjecture right, in three pages (but there is no guessing)——The campaigns themselves will take up as many books; and therefore I apprehend it would be hanging too great a weight of one kind of matter in so flimsy a performance as this, to rhapsodize them, as I once intended, into the body of the work——surely they had better be printed apart——we'll consider the affair——so take the following sketch of them in the meantime.

CHAPTER XXII

When the town, with its works, was finished, my uncle Toby and the corporal began to run their first parallel——not at random, or anyhow——but from the same points and distances the allies had begun to run theirs; and regulating their approaches and attacks by the accounts my uncle Toby received from the daily papers,——they went on, during the whole siege, step by step with the allies.

When the Duke of Marlborough made a lodgment,——my uncle Toby made a lodgment too.——And when the face of a bastion was battered down, or a defence ruined,——the corporal took his mattock and did as much,——and so on;——gaining ground, and making themselves masters of the works one after another, till the town fell into their hands.

To one who took pleasure in the happy state of others,——there could not have been a greater sight in the world than, on a post morning in which a practicable breach had been made by the Duke of Marlborough in the main body of the place,——to have stood behind the hornbeam hedge, and observed the spirit with which my uncle Toby, with Trim behind him, sallied forth;——the one with the *Gazette* in his hand,——the other with a spade on his shoulder to execute the contents.——What an honest triumph in my uncle Toby's looks as he marched up to the ramparts! What intense pleasure swimming in his eye as he stood over the corporal, reading the paragraph ten times over to him, as he was at work, lest, peradventure, he should make the breach an inch too wide,——or leave it an inch too narrow——But when the *chamade* was beat, and the corporal helped my uncle up it, and followed with the colours in his hand, to fix them upon the ramparts——Heaven! Earth! Sea!——but what avails apostrophes?——with all your elements, wet or dry, ye never compounded so intoxicating a draught.

In this track of happiness for many years, without one interruption to it, except now and then when the wind continued to blow due west for a week or ten days together, which detained the Flanders mail, and kept them so long in torture,——but still 'twas the torture of the happy——In this track, I say, did my uncle Toby and Trim move for many years, every year of which, and sometimes every month, from the invention of either the one or the other of them, adding some new conceit or quirk of improvement to their operations, which always opened fresh springs of delight in carrying them on.

The first year's campaign was carried on, from beginning to end, in the plain and simple method I've related.

In the second year, in which my uncle Toby took Liége and Ruremond, he thought he might afford the expense of four handsome drawbridges, of two of which I have given an exact description, in the former part of my work.

At the latter end of the same year he added a couple of gates with portcullises:——These last were converted afterwards into orgues, as the better thing; and during the winter of the same year, my uncle Toby, instead of a new suit of clothes, which he always had at Christmas, treated himself with a handsome sentry box, to stand at the corner of the bowling green, betwixt which point and the foot of the glacis, there was left a little kind of an esplanade for him and the corporal to confer and hold councils of war upon.

——The sentry box was in case of rain.

All these were painted white three times over the ensuing spring, which enabled my uncle Toby to take the field with great splendour.

My father would often say to Yorick, that if any mortal in the whole universe had done such a thing, except his brother Toby, it would have been looked upon by the world as one of the most refined satires upon the parade and prancing manner in which Lewis XIV, from the beginning of the war, but particularly that very year, had taken the field——But 'tis not my brother Toby's nature, kind soul! my father would add, to insult anyone.

——But let us go on.

CHAPTER XXIII

I must observe that although in the first year's campaign, the word *town* is often mentioned,——yet there was no town at that time within the polygon; that addition was not made till the summer following the spring in which the bridges and sentry box were painted, which was the third year of my uncle Toby's campaigns,——when upon his taking Amberg, Bonn, and Rhinberg, and Huy and Limbourg, one after another, a thought came into the corporal's head that to talk of taking so many towns, *without one* TOWN *to show for it,*——was a very nonsensical way of going to work, and so proposed to my uncle Toby that they should have a little model of a town built for them,——to be run up together of slit deals, and then painted, and clapped within the interior polygon to serve for all.

My uncle Toby felt the good of the project instantly, and instantly agreed to it, but with the addition of two singular improvements, of which he was almost as proud as if he had been the original inventor of the project itself.

The one was to have the town built exactly in the style of those of which it was most likely to be the representative: ——with grated windows, and the gable ends of the houses, facing the streets, &c., &c.——as those in Ghent and Bruges, and the rest of the towns in Brabant and Flanders.

The other was not to have the houses run up together, as the corporal proposed, but to have every house independent, to hook on, or off, so as to form into the plan of whatever town they pleased. This was put directly into hand, and many and many a look of mutual congratulation was exchanged between my uncle Toby and the corporal, as the carpenter did the work.

——It answered prodigiously the next summer——the town was a perfect Proteus——It was Landen, and Trerebach, and Santvliet, and Drusen, and Hagenau,——and then it was Ostend and Menin, and Aeth and Dendermond.

——Surely never did any TOWN act so many parts, since Sodom and Gomorrah, as my uncle Toby's town did.

In the fourth year, my uncle Toby, thinking a town looked foolishly without a church, added a very fine one with a steeple.——Trim was for having bells in it;——my uncle Toby said the metal had better be cast into cannon.

This led the way, the next campaign, for half a dozen brass fieldpieces,——to be planted three and three on each side of my uncle Toby's sentry box; and in a short time, these led the way for a train of somewhat larger,——and so on ——(as must always be the case in hobby-horsical affairs) from pieces of half-an-inch bore, till it came at last to my father's jack boots.

The next year, which was that in which Lille was besieged, and at the close of which both Ghent and Bruges fell into our hands,——my uncle Toby was sadly put to it for *proper* ammunition;——I say proper ammunition—— because his great artillery would not bear powder; and 'twas well for the Shandy family they would not——For so full were the papers, from the beginning to the end of the siege, of the incessant firings kept up by the besiegers,——and so heated was my uncle Toby's imagination with the accounts of them, that he had infallibly shot away all his estate.

SOMETHING therefore was wanting, as a succedaneum, especially in one or two of the more violent paroxysms of the siege, to keep up something like a continual firing in the imagination,——and this *something*, the corporal, whose principal strength lay in invention, supplied by an entire new system of battering of his own,——without which this had been objected to by military critics, to the end of the world, as one of the great *desiderata* of my uncle Toby's apparatus.

This will not be explained the worse for setting off, as I generally do, at a little distance from the subject.

CHAPTER XXIV

With two or three other trinkets, small in themselves, but of great regard, which poor Tom, the corporal's unfortunate brother, had sent him over, with the account of his marriage with the Jew's widow——there was

A Montero cap and two Turkish tobacco pipes.

The Montero cap I shall describe by and bye.——The Turkish tobacco pipes had nothing particular in them; they were fitted up and ornamented as usual, with flexible tubes of Morocco leather and gold wire, and mounted at their ends, the one of them with ivory,——the other with black ebony, tipped with silver.

My father, who saw all things in lights different from the rest of the world, would say to the corporal that he ought to look upon these two presents more as tokens of his brother's nicety than his affection.——Tom did not care, Trim, he would say, to put on the cap, or to smoke in the tobacco pipe of a Jew.——God bless your Honour, the corporal would say (giving a strong reason to the contrary),——how can that be?——

The Montero cap was scarlet, of a superfine Spanish cloth, dyed in grain, and mounted all round with fur, except about four inches in the front, which was faced with a light blue, slightly embroidered,——and seemed to have been the property of a Portuguese quartermaster, not of foot, but of horse, as the word denotes.

The corporal was not a little proud of it, as well for its own sake, as the sake of the giver, so seldom or never put it on but upon GALA days; and yet never was a Montero cap put to so many uses; for in all controverted points, whether military or culinary, provided the corporal was sure he was right,——it was either his *oath*,——his *wager*,——or his *gift*.

——'Twas his gift in the present case.

I'll be bound, said the corporal, speaking to himself, to *give* away my Montero cap to the first beggar who comes to the door, if I do not manage this matter to his Honour's satisfaction.

The completion was no further off than the very next morning; which was that of the storm of the counterscarp betwixt the Lower Deule, to the right, and the gate St. Andrew,——on the left, between St. Magdalen's and the river.

As this was the most memorable attack in the whole war, ——the most gallant and obstinate on both sides,——and I must add the most bloody too, for it cost the allies themselves that morning above eleven hundred men,——my uncle Toby prepared himself for it with a more than ordinary solemnity.

The eve which preceded, as my uncle Toby went to bed, he ordered his Ramillie wig, which had laid inside out for many years in the corner of an old campaigning trunk, which stood by his bedside, to be taken out and laid upon the lid of it, ready for the morning;——and the very first thing he did in his shirt, when he had stepped out of bed, my uncle Toby, after he had turned the rough side outwards,——put it on:——This done, he proceeded next to his breeches, and having buttoned the waistband, he forthwith buckled on his sword belt, and had got his sword halfway in,——when he considered he should want shaving, and that it would be very inconvenient doing it with his sword on, ——so took it off:——In assaying to put on his regimental coat and waistcoat, my uncle Toby found the same objection in his wig,——so that went off too:——So that what with one thing, and what with another, as always falls out when a man is in the most haste,——'twas ten o'clock, which was half an hour later than his usual time, before my uncle Toby sallied out.

CHAPTER XXV

My uncle Toby had scarce turned the corner of his yew hedge, which separated his kitchen garden from his bowling green, when he perceived the corporal had began the attack without him.——

Let me stop and give you a picture of the corporal's apparatus; and of the corporal himself in the height of this attack just as it struck my uncle Toby, as he turned towards the sentry box, where the corporal was at work,——for in nature there is not such another,——nor can any combination of all that is grotesque and whimsical in her works produce its equal.

The corporal————

——Tread lightly on his ashes, ye men of genius,——for he was your kinsman:

Weed his grave clean, ye men of goodness,——for he was your brother.——O corporal! had I thee, but now,——now that I am able to give thee a dinner and protection,——how would I cherish thee! thou shouldst wear thy Montero cap every hour of the day, and every day of the week,——and when it was worn out, I would purchase thee a couple like it:——But alas! alas! alas! now that I can do this, in spite of their Reverences——the occasion is lost——for thou art gone;——thy genius fled up to the stars from whence it came;——and that warm heart of thine, with all its generous and open vessels, compressed into a *clod of the valley!*

——But what——what is this, to that future and dreaded page, where I look towards the velvet pall, decorated with the military ensigns of thy master——the first——the foremost of created beings;——where I shall see thee, faithful servant! laying his sword and scabbard with a trembling hand across his coffin, and then returning pale as ashes to the door, to take his mourning horse by the bridle, to follow his hearse, as he directed thee;——where——all my father's systems shall be baffled by his sorrows; and, in spite of his philosophy, I shall behold him, as he inspects the lacquered plate, twice taking his spectacles from off his nose, to wipe away the dew which Nature has shed upon them——When I see him cast in the rosemary with an air of disconsolation, which cries through my ears,——O Toby! in what corner of the world shall I seek thy fellow?

——Gracious powers! which erst have opened the lips of the dumb in his distress, and made the tongue of the stammerer speak plain——when I shall arrive at this dreaded page, deal not with me, then, with a stinted hand.

CHAPTER XXVI

The corporal, who the night before had resolved in his mind to supply the grand *desideratum*, of keeping up something like an incessant firing upon the enemy during the heat of the attack,——had no further idea in his fancy at that time than a contrivance of smoking tobacco against the town, out of one of my uncle Toby's six fieldpieces, which were planted on each side of his sentry box; the means of effecting which occurring to his fancy at the same time, though he had pledged his cap, he thought it in no danger from the miscarriage of his projects.

Upon turning it this way, and that, a little in his mind, he soon began to find out that by means of his two Turkish tobacco pipes, with the supplement of three smaller tubes of wash leather at each of their lower ends, to be tagged by the same number of tin pipes fitted to the touch holes, and sealed with clay next the cannon, and then tied hermetically with waxed silk at their several insertions into the Morocco tube,——he should be able to fire the six fieldpieces all together, and with the same ease as to fire one.——

——Let no man say from what tags and jags hints may not be cut out for the advancement of human knowledge. Let no man who has read my father's first and second *beds of justice* ever rise up and say again from collision of what kinds of bodies, light may, or may not, be struck out, to carry the arts and sciences up to perfection.——Heaven! thou knowest how I love them;——thou knowest the secrets of my heart, and that I would this moment give my shirt——Thou art a fool, Shandy, says Eugenius,——for thou hast but a dozen in the world,——and 'twill break thy set.——

No matter for that, Eugenius; I would give the shirt off my back to be burnt into tinder, were it only to satisfy one feverish enquirer how many sparks at one good stroke a good flint and steel could strike into the tail of it.——Think ye not that in striking these *in*,——he might, peradventure, strike something *out*? as sure as a gun.——

——But this project by the bye.

The corporal sat up the best part of the night in bringing *his* to perfection; and having made a sufficient proof of his cannon, with charging them to the top with tobacco,——he went with contentment to bed.

CHAPTER XXVII

The corporal had slipped out about ten minutes before my uncle Toby, in order to fix his apparatus, and just give the enemy a shot or two before my uncle Toby came. He had drawn the six fieldpieces, for this end, all close up together in front of my uncle Toby's sentry box, leaving only an interval of about a yard and a half betwixt the three, on the right and left, for the convenience of charging, &c.—— and the sake possibly of two batteries, which he might think double the honour of one.

In the rear, and facing this opening, with his back to the door of the sentry box, for fear of being flanked, had the corporal wisely taken his post:——He held the ivory pipe, appertaining to the battery on the right, betwixt the finger and thumb of his right hand,——and the ebony pipe tipped with silver, which appertained to the battery on the left, betwixt the finger and thumb of the other——and with his right knee fixed firm upon the ground, as if in the front rank of his platoon, was the corporal, with his Montero cap upon his head, furiously playing off his two cross batteries at the same time against the counterguard, which faced the counterscarp, where the attack was to be made that morning. His first intention, as I said, was no more than giving the enemy a single puff or two;——but the pleasure of the *puffs*, as well as the *puffing*, had insensibly got hold of the corporal, and drawn him on from puff to puff, into the very height of the attack, by the time my uncle Toby joined him.

'Twas well for my father that my uncle Toby had not his will to make that day.

CHAPTER XXVIII

My uncle Toby took the ivory pipe out of the corporal's hand,——looked at it for half a minute, and returned it.

In less than two minutes my uncle Toby took the pipe from the corporal again, and raised it halfway to his mouth ——then hastily gave it back a second time.

The corporal redoubled the attack;——my uncle Toby smiled,——then looked grave,——then smiled for a moment, ——then looked serious for a long time;——Give me hold of the ivory pipe, Trim, said my uncle Toby——my uncle Toby put it to his lips,——drew it back directly,——gave a peep over the hornbeam hedge;——never did my uncle Toby's mouth water so much for a pipe in his life.——My uncle Toby retired into the sentry box with the pipe in his hand.——

——Dear uncle Toby! don't go into the sentry box with the pipe;——there's no trusting a man's self with such a thing in such a corner.

CHAPTER XXIX

I beg the reader will assist me here, to wheel off my uncle Toby's ordnance behind the scenes,——to remove his sentry box, and clear the theatre, *if possible*, of hornworks and half-moons, and get the rest of his military apparatus out of the way;——that done, my dear friend Garrick, we'll snuff the candles bright,——sweep the stage with a new broom,——draw up the curtain, and exhibit my uncle Toby dressed in a new character, throughout which the world can have no idea how he will act: and yet, if pity be akin to love, ——and bravery no alien to it, you have seen enough of my uncle Toby in these, to trace these family likenesses betwixt the two passions (in case there is one) to your heart's content.

Vain science! thou assists us in no case of this kind—— and thou puzzlest us in every one.

There was, Madam, in my uncle Toby a singleness of heart which misled him so far out of the little serpentine tracks in which things of this nature usually go on; you can—you can have no conception of it: with this, there was a plainness and simplicity of thinking, with such an unmistrusting ignorance of the plies and foldings of the heart of woman;——and so naked and defenceless did he stand before you (when a siege was out of his head) that you might have stood behind any one of your serpentine walks, and shot my uncle Toby ten times in a day, through his liver, if nine times in a day, Madam, had not served your purpose.

With all this, Madam,——and what confounded everything as much on the other hand, my uncle Toby had that unparalleled modesty of nature I once told you of, and which, by the bye, stood eternal sentry upon his feelings, that you might as soon——But where am I going? these reflections crowd in upon me ten pages at least too soon, and take up that time which I ought to bestow upon facts.

CHAPTER XXX

Of the few legitimate sons of Adam whose breasts never felt what the sting of love was——(maintaining, first, all misogynists to be bastards),——the greatest heroes of ancient and modern story have carried off amongst them nine parts in ten of the honour; and I wish for their sakes I had the key of my study out of my draw well, only for five minutes, to tell you their names——recollect them I cannot——so be content to accept of these, for the present, in their stead.——

There was the great king Aldrovandus, and Bosphorus, and Capadocius, and Dardanus, and Pontus, and Asius,——to say nothing of the ironhearted Charles the XIIth, whom the Countess of K***** herself could make nothing of.—— There was Babylonicus, and Mediterraneus, and Polixenes, and Persicus, and Prusicus, not one of whom (except Capadocius and Pontus, who were both a little suspected) ever once bowed down his breast to the goddess——The truth is, they had all of them something else to do——and so had my uncle Toby——till Fate——till Fate, I say, envying his name the glory of being handed down to posterity with Aldrovandus's and the rest,——she basely patched up the peace of Utrecht.

——Believe me, Sirs, 'twas the worst deed she did that year.

CHAPTER XXXI

Amongst the many ill consequences of the treaty of Utrecht, it was within a point of giving my uncle Toby a surfeit of sieges; and though he recovered his appetite afterwards, yet Calais itself left not a deeper scar in Mary's heart than Utrecht upon my uncle Toby's. To the end of his life he never could hear Utrecht mentioned upon any account whatever,——or so much as read an article of news extracted out of the Utrecht *Gazette*, without fetching a sigh, as if his heart would break in twain.

My father, who was a great MOTIVE-MONGER, and consequently a very dangerous person for a man to sit by, either laughing or crying,——for he generally knew your motive for doing both much better than you knew it yourself—— would always console my uncle Toby upon these occasions, in a way which showed plainly he imagined my uncle Toby grieved for nothing in the whole affair, so much as the loss of his hobby-horse.——Never mind, brother Toby, he would say,——by God's blessing we shall have another war break out again some of these days; and when it does,—— the belligerent powers, if they would hang themselves, cannot keep us out of play.——I defy 'em, my dear Toby, he would add, to take countries without taking towns,——or towns without sieges.

My uncle Toby never took this back stroke of my father's at his hobby-horse kindly.——He thought the stroke ungenerous; and the more so, because in striking the horse, he hit the rider too, and in the most dishonourable part a blow could fall; so that upon these occasions, he always laid down his pipe upon the table with more fire to defend himself than common.

I told the reader, this time two years, that my uncle Toby was not eloquent; and in the very same page gave an instance to the contrary:——I repeat the observation, and a fact which contradicts it again.——He was not eloquent, ——it was not easy to my uncle Toby to make long harangues,——and he hated florid ones; but there were occasions where the stream overflowed the man, and ran so counter to its usual course that in some parts my uncle Toby, for a time, was at least equal to Tertullus——but in others, in my opinion, infinitely above him.

My father was so highly pleased with one of these apologetical orations of my uncle Toby's, which he had delivered one evening before him and Yorick, that he wrote it down before he went to bed.

I have had the good fortune to meet with it amongst my father's papers, with here and there an insertion of his own, betwixt two crooks, thus [   ], and is endorsed,

My brother TOBY'S *justification of his own principles and conduct in wishing to continue the war.*

I may safely say, I have read over this apologetical oration of my uncle Toby's a hundred times, and think it so fine a model of defence,——and shows so sweet a temperament of gallantry and good principles in him, that I give it the world, word for word (interlineations and all), as I find it.

CHAPTER XXXII

My uncle TOBY'S apologetical oration

I am not insensible, brother Shandy, that when a man whose profession is arms wishes, as I have done, for war,——it has an ill aspect to the world;——and that, how just and right soever his motives and intentions may be,——he stands in an uneasy posture in vindicating himself from private views in doing it.

For this cause, if a soldier is a prudent man, which he may be without being a jot the less brave, he will be sure not to utter his wish in the hearing of an enemy; for say what he will, an enemy will not believe him.——He will be cautious of doing it even to a friend,——lest he may suffer in his esteem:——But if his heart is overcharged, and a secret sigh for arms must have its vent, he will reserve it for the ear of a brother, who knows his character to the bottom, and what his true notions, dispositions, and principles of honour are: What, I *hope,* I have been in all these, brother Shandy, would be unbecoming in me to say:—— much worse, I know, have I been than I ought,——and something worse, perhaps, than I think: But such as I am, you, my dear brother Shandy, who have sucked the same breasts with me,——and with whom I have been brought up from my cradle,——and from whose knowledge, from the first hours of our boyish pastimes, down to this, I have concealed no one action of my life, and scarce a thought in it——Such as I am, brother, you must by this time know me, with all my vices, and with all my weaknesses too, whether of my age, my temper, my passions, or my understanding.

Tell me then, my dear brother Shandy, upon which of them it is, that when I condemned the peace of Utrecht, and grieved the war was not carried on with vigour a little longer, you should think your brother did it upon unworthy views; or that in wishing for war, he should be bad enough to wish more of his fellow creatures slain,——more slaves made, and more families driven from their peaceful habitations, merely for his own pleasure:——Tell me, brother Shandy, upon what one deed of mine do you ground it? [*The devil a deed do I know of, dear Toby, but one for a hundred pounds, which I lent thee to carry on these cursed sieges.*]

If, when I was a schoolboy, I could not hear a drum beat, but my heart beat with it——was it my fault?——Did I plant the propensity there?——did I sound the alarm within, or Nature?

When Guy, Earl of Warwick, and Parismus and Parismenus, and Valentine and Orson, and the Seven Champions of England were handed around the school,——were they not all purchased with my own pocket money? Was that selfish, brother Shandy? When we read over the siege of Troy, which lasted ten years and eight months,——though with such a train of artillery as we had at Namur, the town might have been carried in a week——was I not as much concerned for the destruction of the Greeks and Trojans as any boy of the whole school? Had I not three strokes of a ferula given me, two on my right hand and one on my left, for calling Helena a bitch for it? Did any one of you shed more tears for Hector? And when King Priam came to the camp to beg his body, and returned weeping back to Troy without it,——you know, brother, I could not eat my dinner.——

——Did that bespeak me cruel? Or because, brother Shandy, my blood flew out into the camp, and my heart panted for war,——was it a proof it could not ache for the distresses of war too?

O brother! 'tis one thing for a soldier to gather laurels, ——and 'tis another to scatter cypress.——[*Who told thee, my dear Toby, that cypress was used by the ancients on mournful occasions?*]

——'Tis one thing, brother Shandy, for a soldier to hazard his own life——to leap first down into the trench, where he is sure to be cut in pieces:——'Tis one thing, from public spirit and a thirst of glory, to enter the breach the first man,——to stand in the foremost rank, and march bravely on with drums and trumpets, and colours flying about his ears:——'Tis one thing, I say, brother Shandy, to do this ——and 'tis another thing to reflect on the miseries of war;——to view the desolations of whole countries, and consider the intolerable fatigues and hardships which the soldier himself, the instrument who works them, is forced (for sixpence a day, if he can get it) to undergo.

Need I be told, dear Yorick, as I was by you, in Le Fever's funeral sermon, *That so soft and gentle a creature, born to love, to mercy, and kindness, as man is, was not shaped for this?*——But why did you not add, Yorick,——if not by NATURE——that he is so by NECESSITY?——For what is war? what is it, Yorick, when fought as ours has been, upon principles of *liberty*, and upon principles of *honour*—— what is it, but the getting together of quiet and harmless people, with their swords in their hands, to keep the ambitious and the turbulent within bounds? And heaven is my witness, brother Shandy, that the pleasure I have taken in these things,——and that infinite delight, in particular, which has attended my sieges in my bowling green, has arose within me, and I hope in the corporal too, from the consciousness we both had that in carrying them on, we were answering the great ends of our creation.

CHAPTER XXXIII

I told the Christian reader——I say *Christian*——hoping he
is one——and if he is not, I am sorry for it——and only
beg he will consider the matter with himself, and not lay
the blame entirely upon this book,——

I told him, Sir——for in good truth, when a man is telling
a story in the strange way I do mine, he is obliged continually to be going backwards and forwards to keep all tight
together in the reader's fancy——which, for my own part,
if I did not take heed to do more than at first, there is so
much unfixed and equivocal matter starting up, with so many
breaks and gaps in it,——and so little service do the stars
afford which, nevertheless, I hang up in some of the darkest
passages, knowing that the world is apt to lose its way, with
all the lights the sun itself at noonday can give it——and
now, you see, I am lost myself!——

——But 'tis my father's fault; and whenever my brains
come to be dissected, you will perceive, without spectacles,
that he has left a large uneven thread, as you sometimes see
in an unsalable piece of cambric, running along the whole
length of the web, and so untowardly, you cannot so much
as cut out a * * (here I hang up a couple of lights again),
——or a fillet, or a thumbstall, but it is seen or felt.——

Quanto id diligentius in liberis procreandis cavendum,
sayeth Cardan. All which being considered, and that you see
'tis morally impracticable for me to wind this round to where
I set out——

I begin the chapter over again.

CHAPTER XXXIV

I told the Christian reader in the beginning of the chapter
which preceded my uncle Toby's apologetical oration,——
though in a different trope from what I shall make use of

now, That the peace of Utrecht was within an ace of creating the same shyness betwixt my uncle Toby and his hobby-horse, as it did betwixt the queen and the rest of the confederating powers.

There is an indignant way in which a man sometimes dismounts his horse, which as good as says to him, "I'll go afoot, Sir, all the days of my life, before I would ride a single mile upon your back again." Now my uncle Toby could not be said to dismount his horse in this manner; for in strictness of language, he could not be said to dismount his horse at all——his horse rather flung him——and somewhat *viciously*, which made my uncle Toby take it ten times more unkindly. Let this matter be settled by state jockeys as they like.——It created, I say, a sort of shyness betwixt my uncle Toby and his hobby-horse.——He had no occasion for him from the month of March to November, which was the summer after the articles were signed, except it was now and then to take a short ride out, just to see that the fortifications and harbour of Dunkirk were demolished, according to stipulation.

The French, were so backwards all that summer in setting about that affair, and Monsieur Tugghe, the deputy from the magistrates of Dunkirk, presented so many affecting petitions to the queen,——beseeching her Majesty to cause only her thunderbolts to fall upon the martial works, which might have incurred her displeasure,——but to spare——to spare the mole, for the mole's sake; which, in its naked situation, could be no more than an object of pity——and the queen (who was but a woman) being of a pitiful disposition,——and her ministers also, they not wishing in their hearts to have the town dismantled, for these private reasons,* * * * *
* * * * * * * * * * * * * * * * *
* * * * * * * * * * * * * * * * ——
* * * * * * * * * * * * * * * * *
* * * * * * * * * * * * * * * * *
* * * * *; so that the whole went heavily on with my uncle Toby; insomuch, that it was not within three full months after he and the corporal had constructed the town, and put it in a condition to be destroyed, that the several commandants, commissaries, deputies, negotiators, and intendants would permit him to set about it.——Fatal interval of inactivity!

The corporal was for beginning the demolition, by making a breach in the ramparts, or main fortifications of the town ——No,——that will never do, corporal, said my uncle

Toby, for in going that way to work with the town, the English garrison will not be safe in it an hour; because if the French are treacherous——They are as treacherous as devils, an' please your Honour, said the corporal——It gives me concern always when I hear it, Trim, said my uncle Toby—— for they don't want personal bravery; and if a breach is made in the ramparts, they may enter it, and make themselves masters of the place when they please:——Let them enter, said the corporal, lifting up his pioneer's spade in both his hands, as if he was going to lay about him with it,——let them enter, an' please your Honour, if they dare.——In cases like this, corporal, said my uncle Toby, slipping his right hand down to the middle of his cane, and holding it afterwards truncheon-wise, with his forefinger extended,——'tis no part of the consideration of a commandant what the enemy dare,——or what they dare not do; he must act with prudence. We will begin with the outworks both towards the sea and the land, and particularly with Fort Louis, the most distant of them all, and demolish it first,——and the rest, one by one, both on our right and left, as we retreat towards the town;——then we'll demolish the mole,——next fill up the harbour,——then retire into the citadel, and blow it up into the air; and having done that, corporal, we'll embark for England.——We are there, quoth the corporal, recollecting himself——Very true, said my uncle Toby——looking at the church.

CHAPTER XXXV

A delusive, delicious consultation or two of this kind, betwixt my uncle Toby and Trim, upon the demolition of Dunkirk——for a moment rallied back the ideas of those pleasures which were slipping from under him:——still—— still all went on heavily——the magic left the mind the weaker——STILLNESS, with SILENCE at her back, entered the solitary parlour, and drew their gauzy mantle over my uncle Toby's head;——and LISTLESSNESS, with her lax fibre and undirected eye, sat quietly down beside him in his armchair. ——No longer Amberg, and Rhinberg, and Limbourg, and Huy, and Bonn, in one year,——and the prospect of Lan-

den, and Trerebach, and Drusen, and Dendermond, the next,
——hurried on the blood:——No longer did saps, and mines,
and blinds, and gabions, and palisadoes keep out this fair
enemy of man's repose:——No more could my uncle
Toby, after passing the French lines, as he eat his egg at
supper, from thence break into the heart of France,——
cross over the Oise, and with all Picardie open behind him,
march up to the gates of Paris, and fall asleep with nothing
but ideas of glory:——No more was he to dream he had
fixed the royal standard upon the tower of the Bastille, and
awake with it streaming in his head.

——Softer visions,——gentler vibrations stole sweetly in
upon his slumbers;——the trumpet of war fell out of his
hands,——he took up the lute, sweet instrument! of all others
the most delicate! the most difficult!——how wilt thou
touch it, my dear uncle Toby?

CHAPTER XXXVI

Now, because I have once or twice said, in my inconsiderate way of talking, That I was confident the following mem-
oirs of my uncle Toby's courtship of widow Wadman, whenever I got time to write them, would turn out one of the
most complete systems both of the elementary and practical
part of love and love-making that ever was addressed to the
world——are you to imagine from thence that I shall set
out with a description of *what love is?* whether part God
and part devil, as Plotinus will have it——
——Or by a more critical equation, and supposing the
whole of love to be as ten——to determine, with Ficinus,
*"How many parts of it——the one,——and how many the
other;"*—or whether it is *all of it one great devil,* from head
to tail, as Plato has taken upon him to pronounce; concerning which conceit of his, I shall not offer my opinion:
——but my opinion of Plato is this: that he appears, from
this instance, to have been a man of much the same temper
and way of reasoning with Dr. Baynyard, who, being a great
enemy to blisters, as imagining that half a dozen of 'em on at
once would draw a man as surely to his grave as a hearse and
six——rashly concluded that the devil himself was nothing

in the world but one great bouncing *Cantharides*.——

I have nothing to say to people who allow themselves this monstrous liberty in arguing, but what Nazianzen cried out (*that is, polemically*) to Philagrius——

"ʼΕυγὲ!" *O rare! 'tis fine reasoning, Sir, indeed!*——"ὅτι φιλοσοφεῖς ἐν Πάθεσί"——*and most nobly do you aim at truth, when you philosophize about it in your moods and passions.*

Nor is it to be imagined, for the same reason, I should stop to enquire whether love is a disease,——or embroil myself with Rhasis and Dioscorides, whether the seat of it is in the brain or liver;——because this would lead me on to an examination of the two very opposite manners in which patients have been treated——the one, of Aetius, who always begun with a cooling clyster of hempseed and bruised cucumbers;——and followed on with thin potations of water lilies and purslane——to which he added a pinch of snuff, of the herb *Hanea;*——and where Aetius durst venture it,—— his topaz ring.

——The other, that of Gordonius, who (in his cap. 15 *de Amore*) directs they should be thrashed, *"ad putorem usque,"* ——till they stink again.

These are disquisitions which my father, who had laid in a great stock of knowledge of this kind, will be very busy with, in the progress of my uncle Toby's affairs: I must anticipate thus much, That from his theories of love (with which, by the way, he contrived to crucify my uncle Toby's mind, almost as much as his amours themselves),——he took a single step into practice;——and by means of a camphorated cerecloth, which he found means to impose upon the tailor for buckram, whilst he was making my uncle Toby a new pair of breeches, he produced Gordonius's effect upon my uncle Toby without the disgrace.

What changes this produced will be read in its proper place: all that is needful to be added to the anecdote is this, ——That whatever effect it had upon my uncle Toby,——it had a vile effect upon the house;——and if my uncle Toby had not smoked it down as he did, it might have had a vile effect upon my father too.

CHAPTER XXXVII

———'Twill come out of itself by and bye.———All I contend for is that I am not *obliged* to set out with a definition of what love is; and so long as I can go on with my story intelligibly, with the help of the world itself, without any other idea to it than what I have in common with the rest of the world, why should I differ from it a moment before the time?———When I can get on no further,———and find myself entangled on all sides of this mystic labyrinth, ———my Opinion will then come in, in course,———and lead me out.

At present, I hope I shall be sufficiently understood, in telling the reader, my uncle Toby *fell in love:*

———Not that the phrase is at all to my liking: for to say a man is *fallen* in love,———or that he is *deeply* in love,——— or up to the ears in love,———and sometimes even *over head and ears in it,*———carries an idiomatical kind of implication that love is a thing *below* a man:———this is recurring again to Plato's opinion, which, with all his divinityship,———I hold to be damnable and heretical;———and so much for that.

Let love therefore be what it will,———my uncle Toby fell into it.

———And possibly, gentle reader, with such a temptation ———so wouldst thou: For never did thy eyes behold, or thy concupiscence covet, anything in this world more concupiscible than widow Wadman.

CHAPTER XXXVIII

To conceive this right,———call for pen and ink———here's paper ready to your hand.———Sit down, Sir, paint her to your own mind———as like your mistress as you can———as
382

unlike your wife as your conscience will let you——'tis all one to me——please but your own fancy in it.

————Was ever anything in nature so sweet!——so exquisite!

——Then, dear Sir, how could my uncle Toby resist it?

Thrice happy book! thou wilt have one page, at least, within thy covers, which MALICE will not blacken, and which IGNORANCE cannot misrepresent.

CHAPTER XXXIX

As Susannah was informed by an express from Mrs. Bridget of my uncle Toby's falling in love with her mistress, fifteen days before it happened,——the contents of which express Susannah communicated to my mother the next day,——it has just given me an opportunity of entering upon my uncle Toby's amours a fortnight before their existence.

I have an article of news to tell you, Mr. Shandy, quoth my

mother, which will surprise you greatly.——

Now my father was then holding one of his second beds of justice, and was musing within himself about the hardships of matrimony, as my mother broke silence.——

"——My brother Toby, quoth she, is going to be married to Mrs. Wadman."

——Then he will never, quoth my father, be able to lie *diagonally* in his bed again as long as he lives.

It was a consuming vexation to my father that my mother never asked the meaning of a thing she did not understand.

——That she is not a woman of science, my father would say——is her misfortune——but she might ask a question.——

My mother never did.——In short, she went out of the world at last without knowing whether it turned *round,* or stood *still.*——My father had officiously told her above a thousand times which way it was,——but she always forgot.

For these reasons a discourse seldom went on much further betwixt them than a proposition,——a reply, and a rejoinder; at the end of which, it generally took breath for a few minutes (as in the affair of the breeches), and then went on again.

If he marries, 'twill be the worse for us,——quoth my mother.

Not a cherry stone, said my father;——he may as well batter away his means upon that, as anything else.

——To be sure, said my mother: so here ended the proposition,——the reply,——and the rejoinder I told you of.

It will be some amusement to him too,——said my father.

A very great one, answered my mother, if he should have children.——

——Lord have mercy upon me,——said my father to himself—— * * * * * * * * * * * * * * *
* * * * * * * * * * * * * * * *
* * * * * * * * * * * * * * * *
* * * * * * * * * * * * * * * *
* * * * * * * * * * *

CHAPTER XL

I am now beginning to get fairly into my work; and by the help of a vegetable diet, with a few of the cold seeds, I make no doubt but I shall be able to go on with my uncle

Toby's story, and my own, in a tolerable straight line.
Now,

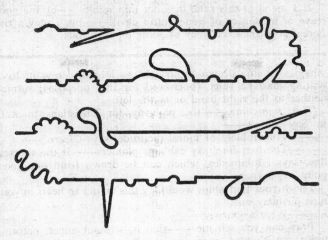

These were the four lines I moved in through my first, second, third, and fourth volumes.——In the fifth volume I have been very good;——the precise line I have described in it being this:

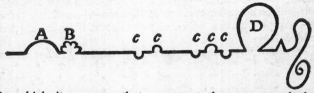

By which it appears, that except at the curve marked A, where I took a trip to Navarre,——and the indented curve B, which is the short airing when I was there with the Lady Baussiere and her page,——I have not taken the least frisk of a digression, till John de la Casse's devils led me the round you see marked D——for as for *c c c c c*, they are nothing but parentheses, and the common *ins* and *outs* incident to the lives of the greatest ministers of state; and when compared with what men have done,——or with my own transgressions at the letters A B D——they vanish into nothing.

In this last volume I have done better still——for from

the end of Le Fever's episode to the beginning of my uncle Toby's campaigns,——I have scarce stepped a yard out of my way.

If I mend at this rate, it is not impossible——by the good leave of his Grace of Benevento's devils——but I may arrive hereafter at the excellency of going on even thus:

---

which is a line drawn as straight as I could draw it, by a writing master's ruler (borrowed for that purpose), turning neither to the right hand or to the left.

This *right line,*——the pathway for Christians to walk in! Say divines——

——The emblem of moral rectitude! says *Cicero*——

——The *best line!* say cabbage planters——is the shortest line, says Archimedes, which can be drawn from one given point to another.——

I wish your Ladyships would lay this matter to heart in your next birthday suits!

——What a journey!

Pray can you tell me,——that is, without anger, before I write my chapter upon straight lines——by what mistake ——who told them so——or how it has come to pass, that your men of wit and genius have all along confounded this line with the line of GRAVITATION?

VOLUME VII

Non enim excursus hic ejus, sed opus ipsum est.
PLIN. Lib. quintus Epistola sexta

CHAPTER I

No——I think I said I would write two volumes every year, provided the vile cough which then tormented me, and which to this hour I dread worse than the devil, would but give me leave——and in another place——(but where, I can't recollect now) speaking of my book as a *machine*, and laying my pen and ruler down crosswise upon the table, in order to gain the greater credit to it——I swore it should be kept a-going at that rate these forty years if it pleased but the fountain of life to bless me so long with health and good spirits.

Now as for my spirits, little have I to lay to their charge ——nay, so very little (unless the mounting me upon a long stick, and playing the fool with me nineteen hours out of the twenty-four, be accusations) that on the contrary, I have much——much to thank 'em for: cheerily have ye made me tread the path of life with all the burdens of it (except its cares) upon my back; in no one moment of my existence, that I remember, have ye once deserted me, or tinged the objects which came in my way either with sable, or with a sickly green; in dangers ye gilded my horizon with hope, and when DEATH himself knocked at my door——ye bade him come again; and in so gay a tone of careless indifference did ye do it, that he doubted of his commission——

"——There must certainly be some mistake in this matter," quoth he.

387

Now there is nothing in this world I abominate worse than to be interrupted in a story——and I was that moment telling Eugenius a most tawdry one, in my way, of a nun who fancied herself a shellfish, and of a monk damned for eating a mussel, and was showing him the grounds and justice of the procedure——

"——Did ever so grave a personage get into so vile a scrape?" quoth Death. Thou hast had a narrow escape, Tristram, said Eugenius, taking hold of my hand as I finished my story——

But there is no *living*, Eugenius, replied I, at this rate; for as this *son of a whore* has found out my lodgings——

——You call him rightly, said Eugenius,——for by sin, we are told, he entered the world——I care not which way he entered, quoth I, provided he be not in such a hurry to take me out with him——for I have forty volumes to write, and forty thousand things to say and do, which nobody in the world will say and do for me, except thyself; and as thou seest he has got me by the throat (for Eugenius could scarce hear me speak across the table) and that I am no match for him in the open field, had I not better, whilst these few scattered spirits remain, and these two spider legs of mine (holding one of them up to him) are able to support me——had I not better, Eugenius, fly for my life? 'tis my advice, my dear Tristram, said Eugenius——then by heaven! I will lead him a dance he little thinks of——for I will gallop, quoth I, without looking once behind me, to the banks of the Garonne; and if I hear him clattering at my heels——I'll scamper away to Mount Vesuvius——from thence to Joppa, and from Joppa to the world's end, where, if he follows me, I pray God he may break his neck——

——He runs more risk *there*, said Eugenius, than thou.

Eugenius's wit and affection brought blood into the cheek from whence it had been some months banished——'twas a vile moment to bid adieu in; he led me to my chaise——*Allons!* said I; the postboy gave a crack with his whip——off I went like a cannon, and in half a dozen bounds got into Dover.

CHAPTER II

Now hang it! quoth I, as I looked towards the French coast ——a man should know something of his own country too, before he goes abroad——and I never gave a peep into

Rochester church, or took notice of the dock of Chatham, or visited St. Thomas at Canterbury though they all three laid in my way——

——But mine, indeed, is a particular case——

So without arguing the matter further with Thomas o' Becket, or anyone else——I skipped into the boat, and in five minutes we got under sail and scudded away like the wind.

Pray, captain, quoth I, as I was going down into the cabin, is a man never overtaken by Death in this passage?

Why, there is not time for a man to be sick in it, replied he——What a cursed liar! for I am sick as a horse, quoth I, already——what a brain!——upside down!——heyday! the cells are broke loose one into another, and the blood, and the lymph, and the nervous juices, with the fixed and volatile salts, are all jumbled into one mass——good G——! everything turns round in it like a thousand whirlpools——I'd give a shilling to know if I shan't write the clearer for it——

Sick! sick! sick! sick!——

——When shall we get to land, captain?——they have hearts like stones——O I am deadly sick!——reach me that thing, boy——'tis the most discomfiting sickness—I wish I was at the bottom——Madam! how is it with you? Undone! undone! un—— O! undone! sir——What, the first time?——No, 'tis the second, third, sixth, tenth time, sir,—— heyday——what a trampling overhead!——hollo! cabin boy! what's the matter——

The wind chopped about! s'Death!——then I shall meet him full in the face.

What luck!——'tis chopped about again, Master——O the devil chop it——

Captain, quoth she, for heaven's sake, let us get ashore.

CHAPTER III

It is a great inconvenience, to a man in a haste, that there are three distinct roads between Calais and Paris, in behalf of which there is so much to be said by the several deputies from the towns which lie along them, that half a day is easily lost in settling which you'll take.

First, the road by Lille and Arras, which is the most about——but most interesting, and instructing.

The second that by Amiens, which you may go if you would see Chantilly——

And that by Beauvais, which you may go if you will.

For this reason a great many choose to go by Beauvais.

CHAPTER IV

"Now before I quit Calais," a travel writer would say, "it would not be amiss to give some account of it."——Now I think it very much amiss——that a man cannot go quietly through a town, and let it alone, when it does not meddle with him, but that he must be turning about and drawing his pen at every kennel he crosses over, merely, o' my conscience, for the sake of drawing it; because, if we may judge from what has been wrote of these things, by all who have *wrote and galloped*——or who have *galloped and wrote*, which is a different way still; or who, for more expedition than the rest, have *wrote galloping*, which is the way I do at present——from the great Addison, who did it with his satchel of school-books hanging at his a—— and galling his beast's crupper at every stroke——there is not a galloper of us all who might not have gone on ambling quietly in his own ground (in case he had any) and have wrote all he had to write, dry shod, as well as not.

For my own part, as heaven is my judge, and to which I shall ever make my last appeal——I know no more of Calais (except the little my barber told me of it, as he was whetting his razor) than I do this moment of Grand Cairo; for it was dusky in the evening when I landed, and dark as pitch in the morning when I set out, and yet by merely knowing what is what, and by drawing this from that in one part of the town, and by spelling and putting this and that together in another——I would lay any travelling odds that I this moment write a chapter upon Calais as long as my arm; and with so distinct and satisfactory a detail of every item which is worth a stranger's curiosity in the town——that you would take me for the town clerk of Calais itself——and where, sir, would be the wonder? was not Democritus, who laughed ten times more than I,——town clerk of Abdera? and was not (I forget his name), who had more discretion than us both, town clerk of Ephesus?——it should be penned

moreover, Sir, with so much knowledge and good sense, and
truth, and precision——

——Nay——if you don't believe me, you may read the
chapter for your pains.

CHAPTER V

Calais, *Calatium, Calusium, Calesium.*

This town, if we may trust its archives, the authority of
which I see no reason to call in question in this place——
was *once* no more than a small village belonging to one of
the first Counts de Guines; and as it boasts at present of
no less than fourteen thousand inhabitants, exclusive of four
hundred and twenty distinct families in the *basse ville,* or
suburbs——it must have grown up by little and little, I suppose, to its present size.

Though there are four convents, there is but one parochial
church in the whole town; I had not an opportunity of
taking its exact dimensions, but it is pretty easy to make a
tolerable conjecture of 'em——for as there are fourteen
thousand inhabitants in the town, if the church holds
them all, it must be considerably large——and if it will not
——'tis a very great pity they have not another——it is
built in form of a cross, and dedicated to the Virgin Mary;
the steeple, which has a spire to it, is placed in the middle
of the church, and stands upon four pillars elegant and
light enough, but sufficiently strong at the same time——
it is decorated with eleven altars, most of which are rather
fine than beautiful. The great altar is a masterpiece in its
kind; 'tis of white marble, and as I was told near sixty feet
high——had it been much higher, it had been as high as
Mount Calvary itself——therefore, I suppose it must be
high enough in all conscience.

There was nothing struck me more than the great Square;
though I cannot say 'tis either well paved or well built;
but 'tis in the heart of the town, and most of the streets,
especially those in that quarter, all terminate in it; could
there have been a fountain in all Calais, which it seems there
cannot, as such an object would have been a great ornament, it is not to be doubted but that the inhabitants would
have had it in the very centre of this square,——not that it
is properly a square,——because 'tis forty feet longer from

391

east to west, than from north to south; so that the French in general have more reason on their side in calling them *Places* than *Squares*, which strictly speaking, to be sure they are not.

The townhouse seems to be but a sorry building, and not to be kept in the best repair; otherwise it had been a second great ornament to this place; it answers however its destination, and serves very well for the reception of the magistrates, who assemble in it from time to time; so that 'tis presumable, justice is regularly distributed.

I have heard much of it, but there is nothing at all curious in the Courgain: 'tis a distinct quarter of the town inhabited solely by sailors and fishermen; it consists of a number of small streets, neatly built and mostly of brick; 'tis extremely populous, but as that may be accounted for from the principles of their diet,——there is nothing curious in that neither.——A traveller may see it to satisfy himself——he must not omit however taking notice of *La Tour de Guet*, upon any account; 'tis so called from its particular destination, because in war it serves to discover and give notice of the enemies which approach the place, either by sea or land;——but 'tis monstrous high, and catches the eye so continually, you cannot avoid taking notice of it, if you would.

It was a singular disappointment to me that I could not have permission to take an exact survey of the fortifications, which are the strongest in the world, and which, from first to last, that is, from the time they were set about by Philip of France, Count of Bologne, to the present war, wherein many reparations were made, have cost (as I learned afterwards from an engineer in Gascony)——above a hundred millions of livres. It is very remarkable that at the *Tête de Gravelenes*, and where the town is naturally the weakest, they have expended the most money; so that the outworks stretch a great way into the champaign, and consequently occupy a large tract of ground.——However, after all that is *said* and *done*, it must be acknowledged that Calais was never upon any account so considerable from itself, as from its situation, and that easy entrance which it gave our ancestors upon all occasions into France: it was not without its inconveniences also; being no less troublesome to the English, in those times, than Dunkirk has been to us, in ours; so that it was deservedly looked upon as the key to both kingdoms, which no doubt is the reason that there have arisen so many contentions who should keep it: of these, the siege of Calais, or rather the blockade (for it was shut up both by land and sea), was the most memorable, as it withstood the efforts of Edward the Third a whole year, and was not terminated at last but by famine and extreme misery; the gallantry of Eustace de St. Pierre, who first offered himself a victim for his fellow citizens, has ranked his name with heroes. As it will not take up above fifty pages, it would be injustice to the reader not to give him a minute account of that romantic transaction, as well as of the siege itself, in Rapin's own words:

CHAPTER VI

——But courage! gentle reader!——I scorn it——'tis enough to have thee in my power——but to make use of the advantage which the fortune of the pen has now gained over thee would be too much——No——! by that all-powerful fire which warms the visionary brain, and lights the spirits through unworldly tracts! ere I would force a helpless creature upon this hard service, and make thee pay, poor soul! for fifty pages which I have no right to sell thee,——naked as I am, I would browse upon the mountains, and smile that the north wind brought me neither my tent or my supper.

——So put on, my brave boy! and make the best of thy way to Boulogne.

CHAPTER VII

——Boulogne!——hah!——so we are all got together—— debtors and sinners before heaven; a jolly set of us——but I can't stay and quaff it off with you——I'm pursued myself like a hundred devils, and shall be overtaken before I can well change horses:——for heaven's sake, make haste——'Tis for high treason, quoth a very little man, whispering as low as he could to a very tall man that stood next him——Or else for murder, quoth the tall man——Well thrown, Size-Ace! quoth I. No, quoth a third, the gentleman has been committing —— ——.

Ah! ma chere fille! said I, as she tripped by, from her

matins——you look as rosy as the morning (for the sun was rising, and it made the compliment the more gracious)—— No; it can't be that, quoth a fourth——(she made a curtsy to me——I kissed my hand) 'tis debt, continued he: 'Tis certainly for debt, quoth a fifth; I would not pay that gentleman's debts, quoth Ace, for a thousand pounds; Nor would I, quoth Size, for six times the sum——Well thrown, Size-Ace, again! quoth I;——but I have no debt but the debt of NATURE, and I want but patience of her, and I will pay her every farthing I owe her——How can you be so hardhearted, MADAM, to arrest a poor traveller going along, without molestation to anyone, upon his lawful occasions? do stop that death-looking, long-striding scoundrel of a scare-sinner, who is posting after me——he never would have followed me but for you——if it be but for a stage or two, just to give me start of him, I beseech you, Madam——do, dear lady——

——Now, in troth, 'tis a great pity, quoth mine Irish host, that all this good courtship should be lost; for the young gentlewoman has been after going out of hearing of it all along——.

——Simpleton! quoth I.

——So you have nothing *else* in Boulogne worth seeing?

——By Jasus! there is the finest SEMINARY for the HUMANITIES——.

——There cannot be a finer, quoth I.

CHAPTER VIII

When the precipitancy of a man's wishes hurries on his ideas ninety times faster than the vehicle he rides in—— woe be to truth! and woe be to the vehicle and its tackling (let 'em be made of what stuff you will) upon which he breathes forth the disappointment of his soul!

As I never give general characters either of men or things in choler, *"the most haste, the worst speed"* was all the reflection I made upon the affair, the first time it happened; ——the second, third, fourth, and fifth time, I confined it respectively to those times, and accordingly blamed only the second, third, fourth, and fifth postboy for it, without carrying my reflections further; but the event continuing to befall me from the fifth, to the sixth, seventh, eighth, ninth, and tenth time, and without one exception, I then could not avoid making a national reflection of it, which I do in these words:

That something is always wrong in a French post chaise upon first setting out.

Or the proposition may stand thus:

A French postillion has always to alight before he has got three hundred yards out of town.

What's wrong now?——*Diable!*——a rope's broke!——a knot has slipt!——a staple's drawn!——a bolt's to whittle! ——a tag, a rag, a jag, a strap, a buckle, or a buckle's tongue want altering.——

Now true as all this is, I never think myself impowered to excommunicate thereupon either the post chaise or its driver——nor do I take it into my head to swear by the living G—, I would rather go a foot ten thousand times—— or that I will be damned if ever I get into another——but I take the matter coolly before me, and consider that some tag, or rag, or jag, or bolt, or buckle, or buckle's tongue will ever be a-wanting, or want altering, travel where I will——so I never chaff, but take the good and the bad as they fall in my road, and get on:——Do so, my lad! said I; he had lost five minutes already, in alighting in order to get at a luncheon of black bread which he had crammed into the chaise pocket, and was remounted and going leisurely on, to relish it the better——Get on, my lad, said I, briskly ——but in the most persuasive tone imaginable, for I jingled a four-and-twenty sous piece against the glass, taking care to hold the flat side towards him, as he looked back: the dog grinned intelligence from his right ear to his left, and behind his sooty muzzle discovered such a pearly row of teeth that Sovereignty would have pawned her jewels for them.——

Just heaven! { What masticators!——
{ What bread!——

and so, as he finished the last mouthful of it, we entered the town of Montreuil.

CHAPTER IX

There is not a town in all France which, in my opinion, looks better in the map than MONTREUIL;——I own, it does not look so well in the book of post roads; but when you come to see it——to be sure it looks most pitifully.

There is one thing however in it at present very hand-some; and that is the innkeeper's daughter: She has been eighteen months at Amiens, and six at Paris, in going through her classes; so knits, and sews, and dances, and does the little coquetries very well.——

——A slut! in running them over within these five minutes that I have stood looking at her, she has let fall at least a dozen loops in a white thread stocking——Yes, yes——I see, you cunning gipsy!——'tis long, and taper——you need not pin it to your knee——and that 'tis your own——and fits you exactly.——

——That Nature should have told this creature a word about a *statue's thumb!*——

——But as this sample is worth all their thumbs——be-sides I have her thumbs and fingers in at the bargain if they can be any guide to me,——and as Janatone withal (for that is her name) stands so well for a drawing——may I never draw more, or rather may I draw like a draught horse, by main strength all the days of my life,——if I do not draw her in all her proportions, and with as de-termined a pencil as if I had her in the wettest drapery.——

——But your Worships choose rather that I give you the length, breadth, and perpendicular height of the great parish church, or a drawing of the façade of the abbey of St. Austreberte, which has been transported from Artois hither——everything is just I suppose as the masons and carpenters left them,——and if the belief in Christ con-tinues so long, will be so these fifty years to come——so your Worships and Reverences may all measure them at your leisures——but he who measures thee, Janatone, must do it now——thou carriest the principles of change within thy frame; and considering the chances of a transitory life, I would not answer for thee a moment; e'er twice twelve months are passed and gone, thou mayest grow out like a pumpkin, and lose thy shapes——or, thou mayest go off like a flower, and lose thy beauty——nay, thou mayest go off like a hussy——and lose thyself.——I would not answer for my aunt Dinah, was she alive——faith, scarce for her picture——were it but painted by Reynolds——

——But if I go on with my drawing, after naming that son of Apollo, I'll be shot——

So you must e'en be content with the original; which, if the evening is fine in passing through Montreuil, you will see at your chaise door, as you change horses: but unless you have as bad a reason for haste as I have——you had better stop:——She has a little of the *devotee:* but that, sir, is a tierce to a nine in your favour——

——L——help me! I could not count a single point: so had been piqued, and repiqued, and capotted to the devil.

CHAPTER X

All which being considered, and that Death moreover might be much nearer me than I imagined——I wish I was at Abbeville, quoth I, were it only to see how they card and spin——so off we set:

*de *Montreuil à Nampont* --- poste et demi
de *Nampont à Bernay* --- poste
de *Bernay à Nouvion* --- poste
de *Nouvion à Abbeville* --- poste

——but the carders and spinners were all gone to bed.

CHAPTER XI

What a vast advantage is travelling! only it heats one; but there is a remedy for that, which you may pick out of the next chapter.

CHAPTER XII

Was I in a condition to stipulate with Death, as I am this moment with my apothecary, how and where I will take his clyster——I should certainly declare against submitting to it before my friends; and therefore, I never seriously think upon the mode and manner of this great catastrophe, which generally takes up and torments my thoughts as much as the catastrophe itself, but I constantly draw the curtain

* Vid. Book of French post roads, page 36, edition of 1762.

across it with this wish, that the Disposer of all things may so order it, that it happen not to me in my own house ——but rather in some decent inn——at home, I know it, ——the concern of my friends, and the last services of wiping my brows and smoothing my pillow, which the quivering hand of pale affection shall pay me, will so crucify my soul that I shall die of a distemper which my physician is not aware of: but in an inn, the few cold offices I wanted would be purchased with a few guineas, and paid me with an undisturbed but punctual attention——but mark. This inn should not be the inn at Abbeville——if there was not another inn in the universe, I would strike that inn out of the capitulation: so

Let the horses be in the chaise exactly by four in the morning——Yes, by four, Sir,——or by Genevieve! I'll raise a clatter in the house shall wake the dead.

CHAPTER XIII

"Make them like unto a wheel," is a bitter sarcasm, as all the learned know, against the *grand tour,* and that restless spirit for making it, which David prophetically foresaw would haunt the children of men in the latter days; and therefore, as thinketh the great Bishop Hall, 'tis one of the severest imprecations which David ever uttered against the enemies of the Lord——and as if he had said, "I wish them no worse luck than always to be rolling about"—— So much motion, continues he (for he was very corpulent), ——is so much unquietness; and so much of rest, by the same analogy, is so much of heaven.

Now, I (being very thin) think differently; and that so much of motion is so much of life, and so much of joy—— and that to stand still, or get on but slowly, is death and the devil——

Hollo! Ho!——the whole world's asleep!——bring out the horses——grease the wheels——tie on the mail——and drive a nail into that moulding——I'll not lose a moment——

Now the wheel we are talking of, and *whereinto* (but not *whereunto,* for that would make an Ixion's wheel of it) he curseth his enemies, according to the bishop's habit of body, should certainly be a post-chaise wheel, whether they were set up in Palestine at that time or not——and my wheel, for the contrary reasons, must as certainly be a cart wheel groaning round its revolution once in an age; and of which sort, were I to turn commentator, I should make no scruple to affirm, they had great store in that hilly country.

I love the Pythagoreans (much more than ever I dare tell my dear Jenny) for their "χωρισμὸν ἀπὸ τοῦ Σώματος, εἰς τὸ καλῶς φιλοσοφεῖν"———their *"getting out of the body, in order to think well."* No man thinks right whilst he is in it; blinded as he must be with his congenial humours, and drawn differently aside, as the bishop and myself have been, with too lax or too tense a fibre———REASON is, half of it, SENSE; and the measure of heaven itself is but the measure of our present appetites and concoctions———

———But which of the two, in the present case, do you think to be mostly in the wrong?

You, certainly, quoth she, to disturb a whole family so early.

CHAPTER XIV

———But she did not know I was under a vow not to shave my beard till I got to Paris;———yet I hate to make mysteries of nothing;———'tis the cold cautiousness of one of those little souls from which Lessius (*lib.* 13, *de moribus divinis, cap.* 24) hath made his estimate, wherein he setteth forth, That one Dutch mile, cubically multiplied, will allow room enouugh, and to spare, for eight hundred thousand millions, which he supposes to be as great a number of souls (counting from the fall of Adam) as can possibly be damned to the end of the world.

From what he has made this second estimate———unless from the parental goodness of God———I don't know———I am much more at a loss what could be in Franciscus Ribbera's head, who pretends that no less a space than one of two hundred Italian miles, multiplied into itself, will be sufficient to hold the like number———he certainly must have gone upon some of the old Roman souls of which he had read, without reflecting how much, by a gradual and most tabid decline, in a course of eighteen hundred years, they must unavoidably have shrunk, so as to have come, when he wrote, almost to nothing.

In Lessius's time, who seems the cooler man, they were as little as can be imagined——

——We find them less *now*——

And next winter we shall find them less again; so that if we go on from little to less, and from less to nothing, I hesitate not one moment to affirm that in half a century, at this rate, we shall have no souls at all; which being the period beyond which I doubt likewise of the existence of the Christian faith, 'twill be one advantage that both of 'em will be exactly worn out together.

Blessed Jupiter! and blessed every other heathen god and goddess! for now ye will all come into play again, and with Priapus at your tails——what jovial times!——but where am I? and into what a delicious riot of things am I rushing? I ——I who must be cut short in the midst of my days, and taste no more of 'em than what I borrow from my imagination——peace to thee, generous fool! and let me go on.

CHAPTER XV

——"So hating, I say, to make mysteries of *nothing*"—— I intrusted it with the postboy, as soon as ever I got off the stones; he gave a crack with his whip to balance the compliment; and with the thill horse trotting, and a sort of an up and a down of the other, we danced it along to Ailly au Clochers, famed in days of yore for the finest chimes in the world; but we danced through it without music——the chimes being greatly out of order——(as in truth they were through all France).

And so making all possible speed, from
Ailly au Clochers, I got to Hixcourt,
from Hixcourt, I got to Pequignay, and
from Pequignay, I got to AMIENS,
concerning which town I have nothing to inform you but what I have informed you once before——and that was—— that Janatone went there to school.

CHAPTER XVI

In the whole catalogue of those whiffling vexations which come puffing across a man's canvass, there is not one of a more teasing and tormenting nature than this particular one which I am going to describe——and for which (unless you travel with an avant-courier, which numbers do in order to prevent it)——there is no help: and it is this.

That be you in never so kindly a propensity to sleep—— though you are passing perhaps through the finest country ——upon the best roads——and in the easiest carriage for doing it in the world——nay, was you sure you could sleep fifty miles straight forwards, without once opening your eyes——nay, what is more, was you as demonstratively satisfied as you can be of any truth in Euclid that you should upon all accounts be full as well asleep as awake—— nay, perhaps better——Yet the incessant returns of paying for the horses at every stage,——with the necessity thereupon of putting your hand into your pocket, and counting out from thence three livres fifteen sous (sous by sous), puts an end to so much of the project, that you cannot execute above six miles of it (or supposing it is a post and a half, that is but nine)——were it to save your soul from destruction.

——I'll be even with 'em, quoth I, for I'll put the precise sum into a piece of paper, and hold it ready in my hand all the way: "Now I shall have nothing to do," said I (composing myself to rest), "but to drop this gently into the postboy's hat, and not say a word."——Then there wants two sous more to drink——or there is a twelve-sous piece of Louis XIV which will not pass——or livre and some odd liards to be brought over from the last stage, which Monsieur had forgot; which altercations (as a man cannot dispute very well asleep) rouse him: still is sweet sleep retrievable; and still might the flesh weigh down the spirit, and recover itself of these blows——but then, by heaven! you have paid but for a single post——whereas 'tis a post and a half; and this obliges you to pull out your book of post roads, the print of which is so very small, it forces you to open your eyes, whether you will or no: then *Monsieur le Curé* offers you a pinch of snuff——or a poor soldier shows you his leg——or a shaveling his box——or the priestess of the cistern will water your wheels——they do not want it——but she swears by her *priesthood* (throwing it back) that they do: ——then you have all these points to argue, or consider over in your mind; in doing of which, the rational powers get so thoroughly awakened——you may get 'em to sleep again as you can.

It was entirely owing to one of these misfortunes, or I had passed clean by the stables of Chantilly——

——But the postillion first affirming, and then persisting in it to my face, that there was no mark upon the two-sous piece, I opened my eyes to be convinced——and seeing the mark upon it, as plain as my nose——I leaped out of the chaise in a passion, and so saw everything at Chantilly in spite.——I tried it but for three posts and a half, but believe 'tis the best principle in the world to travel speedily upon; for as few objects look very inviting in that mood——you have little or nothing to stop you; by which means it was that I passed through St. Dennis, without turning my head so much as on side towards the abbey——

——Richness of their treasury! stuff and nonsense!—— bating their jewels, which are all false, I would not give three sous for any one thing in it, but Jaidas's lantern——nor for that either, only as it grows dark, it might be of use.

CHAPTER XVII

Crack, crack——crack, crack——crack, crack——so this is Paris! quoth I (continuing in the same mood)——and this is Paris!——humph!——Paris! cried I, repeating the name the third time——

The first, the finest, the most brilliant——

——The streets however are nasty;

But it looks, I suppose, better than it smells——crack, crack——crack, crack——What a fuss thou makest! as if it concerned the good people to be informed, That a man with pale face, and clad in black, had the honour to be driven into Paris at nine o'clock at night, by a postillion in a tawny yellow jerkin turned up with red calamanco—— crack, crack——crack, crack——crack, crack——I wish thy whip——

——But 'tis the spirit of thy nation; so crack——crack on.

Ha!——and no one gives the wall!——but in the School of Urbanity herself, if the walls are besh-t——how can you do otherwise?

And prithee when do they light the lamps? What?—— never in the summer months!——Ho! 'tis the time of salads. ——O rare! salad and soup——soup and salad——salad and soup, *encore*——

——'Tis *too much* for sinners.

Now I cannot bear the barbarity of it; how can that unconscionable coachman talk so much bawdy to that lean horse? don't you see, friend, the streets are so villainously narrow that there is not room in all Paris to turn a wheelbarrow? In the grandest city of the whole world, it would not have been amiss if they had been left a thought wider; nay, were it only so much in every single street as that a man might know (was it only for satisfaction) on which side of it he was walking.

One——two——three——four——five——six——seven ——eight——nine——ten.——Ten cooks' shops! and twice the number of barbers'! and all within three minutes' driving! one would think that all the cooks in the world, on some great merrymeeting with the barbers, by joint consent had said——Come, let us all go live at Paris: the French love good eating——they are all *gourmands*——we shall rank high; if their god is their belly——their cooks must be gentlemen: and forasmuch as *the periwig maketh the man*, and the periwig-maker maketh the periwig——*ergo,* would the barbers say, we shall rank higher still——we shall be above you all——we shall be *Capitouls* * at least——*pardi!* we shall all wear swords——

——And so, one would swear (that is by candlelight,—— but there is no depending upon it), they continue to do, to this day.

CHAPTER XVIII

The French are certainly misunderstood:——but whether the fault is theirs, in not sufficiently explaining themselves; or speaking with that exact limitation and precision which one would expect on a point of such importance, and which

* Chief magistrate in Toulouse, etc. etc. etc.

moreover is so likely to be contested by us——or whether the fault may not be altogether on our side, in not understanding their language always so critically as to know "what they would be at"——I shall not decide; but 'tis evident to me, when they affirm, *"That they who have seen Paris have seen everything,"* they must mean to speak of those who have seen it by daylight.

As for candlelight——I give it up——I have said before, there was no depending upon it——and I repeat it again; but not because the lights and shades are too sharp——or the tints confounded——or that there is neither beauty or keeping, &c. . . . for that's not truth——but it is an uncertain light in this respect, That in all the five hundred grand *hôtels* which they number up to you in Paris——and the five hundred good things, at a modest computation (for 'tis only allowing one good thing to a *hôtel*), which by candlelight are best to be *seen, felt, heard, and understood* (which, by the bye, is a quotation from *Lilly*)——the devil a one of us out of fifty can get our heads fairly thrust in amongst them.

This is no part of the French computation: 'tis simply this.

That by the last survey, taken in the year one thousand seven hundred and sixteen, since which time there have been considerable augmentations, Paris doth contain nine hundred streets (*viz.*):

In the quarter called the *City*——there are fifty-three streets.
In St. James of the Shambles, fifty-five streets.
In St. Oportune, thirty-four streets.
In the quarter of the Louvre, twenty-five streets.
In the Palace Royal, or St. Honorius, forty-nine streets.
In Mont Martyr, forty-one streets.
In St. Eustace, twenty-nine streets.
In the Halles, twenty-seven streets.
In St. Dennis, fifty-five streets.
In St. Martin, fifty-four streets.
In St. Paul, or the Mortellerie, twenty-seven streets.
The Greve, thirty-eight streets.
In St. Avoy, or the Verrerie, nineteen streets.
In the Marais, or the Temple, fifty-two streets.
In St. Antony's, sixty-eight streets.
In the Place Maubert, eighty-one streets.
In St. Bennet, sixty streets.
In St. Andrews de Arcs, fifty-one streets.
In the quarter of the Luxembourg, sixty-two streets.
And in that of St. Germain, fifty-five streets, into any of which you may walk; and that when you have seen them

with all that belongs to them, fairly by daylight——their gates, their bridges, their squares, their statues - - - - and have crusaded it moreover through all their parish churches, by no means omitting St. Roche and Sulpice - - - and to crown all, have taken a walk to the four palaces, which you may see either with or without the statues and pictures, just as you choose——

——Then you will have seen——

——but, 'tis what no one needeth to tell you, for you will read it yourself upon the portico of the Louvre, in these words,

* EARTH NO SUCH FOLKS!——NO FOLKS E'ER SUCH A TOWN
AS PARIS IS!——SING, DERRY, DERRY, DOWN.

The French have a gay way of treating everything that is Great; and that is all can be said upon it.

CHAPTER XIX

In mentioning the word *gay* (as in the close of the last chapter), it puts one (*i.e.*, an author) in mind of the word *spleen* ——especially if he has anything to say upon it: not that by any analysis——or that from any table of interest or genealogy, there appears much more ground of alliance betwixt them than betwixt light and darkness, or any two of the most unfriendly opposites in nature——only 'tis an undercraft of authors to keep up a good understanding amongst words, as politicians do amongst men——not knowing how near they may be under a necessity of placing them to each other——which point being now gained, and that I may place mine exactly to my mind, I write it down here——

SPLEEN

This, upon leaving Chantilly, I declared to be the best principle in the world to travel speedily upon; but I gave it only as matter of opinion, I still continue in the same sentiments ——only I had not then experience enough of its working to add this, that though you do get on at a tearing rate, yet you

* Non Orbis gentem, non urbem gens habet ullam
————————ulla parem.

get on but uneasily to yourself at the same time; for which reason I here quit it entirely, and forever, and 'tis heartily at anyone's service——it has spoiled me the digestion of a good supper, and brought on a bilious diarrhaea, which has brought me back again to my first principle on which I set out—— and with which I shall now scamper it away to the banks of the Garonne——

——No;——I cannot stop a moment to give you the character of the people——their genius——their manners—— their customs——their laws——their religion——their government——their manufactures——their commerce—— their finances, with all the resources and hidden springs which sustain them: qualified as I may be, by spending three days and two nights amongst them, and during all that time, making these things the entire subject of my enquiries and reflections——

Still——still I must away——the roads are paved——the posts are short——the days are long——'tis no more than noon——I shall be at Fontainebleau before the king—— ——Was he going there? not that I know——

CHAPTER XX

Now I hate to hear a person, especially if he be a traveller, complain that we do not get on so fast in France as we do in England; whereas we get on much faster, *consideratis considerandis;* thereby always meaning that if you weigh their vehicles with the mountains of baggage which you lay both before and behind upon them——and then consider their puny horses, with the very little they give them——'tis a wonder they get on at all: their suffering is most un-Christian, and 'tis evident thereupon to me that a French post horse would not know what in the world to do, was it not for the two words ****** and ******, in which there is as much sustenance as if you gave him a peck of corn: now as these words cost nothing, I long from my soul to tell the reader what they are; but here is the question——they must be told him plainly, and with the most distinct articulation, or it will answer no end——and yet to do it in that plain way——though their Reverences may laugh at it in the bed-chamber——full well I wot, they will abuse it in the parlour: for which cause, I have been volving and revolving in my fancy some time, but to no purpose, by what clean device or facete contrivance I might so modulate them, that whilst I satisfy *that ear* which the reader chooses to *lend* me——I might not dissatisfy the other which he keeps to himself.

——My ink burns my finger to try——and when I have ——'twill have a worse consequence——it will burn (I fear) my paper.

——No;——I dare not——

But if you wish to know how the Abbess of Andoüillets and a novice of her convent got over the difficulty (only first wishing myself all imaginable success)——I'll tell you without the least scruple.

CHAPTER XXI

The Abbess of Andoüillets, which, if you look into the large set of provincial maps now publishing at Paris, you will find situated amongst the hills which divide Burgundy from Savoy, being in danger of an *Ankylosis* or stiff joint (the *synovia* of her knee becoming hard by long matins) and having tried every remedy————first, prayers and thanksgiving; then invocations to all the saints in heaven promiscuously ——then particularly to every saint who had ever had a stiff leg before her——then touching it with all the relics of the convent, principally with the thigh bone of the man of Lystra, who had been impotent from his youth——then wrapping it up in her veil when she went to bed——then crosswise her rosary——then bringing in to her aid the secular arm, and anointing it with oils and hot fat of animals ——then treating it with emollient and resolving fomentations————then with poultices of marshmallows, mallows, bonus Henricus, white lilies and fenugreek——then taking the woods, I mean the smoke of 'em, holding her scapulary across her lap——then decoctions of wild chicory, water cresses, chervil, sweet cecily, and cochlearia——and nothing all this while answering, was prevailed on at last to try the hot baths of Bourbon——so having first obtained leave of the visitor-general to take care of her existence——she ordered all to be got ready for her journey: a novice of the convent, of about seventeen, who had been troubled with a whitlow in her middle finger, by sticking it constantly into the abbess's cast poultices, &c.——had gained such an interest that, overlooking a sciatical old nun, who might have been set up forever by the hot baths of Bourbon, Margarita, the little novice, was elected as the companion of the journey.

An old calash, belonging to the abbess, lined with green frieze, was ordered to be drawn out into the sun——the gardener of the convent, being chosen muleteer, led out the two old mules to clip the hair from the rump ends of their tails, whilst a couple of lay sisters were busied, the one in darning the lining, and the other in sewing on the shreds of yellow binding, which the teeth of time had unravelled—— the undergardener dressed the muleteer's hat in hot wine lees ——and a tailor sat musically at it, in a shed over against the convent, in assorting four dozen of bells for the harness, whistling to each bell as he tied it on with a throng——

——The carpenter and the smith of Andoüillets held a council of wheels; and by seven, the morning after, all looked spruce, and was ready at the gate of the convent for the hot baths of Bourbon——two rows of the unfortunate stood ready there an hour before.

The Abbess of Andoüillets, supported by Margarita, the novice, advanced slowly to the calash, both clad in white, with their black rosaries hanging at their breasts——

——There was a simple solemnity in the contrast: they entered the calash; and nuns in the same uniform, sweet emblem of innocence, each occupied a window, and as the abbess and Margarita looked up——each (the sciatical poor nun excepted)——each streamed out the end of her veil in the air——then kissed the lily hand which let it go: the good abbess and Margarita laid their hands saint-wise upon their breasts——looked up to heaven——then to them——and looked "God bless you, dear sisters."

I declare I am interested in this story, and wish I had been there.

The gardener, who I shall now call the muleteer, was a little, hearty, broad-set, good-natured, chattering, toping kind of a fellow, who troubled his head very little with the *hows* and *whens* of life; so had mortgaged a month of his conventical wages in a borrachio, or leathern cask of wine, which he had disposed behind the calash, with a large russet-coloured riding coat over it, to guard it from the sun; and as the weather was hot, and he, not a niggard of his labours, walking ten times more than he rode——he found more occasions than those of nature to fall back to the rear of his carriage; till by frequent coming and going, it had so happened that all his wine had leaked out at the *legal* vent of the borrachio, before one half of the journey was finished.

Man is a creature born to habitudes. The day had been sultry——the evening was delicious——the wine was generous ——the Burgundian hill on which it grew was steep——a little tempting bush over the door of a cool cottage at the foot of it hung vibrating in full harmony with the passions ——a gentle air rustled distinctly through the leaves—— "Come——come, thirsty muleteer——come in."

——The muleteer was a son of Adam. I need not say one word more. He gave the mules, each of 'em, a sound lash, and looking in the abbess's and Margarita's faces (as he did it) ——as much as to say, "here I am"——he gave a second good crack——as much as to say to his mules, "get on"——so slinking behind, he entered the little inn at the foot of the hill.

The muleteer, as I told you, was a little, joyous, chirping fellow, who thought not of tomorrow, nor of what had gone before, or what was to follow it, provided he got but his scantling of Burgundy, and a little chitchat along with it; so entering into a long conversation, as how he was chief gardener to the convent of Andoüillets, &c., &c., and out of friendship for the abbess and Mademoiselle Margarita, who was only in her novitiate, he had come along with them from the confines of Savoy, &c. -- &c. -- and as how she had got a white swelling by her devotions——and what a nation of herbs he had procured to mollify her humours, &c., &c., and that if the waters of Bourbon did not mend that leg——she might as well be lame of both——&c., &c., &c.,——He so contrived his story as absolutely to forget the heroine of it ——and with her, the little novice, and what was a more ticklish point to be forgot than both——the two mules; who being creatures that take advantage of the world, inasmuch as their parents took it of them——and they not being in a condition to return the obligation *downwards* (as men and women and beasts are)——they do it sideways, and longways, and backways——and uphill, and downhill, and which way they can.——Philosophers, with all their ethics, have never considered this rightly——how should the poor muleteer then, in his cups, consider it at all? he did not in the least——'tis time we do; let us leave him then in the vortex of his element, the happiest and most thoughtless of mortal men——and for a moment let us look after the mules, the abbess, and Margarita.

By virtue of the muleteer's two last strokes, the mules had gone quietly on, following their own consciences up the hill, till they had conquered about one half of it; when the elder of them, a shrewd crafty old devil, at the turn of an angle, giving a side glance, and no muleteer behind them——

By my fig! said she, swearing, I'll go no further——And if I do, replied the other——they shall make a drum of my hide.——

And so with one consent they stopped thus——

CHAPTER XXII

——Get on with you, said the abbess.

——Wh - - - - ysh——ysh——cried Margarita.

Sh - - - a——shu - u——shu - - u——sh - - aw —— shawed the abbess.

——Whu—v—w——whew—w—w——whuved Margarita, pursing up her sweet lips betwixt a hoot and a whistle.

Thump——thump——thump——obstreperated the Abbess of Andoüillets with the end of her gold-headed cane against the bottom of the calash——

——The old mule let a f——

CHAPTER XXIII

We are ruined and undone, my child, said the abbess to Margarita——we shall be here all night——we shall be plundered——we shall be ravished——

——We shall be ravished, said Margarita, as sure as a gun.

Sancta Maria! cried the abbess (forgetting the *O!*)——why was I governed by this wicked stiff joint? why did I leave the convent of Andoüillets? and why didst thou not suffer thy servant to go unpolluted to her tomb?

O my finger! my finger! cried the novice, catching fire at the word *servant*——why was I not content to put it here, or there, anywhere rather than be in this strait?

——Strait! said the abbess.

Strait——said the novice; for terror had struck their understandings——the one knew not what she said——the other what she answered.

O my virginity! virginity! cried the abbess.

——inity!——inity! said the novice, sobbing.

410

CHAPTER XXIV

My dear mother, quoth the novice, coming a little to herself,——there are two certain words which I have been told will force any horse, or ass, or mule to go up a hill whether he will or no; be he never so obstinate or ill-willed, the moment he hears them uttered, he obeys. They are words magic! cried the abbess, in the utmost horror——No, replied Margarita calmly——but they are words sinful——What are they? quoth the abbess, interrupting her: They are sinful in the first degree, answered Margarita,——they are mortal—— and if we are ravished and die unabsolved of them, we shall both——but you may pronounce them to me, quoth the Abbess of Andoüillets——They cannot, my dear mother, said the novice, be pronounced at all; they will make all the blood in one's body fly up into one's face——But you may whisper them in my ear, quoth the abbess.

Heaven! hadst thou no guardian angel to delegate to the inn at the bottom of the hill? was there no generous and friendly spirit unemployed——no agent in nature, by some monitory shivering, creeping along the artery which led to his heart, to rouse the muleteer from his banquet?——no sweet minstrelsy to bring back the fair idea of the abbess and Margarita, with their black rosaries!

Rouse! rouse!——but 'tis too late——the horrid words are pronounced this moment——

——and how to tell them——Ye who can speak of everything existing, with unpolluted lips——instruct me——guide me——

CHAPTER XXV

All sins whatever, quoth the abbess, turning casuist in the distress they were under, are held by the confessor of our convent to be either mortal or venial: there is no further

411

division. Now a venial sin being the slightest and least of all sins,——being halved——by taking either only the half of it, and leaving the rest——or, by taking it all, and amicably halving it betwixt yourself and another person—— in course becomes diluted into no sin at all.

Now I see no sin in saying, *bou, bou, bou, bou, bou,* a hundred times together; nor is there any turpitude in pronouncing the syllable *ger, ger, ger, ger, ger,* were it from our matins to our vespers: Therefore, my dear daughter, continued the Abbess of Andoüillets——I will say *bou,* and thou shalt say *ger;* and then alternately, as there is no more sin in *fou* then in *bou*——Thou shalt say *fou*—— and I will come in (like fa, sol, la, re, mi, ut, at our complines) with *ter.* And accordingly the abbess, giving the pitch note, set off thus:

Abbess, } Bou - - bou - - bou - -
Margarita, } ——ger, - - ger, - - ger
Margarita, } Fou - - fou - - fou - -
Abbess, } ——ter, - - ter, - - ter.

The two mules acknowledged the notes by a mutual lash of their tails; but it went no further.——'Twill answer by an' by, said the invoice.

Abbess, } Bou- bou- bou- bou- bou- bou-
Margarita, } ——ger, ger, ger, ger, ger, ger.

Quicker still, cried Margarita.

Fou, fou, fou, fou, fou, fou, fou, fou, fou.

Quicker still, cried Margarita.

Bou, bou, bou, bou, bou, bou, bou, bou, bou.

Quicker still——God preserve me! said the abbess—— They do not understand us, cried Margarita——But the devil does, said the Abbess of Andoüillets.

CHAPTER XXVI

What a tract of country have I run!——how many degrees nearer to the warm sun am I advanced, and how many fair and goodly cities have I seen, during the time you have been reading, and reflecting, Madam, upon this story! There's FONTAINEBLEAU, and SENS, and JOIGNY, and AUXERRE, and DIJON, the capital of Burgundy, and CHALLON, and Mâcon, the capital of Mâconese, and a score more upon the road to LYONS——and now I have run them over——I might as well talk to you of so many market towns in the moon, as tell you one word about them: it will be this chapter at the least, if not both this and the next entirely lost, do what I will——

——Why, 'tis a strange story! Tristram.

——Alas! Madam, had it been upon some melancholy lecture of the cross——the peace of meekness, or the contentment of resignation—— I had not been incommoded: or had I thought of writing it upon the purer abstractions of the soul, and that food of wisdom, and holiness, and contemplation upon which the spirit of man (when separated from the body) is to subsist forever——You would have come with a better appetite from it——

——I wish I never had wrote it: but as I never blot anything out——let us use some honest means to get it out of our heads directly.

——Pray reach me my fool's cap——I fear you sit upon it, Madam——'tis under the cushion——I'll put it on—— Bless me! you have had it upon your head this half hour.
——There then let it stay, with a

Fa-ra diddle di
and a fa-ri diddle d
and a high-dum——dye-dum
    fiddle - - - dumb - c.

And now, Madam, we may venture, I hope, a little to go on.

CHAPTER XXVII

——All you need say of Fontainebleau (in case you are asked) is that it stands about forty miles (south *something*) from Paris, in the middle of a large forest——That there is something great in it——That the king goes there once, every two or three years, with his whole court, for the pleasure of the chase——and that during that carnival of sporting, any English gentleman of fashion (you need not forget yourself) may be accommodated with a nag or two, to partake of the sport, taking care only not to outgallop the king——

Though there are two reasons why you need not talk loud of this to everyone.

First, Because 'twill make the said nags the harder to be got; and

Secondly, 'Tis not a word of it true.—*Allons!*

As for SENS——you may dispatch it in a word——
" *'Tis an archiepiscopal see.*"

For JOIGNY——the less, I think, one says of it, the better.

But for AUXERRE——I could go on forever: for in my *grand tour* through Europe, in which, after all, my father (not caring to trust me with anyone) attended me himself, with my uncle Toby, and Trim and Obadiah, and indeed most of the family, except my mother, who being taken up with a project of knitting my father a pair of large worsted breeches——(the thing is common sense)——and she not caring to be put out of her way, she stayed at home at SHANDY HALL, to keep things right during the expedition; in which, I say, my father stopping us two days at Auxerre, and his researches being ever of such a nature that they would have found fruit even in a desert——he has left me enough to say upon AUXERRE: in short, wherever my father went——but 'twas more remarkably so, in this journey through France and Italy, than in any other stages of his life——his road seemed to lie so much on one side of that wherein all other travellers had gone before him——he saw kings and courts and silks of all colours in such strange lights——and his remarks and reasonings upon the characters, the manners and customs of the countries we passed over were so opposite to those of all other mortal men, particularly those of my uncle Toby and Trim——(to say nothing of myself)——and to crown all——the occurrences and scrapes which we were perpetually meeting and getting into, in consequence of his systems and opiniatry ——they were of so odd, so mixed and tragicomical a contexture——That the whole put together, it appears of so different a shade and tint from any tour of Europe which was ever executed——That I will venture to pronounce——the fault must be mine and mine only——if it be not read by all travellers and travel readers till travelling is no more, ——or which comes to the same point——till the world, finally, takes it into its head to stand still.——

———But this rich bale is not to be opened now; except a small thread or two of it, merely to unravel the mystery of my father's stay at AUXERRE.

———As I have mentioned it———'tis too slight to be kept suspended; and when 'tis wove in, there's an end of it.

We'll go, brother Toby, said my father, whilst dinner is coddling———to the abbey of St. Germain, if it be only to see these bodies of which Monsieur Seguier has given such a recommendation.———I'll go see any body, quoth my uncle Toby; for he was all compliance through every step of the journey———Defend me! said my father———they are all mummies———Then one need not shave, quoth my uncle Toby———Shave! no———cried my father———'twill be more like relations to go with our beards on———So out we sallied, the corporal lending his master his arm, and bringing up the rear, to the abbey of St. Germain.

Everything is very fine, and very rich, and very superb, and very magnificent, said my father, addressing himself to the sacristan, who was a young brother of the order of Benedictines———but our curiosity has led us to see the bodies of which Monsieur Seguier has given the world so exact a description.———The sacristan made a bow, and lighting a torch first, which he had always in the vestry ready for the purpose, he led us into the tomb of St. Heribald———This, said the sacristan, laying his hand upon the tomb, was a renowned prince of the house of Bavaria, who under the successive reigns of Charlemagne, Louis le Debonair, and Charles the Bald bore a great sway in the government, and had a principal hand in bringing everything into order and discipline———

Then he has been as great, said my uncle, in the field as in the cabinet———I dare say he has been a gallant soldier ———He was a monk———said the sacristan.

My uncle Toby and Trim sought comfort in each other's faces———but found it not: my father clapped both his hands upon his codpiece, which was a way he had when anything hugely tickled him; for though he hated a monk and the very smell of a monk worse than all the devils in hell———Yet the shot hitting my uncle Toby and Trim so much harder than him, 'twas a relative triumph; and put him into the gayest humour in the world.

———And pray what do you call this gentleman? quoth my father, rather sportingly: This tomb, said the young Benedictine, looking downwards, contains the bones of St.

415

MAXIMA, who came from Ravenna on purpose to touch the body——

——Of St. MAXIMUS, said my father, popping in with his saint before him——they were two of the greatest saints in the whole martyrology, added my father——Excuse me, said the sacristan————'twas to touch the bones of St. Germain, the builder of the abbey——And what did she get by it? said my uncle Toby——What does any woman get by it? said my father——MARTYRDOM, replied the young Benedictine, making a bow down to the ground, and uttering the word with so humble, but decisive, a cadence, it disarmed my father for a moment. 'Tis supposed, continued the Benedictine, that St. Maxima has lain in this tomb four hundred years, and two hundred before her canonization ——'Tis but a slow rise, brother Toby, quoth my father, in this selfsame army of martyrs.——A desperate slow one, an' please your Honour, said Trim, unless one could purchase——I should rather sell out entirely, quoth my uncle Toby——I am pretty much of your opinion, brother Toby, said my father.

——Poor St. Maxima! said my uncle Toby low to himself, as we turned from her tomb: She was one of the fairest and most beautiful ladies either of Italy or France, continued the sacristan——But who the deuce has got lain down here, besides her, quoth my father, pointing with his cane to a large tomb as we walked on——It is St. Optat, Sir, answered the sacristan——And properly in St. Optat placed! said my father: And what is St. Optat's story? continued he. St. Optat, replied the sacristan, was a bishop——

——I thought so, by heaven! cried my father, interrupting him——St. Optat!——how should St. Optat fail? so snatching out his pocketbook, and the young Benedictine holding him the torch as he wrote, he set it down as a new prop to his system of Christian names, and I will be bold to say, so disinterested was he in the search of truth, that had he found a treasure in St. Optat's tomb, it would not have made him half so rich: 'Twas as successful a short visit as ever was paid to the dead; and so highly was his fancy pleased with all that had passed in it,——that he determined at once to stay another day in Auxerre.

——I'll see the rest of these good gentry tomorrow, said my father, as we crossed over the square——And while you are paying that visit, brother Shandy, quoth my uncle Toby ——the corporal and I will mount the ramparts.

CHAPTER XXVIII

——Now this is the most puzzled skein of all——for in this last chapter, as far at least as it has helped me through Auxerre, I have been getting forwards in two different journeys together, and with the same dash of the pen—— for I have got entirely out of Auxerre in this journey which I am writing now, and I am got halfway out of Auxerre in that which I shall write hereafter——There is but a certain degree of perfection in everything; and by pushing at something beyond that, I have brought myself into such a situation as no traveller ever stood before me; for I am this moment walking across the market place of Auxerre with my father and my uncle Toby, in our way back to dinner—— and I am this moment also entering Lyons with my post chaise broke into a thousand pieces——and I am moreover this moment in a handsome pavillion built by Pringello,* upon the banks of the Garonne, which Mons. Sligniac has lent me, and where I now sit rhapsodizing all these affairs.

——Let me collect myself, and pursue my journey.

CHAPTER XXIX

I am glad of it, said I, settling the account with myself as I walked into Lyons——my chaise being all laid higgledy-piggledy with my baggage in a cart, which was moving slowly before me——I am heartily glad, said I, that 'tis all broke to pieces; for now I can go directly by water to Avignon, which will carry me on a hundred and twenty

* The same Don Pringello, the celebrated Spanish architect, of whom my cousin Antony has made such honourable mention in a scholium to the Tale inscribed to his name. Vid. p. 129, small edit.

miles of my journey, and not cost me seven livres——and from thence, continued I, bringing forwards the account, I can hire a couple of mules——or asses, if I like (for nobody knows me), and cross the plains of Languedoc for almost nothing——I shall gain four hundred livres by the misfortune clear into my purse; and pleasure! worth——worth double the money by it. With what velocity, continued I, clapping my two hands together, shall I fly down the rapid Rhone, with the VIVARES on my right hand, and DAUPHINY on my left, scarce seeing the ancient cities of VIENNE, Valence, and Vivieres. What a flame will it rekindle in the lamp, to snatch a blushing grape from the Hermitage and Côte Rôtie, as I shoot by the foot of them? and what a fresh spring in the blood! to behold upon the banks, advancing and retiring, the castles of romance, whence courteous knights have whilom rescued the distressed——and see, vertiginous, the rocks, the mountains, the cataracts, and all the hurry which Nature is in with all her great works about her——

As I went on thus, methought my chaise, the wreck of which looked stately enough at the first, insensibly grew less and less in its size; the freshness of the painting was no more——the gilding lost its lustre——and the whole affair appeared so poor in my eyes——so sorry!——so contemptible! and, in a word, so much worse than the Abbess of Andoüillets' itself——that I was just opening my mouth to give it to the devil——when a pert vamping chaise-undertaker, stepping nimbly across the street, demanded if Monsieur would have his chaise refitted——No, no, said I, shaking my head sideways——Would Monsieur choose to sell it? rejoined the undertaker——With all my soul, said I ——the ironwork is worth forty livres——and the glasses worth forty more——and the leather you may take to live on.

——What a mine of wealth, quoth I, as he counted me the money, has this post chaise brought me in? And this is my usual method of bookkeeping, at least with the disasters of life——making a penny of every one of 'em as they happen to me——

——Do, my dear Jenny, tell the world for me how I behaved under one, the most oppressive of its kind which could befall me as a man proud as he ought to be, of his manhood——

'Tis enough, saidst thou, coming close up to me, as I stood with my garters in my hand, reflecting upon what had *not*

418

passed——'Tis enough, Tristram, and I am satisfied, saidst
thou, whispering these words in my ear, **** ** **** ***
******;——**** ** ****——any other man would have
sunk down to the center——

——Everything is good for something, quoth I.

——I'll go into Wales for six weeks, and drink goat's
whey——and I'll gain seven years longer life for the accident. For which reason I think myself inexcusable for blam-
ing Fortune so often as I have done, for pelting me all my
life long, like an ungracious duchess, as I called her, with so
many small evils: surely if I have any cause to be angry with
her, 'tis that she has not sent me great ones——a score of
good cursed, bouncing losses would have been as good as a
pension to me.

——One of a hundred a year, or so, is all I wish——I
would not be at the plague of paying land tax for a larger.

CHAPTER XXX

To those who call vexations VEXATIONS, as knowing what
they are, there could not be a greater than to be the best
part of a day in Lyons, the most opulent and flourishing
city in France, enriched with the most fragments of antiquity——and not be able to see it. To be withheld upon
any account must be a vexation; but to be withheld *by* a
vexation——must certainly be what philosophy justly calls

VEXATION
upon
VEXATION.

I had got my two dishes of milk coffee (which by the
bye is excellently good for a consumption, but you must boil
the milk and coffee together——otherwise 'tis only coffee
and milk)——and as it was no more than eight in the morning, and the boat did not go off till noon, I had time to see
enough of Lyons to tire the patience of all the friends
I had in the world with it. I will take a walk to the cathedral, said I, looking at my list, and see the wonderful mechanism of this great clock of Lippius of Basil, in the first
place——

Now, of all things in the world, I understand the least of mechanism——I have neither genius, or taste, or fancy—— and have a brain so entirely unapt for everything of that kind, that I solemnly declare I was never yet able to comprehend the principles of motion of a squirrel cage, or a common knife grinder's wheel——though I have many an hour of my life looked up with great devotion at the one—— and stood by with as much patience as any Christian ever could do at the other——

I'll go see the surprising movements of this great clock, said I, the very first thing I do: and then I will pay a visit to the great library of the Jesuits, and procure, if possible, a sight of the thirty volumes of the general history of China, wrote (not in the Tartarian) but in the Chinese language, and in the Chinese character too.

Now I almost knew as little of the Chinese language as I do of the mechanism of Lippius's clockwork; so, why these should have jostled themselves into the two first articles of my list——I leave to the curious as a problem of Nature. I own it looks like one of her Ladyship's obliquities; and they who court her are interested in finding out her humour as much as I.

When these curiosities are seen, quoth I, half addressing myself to my *valet de place,* who stood behind me——'twill be no hurt if we go to the church of St. Ireneus, and see the pillar to which Christ was tied——and after that, the house where Pontius Pilate lived——'Twas at the next town, said the *valet de place*——at Vienne; I am glad of it, said I, rising briskly from my chair, and walking across the room with strides twice as long as my usual pace——"for so much the sooner shall I be at the *tomb of the two lovers.*"

What was the cause of this movement, and why I took such long strides in uttering this——I might leave to the curious too; but as no principle of clockwork is concerned in it ——'twill be as well for the reader if I explain it myself.

CHAPTER XXXI

O! There is a sweet era in the life of man when (the brain being tender and fibrillous, and more like pap than anything else)——a story read of two fond lovers, separated

420

from each other by cruel parents, and by still more cruel
destiny——

Amandus——He

Amanda——She——

each ignorant of the other's course,

He——east

She——west

Amandus taken captive by the Turks, and carried to the
Emperor of Morocco's court, where the Princess of Morocco,
falling in love with him, keeps him twenty years in prison,
for the love of his Amanda——

She——(Amanda) all the time wandering barefoot, and
with dishevelled hair, o'er rocks and mountains enquiring
for Amandus——Amandus! Amandus!——making every hill
and valley to echo back his name——

Amandus! Amandus!

at every town and city sitting down forlorn at the gate——
Has Amandus!——has my Amandus entered?——till,——
going round, and round, and round the world——chance
unexpected bringing them at the same moment of the night,
though by different ways, to the gate of Lyons, their native
city, and each in well-known accents calling out aloud,

Is Amandus
Is my Amanda } still alive?

they fly into each other's arms, and both drop down dead
for joy.

There is a soft era in every gentle mortal's life, where
such a story affords more *pabulum* to the brain than all the
Frusts, and *Crusts,* and *Rusts* of antiquity which travellers
can cook up for it.

——'Twas all that struck on the right side of the colander
in my own, of what Spon and others, in their accounts of
Lyons, had *strained* into it; and finding, moreover, in some
Itinerary, but in what God knows——That sacred to the
fidelity of Amandus and Amanda, a tomb was built without the gates, where to this hour lovers called upon them to
attest their truths,——I never could get into a scrape of
that kind in my life, but this *tomb of the lovers* would
somehow or other come in at the close——nay, such a kind
of empire had it established over me that I could seldom
think or speak of Lyons——and sometimes not so much as
see even a Lyons waistcoat, but this remnant of antiquity
would present itself to my fancy; and I have often said
in my wild way of running on——though I fear with some
irreverence——"I thought this shrine (neglected as it was)

as valuable as that of Mecca, and so little short, except in wealth, of the *Santa Casa* itself that sometime or other, I would go a pilgrimage (though I had no other business at Lyons) on purpose to pay it a visit."

In my list, therefore, of *Videnda* at Lyons, this, though *last*—was not, you see, *least;* so taking a dozen or two of longer strides than usual across my room, just whilst it passed my brain, I walked down calmly into the *basse cour,* in order to sally forth; and having called for my bill ——as it was uncertain whether I should return to my inn, I had paid it——had moreover given the maid ten sous, and was just receiving the dernier compliments of Monsieur Le Blanc, for a pleasant voyage down the Rhône——when I was stopped at the gate——

CHAPTER XXXII

——'Twas by a poor ass who had just turned in with a couple of large panniers upon his back, to collect eleemosynary turnip tops and cabbage leaves; and stood dubious, with his two forefeet on the inside of the threshold, and with his two hinder feet towards the street, as not knowing very well whether he was to go in, or no.

Now, 'tis an animal (be in what hurry I may) I cannot bear to strike——there is a patient endurance of sufferings wrote so unaffectedly in his looks and carriage, which pleads so mightily for him that it always disarms me; and to that degree that I do not like to speak unkindly to him: on the contrary, meet him where I will——whether in town or country——in cart or under panniers——whether in liberty or bondage——I have ever something civil to say to him on my part; and as one word begets another (if he has a little to do as I)——I generally fall into conversation with him; and surely never is my imagination so busy as in framing his responses from the etchings of his countenance—— and where those carry me not deep enough——in flying from my own heart into his, and seeing what is natural for an ass to think——as well as a man, upon the occasion. In truth, it is the only creature of all the classes of beings below me with whom I can do this: for parrots, jackdaws, &c.———I never exchange a word with them———nor with the apes, &c., for pretty near the same reason; they act by rote, as the others speak by it, and equally make me silent: nay, my dog and my cat, though I value them both ———(and for my dog, he would speak if he could)———yet somehow or other, they neither of them possess the talents for conversation———I can make nothing of a discourse with them, beyond the *proposition,* the *reply* and *rejoinder* which terminated my father's and my mother's conversations, in his beds of justice———and those uttered———there's an end of the dialogue———

———But with an ass, I can commune forever.

Come, Honesty! said I,———seeing it was impracticable to pass betwixt him and the gate———art thou for coming in, or going out?

The ass twisted his head round to look up the street———

Well———replied I———we'll wait a minute for thy driver.

———He turned his head thoughtful about, and looked wistfully the opposite way———

I understand thee perfectly, answered I———if thou takest a wrong step in this affair, he will cudgel thee to death——— Well! a minute is but a minute, and if it saves a fellow-creature a drubbing, it shall not be set down as ill spent.

He was eating the stem of an artichoke as this discourse went on, and in the little peevish contentions of nature betwixt hunger and unsavouriness, had dropt it out of his mouth half a dozen times, and picked it up again———God help thee, Jack! said I, thou hast a bitter breakfast on't——— and many a bitter day's labour———and many a bitter blow, I fear, for its wages———'tis all———all bitterness to thee, whatever life is to others.———And now thy mouth, if one knew the truth of it, is as bitter, I dare say, as soot———(for he had cast aside the stem) and thou has not a friend perhaps in all this world that will give thee a macaroon.———In saying this, I pulled out a paper of 'em, which I had just purchased, and gave him one———and at this moment that I am telling it, my heart smites me that there was more of pleasantry in the conceit of seeing *how* an ass would eat a macaroon———than of benevolence in giving him one, which presided in the act.

When the ass had eaten his macaroon, I pressed him to come in———the poor beast was heavy loaded———his legs seemed to tremble under him———he hung rather backwards, and as I pulled at his halter, it broke short in my hand——— he looked up pensive in my face———"Don't thrash me with

423

it——but if you will, you may"——If I do, said I, I'll be d——d.

The word was but one half of it pronounced, like the Abbess of Andoüillets'——(so there was no sin in it)—— when a person, coming in, let fall a thundering bastinado upon the poor devil's crupper, which put an end to the ceremony.

Out upon it!

cried I——but the interjection was equivocal——and, I think, wrong-placed too——for the end of an osier which had started out from the contexture of the ass's pannier had caught hold of my breeches pocket as he rushed by me, and rent it in the most disastrous direction you can imagine——so that the

Out upon it! in my opinion, should have come in here——but this I leave to be settled by

The

REVIEWERS

of

MY BREECHES

which I have brought over along with me for that purpose.

CHAPTER XXXIII

When all was set to rights, I came downstairs again into the *basse cour* with my *valet de place*, in order to sally out towards the tomb of the two lovers, &c.——and was a second time stopped at the gate——not by the ass——but by the person who struck him; and who, by that time, had taken possession (as is not uncommon after a defeat) of the very spot of ground where the ass stood.

It was a commissary sent to me from the post office, with a rescript in his hand for the payment of some six livres odd sous.

Upon what account? said I.——'Tis upon the part of the king, replied the commissary, heaving up both his shoulders——

———My good friend, quoth I———as sure as I am I———
and you are you———

———And who are you? said he.——— ———Don't puzzle
me, said I.

CHAPTER XXXIV

———But it is an indubitable verity, continued I, addressing
myself to the commissary, changing only the form of my as-
severation———that I owe the King of France nothing but my
good will; for he is a very honest man, and I wish him all
health and pastime in the world———

Pardonnez moi———replied the commissary, you are indebted to him six livres four sous, for the next post from
hence to St. Fons, in your rout to Avignon———which being
a post royal, you pay double for the horses and postillion
———otherwise 'twould have amounted to no more than three
livres two sous———

———But I don't go by land, said I.

———You may if you please, replied the commissary———

Your most obedient servant———said I, making him a low
bow———

The commissary, with all the sincerity of grave good breeding———made me one, as low again.———I never was more
disconcerted with a bow in my life.

———The devil take the serious character of these people!
quoth I———(aside) they understand no more of IRONY than
this———

The comparison was standing close by with his panniers
———but something sealed up my lips———I could not pronounce the name———

Sir, said I, collecting myself———it is not my intention to
take post———

———But you may———said he, persisting in his first reply
———you may take post if you choose———

———And I may take salt to my pickled herring, said I, if
I choose———

———But I do not choose———

———But you must pay for it, whether you do or no———

Aye! for the salt, said I (I know)———

425

——And for the post too, added he. Defend me, cried
I——

I travel by water——I am going down the Rhône this
very afternoon——my baggage is in the boat——and I have
actually paid nine livres for my passage——

C'est tout egal——'tis all one, said he.

Bon Dieu! what, pay for the way I go! and for the way I
do *not* go!

——*C'est tout egal,* replied the commissary——

——The devil it is! said I——but I will go to ten thousand
Bastilles first——

O England! England! thou land of liberty, and climate of
good sense, thou tenderest of mothers——and gentlest of
nurses, cried I, kneeling upon one knee, as I was beginning
my apostrophe——

When the director of Madam Le Blanc's conscience, coming in at that instant, and seeing a person in black, with a
face as pale as ashes, at his devotions——looking still paler
by the contrast and distress of his drapery——asked if I
stood in want of the aids of the church——

I go by WATER——said I——and here's another will be
for making me pay for going by OIL.

CHAPTER XXXV

As I perceived the commissary of the post office would have
his six livres four sous, I had nothing else for it but to say
some smart thing upon the occasion, worth the money:

And so I set off thus——

——And pray, Mr. Commissary, by what law of courtesy
is a defenceless stranger to be used just the reverse from
what you use a Frenchman in this matter?

By no means, said he.

Excuse me, said I——for you have begun, sir, with first
tearing off my breeches——and now you want my pocket——

Whereas——had you first taken my pocket, as you do with
your own people——and then left me bare a—d after——
I had been a beast to have complained——

As it is——

——'Tis contrary to the *law of nature*.

——'Tis contrary to *reason*.

——'Tis contrary to the GOSPEL.

But not to this——said he——putting a printed paper into my hand.

PAR LE ROY

—— ——'Tis a pithy prolegomenon, quoth I——and so read on ———— ———— ———— ———— ———— ————
———— ———— ———— ———— ———— ———— ————
———— ———— ———— ———— ———— ———— ————
———— ———— ———— ———— ———— ———— ————

——By all which it appears, quoth I, having read it over, a little too rapidly, that if a man sets out in a post chaise from Paris——he must go on travelling in one all the days of his life——or pay for it.——Excuse me, said the commissary, the spirit of the ordinance is this——That if you set out with an intention of running post from Paris to Avignon, &c., you shall not change that intention or mode of travelling without first satisfying the *fermiers* for two posts further than the place you repent at——and 'tis founded, continued he, upon this, that the REVENUES are not to fall short through your *fickleness*——

——O, by heavens! cried I——if fickleness is taxable in France——we have nothing to do but to make the best peace with you we can——

AND SO THE PEACE WAS MADE;

——And if it is a bad one——as Tristram Shandy laid the cornerstone of it——nobody but Tristram Shandy ought to be hanged.

CHAPTER XXXVI

Though I was sensible I had said as many clever things to the commissary as come to six livres four sous, yet I was determined to note down the imposition amongst my remarks before I retired from the place; so putting my hand into my coat pocket for my remarks——(which, by the bye, may be a caution to travellers to take a little more care of

their remarks for the future) "my remarks were *stolen*"————
Never did sorry traveller make such a pother and racket
about his remarks as I did about mine, upon the occasion.

Heaven! earth! sea! fire! cried I, calling in everything to
my aid but what I should————My remarks are stolen!
————what shall I do?————Mr. Commissary! pray did I drop
any remarks as I stood besides you?————

You dropped a good many very singular ones, replied he
————Pugh! said I, those were but a few, not worth above six
livres two sous————but these are a large parcel————He shook
his head————Monsieur Le Blanc! Madam Le Blanc! did you
see any papers of mine?————you maid of the house! run upstairs————François! run up after her————

————I must have my remarks————they were the best remarks, cried I, that ever were made————the wisest————the
wittiest————What shall I do?————which way shall I turn myself?

Sancho Panza, when he lost his ass's FURNITURE, did not ex-
claim more bitterly.

CHAPTER XXXVII

When the first transport was over, and the registers of the
brain were beginning to get a little out of the confusion into
which this jumble of cross accidents had cast them————it
then presently occurred to me that I had left my remarks in
the pocket of the chaise————and that in selling my chaise,
I had sold my remarks along with it, to the chaise-
vamper.   I
leave this void space that the reader may swear into it any
oath that he is most accustomed to————For my own part, if
ever I swore a *whole* oath into a vacancy in my life, I think
it was into that————*** **** **, said I————and so my remarks through France, which were as full of wit as an egg is
full of meat, and as well worth four hundred guineas as the
said egg is worth a penny————Have I been selling here to a
chaise-vamper————for four *Louis d'Ors*————and giving him
a post chaise (by heaven) worth six into the bargain; had it
been to Dodsley, or Becket, or any creditable bookseller
who was either leaving off business, and wanted a post chaise

——or who was beginning it——and wanted my remarks, and two or three guineas along with them——I could have borne it——but to a chaise-vamper!——show me to him this moment, François,——said I——the *vaiet de place* put on his hat, and led the way——and I pulled off mine, as I passed the commissary, and followed him.

CHAPTER XXXVIII

When we arrived at the chaise-vamper's house, both the house and the shop were shut up; it was the eighth of September, the nativity of the blessed Virgin Mary, mother of God——

——Tantarra - ra - tan - tivi——the whole world was going out a-Maypoling——frisking here——capering there——nobody cared a button for me or my remarks; so I sat me down upon a bench by the door, philosophating upon my condition: by a better fate than usually attends me, I had not waited half an hour, when the mistress came in, to take the papillotes from off her hair, before she went to the May poles——

The French women, by the bye, love Maypoles, *à la folie* ——that is, as much as their nations——give 'em but a Maypole, whether in May, June, July, or September——they never count the times——down it goes——'tis meat, drink, washing, and lodging to 'em——and had we but the policy, an' please your Worships (as wood is a little scarce in France) to send them but plenty of Maypoles——

The women would set them up; and when they had done, they would dance round them (and the men for company) till they were all blind.

The wife of the chaise-vamper stepped in, I told you, to take the papillotes from off her hair——the toilet stands still for no man——so she jerked off her cap, to begin, with them as she opened the door, in doing which, one of them fell upon the ground——I instantly saw it was my own writing——

——O *Seigneur!* cried I——you have got all my remarks upon your head, Madam!——*J'en suis bien mortifiée,* said she——'tis well, thinks I, they have stuck there—for could

429

they have gone deeper, they would have made such confusion in a Frenchwoman's noddle——She had better have gone with it unfrizzled to the day of eternity.

Tenez——said she——so without any idea of the nature of my suffering, she took them from her curls, and put them gravely one by one into my hat——one was twisted this way ——another twisted that——ay! by my faith; and when they are published, quoth I,——

They will be worse twisted still.

CHAPTER XXXIX

And now for Lippius's clock! said I, with the air of a man who had got through all his difficulties——nothing can prevent us seeing that, and the Chinese history, &c., except the time, said François——for 'tis almost eleven——then we must speed the faster, said I, striding it away to the cathedral.

I cannot say, in my heart, that it gave me any concern in being told by one of the minor canons, as I was entering the west door,——That Lippius's great clock was all out of joints, and had not gone for some years——It will give me the more time, thought I, to peruse the Chinese history; and besides, I shall be able to give the world a better account of the clock in its decay than I could have done in its flourishing condition——

——And so away I posted to the college of the Jesuits.

Now it is with the project of getting a peep at the history of China in Chinese characters——as with many others I could mention, which strike the fancy only at a distance; for as I came nearer and nearer to the point——my blood cooled ——the freak gradually went off, till at length I would not have given a cherry stone to have it gratified———The truth was, my time was short, and my heart was at the tomb of the lovers——I wish to God, said I, as I got the rapper in my hand, that the key of the library may be but lost; it fell out as well———

For all the JESUITS *had got the cholic*——and to that degree, as never was known in the memory of the oldest practitioner.

CHAPTER XL

As I knew the geography of the tomb of the lovers, as well as if I had lived twenty years in Lyons, namely, that it was upon the turning of my right hand, just without the gate, leading to the Fauxbourg de Vaise——I dispatched François to the boat, that I might pay the homage I so long owed it, without a witness of my weakness.——I walked with all imaginable joy towards the place——when I saw the gate which intercepted the tomb, my heart glowed within me——

——Tender and faithful spirits! cried I, addressing myself to Amandus and Amanda——long——long have I tarried to drop this tear upon your tomb——I come——I come——

When I came——there was no tomb to drop it upon.

What would I have given for my uncle Toby to have whistled *Lillabullero!*

CHAPTER XLI

No matter how, or in what mood——but I flew from the tomb of the lovers——or rather I did not fly *from* it—— (for there was no such thing existing) and just got time enough to the boat to save my passage;——and e'er I had sailed a hundred yards, the Rhône and the Saône met together, and carried me down merrily betwixt them.

But I have described this voyage down the Rhône before I made it——

——So now I am at Avignon—and as there is nothing to see but the old house in which the Duke of Ormond resided, and nothing to stop me but a short remark upon the place, in three minutes you will see me crossing the bridge upon a mule, with François upon a horse with my portmanteau behind him, and the owner of both striding the way before us with a long gun upon his shoulder, and a sword under his arm, lest peradventure we should run away with his cattle. Had you seen my breeches in entering Avignon——Though you'd have seen them better, I think, as I mounted——you would not have thought the precaution amiss, or found in your heart to have taken it in dudgeon: for my own part, I took it most kindly; and determined to make him a present of them when we got to the end of our journey, for the trouble they had put him to of arming himself at all points against them.

Before I go further, let me get rid of my remark upon Avignon, which is this, That I think it wrong, merely because a man's hat has been blown off his head by chance the first night he comes to Avignon,——that he should therefore say, "Avignon is more subject to high winds than any town in all France;" for which reason I laid no stress upon the accident till I had inquired of the master of the inn about it, who telling me seriously it was so——and hearing, moreover, the windiness of Avignon spoke of in the country about as a proverb——I set it down merely to ask the learned what can be the cause——the consequence I saw——for they are all dukes, marquises, and counts there——the deuce a baron, in all Avignon——so that there is scarce any talking to them, on a windy day.

Prithee, friend, said I, take hold of my mule for a moment——for I wanted to pull off one of my jack boots, which hurt my heel——the man was standing quite idle at the door of the inn, and as I had taken it into my head he was someway concerned about the house or stable, I put the bridle into his hand——so begun with my boot:——when I had finished the affair, I turned about to take the mule from the man, and thank him——

——But Monsieur *le Marquis* had walked in——

CHAPTER XLII

I had now the whole south of France, from the banks of the Rhône to those of the Garonne, to traverse upon my mule at my own leisure——*at my own leisure*——for I had left

Death, the lord knows——and he only——how far behind
me——"I have followed many a man through France," quoth
he——"but never at this mettlesome rate"——Still he followed,——and still I fled him——but I fled him cheerfully
——still he pursued——but like one who pursued his prey
without hope——as he lagged, every step he lost softened
his looks——why should I fly him at this rate?

So notwithstanding all the commissary of the post office
had said, I changed the *mode* of my travelling once more;
and after so precipitate and rattling a course as I had run, I
flattered my fancy with thinking of my mule, and that I
should traverse the rich plains of Languedoc upon his back,
as slowly as foot could fall.

There is nothing more pleasing to a traveller——or more
terrible to travel writers, than a large rich plain; especially if
it is without great rivers or bridges; and presents nothing to
the eye but one unvaried picture of plenty: for after they
have once told you that 'tis delicious! or delightful! (as the
case happens)——that the soil was grateful, and that nature
pours out all her abundance, &c. . . . they have then a large
plain upon their hands, which they know not what to do
with——and which is of little or no use to them but to carry
them to some town; and that town perhaps of little more
but a new place to start from to the next plain——and so
on.

——This is most terrible work; judge if I don't manage my
plains better.

CHAPTER XLIII

I had not gone above two leagues and a half, before the
man with his gun began to look at his priming.

I had three several times loitered *terribly* behind; half a
mile at least every time: once, in deep conference with a
drum-maker, who was making drums for the fairs of
Baucaira and Tarascone——I did not understand the principles——

The second time, I cannot so properly say, I stopped——
for meeting a couple of Franciscans straitened more for time
than myself, and not being able to get to the bottom of what
I was about——I had turned back with them——

The third was an affair of trade with a gossip, for a hand basket of Provence figs for four sous; this would have been transacted at once, but for a case of conscience at the close of it; for when the figs were paid for, it turned out that there were two dozen of eggs covered over with vine leaves at the bottom of the basket——as I had no intention of buying eggs——I made no sort of claim of them——as for the space they had occupied——what signified it? I had figs enow for my money——

——But it was my intention to have the basket——it was the gossip's intention to keep it, without which she could do nothing with her eggs——and unless I had the basket, I could do as little with my figs, which were too ripe already, and most of 'em burst at the side: this brought on a short contention, which terminated in sundry proposals what we should both do——

——How we disposed of our eggs and figs, I defy you, or the devil himself, had he not been there (which I am persuaded he was), to form the least probable conjecture: You will read the whole of it————not this year, for I am hastening to the story of my uncle Toby's amours——but you will read it in the collection of those which have arose out of the journey across this plain——and which, therefore, I call my

PLAIN STORIES.

How far my pen has been fatigued like those of other travellers, in this journey of it over so barren a track——the world must judge——but the traces of it, which are now all set o' vibrating together this moment, tell me 'tis the most fruitful and busy period of my life; for as I had made no convention with my man with the gun as to time——by stopping and talking to every soul I met who was not in a full trot——joining all parties before me——waiting for every soul behind——hailing all those who were coming through crossroads——arresting all kinds of beggars, pilgrims, fiddlers, friars——not passing by a woman in a mulberry tree without commending her legs, and tempting her into conversation with a pinch of snuff————In short, by seizing every handle, of what size or shape soever, which chance held out to me in this journey——I turned my *plain* into a *city*——I was always in company, and with great variety too; and as my mule loved society as much as myself, and had some proposals always on his part to offer to every beast he met——I am confident we could have passed through

Pall Mall or St. James's Street for a month together, with fewer adventures——and seen less of human nature.

O! there is that sprightly frankness which at once unpins every plait of a Languedocian's dress——that whatever is beneath it, it looks so like the simplicity which poets sing of in better days——I will delude my fancy, and believe it is so.

'Twas in the road betwixt Nîmes and Lunel, where there is the best *Muscatto* wine in all France, and which by the bye belongs to the honest canons of MONTPELLIER——and foul befall the man who has drank it at their table who grudges them a drop of it.

——The sun was set——they had done their work; the nymphs had tied up their hair afresh——and the swains were preparing for a carousal——My mule made a dead point ——'Tis the fife and taborin, said I——I'm frightened to death, quoth he——They are running at the ring of pleasure, said I, giving him a prick——By St. Boogar, and all the saints at the backside of the door of purgatory, said he—— (making the same resolution with the Abbess of Andoüillets), I'll not go a step further——'Tis very well, sir, said I——I never will argue a point with one of your family, as long as I live; so leaping off his back, and kicking off one boot into this ditch, and t'other into that——I'll take a dance, said I——so stay you here.

A sunburnt daughter of Labour rose up from the group to meet me as I advanced towards them; her hair, which was a dark chestnut, approaching rather to a black, was tied up in a knot, all but a single tress.

We want a cavalier, said she, holding out both her hands, as if to offer them——And a cavalier ye shall have, said I, taking hold of both of them.

Hadst thou, Nannette, been arrayed like a duchess!

——But that cursed slit in thy petticoat!

Nannette cared not for it.

We could not have done without you, said she, letting go one hand, with self-taught politeness, leading me up with the other.

A lame youth, whom Apollo had recompenced with a pipe, and to which he had added a taborin of his own accord, ran sweetly over the prelude, as he sat upon the bank——Tie me up this tress instantly, said Nannette, putting a piece of string into my hand——It taught me to forget I was a stranger——The whole knot fell down——We had been seven years acquainted.

The youth struck the note upon the taborin——his pipe followed, and off we bounded——"the deuce take that slit!"

The sister of the youth, who had stolen her voice from heaven, sung alternately with her brother——'twas a Gascoigne roundelay.

VIVA LA JOIA!
FIDON LA TRISTESSA!

The nymphs joined in unison, and their swains an octave below them——

I would have given a crown to have it sewed up——Nannette would not have given a sou——*Viva la joia!* was in her lips——*Viva la joia!* was in her eyes. A transient spark of amity shot across the space betwixt us——She looked amiable!——Why could I not live and end my days thus? Just disposer of our joys and sorrows, cried I, why could not a man sit down in the lap of content here——and dance, and sing, and say his prayers, and go to heaven with this nut-brown maid? Capriciously did she bend her head on one side, and dance up insidious——Then 'tis time to dance off, quoth I; so changing only partners and tunes, I danced it away from Lunel to Montpellier——from thence to Pesçnas, Beziers——I danced it along through Narbonne, Carcasson, and Castle Naudairy, till at last I danced myself into Pringello's pavillion, where pulling a paper of black lines, that I might go on straight forwards, without digression or parenthesis, in my uncle Toby's amours——

I begun thus——

VOLUME VIII

CHAPTER I

——But softly——for in these sportive plains, and under this genial sun, where at this instant all flesh is running out piping, fiddling, and dancing to the vintage, and every step that's taken, the judgment is surprised by the imagination, I defy, notwithstanding all that has been said upon *straight lines* * in sundry pages of my book——I defy the best cabbage planter that ever existed, whether he plants backwards or forwards, it makes little difference in the account (except that he will have more to answer for in the one case than in the other)——I defy him to go on coolly, critically, and canonically, planting his cabbages one by one, in straight lines, and stoical distances, especially if slits in petticoats are unsewed up——without ever and anon straddling out, or sidling, into some bastardly digression——In Freeze-land, Fog-land, and some other lands I wot of——it may be done——

But in this clear climate of fantasy and perspiration, where every idea, sensible and insensible, gets vent——in this land, my dear Eugenius——in this fertile land of chivalry and romance, where I now sit, unscrewing my inkhorn to write my uncle Toby's amours, and with all the meanders of JULIA's track in quest of her DIEGO in full view of my study window——if thou comest not and takest me by the hand——

What a work is it likely to turn out!
Let us begin it.

* Vid. Vol. VI, p. 385.

CHAPTER II

It is with LOVE as with CUCKOLDOM——

——But now I am talking of beginning a book, and have long had a thing upon my mind to be imparted to the reader, which, if not imparted now, can never be imparted to him as long as I live (whereas the COMPARISON may be imparted to him any hour in the day)——I'll just mention it, and begin in good earnest.

The thing is this.

That of all the several ways of beginning a book which are now in practice throughout the known world, I am confident my own way of doing it is the best——I'm sure it is the most religious——for I begin with writing the first sentence ——and trusting to Almighty God for the second.

'Twould cure an author forever of the fuss and folly of opening his street door, and calling in his neighbours and friends, and kinsfolk, with the devil and all his imps, with their hammers and engines, &c., only to observe how one sentence of mine follows another, and how the plan follows the whole.

I wish you saw me half starting out of my chair, with what confidence, as I grasp the elbow of it, I look up——catching the idea, even sometimes before it halfway reaches me——

I believe in my conscience I intercept many a thought which heaven intended for another man.

Pope and his Portrait * are fools to me——no martyr is ever so full of faith or fire——I wish I could say of good works too——but I have no
> Zeal or Anger——or
> Anger or Zeal——

And till gods and men agree together to call it by the same name——the errantest TARTUFFE, in science——in politics ——or in religion, shall never kindle a spark within me, or have a worse word, or a more unkind greeting, than what he will read in the next chapter.

---

* Vid. Pope's Portrait.

CHAPTER III

——*Bon jour!*——good morrow!——so you have got your cloak on betimes!——but 'tis a cold morning, and you judge the matter rightly——'tis better to be well mounted than go o' foot——and obstructions in the glands are dangerous—— And how goes it with thy concubine——thy wife——and thy little ones o' both sides? and when did you hear from the old gentleman and lady——your sister, aunt, uncle, and cousins——I hope they have got better of their colds, coughs, claps, toothaches, fevers, stranguries, sciaticas, swellings, and sore eyes.——What a devil of an apothecary! to take so much blood——give such a vile purge——puke——poultice ——plaster——night draught——clyster——blister?——And why so many grains of calomel? Santa Maria! and such a dose of opium! periclitating, *pardi!* the whole family of ye, from head to tail——By my great aunt Dinah's old black velvet mask! I think there was no occasion for it.

Now this being a little bald about the chin, by frequently putting off and on, *before* she was got with child by the coachman——not one of our family would wear it after. To cover the MASK afresh was more than the mask was worth—— and to wear a mask which was bald, or which could be half seen through, was as bad as having no mask at all——

This is the reason, may it please your Reverences, that in all our numerous family, for these four generations, we count no more than one archbishop, a Welsh judge, some three or four aldermen, and a single mountebank——

In the sixteenth century, we boast of no less than a dozen alchemists.

CHAPTER IV

"It is with Love as with Cuckoldom"——the suffering party is at least the *third,* but generally the last in the house who knows anything about the matter: this comes, as all the world knows, from having half a dozen words for one thing; and so long as what in this vessel of the human frame is *Love*——may be *Hatred* in that——*Sentiment* half a yard higher——and *Nonsense*————no, Madam,——not there ——I mean at the part I am now pointing to with my forefinger——how can we help ourselves?

Of all mortal, and immortal men too, if you please, who ever soliloquized upon this mystic subject, my uncle Toby was the worst fitted to have pushed his researches, through such a contention of feelings; and he had infallibly let them all run on, as we do worse matters, to see what they would turn out——had not Bridget's prenotification of them to Susannah, and Susannah's repeated manifestoes thereupon to all the world, made it necessary for my uncle Toby to look into the affair.

CHAPTER V

Why weavers, gardeners, and gladiators——or a man with a pined leg (proceeding from some ailment in the *foot*)—— should ever have had some tender nymph breaking her heart in secret for them are points well and duly settled and accounted for, by ancient and modern physiologists.

A water drinker, provided he is a professed one, and does it without fraud or covin, is precisely in the same predicament: not that, at first sight, there is any consequence or show of logic in it, "That a rill of cold water dribbling through my inward parts should light up a torch in my Jenny's——"

——The proposition does not strike one; on the contrary it seems to run opposite to the natural workings of causes and effects——

But it shows the weakness and imbecility of human reason.

——"And in perfect good health with it?"

——The most perfect——Madam, that friendship herself could wish me——

——"And drink nothing!——nothing but water?"

——Impetuous fluid! the moment thou pressest against the floodgates of the brain——see how they give way!——

In swims CURIOSITY, beckoning to her damsels to follow ——they dive into the centre of the current——

FANCY sits musing upon the bank, and with her eyes following the stream, turns straws and bulrushes into masts and bowsprits——And DESIRE, with vest held up to the knee in one hand, snatches at them, as they swim by her, with the other——

O ye water drinkers! is it then by this delusive fountain that ye have so often governed and turned this world about like a mill wheel——grinding the faces of the impotent——bepowdering their ribs——bepeppering their noses, and changing sometimes even the very frame and face of nature——

——If I was you, quoth Yorick, I would drink more water, Eugenius.——And, if I was you, Yorick, replied Eugenius, so would I.

Which shows they had both read Longinus——

For my own part, I am resolved never to read any book but my own, as long as I live.

CHAPTER VI

I wish my uncle Toby had been a water drinker; for then the thing had been accounted for, That the first moment widow Wadman saw him, she felt something stirring within her in his favour——Something!——something.

——Something perhaps more than friendship——less than love——something——no matter what——no matter where ——I would not give a single hair off my mule's tail, and be obliged to pluck it off myself (indeed the villain has not many to spare, and is not a little vicious into the bargain), to be let by your Worships into the secret——

But the truth is, my uncle Toby was not a water drinker; he drank it neither pure or mixed, or anyhow, or anywhere, except fortuitously upon some advanced posts, where better liquor was not to be had——or during the time he was under cure; when the surgeon telling him it would extend the fibres, and bring them sooner into contact——my uncle Toby drank it for quietness' sake.

Now as all the world knows that no effect in nature can be produced without a cause and as it is as well known that my uncle Toby was neither a weaver——a gardener, or a gladiator——unless as a captain, you will needs have him one——but then he was only a captain of foot——and besides the whole is an equivocation——There is nothing left for us to suppose, but that my uncle Toby's leg——but that will avail us little in the present hypothesis, unless it had proceeded from some ailment *in the foot*——whereas his leg was not emaciated from any disorder in his foot——for my uncle Toby's leg was not emaciated at all. It was a little stiff and awkward, from a total disuse of it, for the three years he lay confined at my father's house in town; but it was plump and muscular, and in all other respects as good and promising a leg as the other.

I declare, I do not recollect any one opinion or passage of my life, where my understanding was more at a loss to make ends meet, and torture the chapter I had been writing, to the service of the chapter following it, than in the present case: one would think I took a pleasure in running into difficulties of this kind, merely to make fresh experiments of getting out of 'em——Inconsiderate soul that thou art! What! are not the unavoidable distresses with which, as an author and a man, thou art hemmed in on every side of thee——are they, Tristram, not sufficient, but thou must entangle thyself still more?

Is it not enough that thou art in debt, and that thou hast ten cartloads of thy fifth and sixth volumes still——still unsold, and art almost at thy wit's ends, how to get them off thy hands.

To this hour art thou not tormented with the vile asthma thou gattest in skating against the wind in Flanders? and is it but two months ago that in a fit of laughter, on seeing a cardinal make water like a chorister (with both hands), thou breakest a vessel in thy lungs, whereby, in two hours, thou lost as many quarts of blood; and hadst thou lost as much more, did not the faculty tell thee——it would have amounted to a gallon?——

CHAPTER VII

——But for heaven's sake, let us not talk of quarts or gallons——let us take the story straight before us; it is so nice and intricate a one, it will scarce bear the transposition of a single tittle; and somehow or other, you have got me thrust almost into the middle of it——

——I beg we may take more care.

CHAPTER VIII

My uncle Toby and the corporal had posted down with so much heat and precipitation, to take possession of the spot of ground we have so often spoke of, in order to open their campaign as early as the rest of the allies, that they had forgot one of the most necessary articles of the whole affair; it was neither a pioneer's spade, a pickaxe, or a shovel——

——It was a bed to lie on: so that as Shandy Hall was at that time unfurnished; and the little inn where poor Le Fever died not yet built; my uncle Toby was constrained to accept of a bed at Mrs. Wadman's, for a night or two, till Corporal Trim (who to the character of an excellent valet, groom, cook, seamster, surgeon, and engineer, superadded that of an excellent upholsterer too) with the help of a carpenter and a couple of tailors, constructed one in my uncle Toby's house.

A daughter of Eve, for such was widow Wadman, and 'tis all the character I intend to give of her——

——"*That she was a perfect woman,*" had better be fifty leagues off——or in her warm bed——or playing with a case knife——or anything you please——than make a man the object of her attention, when the house and all the furniture is her own.

There is nothing in it out of doors and in broad daylight, where a woman has a power, physically speaking, of viewing a man in more lights than one——but here, for her soul, she can see him in no light without mixing something of her own goods and chattels along with him——till by reiterated acts of such combinations, he gets foisted into her inventory——

——And then good night.

But this is not matter of SYSTEM; for I have delivered that above——nor is it matter of BREVIARY——for I make no man's creed but my own——nor matter of FACT——at least that I know of; but 'tis matter copulative and introductory to what follows.

CHAPTER IX

I do not speak it with regard to the coarseness or cleanness of them——or the strength of their gussets——but pray do not night shifts differ from day shifts as much in this particular as in anything else in the world, That they so far exceed the others in length that when you are laid down in them, they fall almost as much below the feet as the day shifts fall short of them?

Widow Wadman's night shifts (as was the mode I suppose in King William's and Queen Anne's reigns) were cut however after this fashion; and if the fashion is changed (for in Italy they are come to nothing),——so much the worse for the public; they were two Flemish ells and a half in length; so that allowing a moderate woman two ells, she had half an ell to spare, to do what she would with.

Now from one little indulgence gained after another, in the many bleak and decemberly nights of a seven years' widowhood, things had insensibly come to this pass, and for the two last years had got established into one of the ordinances of the bedchamber——That as soon as Mrs. Wadman was put to bed, and had got her legs stretched down to the bottom of it, of which she always gave Bridget notice——Bridget with all suitable decorum, having first opened the bedclothes at the feet, took hold of the half ell of cloth we are speaking of, and having gently, and with both her hands, drawn it downwards to its furthest extension, and then contracted it again sidelong by four or five even plaits, she took a large corking pin out of her sleeve, and with the point directed towards her, pinned the plaits all fast together a little above the hem; which done, she tucked all in tight at the feet, and wished her mistress a good night.

This was constant, and without any other variation than this: that on shivering and tempestuous nights, when Bridget untucked the feet of the bed, &c., to do this——she consulted no thermometer but that of her own passions; and so performed it standing——kneeling——or squatting, according to the different degrees of faith, hope, and charity she was in, and bore towards her mistress that night. In every

444

other respect the *etiquette* was sacred, and might have vied with the most mechanical one of the most inflexible bed-chamber in Christendom.

The first night, as soon as the corporal had conducted my uncle Toby upstairs, which was about ten——Mrs. Wadman threw herself into her armchair, and crossing her left knee with her right, which formed a resting place for her elbow, she reclined her cheek upon the palm of her hand, and leaning forwards, ruminated till midnight upon both sides of the question.

The second night she went to her bureau, and having ordered Bridget to bring her up a couple of fresh candles and leave them upon the table, she took out her marriage settlement, and read it over with great devotion; and the third night (which was the last of my uncle Toby's stay), when Bridget had pulled down the night shift, and was assaying to stick in the corking pin——

——With a kick of both heels at once, but at the same time the most natural kick that could be kicked in her situation—— for supposing * * * * * * * * * to be the sun in its meridian, it was a northeast kick——she kicked the pin out of her fingers——the *etiquette* which hung upon it, down ——down it fell to the ground, and was shivered into a thousand atoms.

From all which it was plain that widow Wadman was in love with my uncle Toby.

CHAPTER X

My uncle Toby's head at that time was full of other matters, so that it was not till the demolition of Dunkirk, when all the other civilities of Europe were settled, that he found leisure to return this.

This made an armistice (that is, speaking with regard to my uncle Toby——but with respect to Mrs. Wadman, a vacancy)——of almost eleven years. But in all cases of this nature, as it is the second blow, happen at what distance of time it will, which makes the fray——I choose for that reason to call these the amours of my uncle Toby with Mrs.

Wadman, rather than the amours of Mrs. Wadman with my uncle Toby.

This is not a distinction without a difference.

It is not like the affair of *an old hat cocked*——and *a cocked old hat,* about which your Reverences have so often been at odds with one another——but there is a difference here in the nature of things——

And let me tell you, gentry, a wide one too.

CHAPTER XI

Now as widow Wadman did love my uncle Toby——and my uncle Toby did not love widow Wadman, there was nothing for widow Wadman to do, but to go on and love my uncle Toby——or let it alone.

Widow Wadman would do neither the one or the other——

——Gracious heaven!——but I forget I am a little of her temper myself; for whenever it so falls out, which it sometimes does about the equinoxes, that an earthly goddess is so much this, and that, and t'other that I cannot eat my breakfast for her——and that she careth not three halfpence whether I eat my breakfast or no——

——Curse on her! and so I send her to Tartary, and from Tartary to Terra del Fuego, and so on to the devil: in short there is not an infernal niche where I do not take her divinityship and stick it.

But as the heart is tender, and the passions in these tides ebb and flow ten times in a minute, I instantly bring her back again; and as I do all things in extremes, I place her in the very centre of the milky way——

Brightest of stars! thou wilt shed thy influence upon some-one——

——The deuce take her and her influence too——for at that word I lose all patience——much good may it do him!

——By all that is hirsute and gashly! I cry, taking off my furred cap, and twisting it round my finger——I would not give sixpence for a dozen such!

——But 'tis an excellent cap too (putting it upon my head, and pressing it close to my ears)——and warm——and soft; especially if you stroke it the right way——but alas! that will never be my luck——(so here my philosophy is shipwrecked again)

——No; I shall never have a finger in the pie (so here I break my metaphor)——

Crust and crumb
Inside and out
Top and bottom——I detest it, I hate it, I repudiate it—— I'm sick at the sight of it——

'Tis all pepper,
     garlic,
     staragen,
     salt, and
     devil's dung——by the great archcook of cooks, who does nothing, I think, from morning to night, but sit down by the fireside and invent inflammatory dishes for us, I would not touch it for the world——

O Tristram! Tristram! cried Jenny.

O Jenny! Jenny! replied I, and so went on with the twelfth chapter.

CHAPTER XII

——"Not touch it for the world" did I say——

Lord, how I have heated my imagination with this metaphor!

CHAPTER XIII

Which shows, let your Reverences and Worships say what you will of it (for as for *thinking*——all who *do* think—— think pretty much alike, both upon it and other matters) ——LOVE is certainly, at least alphabetically speaking, one of the most

A gitating

B   ewitching
C   onfounded
D   evilish affairs of life——the most
E   xtravagant
F   utilitous
G   alligaskinish
H   andy-dandyish
I   racundulous (there is no K to it) and
L   yrical of all human passions: at the same time, the most
M   isgiving
N   innyhammering
O   bstipating
P   ragmatical
S   tridulous
R   idiculous——though by the bye the R should have gone
first——But in short 'tis of such a nature, as my father once
told my uncle Toby upon the close of a long dissertation
upon the subject——"You can scarce," said he, "combine
two ideas together upon it, brother Toby, without an hypal-
lage"——What's that? cried my uncle Toby.

The cart before the horse, replied my father——

——And what has he to do there? cried my uncle
Toby——

Nothing, quoth my father, but to get in——or let it alone.

Now widow Wadman, as I told you before, would do neither the one or the other.

She stood however ready harnessed and caparisoned at
all points to watch accidents.

CHAPTER XIV

The Fates, who certainly all foreknew of these amours of
widow Wadman and my uncle Toby, had, from the first creation of matter and motion (and with more courtesy than
they usually do things of this kind), established such a chain
of causes and effects hanging so fast to one another, that it
was scarce possible for my uncle Toby to have dwelt in any
other house in the world, or to have occupied any other garden in Christendom, but the very house and garden which
joined and laid parallel to Mrs. Wadman's; this, with the ad-

vantage of a thick-set arbour in Mrs. Wadman's garden, but planted in the hedgerow of my uncle Toby's, put all the occasions into her hands which Love-militancy wanted; she could observe my uncle Toby's motions, and was mistress likewise of his councils of war; and as his unsuspecting heart had given leave to the corporal, through the mediation of Bridget, to make her a wicker gate of communication to enlarge her walks, it enabled her to carry on her approaches to the very door of the sentry box; and sometimes out of gratitude, to make the attack, and endeavour to blow my uncle Toby up in the very sentry box itself.

CHAPTER XV

It is a great pity——but 'tis certain from every day's observation of man, that he may be set on fire like a candle, at either end——provided there is a sufficient wick standing out; if there is not——there's an end of the affair; and if there is——by lighting it at the bottom, as the flame in that case has the misfortune generally to put out itself——there's an end of the affair again.

For my part, could I always have the ordering of it which way I would be burnt myself——for I cannot bear the thoughts of being burnt like a beast——I would oblige a housewife constantly to light me at the top; for then I should burn down decently to the socket; that is, from my head to my heart, from my heart to my liver, from my liver to my bowels, and so on by the mesaraic veins and arteries, through all the turns and lateral insertions of the intestines and their tunicles to the blind gut——

——I beseech you, Dr. Slop, quoth my uncle Toby, interrupting him as he mentioned the *blind gut,* in a discourse with my father the night my mother was brought to bed of me——I beseech you, quoth my uncle Toby, to tell me which is the blind gut; for, old as I am, I vow I do not know to this day where it lies.

The *blind gut,* answered Dr. Slop, lies betwixt the *Ileum* and *Colon*——

——In a man? said my father.

449

——'Tis precisely the same, cried Dr. Slop, in a woman——

That's more than I know, quoth my father.

CHAPTER XVI

——And so to make sure of both systems, Mrs. Wadman predetermined to light my uncle Toby neither at this end or that; but like a prodigal's candle, to light him, if possible, at both ends at once.

Now, through all the lumber rooms of military furniture, including both of horse and foot, from the great arsenal of Venice to the Tower of London (exclusive), if Mrs. Wadman had been rummaging for seven years together, and with Bridget to help her, she could not have found any one *blind* or *mantelet* so fit for her purpose as that which the expediency of my uncle Toby's affairs had fixed up ready to her hands.

I believe I have not told you——but I don't know——possibly I have——be it as it will, 'tis one of the number of those many things which a man had better do over again than dispute about it——That whatever town or fortress the corporal was at work upon, during the course of their campaign my uncle Toby always took care on the inside of his sentry box, which was towards his left hand, to have a plan of the place, fastened up with two or three pins at the top, but loose at the bottom, for the conveniency of holding it up to the eye, &c. . . . as occasions required; so that when an attack was resolved upon, Mrs. Wadman had nothing more to do, when she had got advanced to the door of the sentry box, but to extend her right hand; and edging in her left foot at the same movement, to take hold of the map or plan, or upright, or whatever it was, and with outstretched neck meeting it halfway,——to advance it towards her; on which my uncle Toby's passions were sure to catch fire——for he would instantly take hold of the other corner of the map in his left hand, and with the end of his pipe in the other, begin an explanation.

When the attack was advanced to this point,——the world will naturally enter into the reasons of Mrs. Wadman's next stroke of generalship——which was to take my uncle Toby's tobacco pipe out of his hand as soon as she possibly could; which, under one pretence or other, but generally that of pointing more distinctly at some redoubt or breastwork in the map, she would effect before my uncle Toby (poor soul!) had well marched above half a dozen toises with it.

——It obliged my uncle Toby to make use of his forefinger.

The difference it made in the attack was this, That in going upon it, as in the first case, with the end of her forefinger against the end of my uncle Toby's tobacco pipe, she might have travelled with it along the lines from Dan to Beersheba, had my uncle Toby's lines reached so far, without any effect: For as there was no arterial or vital heat in the end of the tobacco pipe, it could excite no sentiment——it could neither give fire by pulsation——or receive it by sympathy——'twas nothing but smoke.

Whereas, in following my uncle Toby's forefinger with hers, close through all the little turns and indentings of his works—pressing sometimes against the side of it——then treading upon its nail——then tripping it up——then touching it here——then there, and so on——it set something at least in motion.

This, though slight skirmishing, and at a distance from the main body, yet drew on the rest; for here, the map usually falling with the back of it close to the side of the sentry box, my uncle Toby, in the simplicity of his soul, would lay his hand flat upon it, in order to go on with his explanation; and Mrs. Wadman, by a manoeuvre as quick as thought, would as certainly place hers close besides it; this at once opened a communication large enough for any sentiment to pass or re-pass which a person skilled in the elementary and practical part of love-making has occasion for——

By bringing up her forefinger parallel (as before) to my uncle Toby's——it unavoidably brought the thumb into action——and the forefinger and thumb being once engaged, as naturally brought in the whole hand. Thine, dear uncle Toby! was never now in its right place——Mrs. Wadman had it ever to take up, or, with the gentlest pushings, protrusions, and equivocal compressions that a hand to be removed is capable of receiving——to get it pressed a hairbreadth of one side out of her way.

Whilst this was doing, how could she forget to make him sensible that it was her leg (and no one's else), at the bottom of the sentry box, which slightly pressed against the calf of

451

his——So that my uncle Toby being thus attacked and sore pushed on both his wings——was it a wonder if, now and then, it put his centre into disorder?——

——The deuce take it! said my uncle Toby.

CHAPTER XVII

These attacks of Mrs. Wadman you will readily conceive to be of different kinds; varying from each other like the attacks which history is full of, and from the same reasons. A general looker on would scarce allow them to be attacks at all ——or if he did, would confound them all together——but I write not to them: it will be time enough to be a little more exact in my descriptions of them as I come up to them, which will not be for some chapters; having nothing more to add in this, but that in a bundle of original papers and drawings which my father took care to roll up by themselves, there is a plan of Bouchain in perfect preservation (and shall be kept so, whilst I have power to preserve anything), upon the lower corner of which, on the right-hand side, there is still remaining the marks of a snuffy finger and thumb, which there is all the reason in the world to imagine were Mrs. Wadman's; for the opposite side of the margin, which I suppose to have been my uncle Toby's, is absolutely clean: This seems an authenticated record of one of these attacks; for there are vestigia of the two punctures, partly grown up, but still visible, on the opposite corner of the map, which are unquestionably the very holes through which it has been pricked up in the sentry box——

By all that is priestly! I value this precious relic, with its *stigmata* and *pricks,* more than all the relics of the Romish church——always excepting, when I am writing upon these matters, the pricks which entered the flesh of St. Radagunda in the desert, which in your road from FESSE to CLUNY, the nuns of that name will show you for love.

CHAPTER XVIII

I think, an' please your Honour, quoth Trim, the fortifications are quite destroyed——and the basin is upon a level with the mole——I think so too, replied my uncle Toby with a sigh half suppressed——but step into the parlour, Trim, for the stipulation——it lies upon the table.

It has lain there these six weeks, replied the corporal, till this very morning that the old woman kindled the fire with it——

——Then, said my uncle Toby, there is no further occasion for our services. The more, an' please your Honour, the pity, said the corporal; in uttering which, he cast his spade into the wheelbarrow, which was beside him, with an air the most expressive of disconsolation that can be imagined, and was heavily turning about to look for his pickaxe, his pioneer's shovel, his pickets and other little military stores, in order to carry them off the field——when a heigh ho! from the sentry box, which, being made of thin slit deal, reverberated the sound more sorrowfully to his ear, forbad him.

——No, said the corporal to himself, I'll do it before his Honour rises tomorrow morning; so taking his spade out of the wheelbarrow again, with a little earth in it, as if to level something at the foot of the glacis——but with a real intent to approach nearer to his master, in order to divert him—— he loosened a sod or two——pared their edges with his spade, and having given them a gentle blow or two with the back of it, he sat himself down close by my uncle Toby's feet, and began as follows.

CHAPTER XIX

It was a thousand pities——though I believe, an' please your Honour, I am going to say but a foolish kind of a thing for a soldier——

A soldier, cried my uncle Toby, interrupting the corporal, is no more exempt from saying a foolish thing, Trim, than a man of letters——But not so often, an' please your Honour, replied the corporal——My uncle Toby gave a nod.

It was a thousand pities then, said the corporal, casting his eye upon Dunkirk, and the mole, as Servius Sulpicius, in returning out of Asia (when he sailed from Aegina towards Megara) did upon Corinth and Piraeus——

——"It was a thousand pities, an' please your Honour, to destroy these works——and a thousand pities to have let them stood."——

——Thou art right, Trim, in both cases, said my uncle Toby——This, continued the corporal, is the reason that from the beginning of their demolition to the end——I have never once whistled, or sung, or laughed, or cried, or talked of past-done deeds, or told your Honour one story good or bad——

——Thou hast many excellencies, Trim, said my uncle Toby, and I hold it not the least of them, as thou happenest to be a storyteller, that of the number thou hast told me, either to amuse me in my painful hours, or divert me in my grave ones——thou hast seldom told me a bad one——

——Because, an' please your Honour, except one of a *King of Bohemia and his seven castles,*——they are all true; for they are about myself——

I do not like the subject the worse, Trim, said my uncle Toby, on that score: But prithee what is this story? thou hast excited my curiosity.

I'll tell it your Honour, quoth the corporal directly—— Provided, said my uncle Toby, looking earnestly towards Dunkirk and the mole again——provided it is not a merry one; to such, Trim, a man should ever bring one half of the entertainment along with him; and the disposition I am in at present would wrong both thee, Trim, and thy story——It is not a merry one by any means, replied the corporal——Nor would I have it altogether a grave one, added my uncle Toby ——It is neither the one nor the other, replied the corporal, but will suit your Honour exactly——Then I'll thank thee for it with all my heart, cried my uncle Toby, so prithee begin it, Trim.

The corporal made his reverence; and though it is not so easy a matter as the world imagines to pull off a lank Montero cap with grace——or a whit less difficult, in my conceptions, when a man is sitting squat upon the ground, to make a bow so teeming with respect as the corporal was wont, yet by suffering the palm of his right hand, which was towards his master, to slip backward upon the grass, a little beyond his body, in order to allow it the greater sweep——and by an unforced compression, at the same time, of his cap with the thumb and the two forefingers of his left, by which the di-ameter of the cap became reduced, so that it might be said rather to be insensibly squeezed——than pulled off with a flatus——the corporal acquitted himself of both in a better manner than the posture of his affairs promised; and having hemmed twice, to find in what key his story would best go, and best suit his master's humour——he exchanged a single look of kindness with him, and set off thus.

The story of the King of Bohemia
and his seven castles.

There was a certain King of Bo -- he——

As the corporal was entering the confines of Bohemia, my uncle Toby obliged him to halt for a single moment; he had set out bareheaded, having, since he pulled off his Montero cap in the latter end of the last chapter, left it lying beside him on the ground.

——The eye of Goodness espieth all things——so that be-fore the corporal had well got through the first five words of his story, had my uncle Toby twice touched his Montero cap with the end of his cane, interrogatively——as much as to say, Why don't you put it on, Trim? Trim took it up with the most respectful slowness, and casting a glance of humilia-tion, as he did it, upon the embroidery of the forepart, which, being dismally tarnished and frayed moreover in some of the principal leaves and boldest parts of the pattern, he laid it down again betwixt his two feet, in order to moralize upon the subject.

——'Tis every word of it but too true, cried my uncle Toby, that thou art about to observe——

"Nothing in this world, Trim, is made to last forever."

——But when tokens, dear Tom, of thy love and remem-brance wear out, said Trim, what shall we say?

There is no occasion, Trim, quoth my uncle Toby, to say anything else; and was a man to puzzle his brains till Doom's day, I believe, Trim, it would be impossible.

The corporal perceiving my uncle Toby was in the right, and that it would be in vain for the wit of man to think of extracting a purer moral from his cap, without further attempting it, he put it on; and passing his hand across his forehead to rub out a pensive wrinkle, which the text and the doctrine between them had engendered, he returned, with the same look and tone of voice, to his story of the King of Bohemia and his seven castles.

The story of the King of Bohemia and his seven castles, continued

There was a certain King of Bohemia, but in whose reign, except his own, I am not able to inform your Honour——I do not desire it of thee, Trim, by any means, cried my uncle Toby.

——It was a little before the time, an' please your Honour, when giants were beginning to leave off breeding;—— but in what year of our Lord that was——

——I would not give a halfpenny to know, said my uncle Toby.

——Only, an' please your Honour, it makes a story look the better in the face——

——'Tis thy own, Trim, so ornament it after thy own fashion; and take any date, continued my uncle Toby, looking pleasantly upon him——take any date in the whole world thou choosest, and put it to——thou art heartily welcome——

The corporal bowed; for of every century, and of every year of that century, from the first creation of the world down to Noah's flood; and from Noah's flood to the birth of Abraham; through all the pilgrimages of the patriarchs, to the departure of the Israelites out of Egypt——and throughout all the Dynasties, Olympiads, Urbeconditas, and other memorable epochas of the different nations of the world, down to the coming of Christ, and from thence to the very moment in which the corporal was telling his story——had my uncle Toby subjected this vast empire of time and all its abysses at his feet; but as MODESTY scarce touches with a finger what LIBERALITY offers her with both hands open—— the corporal contented himself with the very *worst year* of the whole bunch; which, to prevent your Honours of the Majority and Minority from tearing the very flesh off your bones in contestation, "Whether that year is not always the last cast year of the last cast almanac"——I tell you plainly it was; but from a different reason than you wot of——

——It was the year next him——which being the year of
our Lord seventeen hundred and twelve, when the Duke of
Ormond was playing the devil in Flanders——the corporal
took it, and set out with it afresh on his expedition to Bohemia.

The story of the King of Bohemia and
his seven castles, continued

In the year of our Lord one thousand seven hundred and
twelve, there was, an' please your Honour——

——To tell thee truly, Trim, quoth my uncle Toby, any
other date would have pleased me much better, not only on
account of the sad stain upon our history that year, in marching off our troops, and refusing to cover the siege of Quesnoi,
though Fagel was carrying on the works with such incredible
vigour——but likewise on the score, Trim, of thy own story;
because if there are——and which, from what thou hast
dropt, I partly suspect to be the fact——if there are giants in
it——

There is but one, an' please your Honour——

——'Tis as bad as twenty, replied my uncle Toby——thou
shouldst have carried him back some seven or eight hundred
years out of harm's way, both of critics and other people;
and therefore I would advise thee, if ever thou tellest it
again——

——If I live, an' please your Honour, but once to get
through it, I will never tell it again, quoth Trim, either to
man, woman, or child——Poo——poo! said my uncle Toby
——but with accents of such sweet encouragement did he
utter it that the corporal went on with his story with more
alacrity than ever.

The story of the King of Bohemia and
his seven castles, continued

There was, an' please your Honour, said the corporal, raising
his voice and rubbing the palms of his two hands cheerily
together as he begun, a certain King of Bohemia——

——Leave out the date entirely, Trim, quoth my uncle
Toby, leaning forwards, and laying his hand gently upon the
corporal's shoulder to temper the interruption——leave it out
entirely, Trim; a story passes very well without these niceties,

unless one is pretty sure of 'em——Sure of 'em! said the corporal, shaking his head——

Right, answered my uncle Toby; it is not easy, Trim, for one bred up as thou and I have been to arms, who seldom looks further forwards than to the end of his musket, or backwards beyond his knapsack, to know much about this matter——God bless your Honour! said the corporal, won by the *manner* of my uncle Toby's reasoning as much as by the reasoning itself; he has something else to do; if not on action, or a march, or upon duty in his garrison——he has his firelock, an' please your Honour, to furbish——his accoutrements to take care of——his regimentals to mend——himself to shave and keep clean, so as to appear always like what he is upon the parade; what business, added the corporal triumphantly, has a soldier, an' please your Honour, to know anything at all of *geography*?

——Thou wouldst have said *chronology*, Trim, said my uncle Toby; for as for geography, 'tis of absolute use to him; he must be acquainted intimately with every country and its boundaries where his profession carries him; he should know every town and city, and village and hamlet, with the canals, the roads and hollow ways which lead up to them; there is not a river or a rivulet he passes, Trim, but he should be able at first sight to tell thee what is its name——in what mountains it takes its rise——what is its course——how far it is navigable——where fordable——where not; he should know the fertility of every valley, as well as the hind who ploughs it; and be able to describe, or, if it is required, to give thee an exact map of all the plains and defiles, the forts, the acclivities, the woods and morasses through and by which his army is to march; he should know their produce, their plants, their minerals, their waters, their animals, their seasons, their climates, their heats and cold, their inhabitants, their customs, their language, their policy, and even their religion.

Is it else to be conceived, corporal, continued my uncle Toby, rising up in his sentry box, as he began to warm in this part of his discourse——how Marlborough could have marched his army from the banks of the Maas to Belburg; from Belburg to Kerpenord——(here the corporal could sit no longer) from Kerpenord, Trim, to Kalsaken; from Kalsaken to Newdorf; from Newdorf to Landenbourg; from Landenbourg to Mildenheim; from Mildenheim to Elchingen; from Elchingen to Gingen; from Gingen to Balmerchoffen; from Balmerchoffen to Skellenburg, where he broke in upon the enemy's works; forced his passage over the Danube;

458

crossed the Lech——pushed on his troops into the heart of the empire, marching at the head of them through Friburg, Hokenwert, and Schonevelt, to the plains of Blenheim and Hochstet?——Great as he was, corporal, he could not have advanced a step, or made one single day's march, without the aids of *geography*——As for *chronology,* I own, Trim, continued my uncle Toby, sitting down again coolly in his sentry box, that of all others, it seems a science which the soldier might best spare, was it not for the lights which that science must one day give him, in determining the invention of powder; the furious execution of which, renversing everything like thunder before it, has become a new era to us of military improvements, changing so totally the nature of attacks and defences both by sea and land, and awakening so much art and skill in doing it, that the world cannot be too exact in ascertaining the precise time of its discovery, or too inquisitive in knowing what great man was the discoverer, and what occasions gave birth to it.

I am far from controverting, continued my uncle Toby, what historians agree in, that in the year of our Lord 1380, under the reign of Wenceslaus, son of Charles the Fourth ——a certain priest, whose name was Schwartz, showed the use of powder to the Venetians, in their wars against the Genoese; but 'tis certain he was not the first; because if we are to believe Don Pedro, the Bishop of Leon——How came priests and bishops, an' please your Honour, to trouble their heads so much about gunpowder?——God knows, said my uncle Toby——his providence brings good out of everything ——and he avers, in his chronicle of King Alphonsus, who reduced Toledo, That in the year 1343, which was full thirty-seven years before that time, the secret of powder was well known, and employed with success, both by Moors and Christians, not only in their seacombats, at that period, but in many of their most memorable sieges in Spain and Barbary ——And all the world knows that Friar Bacon had wrote expressly about it, and had generously given the world a receipt to make it by, above a hundred and fifty years before even Schwartz was born——And that the Chinese, added my uncle Toby, embarrass us, and all accounts of it still more, by boasting of the invention some hundreds of years even before him——

——They are a pack of liars, I believe, cried Trim—— ——They are somehow or other deceived, said my uncle Toby, in this matter, as is plain to me from the present miserable state of military architecture amongst them; which

459

consists of nothing more than a fosse with a brick wall without flanks——and for what they give us as a bastion at each angle of it, 'tis so barbarously constructed that it looks for all the world—— —— Like one of my seven castles, an' please your Honour, quoth Trim.

My uncle Toby, though in the utmost distress for a comparison, most courteously refused Trim's offer——till Trim telling him he had half a dozen more in Bohemia, which he knew not how to get off his hands——my uncle Toby was so touched with the pleasantry of heart of the corporal——that he discontinued his dissertation upon gunpowder——and begged the corporal forthwith to go on with his story of the King of Bohemia and his seven castles.

The story of the King of Bohemia and his seven castles, continued

This *unfortunate* King of Bohemia, said Trim——Was he unfortunate then? cried my uncle Toby, for he had been so wrapt up in his dissertation upon gunpowder and other military affairs that, though he had desired the corporal to go on, yet the many interruptions he had given dwelt not so strong upon his fancy as to account for the epithet——Was he *unfortunate* then, Trim? said my uncle Toby, pathetically ——The corporal, wishing first the *word* and all its synonyms at the devil, forthwith began to run back in his mind the principal events in the King of Bohemia's story; from every one of which, it appearing that he was the most fortunate man that ever existed in the world——it put the corporal to a stand: for not caring to retract his epithet——and less, to explain it——and least of all, to twist his tale (like men of lore) to serve a system——he looked up in my uncle Toby's face for assistance——but seeing it was the very thing my uncle Toby sat in expectation of himself——after a hum and a haw, he went on——

The King of Bohemia, an' please your Honour, replied the corporal, was *unfortunate,* as thus——That taking great pleasure and delight in navigation and all sort of sea affairs ——and there *happening* throughout the whole kingdom of Bohemia to be no seaport town whatever——

How the deuce should there——Trim? cried my uncle Toby; for Bohemia being totally inland, it could have happened no otherwise——It might, said Trim, if it had pleased God——

460

My uncle Toby never spoke of the being and natural attributes of God but with diffidence and hesitation——

——I believe not, replied my uncle Toby, after some pause ——for being inland, as I said, and having Silesia and Moravia to the east; Lusatia and Upper Saxony to the north; Franconia to the west; and Bavaria to the south: Bohemia could not have been propelled to the sea, without ceasing to be Bohemia——nor could the sea, on the other hand, have come up to Bohemia, without overflowing a great part of Germany, and destroying millions of unfortunate inhabitants who could make no defence against it——Scandalous! cried Trim——Which would bespeak, added my uncle Toby, mildly, such a want of compassion in him who is the father of it——that, I think, Trim,——the thing could have happened no way.

The corporal made the bow of unfeigned conviction; and went on.

Now the King of Bohemia with his queen and courtiers *happening* one fine summer's evening to walk out——Aye! there the word *happening* is right, Trim, cried my uncle Toby; for the King of Bohemia and his queen might have walked out, or let it alone;——'twas a matter of contingency, which might happen, or not, just as chance ordered it.

King William was of an opinion, an' please your Honour, quoth Trim, that everything was predestined for us in this world; insomuch, that he would often say to his soldiers that "every ball had its billet." He was a great man, said my uncle Toby——And I believe, continued Trim, to this day that the shot which disabled me at the battle of Landen was pointed at my knee for no other purpose but to take me out of his service, and place me in your Honour's, where I should be taken so much better care of in my old age——It shall never, Trim, be construed otherwise, said my uncle Toby.

The heart both of the master and the man were alike subject to sudden overflowings;——a short silence ensued.

Besides, said the corporal, resuming the discourse——but in a gayer accent——if it had not been for that single shot, I had never, an' please your Honour, been in love——

So, thou wast once in love, Trim! said my uncle Toby, smiling——

Souse! replied the corporal——over head and ears! an' please your Honour. Prithee when? where?——and how came it to pass?——I never heard one word of it before, quoth my uncle Toby:——I dare say, answered Trim, that every drummer and serjeant's son in the regiment knew of it

——It's high time I should——said my uncle Toby.

Your Honour remembers with concern, said the corporal, the total rout and confusion of our camp and army at the affair of Landen; everyone was left to shift for himself; and if it had not been for the regiments of Wyndham, Lumley, and Galway, which covered the retreat over the bridge of Neerspeeken, the king himself could scarce have gained it ——he was pressed hard, as your Honour knows, on every side of him——

Gallant mortal! cried my uncle Toby, caught up with enthusiasm——this moment, now that all is lost, I see him galloping across me, corporal, to the left, to bring up the remains of the English horse along with him to support the right, and tear the laurel from Luxembourg's brows, if yet 'tis possible——I see him with the knot of his scarf just shot off, infusing fresh spirits into poor Galway's regiment ——riding along the line——then wheeling about, and charging Conti at the head of it——Brave! brave by heaven! cried my uncle Toby——he deserves a crown——As richly as a thief a halter, shouted Trim.

My uncle Toby knew the corporal's loyalty;——otherwise the comparison was not at all to his mind——it did not altogether strike the corporal's fancy when he had made it—— but it could not be recalled——so he had nothing to do but proceed.

As the number of wounded was prodigious, and no one had time to think of anything but his own safety——Though Talmash, said my uncle Toby, brought off the foot with great prudence——But I was left upon the field, said the corporal. Thou wast so; poor fellow! replied my uncle Toby ——So that it was noon the next day, continued the corporal, before I was exchanged, and put into a cart with thirteen or fourteen more, in order to be conveyed to our hospital.

There is no part of the body, an' please your Honour, where a wound occasions more intolerable anguish than upon the knee——

Except the groin, said my uncle Toby. An' please your Honour, replied the corporal, the knee, in my opinion, must certainly be the most acute, there being so many tendons and what-d'ye-call-'ems all about it.

It is for that reason, quoth my uncle Toby, that the groin is infinitely more sensible——there being not only as many tendons and what-d'ye-call-'ems (for I know their names as little as thou dost)——about it——but moreover * * *——

Mrs. Wadman, who had been all the time in her arbour

462

——instantly stopped her breath——unpinned her mob at the chin, and stood up upon one leg——

The dispute was maintained with amicable and equal force betwixt my uncle Toby and Trim for some time; till Trim at length recollecting that he had often cried at his master's sufferings, but never shed a tear at his own——was for giving up the point, which my uncle Toby would not allow——'Tis a proof of nothing, Trim, said he, but the generosity of thy temper——

So that whether the pain of a wound in the groin (*Caeteris paribus*) is greater than the pain of a wound in the knee——or

Whether the pain of a wound in the knee is not greater than the pain of a wound in the groin——are points which to this day remain unsettled.

CHAPTER XX

The anguish of my knee, continued the corporal, was excessive in itself; and the uneasiness of the cart, with the roughness of the roads, which were terribly cut up——making bad still worse——every step was death to me: so that with the loss of blood, and the want of caretaking of me, and a fever I felt coming on besides——(Poor soul! said my uncle Toby) all together, an' please your Honour, was more than I could sustain.

I was telling my sufferings to a young woman at a peasant's house, where our cart, which was the last of the line, had halted; they had helped me in, and the young woman had taken a cordial out of her pocket and dropped it upon some sugar, and seeing it had cheered me, she had given it me a second and a third time——So I was telling her, an' please your Honour, the anguish I was in, and was saying it was so intolerable to me that I had much rather lie down upon the bed, turning my face towards one which was in the corner of the room——and die, than go on——when, upon her attempting to lead me to it, I fainted away in her arms. She was a good soul! as your Honour, said the corporal, wiping his eyes, will hear.

I thought *love* had been a joyous thing, quoth my uncle Toby.

'Tis the most serious thing, an' please your Honour (sometimes), that is in the world.

By the persuasion of the young woman, continued the corporal, the cart with the wounded men set off without me: she had assured them I should expire immediately if I was put into the cart. So when I came to myself——I found myself in a still, quiet cottage, with no one but the young woman, and the peasant and his wife. I was laid across the bed in the corner of the room, with my wounded leg upon a chair, and the young woman beside me, holding the corner of her handkerchief dipped in vinegar to my nose with one hand, and rubbing my temples with the other.

I took her at first for the daughter of the peasant (for it was no inn)——so had offered her a little purse with eighteen florins, which my poor brother Tom (here Trim wiped his eyes) had sent me as a token, by a recruit, just before he set out for Lisbon——

——I never told your Honour that piteous story yet——here Trim wiped his eyes a third time.

The young woman called the old man and his wife into the room, to show them the money, in order to gain me credit for a bed and what little necessaries I should want, till I should be in a condition to be got to the hospital——Come then! said she, tying up the little purse——I'll be your banker——but as that office alone will not keep me employed, I'll be your nurse too.

I thought by her manner of speaking this, as well as by her dress, which I then began to consider more attentively——that the young woman could not be the daughter of the peasant.

She was in black down to her toes, with her hair concealed under a cambric border, laid close to her forehead: she was one of those kind of nuns, an' please your Honour, of which, your Honour knows, there are a good many in Flanders which they let go loose——By thy description, Trim, said my uncle Toby, I dare say she was a young Beguine, of which there are none to be found anywhere but in the Spanish Netherlands——except at Amsterdam——they differ from nuns in this, that they can quit their cloister if they choose to marry; they visit and take care of the sick by profession——I had rather, for my own part, they did it out of good nature.

——She often told me, quoth Trim, she did it for the love of Christ——I did not like it.——I believe, Trim, we are both wrong, said my uncle Toby——we'll ask Mr. Yorick

464

about it tonight at my brother Shandy's——so put me in mind, added my uncle Toby.

The young Beguine, continued the corporal, had scarce given herself time to tell me "she would be my nurse," when she hastily turned about to begin the office of one, and prepare something for me——and in a short time——though I thought it a long one——she came back with flannels, &c., &c., and having fomented my knee soundly for a couple of hours, &c., and made me a thin basin of gruel for my supper——she wished me rest, and promised to be with me early in the morning.——She wished me, an' please your Honour, what was not to be had. My fever ran very high that night——her figure made sad disturbance within me ——I was every moment cutting the world in two——to give her half of it——and every moment was I crying, That I had nothing but a knapsack and eighteen florins to share with her——The whole night long was the fair Beguine, like an angel, close by my bedside, holding back my curtain and offering me cordials——and I was only awakened from my dream by her coming there at the hour promised, and giving them in reality. In truth, she was scarce ever from me, and so accustomed was I to receive life from her hands that my heart sickened, and I lost colour, when she left the room: and yet, continued the corporal (making one of the strangest reflections upon it in the world)——

——*"It was not love"*——for during the three weeks she was almost constantly with me, fomenting my knee with her hand, night and day——I can honestly say, an' please your Honour——that * * * * * * * * * * * * * * * * once.

That was very odd, Trim, quoth my uncle Toby——

I think so too——said Mrs. Wadman.

It never did, said the corporal.

CHAPTER XXI

——But 'tis no marvel, continued the corporal——seeing my uncle Toby musing upon it——for Love, an' please your Honour, is exactly like war, in this: That a soldier, though he has escaped three weeks complete o' Saturday night,——

may nevertheless be shot through his heart on Sunday morning——*It happened so here,* an' please your Honour, with this difference only——that it was on Sunday in the afternoon when I fell in love all at once with a siserara——it burst upon me, an' please your Honour, like a bomb—— scarce giving me time to say, "God bless me."

I thought, Trim, said my uncle Toby, a man never fell in love so very suddenly.

Yes, an' please your honour, if he is in the way of it—— replied Trim.

I prithee, quoth my uncle Toby, inform me how this matter happened.

——With all pleasure, said the corporal, making a bow.

CHAPTER XXII

I had escaped, continued the corporal, all that time from falling in love, and had gone on to the end of the chapter, had it not been predestined otherwise——there is no resisting our fate.

It was on a Sunday, in the afternoon, as I told your Honour——

The old man and his wife had walked out——

Everything was still and hush as midnight about the house——

There was not so much as a duck or a duckling about the yard——

——When the fair Beguine came in to see me.

My wound was then in a fair way of doing well——the inflammation had been gone off for some time, but it was succeeded with an itching both above and below my knee, so insufferable that I had not shut my eyes the whole night for it.

Let me see it, said she, kneeling down upon the ground parallel to my knee, and laying her hand upon the part below it——It only wants rubbing a little, said the Beguine; so covering it with the bedclothes, she began with the forefinger of her right hand to rub under my knee, guiding her forefinger backwards and forwards by the edge of the flannel which kept on the dressing.

In five or six minutes I felt slightly the end of her second finger——and presently it was laid flat with the other, and she continued rubbing in that way round and round for a good while; it then came into my head that I should fall in love——I blushed when I saw how white a hand she had ——I shall never, an' please your Honour, behold another hand so white whilst I live——

——not in that place, said my uncle Toby——

Though it was the most serious despair in nature to the corporal——he could not forbear smiling.

The young Beguine, continued the corporal, perceiving it was of great service to me——from rubbing, for some time, with two fingers——proceeded to rub, at length, with three ——till by little and little she brought down the fourth, and then rubbed with her whole hand: I will never say another word, an' please your Honour, upon hands again——but it was softer than satin——

——Prithee, Trim, commend it as much as thou wilt, said my uncle Toby; I shall hear thy story with the more delight ——The corporal thanked his master most unfeignedly; but having nothing to say upon the Beguine's hand but the same over again——he proceeded to the effects of it.

The fair Beguine, said the corporal, continued rubbing with her whole hand under my knee——till I feared her zeal would weary her——"I would do a thousand times more," said she, "for the love of Christ"——In saying which she passed her hand across the flannel, to the part above my knee, which I had equally complained of, and rubbed it also.

I perceived, then, I was beginning to be in love——

As she continued rub-rub-rubbing——I felt it spread from under her hand, an' please your Honour, to every part of my frame——

The more she rubbed, and the longer strokes she took—— the more the fire kindled in my veins——till at length, by two or three strokes longer than the rest——my passion rose to the highest pitch——I seized her hand——

——And then, thou clappedst it to thy lips, Trim, said my uncle Toby——and madest a speech.

Whether the corporal's amour terminated precisely in the way my uncle Toby described it is not material; it is enough that it contained in it the essence of all the love-romances which ever have been wrote since the beginning of the world.

CHAPTER XXIII

As soon as the corporal had finished the story of his amour
——or rather my uncle Toby for him——Mrs. Wadman
silently sallied forth from her arbour, replaced the pin in her
mob, passed the wicker gate, and advanced slowly towards
my uncle Toby's sentry box: the disposition which Trim had
made in my uncle Toby's mind was too favourable a crisis to
be let slipped——

——The attack was determined upon: it was facilitated
still more by my uncle Toby's having ordered the corporal
to wheel off the pioneer's shovel, the spade, the pickaxe,
the pickets, and other military stores which lay scattered
upon the ground where Dunkirk stood——The corporal had
marched——the field was clear.

Now consider, Sir, what nonsense it is, either in fighting, or
writing, or anything else (whether in rhyme to it, or not)
which a man has occasion to do——to act by plan: for if ever
Plan, independent of all circumstances, deserved registering
in letters of gold (I mean in the archives of Gotham)——it
was certainly the PLAN of Mrs. Wadman's attack of my
uncle Toby in his sentry box, BY PLAN——Now the Plan
hanging up in it at this juncture being the Plan of Dunkirk
——and the tale of Dunkirk a tale of relaxation, it opposed
every impression she could make: and besides, could she
have gone upon it——the manoeuvre of fingers and hands in
the attack of the sentry box was so outdone by that of the
fair Beguine's in Trim's story——that just then, that particular attack, however successful before——became the most
heartless attack that could be made——

O! let woman alone for this. Mrs. Wadman had scarce
opened the wicker gate, when her genius sported with the
change of circumstances.

——She formed a new attack in a moment.

CHAPTER XXIV

——I am half distracted, Captain Shandy, said Mrs. Wadman, holding up her cambric handkerchief to her left eye, as she approached the door of my uncle Toby's sentry box——a mote——or sand——or something——I know not what, has got into this eye of mine——do look into it——it is not in the white——

In saying which, Mrs. Wadman edged herself close in beside my uncle Toby, and squeezing herself down upon the corner of his bench, she gave him an opportunity of doing it without rising up————Do look into it——said she.

Honest soul! thou didst look into it with as much innocency of heart as ever child looked into a raree-show box; and 'twere as much a sin to have hurt thee.

——If a man will be peeping of his own accord into things of that nature——I've nothing to say to it——

My uncle Toby never did: and I will answer for him that he would have sat quietly upon a sofa from June to January (which, you know, takes in both the hot and cold months), with an eye as fine as the Thracian * Rhodope's besides him, without being able to tell whether it was a black or a blue one.

The difficulty was to get my uncle Toby to look at one at all.

'Tis surmounted. And

I see him yonder with his pipe pendulous in his hand, and the ashes falling out of it——looking——and looking ——then rubbing his eyes——and looking again, with twice the good nature that ever Galileo looked for a spot in the sun.

——In vain! For by all the powers which animate the organ ——widow Wadman's left eye shines this moment as lucid as her right——there is neither mote, or sand, or dust, or chaff, or speck, or particle of opaque matter floating in it—— There is nothing, my dear paternal uncle! but one lambent

---

* Rhodope Thracia tam inevitabili fascino instructa, tam exacte oculis intuens attraxit, ut si in illam quis incidesset, fieri non posset, quin caperetur.——I know not who.

delicious fire, furtively shooting out from every part of it, in all directions, into thine——

——If thou lookest, uncle Toby, in search of this mote one moment longer——thou art undone.

CHAPTER XXV

An eye is for all the world exactly like a cannon, in this respect: That it is not so much the eye or the cannon, in themselves, as it is the carriage of the eye——and the carriage of the cannon, by which both the one and the other are enabled to do so much execution. I don't think the comparison a bad one: However, as 'tis made and placed at the head of the chapter, as much for use as ornament, all I desire in return is that whenever I speak of Mrs. Wadman's eyes (except once in the next period) that you keep it in your fancy.

I protest, Madam, said my uncle Toby, I can see nothing whatever in your eye.

It is not in the white, said Mrs. Wadman; my uncle Toby looked with might and main into the pupil——

Now of all the eyes which ever were created——from your own, Madam, up to those of Venus herself, which certainly were as venereal a pair of eyes as ever stood in a head ——there never was an eye of them all so fitted to rob my uncle Toby of his repose as the very eye at which he was looking——it was not, Madam, a rolling eye——a romping or a wanton one——nor was it an eye sparkling——petulant or imperious——of high claims and terrifying exactions, which would have curdled at once that milk of human nature of which my uncle Toby was made up——but 'twas an eye full of gentle salutations——and soft responses——speaking ——not like the trumpet stop of some ill-made organ, in which many an eye I talk to holds coarse converse——but whispering soft——like the last low accents of an expiring saint——"How can you live comfortless, Captain Shandy, and alone, without a bosom to lean your head on——or trust your cares to?"

It was an eye——

But I shall be in love with it myself, if I say another word about it.

——It did my uncle Toby's business.

CHAPTER XXVI

There is nothing shows the characters of my father and my uncle Toby in a more entertaining light than their different manner of deportment, under the same accident——for I call not love a misfortune, from a persuasion that a man's heart is ever the better for it——Great God! what must my uncle Toby's have been, when 'twas all benignity without it.

My father, as appears from many of his papers, was very subject to this passion before he married——but from a little subacid kind of drollish impatience in his nature, whenever it befell him, he would never submit to it like a Christian; but would pish, and huff, and bounce, and kick, and play the devil, and write the bitterest philippics against the eye that ever man wrote——there is one in verse upon somebody's eye or other, that for two or three nights together had put him by his rest; which in his first transport of resentment against it, he begins thus:

> "A devil 'tis——and mischief such doth work
> As never yet did Pagan, Jew, or Turk." *

In short, during the whole paroxysm, my father was all abuse and foul language, approaching rather towards malediction——only he did not do it with as much method as Ernulphus——he was too impetuous; nor with Ernulphus's policy——for though my father, with the most intolerant spirit, would curse both this and that, and everything under heaven, which was either aiding or abetting to his love—— yet never concluded his chapter of curses upon it, without cursing himself in at the bargain, as one of the most egregious fools and coxcombs, he would say, that ever was let loose in the world.

My uncle Toby, on the contrary, took it like a lamb——sat

* This will be printed with my father's life of Socrates, etc, etc.

still and let the poison work in his veins without resistance
——in the sharpest exacerbations of his wound (like that on
his groin) he never dropt one fretful or discontented word
——he blamed neither heaven nor earth——or thought or
spoke an injurious thing of anybody, or any part of it; he sat
solitary and pensive with his pipe——looking at his lame leg
——then whiffing out a sentimental heigh ho! which mixing
with the smoke, incommoded no one mortal.

He took it like a lamb——I say.

In truth he had mistook it at first; for having taken a ride
with my father, that very morning, to save if possible a beautiful wood, which the dean and chapter were hewing down to
give to the poor; * which said wood being in full view of my
uncle Toby's house, and of singular service to him in his
description of the battle of Wynendale——by trotting on too
hastily to save it——upon an uneasy saddle——worse horse,
&c., &c. . . . it had so happened that the serious part of the
blood had got betwixt the two skins, in the nethermost part
of my uncle Toby——the first shootings of which (as my
uncle Toby had no experience of love) he had taken for a
part of the passion——till the blister breaking in the one
case——and the other remaining——my uncle Toby was
presently convinced that his wound was not a skin-deep
wound——but that it had gone to his heart.

CHAPTER XXVII

The world is ashamed of being virtuous——My uncle Toby
knew little of the world; and therefore when he felt he was
in love with widow Wadman, he had no conception that the
thing was any more to be made a mystery of than if Mrs.
Wadman had given him a cut with a gaped knife across his
finger: Had it been otherwise——yet as he ever looked upon
Trim as a humble friend, and saw fresh reasons every day of
his life to treat him as such——it would have made no
variation in the manner in which he informed him of the
affair.

"I am in love, corporal!" quoth my uncle Toby.

* Mr. Shandy must mean the poor *in spirit;* inasmuch as
they divided the money among themselves.

CHAPTER XXVIII

In love!——said the corporal——your Honour was very well
the day before yesterday, when I was telling your Honour
the story of the King of Bohemia——Bohemia! said my uncle
Toby - - - - musing a long time - - - What became of that
story, Trim?

——We lost it, an' please your Honour, somehow betwixt
us——but your Honour was as free from love, then, as I am
——'twas just whilst thou wentst off with the wheelbarrow
——with Mrs. Wadman, quoth my uncle Toby——She has
left a ball here——added my uncle Toby——pointing to his
breast——

——She can no more, an' please your Honour, stand a
seige than she can fly——cried the corporal——

——But as we are neighbours, Trim;——the best way I
think is to let her know it civilly first——quoth my uncle
Toby.

Now if I might presume, said the corporal, to differ from
your Honour——

——Why else do I talk to thee, Trim, said my uncle Toby,
mildly——

——Then I would begin, an' please your Honour, with
making a good thundering attack upon her, in return——and
telling her civilly afterwards——for if she knows anything of
your Honour's being in love, beforehand——L—d help her!
——she knows no more at present of it, Trim, said my uncle
Toby——than the child unborn——

Precious souls!——

Mrs. Wadman had told it, with all its circumstances, to
Mrs. Bridget twenty-four hours before; and was at that very
moment sitting in council with her, touching some slight mis-
givings with regard to the issue of the affair, which the devil,
who never lies dead in a ditch, had put into her head——
before he would allow half time to get quietly through her
Te Deum——

I am terribly afraid, said widow Wadman, in case I should
marry him, Bridget——that the poor Captain will not enjoy
his health, with the monstrous wound upon his groin——

It may not, Madam, be so very large, replied Bridget, as you think——and I believe besides, added she——that 'tis dried up——

——I could like to know——merely for his sake, said Mrs. Wadman——

——We'll know the long and the broad of it, in ten days ——answered Mrs. Bridget, for whilst the Captain is paying his addresses to you——I'm confident Mr. Trim will be for making love to me——and I'll let him as much as he will—— added Bridget——to get it all out of him——

The measures were taken at once——and my uncle Toby and the corporal went on with theirs.

Now, quoth the corporal, setting his left hand akimbo, and giving such a flourish with his right as just promised success ——and no more——if your Honour will give me leave to lay down the plan of this attack——

——Thou wilt please me by it, Trim, said my uncle Toby, exceedingly——and as I foresee thou must act in it as my *aide de camp*, here's a crown, corporal, to begin with, to steep thy commission.

Then, an' please your Honour, said the corporal (making a bow first for his commission)——we will begin with getting your Honour's laced clothes out of the great campaign trunk, to be well aired, and have the blue and gold taken up at the sleeves——and I'll put your white Ramillie wig fresh into pipes——and send for a tailor, to have your Honour's thin scarlet breeches turned——

——I had better take the red plush ones, quoth my uncle Toby——They will be too clumsy——said the corporal.

CHAPTER XXIX

——Thou wilt get a brush and a little chalk to my sword ——'Twill be only in your Honour's way, replied Trim.

CHAPTER XXX

——But your Honour's two razors shall be new set——
and I will get my Montero cap furbished up, and put on poor
Lieutenant Le Fever's regimental coat, which your Honour
gave me to wear for his sake——and as soon as your Honour is clean-shaved——and has got your clean shirt on, with
your blue and gold, or your fine scarlet——sometimes one
and sometimes t'other——and everything is ready for the
attack——we'll march up boldly, as if 'twas to the face of a
bastion; and whilst your Honour engages Mrs. Wadman in
the parlour, to the right——I'll attack Mrs. Bridget in the
kitchen, to the left; and having seized that pass, I'll answer
for it, said the corporal, snapping his fingers over his head
——that the day is our own.

I wish I may but manage it right, said my uncle Toby——
but I declare, corporal, I had rather march up to the very edge
of a trench——

——A woman is quite a different thing——said the corporal.

——I suppose so, quoth my uncle Toby.

CHAPTER XXXI

If anything in this world which my father said could have
provoked my uncle Toby, during the time he was in love, it
was the perverse use my father was always making of an expression of Hilarion the hermit; who, in speaking of his ab-
stinence, his watchings, flagellations, and other instrumental
parts of his religion——would say——though with more facetiousness than became an hermit——"That they were the
means he used to make his *ass* [meaning his body] leave
off kicking."

It pleased my father well; it was not only a laconic way

of expressing——but of libelling, at the same time, the desires and appetites of the lower part of us; so that for many
years of my father's life, 'twas his constant mode of expression——he never used the word *passions* once——but *ass*
always instead of them——So that he might be said truly to
have been upon the bones, or the back of his own ass, or else
of some other man's, during all that time.

I must here observe to you the difference betwixt

My father's ass

and my hobby-horse——in order to keep characters
as separate as may be in our fancies as we go along.

For my hobby-horse, if you recollect a little, is no way a
vicious beast; he has scarce one hair or lineament of the ass
about him——'Tis the sporting little filly-folly which carries
you out for the present hour——a maggot, a butterfly, a picture, a fiddlestick——an uncle Toby's siege——or an *anything,* which a man makes a shift to get a stride on, to canter
it away from the cares and solicitudes of life——'Tis as useful a beast as is in the whole creation——nor do I really see
how the world could do without it——

——But for my father's ass——oh! mount him——
mount him——mount him——(that's three times, is it not?)
——mount him not:——'tis a beast concupiscent——and
foul befall the man who does not hinder him from kicking.

CHAPTER XXXII

Well! dear brother Toby, said my father, upon his first seeing
him after he fell in love——and how goes it with your
Ass?

Now my uncle Toby thinking more of the *part* where he
had had the blister than of Hilarion's metaphor——and our
preconceptions having (you know) as great a power over the
sounds of words as the shapes of things, he had imagined
that my father, who was not very ceremonious in his choice
of words, had enquired after the part by its proper name; so
notwithstanding my mother, Dr. Slop, and Mr. Yorick were
sitting in the parlour, he thought it rather civil to conform to
the term my father had made use of than not. When a man
is hemmed in by two indecorums, and must commit one of

'em——I always observe——let him choose which he will, the world will blame him——so I should not be astonished if it blames my uncle Toby.

My a—, quoth my uncle Toby, is much better——brother Shandy——My father had formed great expectations from his ass in this onset; and would have brought him on again; but Dr. Slop setting up an intemperate laugh——and my mother crying out L—— bless us!——it drove my father's ass off the field——and the laugh then becoming general ——there was no bringing him back to the charge, for some time——

And so the discourse went on without him.

Everybody, said my mother, says you are in love, brother Toby——and we hope it is true.

I am as much in love, sister, I believe, replied my uncle Toby, as any man usually is——Humph! said my father—— and when did you know it? quoth my mother——

——When the blister broke, replied my uncle Toby.

My uncle Toby's reply put my father into good temper ——so he charged o' foot.

CHAPTER XXXIII

As the ancients agree, brother Toby, said my father, that there are two different and distinct kinds of *love,* according to the different parts which are affected by it——the Brain or Liver——I think when a man is in love, it behoves him a little to consider which of the two he is fallen into.

What signifies it, Brother Shandy, replied my uncle Toby, which of the two it is, provided it will but make a man marry, and love his wife, and get a few children.

——A few children! cried my father, rising out of his chair, and looking full in my mother's face, as he forced his way betwixt hers and Dr. Slop's——a few children! cried my father, repeating my uncle Toby's words as he walked to and fro——

——Not, my dear brother Toby, cried my father, recovering himself all at once, and coming close up to the back of my uncle Toby's chair——not that I should be sorry hadst thou a score——on the contrary I should rejoice——and be

477

as kind, Toby, to every one of them as a father——

My uncle Toby stole his hand unperceived behind his chair. to give my father's a squeeze——

——Nay, moreover, continued he, keeping hold of my uncle Toby's hand——so much dost thou possess, my dear Toby, of the milk of human nature, and so little of its asperities——'tis piteous the world is not peopled by creatures which resemble thee; and was I an Asiatic monarch, added my father, heating himself with his new project——I would oblige thee, provided it would not impair thy strength——or dry up thy radical moisture too fast——or weaken thy memory or fancy, brother Toby, which these gymnics inordinately taken are apt to do——else, dear Toby, I would procure thee the most beautiful women in my empire, and I would oblige thee, *nolens volens,* to beget for me one subject every *month*——

As my father pronounced the last word of the sentence ——my mother took a pinch of snuff.

Now I would not, quoth my uncle Toby, get a child, *nolens volens,* that is, whether I would or no, to please the greatest prince upon earth——

——And 'twould be cruel in me, brother Toby, to compel thee, said my father——but 'tis a case put to show thee that it is not thy begetting a child——in case thou shouldst be able——but the system of Love and marriage thou goest upon, which I would set thee right in——

There is at least, said Yorick, a great deal of reason and plain sense in Captain Shandy's opinion of love; and 'tis amongst the ill-spent hours of my life which I have to answer for, that I have read so many flourishing poets and rhetoricians in my time, from whom I never could extract so much——

I wish, Yorick, said my father, you had read Plato; for there you would have learnt that there are two LOVES——I know there were two RELIGIONS, replied Yorick, amongst the ancients——one——for the vulgar, and another for the learned; but I think ONE LOVE might have served both of them very well——

It could not, replied my father——and for the same reasons: for of these LOVES, according to Ficinus's comment upon Valesius, the one is *rational*——

——the other is *natural*——

the first ancient——without mother——where Venus had nothing to do: the second, begotten of Jupiter and Dione——

——Pray, brother, quoth my uncle Toby, what has a man

who believes in God to do with this? My father could not stop to answer, for fear of breaking the thread of his discourse——

This latter, continued he, partakes wholly of the nature of Venus.

The first, which is the golden chain let down from heaven, excites to love heroic, which comprehends in it, and excites to the desire of philosophy and truth——the second excites to *desire*, simply——

——I think the procreation of children as beneficial to the world, said Yorick, as the finding out the longitude——

——To be sure, said my mother, *love* keeps peace in the world——

——In the *house*——My dear, I own——

——It replenishes the earth, said my mother——

But it keeps heaven empty——my dear, replied my father.

——'Tis Virginity, cried Slop, triumphantly, which fills paradise.

Well pushed, nun! quoth my father.

CHAPTER XXXIV

My father had such a skirmishing, cutting kind of a slashing way with him in his disputations, thrusting and ripping, and giving everyone a stroke to remember him by in his turn ——that if there were twenty people in company——in less than half an hour he was sure to have every one of 'em against him.

What did not a little contribute to leave him thus without an ally was that if there was any one post more untenable than the rest, he would be sure to throw himself into it; and to do him justice, when he was once there, he would defend it so gallantly that 'twould have been a concern, either to a brave man, or a good-natured one, to have seen him driven out.

Yorick, for this reason, though he would often attack him ——yet could never bear to do it with all his force.

Dr. Slop's VIRGINITY, in the close of the last chapter, had got him for once on the right side of the rampart; and he was beginning to blow up all the convents in Christendom about Slop's ears, when Corporal Trim came into the parlour to inform my uncle Toby that his thin scarlet breeches, in which the attack was to be made upon Mrs. Wadman, would not do; for that the tailor, in ripping them up, in order to turn them, had found they had been turned before——Then turn them again, brother, said my father rapidly, for there will be many a turning of 'em yet before all's done in the affair——They are as rotten as dirt, said the corporal——Then by all means, said my father, bespeak a new pair, brother——for though I know, continued my father, turning himself to the company, that widow Wadman has been deeply in love with my brother Toby for many years, and has used every art and circumvention of woman to outwit him into the same passion, yet now that she has caught him——her fever will be past its height——

——She has gained her point.

In this case, continued my father, which Plato, I am persuaded, never thought of——Love, you see, is not so much a SENTIMENT as a SITUATION, into which a man enters, as my brother Toby would do, into a *corps*——no matter whether he loves the service or no——being once in it——he acts as if he did; and takes every step to show himself a man of prowess.

The hypothesis, like the rest of my father's, was plausible enough, and my uncle Toby had but a single word to object to it——in which Trim stood ready to second him——but my father had not drawn his conclusion——

For this reason, continued my father (stating the case over again), notwithstanding all the world knows that Mrs. Wadman *affects* my brother Toby——and my brother Toby contrariwise *affects* Mrs. Wadman, and no obstacle in nature to forbid the music striking up this very night, yet will I answer for it that this selfsame tune will not be played this twelve-month.

We have taken our measures badly, quoth my uncle Toby, looking up interrogatively in Trim's face.

I would lay my Montero cap, said Trim——Now Trim's Montero cap, as I once told you, was his constant wager; and having furbished it up that very night, in order to go upon the attack——it made the odds look more considerable——I would lay, an' please your Honour, my Montero cap to a shilling——was it proper, continued Trim (making a bow), to offer a wager before your Honours——

——There is nothing improper in it, said my father—— 'tis a mode of expression; for in saying thou wouldst lay thy

Montero cap to a shilling——all thou meanest is this——
that thou believest——

——Now, What dost thou believe?

That widow Wadman, an' please your Worship, cannot
hold it out ten days——

And whence, cried Slop, jeeringly, hast thou all this knowledge of woman, friend?

By falling in love with a popish clergywoman, said Trim.

'Twas a Beguine, said my uncle Toby.

Dr. Slop was too much in wrath to listen to the distinction; and my father taking that very crisis to fall in helter-
skelter upon the whole order of Nuns and Beguines, a set of
silly, fusty baggages——Slop could not stand it——and my
uncle Toby having some measures to take about his breeches
——and Yorick about his fourth general division——in
order for their several attacks next day——the company
broke up: and my father being left alone, and having half
an hour upon his hands betwixt that and bedtime, he called
for pen, ink, and paper, and wrote my uncle Toby the following letter of instructions.

My dear brother Toby,

What I am going to say to thee is upon the nature of women,
and of love-making to them; and perhaps it is as well for thee
——though not so well for me——that thou hast occasion
for a letter of instructions upon that head, and that I am able
to write it to thee.

Had it been the good pleasure of him who disposes of our
lots——and thou no sufferer by the knowledge, I had been
well content that thou shouldst have dipped the pen this moment into the ink, instead of myself; but that not being the
case—— ——Mrs. Shandy being now close besides me,
preparing for bed——I have thrown together without order,
and just as they have come into my mind, such hints and
documents as I deem may be of use to thee; intending, in
this, to give thee a token of my love; not doubting, my dear
Toby, of the manner in which it will be accepted.

In the first place, with regard to all which concerns religion in the affair——though I perceive from a glow in my
cheek that I blush as I begin to speak to thee upon the subject, as well knowing, notwithstanding thy unaffected secrecy,
how few of its offices thou neglectest——yet I would remind
thee of one (during the continuance of thy courtship) in a

particular manner, which I would not have omitted; and that is, never to go forth upon the enterprise, whether it be in the morning or the afternoon, without first recommending thyself to the protection of Almighty God, that he may defend thee from the evil one.

Shave the whole top of thy crown clean, once at least every four of five days, but oftener if convenient; lest in taking off thy wig before her, through absence of mind, she should be able to discover how much has been cut away by Time——how much by Trim.

——'Twere better to keep ideas of baldness out of her fancy. Always carry it in thy mind, and act upon it, as a sure maxim, Toby——

"That women are timid:" And 'tis well they are——else there would be no dealing with them.

Let not thy breeches be too tight, or hang too loose about thy thighs, like the trunk hose of our ancestors.

——A just medium prevents all conclusions.

Whatever thou hast to say, be it more or less, forget not to utter it in a low soft tone of voice. Silence, and whatever approaches it, weaves dreams of midnight secrecy into the brain: For this cause, if thou canst help it, never throw down the tongs and poker.

Avoid all kinds of pleasantry and facetiousness in thy discourse with her, and do whatever lies in thy power, at the same time, to keep from her all books and writings which tend thereto: there are some devotional tracts, which if thou canst entice her to read over——it will be well: but suffer her not to look into Rabelais, or Scarron, or *Don Quixote*——

——They are all books which excite laughter; and thou knowest, dear Toby, that there is no passion so serious as lust.

Stick a pin in the bosom of thy shirt before thou enterest her parlour.

And if thou are permitted to sit upon the same sofa with her, and she gives thee occasion to lay thy hand upon hers ——beware of taking it——thou canst not lay thy hand on hers but she will feel the temper of thine. Leave that, and as many other things as thou canst, quite undetermined; by so doing, thou wilt have her curiosity on thy side; and if she is not conquered by that, and thy Ass continues still kicking, which there is great reason to suppose——Thou must begin with first losing a few ounces of blood below the ears, according to the practice of the ancient Scythians, who cured

482

the most intemperate fits of the appetite by that means.

Avicenna, after this, is for having the part anointed with the syrup of hellebore, using proper evacuations and purges ——and I believe rightly. But thou must eat little or no goat's flesh, nor red deer——nor even foal's flesh by any means; and carefully abstain——that is, as much as thou canst, from peacocks, cranes, coots, didappers, and water hens——

As for thy drink——I need not tell thee, it must be the infusion of VERVAIN, and the herb HANEA, of which Aelian relates such effects——but if thy stomach palls with it—— discontinue it from time to time, taking cucumbers, melons, purslane, water lilies, woodbine, and lettuce, in the stead of them.

There is nothing further for thee, which occurs to me at present——

——Unless the breaking out of a fresh war——So wishing everything, dear Toby, for the best,

I rest thy affectionate brother,

WALTER SHANDY

CHAPTER XXXV

Whilst my father was writing his letter of instructions, my uncle Toby and the corporal were busy in preparing everything for the attack. As the turning of the thin scarlet breeches was laid aside (at least for the present), there was nothing which should put it off beyond the next morning; so accordingly it was resolved upon, for eleven o'clock.

Come, my dear, said my father to my mother——'twill be but like a brother and sister, if you and I take a walk down to my brother Toby's——to countenance him in this attack of his.

My uncle Toby and the corporal had been accoutred both some time, when my father and mother entered, and the clock striking eleven, were that moment in motion to sally forth——but the account of this is worth more than to be wove into the fag end of the eighth volume of such a work as this.——My father had no time but to put the letter of in-

structions into my uncle Toby's coat pocket——and join
with my mother in wishing his attack prosperous.

I could like, said my mother, to look through the keyhole
out of *curiosity*——Call it by its right name, my dear, quoth
my father——

And look through the keyhole as long as you will.

484

Si quid urbaniusculè lusum a nobis, per Musas et Charitas et omnium poetarum Numina, Oro te, ne me malè capias.

A
DEDICATION

TO A

GREAT MAN

Having, *a priori*, intended to dedicate *The Amours of my uncle Toby* to Mr. ***——I see more reasons, *a posteriori*, for doing it to Lord *******.

I should lament from my soul, if this exposed me to the jealousy of their Reverences; because, *a posteriori*, in Court Latin, signifies the kissing hands for preferment——or any thing else——in order to get it.

My opinion of Lord ******* is neither better nor worse than it was of Mr. ***. Honours, like impressions upon coin, may give an ideal and local value to a bit of base metal; but Gold and Silver will pass all the world over without any other recommendation than their own weight.

The same good will that made me think of offering up half an hour's amusement to Mr. *** when out of place—operates more forcibly at present, as half an hour's amusement will be more serviceable and refreshing after labour and sorrow than after a philosophical repast.

Nothing is so perfectly *Amusement* as a total change of ideas; no ideas are so totally different as those of Ministers, and innocent Lovers: for which reason, when I come to talk of Statesmen and Patriots, and set such marks upon them as will prevent confusion and mistakes concerning them for the future——I propose to dedicate that Volume to some gentle Shepherd,

Whose Thoughts proud Science never taught to stray,
Far as the Statesman's walk or Patriot way;

485

Yet *simple Nature* to his hopes had given
Out of a cloud-capped head a humbler heaven;
Some *untamed* World in depth of woods embraced——
Some happier Island in the watery waste——
And where admitted to that equal sky,
His *faithful Dogs* should bear him company.

In a word, by thus introducing an entire new set of objects
to his Imagination, I shall unavoidably give a *Diversion* to
his passionate and lovesick Contemplations. In the meantime,
I am

The AUTHOR

VOLUME IX

CHAPTER I

I call all the powers of time and chance, which severally check us in our careers in this world, to bear me witness that I could never yet get fairly to my uncle Toby's amours till this very moment that my mother's *curiosity,* as she stated the affair,——or a different impulse in her, as my father would have it——wished her to take a peep at them through the keyhole.

"Call it, my dear, by its right name," quoth my father, "and look through the keyhole as long as you will."

Nothing but the fermentation of that little subacid humour which I have often spoken of in my father's habit could have vented such an insinuation——he was however frank and generous in his nature, and at all times open to conviction; so that he had scarce got to the last word of this ungracious retort, when his conscience smote him.

My mother was then conjugally swinging with her left arm twisted under his right, in such wise that the inside of her hand rested upon the back of his——she raised her fingers, and let them fall——it could scarce be called a tap; or if it was a tap——'twould have puzzled a casuist to say whether 'twas a tap of remonstrance, or a tap of confession: my father, who was all sensibilities from head to foot, classed it right——Conscience redoubled her blow——he turned his face suddenly the other way, and my mother, supposing his body was about to turn with it in order to move homewards, by a cross movement of her right leg, keeping her left as its centre, brought herself so far in front that as he turned his

487

head, he met her eye————Confusion again! he saw a thousand reasons to wipe out the reproach, and as many to reproach himself————a thin, blue, chill, pellucid crystal with all its humours so at rest, the least mote or speck of desire might have been seen at the bottom of it, had it existed————it did not————and how I happen to be so lewd myself, particularly a little before the vernal and autumnal equinoxes———— heaven above knows————My mother————Madam————was so at no time, either by nature, by institution, or example.

A temperate current of blood ran orderly through her veins in all months of the year, and in all critical moments both of the day and night alike; nor did she superinduce the least heat into her humours from the manual effervescencies of devotional tracts, which having little or no meaning in them, nature is ofttimes obliged to find one————And as for my father's example! 'twas so far from being either aiding or abetting thereunto, that 'twas the whole business of his life to keep all fancies of that kind out of her head————Nature had done her part to have spared him this trouble; and what was not a little inconsistent, my father knew it————And here am I sitting, this 12th day of August, 1766, in a purple jerkin and yellow pair of slippers, without either wig or cap on, a most tragicomical completion of his prediction "That I should neither think nor act like any other man's child, upon that very account."

The mistake of my father was in attacking my mother's motive, instead of the act itself: for certainly keyholes were made for other purposes; and considering the act as an act which interfered with a true proposition, and denied a keyhole to be what it was————it became a violation of nature; and was so far, you see, criminal.

It is for this reason, an' please your Reverences, That keyholes are the occasions of more sin and wickedness than all other holes in this world put together.

————which leads me to my uncle Toby's amours.

CHAPTER II

Though the corporal had been as good as his word in putting my uncle Toby's great Ramillie wig into pipes, yet the time was too short to produce any great effects from it: it had lain many years squeezed up in the corner of his old campaign trunk; and as bad forms are not so easy to be got the better of, and the use of candle ends not so well understood, it was not so pliable a business as one would have wished. The corporal, with cheery eye and both arms extended, had fallen back perpendicular from it a score times, to inspire it, if possible, with a better air——had SPLEEN given a look at it, 'twould have cost her Ladyship a smile——it curled everywhere but where the corporal would have it; and where a buckle or two, in his opinion, would have done it honour, he could as soon have raised the dead.

Such it was——or rather such would it have seemed upon any other brow; but the sweet look of goodness which sat upon my uncle Toby's assimilated everything around it so sovereignly to itself, and Nature had moreover wrote GENTLEMAN with so fair a hand in every line of his countenance, that even his tarnished gold-laced hat and huge cockade of flimsy taffeta became him; and though not worth a button in themselves, yet the moment my uncle Toby put them on, they became serious objects, and altogether seemed to have been picked up by the hand of Science to set him off to advantage.

Nothing in this world could have co-operated more powerfully towards this than my uncle Toby's blue and gold—— *had not Quantity in some measure been necessary to Grace:* in a period of fifteen or sixteen years since they had been made, by a total inactivity in my uncle Toby's life, for he seldom went further than the bowling green——his blue and gold had become so miserably too strait for him that it was with the utmost difficulty the corporal was able to get him into them: the taking them up at the sleeves was of no advantage.——They were laced however down the back, and at the seams of the sides, &c., in the mode of King William's reign; and to shorten all description, they shone so bright against the sun that morning, and had so metallic and doughty an air with them, that had my uncle Toby thought of attacking in armour, nothing could have so well imposed upon his imagination.

As for the thin scarlet breeches, they had been unripped by the tailor between the legs, and left at *sixes and sevens*——
——Yes, Madam,——but let us govern our fancies. It is enough they were held impracticable the night before, and as there was no alternative in my uncle Toby's wardrobe, he sallied forth in the red plush.

The corporal had arrayed himself in poor Le Fever's regimental coat; and with his hair tucked up under his Montero cap, which he had furbished up for the occasion, marched three paces distant from his master: a whiff of military pride had puffed out his shirt at the wrist; and upon that, in a black leather thong clipped into a tassel beyond the knot, hung the corporal's stick——My uncle Toby carried his cane like a pike.

——It looks well at least, quoth my father to himself.

CHAPTER III

My uncle Toby turned his head more than once behind him, to see how he was supported by the corporal; and the corporal, as oft as he did it, gave a slight flourish with his stick——but not vapouringly; and with the sweetest accent of most respectful encouragement, bid his Honour "never fear."

Now my uncle Toby did fear; and grievously too: he knew not (as my father had reproached him) so much as the right end of a Woman from the wrong, and therefore was never altogether at his ease near any one of them——unless in sorrow or distress; then infinite was his pity; nor would the most courteous knight of romance have gone further, at least upon one leg, to have wiped away a tear from a woman's eye; and yet excepting once that he was beguiled into it by Mrs. Wadman, he had never looked steadfastly into one; and would often tell my father, in the simplicity of his heart, that it was almost (if not alout) as bad as talking bawdy.——

——And suppose it is? my father would say.

CHAPTER IV

She cannot, quoth my uncle Toby, halting, when they had marched up to within twenty paces of Mrs. Wadman's door ——she cannot, corporal, take it amiss.——

——She will take it, an' please your Honour, said the corporal, just as the Jew's widow at Lisbon took it of my brother Tom.——

——And how was that? quoth my uncle Toby, facing quite about to the corporal.

Your Honour, replied the corporal, knows of Tom's misfortunes; but this affair has nothing to do with them any further than this, That if Tom had not married the widow ——or had it pleased God after their marriage that they had but put pork into their sausages, the honest soul had never been taken out of his warm bed, and dragged to the Inquisition——'Tis a cursed place——added the corporal, shaking his head,——when once a poor creature is in, he is in, an' please your Honour, forever.

'Tis very true, said my uncle Toby, looking gravely at Mrs. Wadman's house, as he spoke.

Nothing, continued the corporal, can be so sad as confinement for life——or so sweet, an' please your Honour, as liberty.

Nothing, Trim——said my uncle Toby, musing——

Whilst a man is free——cried the corporal, giving a flourish with his stick thus——

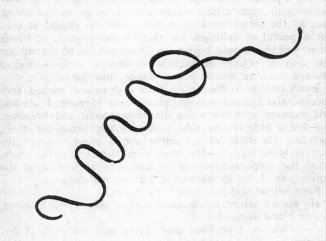

A thousand of my father's most subtle syllogisms could not have said more for celibacy.

My uncle Toby looked earnestly towards his cottage and his bowling green.

The corporal had unwarily conjured up the Spirit of calculation with his wand; and he had nothing to do, but to conjure him down again with his story, and in this form of Exorcism, most unecclesiastically did the corporal do it.

CHAPTER V

As Tom's place, an' please your Honour, was easy——and the weather warm——it put him upon thinking seriously of settling himself in the world; and as it fell out about that time that a Jew who kept a sausage shop in the same street had the ill luck to die of a strangury, and leave his widow in possession of a rousing trade——Tom thought (as everybody in Lisbon was doing the best he could devise for himself) there could be no harm in offering her his service to carry it on: so without any introduction to the widow, except that of buying a pound of sausages at her shop——Tom set out—— counting the matter thus within himself, as he walked along; that let the worst come of it that could, he should at least get a pound of sausages for their worth——but, if things went well, he should be set up; inasmuch as he should get not only a pound of sausages——but a wife——and a sausage shop, an' please your Honour, into the bargain.

Every servant in the family, from high to low, wished Tom success; and I can fancy, an' please your Honour, I see him this moment with his white dimity waistcoat and breeches, and hat a little o' one side, passing jollily along the street, swinging his stick, with a smile and a cheerful word for everybody he met:——But alas! Tom! thou smilest no more, cried the corporal, looking on one side of him upon the ground, as if he apostrophized him in his dungeon.

Poor fellow! said my uncle Toby, feelingly.

He was an honest, lighthearted lad, an' please your Honour, as ever blood warmed——

——Then he resembled thee, Trim, said my uncle Toby, rapidly.

The corporal blushed down to his fingers' ends——a tear of sentimental bashfulness——another of gratitude to my

492

uncle Toby——and a tear of sorrow for his brother's misfortunes started into his eye and ran sweetly down his cheek together; my uncle Toby's kindled as one lamp does at another; and taking hold of the breast of Trim's coat (which had been that of Le Fever's) as if to ease his lame leg, but in reality to gratify a finer feeling——he stood silent for a minute and a half; at the end of which he took his hand away, and the corporal, making a bow, went on with his story of his brother and the Jew's widow.

CHAPTER VI

When Tom, an' please your Honour, got to the shop, there was nobody in it but a poor Negro girl, with a bunch of white feathers slightly tied to the end of a long cane, flapping away flies——not killing them.——'Tis a pretty picture! said my uncle Toby——she had suffered persecution, Trim, and had learnt mercy——

——She was good, an' please your Honour, from nature as well as from hardships; and there are circumstances in the story of that poor friendless slut that would melt a heart of stone, said Trim; and some dismal winter's evening, when your Honour is in the humour, they shall be told you with the rest of Tom's story, for it makes a part of it——

Then do not forget, Trim, said my uncle Toby.

A Negro has a soul? an' please your Honour, said the corporal (doubtingly).

I am not much versed, corporal, quoth my uncle Toby, in things of that kind; but I suppose God would not leave him without one, any more than thee or me——

——It would be putting one sadly over the head of another, quoth the corporal.

It would so, said my uncle Toby. Why then, an' please your Honour, is a black wench to be used worse than a white one?

I can give no reason, said my uncle Toby——

——Only, cried the corporal, shaking his head, because she has no one to stand up for her——

——'Tis that very thing, Trim, quoth my uncle Toby,—— which recommends her to protection——and her brethren with her; 'tis the fortune of war which has put the whip into our hands *now*——where it may be hereafter, heaven knows! ——but be it where it will, the brave, Trim! will not use it unkindly.

——God forbid, said the corporal.

Amen, responded my uncle Toby, laying his hand upon his heart.

The corporal returned to his story, and went on——but with an embarrassment in doing it which here and there a reader in this world will not be able to comprehend; for by the many sudden transitions all along, from one kind and cordial passion to another, in getting thus far on his way, he had lost the sportable key of his voice which gave sense and spirit to his tale: he attempted twice to resume it, but could not please himself; so giving a stout hem! to rally back the re-treating spirits, and aiding Nature at the same time with his left arm akimbo on one side, and with his right a little ex-tended, supporting her on the other——the corporal got as near the note as he could; and in that attitude, continued his story.

CHAPTER VII

As Tom, an' please your Honour, had no business at that time with the Moorish girl, he passed on into the room be-yond to talk to the Jew's widow about love——and his pound of sausages; and being, as I have told your Honour, an open, cheery-hearted lad, with his character wrote in his looks and carriage, he took a chair, and without much apol-ogy, but with great civility at the same time, placed it close to her at the table, and sat down.

There is nothing so awkward as courting a woman, an' please your Honour, whilst she is making sausages——So Tom began a discourse upon them; first gravely,——"as how they were made——with what meats, herbs, and spices"—— Then a little gayly——as, "With what skins——and if they never burst——Whether the largest were not the best"—— and so on——taking care only, as he went along, to season what he had to say upon sausages rather under, than over; ——that he might have room to act in——

It was owing to the neglect of that very precaution, said my uncle Toby, laying his hand upon Trim's shoulder, that Count de la Motte lost the battle of Wynendale: he pressed too speedily into the wood; which if he had not done, Liele had not fallen into our hands, nor Ghent and Bruges, which both followed her example; it was so late in the year, continued my uncle Toby, and so terrible a season came on, that if things had not fallen out as they did, our troops must have perished in the open field.——

——Why, therefore, may not battles, an' please your Honour, as well as marriages, be made in heaven?——My uncle Toby mused.——

Religion inclined him to say one thing, and his high idea of military skill tempted him to say another; so not being able to frame a reply exactly to his mind——my uncle Toby said nothing at all; and the corporal finished his story.

As Tom perceived, an' please your Honour, that he gained ground, and that all he had said upon the subject of sausages was kindly taken, he went on to help her a little in making them.——First, by taking hold of the ring of the sausage whilst she stroked the forced meat down with her hand——then by cutting the strings into proper lengths, and holding them in his hand, whilst she took them out one by one—— then, by putting them across her mouth, that she might take them out as she wanted them——and so on from little to more, till at last he adventured to tie the sausage himself, whilst she held the snout.——

——Now a widow, an' please your Honour, always chooses a second husband as unlike the first as she can: so the affair was more than half settled in her mind before Tom mentioned it.

She made a feint however of defending herself, by snatching up a sausage:——Tom instantly laid hold of another——

But seeing Tom's had more gristle in it——

She signed the capitulation——and Tom sealed it; and there was an end of the matter.

CHAPTER VIII

All womankind, continued Trim (commenting upon his story), from the highest to the lowest, an' please your Honour, love jokes; the difficulty is to know how they choose to have them cut; and there is no knowing that, but by trying as we do with our artillery in the field, by raising or letting down their breeches, till we hit the mark.——

——I like the comparison, said my uncle Toby, better than the thing itself——

——Because your Honour, quoth the corporal, loves glory more than pleasure.

I hope, Trim, answered my uncle Toby, I love mankind more than either; and as the knowledge of arms tends so apparently to the good and quiet of the world——and particularly that branch of it which we have practised together in our bowling green has no object but to shorten the strides of AMBITION, and intrench the lives and fortunes of the *few,* from the plunderings of the *many*——whenever that drum beats in our ears, I trust, corporal, we shall neither of us want so much humanity and fellow-feeling as to face about and march.

In pronouncing this, my uncle Toby faced about, and marched firmly as at the head of his company——and the faithful corporal, shouldering his stick, and striking his hand upon his coat skirt as he took his first step——marched close behind him down the avenue.

——Now what can their two noddles be about? cried my father to my mother——by all that's strange, they are besieging Mrs. Wadman in form, and are marching round her house to mark out the lines of circumvallation.

I dare say, quoth my mother——————But stop, dear Sir——for what my mother dared to say upon the occasion ——and what my father did say upon it——with her replies and his rejoinders, shall be read, perused, paraphrased, commented and discanted upon——or to say it all in a word, shall be thumbed over by Posterity in a chapter apart——I say, by Posterity——and care not if I repeat the word again ——for what has this book done more than the Legation of

Moses or the Tale of a Tub, that it may not swim down the gutter of Time along with them?

I will not argue the matter: Time wastes too fast: every letter I trace tells me with what rapidity Life follows my pen; the days and hours of it, more precious, my dear Jenny! than the rubies about thy neck, are flying over our heads like light clouds of a windy day, never to return more——everything presses on——whilst thou are twisting that lock, ——see! it grows grey; and every time I kiss thy hand to bid adieu, and every absence which follows it, are preludes to that eternal separation which we are shortly to make.——

——Heaven have mercy upon us both!

CHAPTER IX

Now, for what the world thinks of that ejaculation——I would not give a groat.

CHAPTER X

My mother had gone with her left arm twisted in my father's right, till they had got to the fatal angle of the old garden wall where Dr. Slop was overthrown by Obadiah on the coach horse: as this was directly opposite to the front of Mrs. Wadman's house, when my father came to it, he gave a look across; and seeing my uncle Toby and the corporal within ten paces of the door, he turned about——Let us just stop a moment, quoth my father, and see with what ceremonies my brother Toby and his man Trim make their first entry——it will not detain us, added my father, a single minute:——No matter if it be ten minutes, quoth my mother.

——It will not detain us half a one, said my father.

The corporal was just then setting in with the story of his brother Tom and the Jew's widow: the story went on——and

on——it had episodes in it——it came back, and went on
——and on again; there was no end of it——the reader
found it very long——

——G— help my father! he pished fifty times at every
new attitude, and gave the corporal's stick, with all its
flourishings and danglings, to as many devils as chose to
accept of them.

When issues of events like these my father is waiting for
are hanging in the scales of fate, the mind has the advantage
of changing the principle of expectation three times, without
which it would not have power to see it out.

Curiosity governs the *first moment;* and the second moment is all economy to justify the expense of the first——
and for the third, fourth, fifth, and sixth moments, and so on
to the day of judgment——'tis a point of HONOUR.

I need not be told that the ethic writers have assigned this
all to Patience; but that VIRTUE, methinks, has extent of
dominion sufficient of her own, and enough to do in it, without invading the few dismantled castles which HONOUR has
left him upon the earth.

My father stood it out as well as he could with these three
auxiliaries to the end of Trim's story; and from thence to the
end of my uncle Toby's panegyric upon arms, in the chapter following it; when seeing that instead of marching up to
Mrs. Wadman's door, they both faced about and marched
down the avenue diametrically opposite to his expectation
——he broke out at once with that little subacid soreness of
humour which, in certain situations, distinguished his character from that of all other men.

CHAPTER XI

——"Now what can their two noddles be about?" cried my
father - - &c. - - - -

I dare say, said my mother, they are making fortifications——

——Not on Mrs. Wadman's premises! cried my father,
stepping back——

I suppose not, quoth my mother.

I wish, said my father, raising his voice, the whole science

of fortification at the devil, with all its trumpery of saps, mines, blinds, gabions, faussebrayes, and cuvettes——
——They are foolish things——said my mother.

Now she had a way, which, by the bye, I would this moment give away my purple jerkin, and my yellow slippers into the bargain, if some of your Reverences would imitate ——and that was never to refuse her assent and consent to any proposition my father laid before her, merely because she did not understand it, or had no ideas to the principal word, or term of art, upon which the tenet or proposition rolled. She contented herself with doing all that her godfathers and godmothers promised for her——but no more; and so would go on using a hard word twenty years together ——and replying to it too, if it was a verb, in all its moods and tenses, without giving herself any trouble to enquire about it.

This was an eternal source of misery to my father, and broke the neck, at the first setting out, of more good dialogues between them than could have done the most petulant contradiction——the few which survived were the better for the cuvettes——

——"They are foolish things," said my mother.

——Particularly the cuvettes, replied my father.

'Twas enough——he tasted the sweet of triumph——and went on.

——Not that they are, properly speaking, Mrs. Wadman's premises, said my father, partly correcting himself——because she is but tenant for life——

——That makes a great difference——said my mother——

——In a fool's head, replied my father——

Unless she should happen to have a child——said my mother——

——But she must persuade my brother Toby first to get her one——

——To be sure, Mr. Shandy, quoth my mother.

——Though if it comes to persuasion——said my father ——Lord have mercy upon them.

Amen: said my mother, *piano*.

Amen: cried my father, *fortissimo*.

Amen: said my mother again——but with such a sighing cadence of personal pity at the end of it, as discomfited every fibre about my father——he instantly took out his almanac; but before he could untie it, Yorick's congregation coming out of church became a full answer to one half of his business with it——and my mother telling him it was a sacrament day——left him as little in doubt as to the other part ——He put his almanac into his pocket.

The first Lord of the Treasury, thinking of *ways and means*, could not have returned home with a more embarrassed look.

CHAPTER XII

Upon looking back from the end of the last chapter and surveying the texture of what has been wrote, it is necessary that upon this page and the five * following, a good quantity of heterogeneous matter be inserted, to keep up that just balance betwixt wisdom and folly without which a book would not hold together a single year: nor is it a poor creeping digression (which but for the name of, a man might continue as well going on in the king's highway) which will do the business——no; if it is to be a digression, it must be a good frisky one, and upon a frisky subject too, where neither the horse or his rider are to be caught, but by rebound.

The only difficulty is raising powers suitable to the nature of the service: FANCY is capricious——WIT must not be searched for——and PLEASANTRY (good-natured slut as she is) will not come in at a call, was an empire to be laid at her feet.

——The best way for a man is to say his prayers——

Only if it puts him in mind of his infirmities and defects as well ghostly as bodily——for that purpose, he will find himself rather worse after he has said them than before——for other purposes, better.

For my own part there is not a way either moral or mechanical under heaven that I could think of, which I have not taken with myself in this case: sometimes by addressing myself directly to the soul herself, and arguing the point over and over again with her upon the extent of her own faculties——

——I never could make them an inch the wider——

Then by changing my system, and trying what could be made of it upon the body, by temperance, soberness, and

* Five in the original edition.

500

chastity: These are good, quoth I, in themselves——they are good, absolutely;——they are good, relatively;——they are good for health——they are good for happiness in this world ——they are good for happiness in the next——

In short, they were good for everything but the thing wanted; and there they were good for nothing, but to leave the soul just as heaven made it: as for the theological virtues of faith and hope, they give it courage; but then that sniveling virtue of Meekness (as my father would always call it) takes it quite away again, so you are exactly where you started.

Now in all common and ordinary cases, there is nothing which I have found to answer so well as this——

——Certainly, if there is any dependence upon Logic, and that I am not blinded by self-love, there must be something of true genius about me, merely upon this symptom of it, that I do not know what envy is: for never do I hit upon any invention or device which tendeth to the furtherance of good writing, but I instantly make it public; willing that all mankind should write as well as myself.

——Which they certainly will, when they think as little.

CHAPTER XIII

Now in ordinary cases, that is, when I am only stupid, and the thoughts rise heavily and pass gummous through my pen——

Or that I am got, I know not how, into a cold unmetaphorical vein of infamous writing, and cannot take a plumb lift out of it *for my soul;* so must be obliged to go on writing like a Dutch commentator to the end of the chapter, unless something be done——

——I never stand conferring with pen and ink one moment; for if a pinch of snuff or a stride or two across the room will not do the business for me——I take a razor at once; and having tried the edge of it upon the palm of my hand, without further ceremony, except that of first lathering my beard, I shave it off; taking care only if I do leave a hair, that it be not a grey one: this done, I change my shirt—— put on a better coat——send for my last wig——put my topaz ring upon my finger; and in a word, dress myself from one end to the other of me, after my best fashion.

Now the devil in hell must be in it, if this does not do: for consider, Sir, as every man chooses to be present at the shaving of his own beard (though there is no rule without an exception) and unavoidably sits over against himself the whole time it is doing, in case he has a hand in it——the Situation, like all others, has notions of her own to put into the brain.——

——I maintain it, the conceits of a rough-bearded man are seven years more terse and juvenile for one single operation; and if they did not run a risk of being quite shaved away, might be carried up by continual shavings to the highest pitch of sublimity——How Homer could write with so long a beard, I don't know——and as it makes against my hypothesis, I as little care——But let us return to the Toilet.

Ludovicus Sorbonensis makes this entirely an affair of the body (ἐξωτερικὴ πρᾶξις) as he calls it———but he is deceived: the soul and body are joint sharers in everything they get: A man cannot dress, but his ideas get clothed at the same time; and if he dresses like a gentleman, every one of them stands presented to his imagination, genteelized along with him——so that he has nothing to do but take his pen, and write like himself.

For this cause, when your Honours and Reverences would know whether I writ clean and fit to be read, you will be able to judge full as well by looking into my Laundress's bill, as my book: there was one single month in which I can make it appear that I dirtied one-and-thirty shirts with clean writing; and, after all, was more abused, cursed, criticised and confounded, and had more mystic heads shaken at me, for what I had wrote in that one month, than in all the other months of that year put together.

——But their Honours and Reverences had not seen my bills.

CHAPTER XIV

As I ever had any intention of beginning the Digression I am making all this preparation for, till I come to the 15th chapter——I have this chapter to put to whatever use I think proper——I have twenty this moment ready for it——I could write my chapter of Buttonholes in it——

Or my chapter of *Pishes,* which should follow them——

Or my chapter of *Knots,* in case their Reverences have done with them——they might lead me into mischief: the safest way is to follow the tract of the learned, and raise objections against what I have been writing, though I declare beforehand, I know no more than my heels how to answer them.

And first, it may be said, there is a pelting kind of *thersitical* satire, as black as the very ink 'tis wrote with——(and by the bye, whoever says so is indebted to the muster-master general of the Grecian army, for suffering the name of so ugly and foul-mouthed a man as Thersites to continue upon his roll——for it has furnished him with an epithet)—— in these productions, he will urge, all the personal washings and scrubbings upon earth do a sinking genius no sort of good——but just the contrary, inasmuch as the dirtier the fellow is, the better generally he succeeds in it.

To this, I have no other answer——at least ready——but that the Archbishop of Benevento wrote his *nasty* Romance of the *Galateo,* as all the world knows, in a purple coat, waistcoat, and purple pair of breeches; and that the penance set him of writing a commentary upon the book of the Revelations, as severe as it was looked upon by one part of the world, was far from being deemed so by the other, upon the single account of that *Investment.*

Another objection to all this remedy is its want of universality; forasmuch as the shaving part of it, upon which so much stress is laid, by an unalterable law of nature excludes one half of the species entirely from its use: all I can say is that female writers, whether of England, or of France, must e'en go without it——

As for the Spanish ladies——I am in no sort of distress——

CHAPTER XV

The fifteenth chapter is come at last; and brings nothing with it but a sad signature of "How our pleasures slip from under us in this world;"

For in talking of my digression——I declare before heaven I have made it! What a strange creature is mortal man! said she.

'Tis very true, said I——but 'twere better to get all these things out of our heads, and return to my uncle Toby.

CHAPTER XVI

When my uncle Toby and the corporal had marched down to the bottom of the avenue, they recollected their business lay the other way; so they faced about and marched up straight to Mrs. Wadman's door.

I warrant your Honour, said the corporal, touching his Montero cap with his hand, as he passed him in order to give a knock at the door——My uncle Toby, contrary to his invariable way of treating his faithful servant, said nothing good or bad: the truth was, he had not altogether marshalled his ideas; he wished for another conference, and as the corporal was mounting up the three steps before the door—— he hemmed twice——a portion of my uncle Toby's most modest spirits fled, at each expulsion, towards the corporal; he stood with the rapper of the door suspended for a full minute in his hand, he scarce knew why. Bridget stood perdue within, with her finger and her thumb upon the latch, benumbed with expectation; and Mrs. Wadman, with an eye ready to be deflowered again, sat breathless behind the window curtain of her bedchamber, watching their approach.

Trim! said my uncle Toby——but as he articulated the word, the minute expired, and Trim let fall the rapper.

My uncle Toby, perceiving that all hopes of a conference were knocked on the head by it——whistled *Lillabullero*.

CHAPTER XVII

As Mrs. Bridget's finger and thumb were upon the latch, the corporal did not knock as oft as perchance your Honour's tailor——I might have taken my example something nearer home; for I owe mine some five-and-twenty pounds at least, and wonder at the man's patience——

——But this is nothing at all to the world: only 'tis a cursed thing to be in debt; and there seems to be a fatality in the exchequers of some poor princes, particularly those of our house, which no Economy can bind down in irons: for my own part, I'm persuaded there is not any one prince, prelate, pope, or potentate, great or small, upon earth, more desirous in his heart of keeping straight with the world than I am——or who takes more likely means for it. I never give above half a guinea——or walk with boots——or cheapen toothpicks——or lay out a shilling upon a bandbox the year round; and for the six months I'm in the country, I'm upon so small a scale that with all the good temper in the world, I outdo Rousseau, a bar length——for I keep neither man or boy, or horse, or cow, or dog, or cat, or anything that can eat or drink, except a thin poor piece of a Vestal (to keep my fire in) and who has generally as bad an appetite as myself——but if you think this makes a philosopher of me—— I would not, my good people! give a rush for your judgments.

True philosophy——but there is no treating the subject whilst my uncle is whistling *Lillabullero*.

——Let us go into the house.

CHAPTER XVIII

CHAPTER XIX

CHAPTER XX

         * * * * * * * * * * * * * * *
 * * * * * * * * * * * * * * * * *
 * * * * * * * * * *
 * * * * * * * * * * * * * * * * *
 * * * * * * * * * * * * * * * * *
 * * * * * * * * * * * * * * * * *
 * * * * * * * *

——You shall see the very place, Madam, said my uncle
Toby.

Mrs. Wadman blushed——looked towards the door——
turned pale——blushed slightly again——recovered her natural colour——blushed worse than ever; which for the sake
of the unlearned reader, I translate thus——

"L—d! I cannot look at it——
What would the world say if I looked at it?
I should drop down, if I looked at it——
I wish I could look at it——
There can be no sin in looking at it.
——I will look at it."

Whilst all this was running through Mrs. Wadman's imagination, my uncle Toby had risen from the sofa, and got to
the other side of the parlour door, to give Trim an order
about it in the passage——

 * * * * * * * * * * * * * * * *
 * * * * *   ——I believe it is in the garret, said my
uncle Toby——I saw it there, an' please your Honour, this
morning, answered Trim——Then prithee, step directly for
it, Trim, said my uncle Toby, and bring it into the parlour.

The corporal did not approve of the orders, but most
cheerfully obeyed them. The first was not an act of his will
——the second was; so he put on his Montero cap, and went
as fast as his lame knee would let him. My uncle Toby returned into the parlour, and sat himself down again upon the
sofa.

——You shall lay your finger upon the place——said my
uncle Toby.——I will not touch it, however, quoth Mrs.
Wadman to herself.

This requires a second translation:——it shows what little knowledge is got by mere words——we must go up to the first springs.

Now in order to clear up the mist which hangs upon these three pages, I must endeavour to be as clear as possible myself.

Rub your hands thrice across your foreheads——blow your noses——cleanse your emunctories——sneeze, my good people!——God bless you——

Now give me all the help you can.

CHAPTER XXI

As there are fifty different ends (counting all ends in——as well civil as religious) for which a woman takes a husband, she first sets about and carefully weighs, then separates and distinguishes in her mind, which of all that number of ends is hers: then by discourse, enquiry, argumentation, and inference, she investigates and finds out whether she has got hold of the right one——and if she has——then, by pulling it gently this way and that way, she further forms a judgment, whether it will not break in the drawing.

The imagery under which Slawkenbergius impresses this upon his reader's fancy, in the beginning of his third decad, is so ludicrous that the honour I bear the sex will not suffer me to quote it——otherwise 'tis not destitute of humour.

She first, saith Slawkenbergius, stops the ass, and holding his halter in her left hand (lest he should get away) she thrusts her right hand into the very bottom of his pannier to search for it——For what?——you'll not know the sooner, quoth Slawkenbergius, for interrupting me——

"I have nothing, good Lady, but empty bottles," says the ass.

"I'm loaded with tripes," says the second.

——And thou art little better, quoth she to the third; for nothing is there in thy panniers but trunk hose and pantofles ——and so to the fourth and fifth, going on one by one through the whole string, till coming to the ass which carries it, she turns the pannier upside down, looks at it—— considers it——samples it——measures it——stretches it

507

——wets it——dries it——then takes her teeth both to the warp and weft of it——
——Of what? for the love of Christ!

I am determined, answered Slawkenbergius, that all the powers upon earth shall never wring that secret from my breast.

CHAPTER XXII

We live in a world beset on all sides with mysteries and riddles——and so 'tis no matter——else it seems strange that Nature, who makes everything so well to answer its destination, and seldom or never errs, unless for pastime, in giving such forms and aptitudes to whatever passes through her hands, that whether she designs for the plough, the caravan, the cart——or whatever other creature she models, be it but an ass's foal, you are sure to have the thing you wanted; and yet at the same time should so eternally bungle it as she does, in making so simple a thing as a married man.

Whether it is in the choice of the clay——or that it is frequently spoiled in the baking; by an excess of which a husband may turn out too crusty (you know) on one hand ——or not enough so, through defect of heat, on the other ——or whether this great Artificer is not so attentive to the little Platonic exigencies *of that part* of the species for whose use she is fabricating *this*——or that her Ladyship sometimes scarce knows what sort of a husband will do—— I know not: we will discourse about it after supper.

It is enough that neither the observation itself, or the reasoning upon it, are at all to the purpose——but rather against it; since with regard to my uncle Toby's fitness for the marriage state, nothing was ever better: she had formed him of the best and kindliest clay——had tempered it with her own milk, and breathed into it the sweetest spirit——she had made him all gentle, generous, and humane——she had filled his heart with trust and confidence, and disposed every passage which led to it for the communication of the tenderest offices——she had moreover considered the other causes for which matrimony was ordained——

And accordingly * * * * * * * * * *

508

* * * * * * * * * * * * * * * *
* * * * * * * * * * * * * * * *
* * * *.

The DONATION was not defended by my uncle Toby's wound.

Now this last article was somewhat apocryphal; and the devil, who is the great disturber of our faiths in this world, had raised scruples in Mrs. Wadman's brain about it; and like a true devil as he was, had done his own work at the same time, by turning my uncle Toby's Virtue thereupon into nothing but *empty bottles, tripes, trunk hose,* and *pantofles.*

CHAPTER XXIII

Mrs. Bridget had pawned all the little stock of honour a poor chambermaid was worth in the world, that she would get to the bottom of the affair in ten days; and it was built upon one of the most concessible *postulata* in nature: namely, that whilst my uncle Toby was making love to her mistress, the corporal could find nothing better to do than make love to her——"*And I'll let him as much as he will,*" said Bridget, "*to get it out of him.*"

Friendship has two garments; an outer, and an under one. Bridget was serving her mistress's interests in the one—— and doing the thing which most pleased herself in the other; so had as many stakes depending upon my uncle Toby's wound as the devil himself——Mrs. Wadman had but one ——and as it possibly might be her last (without discouraging Mrs. Bridget, or discrediting her talents), was determined to play her cards herself.

She wanted not encouragement: a child might have looked into his hand——there was such a plainness and simplicity in his playing out what trumps he had——with such an unmistrusting ignorance of the *tenace*——and so naked and defenceless did he sit upon the same sofa with widow Wadman, that a generous heart would have wept to have won the game of him.

Let us drop the metaphor.

CHAPTER XXIV

——And the story too——if you please: for though I have all along been hastening towards this part of it, with so much earnest desire, as well knowing it to be the choicest morsel of what I had to offer to the world, yet now that I am got to it, anyone is welcome to take my pen, and go on with the story for me that will——I see the difficulties of the descriptions I'm going to give——and feel my want of powers.

It is one comfort at least to me that I lost some fourscore ounces of blood this week in a most uncritical fever which attacked me at the beginning of this chapter; so that I have still some hopes remaining it may be more in the serous or globular parts of the blood than in the subtile *aura* of the brain——be it which it will——an Invocation can do no hurt——and I leave the affair entirely to the *invoked,* to inspire or to inject me according as he sees good.

THE INVOCATION

Gentle Spirit of sweetest humour, who erst didst sit upon the easy pen of my beloved CERVANTES; Thou who glidedst daily through his lattice, and turnedst the twilight of his prison into noonday brightness by thy presence——tingedst his little urn of water with heaven-sent Nectar, and all the time he wrote of Sancho and his master, didst cast thy mystic mantle o'er his withered * stump, and wide extended it to all the evils of his life——

——Turn in hither, I beseech thee!——behold these breeches!——they are all I have in the world——that piteous rent was given them at Lyons——

My shirts! see what a deadly schism has happened amongst 'em——for the laps are in Lombardy, and the rest of 'em here——I never had but six, and a cunning gypsy of a laundress at Milan cut me off the fore laps of five——To do her justice, she did it with some consideration——for I was returning *out* of Italy.

* He lost his hand at the battle of Lepanto.

And yet, notwithstanding all this, and a pistol tinderbox which was moreover filched from me at Siena, and twice that I paid five Pauls for two hard eggs, once at Raddicoffini, and a second time at Capua——I do not think a journey through France and Italy, provided a man keeps his temper all the way, so bad a thing as some people would make you believe: there must be *ups* and *downs,* or how the deuce should we get into valleys where Nature spreads so many tables of entertainment.——'Tis nonsense to imagine they will lend you their *voitures* to be shaken to pieces for nothing; and unless you pay twelve sous for greasing your wheels, how should the poor peasant get butter to his bread?——We really expect too much——and for the livre or two above par for your suppers and bed——at the most they are but one shilling and ninepence halfpenny——who would embroil their philosophy for it? for heaven's and for your own sake, pay it——pay it with both hands open, rather than leave *Disappointment* sitting drooping upon the eye of your fair Hostess and her Damsels in the gateway, at your departure ——and besides, my dear Sir, you get a sisterly kiss of each of 'em worth a pound——at least I did——

——For, my uncle Toby's amours running all the way in my head, they had the same effect upon me as if they had been my own——I was in the most perfect state of bounty and good will; and felt the kindliest harmony vibrating within me, with every oscillation of the chaise alike; so that whether the roads were rough or smooth, it made no difference; everything I saw, or had to do with, touched upon some secret spring either of sentiment or rapture.

——They were the sweetest notes I ever heard; and I instantly let down the foreglass to hear them more distinctly ——'Tis Maria, said the postillion, observing I was listening ——Poor Maria, continued he (leaning his body on one side to let me see her, for he was in a line betwixt us), is sitting upon a bank playing her vespers upon her pipe, with her little goat beside her.

The young fellow uttered this with an accent and a look so perfectly in tune to a feeling heart, that I instantly made a vow I would give him a four-and-twenty-sous piece, when I got to Moulins——

——And who is *poor* Maria? said I.

The love and pity of all the villages around us, said the postillion——it is but three years ago, that the sun did not shine upon so fair, so quick-witted and amiable a maid; and better fate did Maria deserve than to have her Banns forbid, by the intrigues of the curate of the parish who published them——

He was going on, when Maria, who had made a short pause, put the pipe to her mouth and began the air again ——they were the same notes;——yet were ten times sweeter: It is the evening service to the Virgin, said the young man——but who has taught her to play it——or how she came by her pipe, no one knows; we think that heaven has assisted her in both; for ever since she has been unsettled in her mind, it seems her only consolation——she has never once had the pipe out of her hand, but plays that *service* upon it almost night and day.

The postillion delivered this with so much discretion and natural eloquence, that I could not help deciphering something in his face above his condition, and should have sifted out his history, had not poor Maria's taken such full possession of me.

We had got up by this time almost to the bank where Maria was sitting: she was in a thin white jacket with her hair, all but two tresses, drawn up into a silk net, with a few olive leaves twisted a little fantastically on one side——she was beautiful; and if ever I felt the full force of an honest heartache, it was the moment I saw her——

——God help her! poor damsel! Above a hundred masses, said the postillion, have been said in the several parish churches and convents around, for her,——but without effect; we have still hopes, as she is sensible for short intervals, that the Virgin at last will restore her to herself; but her parents, who know her best, are hopeless upon that score, and think her senses are lost forever.

As the postillion spoke this, Maria made a cadence so melancholy, so tender and querulous, that I sprung out of the chaise to help her, and found myself sitting betwixt her and her goat before I relapsed from my enthusiasm.

Maria looked wistfully for some time at me, and then at her goat——and then at me——and then at her goat again, and so on, alternately——

——Well, Maria, said I softly——What resemblance do you find?

I do intreat the candid reader to believe me, that it was from the humblest conviction of what a *Beast* man is—— that I asked the question; and that I would not have let fallen an unseasonable pleasantry in the venerable presence of Misery, to be entitled to all the wit that ever Rabelais scattered——and yet I own my heart smote me, and that I so smarted at the very idea of it, that I swore I would set up for Wisdom and utter grave sentences the rest of my days ——and never——never attempt again to commit mirth with man, woman, or child, the longest day I had to live.

As for writing nonsense to them——I believe there was a reserve——but that I leave to the world.

Adieu, Maria!——adieu, poor hapless damsel!——sometime, but not *now,* I may hear thy sorrows from thy own lips——but I was deceived; for that moment she took her pipe and told me such a tale of woe with it, that I rose up, and with broken and irregular steps walked softly to my chaise.

——What an excellent inn at Moulins!

CHAPTER XXV

When we have got to the end of this chapter (but not before) we must all turn back to the two blank chapters, on the account of which my honour has lain bleeding this half hour ——I stop it, by pulling off one of my yellow slippers and throwing it with all my violence to the opposite side of my room, with a declaration at the heel of it——

——That whatever resemblance it may bear to half the chapters which are written in the world, or, for aught I know, may be now writing in it——that it was as casual as the foam of Zeuxis his horse: besides, I look upon a chapter which has *only nothing in it* with respect; and considering what worse things there are in the world——That it is no way a proper subject for satire——

——Why then was it left so? And here, without staying for my reply, shall I be called as many blockheads, numskulls, doddypoles, dunderheads, ninny-hammers, goosecaps, joltheads, nincompoops, and sh--t-a-beds——and other unsavory appellations, as ever the cake-bakers of Lerné cast in the teeth of King Gargantua's shepherds——And I'll let them do it, as Bridget said, as much as they please; for how was it possible they should foresee the necessity I was under of writing the 25th chapter of my book before the 18th, &c.?

————So I don't take it amiss————All I wish is that it may be a lesson to the world, *"to let people tell their stories their own way."*

The Eighteenth Chapter

As Mrs. Bridget opened the door before the corporal had well given the rap, the interval betwixt that and my uncle Toby's introduction into the parlour was so short that Mrs. Wadman had but just time to get from behind the curtain ————lay a Bible upon the table, and advance a step or two towards the door to receive him.

My uncle Toby saluted Mrs. Wadman, after the manner in which women were saluted by men in the year of our Lord God one thousand seven hundred and thirteen————then facing about, he marched up abreast with her to the sofa, and in three plain words————though not before he was sat down ————nor after he was sat down————but as he was sitting down, told her, *"he was in love"*————so that my uncle Toby strained himself more in the declaration than he needed.

Mrs. Wadman naturally looked down, upon a slit she had been darning up in her apron, in expectation, every moment, that my uncle Toby would go on; but having no talents for amplification, and LOVE moreover of all others being a subject of which he was the least a master————When he had told Mrs. Wadman once that he loved her, he let it alone, and left the matter to work after its own way.

My father was always in raptures with this system of my uncle Toby's, as he falsely called it, and would often say that could his brother Toby to his process have added but a pipe of tobacco————he had wherewithal to have found his way, if there was faith in a Spanish proverb, towards the hearts of half the women upon the globe.

My uncle Toby never understood what my father meant; nor will I presume to extract more from it than a condemnation of an error which the bulk of the world lie under———— but the French, every one of 'em to a man, who believe in it, almost as much as the REAL PRESENCE, *"That talking of love is making it."*

————I would as soon set about making a black pudding by the same receipt.

Let us go on: Mrs. Wadman sat in expectation my uncle Toby would do so, to almost the first pulsation of that minute wherein silence on one side or the other generally becomes indecent: so edging herself a little more towards him, and raising up her eyes, sub-blushing, as she did it——she took up the gauntlet——or the discourse (if you like it better) and communed with my uncle Toby, thus.

The cares and disquietudes of the marriage state, quoth Mrs. Wadman, are very great. I suppose so——said my uncle Toby; and therefore when a person, continued Mrs. Wadman, is so much at his ease as you are——so happy, Captain Shandy, in yourself, your friends, and your amusements—— I wonder what reasons can incline you to the state——

——They are written, quoth my uncle Toby, in the Common Prayer Book.

Thus far my uncle Toby went on warily, and kept within his depth, leaving Mrs. Wadman to sail upon the gulf as she pleased.

——As for children——said Mrs. Wadman——though a principal end perhaps of the institution, and the natural wish, I suppose, of every parent——yet do not we all find they are certain sorrows, and very uncertain comforts? and what is there, dear sir, to pay one for the heartaches—— what compensation for the many tender and disquieting apprehensions of a suffering and defenceless mother who brings them into life? I declare, said my uncle Toby, smit with pity, I know of none; unless it be the pleasure which it has pleased God——

A fiddlestick! quoth she.

Chapter the Nineteenth

Now there are such an infinitude of notes, tunes, cants, chants, airs, looks, and accents with which the word *fiddlestick* may be pronounced in all such causes as this, every one of 'em impressing a sense and meaning as different from the other as *dirt* from *cleanliness*——That casuists (for it is an affair of conscience on that score) reckon up no less than fourteen thousand in which you may do either right or wrong.

Mrs. Wadman hit upon the *fiddlestick* which summoned up all my uncle Toby's modest blood into his cheeks——so feeling within himself that he had somehow or other got beyond his depth, he stopt short; and without entering further either into the pains or pleasures of matrimony, he laid his hand upon his heart, and made an offer to take them as they were, and share them along with her.

515

When my uncle Toby had said this, he did not care to say it again; so casting his eye upon the Bible which Mrs. Wadman had laid upon the table, he took it up; and popping, dear soul! upon a passage in it, of all others the most interesting to him——which was the siege of Jericho——he set himself to read it over——leaving his proposal of marriage, as he had done his declaration of love, to work with her after its own way. Now it wrought neither as an astringent or a loosener; nor like opium, or bark, or mercury, or buckthorn, or any one drug which nature had bestowed upon the world——in short, it worked not at all in her; and the cause of that was that there was something working there before ——Babbler that I am! I have anticipated what it was a dozen times; but there is fire still in the subject——*allons*.

CHAPTER XXVI

It is natural for a perfect stranger who is going from London to Edinburgh to enquire, before he sets out, how many miles to York; which is about the half way——nor does anybody wonder if he goes on and asks about the Corporation, &c. - -

It was just as natural for Mrs. Wadman, whose first husband was all his time afflicted with a Sciatica, to wish to know how far from the hip to the groin; and how far she was likely to suffer more or less in her feelings in the one case than in the other.

She had accordingly read Drake's anatomy from one end to the other. She had peeped into Wharton upon the brain, and borrowed Graaf upon the bones and muscles; * but could make nothing of it.

She had reasoned likewise from her own powers——laid down theorems——drawn consequences, and come to no conclusion.

To clear up all, she had twice asked Dr. Slop, "if poor Captain Shandy was ever likely to recover of his wound——?"

——He is recovered, Dr. Slop would say——

What! quite?

* This must be a mistake in Mr. Shandy; for Graaf wrote upon the pancreatic juice, and the parts of generation.

516

——Quite, Madam——

But what do you mean by a recovery? Mrs. Wadman would say.

Dr. Slop was the worst man alive at definitions; and so Mrs. Wadman could get no knowledge: in short, there was no way to extract it, but from my uncle Toby himself.

There is an accent of humanity in an enquiry of this kind which lulls SUSPICION to rest——and I am half persuaded the serpent got pretty near it, in his discourse with Eve; for the propensity in the sex to be deceived could not be so great that she should have boldness to hold chat with the devil without it——But there is an accent of humanity—— how shall I describe it?——'tis an accent which covers the part with a garment, and gives the enquirer a right to be as particular with it as your body surgeon.

"——Was it without remission?——

"——Was it more tolerable in bed?

"——Could he lie on both sides alike with it?

"——Was he able to mount a horse?

"——Was motion bad for it?" *et cetera,* were so tenderly spoke to, and so directed towards my uncle Toby's heart, that every item of them sunk ten times deeper into it than the evils themselves——but when Mrs. Wadman went round about by Namur to get at my uncle Toby's groin; and engaged him to attack the point of the advanced counterscarp, and *pêle-mêle* with the Dutch to take the counterguard of St. Roch, sword in hand——and then with tender notes playing upon his ear, led him all bleeding by the hand out of the trench, wiping her eye as he was carried to his tent—— Heaven! Earth! Sea!——all was lifted up——the springs of nature rose above their levels——an angel of mercy sat besides him on the sofa——his heart glowed with fire——and had he been worth a thousand, he had lost every heart of them to Mrs. Wadman.

——And whereabouts, dear Sir, quoth Mrs. Wadman, a little categorically, did you receive this sad blow?——In asking this question, Mrs. Wadman gave a slight glance towards the waistband of my uncle Toby's red plush breeches, expecting naturally, as the shortest reply to it, that my uncle Toby would lay his forefinger upon the place——It fell out otherwise——for my uncle Toby having got his wound before the gate of St. Nicolas, in one of the traverses of the trench, opposite to the salient angle of the demibastion of St. Roch, he could at any time stick a pin upon the identical spot of ground where he was standing when the stone struck

517

him: this struck instantly upon my uncle Toby's sensorium
——and with it, struck his large map of the town and citadel of Namur and its environs, which he had purchased and
pasted down upon a board by the corporal's aid, during his
long illness——it had lain with other military lumber in the
garret ever since, and accordingly the corporal was detached
into the garret to fetch it.

My uncle Toby measured off thirty toises, with Mrs. Wadman's scissors, from the returning angle before the gate of
St. Nicolas; and with such a virgin modesty laid her finger
upon the place, that the goddess of Decency, if then in being
——if not, 'twas her shade——shook her head, and with a
finger wavering across her eyes——forbid her to explain the
mistake.

Unhappy Mrs. Wadman!——

——For nothing can make this chapter go off with spirit
but an apostrophe to thee——but my heart tells me that in
such a crisis, an apostrophe is but an insult in disguise, and
ere I would offer one to a woman in distress——let the
chapter go to the devil; provided any damned critic *in keeping* will be but at the trouble to take it with him.

CHAPTER XXVII

My uncle Toby's Map is carried down into the kitchen.

CHAPTER XXVIII

——And here is the Maas——and this is the Sambre, said
the corporal, pointing with his right hand extended a little
towards the map, and his left upon Mrs. Bridget's shoulder
——but not the shoulder next him——and this, said he, is
the town of Namur——and this the citadel——and there lay
the French——and here lay his Honour and myself——and
in this cursed trench, Mrs. Bridget, quoth the corporal, tak-

518

ing her by the hand, did he receive the wound which crushed him so miserably *here*——In pronouncing which he slightly pressed the back of her hand towards the part he felt for ——and let it fall.

We thought, Mr. Trim, it had been more in the middle ——said Mrs. Bridget——

That would have undone us forever——said the corporal.

——And left my poor mistress undone too——said Bridget.

The corporal made no reply to the repartee, but by giving Mrs. Bridget a kiss.

Come——come——said Bridget——holding the palm of her left hand parallel to the plane of the horizon, and sliding the fingers of the other over it, in a way which could not have been done, had there been the least wart or protuberance ——'Tis every syllable of it false, cried the corporal, before she had half finished the sentence——

——I know it to be fact, said Bridget, from credible witnesses.

——Upon my honour, said the corporal, laying his hand upon his heart, and blushing as he spoke with honest resentment——'tis a story, Mrs. Bridget, as false as hell——Not, said Bridget, interrupting him, that either I or my mistress care a halfpenny about it, whether 'tis so or no——only that when one is married, one would choose to have such a thing by one at least——

It was somewhat unfortunate for Mrs. Bridget, that she had begun the attack with her manual exercise; for the corporal instantly * * * * * * * * * * * *
* * * * * * * * * * * * * *
* * * * * * * * * * * * * *
* * * *.

CHAPTER XXIX

It was like the momentary contest in the moist eyelids of an April morning, "Whether Bridget should laugh or cry."

She snatched up a rolling pin——'twas ten to one she had laughed——

She laid it down——she cried; and had one single tear of

519

'em but tasted of bitterness, full sorrowful would the corporal's heart have been that he had used the argument; but the corporal understood the sex, a *quart major to a terce* at least better than my uncle Toby, and accordingly he assailed Mrs. Bridget after this manner.

I know, Mrs. Bridget, said the corporal, giving her a most respectful kiss, that thou are good and modest by nature, and art withal so generous a girl in thyself that, if I know thee rightly, thou wouldst not wound an insect, much less the honour of so gallant and worthy a soul as my master, wast thou sure to be made a countess of——but thou hast been set on, and deluded, dear Bridget, as is often a woman's case, "to please others more than themselves——"

Bridget's eyes poured down at the sensations the corporal excited.

——Tell me——tell me then, my dear Bridget, continued the corporal, taking hold of her hand, which hung down dead by her side,——and giving a second kiss——whose suspicion has misled thee?

Bridget sobbed a sob or two——then opened her eyes——the corporal wiped 'em with the bottom of her apron——she then opened her heart and told him all.

CHAPTER XXX

My uncle Toby and the corporal had gone on separately with their operations the greatest part of the campaign, and as effectually cut off from all communication of what either the one or the other had been doing, as if they had been separated from each other by the Maas or the Sambre.

My uncle Toby, on his side, had presented himself every afternoon in his red and silver, and blue and gold, alternately, and sustained an infinity of attacks in them, without knowing them to be attacks——and so had nothing to communicate——

The corporal, on his side, in taking Bridget, by it had gained considerable advantages——and consequently had much to communicate——but what were the advantages——as well as what was the manner by which he had seized them, required so nice an historian that the corporal durst not venture upon it; and as sensible as he was of glory, would rather have been contented to have gone bareheaded and without laurels forever, than torture his master's modesty for a single moment——

——Best of honest and gallant servants!——But I have apostrophized thee, Trim! once before——and could I apotheosize thee also (that is to say) with good company—— I would do it *without ceremony* in the very next page.

CHAPTER XXXI

Now my uncle Toby had one evening laid down his pipe upon the table, and was counting over to himself upon his finger ends (beginning at his thumb) all Mrs. Wadman's perfections one by one; and happening two or three times together, either by omitting some, or counting others twice over, to puzzle himself sadly before he could get beyond his middle finger——Prithee, Trim! said he, taking up his pipe again,——bring me a pen and ink: Trim brought paper also.

Take a full sheet——Trim! said my uncle Toby, making a sign with his pipe at the same time to take a chair and sit down close by him at the table. The corporal obeyed—— placed the paper directly before him——took a pen and dipped it in the ink.

——She has a thousand virtues, Trim! said my uncle Toby——

Am I to set them down, an' please your Honour? quoth the corporal.

——But they must be taken in their ranks, replied my uncle Toby; for of them all, Trim, that which wins me most, and which is a security for all the rest, is the compassionate turn and singular humanity of her character——I protest, added my uncle Toby, looking up, as he protested it, towards the top of the ceiling——That was I her brother, Trim, a thousandfold, she could not make more constant or more tender enquiries after my sufferings——though now no more.

The corporal made no reply to my uncle Toby's protestation, but by a short cough——he dipped the pen a second time into the inkhorn; and my uncle Toby, pointing with the end of his pipe as close to the top of the sheet at the left-hand corner of it as he could get it——the corporal wrote down the word

HUMANITY - - - - - - - - - - - - - thus.

Prithee, corporal, said my uncle Toby, as soon as Trim had done it——how often does Mrs. Bridget enquire after the wound on the cap of thy knee, which thou receivedst at the battle of Landen?

She never, an' please your Honour, enquires after it at all.

That, corporal, said my uncle Toby, with all the triumph the goodness of his nature would permit——That shows the difference in the character of the mistress and maid——had the fortune of war allotted the same mischance to me, Mrs. Wadman would have enquired into every circumstance relating to it a hundred times——She would have enquired, an' please your Honour, ten times as often about your Honour's groin——The pain, Trim, is equally excruciating,——and Compassion has as much to do with the one as the other——

——God bless your Honour! cried the corporal——what has a woman's compassion to do with a wound upon the cap of a man's knee? had your Honour's been shot into ten thousand splinters at the affair of Landen, Mrs. Wadman would have troubled her head as little about it as Bridget; because, added the corporal, lowering his voice and speaking very distinctly, as he assigned his reason——

"The knee is such a distance from the main body—— whereas the groin, your Honour knows, is upon the very *curtain* of the *place*."

My uncle Toby gave a long whistle——but in a note which could scarce be heard across the table.

The corporal had advanced too far to retire——in three words he told the rest——

My uncle Toby laid down his pipe as gently upon the fender as if it had been spun from the unravellings of a spider's web——

——Let us go to my brother Shandy's, said he.

CHAPTER XXXII

There will be just time, whilst my uncle Toby and Trim are walking to my father's, to inform you that Mrs. Wadman had, some moons before this, made a confidant of my mother; and that Mrs. Bridget, who had the burden of her own, as well as her mistress's secret to carry, had got happily delivered of both to Susannah behind the garden wall.

As for my mother, she saw nothing at all in it to make the least bustle about——but Susannah was sufficient by herself, for all the ends and purposes you could possibly have, in exporting a family secret; for she instantly imparted it by signs to Jonathan——and Jonathan by tokens to the cook, as she was basting a loin of mutton; the cook sold it with some kitchen fat to the postillion for a groat, who tucked it with the dairy maid for something of about the same value ——and though whispered in the hayloft, FAME caught the notes with her brazen trumpet and sounded them upon the housetop——In a word, not an old woman in the village or five miles round, who did not understand the difficulties of my uncle Toby's siege, and what were the secret articles which had delayed the surrender.——

My father, whose way was to force every event in nature into an hypothesis, by which means never man crucified TRUTH at the rate he did——had but just heard of the report as my uncle Toby set out; and catching fire suddenly at the trespass done his brother by it, was demonstrating to Yorick, notwithstanding my mother was sitting by——not only, "That the devil was in women, and that the whole of the affair was lust;" but that every evil and disorder in the world, of what kind or nature soever, from the first fall of Adam, down to my uncle Toby's (inclusive), was owing one way or other to the same unruly appetite.

Yorick was just bringing my father's hypothesis to some temper, when my uncle Toby entering the room with marks of infinite benevolence and forgiveness in his looks, my father's eloquence rekindled against the passion——and as he was not very nice in the choice of his words when he was wroth——as soon as my uncle Toby was seated by the fire, and had filled his pipe, my father broke out in this manner.

CHAPTER XXXIII

——That provision should be made for continuing the race of so great, so exalted and godlike a Being as man——I am far from denying——but philosophy speaks freely of everything; and therefore I still think and do maintain it to be a pity that it should be done by means of a passion which bends down the faculties, and turns all the wisdom, contemplations, and operations of the soul backwards——a passion, my dear, continued my father, addressing himself to my mother, which couples and equals wise men with fools, and makes us come out of caverns and hiding places more like satyrs and four-footed beasts than men.

I know it will be said, continued my father (availing himself of the Prolepsis), that in itself, and simply taken——like hunger, or thirst, or sleep——'tis an affair neither good or bad——or shameful or otherwise.——Why then did the delicacy of Diogenes and Plato so recalcitrate against it? and wherefore, when we go about to make and plant a man, do we put out the candle? and for what reason is it that all the parts thereof——the congredients——the preparations—— the instruments, and whatever serves thereto, are so held as to be conveyed to a cleanly mind by no language, translation, or periphrasis whatever?

——The act of killing and destroying a man, continued my father, raising his voice——and turning to my uncle Toby—— you see, is glorious——and the weapons by which we do it are honourable——We march with them upon our shoulders ——We strut with them by our sides——We gild them—— We carve them——We inlay them——We enrich them—— Nay, if it be but a *scoundrel* cannon, we cast an ornament upon the breech of it.——

——My uncle Toby laid down his pipe to intercede for a better epithet——and Yorick was rising up to batter the whole hypothesis to pieces——

——When Obadiah broke into the middle of the room with a complaint, which cried out for an immediate hearing.

The case was this:

My father, whether by ancient custom of the manor, or as impropriator of the great tithes, was obliged to keep a Bull for the service of the Parish, and Obadiah had led his cow upon a *pop visit* to him one day or other the preceding summer——I say, one day or other——because as chance would have it, it was the day on which he was married to my father's housemaid——so one was a reckoning to the other. Therefore when Obadiah's wife was brought to bed——Obadiah thanked God——

——Now, said Obadiah, I shall have a calf: so Obadiah went daily to visit his cow.

She'll calve on Monday——on Tuesday——on Wednesday at the farthest——

The cow did not calve——no——she'll not calve till next week——the cow put it off terribly——till at the end of the sixth week Obadiah's suspicions (like a good man's) fell upon the Bull.

Now the parish being very large, my father's Bull, to speak the truth of him, was no way equal to the department; he had, however, got himself, somehow or other, thrust into employment——and as he went through the business with a grave face, my father had a high opinion of him.

——Most of the townsmen, an' please your Worship, quoth Obadiah, believe that 'tis all the Bull's fault——

——But may not a cow be barren? replied my father, turning to Dr. Slop.

It never happens, said Dr. Slop, but the man's wife may have come before her time naturally enough——Prithee has the child hair upon his head?——added Dr. Slop——

——It is as hairy as I am, said Obadiah.——Obadiah had not been shaved for three weeks——Wheu - - u - - - - u - - - - - - - - cried my father, beginning the sentence with an exclamatory whistle——and so, brother Toby, this poor Bull of mine, who is as good a Bull as ever p–ssed, and might have done for Europa herself in purer times——had he but two legs less, might have been driven into Doctors Commons and lost his character——which to a Town Bull, brother Toby, is the very same thing as his life——

L - - d! said my mother, what is all this story about?——

A COCK and a BULL, said Yorick——And one of the best of its kind I ever heard.

AFTERWORD

TRISTRAM SHANDY'S ANTI-BOOK

"Of all the cants which are canted in this canting world —though the cant of hypocrites may be the worst—the cant of criticism is the most tormenting!" So says Tristram Shandy. With Shandy standing behind one's chair, what can one ("*i.e.*, an author," says Tristram, making fun of writers who say *one* when they mean *I*)—with Tristram at my elbow, probably, like Uncle Toby, whistling "Lillabulero," what can I say about *The Life and Opinions of Tristram Shandy, Gent.*, by the Reverend Mr. Laurence Sterne? There are certain stock things that can be said, that have been said. The pattern of criticism was set with the publication of the first two volumes in 1760. At about that time, Samuel Richardson, the fame of having protected Pamela's virtue for so many pages heavy about his shoulders, wrote, in the guise of a young lady in London, that the book was built of "unaccountable wildness; whimsical incoherencies; uncommon indecencies. . . ." *Tristram Shandy* was to be much loved and much laughed at, but the author was to be harried for structural perversities, apparently as arbitrary as e. e. cummings' predilection for the lower case. Although we have come to accept the notion that there is method in Sterne's chaos, the criticism—somewhat watered—still persists. George Sherburn wrote in *The Restoration and Eighteenth Century* (1948), his volume of *A Literary History of England:* "One tolerates his use of blank pages, black pages, and marbled pages, his placing his preface in the middle of the book, his dots, dashes, and index hands, and other tricks that Joseph Addison would have classed as 'false wit.' "

Judging from his letters and the later volumes of the book itself, Sterne was as sensitive to the criticism aimed at *Tristram Shandy* as any author is likely to be. The entire work is sprinkled with asides to critics, advice to critics, quarrels with critics, defenses against critics. At one point in the last volume, for example, Tristram refuses to praise the widow Wadman, even though he is convinced that an apostrophe would be the making of his chapter: "let the chapter go to the devil; provided any damned critic in keeping will be but at the trouble to take it with him." The criticism of *Tristram Shandy* and the author's annoyance at it thus become one of the jokes in the book. Today, however, Tristram appears to be facing quite another indignity, one that would have been less easy for the author to absorb, even though, not quite seriously, he had predicted its coming:

> As my life and opinions are likely to make some noise in the world, and, if I conjecture right, will take in all ranks, professions, and denominations of men whatever, —be no less read than the *Pilgrim's Progress* itself—and in the end, prove the very thing which Montaigne dreaded his Essays should turn out, that is, a book for a parlour-window. . . .

The prophecy has proven itself. In the eighteenth century Sterne was often attacked, but more often read; today his novel is an accepted classic, but in the acceptance (turn away, Mr. Shandy) lies good-humored indifference. A casual, nonstatistical inquiry indicates that of all the books that call forth easy protestations of love—excepting probably Robert Burton's *The Anatomy of Melancholy*—Sterne's novel must be the least read. The modern reader, like the lady whom Tristram reprimands for "reading straight forwards, more in quest of adventures, than of the deep erudition and knowledge," is likely to become impatient, not just with the tricks that offend Professor Sherburn (as Joseph Addison), but with the digressive structure—the starts and stops, the interruptions, the false promises, the asides. Yet, digressions are "the life, the soul of reading," as Tristram says; "take them out of this book, for instance,—you might as well take the book along with them. . . ." In this sentence, Sterne is doing more than laughing at Tristram's apparently pointless garrulity. He is pointing out that the digressions, like the mechanical surprises, are basic to the form and intention of *Tristram Shandy,* that those devices which annoy and repel some readers are precisely the instruments that make the book most attractive.

More than a century ago Walter Bagehot tried to rule out the possibility of a pattern in Sterne's novel: "No analysis or account of 'Tristram Shandy' could be given which would suit the present generation; being, indeed, a book without a plan or order, it is in every generation unfit for analysis." The present present generation (Bagehot could not have known) can find plan or order in any work, given the inclination and a little careful distortion. With *Tristram Shandy* definition, not distortion, is needed—for *plan* or *order,* read *attitude.* The nine volumes with all their twists and turns are held together by the fact that they are so obviously products of a single imagination and a single method, which is, I suppose, what Sterne meant when he wrote to David Garrick (sending him the first two volumes): "'tis however a picture of myself, & so far may bid the fairer for being an Original." *Tristram Shandy* is Sterne's comic view of the world and of his own place in it. The recurring references to Cervantes and Rabelais, the writers from whom he seems to have gained the greatest inspiration and the most enjoyment, imply what Sterne is trying to do in the novel. He is specific about it in a letter to Robert Dodsley, his first publisher: "The Plan, as you will percieve [*sic*], is a most extensive one,—taking in, not only, the Weak part of the Sciences, in wch the true point of Ridicule lies—but every Thing else, which I find Laugh-at-able in my way. . . ." It is impossible to read very far in *Tristram Shandy* without realizing that Sterne finds laugh-at-able all human pretension—social, intellectual, artistic, personal—and, by extension, all human activity. He is not an angry satirist; his laughter is good humored. He knows, as he says in his sermon, "The Levite and His Concubine," that "certainly there is a difference between *Bitterness* and *Saltness,*—that is,—between the malignity and the festivity of wit."

Sterne's use of digression cannot be explained simply by recognizing that his book reflects the humorist's laughing fondness (with only occasional dips into venom) for men and the preposterous ways in which they think, talk, and act. He can raise laughter at the foibles of human behavior by describing a brief scene; he can mock a man's special knowledge (his hobby-horse) by parody or quotation. The endless interruption serves these two comic methods by giving them greater employment, by dragging more and more subjects in by the heels. Sterne's digression, however, does more than open doors. It is a comic method itself and its butt is Sterne and his novel. He can best make fun of himself and the incredible idea that he, like all the other hobby-horse riders, is writing a book, by defying every convention of the eighteenth-century novel and memoir (of which *Tristram Shandy* is a distant relative), by going beyond the defiance even—by breaking his work into fragments that shoot off in all directions. *Tristram Shandy* is essentially an anti-book. When that fact is recognized, every irrelevance becomes relevant, not to the book's plot, but to its narrator-hero, Sterne's instrument for achieving order by making disorder, for displaying a mind by pretending that minds are so beset by vagaries that their likenesses can never be caught.

Before looking at the ways in which Sterne avoids telling his story, I should point out that there is a story to be told, that *Tristram Shandy* has a plot. Supposedly the novel was to describe the life (and the opinions) of a country gentleman whose character had been formed by a number of accidents that befell him before, at, or shortly after his birth. The nine volumes (published two at a time between 1760 and 1767) never get the narrator-hero beyond his childhood. The first four volumes form the most obvious unit; primarily concerned with getting Tristram born and named, the real or nondigressive action of these volumes takes place within a year. There are four main incidents—the begetting of Tristram, the decision that his mother shall have her lying-in in the country, the mashing of his nose by Dr. Slop's forceps and the mix-up at the christening which gives him his name—which serve as anchors to hold in place the rest of the material—the story of Yorick, the presentation of Uncle Toby and Corporal Trim and their passion for playing soldier, the ideas of Tristram's father, Yorick's sermon, and the asides of the narrator. The fifth and sixth volumes jump to Tristram's childhood, using the death of his brother Bobby, the preparation of Mr. Shandy's educational system (the *Tristra-paedia*), and the unfortunate affair of the falling window which gives Tristram an accidental circumcision as the weak wall of plot on which to hang the comic decoration. The three years that passed between the publication of Volumes V and VI (1762) and Volumes VII and VIII (1765) took Sterne to France in search of health, which he never found. The seventh volume is a complete digression, an account of the narrator's sudden trip to France to escape death, the result probably of an inability to get on with the book as he had planned it. The eighth volume takes up the story of Uncle Toby's courting of the widow Wadman, hinted at in Volume I, promised in Volume III and begun at the end of Volume VI, and the ninth volume, published singly, finishes the courtship. The novel ended at this point not because it had come to a conclusion in any conventional sense, but because Sterne had turned to his *A Sentimental Journey through France and Italy* and because he died before he could turn back to Tristram—as he suggested he would in a letter written in 1766.

These few high points in Tristram's embryonic and infant life and the courtship of Uncle Toby (a flashback to the year before Tristram was born) are held together by continual glances ahead and to the rear. They are the beads through which the string of the narrative is to run, but it is Sterne's business to knot the string as often as possible between beads, to loop it, tangle it, break it completely, and retie it as neatly as possible. To drag his feet between incidents, Sterne uses four kinds of interruption: (1) conversation with imagined readers; (2) false starts, promises that are never kept; (3) the structural play that Professor Sherburn lists; and (4) digressions which often, like Chinese boxes, become digressions within digressions within digressions. The conversations with the reader are simply overextensions of the eighteenth-century fondness for speaking directly to the audience. Where Fielding might introduce a chapter by taking his readers into his confidence, Sterne is more likely to command them ("Lay down the book, and I will allow you half a day to give a probable guess at the grounds of this procedure"), to ask their advice ("What would your worships have me do in this case?") and to get it ("Tell it, Mr. Shandy, by all means.—You are a fool, Tristram, if you do"), to discuss their competence as readers, to give them age, sex, position, personality. At one point, he sends the inattentive lady back to reread a chapter because he is convinced that she has missed an important point: "I told you in it, That my mother was not a papist.—Papist! You told me no such thing, Sir."

A variation on this familiarity with the reader is Sterne's continued assurance that a matter will be made clear farther on, that a story will be told in a later volume, that a character will finally be explained. It is possible that some of the hints would have materialized, like Toby's affair with Mrs. Wadman, had the book really run on to more volumes, but it is apparent throughout that Sterne is starting hares that he has no intention of running to ground. He promises chapters on chambermaids and buttonholes, although later he begs off, asking if he might substitute a chapter on chapters instead. Tristram often looks forward to his account of his travels with Mr. Noddy, but since Tristram never gets out of childhood, Mr. Noddy never becomes more than a name. The most pervasive of Sterne's false starts is Jenny, a character to whom he often speaks or whose actions he describes, but who is never identified. She appears casually in the first volume, where Tristram stops to reprimand the reader for jumping to conclusions in assuming that he must be married because he addresses a "dear, dear Jenny." Jenny may be his kept mistress, his child, a friend of the opposite sex, he suggests, but although Jenny is still turning up in the ninth volume, she is still carefully unidentified.

The structural and typographical trickery is more than the adolescent high spirits that some of Sterne's critics have implied that it is. His mechanical jokes are not always funny and they are sometimes used too repetitiously, but even more than the unresolved promises and the arguments with imaginary readers, they are aimed at the pretensions and the fastidiousness of both readers and writers. The book is sprinkled with asterisks to replace material which ostensibly Sterne considers too delicate for the ears of his readers. Since he often uses the word *spade,* and not ******,* when he means *spade,* the scattering of asterisks is, in fact, a laugh at the gentility which insisted that its mild scatology and pornography are more becoming dressed in typographical veils. Sterne's mock nicety is most evident in the wonderfully funny scene in which the hot chestnut rolls into the open fly of Phutatorius, at the gathering of the divines; "Zounds!" cries Phutatorius, and then, "Z—ds!" Similarly, Sterne's placing of the dedication in the eighth chapter of the first volume and the preface in the middle of Volume III is not sheer perversity; in playing with their position in his novel, he satirizes the whole process of dedications and prefaces, just as the matter of the first thrusts at the venality of dedications and of the second at the pomposity of prefaces.

Sterne is structually most cavalier in his treatment of chapters. Their length has nothing to do with the material they contain; occasionally a single sentence or a very short paragraph becomes a complete chapter. Even when he restrains the digressions, he often, for no apparent reason, breaks a single incident into several chapters. "A sudden impulse comes across me," he explains, "drop the curtain, Shandy—I drop it—Strike a line here across the paper, Tristram—I strike it—and hey for a new chapter." He leaves one chapter blank so that the reader can fill in his own description of Mrs. Wadman, just as, at another spot, he leaves a space for the reader to swear in. He passes over two chapters because his Uncle Toby is whistling and he cannot concentrate and then, pages later, inserts the missing chapters under their original numbers, going back to pick up the material that he left out. He leaves out a chapter in the fourth volume because its description of the journey of Mr. Shandy and Toby is so beautifully done that it will make the rest of the book weak by comparison. "A dwarf who brings a standard along with him to measure his own size—take my word, is a dwarf in more articles than one. —And so much for tearing out of chapters." Sterne's toying with the length, position, even the necessity of chapters is more than harmless personal pleasure, although he obviously enjoys the joke involved. It is a slap at the order implied in the division of material into suitable working units. It is a demonstration of his claim, made early in the book when he introduces and dismisses Horace: "for in writing what I have set about, I shall confine myself neither to his rules, nor to any man's rules that ever lived."

The first three of Sterne's interruptive methods contribute to the planned disorder of his book, but, by comparison with the fourth, they are merely surface mannerisms. Digression ("the life, the soul") is obviously basic to the structure of a novel that is going to take until the middle of its third volume to get its hero born. Sterne's digressions are not the conventional, neat insertions of picaresque novels, like the goat-herd's story in *Don Quixote* or Mr. Wilson's account of his misspent youth in *Joseph Andrews*. *Tristram Shandy* does have such set pieces—Slawkenbergius's tale about the man with the long nose—but these are as subject to interruption as anything else in the book. Trim's story of the King of Bohemia and his seven castles, for example, is halted first in an attempt to date the action, then to allow Toby to discuss the origin of gunpowder, next to let Trim describe his wound and his love for the young Beguine. "What became of that story, Trim?" asks Toby pages later. "We lost it, an' please your honour, somehow betwixt us. . . ." Sterne's digressive technique can be seen at its most flamboyant when he interrupts a remark of Uncle Toby's ("I think, says he") near the beginning of Volume I, Chapter XXI. The narrator leaves Toby's words hanging in the air while he proceeds to describe the speaker, a description that is stopped immediately by some general remarks on climate and writing. Having returned to Uncle Toby's history and character, Sterne (or Tristram) gets involved in the story of Aunt Dinah and the coachman, with some side remarks on formal argumentation. What with a chapter on disgressions, a chapter on ways of drawing character ("I have a strong propensity in me to begin this chapter very nonsensically") and a minute and roundabout account of Uncle Toby's wound in the groin, his convalescence, his preoccupation with fortification and his servant Trim, it is not until Volume II, Chapter VI that the poor man finished his sentence: "I think, replied he,—it would not be amiss, brother, if we rung the bell." In his chapter on digressions, Sterne offers his own explanation, at once comic and accurate, of his digressive method. He finds "truly pitiable" the ordinary author. "For, if he begins a digression,—from that moment, I observe, his whole work stands stock still;—and if he goes on with his main work,—then there is an end of his digression." As for himself, "I have constructed the main work and the adventitious parts of it with such intersections, and have so complicated and involved the digressive and progressive movements, one wheel within another, that the whole machine, in general, has been kept a-going. . . ." The splendor of Sterne's digressions, aside from their intrinsic wit and humor, is that they do keep the machine a-going even while they appear to be poking sticks in the spokes of its wheels; they get Tristram's story told even while they seem to be insisting that storytelling is as laughable an activity for a man as any other.

If *Tristram Shandy* as a whole, its structure and its style, becomes Sterne's humorous view of himself and his world, there are within it specific satirical thrusts at the conventional butts of satire, at "the Weak part of the Sciences, in wch the true point of Ridicule lies." Toward the end of the fourth volume, Tristram comments on the wild ride he has taken through the first four volumes of his life and admits cheerfully that some bystanders have been brushed as he passed by:

> Now ride at this rate with what good intention and resolution you may—'tis a million to one you'll do someone a mischief, if not yourself—He's flung—he's off—he's lost his hat—he's down—he'll break his neck—see!—if he has not galloped full among the scaffolding of the undertaking critics!—he'll knock his brains out against some of their posts—he's bounced out!—look—he's now riding like a madcap full tilt through a whole crowd of painters, fiddlers, poets, biographers, physicians, lawyers, logicians, players, schoolmen, churchmen, statesmen, soldiers, casuists, connoisseurs, prelates, popes, and engineers—Don't fear, said I—I'll not hurt the poorest jackass upon the king's highway —But your horse throws dirt; see you've splashed a bishop —I hope in God, 'twas only Ernulphus, said I.—But you have squirted full in the faces of Mess. Le Moyne, De Romigny, and De Marcilly, doctors of the Sorbonne.—That was last year, replied I.—But you have trod this moment upon a king.—Kings have bad times on't, said I, to be trod upon by such people as me.

Tristram's horse is not quite so out of control as he makes it sound in this paragraph; Sterne holds the reins and if Tristram rides close enough to splash a bishop, it is because Sterne sees something in the bishop that is obviously splashable. Yet, it is certainly true that he has no intention of hurting the "poorest jackass" on the road. Sterne's satire is not the reforming anger of Ben Jonson or Jonathan Swift; it is the good-natured satire of a man who is amused at jackasses, expects them to go on being jackasses, and is cheerfully willing to admit that he is something of a jackass himself. Oliver Goldsmith accused Sterne of having "contempt for all but himself, smiling without a jest, and without wit professing vivacity." "Contempt" is too harsh a word for Sterne's amusement at men, and Goldsmith is quite inaccurate when he suggests that Sterne exempts himself from the general laughter. Not only is he a butt implicitly; he is one specifically. Sterne uses one of his own sermons, "The Abuses of Conscience Considered," when he reaches the scene in *Tristram Shandy* in which the sermon is to become the target of satire.

The specific objects of Sterne's satire are no longer of interest to anyone except scholars and antiquarians. He was obviously attracted to arcane volumes of all kinds, treatises written in the excluding jargon of the professions, the special language of what Gerard Manley Hopkins called, in another context, "áll trádes, their gear and tackle and trim." Sometimes Sterne quotes directly from his sources, as when he gives, in Latin and English, the anathema of Ernulphus, the twelfth-century Bishop of Rochester. Sometimes he parodies; sometimes he invents. The book is awash with references, both genuine and fictitious; the classical authors are called on to uphold positions they may or may not have supported. This ambiguous richness has been a blessing to academic detectives who have hunted out sources with diligence; Wilbur L. Cross's standard biography of Sterne discusses a number of the works that found their way into Sterne's mind and book, particularly those that gave Uncle Toby his military knowledge, and since the Cross biography was published in 1929, other scholars have continued to work over the body of Tristram Shandy in an attempt to identify the marks on it. This process, which would probably have amused Sterne, is the business of scholarship, but it can have very little importance to the general reader of *Tristram Shandy*. Uncle Toby and his sieges are not more or less funny when the reader knows that there was a Comte de Pagan and that Sterne had read (had heard of, at least) his *Traité des Fortifications* (1645). Actually the list of readings that Sterne gives for Uncle Toby in *Tristram Shandy* becomes a little wearing, even when we know that they are real; it is the situation that is funny: that a man with a wound in his groin has to read treatises dating back two centuries to explain what has happened to him. Toby is funny because, like Don Quixote, he is a man possessed by his reading, and his descriptions are funny (the *double entendre* aside) because they ridicule the kind of military writing which displays a garrulous concern for detail and terminology and an indifference to the human activity of the battlefield. One of the few times that Sterne becomes acid in *Tristram Shandy* and the only time the acidity splashes on Uncle Toby is when he casually comments on a battle that Toby is about to re-enact in his own backyard:

> As this was the most memorable attack in the whole war,— the most gallant and obstinate on both sides,—and I must add the most bloody too, for it cost the allies themselves that morning above eleven hundred men,—my uncle Toby prepared himself for it with a more than ordinary solemnity.

Sterne uses a variety of methods of mocking the preten-

536

sions that he wants to explode. One of the most consistent and most effective is to turn the specialist's knowledge over to Walter Shandy and let him run it quickly into absurdity. Mr. Shandy is fascinated by matters medical, theological, philosophical; he is addicted to argument and explanation. As a result, he presents his theories about the importance of an uninterrupted begetting, of a feet-first birth, of a long nose, of a name with implicit power to greatness, and of the auxiliary verb as the key to education with the proper consideration of the authorities and the rejection or acceptance of them. In the course of Mr. Shandy's thinking, the medical theorist, the theologian, and the philosopher become so removed from practical matters that their disciplines become ridiculous. In some of its details, the scholastic argumentation that Walter Shandy plays havoc with is no longer pertinent, but it is a relatively simple matter to recognize that the satire is easily transferable to our own time, to the sometimes picayune concerns of the literary critic, the analytic philosopher, the educationist, and the social scientist. In turning Walter Shandy loose on those disciplines that are supposedly most concerned with men but which have invented a special language that excludes the bulk of men, Sterne has created a situation that is valid far beyond Mr. Shandy's immediate cogitations. There are always small bands of men who take shelter in the bastions of jargon and run up flags of complacency; there is always the need of a Walter Shandy to blow up these redoubts, not by attacking them but simply by entering them.

Although Walter Shandy is Sterne's chief satirical weapon, he has others. One is the simple statement, sometimes in the mouth of a character, sometimes from the narrator himself, which in summarizing a pompous passage destroys the material it is concerned with. The best example follows the article in his mother's marriage-settlement that Tristram quotes in Volume I. The article, full of the repetitions, the re-identifications, the *to wits* and *whereases* that are standard for a satire on the legal style, runs for three tiresome pages (present ed.); at the end Tristram adds, "In three words—'My mother was to lay in, (if she chose it) in London.'" A third device of Sterne's, the one that he uses with his own sermon, is to present the material that is to be laughed at in a dramatic situation in which the behavior of the characters points up the absurdity of what is being said. Sterne's sermon is not absurd in itself; it lacks the ornateness of classical and theological reference that would have made of it the kind of joke that we get in the philosophical ruminations of Mr. Shandy. "The Abuses of Conscience Considered," like most of Sterne's sermons, is a straightforward pleading for morality, touched here and there with evidences that it was written by the author of *Tristram Shandy*, but for the most part it is simply competently dull. Sterne thought enough of it to have it printed later in a volume of his sermons. He is, then, not specifically satirizing the material or the style of his sermon; he is satirizing the whole idea that one man—especially himself —should get up and preach morality at another. This becomes clear as we realize that Sterne is more interested in the delivery of the sermon and its reception than he is in the sermon itself. He takes great pains to get Corporal Trim in the correct oratorical position to read the sermon; he allows frequent interruptions from Mr. Shandy, Uncle Toby, and Dr. Slop; he lets the sermon anger the Roman Catholic doctor and then put him to sleep; he makes Trim break down before the end of the sermon, convinced that the general description of the Inquisition is a factual account of what has befallen his unfortunate brother Tom, and give way to Mr. Shandy, who finishes the reading. Although some of the eighteenth-century reviewers expressed an admiration for the sermon itself, the actual effect of the scene is to lose the sermon in its reading. So much for the preaching of morality, Sterne seems to say.

Although *Tristram Shandy* is spotted with laughter at particular professions and disciplines, it is filled also with thrusts at a more general erudition, the kind of intellectual ornamentation that eighteenth-century authors delighted in and that modern authors use almost as frequently but more self-consciously, the learned additions that are dragged in by the heels, like my introduction of Gerard Manley Hopkins three paragraphs back. Sterne makes fun of this kind of pretension by allowing his narrator to call up classical analogies which he only vaguely remembers. The most extended example comes after the death of his brother Bobby when Tristram runs through a whole list of authors, pagan and Christian, ancient and modern, in an attempt to put his finger on the depiction of grief that best describes Walter Shandy's reaction to his son's death. At another point, Tristram says of one of his learned references, "I have not the time to look into Saxo-Grammaticus's Danish history to know the certainty of this;—but if you have leisure, and can easily get at the book, you may do it full as well yourself." Tristram's pose, the knower who is not really certain that he knows, is the standard comic way of satirizing the writer who is happier with a quotation than with a straightforward observation.

There are two aspects of Sterne—Sterne the sentimental and Sterne the prurient—that deserve special consideration. To some of Sterne's critics, in his own and later centuries, his sentiment has seemed the most admirable thing in his book and his bawdy the most deplorable. This kind of criticism implies that neither the sentiment nor the bawdy quite belongs in *Tristram Shandy,* and such an implication is false. Sterne uses both kinds of writing in a special way in his novel, so that the sentiment does not become sentimental and the bawdy does not become dirty.

Sterne's sentiment is neither the utilitarian nicety of Sir Richard Steele nor the genteel glorying in a polite emotion for the emotion's sake that characterized the sentimentalists who sighed over his counting the pulse of the lovely glove seller in *A Sentimental Journey.* His biography is full of attachments to ladies, sentimental affairs that never apparently went beyond the letter-writing stage; yet although he affected passions, and perhaps believed in the affectation, he never ceased to see himself, even in his letters to the ladies, as something of a comic figure. *Tristram Shandy* has its sentimental, its pathetic passages, but even the most celebrated of them—the death of Le Fever—is not pure pathos. Much was made when Volume VI first appeared of the exquisiteness of the line that follows on Uncle Toby's oath ("He shall not die, by G——") on hearing that Le Fever must die: "The Accusing Spirit which flew up to heaven's chancery with the oath blushed as he gave it in;—and the Recording Angel, as he wrote it down, dropped a tear upon the word, and blotted it out forever." It was possible for the eighteenth century to take this kind of excess seriously, even though it is hard to do so today, but there is evidence that Sterne, although he was eighteenth-century enough to write it, was realistic enough to know that it was humorous. The scene in which Toby speaks his oath is one in which he is struggling, half-in, half-out of bed, marching forward, one shoe off, one on, at each repetition of "He shall march," and shouting hopeful defiance above each of Trim's matter-of-fact statements that the lieutenant must die. The scene is essentially comic, and all the pathos of the dying lieutenant and Uncle Toby's concern for him cannot erase the comedy. There is no laughter in the story of Le Fever, but there are smiles at least because Toby and Trim insist on being Toby and Trim even at the dying man's bedside. Sterne never sees any action simply through the eyes of the actor and, as a result, even his sentiment is tinged with a mild and loving mockery.

In the same way, the other pathetic or potentially pathetic scenes are touched with comedy. Yorick's death is lightened by the high rhetoric of Eugenius at his bedside, by the byplay with the night cap as the parson says farewell, and by the presentation of the inscription on his grave: "Alas, poor Yorick!" The death of Bobby is completely lost in the classic definitions of Mr. Shandy and the scene in the kitchen in which Trim moralizes (a below-stairs Mr. Shandy) and Susannah can think of nothing except the green satin nightgown which will come to her when Mrs. Shandy goes into mourning. As the pathetic scenes are touched into comedy by the behavior of the characters who play them, so Sterne's flights of sentimental rhetoric are consciously undercut when he gives lavishly of his eloquence, only to withdraw the gift with a single capping sentence. He ends an apostrophe on the simple worth of Trim with "O Trim! would to heaven thou had'st a better historian!—would thy historian had a better pair of breeches!" In the last volume, he follows a paragraph, addressed to Jenny, on the sadness and shortness of life with a one-sentence chapter: "Now, for what the world thinks of that ejaculation—I would not give a groat." Sterne is too much of a realist to take his sentiment and his pathos without comedy; the impulse that produced *Tristram Shandy*, the inclination to laugh in delight at the strange humors of the world, operates on Sterne the sentimentalist, just as it operates on Sterne the writer and Sterne the preacher.

Sterne's "uncommon indecencies," as Richardson called them, are absorbed into the texture of *Tristram Shandy* as surely as his sentiment is. Thackeray, in his famous hatcheting essay on Sterne in *The English Humourists of the Eighteenth Century*, speaks of "that dreary *double entendre*" and complains that the "foul Satyr's eyes leer out of the leaves constantly." Some of Sterne's readers who are not so fastidious as Richardson and Thackeray were, and I am one of them, are likely to find the *double entendre* almost as funny as Sterne himself obviously did. In the description of the terrible accident in which Trim and Bridget break down the bridge in Toby's garden the slapstick of the scene is heightened by the fact that the author appears to be talking about a completely different kind of maneuver than the surface meaning of his words denotes. If this scene is in the novel for its own sake, there are others in which the *double entendre* heightens the satire. That the monumental nose in

Slawkenbergius's tale may be no nose at all gives more than a prurient fillip to the story; the double meaning makes that much more ridiculous the curiosity of the townspeople of Frankfort and the abstruse university arguments on the reality or the falseness of the nose. In the same way, the Italian wind-instrument ("I dare not mention the name of the instrument in this place") that Sterne introduces into his scholary analysis of the ways of drawing character emphasizes the foolishness of the whole discussion. If the more accepting reader has a complaint against Sterne, it is not that he uses *double entendre*, but that he sometimes, almost coyly, insists on hinting that the reader may miss something. These suggestions, however, like the passages they accompany, are aimed at the kind of nicety that likes references to the bedroom and the bathroom if they are cloaked in polite enough language. "Why the most natural actions of a man's life should be called his Non-naturals,—is another question," says Tristram. At the end of his story about the court of Navarre, in which the word *whiskers* gains a double meaning and then reverts to a single meaning, although not the denotative one, Sterne comments on the kind of thinking that is the real butt of all his *double entendre:* "And when the extremes of delicacy, and the beginnings of concupiscence, hold their next provincial chapter together, they may decree that bawdy also."

If Sterne worked only in hints, suggestions, double meanings, he might in one sense deserve the prurient label that is sometimes fastened on him. In *Tristram Shandy,* however, the dainty suggestions are balanced with downright frankness. In a letter to William Warburton, who had offered Sterne unwanted advice on how to make his novel more acceptable to the tender-minded, Sterne says, "I may find it very hard, in writing such a book as 'Tristram Shandy' to mutilate everything in it down to the prudish humour of every particular." He finds mutilation not hard, but impossible, for he is working not in genteel comedy, but in an older tradition that takes in the Elizabethans, his beloved Rabelais, and the first important comedian, Aristophanes. He is the kind of comic writer who does not put on blinkers, does not choose to work a small plot delicately. For this reason, he takes the reader to the Shandy bedside at the moment of Tristram's begetting to hear Mrs. Shandy say, "Pray, my Dear, have you not forgot to wind up the clock?" He lets the window fall on the exposed Tristram and lets the hot chestnut roll into the front of Phutatorius' trousers. He makes the widow Wadman worry greatly about the extent of the wound in Uncle Toby's groin. He understands and uses low comedy, and by allowing his characters to moralize, philosophize, and categorize all around these actions, he makes clear and comic the dichotomy between the functions and passions of the body and the idealizing vagaries of the mind.

Sterne also uses the frankly sexual and scatalogical, as he sometimes uses his *double entendre,* as a satirical device. A bald line at the end of a pompous passage can bring the pretentious down from its self-supplied pedestal. After printing in French the discussion by the doctors of the Sorbonne on the methods by which a child may be baptized while still in its mother's womb, Tristram suggests that baptizing all the homunculi at once might be a safer and more effective course: "And provided, in the second place, That the thing can be done, which Mr. Shandy apprehends it may, *par le moyen d'une* petite canulle, and *sans faire aucun tort au père.*" Similarly Uncle Toby puts an end to a discussion between Walter Shandy and Yorick on prodigies and the ages at which they first make their genius known. The two disputants, displaying their learning, attempt to cap each other's examples, moving with each exemplary prodigy to an earlier age. Yorick finally tops Mr. Shandy. "But you forget the great Lipsius, quoth Yorick, who composed a work the day he was born." But the victory is Uncle Toby's. "They should have wiped it up, said my uncle Toby, and said no more about it." These lines are the verbal equivalent of the dung beetle on which Trygaeus flies to heaven in Aristophanes' *Peace.* Sterne does not use his "uncommon indecencies" exactly as Aristophanes and Rabelais did before him, but, like the earlier comic writers, he uses them for more than their own sake. He is not a teller of dirty stories; he is a humorist who is aware that men do not spend the whole of their lives in drawing-rooms.

For the bulk of this essay I have been concerned with *Tristram Shandy* as one man's laughing attempt to look closely at the world he lived in. From time to time, I have referred to the book as a "novel"—the label it customarily wears. Since little of the material and method discussed above has close relevance to that genre, I should perhaps say something about *Tristram Shandy* as a novel. Although it looks back to *Don Quixote* and forward to *Ulysses,* it is plainly unlike most of its generic brothers. It can best be described in Huey Long's famous words: "Just say I'm *sui generis,* and let it go at that."

Without attempting a detailed explanation of what I think

constitutes a novel, I should like to suggest that in two important ways *Tristram Shandy* fits that genre. Sterne creates genuine characters and places them in a concrete setting, and when he chooses to put aside digression, he involves his characters in dramatic situations that forward whatever plot the book has. Although the reader is likely to come away from *Tristram Shandy* with a generalized sense of the bemused and amused view of the world that is the book's primary quality, the specific things that stick in his mind are probably the characters, Tristram's relatives and neighbors, rather than the satiric points that Sterne makes. When Ignatius Sancho, the ex-slave, wrote to Sterne, "I declare I would walk ten miles in the dog days, to shake hands with the honest Corporal," he was expressing the kind of fondness for Trim, and for Uncle Toby, that Sterne's readers have always come away with. The reason is that Trim and Toby are so carefully delineated in the course of the book—their habits, their foibles, their tics, their little vanities, their strong loyalties—that they become more than the caricatures they would have been had Sterne allowed them simply to represent their primary passion for mock warfare and left them at that. The other figures—Mr. and Mrs. Shandy, Yorick, Dr. Slop, the widow Wadman—are as completely presented; starting with a particular characteristic —Mr. Shandy's fondness for argumentation, Mrs. Shandy's happy inability to grasp any idea, Yorick's cheerful irreverence—Sterne builds on and around it until a palpable character emerges. Even the minor characters—the disputing divines, the gossiping servants—take on flesh. Sterne, like Dickens, uses comic overstatement in painting his characters, but he never allows them to become stereotypes. They are human enough to need a place to live. Sterne provides a real countryside, real houses and gardens and, what is more important, real relationships for them to thrive in. His use of detail provides the furnishings (material and emotional) that make the settings believable. The reader not only hears the squeaking hinge on the Shandy parlor door and sees the converted bowling green where Toby and Trim hold their maneuvers; he knows clearly the relationship of Mr. Shandy to his wife and his brother, of Dr. Slop to the neighborhood, of Yorick to his parishioners, of the servants to the Shandy family, of Trim to Uncle Toby.

One of the reasons that the characters are such solid creations is that Sterne places them, and often arrests them, in scenes that define them dramatically. When Hogarth chose to draw Trim reading Yorick's sermon for a second edition

543

of Volume I, he picked a scene that had already caught Trim as clearly as a painter could. The novel is full of such scenes: Yorick riding into the village on his skinny horse, Mrs. Shandy stooping at the keyhole, Mr. Shandy reaching for his handkerchief, Obadiah riding wildly with Dr. Slop's bag flying at his neck, Uncle Toby looking for a mote in Mrs. Wadman's eye, Trim dropping his hat to illustrate the transience of human life. These are short scenes in which the gestures of the actors are indications of personality. In the more sustained narrative passages—Uncle Toby's courtship, for instance—the characters are revealed more fully, but they never act in a way that contradicts anything that the reader knows of their history or their mannerisms. Sterne gets all the humorous and satiric effects that he wants from his characters, not at their expense.

Those short scenes in which the characters are allowed to act can do more than put the actors on display. When Sterne chooses to let the digression rest, he can advance the narrative action of the novel with a few sentences—a gesture, an alarm, a confrontation, a line of dialogue. He knows, as good novelists always do, that action is at the heart of every novel, although in *Tristram Shandy*, unlike most novels, the action is not going anywhere in particular. There are temporary stops—the birth of Tristram, the death of Bobby, Uncle Toby's breaking off with Mrs. Wadman—but there is no final destination. The end of *Tristram Shandy* is that there shall be no end. In this sense—for all that is novelistic about it—it is an anti-novel as much as it is an anti-book.

With Tristram still at my shoulder, his whisper of cant still in my ear, I had better drop all this talk of anti-novel and anti-book, and go back to the work itself. At the end of the last volume, after Toby has escaped Mrs. Wadman, Obadiah comes into the Shandy parlor to complain that Mr. Shandy's bull has failed to provide his cow with a calf. Obadiah's accusation sets Mr. Shandy off on one of his rhetorical flights, which is interrupted, as they so often are, by Mrs. Shandy's failure to understand what is going on:

L——d! said my mother, what is all this story about?——
A COCK and a BULL, said Yorick——And one of the best of its kind I ever heard.

And so it is.

GERALD WEALES

SELECTED BIBLIOGRAPHY

OTHER WORKS BY STERNE

A Political Romance (The History of a Good Warm Watch-Coat), 1759
Sermons of Mr. Yorick, 1760-69
A Sentimental Journey through France and Italy, 1768
Journal to Eliza, 1775

BIOGRAPHY AND CRITICISM

Cross, Wilbur L. *The Life and Times of Laurence Sterne*. 3rd rev. ed. New Haven: Yale University Press; London: Oxford University Press, 1929.

Curtis, Lewis Perry. *The Politicks of Laurence Sterne*. New York & London: Oxford University Press, 1929.
————(ed.). *The Letters of Laurence Sterne*. New York & London: Oxford University Press, 1935.

Fredman, Alice Green. *Diderot and Sterne*. New York: Columbia University Press; London: Oxford University Press, 1955.

Howes, A. B. *Yorick and the Critics: Sterne's Reputation in England, 1760-1868*. New Haven: Yale University Press, 1958.

More, P. E. "Sterne," *Shelburne Essays*. 3rd Series. Boston: Houghton Mifflin Company, 1906.

Priestley, J. B. "The Brothers Shandy," *The English Comic Characters*. New York: Dodd, Mead & Company, Inc., 1925.

Quennell, Peter. *Profane Virtues: Four Studies of the Eighteenth Century*. New York: The Viking Press, Inc., 1945.

Read, Herbert. "Sterne," *The Sense of Glory: Essays in Criticism*. London: Cambridge University Press, 1929; New York: Harcourt, Brace & Company, Inc., 1930.

Thackeray, William M. "Sterne and Goldsmith," *English Humorists of the Eighteenth Century*. New York: The Macmillan Company, 1910.

Traugott, John. *Tristram Shandy's World: Sterne's Philosophical Rhetoric*. Berkeley: University of California Press, 1954; London: Cambridge University Press, 1955.

Watkins, Walter B.C. *Perilous Balance*. (pap.). Cambridge, Mass.: Walker-de Berry, Inc., 1961.

Yoseloff, Thomas. *A Fellow of Infinite Jest*. New York: Prentice-Hall, Inc., 1945.

A NOTE ON THE TEXT

The present text of *Tristram Shandy* is based on the first London edition of each of the nine volumes of the book, published over a period extending from 1760 to 1767. Sterne's typographic devices have been retained throughout. Spelling and punctuation have been brought into conformity with modern British usage.